# THE WAY IT WAS

## A Novel of the Civil War

G. R. Tredway

VANTAGE PRESS
New York

This book is a work of fiction and, except for certain well-known historical figures, all characters are fictitious and the resemblance to any actual person purely coincidental.

FIRST EDITION



Published by Vantage Press, Inc.
516 West 34th Street, New York, New York 10001

Manufactured in the United States of America
ISBN: 0-533-10733-4

Library of Congress Catalog Card No.: 93-94034

0 9 8 7 6 5 4 3 2 1

In memory of my sister, Juanita M. Tredway, 1925–1991,
and of my parents, George R. Tredway, 1884–1958, and
Pearl C. Tredway, 1886–1979.

Maybe it shouldn't have been this way.
Maybe we wish it hadn't been this way,
but
this is *the way it was.*

# THE WAY IT WAS

# 1

April of 1861 was like April usually is in southern Indiana. Periods of pleasantly warm weather heralding spring alternated with brief returns of winter, with freezes and even snow. During one of these warm spells about the middle of the month, a man was plowing in a field only a few years cleared from the forest surrounding it. This made the plowing hard. Roots still remained and a few sprouts had come up despite previous cultivation. The mules had to strain, and the plowman kept the point deep and straight only with considerable effort. The popping and snapping of roots broke through the soft sound of the plow and the subdued stamp of the mules' hooves.

A horseman appeared on the path that came out of the woods and bounded the field on the north. He stopped at the end of the field, dismounted, and tied his reins to a small tree at the edge of the woods. He sat on the fence and waited.

The plowman saw him at once but could not take his hands from the plow and continued doggedly on his circuit with no sign of recognition. His tall, slender body with the narrow hips and broad shoulders characteristic of his people was tiring, and he welcomed the opportunity to stop. He had been plowing since sunup, and it was now early afternoon.

When the plowman reached the man on the fence and stopped, the man got down and asked cheerily, "How air ye, Tom? I see yo're plowin' awreddy." He was a short, heavily built fellow in his late thirties, black-haired and swarthy.

"Oh, I'm all right," was the reply. "Had to get this field plowed before the weather turns bad again." He took off his hat and wiped his brow with his sleeve, the sweat showing darkly in the edge of his fair hair. "How're you, Jake?"

"Doin' fine. No farmin' this year, I guess. I'm helpin' raise a comp'ny fer th' war."

"That's what I've heard."

"How 'bout jinin' hit, Tom? We'd shore like t' have th' best shot in Dubois County in hit." Jake laughed. "Y' know, yore string always measured out shorter'n enybody else's at ever' shootin' match we've had th' last few years."

"I'm supposed to get married in June, Jake."

"Yeah, you an' Sally. She'd wait fer ye, Tom."

Tom laughed a little bitterly. "I guess she would. She's been waitin' for a long time now, till I got land and got set up." He sighed and wiped his brow again. "I've got that old Haskins house on my south forty fixed up so we can live in it till I can build a new one. I was goin' to do that this winter."

"Y' could hurry hit up a little an' git hitched up 'fore ye go," suggested Jake.

Tom shook his head. "No, if I go, I don't want to go in a married man. I don't want anybody but myself to worry about."

Jake nodded and sighed. "I know what y' mean. I don't s'pect I'd be goin' if'n Zeldy wuz still 'live." Zelda had been Jake's wife.

Tom put his hands on his hips and looked directly at Jake. "There're other things, too. There's a lot about this war I don't understand, and some of what I do understand, I don't like."

"That's th' way hit is with most uv us I guess, 'ceptin' th' Republicans, but hit's fer th' Union. Whoever's t' blame fer hit an' whyever they done hit, th' Union's been busted up an' hit's got t' be put back t'gether agin." Jake nodded gravely. "An' th' only way t' do hit now is fight them Secesh an' make 'em come back."

"There *were* other ways to do it without fightin'. You know who killed that compromise that Crittenden got up. If it'd passed, there wouldn't be any war."

"Yep, I know. Th' Republicans killed hit. An' maybe they wuz other ways t' do hit, but they hain't no more now that th' shootin's started." Jake's voice had the ring of conviction.

"Our governor, Morton, he did his part t' kill that Crittenden compromise. He knew that if they let the South have part of th' territories, it'd bust up his party. He'd rather bust up his country than his party, even if it means a war." He snorted angrily. "Now he wants us Democrats t' help fight it."

"I know men that'd git mad at what yo're sayin'," said Jake a little shortly. "They'd call y' a Tory er a traitor."

Tom bridled. "Are you callin' me that, Jake?"

Jake blinked. "No, I ain't. I know you ain't one. Yo're jist puzzled an' troubled." His tone became conciliatory. "I've been one uv yore neighbors ever' since y' wuz a little tike. I wuz with yore pa's brother Bill in Mexico. I picked him up atter th' battle an' helped bury him. I ain't got no better fren' in th' world than yore pa."

Tom subsided, and Jake went on. "I know how y' feel, Tom. A lot uv what y' say is so; but I've thought hit over, an' they hain't nothin' t' do now but fight."

Tom wasn't done. "Those Republicans. They carried on about slavery and keepin' it out of th' territories and finally scared th' South out of th' Union. And now they want us Democrats t' fight t' make it come back."

Jake sighed. "Now, Tom—"

Tom cut him off. "My mother's got people in Virginia, you know. There's her brother Henry. He went there t' visit several years ago and married and stayed. It's hard t' have t' fight your own kin, 'specially when they think they're right and you think they might be, too."

"A lot uv us has people in th' South," replied Jake with a nod, "but they're Rebels now, an' fixin' t' bust this country up fer good. We jist cain't let 'em do hit. Hit'll be better fer them, too, if'n we kin make 'em come back inta th' Union. They ain't gonna do no good tryin' t' be a country by theirselves."

Tom silently contemplated the woods, so Jake went on. "B'lieve me, Tom, I know how y' feel 'cause I usta feel 'bout th' same way. But hit's gotta be done. Hit's jist one uv them things that's gotta be done."

Tom changed the subject. "Are you goin' t' be captain of this company?"

"Naw, Mark Dixon is. I'm jist helpin' him. He wanted me t' see you 'cause I knowed ye better."

"Mark Dixon, huh! His old daddy's th' blackest Republican in th' country. He's been for fightin' th' South all along. At least he was always against settlin' with 'em any other way." Tom paused and shook his head. "And I never did cotton t' Mark. He always acted too stuck up."

"Aw, you jist don't know Mark well's I do," Jake assured him. "He ain't really stuck up. Hit's jist that he's always had fine clothes an' a fine horse an' never 'sociated 'round very much."

A pause followed. "He's been back east t' college an' all, y' know," added Jake.

"Well, I've been t' college, too, even if I didn't go back east t' one," said Tom. He looked at Jake questioningly. "Do you think he knows anything about soldiering?"

"I don't 'spect he does yet, but he will. He's a smart feller, an' he's been studyin' a book on tactics, one by a feller named Hardy er Hardee er somethin' like that."

"What'll you be, Jake, just a private?"

"Naw, I'm gonna be sargint major."

"You were in th' Mexican War. You know more about soldierin' than he does. You ought t' be captain."

"No, sir. I ain't no gentleman, an' an officer's got t' be a gentleman. I ain't got no edycation er nothin', y' know. I'm jist a farmer, an' a little one at that."

"That shouldn't make any difference."

"Hit does, though. Officers is gotta be gentlemen, an' that's somethin' I ain't."

"Well, Mark Dixon's sure enough a gentleman, if bein' a gentleman only means a man doesn't work for a livin'," said Tom with an air of resignation. "He don't even work in his daddy's store."

"Y' know," said Jake, "you oughta 'ply fer a commission an' be an officer. You been t' college, an' you've teached school. I 'spect you'd git one if'n ye'd 'ply."

Tom shook his head. "No, even if I do decide t' go, I don't want t' start out bein' an officer. I don't know th' first thing about soldierin'. I'd just get my men killed or something." He looked at Jake quizzically. "You know, that's what worries me about Mark Dixon."

"Oh, somebody's gotta be cap'n, an' he's took th' lead in signin' men up an' all. That's th' way they give cap'ns' commissions out, I guess. Y' raise a comp'ny an' yo're a cap'n."

There was a pause. Jake wanted to bring on a conclusion, so he asked, "Well, what 'bout hit, Tom? Can I count on ye?"

"You'll be sergeant major, you say?"

Jake nodded. "Yeah, an' that's purty close t' bein' cap'n. Enyhow, th' sargint major does most uv th' work."

Tom shifted his feet, his hands on his hips, and again looked off into the woods. "Well, I've got t' talk t' Sally about it and Pa, too; and I want t' do a little more thinkin' myself." He turned back to the older man. "How soon d'you have t' know?"

Jake sensed he had won. Tom would go, regardless of what anyone said or how much thinking he did. "Well, we're havin' a war meetin' at Celestine Thursday night t' fill up th' comp'ny. You kin wait till then an' make up yore mind. If'n y' comes up when they makes th' call, ye'll go. If'n ye don't, ye won't."

"We'll see," replied Tom.

Jake went to untie his horse. He mounted and said, "Well, we'll see ye at Celestine."

"Like I say, we'll see," was the only reply Jake got.

Jake rode away with a grin and a wave, and Tom went back to his plow. His mind was no longer on his work, though, and he had the air of a man making an important decision.

John Traylor's house sat just below the ridge top at the edge of the forest. A few of the primordial trees had been left to shade the front, and although it was a sizable two-story house, the trees dwarfed it. In front, cleared land ran down a gentle slope to a creek, which was cleared on both sides to the ridge crests that confined its valley. Good fences, white-washed buildings, and a general appearance of tidiness testified to a well-kept farm.

It was suppertime and the family sat around the table in the kitchen. John sat at the head of the table, flanked by his wife, Sarah, and Tom, their older son. Billy, the younger, sat at the foot. As they ate, the men talked of their work.

"How was it, plowin' in that new field t'day, Tom?" asked his father.

"Pretty hard. There're some roots in it yet, and a few sprouts have come up."

Billy spoke up. "Farmin' is hard work. I never could unnerstan' why y' give up school teachin' fer farmin', 'speshully atter goin' t' college up t' Bloomington two hull winters."

Tom grunted. "School teachin's not all that easy, and it keeps a fellow inside too much. I'd a whole lot rather farm. I just taught long enough t' get money t' buy land."

Billy only shook his head in puzzlement. He was ruddy and fair like his father and brother and, although not so heavy, was nearly as tall as both his elders.

"Well, I don't blame you, Tom," said his father. "I couldn't stand havin' to stay indoors with a bunch of pesky younguns myself." He shook his head. "I didn't think you'd stay with teachin' very long, but you were always so good in school and read so much that I wanted you t' go t' college fer a spell anyhow."

They ate in silence for a time, as though what they had been talking about was not what was really on their minds. "Sarah," said the father at length, "we're out of bread. Go fetch some more." Sarah looked almost too young and trim to be his wife.

The mother arose to comply, and as soon as she was gone, John asked, "Well, Tom, what're you goin' to do? You're twenty-one and have got t' decide for yourself."

"I've been deciding. I guess I'll go."

"I'm goin', too!" announced Billy.

His mother had returned in time to hear. She dropped the plate with a crash and burst into tears. "Oh, Lord, spare me that! Not both of my boys!"

The men looked at one another with pained consternation. “John!” sobbed the mother. “You've got t' keep Billy anyhow, even if Tom's got t' go!”

John turned to his younger son. “I didn't know you had any such notion, Billy.”

“Well, I do. I'm goin' on eighteen. I'm big 'nough. Me an' Tom can go t'gether, an' he kin look out fer me. An' I kin look out fer him,” he added hastily.

Sarah tried a practical approach. “John, it'll be awful hard on you doin' all th' work on th' farm yourself, with that new field and all.” Her lips trembled, but she had stopped crying, and the men looked relieved.

“Oh, that needn't stop anyone. I can do th' work all right. I done it b'fore th' boys was big enough t' help. A stiff leg don't keep a man from workin', only from marchin'. If it hadn't been for my leg, I'd a gone t' Mexico.”

Sarah broke out afresh. “Mexico! Mexico!” she cried. “Your brother Bill went, an' he was killed! That's what'll happen t' Tom an' Billy if they go t' this war!” She stopped to weep, then cried, “John, John, you've got t' stop them! Billy anyhow! He's my baby!”

Billy was indignant. “I ain't no baby! I'm 'most as tall as Tom, ain't I? I kin march an' shoot, an' that's all soldiers do!”

Tom spoke up. “Billy, you shouldn't go. You're not strong enough yet, and soldierin's a hard life. You've got to march twenty or thirty miles a day sometimes, and that's carryin' a heavy load, a pack, rifle, ammunition, and a lot of other stuff. You've got to sleep out in th' weather and all. You've heard th' men who went to Mexico talk.”

“Tom's right,” affirmed the father. “A soldier's life is awful hard, and it takes a strong man t' stand it.” He nodded emphatically. “You're not a strong man yet.”

“I ain't no strong man like you an' Tom,” admitted Billy, “but they ain't no hard work in th' army, jist marchin' an' shootin'. I can walk as fer as enyone an' shoot better'n most fellers, cain't I, Tom?”

“You're a good shot all right,” replied Tom, “and you can walk as far as anyone, but walkin's not marchin' and sleepin' out in th' weather.”

Billy was insistent. “If I cain't go with Tom, I'll go enyhow.” He played his trump. “Wouldn't y' ruther I'd go with Tom than a bunch of fellers who didn't know me er enything!”

Billy had scored. His father's face fell, and Tom frowned thoughtfully.

"You're just a baby!" cried his mother. "It hasn't been long since I carried you in my arms. . . ." Her voice trailed off into sobs.

"I've said all I'm gonna say." Billy pushed back his chair. "I'm goin', whether with Tom er not."

"Listen here, young man," warned his father, "you're not eighteen yet, an' I'll have somethin' t' say 'bout your goin'."

"I'll be eighteen in December," Billy reminded him, "an' you cain't keep me frum goin' then!" He had scored and he knew it.

His mother took the floor. "Let me have my say," she began in a quavering voice. "I never have anything t' say 'bout you menfolks business, but I'm goin' t' have my say this time."

"Go ahead, Sarah," said John. He frowned at Billy. "Maybe you can talk some sense into this young idjit's head."

Sarah's voice lost its quaver and gained strength. "There's no need for either of you t' go. It's th' Republicans an' that old Lincoln. They started it. I've heard you say that yourself, John. Let them fight it. That old Lincoln's done it, eggin' them South C'lina men on till they started shootin' at that fort down there. Let them fight it. Us Democrats had no part in it. If Douglas'd won th' 'lection last fall, there wouldn't be any 'cession or any war. I've heard you say that, too, John, you an' Tom both."

Tom tried to interrupt, but she waved him down. "Us women don't have any say 'bout anything. We just wait an' weep, but it's our sons—our men—who go 'way an' get killed, though." She turned to her husband. "Remember how your mother worried about Bill, an' how it 'fected her when she heard he'd been killed way down there in Mexico?"

"But, Mother," John replied, "not ever'body who went got killed! Why, there's—"

His wife interrupted. "You said I could have my say!" she shrilled.

John only nodded glumly, so she went on. "If it was left t' us wives an' mothers, there wouldn't be any wars, 'ceptin' maybe with Indians. I know Southern women feel th' same way. It's just you men! You just like t' fight an' kill! John, you'd have gone t' Mexico an' left me with th' two little boys if it hadn't been for that knee you hurt loggin'!"

The men had become embarrassed and perturbed. "Now, Mother—" John began.

"Don't 'now, Mother' me!" she cried. "You're th' father of these boys!"

She threw her apron over her face and started to flee the room. Her husband caught her with an easy motion and pulled her back to the table like a man might retrieve a blowing cloth. "Come on now, Sarah! Set down and act sensible. We've had 'nough of this!"

The mother gave up and resumed her seat, but she kept her eyes on the table, sobbing softly and wiping tears with her apron.

"Men are men an' women are women," sighed John. "Th' dear creatures just cain't see things like we do."

"Yeah, there's things you wimmin jist don't unnerstan'," began Billy, "an' us men—"

His father cut him off. "You just keep quiet, young man, an' let me do th' talkin'."

Billy's eyes widened and he bobbed his head.

"There's a war goin' on," John continued solemnly, "and your mother's right about th' startin' of it. I don't deny that. I've said th' same things myself a hundred times, I expect; but it's started, and it don't matter anymore who started it or why. It's got t' be fought an' th' Union put back t'gether, or we're all gone under." He turned to his elder son. "Me an' Tom has done a lot of talkin' an' a heap more thinkin' about it, haven't we?"

Tom nodded. "I don't feel good about it, but it's got to be done. We'd starve to death way up here, cut off from New Orleans; and once it's started, there'll be no end to it. Each state will set up for itself, and we'll always be quarrelin' and fightin' with one another, like in Europe." He looked thoughtfully at his brother. "I guess maybe Billy had better go with me. We can join this company Mark Dixon's gettin' up, and we'll be together. He'll go sooner or later anyhow, because this war's goin' to last a long time. It won't be quick and easy like a lot of people think."

His mother broke in. "What about my folks in Virginia, John? My brother Henry lives there, an' he's not much older'n Tom. Are you gonna let your boys go fight them?"

John bowed his head. "I guess they will if your folks go against th' Union." He looked up and added hopefully, "They might not, though. There's a lot of Union men in th' South."

"They'll all fight when you come down on them, Union men or not!" insisted the mother. "Anyone'll fight t' protect his home an' people!" Her husband looked gloomily at the table, and Tom shifted uneasily in his chair.

Sarah knew she had raised a good point and went ahead with it. "I've got cousins an' even a brother that you're sendin' our boys to fight an' kill, John! Can you 'magine anything worse'n that?"

"It's not likely," replied John lamely. "There'll be thousands of men, all mixed up, an' they prob'ly won't ever see one another. And," he went on more positively, "Henry might come back an' join us, an' th' others might not go fight."

The mother broke into sobs again. "You've been listenin' t' those black Republicans like that ol' man Dixon again! You know that's not so. They're all liars, from ol' Lincoln on down. And they're abolish! They just want to free th' niggers, so they can come up here an' go t' school with our children an' marry white folks! That's th' Republicans for you! I've heard you say so yourself, John!"

The father was embarrassed. "I've said a good many things, an' some of 'em was so an' some wasn't. Things are diff'rent now, though."

Sarah broke into a fresh fit of weeping.

"Mother, Mother," said John softly, "you've got t' stop this. These boys are gonna go, an' we'll just have t' 'cept it."

She jumped up and ran from the room trailing tears and lamentations, her face buried in her apron. This time John made no attempt to stop her. Only Billy seemed pleased by what had happened, but he did his best to hide it.

# 2

The meeting would be far too large for the little schoolhouse, so it was held in the grove of trees in front. Wood had been gathered and several fires built to provide illumination. Candle lanterns hung along the front of the schoolhouse lighted the speakers' platform, especially built for the occasion. Normally the meeting would have been held during the day, but it was planting time and many wouldn't have been able to come.

Tom and Billy were in the middle of the crowd, most of whom took the meeting as a social occasion. People talked and gossiped in groups. Certain young men paraded about with an air of importance, occasionally stopping to talk or flirt with girls. Children shouted and played. The leaping flames of the fires lighted up the tree limbs overhead, at times making them resemble the ribs of high vaulted arches holding up the great dome of darkness. The alternation of light and shadow made people seem to be moving when they were still. Sometimes it made laughing faces look serious and serious ones look mirthful.

"I wish Pa had come with us," sighed Billy. "This is th' first meetin' like this he's missed."

"Ma's pretty bad off," replied Tom, "mostly on account of you. He thought he ought t' stay home with her."

Billy had no reply. He only shrugged and sighed again.

A knot of young men shoved up alongside, talking and jostling. A gangly, pop-eyed fellow wearing loose linsey-woolsey and a floppy hat was the noisiest among them.

When he wasn't talking, he was going from one foot to another, hunching his shoulders and grimacing with his mouth. He was charged with nervous energy.

"Why don't you fellers go up closer?" a huge, heavily bearded man asked him. "We won't be able t' hear nothin' with you-uns carryin' on like that."

"Oh, hi, Burk!" said the gangly one, grinning. "Why don't y' come out from b'hind that bresh pile so folks kin see what y' look like?" He and his companions broke into guffaws at the reference to Burk's beard.

"I guess that'll hold ye, Burk," said one of them. "Harve Akers has always got a comeback."

Suddenly Harve noticed Tom and Billy. "Well, look who's hyar! Who would've thought it?"

"Why shouldn't we be here?" demanded Tom. "Almost everybody else is."

Harve's perpetual loose-mouthed grin spread wider. "Glad t' see y' hyar, Tom, an' you, too, Billy! Air ye goin' up?"

"I'm thinking about it," replied Tom. "Are you?"

"Shore am. I was th' first feller to put his name down." He laughed like it was a joke.

Billy spoke up. "Well, that's jist 'cause you work in ol' man Dixon's store. He'd a fired ye if'n ye hadn't."

Harve didn't take offense. "Nothin' to it! Nothin' to it! I'm th' feller that give Mark Dixon th' notion t' raise a comp'ny. I'd ruther fight than work any day!" His laugh resembled the neigh of a wind-broken horse.

"Lissen now," broke in Burk. "Let's all quiet down so we kin hear when th' speakin' starts."

"Well, hit ain't started yit," replied Akers cockily. "Don't holler till ye'er hurt, y' big ol' ox!" He and his friends hee-hawed gleefully. Burk only folded his massive arms and shook his head.

There was motion in the front. Akers was all eyes. "There they are!" he exclaimed. Suddenly he was seized with dissatisfaction. "C'mon, you fellers, we kin git a lot closer'n this." He and his companions pushed forward into the crowd and were soon lost to view.

"I'm shore glad he's gone," sighed a man nearby. "I never seen sich a noisy, feather-headed feller."

"Yeah, an' he's drinkin', too," a woman said. "I smelt likker on him."

Suddenly Tom felt movement close to him and looked down to see a young woman smiling up at him. "Hello, Tom," she said softly. She was a beautiful girl, with wavy golden hair, finely molded features, and eyes that were a deep blue in good light.

"Sally!" exclaimed Billy. Tom said nothing.

"I was just waitin' for those fellows t' go away," she continued, still looking up at Tom. "I knew they would. That Harve Akers has got t' be in th' middle of everything." She leaned closer and whispered, "I just can't stand him."

"I hear there're other fellows you *can* stand, like Mark Dixon," said Tom gruffly.

Sally took his arm. "I wondered why you hadn't been over," she said. "That's why I hunted you up tonight."

Tom looked off into the crowd. "A man doesn't want th' woman he's supposed t' marry seein' someone else."

"Oh, Tom," sighed Sally, "he just came over one evenin', and Pa couldn't very well turn him away. Nobody asked him to come."

Tom knew the people around them could hear, but it couldn't be helped. "*You* didn't have t' talk t' him!" he accused, doing his best to keep his voice low.

"I didn't, hardly at all!" protested Sally. "I went in th' kitchen right away and didn't come out till Mark was leavin', when Pa called me. And it was Pa who asked him to come back, not me. He owes ol' Calvin a lot of money, you know."

Billy was disgusted and moved away. He still thought interest in women was a weakness.

Tom was somewhat mollified. "I'm glad t' hear that, but I'm all ready t' call Mark Dixon out. He knows you're my girl. Everybody knows that."

"I don't think he does," replied Sally. "He's been gone back east to school, you know. I tried to tell him, but I don't know if he understood."

"Well, I'll make him understand. I'm not going t' stand for it."

"Oh, Tom, don't go fightin' him or anything! Ol' Calvin Dixon'll have the law on you! He's always haulin' somebody into court, and Mark's goin' t' be a lawyer, they say."

"I don't care about that," said Tom grimly. "I'm goin' to see Mr. Mark Dixon just as soon as he gets back from Indianapolis." He snorted. "I just wish I'd found out about it before he left."

Sally was frightened. "I'll tell him, Tom. I'll tell him if he ever comes back. I don't want you gettin' into trouble over it." She squeezed his arm again. "I don't think he'll come back, though. I did my best t' show I didn't want t' see him."

Tom pondered. Although he hadn't said anything about it, he had almost changed his mind about joining Mark's company when he had heard about his going to see Sally, because it made a confrontation with him inevitable. He didn't want to back out, though, because it would disappoint Billy and might even be interpreted as cowardice. Maybe just letting Sally take care of it was the best way out, and there was no doubt now that she would.

"Oh, all right, then," he replied, "but I don't want him gettin' th' idea he can walk all over me."

"Oh, he won't," Sally assured him. "If he comes again, it'll be the last time. I don't care what Pa says."

"That'll still be twice too much," said Tom grumpily.

Sally changed the subject. "Well," she sighed, "I guess you'll be goin' up when they make th' call tonight."

Tom was glad she was resigned to it. He had feared tears and lamentations. "Yes, I guess I'll go up."

She sighed tremulously. "June was so close."

Tom took her hand and whispered in her ear, "I'm sorry, sweetheart. I'm sorry."

"We've waited so long," she went on. "Couldn't we—"

He didn't want anyone to hear what she was going to say and cut her off. "No, Sally, we can't," he whispered fiercely. "A man goin' away t' war's got no business gettin' married!"

She bowed her head, and although no one could see it, a tear stole down her cheek. "Well, if . . . if you men can go, I . . . guess us women can wait." Her tone belied the brave words.

"I'll explain it all t' you on our way back home. We'll go with you an' your folks."

"Oh, we're not goin' back home tonight," she said sadly. "We're staying at Uncle Pleas's house, just out th' road. Pa said it was too far to go back after dark."

"Well, I'm not goin' 'round Pleas Napier's house," said Tom emphatically. "He's had it in for us for four, five years now, ever since Pa got up that bunch who busted up that abolition meetin' Pleas was head of down at Huntingburg. He'd order me off."

Sally nodded. "I know, Tom, but that wasn't any abolition meetin'. Those two fellows Uncle Pleas got t' come up from Evansville t' speak were just Republicans out 'lectioneerin'. Wouldn't any abolish ever come t' Dubois County; you know that."

"Well, nobody knew the difference between Republicans and abolish back then, and Pleas wouldn't deny they were abolish." Tom shook his head. "I just can't stand that man. I never could."

"Uncle Pleas is no abolish, Tom," protested Sally. "He's just kinda queer. Pa says he was always that way. He'd be for somethin' just because ever'body else was against it." She paused and looked back in the crowd. "I've got t' go now, Tom, or Pa'll be lookin' for me." She dropped his hand.

"I'd go with you if you wasn't for Pleas," said Tom.

She looked at him sadly. "You won't be leavin' right away, will you, after you go up tonight?"

"No, it'll probably be a couple of weeks yet. They have to get ready for us up at Indianapolis."

Sally nodded. "So you'll be comin' over to see me right away, won't you?"

"Tomorrow night; all right?" He took her hand again.

"Tomorrow night, then." She smiled, squeezed his hand, and was gone.

Looking after her, Tom found his view blocked by Burk's gigantic hulk. The big man winked solemnly at him, his yellow beard gleaming in the firelight. He had undoubtedly heard a good deal, but he was no gossip. Proceedings had started on the platform, so Tom asked, "Did we make too much noise, Burk?"

"Naw, a feller an' his gal never makes too much noise," rumbled the giant.

"You oughta get yourself one, Burk. There's plenty of them around."

"None uv 'em 'd ever be int'rested in me, Tom; enyhow, none uv 'em ever has been." He sighed with a heave of his massive chest. "I'm jist too big an' ugly, I guess."

"Just wait, Burk," said Tom as Billy resumed his place beside him. "There's a lid for every kettle, you know."

"I'm glad she's gone," muttered Billy. "We couldn't of heered nothin', an' you wouldn't 've paid no 'tention t' nothin' but her."

"You'll grow up someday," rejoined Tom gruffly.

Billy's attention was on the platform, and he made no reply. A tall, imposing man who had just joined the group there was coming forward to face the crowd. He was the Honorable Benjamin Baker, who represented the district in Congress. Someone knocked on the side of the schoolhouse with a stick of wood, but there was no need to. The noise died rapidly away as Baker stopped and looked out over the crowd. His handsome clean-shaven face bore the expression of a man who was accustomed to speaking and being listened to, and there was scarcely a whisper by the time he began.

"Ladies and gentlemen," came the deep, well-modulated voice, "I apologize for my late arrival, but my train was a little late coming into Shoals Station, and the gentleman who was to have a horse saddled and waiting for me had forgotten about it." Although his voice didn't seem loud, it carried to the outer fringe of the crowd.

He paused briefly. "The gentlemen who organized this meeting have asked me to serve as its chairman and to give the concluding address. If there are no objections—"

A raffish voice broke in. "Whar's yore fren', ol' Bill Bowles?" It was Harve Akers.

Boisterous laughter arose from those clustered about Akers. "Still runnin' from Booney Vistey!" shouted one of them. There were whoops and more boisterous laughter from the group.

Baker regarded the noisemakers coldly, and they subsided. "Dr. Bowles was not invited to this meeting. He is not present. Does that answer your question, my friend?"

"Then how come yo're hyar?" demanded Akers. "Yo're a 'cessionist jist like he is!"

Akers' interjection didn't go over very well. Shouts of anger and disapproval arose from the crowd. "Throw him out!" bellowed someone toward the front. A roar of approval followed.

Baker was equal to the occasion. "Now, now, let's not be so hard on this poor fellow," he said in mock sympathy. "His brain is addled, as everybody knows. His friends should look after him better."

An uproar of laughter and shouts of ridicule followed. "That's tellin' him!" "That oughta hold you, Akers!" "He ain't got no brain t' be addled!" came successive shouts.

The crowd was convulsed with laughter. Billy laughed so hard he had to clutch Tom for support. Even Burk grinned and rumbled in his chest.

Baker extended his arms and the multitude quieted. Nothing more was heard of the troublemakers, and Baker introduced the first speaker. He was Mr. Calvin Dixon, a small, thin man in his fifties with a sharp face and glittering dark eyes.

"Why air they startin' with that dried up ol' wart?" wondered Billy aloud.

"Folks will listen to him," replied Tom. "I expect half of 'em owe him money."

Dixon spoke in a high, nasal voice. "I wasn't born an' raised in this part of th' country," he began, "or in th' South like a lot of you folks. I come here from Connecticut, which makes me a Yankee, but I ain't really one. I've been livin' 'mongst you fer thirty year now, keepin' store mostly, so I've growed outa it."

Chuckles arose from the crowd, but someone nearby said, "I'll be durned if'n he has!"

"I'm a real native of th' Pocket now," Dixon went on, "an' I feel a lot like you do 'bout th' Yankees. Too many of 'em are abolitionists, an' they meddle in other folks' bisniss too much."

He paused while murmurs of approval ran through the crowd. "But I'm gonna tell you something'!" he shouted. "Things ain't like they usta be! Our ol' friends down South have broke up th' Union, an' th' Yankees is gonna help put it back t'gether agin!" He looked around as if to invite contradiction, but there was none.

"I'm an ol' Whig, too," confessed Dixon. "There never was many Whigs 'round here, an' I used t' git kinda lonesome sometimes. I think we used t' git a few dozen votes in th' county 'lections, an' we never done much better in th' district. I know we always got beat, an' got beat bad."

The crowd chuckled appreciatively. "Then," Dixon went on, "I jined th' Republicans when they come 'long back six er seven year ago, but we didn't do much better." He turned to Baker, who was seated behind and to his left. "We always put up a fight, though, didn't we, Yer Honor?"

Baker nodded and smiled while the crowd showed its appreciation.

Dixon turned back to his audience. "Most of you people didn't know what t' make of us Republicans at first." He paused and smilingly surveyed the crowd. "I rec'lect that meetin' we had, er tried t' have, down at Huntingburg four er five year ago. That was a hot ol' time," he said ruefully, "an' I 'spect them two men Pleas Napier got t' come up from Evansville is runnin' yet." The crowd remembered, too. A tumult of laughter, backslapping, and humorous reminiscenses broke out.

The little man suddenly became serious. "But you know, er oughta know by now, that us Republicans ain't abolitionists. Maybe we got some in our party; but a dog gits fleas, y' know, an' he cain't help hit." The crowd showed that the speaker had scored a point.

Dixon raised his voice. "But our fightin' an' carryin' on 'bout politics oughta all stop now! There shouldn't be no Republicans or Democrats no more! We oughta all fergit our past diff'runces an' come t'gether in a great Union party, like Gov'nor Morton says, a party with only one purpose!" He waved his arms and shrieked at the top of his lungs, "An' that purpose is t' restore th' Union as our forefathers made it!" Shouts of approval and loud applause followed.

"We hear a lot 'bout abolitionists an' 'bolishin' slavery," Dixon said, "but there's no danger of that. Didn't Pres'dent Lincoln promise t' leave slavery 'lone in his 'naugural address?"

"He shore did!" shouted someone.

"There won't be any abolishin' of slavery," promised Dixon. "We don't need t' worry 'bout th' niggers bein' freed an' leavin' th' South an' comin' up here t' fill our jails an' poorhouses an' steal our p'sessions an' m'lest our wimmin." He bobbed his head for emphasis. "Th' niggers'll jist go on bein' slaves, an' they'll stay in th' South." A roar of approval swept the crowd, followed by prolonged cheering. The speaker had dealt successfully with what was obviously a major concern of his audience.

Dixon made several attempts before he could make himself heard again. "Abolishin' slavery'd wreck th' country!" he shouted at the top of his lungs. "Th' border states'd all jine th' Confed'rits, an' our men'd all leave th' army an' come home! There wouldn't be any army t' fight th' Rebels with, an' th' Union'd be gone f'rever!" He paused to catch his breath, then shrieked, "Our boys'll fight t' save th' Union but not t' free th' slaves!"

The crowd's reaction dwarfed all previous ones. The cheering went on and on. Dixon could only stand and wait. Finally the uproar subsided enough for him to go on. "Don't you think Mr. Lincoln knows that? Don't you think th' leadin' men in Congress knows that? 'Course they do! They'll keep th' abolitionists shut up in th' cellar till it's all over, an' then they oughta be took out an' hung!"

"Hang 'em now!" shouted someone. "They caused all th' trouble!" The crowd expressed vociferous agreement.

Dixon turned to another subject. "Then there's constitootional rights. I hear a lot 'bout 'em. I've heered an' read that Lincoln's gonna make hisself a dictator an' 'rest people 'thout warrants an' hold 'em 'thout trials like them kings an' emp'rors in Europe do. That's 'cause of what had t' be done in Maryland an' 'round th' capital of our country." Dixon waved his arms. "That's all nonsense! Only traitors have t' be 'rested an' treated like that, an' there ain't no traitors in th' North, is there?"

"No! No!" came from several places in the crowd.

"I kin say th' same 'bout states' rights. Some people seems skeered 'bout them, too. They say it's 'gin states' rights under th' Constitootion t' coerce a sov're'n state." He paused for effect, then asked dramatically, "Well, how're ye gonna restore th' Union now 'lessen ye coerce them sov're'n states that has seceded an' set up that Confed'racy?"

"You cain't! Hit cain't be done!" came shouts from the crowd.

"They say," Dixon went on, "that th' fed'ral gov'ment'll subjugate th' states an' rule th' whole country like Looey th' Fourteenth done in France, an' tell us what t' eat an' drink an' think, an' even take over our schools." He paused and nodded. "You needn't be skeered 'bout enything like that. That'd undo th' revolution 'gin England. It'd be like bein' ruled by Parl'ment from three thousan' miles away. Folks'd have no say a'tall 'bout what th' gov'ment done. It could do enything it wanted to 'em." He paused again. "Nobody wants enything like that, nobody," he went on to demonstrations of approval from the crowd.

Dixon was ready to conclude. "We all oughta remember that this here war's fer th' Constitootion," he said solemnly. "Now," he said dramatically, "how kin a war t' uphold th' Constitootion distroy it?"

Loud and prolonged applause broke out as the little man nodded, smiled, and returned to his seat. Congressman Baker had him stand again, which carried the applause on and on.

Tom was impressed and the behavior of the crowd showed that it was, too. Tom would never have thought the fellow had it in him. He had dealt with every major concern his audience had about the war and done so very successfully.

Billy wasn't impressed, though. "When're they gonna quit this speechifyin' an' git down t' bisniss?" he asked impatiently.

A succession of other speakers followed. Most of them spoke only briefly, and none of them said anything new. The people grew restless and there was much moving about and talking in low tones. Finally the time came, and the noise and movement died away. Quiet and an air of expectation greeted Congressman Baker as he came forward to speak.

"Tonight," he began, "I presume to speak in the name of the people of the First Congressional District and of Dubois County. The people of the district have sent me to represent them in Congress four times in succession, and Dubois County has always given me my largest majorities."

"We'll do it again!" shouted someone toward the front, and the crowd noisily affirmed the pledge.

Baker bowed and smiled appreciatively. "This meeting," he went on, "is to raise a company of infantry to fight to restore the Union. As a Democrat, I heartily support a war for that purpose, and I am sure you do the same."

Applause commenced, but Baker didn't permit it to build up. "Some say," he continued, "that the Union could have been restored peacefully if our leaders had been willing to unbend a little. I have said that myself. However true that once was, I think we can agree that it is no longer true. Now the Union can be restored *only by going through the red gates of war!*"

The crowd roared its agreement.

"If we fail to support a war for the Union, we will become a divided country." Baker paused and nodded significantly. "And the parts into which the Union is already divided may themselves divide, as talk of a Northwest Confederacy shows." The crowd seemed stricken at the thought.

Baker raised his voice. "Unless the Union is restored, this great nation may break up into a number of small countries, all sunk in poverty and incapable of defending themselves against predatory foreign powers." He shook his head sadly. "I refer you to our fellow citizens from Germany, who stand among us now." He shot his arms into the air and shouted, "Ask them what it's like to live in a divided country! Ask them what it's like to have your land invaded, your crops destroyed, your barns and houses burned, and your womenfolk ravished!" Shouts of endorsement in both German and English arose all over the crowd. It was the first noticeable response from the Germans present.

Baker took up another subject. "This war *is not* for the abolition of slavery; most assuredly it is not. If I thought it was," he shouted, "I would not support it for a minute!" He paused while cries of agreement went up in his audience, then went on. "I would rather," he shouted vehemently, "live in a country the size of a postage stamp, have only crusts for my daily fare, and have nothing but rags to hide my nakedness, then have a horde of freed Negroes pouring into our state to corrupt and debase our people!" Applause broke out, but he again overrode it. "I would rather live under the despotism of a Napoléon or a Frederick William than amid the crime and degeneracy of a society in which the races mix!" His voice was nearly drowned out toward the last by such an uproar of applause that it seemed almost every person present had joined in at the top of his lungs. Baker could only pace the platform until it began to subside.

Finally he was able to resume. "There are no abolitionists among you. There are none in the First District, except for a few perverted souls despised and ostracized by their neighbors. Most of the abolitionists we have in Indiana are those fool Quakers up in the Fifth District."

Emphatic booing and shouts of censure came from the crowd. "Hang ol' Julian!" bellowed a deep bass voice above the uproar. Vociferous shouts of endorsement followed.

"I see you do not approve of my colleague in Congress from the Fifth District, Mr. George Washington Julian," said Baker smilingly. "Neither do I. I only wish he had been named after someone else. It is ironic, most ironic, that a man who has done as much as anyone to destroy our country should bear the name of the great man who was its father." The crowd expressed its agreement in no uncertain terms.

"Mr. Julian and his fellow abolitionists have much to answer for," Baker went on. "Their insane raving about slavery is what has caused this war. *They* scared the people of the South into seeking safety in secession and independence. *They* broke up the Union. Now," he went on angrily, "we must fight our Southern brethren, and kill them and be killed by them, to compel them to return to a Union the abolitionists scared them into leaving!"

The crowd raged at the prospect.

"And what do we find now?" Baker went on scathingly. "It seems that most of these abolitionists refuse to fight in a war they caused. They say they are men of high moral principles who oppose taking human life. They will sit piously and safely at home while thousands of other men, who only wanted to live in peace, slaughter one another in a war they had no part in causing!" The rage of the crowd was unbounded.

Baker tried several times to make himself heard. Finally he was able to. "I wonder," he asked sarcastically, "how many Quakers will answer our worthy governor's call for troops to put down the rebellion?"

Scornful laughter and contemptuous hoots resounded. "None! None! Nary a one!" and like shouts went up.

Baker went to another subject. "On your behalf," he began, "I solemnly warn the powers that be—the president, our governor, and the leading men in Congress—that they must remain true to their pledge that this war is *only* to restore the Union." He nodded solemnly. "As our first speaker so ably said, our young men *will* fight to restore the Union, but *not* to free the slaves; and we who will stay at home will be behind them one hundred percent!"

Cheering and shouts of approval swept the crowd, and it was several moments before Baker could resume. "I also warn the powers that be," he intoned, "that they must pay the most scrupulous respect to our personal liberties under the Constitution." He paused significantly as a hush settled over the crowd. "In the past," he went on, "great revolutions, such as our government now faces, have led to despotism. The jails have been filled with men arrested only for their political opinions. The gutters have run with the blood of men who only opposed tyranny."

The people were awestruck and the hush continued. "I have always been a student of history," Baker resumed, "and I learned long ago that history has many dark and bloody pages. Let us pray that the history of our times has no more than its share. Whether it will or not depends on the men who won control of our state and national governments in the elections last fall."

Although the people remained quiet, Baker regarded them silently for a time before going on. "May God guide their footsteps aright, for if they stray, if they depart from the goals which have won our support for the war, and for which our young men go to risk their lives, they will have betrayed us and them!" He paused dramatically, raised an arm, and thundered, "If they do, we will hurl them from power as our fathers did George the Third of England!"

"Hear! Hear!" resounded from the crowd.

"Tell ol' Linkun that!" shouted someone.

A hum of conversation indicated the speaker had uncovered a major concern of his audience.

Baker turned to the other men on the platform. They exchanged nods, and he again faced the crowd. "Now to our principal concern tonight." He paused and looked over the crowd. "I see among you many young men. God never made better ones. They are our future. Their stout arms, their strong backs, and their keen minds will raise us to prosperity and plenty. They are the fathers of future generations of men and women who will carry our nation to power and greatness."

Baker paused, then went on. "But before anything else, they must perform what may be their greatest task, the noble work of restoring our Union. All over the state young men are rushing forward to enlist in this just and righteous cause, to save the precious heritage our fathers bought with their life's blood. The young men of the First Congressional District are among the foremost, and those of Dubois County will be second to none. I am as certain of that as I am that God made the heavens and the earth, for no finer, no stronger, no braver young men ever lived than those I see before me tonight."

Baker was no longer the polished speaker who played on the emotions of his audience. He spoke from the heart and actually seemed close to tears. The crowd displayed similar emotions. Women wept openly and many a man wiped furtive tears. Almost every man of military age was regarded with something akin to worship.

Billy was so strongly affected he had to blink back the tears so unbecoming to a young warrior. Tom was hard put to keep a cool demeanor. He felt his pulse pounding and heard his ears singing. The flushed faces and self-conscious movements of other young men made him wonder if he looked as foolish as they did.

An old woman laid hands on Tom and sobbed, "God bless you brave boys!"

He could only say, "Thank you, Aunt Mandy, thank you," and felt silly for doing so.

Baker waited for the tumult to subside, as though it was a storm that had to pass of its own accord. Knocking on the schoolhouse had no effect. Finally Baker spoke, his magnificent voice acting like oil on the troubled waters.

"We must have room in front! We must make room for the volunteers! Move back in front, please!"

Self-appointed aides went into the crowd, and gradually the multitude receded like the tide from a beach, leaving a clear space in front.

Baker conferred with the others on the platform, then stepped forward again. "Mr. Mark Dixon, who has taken the lead in raising this company, is absent in Indianapolis on military business. He will be represented by Mr. Jacob Bower, whom many of you know."

Jake came forward. He looked strange in an ill-fitting suit and a hat that was too small for him, but his sturdy form had assumed a soldierly bearing. Baker spoke briefly with him, then turned to the crowd.

"We have come to the solemn moment." The people quieted abruptly. "The young men who will go to fight for the Union will please give their attention to Mr. Bower."

Baker stepped back and Jake took his place. "Will them that has give their names already, an' them that wants t' give their names t'night, come t' th' front!"

The crowd was wracked with turmoil. Whirlpools and eddies disgorged young men who made their way forward. As they started to move, Burk laid his hands on Billy and Tom. "Let me git in front an' make way."

Hands, blessings, and demonstrations of respect and affection were showered on the other men moving forward, but Billy and Tom were so overshadowed by Burk that no one seemed to notice them. The people moved back in awe from the giant's path.

As the men reached the front, Jake and several assistants divided them into two groups. Those who had already given their names were lined up in front of the crowd. The others took places in a line that moved to where Calvin Dixon waited with pen, ink, and a store ledger on the edge of the platform.

Each man signed his name before he filed past Dixon. A few couldn't write and only made marks after which Dixon wrote their names. They could see nothing of the crowd because of the men who had already signed.

Burk came to the platform, took the pen and dipped it, then promptly broke it when he started to write. He was very embarrassed.

"Dern it, Burk!" scolded Dixon. "Yo're always breakin' somethin! They jist don't make things fer th' likes of you! Here, lemme git 'nother pen." He fished one from his pocket. "Here now, be keerful with this one."

Burk took the pen and scrawled his name with great care.

Tom was seized with a strange waggishness when his turn came. "You sure we're not signin' a mortgage or somethin'? Here, let me read what it says."

Dixon cackled. "This is th' biggest mor'gage you'll ever sign! It says: 'I hereby pledge t' serve in th' comp'ny of infantry bein' raised by Mark Dixon.' " He looked at Tom with a thin smile. "Yo're mor'gagin' yore life, y' know that?"

"Oh, I was afraid it might be my property or somethin'," replied Tom. "As long as it's just my life, I don't care."

His intended joke didn't go over very well. What laughter followed sounded a little forced, like no one had thought of it that way before. When Tom signed, he noticed that Burk's name was Carl Burkhart. He had always thought it was just Burk.

As they finished signing they were lined up behind the men who were already standing before the crowd. Tom's six feet enabled him to see over the heads of the men in front. The people wore serious and sorrowful expressions. Feminine sobbing and wailing sounded intermittently. An old man whose snow white hair and beard contrasted with his weathered face stood as straight as a ramrod directly in front. He was old Uncle Charley Polson, a veteran of the War of 1812, and his grandson Jim was among the volunteers.

When all the men had taken their places, Baker announced that the Reverend Howard Stevens would conclude the meeting with a prayer.

A tall, bony man stumped forward on a wooden leg, a souvenir of the Battle of Buena Vista in Mexico fourteen years before. He was dressed in a black broadcloth suit, and the leg striking the platform made hollow, reverberating sounds at precise intervals, like the knocking of doom. A deathlike stillness settled over the multitude.

"Let us bow our heads," began Stevens in a deep, sepulchral voice. "Oh Lord," he prayed, "bless these young men who go forth to fight for the Union. Be with them in the hour of battle, when the bullets and the sabers strike, and the angel of death hovers over the bloody field."

A low, moaning sound swept over the crowd.

"We cannot ask Thee, dear God, to bring all of them back to us. Some must fall, as we who have been to war well know. But we do ask Thee to take those that fall to be with Thee in Heaven, and to strengthen our souls that we may bear the fearful loss."

He paused amid a deep silence broken only by a convulsive, smothered sob from somewhere in the crowd. "Amen!" he intoned.

The meeting was over.

# 3

The Honorable Benjamin Baker reined up before the house and dismounted. It was an imposing structure of two stories with a columned porch in front and many rooms. Large trees only just coming into full leaf surrounded it on three sides. On the fourth was a tastefully laid out rose garden with neat graveled walks. A wizened old man appeared to take his horse.

"Is Doctor Bowles in?" asked Baker.

"Yes, Yer Honor," was the reply. "He don't git 'round much anymore. Jist knock."

"You needn't unsaddle the horse," instructed Baker. "Just feed and water him. I won't be long."

The old man nodded and led the horse away.

Baker reached for the big brass knocker on the door, but before he could touch it the door opened. A tall, dignified man in his sixties wearing a linen duster stood before him. He had a mane of snow white hair and was clean-shaven. "Ben!" he said in pleased surprise. "Come in! Come in! I wasn't expecting you." Except for a nose that was a little too long and a jaw that receded somewhat, the doctor was a handsome man.

"I'm on my way back to Shoals Station from Celestine and couldn't go by without stopping. You're looking well, Doctor."

"Thank you. I'm glad I can say the same for you." Bowles led the way into his study and gestured to a chair. "Have a seat." The doctor remained standing. "How would you like a glass of cold beer on this hot day? Real German beer. I have a keg brought up from Jasper every now and then during hot weather. They really know how to make beer down there, those Germans do."

"Nothing would suit me better. Trot it out. Those Germans are good Democrats, too, almost all of them."

Bowles went to the door and called, "Two glasses of beer, please, Clara!" Someone answered unintelligibly from down the hall.

The room was as Baker remembered it. The walls were lined with shelves of books, many of them large leather-bound tomes with gold lettering. The carpet would have done credit to a Turkish grand vizier, and the furniture went with it.

Bowles returned and seated himself. "I guess we are in for our first really hot spell, though it's still May."

"Yes, it's hot already today, and the whole summer is before us. It's pleasantly cool in the house, though."

"I built it to be. Two stories, big windows, and high ceilings. My wife is familiar with architecture for warm climates."

"How is Mrs. Bowles?"

"Very well, by her letters. She had to go to Louisiana on some business matters early last month. She owns property there."

"Any trouble getting back?"

"Yes, but she's on her way. I expect her by the end of the week. They're not interfering with northward traffic, at least not yet."

An old woman entered with the beer. She was exactly the age and type of the old man who had met Baker and was, in fact, his wife.

"Thank you, Clara," said Bowles.

The men took their glasses and drank.

"That's good beer," said Baker, "and very, very cold."

"I keep it in the icehouse. It's the best; old Hagenheimer makes it. He was a brewer in Germany, and his father before him, and his father's father, he says."

"I don't doubt it," replied Baker after another swallow. "I haven't had such good beer since I was at Ferdinand during the late campaign."

Then drank in silence for a few minutes.

"I'm surprised you came to see me," said the doctor as they set their empty glasses down. "You're risking your reputation for loyalty, you know. I'm in very bad repute anymore. 'Tory' is about the kindest thing I am called."

"So I understand. My friends are my friends, though, and politics won't turn me from them, even what might be called matters of state."

"I had a report on your meeting at Celestine last night. I understand it was quite enthusiastic."

"Yes, we finished raising an entire company, with some to spare."

"I also understand my name was again taken in vain."

Baker chuckled. "Yes, that was the first thing I had to contend with."

The doctor arose and paced about. "It's been over fourteen years now, and still they call me a coward. I didn't run at Buena Vista, but my regiment did, all but the company I raised myself. Why won't they admit that and stop this business?"

"I've told you before, Doctor. People have to either throw the shame on you or take it on themselves, so they throw it on you. That's human nature."

"It's been proved time and time again. The court of inquiry exonerated me and in fact commended me for bravery." He paced some more. "Then there are the men of my company, those that survived. There are Howard Stevens, Jake Bower, and a dozen others who still live around here. They don't shrink from telling the truth. We beat back three cavalry charges, and only about a third of us were still on our feet when Jeff Davis led his Second Mississippi in the counterattack that saved us."

"I know all that. Everybody knows all that. But it doesn't make any difference. People will believe what they want to believe, and they want to believe that you led the Second Indiana in ignominious flight from Santa Anna's cavalry. Nothing will change it. You might as well resign yourself to it."

Bowles sighed and shook his head. "People are simply not rational beings. They're governed entirely by their emotions. I see evidence of that all about me now."

"That is one of the first things a man in public life learns," agreed Baker. "But it may be for the good as well as for the bad. They are much aroused now."

"How well I know that," replied the doctor. He returned to his chair, leaned back, and looked at the ceiling. "But I do not agree that it is for the good now."

"You haven't changed your mind, even now? I had hoped you had."

"No," said Bowles heavily, "I cannot; I am not governed by my emotions. I see things too clearly."

"What do you see that I do not?"

"I can see the past, and in it I see the future. I am a student of history, as you are, but have the advantage of being isolated from public affairs. I can reflect. You cannot. You are too much caught up in the events of our time."

"Perhaps it is only that I know what is going on and you do not." Baker looked at his friend challengingly.

"You are too much exposed to the storms sweeping the public. You have been torn loose from your moorings."

"You are a difficult man to argue with, Doctor."

Bowles sat forward in his chair, a frown of concentration on his face. "Those Republicans are old Whigs, most of them. Look at Lane, or Lincoln. Their party died as dead as the dodo after they couldn't elect even Scott in '52. If you can't elect a military hero in this country, you can't elect anyone. Then none of them had ever had anything.

They were always a minority here in the West, fighting with their backs to the wall for dear life itself. Only once in a while would they get a few crumbs. What did Lincoln have to show for twenty years in politics as a Whig? A single two-year term in Congress. That's all, except for a few years in the Illinois legislature, but those weren't even crumbs. Lean, lanky, and hungry, that's what they were, always on the outside, looking in while we Democrats feasted. Don't you remember?"

"I remember we Democrats used to have things all our own way. We do not anymore."

"They tried the antiforeign movement, Know-Nothingism. They tried temperance. They were desperate after the Whig party died out. They would try anything. Then this issue of slavery in the territories came up in Kansas. They tried it, like they had Know-Nothingism and temperance, but it turned out to be a gold mine. They found they could get up a lot more enthusiasm over saving the territories from slavery than with things like protective tariffs and national banking. But it was dangerous; they knew that. Several of them hung back, like old Dick Thompson at Terre Haute and Tom Slaughter down in Harrison County. They knew the South would eventually rebel and leave the Union if they pushed it far enough to win the North and take over the national government."

"I tend to believe they deceived themselves on that score," interjected Baker.

"I have known Henry S. Lane for thirty years. He is incapable of self-deception. I don't know Lincoln, but I'll bet he's even more coolheaded and calculating than Lane. Look how he eliminated Seward, Chase, and Bates at their Chicago convention and took the nomination. They never knew what hit them."

"Your acquaintance among our senior politicians is more extensive than mine."

Bowles got up and began pacing about. "Keeping slavery out of the territories! They knew there was no more chance of that than slavery on the moon. What could you do with slaves in New Mexico? Raise cactus and rattlesnakes?"

Baker chuckled. "I hardly think that would pay."

Bowles went on pacing. "They scared the people with this bogeyman, convinced them that the planters and their slaves would take over the territories and keep free white men from moving west and getting land. They knew that would never happen. They built up their party by deception and fakery." The doctor took his seat again. "Then the day of reckoning came. They won and the South began to secede. They could have stopped it by merely agreeing that New Mexico would be open to slavery. That would have soothed Southern pride and assured Southerners that they were dealing with moderate and reasonable men." Bowles's voice rose. "But they couldn't do it, or it would destroy their party! It would have been an admission that there had never been any danger of slavery in the territories, and that they had been consciously and deliberately deceiving the people all the time. They would have been put back to where they were when they were Whigs. So, they put their party before their country and stood fast. Now we have a war." Bowles got up again. "Sometimes I even think they wanted a war. Their reason for being, keeping slavery out of the territories, disappeared when they won the election. They needed another issue to prop up their party and keep it going. And what could have more appeal to the masses than a war to restore the Union?"

Baker shook his head. "I thoroughly agree with much of what you've said, Doctor. I have no love for the Republicans." He leaned forward and looked at his friend intently. "But that does not touch upon the principal issue of the present; restoring the Union. I grant that the Republicans are mainly responsible for the present state of affairs." Baker raised his voice for emphasis. "But the Union *must be restored,* and as things now stand, that can only be done on the field of battle."

"I understand you put one thing above restoring the Union at Celestine last night." Bowles sat down again.

Baker was startled. "What?"

"As it was reported to me, you said you would rather live in a country the size of a postage stamp than—"

"Oh yes!" exclaimed Baker. "The abolition of slavery."

"You think there is no danger of that?" The doctor fastened his eyes on Baker's.

"Of course not."

"It will come," said Bowles with conviction. "You will see. Once the war gets under way proper, and blood is shed, the people will get more and more aroused. If it lasts long enough, they will finally get to hate the South so much they will want to destroy it entirely, slavery and all. The Republicans will carefully cultivate this. They envision a country of factories, warehouses, and railroads, a country in which slavery has no place. They will also see how the issue of human freedom will add nobility to their cause in Europe and in much of the North."

"The people will never stand for it!" said Baker emphatically, but Bowles could tell he was perturbed.

"Yes, slavery will go," the doctor went on. "Slaves will become freemen, free to go anywhere they desire. They will aspire to all the rights of freemen. They will get these rights, although it may take a century or two. They will have the help of the preachers, the philosophers and the literati. There may be blood, but it will come in the end, because the pressure will never let up. It will be like gravity, and the people will eventually tire and give in. First will come the right to vote and to hold public office. Then the right to use all places of public accommodation, including the schools." Bowles leaned forward and looked earnestly at his friend. "Ben, I will not see it. You will not see it. Your children will not see it, and perhaps not even their children. But someday, someday, if the North wins the war, white women will take black men all over this country, even here in French Lick Springs."

Baker shook off his perturbation. Bowles had gone too far. "I respect you too much to say you talk nonsense, my friend. But what you say is preposterous. You are too isolated, and you brood too much."

Bowles smiled sadly. "I'm certainly isolated. You could even say I am besieged. Perhaps I brood, although I prefer to believe that I think."

Baker pulled out his watch. "I must go. I hadn't intended to stay so long, and will have to push my horse to get back to Shoals Station in time."

"You are speaking at another meeting?"

"Yes, at Terre Haute, tomorrow night. It's Voorhees' district, but he pleaded business and they persuaded me to do it." He arose from his chair.

Bowles went to a window and called for Baker's horse to be brought, then accompanied his friend to the door. "We go, each according to his lights," he said laconically.

Baker did not reply. They reached the porch and waited for the horse.

"Take care," said Baker as the animal was brought up.

Bowles pulled aside his duster and showed a revolver in his belt. "I will. This is my companion, night and day."

Baker whistled. "I didn't realize it was that bad."

"My life is threatened almost daily."

"Perhaps you should leave the country until the war excitement dies down."

The doctor's lip curled. "I'll never run. I'll die first. I'm the hero of Buena Vista, you know," he added bitterly.

Baker shook his head, mounted his horse, and rode away with only a wave of his hand. Bowles watched him until he was out of sight, then went back into the house.

# 4

It was dark when Tom rode up to the house, dismounted, and hitched his horse to a small tree in front. A man inside heard him and came out the front door. The light from inside showed him to be a small fellow, slender and sandy-haired, with a listless air about him.

"Come on in, Tom!" he called. "Sally's 'spectin' ye."

"Howdy, Mr. Napier. How are you?"

"All right, I reckon. Ain't been sleepin' too good, though. All th' 'citement 'bout th' war, I reckon." As Tom walked up to him, he said, "I hear you fellers air leavin' fer Injinap'lis t'morra."

"Yes, I guess we're finally going."

Napier opened the door and they went inside. "I never 'lowed yer pa'd let Billy go."

Tom took off his hat and hung it on a peg. "Well, he wouldn't have, but then Billy swore he was going as soon as he was eighteen, in December, and Pa figured he'd better go with me if he was going anyhow."

Sally entered from the kitchen in back. Tom had never seen her so beautiful. She was a little flushed, and her rose-petal lips were slightly open, revealing the tips of her even, white teeth. Her golden hair was put up in a neat roll, showing her shapely little ears and the delicate outline of her jaw. From her waist up her dress fitted like a glove, and her deep blue eyes regarded him lovingly. "I'm glad to see you, Tom," she said softly.

"And I'm glad to see you, Sally," he replied. "It'll probably be the last time in a long time."

"I know," she replied sadly as she came to meet him. Tom took her hand and they looked into each other's eyes until her father cleared his throat abruptly.

"Have a seat, Tom," he said. "Th' ol' lady'll be out d'rectly."

"She's here now," said a woman from the doorway of the kitchen as Tom and Sally seated themselves on a couch. It was Mrs. Napier and it was easy to see where Sally had gotten her beauty. Although well into middle age, the mother was still a "looker," in local parlance.

People had always wondered why she had married little Mort Napier, an insignificant fellow who would never amount to anything.

"Howdy, Mrs. Napier," said Tom as he got to his feet. "I hope you're well."

"Oh, I'm fine, Tom. Go on an' set back down. I've got some work t' do yet out in th' kitchen, Sally's work." She smiled indulgently at her daughter. "She ain't hardly been able t' do enything t'day, too nervous an' all."

Sally looked down and her flush deepened.

"Well, in these days just about everybody's nervous, I guess," Tom replied. "You go ahead and don't mind me." He resumed his seat and he and Sally fell to looking at each other again.

"Humph." It was Sally's father again, but the couple paid him no heed. "Well," he said at length as he got up from his chair, "I've gotta go out t' th' barn a minit t' look 'bout a new calf."

"Yes, sir," replied Tom. "We'll see you when you get back."

Napier went back through the kitchen. "Whar's m' coat?" they heard him ask; then the outside door in the kitchen opened and closed.

Shortly Mrs. Napier appeared in the doorway. "I'm goin', too," she announced. "Hit's a lil' heifer and I wanta make shore hit's all right. Y' cain't trust menfolks 'bout sich things."

"Yes'm," said Tom, "I guess you're right about that." Mrs. Napier disappeared and the door went through its cycle again.

"Well, Sally," Tom began, "we're leaving tomorrow. Word just came today."

"I know," she sighed, her eyes glowing strangely. "We heard."

"I expect to be gone a long time, three years," he said heavily.

"I'll wait for you, Tom," she said as she reached for his hand and leaned toward him. Her nearness affected him strongly.

"It's for the future, Sally, the future of our country, and our children. I want them to live in a big country that's all in one piece, so they won't be quarreling and having wars all the time, like in Europe."

"Our children, our babies," she said softly as she brought her face close to his. He was drawn to her, and the touch of her cheek sent a thrill through him. She moved closer and he could feel her firm little breasts against his shoulder.

Suddenly he drew back. "We can't be carrying on like this! We're not married yet! You'd think we'd been meetin' in th' woods, like Jim Keelson an' that Evans girl that had t' get married last year!"

Sally wasn't put off. She leaned close again and her arm stole about him. "I'd meet you in th' woods, Tom," she said breathlessly as she nestled close to him.

Tom arose abruptly. "You shouldn't talk like that, Sally! What's got into you? We're respectable people!"

Sally looked up at him. Her lips were parted and her eyes were wide. "There might never be any babies, Tom," she said tremulously. "You might not come back, like most of the men from 'round here that went to Mexico."

Tom turned away and began pacing the floor. "Maybe we should've got married before this," he said in an agitated voice, "but I just don't think a man goin' off to war should get married. It's a worry to him, an' he might not want t' fight, thinkin' 'bout his wife, an' his fam'ly." He stopped pacing and his voice gained assurance as he faced her again. "But I'll get back; I'm sure of it. No bullet will ever be molded that'll kill me. I'll be back, and then we'll be married, after it's all over."

He saw tears start down her cheeks and was devastated. He knelt before her and sought her hand. "Here now, don't cry, Sally; don't cry," he pleaded. Then he felt tears come to his own eyes. What was wrong with him? He hadn't cried since he was a baby.

"Oh, oh," she sobbed, "it was so close, only till June, and we've been waiting so long—"

The back door opened and Tom got up. By the time the Napiers had put away their coats and come back into the room, Tom was at one end of the couch and Sally at the other.

# 5

Tom and Billy were to leave for Indianapolis, where the regiment was assembling, that morning, and the house had been a bustle of activity since before dawn. One of the problems had been their mother's insistence that they take things besides what Jake had told them to bring. It wasn't just socks and enough underwear to last for a year, but nightshirts and cooking utensils. All Tom would take was a change of clothing, enough cooked food for two meals, a small skillet, and a tin pot.

"That Jake Bower don't know everything," the mother sniffed. "He's all puffed up now, runnin' around all over the county with Mark Dixon and Mr. Rivers, tellin' ever'body what to do. He was just a farmer a few months ago, no better'n anybody else."

After they were ready they sat on the front porch in view of the road and waited. The sun was well up and its rays slanted like golden arrows through the trees.

Billy couldn't sit still. After a while he got up and started walking about. "I wisht they'd come," he said impatiently. "We been waitin' over two months fer them t' git things ready up at Indianap'lis, an' I'm sick an' tired uv waitin', sick an' tired uv hit."

"Well, there was a lot to do, getting guns and uniforms and equipment," said Tom. "Colonel Rivers said he wasn't going to take us up there till everything was ready. There's no sense in just going up there to sit around."

"That Rivers'll make you a good colonel," the father assured them. "He was a cap'n in Mexico, in a Kentucky reg'ment, an' they say he was in th' army for a while after that, before he came up here 'n' settled down there in Posey County."

Billy continued to pace the floor. "Looks like we coulda gone up thar an' done somethin'," he grumbled.

"Don't be in such a hurry, Billy," admonished Tom. "They took us for three years, and we'll be gone a long time."

"Forever, maybe," mourned the mother.

"Don't look at it like that, Sarah," said her husband. "Keep hold of yourself now. You've been doin' purty well here lately."

"That was mainly 'cause I kept hoping they'd forget it up there, or they'd decide to quit fighting or something." She looked sadly at the floor.

"Don't start up agin' now, Ma," interjected Billy. "We gotta go. You know that. We done signed up. An' don't be tellin' Tom t' take keer uv me. I've heered 'nough uv that. Ye'd think I wuz jist a baby t' hear ye talk."

"That's no way to talk to your mother," reproved his father. "It's only natural for a mother to feel thataway about her youngest, that's really just a boy yet. We're only lettin' you go so you can go with Tom 'stead of by yourself. We could've kept you by tellin' 'em you wasn't eighteen yet."

"Yeah, I know, I know. I've heered that a hunert times, too." Billy walked toward the road. "I'm gonna go see if they're comin'."

They watched him go. When he was out of hearing his mother said softly, "Tom."

"Yeah, Ma?"

"Take good care of Billy, Tom. He's so young, and he don't know about bad women and such. You'll be in with a big bunch of men, and there'll be bad ones among them, drinkin' an' gamblin' and carryin' on."

"I will, Ma," promised Tom, "and Billy will pay attention to me. He's a good boy that way."

"Help him on the march," she went on, "and in battle . . . in battle—" her voice trailed off into sobs.

John put his arm around her. "Now, Sarah, don't start carryin' on again. These boys will be all right. You don't want them to go away rememberin' you crying' an' carryin' on, do you?"

Sarah regained control and sat watching Billy for a time. He was pacing up and down the road, occasionally stopping to throw rocks at trees. "No," she said in a trembling voice, "I don't want them to remember me like that. I just hope and pray I'll see them again, and that they'll come home safe and sound."

"We will, Ma," Tom assured her. He saw for the first time that she was growing old. She had always looked so young and fresh that strangers had been known to take her for his sister, or his wife. They wouldn't anymore. She was still youthfully slender, her face unwrinkled and her hair reddish-blond, but the freshness was gone. It made a tremendous difference, and it startled him to think that the change had occurred only since early spring. It was as though she had began to fade like the forest flowers that come in March and die in May.

"There's something else, Tom," she said with a tremor in her voice. "You remember my brother Henry, don't you, what he looked like, with his big red beard, when he visited with us two years ago? You'd know him if you saw him, wouldn't you, Tom?"

"Of course I would, Ma. I'd know Henry a mile off."

"You know that letter we got. He's joined up with them." Her voice began to quiver.

"I know what you're thinkin', Sarah," interjected her husband. "Don't worry now. Henry's in the cavalry. They won't be fightin' with foot soldiers like Tom an' Billy is goin' to be." He turned to Tom. "Ain't that right, Tom?"

"Yeah, that's right. Cavalry's just used for scoutin' mostly. When they fight, it's just against other cavalry."

"I don't know anything about all that," replied Sarah. "I just know he'll be your enemy and you'll be his. And then there's all my cousins in Virginia—"

"You're goin' to have to stop worryin' about that, Sarah. You'll just make yourself sick. They'll be thousands of them, all mixed up, and there's almost no chance they'll ever come up against Tom and Billy." He put his arm about his wife to comfort her. "Now, there's a big bunch of men goin' from this county," he went on, "a hundred of 'em. Twenty-five from this township, boys that have knowed each other all their lives. They'll stick together and get through it all right."

"Yeah," interjected Tom. "We're all cut from the same cloth, except the Germans from further down in the county. And they're good boys, too. It's just that we never mixed with them much. Most of them don't know a word of English."

John laughed. "They'll have to learn English commands, anyhow, but that oughtn't to be too hard. Just a few words. Somebody said half of the comp'ny will be Germans. I never would have expected that."

"Me neither," replied Tom. "Most of them weren't even born in this country, and those that were have grown up speakin' German and thinkin' German just like they'd been born over there."

"They say some of them was in the army in Germany and know all about soldierin'. One of them was even an officer."

"Who says?" asked Tom.

"Jake told me. He's gonna use 'em t' drill th' rest of you. Nobody but him in the whole company has any experience, and he says he can't do it all." John laughed again. "Said if they can't learn English, you-all will have to learn German."

The mother sat sunk in sadness all the while, paying no attention to what was said and staring unseeingly at the floor of the porch. Her depression lay like a blanket over them all, even on Billy across the road. Tom essayed to lift it. "Smile for me, Ma. Pa says you always look so pretty when you smile."

Sarah tried her best, but it was so strained it was really not a smile at all. Her bosom heaved, but she controlled herself. Her husband wordlessly embraced her, and she rested her head on his chest.

Tom was embarrassed and looked away, watching Billy throw rocks.

"Tom," his father said at length, "I been meanin' to ask you about goin' over to Napier's last night. Sally's goin' to wait for you, isn't she?"

Tom nodded affirmatively but said nothing.

"It's a shame," sighed the mother. "Here you were goin' to get married th' last of June, not even a week off now. You've got that old Haskins house all fixed up t' live in. You've even bought another team of mules and that wheat-harvestin' machine."

"Oh, Pa can use the mules and that harvester. The same with th' rest of my tools. And that house can wait. I was just goin' t' live in it till I could build a new one this winter. I didn't spend much money on it anyhow."

"I'll deed that south forty t' you as soon as you come back," said his father. "When you put that with that adjoinin' eighty acres you bought from Haskins, you'll have a nice farm. Eighty acres cleared and most of it bottomland."

"What about their new house?" asked the mother.

John chuckled. "I wasn't goin' t' tell him about that. It was supposed t' be a surprise."

"What about a new house?" asked Tom.

"Oh well, I might as well tell you," sighed his father. "I'm goin' t' tear down that old Haskins house and build you a new one where it is. Old Dan Martin is goin' t' help me, and we'll build it like Sally wants." He laughed and slapped his knee. "Eight rooms we're countin' on, a big house for a big family."

Tom grinned. "I see you're countin' on a lot of grandchildren." He nodded and laughed. "I'll try not to disappoint you."

Even the mother laughed a little before John went on. "Old Dan Martin's 'bout th' best house builder in these parts, and you've got a good location, there on that south hillside out of th' winter wind and in the sun when th' leaves are off. You've got a good spring, too, not fifty feet away. I'll dig it out and line it with rock; then I'll build a springhouse over it."

"That'll be too much work, Pa, and it'll cost you a lot of money. 'Course I'll pay you for it—"

John interrupted, "Oh, no, you won't! It's th' least I can do for you, considerin' how you've helped me all these years."

Tom started to speak, but his father cut him off. "And don't worry about th' work! I'll just not plant as much as I have been, and I never have much to do in th' winter anyhow. That's when we'll do th' buildin', and I'll have it all ready for you an' Sally t' move in when you come back."

"If he comes back," said Sarah half to herself, looking bleakly at the floor.

Her husband ignored the regression. "It'll be a lot better'n what I had when I started out, Tom. I just had forty acres and a little old log cabin with two rooms."

"I wish we were back in that little old log cabin," said the mother fervently, "and the two boys was little again instead of going off to war." She sighed. "Those were happy days. There wasn't any Republicans or any secession and war then. I just wish those Republicans had never been heard of."

Billy yelled and came running from the road. "They're comin'! They're comin'! I seen 'em down the road!"

"Are you sure?" asked Tom. "It might be somebody else."

"Hit's them fer shore," panted Billy. "I could see Burk in the bunch."

"Yeah, you can see him a mile off," said the father. "It's them all right."

Everybody got up but the mother, whose bosom was heaving again. "Mother, Mother," said her husband gently. "Get up now. The boys are leavin'. Don't you want to go to the road with them?"

Sarah compressed her lips and rose. As they walked toward the road she said in a tremulous voice, "Be sure and write, Tom, and you, too, Billy. It'll be a big help if we can hear from you now and then."

"We will," assured Tom. "We'll write every week. I'll write one week and Billy the next."

"There'll be times when you can't," said John, "when you're marchin' an' fightin'. Just write when you can after you leave Indianapolis."

They reached the road and waited, watching the group approach, with Burk standing out like a mother hen among her chicks.

"Air ye all ready to go?" called a slender dark youth among them as they drew near. He was Johnny Conrad, the neighbors' son.

"Yep, all ready," replied Billy eagerly.

"You're walkin to Shoals Station, then takin' the train?" asked his father.

"That's right," replied Johnny. "We could've got wagins, but Jake said hit'd be a good idy t' walk an' begin t' git used t' marchin'. We'll git t'gether with the rest of th' company at Shoals Station. Diff'runt bunches frum diff'runt places is goin' diff'runt ways."

"Them Germans frum down 'round Jasper has got a long ways t' go, fifteen er twenty mile, I guess," said John.

"Well, we gotta git goin'," said Burk apologetically. Jake had put him in charge of the group.

The father shook hands with his two sons, and the mother embraced them. She clung to Billy until he began to squirm. Much to her family's relief, she bore up bravely otherwise.

As the group started off, the father said jocularly, "You see that these boys behave, Burk. Whup 'em if they won't."

Burk grinned but said nothing.

John and Sarah Taylor stood in the road watching the men march away. Just before they reached a curve that would take them out of sight, Tom and Billy turned and waved without breaking their stride. They were gone, as though the forest had swallowed them. John put his arm around his wife, and they walked slowly back to their empty and lonely house.

# 6

The regiment was quartered in buildings formerly used for the exhibition of livestock at the state fairgrounds near Indianapolis. Little had been done in the way of conversion during the warm spring and summer months. Hay was still much in evidence but was now used for bedding rather than for feed.

Tom, Billy, and some of their friends sat before their quarters in the early evening talking and smoking. It had been a hard day's drilling, and now they were resting.

A man came from between the buildings and headed toward them. "Howdy, fellers!"

"Well, if hit ain't George Sanders!" exclaimed Johnny Conrad. "Have they fin'ly let ye outa th' horspital, George?"

"Yep, fin'ly let me go." George put down a box he was carrying and sat on it. He was a slender blond fellow of average height.

"How're you feeling?" asked Tom.

"Purty good. I been over th' runnin' off fer over a week now, but I jist couldn't git my stren'th back." He sighed. "I jist reported t' Jake, an' he says I got a lot t' larn."

"Well, yore place in th' hay's still thar, an' I hid yore waterproof 'way so nobody'd steal hit," said Johnny. "Y' want me t' git hit out fer ye?"

"Naw, naw, I'm sick uv layin' 'round. I'll stay up an' talk. I gotta find out what's been goin' on since I been gone." He produced a pipe. "Enybody got eny terbaccer?"

Tom handed George a plug. He crumbled the end of it into his pipe, then gave it back. "Thank ye, Tom." He lit his pipe and puffed contentedly. "I'm shore glad t' be back. Horspitals is awful places."

"How's that?" asked Ben Noble through his black beard.

"Cain't do nothin'. Lay 'round all th' time. Ever'body sick an' men a-dyin'."

"Many of 'em die?"

"A good many, brain fever mostly. Some frum measles."

"Yeah, I heard brain fever wuz bad, mostly in th' Thirty-first."

"Hit's 'bout played out now. No new fellers sick with hit fer over a week now. Measles is bad, though."

"Well, measles is bad, but they gin'rally don't kill ye, an' that brain fever does." Noble shook his head gravely. "I'm shore glad we didn't git hit in our reg'ment."

"Well, what's been goin' on?" asked George. "We'd jist got our rifles an' uniforms when I took sick, an' wuz gittin' reddy t' 'lect lootenants an' sargints."

"Oh, they wuzn't eny 'lection!" laughed Billy. "Th' colonel put a stop to hit jist 's soon's he found out 'bout hit. He said th' army wuz no place fer 'lections, an' he didn't keer how many uv th' other reg'ments done hit. He let th' ones that'd raised comp'nies be cap'ns all right, but he 'pinted all th' lootenants till they gits their commissions. He let th' cap'ns pick th' sargints an' corp'rils."

"How'd them fellers that wuz goin' 'round 'lectioneerin' like hit?" asked George.

"They didn't like hit a'tall," replied Ben, "an' some uv 'em went t' see th' colonel 'bout hit." He laughed. "They didn't have no more t' say 'bout hit atter that, though, nary a word!"

George nodded and puffed his pipe. "He done right in that. Y' cain't 'lect officers an' sich like y' do county 'sessers er somethin'. Too many blatherskites'd git 'lected if'n ye did."

Everyone seemed to agree with him. "Well, what else y'been doin'?" asked George.

"Drillin', drillin', an' more drillin'," replied Billy. "We're real soljers now. Y' oughta see us drill. Th' colonel says we're th' best comp'ny in th' reg'ment."

"Jake an' his Dutch drillmasters done that," interjected Ab Inman, a tall, lanky, lantern-jawed fellow. "Cap'n Dixon ain't drilled us but twice, an' he didn't do too good at hit when he did. Got us all mixed up once."

"Dutch drillmasters?" queried Sanders.

"Germans," replied Ab. "Ha'f th' comp'ny's Germans, y'know, an' some uv 'em wuz in th' army over thar. Lootenant Mertens wuz an officer, an' Kemper's 'nother'n, only he wuzn't no officer. He's our platoon sargint, an' he's some feller."

"Yeah? What d'ya mean?"

"Fifteen year in th' Prussian army. He knows drill like a book, only he ain't too good speakin' English." Ab laughed shortly. "Sometimes he fergits an' gives th' commands in German, an' only th' Germans follers 'em, when he's drillin' th' comp'ny enyhow. Th' rest uv us jist stands thar." He cackled gleefully. "Hit's a sight!"

"Oh, I kin foller 'em," interjected Billy. "I know 'em all."

"Yeah, I've noticed that," remarked Noble. "How d'ye do hit? I cain't understan' a word uv hit."

"Jist payin' close 'tention, an' Fred Anders is teachin' me German, a little 'long. He's frum Jasper, an' his pa's a doctor."

"Yeah, I've noticed y' with him a lot. How old is he, enyhow? He don't look t' be 's old 's you air."

"Oh, he is. He's nigh on two year older'n me. He went to a university in Germany."

"This Kemper, y' say he's our platoon sargint?" asked George.

"Yeah. Th' colonel's divided th' comp'nies up inta platoons, four uv 'em, twenty-five men in each one, an' ever'one has a sargint an' a corp'ril. We ain't got two sections in each comp'ny with two platoons in 'em an' officers commandin' 'em like we're s'posed t' have. Hit's on 'count uv not havin' 'nough officers."

"How come we ain't got 'nough officers?" George wanted to know.

" 'Cause th' gov'nor wouldn't let all th' men th' colonel picked t' be officers git commissions," Ab told him. "He wants t' pick 'em hisself, an' they say him an' th' colonel had a big argyment 'bout hit."

"He's jist politickin', that Morton is!" exclaimed Ben. "That's why he wants t' have a say 'bout pickin' officers."

"Yeah, I guess politishuns'll be politishuns, war er not," allowed George. He went on before anyone could take the subject further, "Now, if'n Kemper's our sargint, who's our corp'ril?"

"Tom is, on 'count uv bein' good at drill an' shootin'. Cain't y' see them stripes on his arm?"

Tom laughed and held up his arm for George to see. "Oh, a corporal's just a file closer, that's all."

Billy was very proud of his brother. "Aw now, they's a lot more to hit than that! Yo're in charge uv th' quarters an' next only t' Sargint Kemper in th' platoon, an' you drill us 's much's he does. Jake even had y' drill th' hull com'ny once, an' you done real good at hit."

"Whar is Kemper?" asked George. "Don't he stay with you-uns?"

"Naw," replied Billy. "Th' sargints has got speshul quarters, jist like th' officers."

"How d'ye git 'long with them Germans?" was George's next question.

"Aw, jist fine," answered Ben. "Course they ain't none uv 'em speaks hardly any English 'ceptin Lootenant Mertens an' Anders, an' they stays purty well to theirselfs." He looked at Billy. "Billy's got t' know 'em better'n enybody, I guess."

"Y'know," confided Billy, "I never knowed a one uv 'em, er eything 'bout 'em, till we come up hyar, but they're real fine fellers once y' git t' know 'em."

"That's right," agreed Ab. "I've lived right 'cross th' Padoky River frum 'em all my life. Knowed a bunch uv 'em real well. But y' know," he went on, "I never got t' whar I could unnerstan' their talkin' very well, an' I jist cain't unnerstan' how Billy's larnt hit s' good. He's gittin' so he kin even talk hit."

"He's just that way," said Tom. "He learns everything and never forgets anything. He's just got a mind like that. I found that out when I had him in school those two years I taught."

"Y' better watch out, Billy, er ye'll git t' be a reg'lar Dutchman," warned Johnny laughingly.

"Aw, I could do worse, I guess," replied Billy.

"I've seen Billy writin' some letters that wuzn't t' his ma 'n' pa, too," snickered Ab.

"Who was they to?" asked Ben.

Ab grinned slyly. "Y' better ask him."

Billy made a clean breast of it. "Aw, I jist got t' writin' t' Fred's sister. Hit don't mean nothin'. I ain't never even seen her." He couldn't hide his embarrassment, though, which led to a round of sly grinning and winking among the others.

Burk suddenly spoke up. "What I like 'bout th' Germans is their beer, like what they brung up hyar from Jasper last week." He so seldom had anything to say that everyone was startled, and Tom decided he must really like the stuff.

"What's that 'bout bringin' beer up hyar?" asked George.

Tom filled him in. "Old Mr. Hagenheimer that makes beer down at Jasper sent some up to the whole company. Brought it up in a wagon, three big kegs of it. Five days it took them."

"I shore wisht they'd send some more," sighed Ab. "That wuz th' best beer that wuz ever made."

"Fred Anders says they're makin' up t' send up 'nother batch," Billy told them.

"H'ray! H'ray!" shouted several.

Even Burk grinned and rumbled in his chest.

"I jist hope hit gits hyar 'fore we leave er somethin'," breathed Ab.

"Say, whar's Harve Akers?" asked Sanders. "Hit's strange not t' hear him carryin' on."

"He stays 'way frum us enymore," replied Conrad. "He's skeered uv Burk."

"What'd ye do t' him, Burk?" Sanders asked.

Burk only grunted, so Johnny undertook to tell. "He jerked him up by his coat collar an' shook him real good once."

"What fer?" asked George eagerly.

Tom broke in in order to spare Burk. "Oh, you know Akers, how he can get on a man's nerves." Tom knew it had been because Harve was always showing off by making Burk the butt of his jokes and getting others to laugh at him. Back home Burk had been able to avoid Harve, but the big fellow had known he could no longer do that and had decided to put an end to it.

"Y' oughta seen hit," laughed Billy. "Ol' Burk helt him out thar an' shook him till his teeth rattled."

"Well, I cain't say that I miss th' feller," said Sanders. "He shore kin be wearin' on a man."

Billy suddenly lay back and heaved a great sigh. "I'm shore gittin' awful tard uv playin' soljer! I'm all reddy t' go fight th' rebels."

"You'll git yore bellyful soon 'nough," replied Sanders. "Hit ain't no circus. I larned that frum one uv them ninety-day men that wuz in th' horspital. They wuz in western Virginny back in th' spring an' fit th' Rebels, y' know."

"Yeah, them Rebels kin shore fight," added Ab. "Look what they done t' us at Bull Run. Licked us good. Our men throwed 'way their rifles an' run like turkeys, all th' way back t' Washin'ton."

"Aw," scoffed Billy, "them wuz Easterners, abolish frum Boston an' Noo Yawk an' sich places. Western men'll never run like that, not Indiany men frum th' Pocket enyhow."

"We'll see th' elephant one uv these days," warned Noble. "Then we'll find out fer shore."

The group was impressed and took time to reflect.

Billy broke the silence. "I'd shore like t' see Injinap'lis 'fore we leaves hyar."

"None of that," said Tom emphatically. "You'd see nothin' but bad whiskey and worse women."

"Now, Tom," protested Billy, "you know they's good people in Injinap'lis, 's good 's enywhar, an' I ain't gonna drink no likker."

"Oh, there's good people in Indianapolis," admitted Tom, "and good women, too, but no soldier's ever goin' t' see 'em. Nobody'll have anything to do with soldiers 'cause of the way they carry on, nobody decent anyhow."

"I don't blame 'em," agreed Ben. "I never seen sich wild boys, drinkin' an' fightin' an' carryin' on."

"Hit's 'cause they're 'way frum home, an' nobody that knows 'em er their folks'll see 'em," explained Sanders. "That's why they're so wild."

"That Harve Akers an' his bunch is 'bout th' worst, I 'spect," said Ab. "I'll bet that's whar they air now, snuck past th' guard an' in town."

"Yeah, they say Harve's got a gurl in thar, stays with her ever' time he's in town," added Ben Noble.

"She's with Harve when she ain't with someone else," Ab informed them, "an' fer money, too."

Billy's eyes bulged. "Y' mean she's a whore?"

"Not 'zackly, I guess. She jist goes at hit when she needs money. Harve's free, I reckon."

A hurrying figure materialized in the twilight. "Hit's Fred Anders," said Billy. "What's yore hurry, Fred?" he called.

Fred was slender, and blond and looked too young to be in the army. "I haf news, boys, goot news!"

Everybody sat up like they were jerked by strings. Fred was Colonel Rivers's clerk and always knew what was going on.

"What?" came the excited query.

"Ve are going! Ve are going! To de var!"

"T' th' war? When? Whar?"

"In tree days ve go, to Wirginia!"

"Virginny! In three days! How d'ye know?"

"I haf de orders seen, from Thomas A. Schott, it vas, to de colonel, *und* I wride de reply!" Fred was really excited. His English was normally so good he scarcely had an accent.

"Frum Scott! Why, he's th' gin'ral in chief!"

"No, iss anodder Schott. He iss de . . . de assist-assistant to de secretary of var."

"Th' 'sistant sec'etary uv war! He's even higher up!" Billy threw his cap into the air. "Whoopee, boys! This is hit, shore 'nough!"

The men were all jumping and shouting, and Tom found himself tingling with excitement, although the news was what he had been expecting for a long time.

# 7

The meeting was at French Lick in Orange County, but as it was close by several men from northern Dubois County had come, John Traylor and three of his neighbors among them. Dr. Bowles was to be the main speaker, and they wanted to hear what he had to say. Most people thought he had not changed his attitude since before the war began, when he had last been heard from in public. Only a few professed to believe he had, but all wanted to hear.

Several hundred people had gathered in a grove of trees in a bottom near town. A platform with room for several people and a bench at the back had been erected, so the speakers would not use stumps. Someone said the men who worked on Bowles' big farm had put it up. It was a late summer afternoon in the first year of the war and hot enough to make the shade of the trees welcome. It was also very dry, and some of the leaves were beginning to turn.

There were very few women in the crowd and even fewer children, an ominous sign. Many men present had sons in the army and might make trouble unless the doctor had changed his views. More serious were rumors that Republicans would come from outside the area to break up the meeting, as they had several others since the war had begun. A phalanx of rough-looking characters toward the front, most of them strangers, was pointed out as proof the rumors were true. People said they were mostly from the northern part of Orange County, where there were a good many Republicans. Their behavior was purposeful and menacing, but attempts to draw them out by pointed remarks about "abolish" and "nigger lovers" met with no success. A tall well-dressed young man seemed to be their leader. He was identified as Tom Cartwright, whose father ran a store in Paoli and was about the only Republican in town.

Punctually at two o'clock several men mounted the platform, Dr. Bowles' tall figure and silver hair prominent among them. All seated themselves but a short, fat fellow who perspired profusely and seemed very nervous. He came forward and began to speak.

"Th' gen'min who 'ranged this meetin' ast me t' be temp'rary cheerman," he began, " 'n' t' 'range fur th' 'pointment uv th' perm'nant officers." He stopped and looked doubtfully at his audience as though expecting objections, but there were none. The speaker swallowed convulsively, then produced a handkerchief and wiped his face.

He put away the handkerchief and shifted his feet. "I wants t' say sumpin' 'fore we starts," he began. "Ain't nobody told me t' say hit, but I think I oughta." His eyes roved over the crowd, coming to rest on the front. "We still lives in th' United States uv Ameriky, an' th' Constitootion ain't been repealed er nuthin." He seemed to gather confidence as he spoke. "We got th' freedom uv speech yit, an' freedom of th' press, too. I wants y'all to 'member that an' not start actin' like a man cain't speak his piece no more jist 'cause they's a war on." He paused and nodded for emphasis.

"Shore, shore!" called a deep voice. "We knows all that. Them abolish up front thar ain't gonna start nothin'. They'll git their heads knocked in if they does." The speaker was a big, hulking fellow who carried a stick much too large for walking. The strangers turned to size him up. Cartwright nervously dabbed his brow with a snowy handkerchief, and his companions looked impressed.

John Conrad, Sr., snickered. "Them fellers wuz brought down here t' break up th' meetin', I'll bet," he said to Traylor. "Now they're wishin' they hadn't come."

Traylor nodded agreement. "They've got into deep water, a whole lot deeper than they 'spected."

"Yeah," chuckled Rob Sanders, "lookit young Cartwright. He's wishin' he'd never lissened t' his ol' daddy 'bout this."

"I don't 'spect t' agree with a lot that's gonna be said here," called John Traylor loudly, "but I ain't havin' no nigger-lovin' abolish Republicans comin' down here, shovin' folks 'round, n' telling' em what t' say!" There were expressions of agreement.

"That's what I say," affirmed Uncle Charley Polson, his white beard wagging. "I fit King George uv England fur that."

The fat man on the platform spoke up, his nervousness entirely gone. "Now let's git on with our business." They did. Nominations were called for, made, and voted on. Dr. Bowles was elected permanent chairman. While this was going on there was a good deal of moving about in the crowd and the strangers found themselves surrounded by what seemed to be the largest men present. One of them was John Traylor, and Uncle Charley Polson didn't let his seventy-odd years keep him back.

Bowles came forward and faced the crowd. The cut and quality of his clothing were the best. Despite the heat, he wore a fine frock coat, closely buttoned. A close scrutiny would have discerned a bulge on his right hip.

"I am honored," he began, "to have been elected chairman of a meeting of the *freemen* of this area." The crowd showed appreciation of his emphasis. "Let us hope," he added significantly, "that we remain *freemen*." The emphasis was again appreciated.

Before he could continue, one of the strangers shouted, "Booney Vistey!" and the others whooped and guffawed.

The doctor regarded the heckler. "Were you at Buena Vista, my friend?"

"Naw, but I know men what wuz!" There were more whoops and guffaws.

"No, you were not at Buena Vista, and I doubt if you know men that were, unless you know some Democrats." Bowles nodded sagely. "You were a Whig, and you didn't go because the Whigs were against the war. They hoped the wretched mongrel Mexicans would win." He let it sink in. "And now the Whigs are all Republicans!"

"The Republicans are all for this war," shouted Cartwright, "and the loyal Democrats are too! There's Tories an' traitors that ain't, though!"

Bowles studied Cartwright and his companions. "If you're so strongly for the war, why aren't you in the army?" he asked coldly. "You're military age, and most of your friends are, too. Why don't you go?" he challenged.

The group was angered. "We gotta stay home an' watch men like you—" began Cartwright hotly, but the stick that was too large for walking was suddenly thrust forcefully through the press and against his shoulder.

"Shet up, you," growled the bearer. "An' th' 'rest uv you, too," he added, raising his voice. "I come t' hear th' speakin', an' I aims t' hear it!" He glowered at them. "If'n I hears eny more outa you, they's gonna be trouble an' plenty of it."

Cartwright rubbed his shoulder but said nothing. His friends shifted nervously about, their eyes roving like those of trapped animals. No more was heard from them, and soon they began to slip away. Before the meeting was very far along they were all gone, Cartwright included.

Bowles resumed speaking. "My friends, we live in troubled times. There is so much clamor and hurly-burly that it is hard for a man to think, and even harder for him to think clearly." He paused and looked out over the crowd briefly.

"But we must think, and think clearly. We must not let ourselves be distracted by these cries of 'Tory' and 'traitor' coming from men who don't want us to think, but only to rush madly after them, wherever they lead us." He paced the platform briefly. "If we rush unthinkingly after them, I fear we will see the free institutions of the founding fathers come crashing down upon us, and we will have aided in their destruction."

The crowd was suitably impressed.

"I suppose," he continued, "I study history as much as anyone." He paused and surveyed the crowd. "The atmosphere of our times reminds me of the French Revolution, which brought the reign of terror, guillotines, and mass executions."

The crowd shuddered.

"Let us all hope," he intoned, "that such bloody scenes are not repeated in the United States of America in the months ahead." He stopped and looked reflective. "One can see indications that this may be, however. We have Marats and Robespierres among our public figures today. There are men who call for vengeance, for confiscating of property, for executions, and," Bowles paused for emphasis, "for an uprising of the slaves!" The crowd was struck with horror.

"Julian!" shouted someone. "He's one of 'em!"

"Yes," replied Bowles sorrowfully, "we even have men in Indiana who call for these things, but there is nothing we can do about whom those bloody-minded Quakers up in the Fifth District send to Congress, those idealistic, humanitarian pacifists up there, those devoted followers of the teachings of Christ, who so strongly oppose the shedding of blood." His voice dripped with sarcasm.

"Jist their blood, that's all!" shouted a strident voice.

The doctor smiled. "I'm afraid that's about what it amounts to." He paced the platform. "I used to respect the Quakers," he went on, "but no more. I gave them credit for sincerity. That was my mistake. If they were sincere," he said, his voice rising, "if they were not the most arrant hypocrites God ever saw, they would be shouting for peace, for a stop to the fighting and bloodshed, instead of calling for war, for blood, even for extermination!" The crowd agreed vociferously.

Bowles paced the platform for a time. Suddenly he stopped and faced the crowd. "I am not a Quaker," he began, "but I am for peace; I wish this unnatural, fratricidal war, which is taking so many young lives, would cease."

There were shouts of disagreement. "Hey! Hold on there!" called someone.

Bowles held up his hands. "Please, hear me out!"

The crowd quieted.

"You are free," he continued, "to disagree with me, but I will tell you why I favor an immediate armistice in this war." He paused and ran his eyes over the crowd. "I look at the faces of men who have sons in the army, many of them." He nodded sorrowfully. "I fear that if the war goes on, many of them will perish, and their bones will molder on faraway fields."

Many were impressed and rendered thoughtful.

"But we gotta restore th' Union!" cried John Traylor. "My boys went for that, an' it can't be done 'thout th' sheddin' of blood, maybe even theirs!"

"Yeah," agreed Rob Sanders. "Them Confed'rits hain't gonna jist s'render 'n' come back inter th' Union!" There were shouts of agreement.

Bowles waited until the noise ended. "Your boys went to save the Union, John, and Robert, and no finer boys ever lived. I know them, all three of them. In fact, I brought them into the world. There are others. Many of you have sons who have offered their lives for the Union. They are fine young men, all of them, the bravest and the best."

He turned and paced the platform, his hands behind his back and his head bowed. Suddenly he stopped, wheeled, and raised a hand. "But neither you nor I nor they will decide if they go on fighting only for the Union, or for other goals as well. The Republicans will decide that!" he shouted. "Lincoln, Lane, Julian, Seward, Stevens, and men like that will decide if other things are to be fought for!"

"What other things?" someone wanted to know.

"To subjugate the states to the federal government, to establish control of the country's economy by the bankers and manufacturers of New England, and," he paused dramatically, "to abolish slavery!"

"But they've promised—" began someone.

"Do you believe Republican promises? Do you believe they are honest and sincere?"

The man was struck with doubt. "Well, I dunno—"

Bowles laughed scornfully. "The truth is the Republicans are the worst set of political tricksters and demagogues this country has ever seen."

The people were struck dumb by the thought and stood gaping.

Bowles went on. "They have promised you, promised you faithfully, that the war would be *only* to restore the Union, not to subjugate the states, or free the slaves." He nodded and set his lips. "But," he shouted, "their promises are worthless!" He faced the crowd, his eyes wide and face glowing. "I know that; you know that." He lowered his voice. "Let's examine the honesty and sincerity of these Republicans." He paced briefly. "What did they build up their party on?" He waited for an answer.

"Keepin' slavery out uv th' territories!" shouted someone.

"Yes, that's it, keeping slavery out of the territories so there would be no more slave states. They went on and on about that. Slavery was going to spread all over the territories, and keep white farmers out of them, and strengthen the power of the slave states so much that they would force slavery on the free states. That's what Lincoln said when he ran for the Senate in '58, isn't it? Didn't he say that a house divided against itself cannot stand, that this country cannot exist half-slave and half-free?"

"Yep, that's what he said," admitted someone.

"That was how they scared the people into stampeding into their party by the thousands and scores of thousands. They, the Republicans, promised to save the country, the whole country, from the curse of slavery. A desperate fight by the people of the free states was necessary to save it, and they would lead this fight."

Bowles stopped and studied his audience. "Then," he asked, "what was the first thing they did when enough Southern states had left the Union to give them majorities in both houses of Congress? Remember now, this was their first chance to save the territories, and eventually the whole country, from being taken over by slavery." He paused dramatically. "What did they do? Did they pass a law prohibiting slavery in the territories?"

"Naw, they didn't," was the reply. "They ain't done it yet!"

"What did they do, then?" No one had an answer. "Well, I'll tell you what they did. They passed a protective tariff bill so New England manufacturers could charge you higher prices and make more money! That's what they did!"

The doctor turned and paced the platform while it sank in, then faced the crowd again. "They knew there was *no need* to prohibit slavery in the territories. It could never go into any of them. Slavery can't go where cotton won't grow, and it won't grow in any of the territories. That was just their bogeyman, to scare the people with, and get elected to office, so they could pass a bill that would take money out of your pockets and put it into the pockets of Yankee cloth makers and ironmongers."

Bowles turned aside and paced the platform again. He stopped. "That's why I have no faith in Republican sincerity and honesty. That's why I put no stock in their promises. That's why no one can believe the *Lincolns,* the Mortons, the Lanes, the Colfaxes, and all of them.

They promise to fight the war *only* to restore the Union, and to leave slavery alone where it exists, to keep the Negroes from leaving the South to come up here and live among us." His voice rose a note, and he gestured emphatically. "They promise you this only to enlist your support for the war and lure your sons into the army. Now that they have you, they are deciding when to announce *what else* the war will be fought for!"

"What else?" asked someone challengingly.

"Ask George W. Julian and men of his ilk. They can tell you. I have no more to say." With that Bowles took a seat.

A hum of anxious conversation swept the crowd. Men wore troubled faces. The doctor had scored and he knew it.

Bowles was delayed after the meeting. When he arrived home he noticed movement in the shadow of the trees in front. He dismounted instantly on the other side of his horse and drew his revolver. "Hit's jist me, Doc—Jake Cox," came a voice. The doctor holstered the weapon as the wizened little man came to take his horse. Afterward he went back where Cox waited. He was the man who had carried the big stick at the meeting.

"Hello, Jacob," said Bowles. "I appreciate your squelching those Republicans Cartwright sent down here. They would have caused trouble."

"Oh, t'wuzn't nothin'," replied Cox. "I wuz hopin' they'd put up a fight." He nodded grimly. "Then we'd a larned 'em a lesson."

"Well, I'm glad we had no trouble. The Republicans would have made a big thing of it."

Cox changed the subject. "Well, I'm leavin' t'morra."

"You have everything arranged?"

"Yep. M' propity is all in m' wife's name now; they oughtn't t' be able t' take it."

"You still have my letter to General Pillow and the list of places where you can stop until you get into Tennessee?"

"Yep, still got 'em."

"Be careful with them, even the list. My handwriting would be recognized, and aiding and encouraging men to go south and join the Confederate army is a serious offense."

"I'll be keerful." Cox paused a moment. "You'll look after m' wife an' take keer o' things, won't ye, Doc?" He sounded anxious.

"Of course I will," Bowles assured him. "You needn't worry about a thing. If they try to take your property or anything, I'll get the best lawyer in the country."

Cox was reassured. "I sure 'preciate it, Doc. I hate t' leave m' wife all 'lone 'gin somethin' like that."

Bowles extended his hand. "Good luck, Jacob, and remember, you'll be fighting for the salvation of the whole country. Unless the South wins, the white race is doomed."

Cox took Bowles's hand in a crushing grip. "I cain't say hit like you kin," he said fervently, "but I'm shore I'm doin' the right thing."

Afterward Cox faded back under the trees and Bowles went toward the house.

# 8

The regiment had broken camp and was on its way to war. It marched through the streets of Indianapolis toward the Governor's Circle, where there was to be a ceremony before it went on to entrain. There would be a flag presentation and a farewell speech by Congressman Baker, substituting for the governor, who was in Washington on urgent business.

It was harvesttime and notice had been short, so few friends and relatives would be present. The regiment had no band because Colonel Rivers scorned bands as useless encumbrances, but one had been borrowed and would be waiting at the circle. It was from an all-German regiment and was supposed to be the best there was.

The men marched in step, their footfalls sounding like a great muffled drum. They wore full field equipment. Packs, precisely folded and fastened, were on their backs, and canteens swung by their sides. Around their waists were dark leather ammunition pouches and sword bayonets in scabbards. Their dark blue caps and coats with light blue trousers were in sober contrast to the colorful uniforms of earlier units.

Always before, the march of a regiment through the streets had been like a holiday event, with the men rarely in step and seldom staying in ranks. They would grin, wave, and call out, generally to people they had never seen before. The people along the line of march would cheer and call back. This time it was different. The men marched in precise step and alignment, eyes forward and faces set in expressions of blank sobriety. The overtures of the spectators met with no response and soon ceased.

When the regiment reached the circle, the men marched around half its circumference, then halted and faced front in answer to sharp commands. They saw before them an elevated platform fronting the old governor's mansion, now empty and becoming dilapidated. The colonel put them at rest in place, then joined the group on the platform, which included Congressman Baker and a young woman.

She was a beautiful brunette, dressed fashionably but tastefully, and was the immediate target of a thousand admiring male eyes. She maintained a quiet composure, looking steadily over the heads of the men in front.

To the right of the platform, the band struck up with a thump of drums and a blare of brass. The men stood listening to the music with their rifles at the trail. The band played a lilting march and more than lived up to its reputation. Tom had never heard one that could compare with it.

A crowd had begun to collect in the unoccupied part of the circle, and people were standing in front of the surrounding buildings and at their windows. Their numbers grew rapidly until almost every space was filled, probably because of the excellence of the music, since departing regiments had become commonplace. The only person from home Tom ever saw was Calvin Dixon, who stood close to the platform. He had no crops or livestock to keep him away.

The band finished its first number, and the director turned to bow toward the regiment. He was a tall, thin, aesthetic-looking captain who wore glasses. The bandsmen behaved much like the men drawn up before them and handled their instruments with proficiency and precision, almost like they were weapons.

The ceremony began with a short speech by one of several men on the platform with Baker. It was a conventional patriotic speech such as everyone had already heard enough of, and Tom was glad it was short. Another followed with a similar effort. They were both state officials, but none of the men knew them. Republicans were too scarce in the part of the state they came from to ever get important state offices.

Everyone knew Baker, and interest reawakened when he came forward. He looked more serious than usual but was as impressive and well dressed as ever. "In the absence of the governor," he began, "I have been honored with the request that I address this regiment on its departure for the field." He paused and looked somberly at the men standing in front of him. "I think," he continued, "that I would have been the proper person to speak on this occasion anyhow. Your regiment was raised exclusively in the Pocket, that corner of southwest Indiana which I have represented in Congress for many years." He looked at them thoughtfully. "I know many of you, despite our differences in age. I know most of your parents, and all your grandparents who are still among the living."

He turned aside and paced the platform briefly, then faced his audience again. "I was brought to the Pocket nearly fifty years ago as a babe in my mother's arms and have lived there ever since. I know its people, and its green hills and broad bottoms are as familiar to me as the palm of my hand."

He paused reflectively. "You men come from counties like Martin and Posey, Spencer and Knox. Each of the companies in your regiment was raised in a county in the First Congressional District. Each platoon, I understand, was raised in a township or a neighborhood in a county. Most of you have grown up with your comrades, and their parents are friends and neighbors."

He paused and looked down. "I know this is true of my sons, three of whom are in the Daviess County company, because that is where I make my home." He looked at the men earnestly. "I think your regiment should bear a designation other than that of your number and state. I want to know you as 'the Pride of the Pocket,' because that is what you are. You are our finest, our bravest, and our best." He raised his hand and his voice. "I therefore christen you, 'the Pride of the Pocket'!"

Applause began among the spectators but soon died away. "Like all your fathers," Baker went on somberly, "I dread sending my sons far away to risk life and limb, perhaps never to return." He paused and nodded grimly. "But mine wanted to go, and I would have recognized them as my sons no longer if they had not."

He paced the platform again, head down. "But believe me," he said without looking up, "only a mother could have deeper feelings than a father when his sons go away to war."

Baker stopped and faced his audience again but paused a long time amid a silence broken only by the noise from the streets. "But I send my sons, and your fathers send you and you go freely, to fight to restore our precious Union, and give your lives for it if you must."

He gazed at the men soberly, his eyes seeming to search every face, then went on in his great organ voice. "I bid you farewell. May God bless and protect you, and bring those of you back to us whom He, in His wisdom, sees fit to spare."

Baker was done, but he stood before them for long moments, looking at their faces as though to print them indelibly on his memory before turning away to resume his seat. It was as though he knew he would never see most of them again.

The band played another selection, this one sounding like a hymn or part of an opera. It was breathlessly beautiful, and the people, soldiers and citizens alike, stood entranced until it was over.

Colonel Rivers and the beautiful brunette came forward. She bore what was obviously a flag bound about the upper part of its staff. Rivers was of medium height and heavily built. Gray sprinkled his short black beard. "Men," he began in his deep, resonant voice, "I present to you my daughter, Carolyn." He smiled. "She is closely connected to our regiment. Not only is she my daughter; she is affianced to one of the young men standing among you." Everyone knew it was Lt. Marcus Allen of the Posey County company.

The colonel stepped back and Carolyn faced the regiment alone, a little less poised than before. "Thank you, Father, for your *very clever* introduction." She essayed a smile, and Tom thought she was the most beautiful woman he had ever seen. Her white skin, black hair, and blue eyes made an entrancing contrast, and her voice was enough to thrill a dead man. She was really no prettier than Sally, but her slender figure and lovely face had a poise and presence Mort Napier's daughter would never know.

"I represent," she went on, "the ladies of the first Congressional District, who will remain behind, to pray for you and wait for you, while you go forth to fight for our beloved Union." She had obviously memorized her speech, but she was delivering it very well.

"Hopefully," she went on, "we will someday welcome you back to your homes and loved ones, *all of you.* Even if that is too much to expect, it is not too much to hope." She paused and looked at her audience out of those deep blue eyes. Tom thought he heard a great, subdued sigh of rapture rise from around him.

"We ladies charge you, as 'the Pride of the Pocket'," the clarion voice went on, "with the honor of the First Congressional District of the state of Indiana." She reached up and deftly unbound the flag, then, pivoting the staff on the floor, threw it out to full spread, where it remained momentarily before falling back in folds along the staff. It was a beautiful indigo blue with fringe and lettering in gleaming gold braid. No one knew at the time that the colonel had no more use for flags than he did bands and that this one would be seen only at formal parades and inspections.

Carolyn thrust the staff toward the colonel. "To you, sir, the commander of this regiment and my honored father, we entrust this banner." Rivers took the staff and she concluded, "May it ever wave in victory and never be furled in defeat." She turned and bowed to the men, then gracefully returned to her seat.

Rivers faced his men, the flag by his side. "I speak for the regiment I have the honor to command, in reply to the ladies whose fair hands have wrought this beautiful banner." He turned and bowed to his daughter, then faced front again. "I am sure," he went on, "that I speak for every man standing before me attired in the garb of war when I pledge most solemnly to those ladies who have bestowed on us this beautiful banner that we will discharge the obligation it lays upon us, at the cost of our lives if we must."

Rivers paused and ran his eyes over his men. "I pledge," he went on, "that we will fight to the death for our honor, as well as that of our ladies, as did our fathers in the olden time, when men wore armor and fought with swords and lances."

He stood silent and impassive for a moment, looking very imposing in his uniform of darkest blue. His boots, belt, and holster only gleamed softly, and the big service sword he wore was no more colorful. The only sparkles came from the silver eagles on his shoulders and the gold insignia on his hat.

Rivers concluded, "I say this because without honor a man is not a man, and life is not worthwhile."

As the colonel came down from the platform, Tom doubted if he had ever been more impressed by any speech he had ever heard.

Rivers handed the flag to a sergeant and took position in front of the regiment.

"*Attention!*" The men snapped erect.

"Present *arms!*" The rifles leapt up at the same precise instant and were held at exactly the same vertical angle.

The colonel wheeled to face the platform and came to the salute. One thousand men stood like statues graven in stone while the band played a solemn, measured tune. Tom's eyes sought out Carolyn Rivers. She stood apart, her lovely face framed by her raven hair, her slender, graceful figure erect. Her eyes were on the Posey County company, and she looked very beautiful and very sad.

The band played only briefly, then left the stand and took its place at what would be the front of the column. All the while the serried rows of rifles remained at present arms and not a man moved a muscle.

"Order *arms!*" A thousand rifle butts crashed to the ground at precisely the same instant, making an appalling sound, like a giant striking the earth with an enormous club. The spectators stood with whitened faces, and the whole city seemed struck with awe.

"Right shoulder, *arms!*" One thousand rifles leapt up in smooth, perfectly coordinated movements and came to rest on a thousand right shoulders.

"Right *face!*" The men wheeled simultaneously to the right, and a thousand hobnailed left shoes swung through short arcs and crashed to the ground.

"For'ard, *march!*" The men stepped off at the same instant and the band struck up with a dull thump of drums and a subdued blare of brass. The people got out of the way, and the regiment made a circuit of the circle before turning off on the street leading to where the trains waited.

Spectators lined the streets for several blocks and passersby stopped to watch, but there were still no demonstrations like there had always been before. The people stood silently facing the line of march. Even the children were subdued and stood gazing wide-eyed.

Perhaps it was because of the music. The drums thumped a slow, measured beat without reverberations or echo, and the muted horns carried a melody combining joy and sadness, anticipation and foreboding, in a rhythm so harmonious it was unearthly.

Perhaps the silence was because the regiment was the best drilled and disciplined unit the people had seen so far. It was a great blue machine, its thousand parts moving with such mechanical precision that they scarcely seemed to be men. A thousand left arms swung together and a thousand feet struck the street at exactly the same instant with each step. A thousand dully gleaming rifles slanted at precisely the same angle on a thousand shoulders.

For whatever reason, the somber atmosphere continued all the way. It was as though the people sensed that few of these thousand pairs of eyes, fixed solemnly forward in a thousand fresh young faces, would ever see those green hills and broad bottoms between the Ohio and the Wabash again.

# 9

It was spring and everyone expected the regiment to leave its winter quarters soon. Movement was in the air as the April sun warmed the earth, the grass greened, and the trees budded out. The camp was on a flat-topped ridge overlooking a long clear valley. It was otherwise surrounded by woods, but the trees were not the primeval giants of southern Indiana. They were the second-and third-growth specimens of an area settled for nearly two centuries, and had been much thinned near camp for firewood and building material.

The men spent most of the winter in log huts they had built themselves. The roofs were canvas relics of the big tents they had lived in until cold weather had driven them out. They had since been issued rectangular pieces of canvas, two of which buttoned together to form open-ended two-man shelter tents for use in the field.

The huts all had fireplaces. Most chimneys were made of mud and sticks, but a few boasted ones of stone. They looked much alike, and each company's huts were regularly spaced along both sides of paths leading off from the road that ran through the middle of camp. Most of the officers still lived and messed in large tents, but all had been floored, framed, and furnished with stoves for heat.

The men stood in groups along the path in front of their huts, Tom, Billy, and their friends among them. There was a general air of expectancy. Ammunition had been issued a week before, and the previous evening the men had cooked three days' rations. They had done that once before and nothing had come of it, but rumor had it that this time would be different.

"No drill t'day," remarked Billy. "That means somethin'."

"Yeah, hit shore does," agreed Ab Inman. "We'd of been out on th' drill field b'fore now if'n hit didn't."

"Th' colonel wouldn't waste a good day like this," observed Tom with a look at the clear sky. "I guess we've drilled three times as much as any other regiment in th' brigade."

"We shore have," vowed Ab. "Th' t'other three reg'ments ain't been out more'n two er three times since th' weather broke, an' we've been out ever' day."

"They'll ketch hit when th' gin'ral has brigade drill an' inspection like they been sayin' he wuz gonna do," forecast George Sanders.

"Wal, I don't think he's gonna inspect *his* men," drawled Ab. "I think he's gonna go inspect th' Rebels an' see how they kin fight."

"Hit's 'bout time!" exclaimed Billy. "Hit'll soon be a hull year since we been in th' army, an' we ain't seen a Rebel yit."

"I 'spect we'll see 'nough uv 'em 'fore hit's over," sighed George.

"Yeah, we gotta git goin' with this hyar war," interjected Johnny Conrad. "We gotta git hit over with so we kin go back home."

Tom agreed. "Yeah, it's plowin' and plantin' time now, and I want to be back home when it comes next spring." He mostly wanted to get back so he could marry Sally, but he didn't want to say anything about that.

"Oh, lawsy," sighed Ab. "Y' know, I keep thinkin' 'bout how hit feels t' hold th' plow in th ground with th' hosses pullin', an' how th' ground smells when y' first break hit."

"An' burnin' bresh!" exclaimed Ben Noble. "When I smelt that fire that got out in that thicket by Comp'ny C t'other mornin' early, I wuz 'bout haf-'sleep an' thought I wuz burnin' weeds outa th' garden for Ma."

The men stood silently for a time, avoiding each other's eyes and looking away into the woods or down into the valley.

Sudden shouting down the path toward the road attracted their attention. A burly sergeant with a short, grizzled beard and bright blue eyes set in a weathered face advanced toward them. *"Kompanie,* fall oudt! Fall oudt!" he bellowed. *"Alle* de *Kompanie,* fall oudt, *mit* packs *und alle* equipmendt! Fall oudt! *Mach schnell!"*

Many of the men didn't understand his last words, but they all knew what he meant and ran for their huts. He was Sgt. Dieter Kemper of the Second Platoon, the one Tom and Billy belonged to, sent out by Sergeant Major Bower to put the whole company on notice.

"Whooppee!" exulted Billy. "We're goin' fer shore this time!"

Inside the hut the men scrambled about for their equipment. "Whar's my bay'net?" demanded Ab in exasperation as he buckled on his belt, his eyes roving about the hut.

"Stuck 'tween th' logs, there over your bunk," replied Tom.

Ab grabbed the bayonet and stuck it in his scabbard. The men had sword bayonets, which made good knives, instead of the usual type, which had rings to fit over the rifle muzzles and were good only for candlesticks.

As Billy started to put on his belt, one of his ammunition pouches dropped to the dirt floor under Burk's feet. "Watch out, Burk!" warned Billy. "Don't step on my pouch thar!"

Burk stepped back and collided with Ab, who was starting out with pack and rifle. The hut was too small for much moving around. Ab recovered his balance and hurried on out the doorway.

Burk already had one piece of canvas ready to roll up and strap on top of his pack when he produced another and rolled them together.

"How come y' got two tent halves, Burk?" asked Billy.

"Ain't gonna be 'nough room in one uv these lil' tents for me an' another feller," was the rumbled reply.

"Yeah, I guess yo're right," laughed Billy as he hefted his pack. "Whoever 'twuz 'd prob'ly git mashed if'n y' ever rolled over."

The men emerged from their huts carrying their packs, large affairs that combined knapsack and haversack. There had been an acute shortage of those two items back at Indianapolis, and tentmakers had made substitutes at the colonel's specification. The men liked them a lot better because one pack was easier to handle than two.

The men slung their packs and fastened the straps to their belts in front, then helped one another fasten them in back. They were scarcely done with them when, "Sekun Platoon! Sekun Platoon! Fall een! Fall een!" resounded among the huts.

The other platoon sergeants followed Kemper's example, and soon the path in front of the company's huts was transformed from a scene of confused activity into regular ranks of men with packs on their backs, canteens at their sides, and rifles at the trail.

Kemper's platoon was first, though. It was always first in everything. It was the best in the whole company, if not the whole regiment, and his men were proud of it. It had taken a little time to get used to him and his mangled English and some of the men had grumbled that he was too hard on them, but they looked at it differently now and were given to boasting what a "tough sargint" they had.

He really wasn't tough in the sense that he was rough and brutal, though. Tom had often wondered how Kemper could manage his men like he did without the noise and bluster of most of the other sergeants. He guessed he was just a natural leader, that and all the experience he had in the old country.

Tom had also wondered why Kemper had thrown away fifteen years' military service there and come to America. It wasn't until he got better acquainted with some of the Germans who had known him before the war that he found out.

Kemper had a younger brother with a bad case of consumption and was persuaded that if he took him to America, the climate would give him a better chance of getting well. Neither of them was married, so they came over and settled on White River near Haysville, where they bought a farm. Kemper's brother got worse, though, and died in a few years, just before the war broke out. Kemper had sold the farm and was on the point of going back to the old country, but had let some friends talk him into enlisting with them because he had so much experience and would make them a good leader.

There had been several other veterans of service in Germany in the two platoons raised in the southern part of the county, though, and Kemper was the only one who knew any English at all. When it turned out that the Second Platoon had no one with any military experience, Kemper had been put in charge of it, although there wasn't a German in it.

Captain Dixon and Sergeant Major Bower shortly came down the path and began an inspection. Things didn't go well in the First Platoon, where one man was short an ammunition pouch. Jake had a few words with the fellow, and Tom imagined he would also have a few with his sergeant, a lanky, easygoing fellow named Hall who was inclined to overlook small things.

When the turn of the Second Platoon came, Tom noticed that Dixon was resplendent in a new uniform complete with sword and revolver. He had also grown a small mustache, which went well with his dark, aquiline features. It gave Tom a sinking sensation to realize that women must think Dixon a handsome man.

As they passed along the road, Jake looked everyone over carefully, but Dixon seemed to pay no attention until they were behind Burk. Then he stopped and said, "This man has two shelter halves."

"Yes sir," replied Jake. "He's s' big he's gotta have a tent all by hisself. I got him 'nother one."

Dixon looked at Burk like he had never seen him before, then passed on. He and Jake finished the inspection, then came back and stopped before Kemper, standing at attention like a granite boulder at the head of the front rank. "Carry on, Sergeant."

Kemper came to present arms. *"Jawohl, Herr Hauptmann!"* He had forgotten himself and lapsed into German, as he often did.

Tom thought Dixon grimaced slightly at being addressed in German, but he only returned the salute and passed on. After all, Kemper was the best sergeant he had, and he probably realized he wouldn't have kept his company without men like him. Colonel Rivers had weeded out better officers than he was.

Tom knew the inspection of the other two platoons wouldn't take long. They were entirely German, and their commander, Lieutenant Mertens, and both his sergeants were veterans of service in the old country. Their men were freely admitted to be the best disciplined and most tractable in the regiment, and they always shone at inspections.

Kemper put his men at rest in place, and they waited until Dixon and Jake came back. When they did, they took position halfway along the company's front and looked toward the road that ran through the camp.

Soon there were shouted commands from where the other companies were on up the road. Beginning with the farthest one, they went to right shoulder arms, wheeled to face the road, and when their turn came, entered in to form a column that moved toward where Dixon's company waited to take its place at the rear.

When it did, the column flowed on down the road and out into the valley like a great blue ribbon. The regiment was on its way to meet the enemy, and Tom felt a strange, exhilarating excitement, like he imagined he would feel when he got married.

# 10

Since it had left winter camp, the regiment had been marching steadily for nearly two weeks as part of the brigade. The marching was hard, even after the men got accustomed to it, but they wouldn't have minded if it made any sense.

It didn't, though. They marched and marched and then countermarched over the route they had covered before. They went off on side roads and then came back. Sometimes they left the road and marched across country, often to get around towns, which were generally avoided for some reason. Several times they joined the division and then left it. Once they even joined the corps, or at least rumor said they had.

When it rained they got wet, and when the sun came out they dried. The only good thing about it was the scenery. They were operating in the Shenandoah Valley, which had great blue walls of mountains on both sides, although you could rarely see both of them. Eventually the men found themselves in a part of the valley that was split by a great, mountainous ridge.

They were chasing a Rebel general named Jackson who had the nickname of Stonewall, and the men soon acquired a grudging admiration for him. Several different forces, each larger than his, were after him, but he could never be cornered. He marched so fast they wondered how his men could stand it. There was no way of telling where he could be from one day to the next. He was here; he was there; he was everywhere. They might have thought he was nowhere, except that parts of the army ran into him from time to time, and generally got the worst of it.

Jackson always seemed to know where his enemies were, and it wasn't hard to see why. Scarcely a day went by that his cavalry wasn't sighted hovering about the column. At first the gray-clad troopers were the objects of great curiosity and the higher officers would study them with field glasses, but everyone soon got used to them and paid no attention, like flies in the summertime.

The marching and countermarching put the regiment at the head of the column one day, and the next morning things began to change.

Soon after the march began, Hall's and Kemper's platoons were taken out, double-timed past the rest of the regiment, and deployed as skirmishers several hundred yards ahead. Hall's men went to the right of the road and Kemper's to the left. In the meantime, the regiment deployed off the road into line of battle and followed them. The other three regiments remained on the road in column until there was a sharp turn to the right. Then everybody struck out straight ahead cross country, skirmishers, line of battle, and column.

All this meant that the enemy was close, and Tom knew he would be one of the first to see him. Tom moved forward holding his rifle at the ready with his thumb on the hammer, expecting to see men in gray behind every copse and wall. Keeping alignment and interval turned out to be a lot harder than when the platoon had been deployed as skirmishers on the drill field. He was on the extreme right and had to watch carefully because the rest of the platoon guided on him, particularly after they left the road. He tended to drift too close to Billy on his left and set too fast a pace unless he was careful. Gradually it became monotonous and he had to keep reminding himself that they might meet the enemy at any time.

Kemper's men advanced along a gradual slope that came down from some woods running along the top of a low ridge to the left. At first they crossed well-kept fields, many of them planted in wheat or corn, separated by four-foot-high stone walls the men had to climb over. Tom was glad when the field was in grass, because he didn't like trampling the wheat or corn. The wheat was well grown for that time of year, but the corn was just putting up pale green shoots an inch or so high.

After a while there were no more cultivated fields and the grassy ones began to sprout bushes, briers, and even small trees. They became more and more overgrown and had dense thickets and brier patches. The walls became tumbledown, often with gaps that could be walked through or so low you could step over them. The only houses and other buildings Tom saw were down along the road, and they became progressively scarcer.

Kemper ranged along behind the line as it moved, but he had it easy. He could avoid the thickets and brier patches, and his men were so well drilled he rarely had to say anything about alignment or interval.

Suddenly a farmstead appeared in the growth ahead, the first buildings they had encountered since leaving the road. It looked like it would be a good place for a Rebel outpost, and they advanced cautiously, eyes on windows and corners, rifles at the ready. It was in line with Tom and Billy, so Kemper came down to join them. They came closer and closer, but nothing happened. The house was dilapidated and the windows stared vacantly. There was a little portico in front, but the floor had fallen in, and weeds thrust up through the dense mat of grass around it. Of all the buildings, only the barn was in good repair and looked like it still might be in use.

When they reached the buildings, Kemper halted his men. Hall did the same and came up to join him. Kemper went through the barn and Hall the house. The other buildings were too small and tumble-down to bother with. Neither of them found anything, but when they came out Captain Dixon came up from the rear and joined them. They started talking, but Tom was too far away to hear what they said. The line of battle had halted, too. Tom couldn't see it for the growth, but he couldn't hear the noise of its advances any longer.

While they waited, Tom looked up the line to his left. Although he couldn't see many of the closer ones, he could see the men on the end up the slope at the edge of the woods. Some of them had come together during the halt, probably Harve Akers and some of his friends.

Billy stood close to Tom with his legs apart, holding his rifle loosely. He always looked strange to Tom with the big rifle and all the accouterments of war strapped on his slender form, but he had stood up splendidly on the march. Tom had expected to have to help him, carrying his rifle and maybe even his pack, but there had never been any need for it.

Dixon and the two sergeants ended their conversation and moved apart. Suddenly Hall threw up his arms and disappeared from sight into a startled yell. Tom was astounded and started running over. By the time he got there, Kemper and Billy were helping Hall out of an old well that had been invisible in the grass. By the time Dixon reached them, Hall was sitting on the ground grimacing with pain and taking off a shoe. "Sprung my damn ankle!" he exclaimed disgustedly.

Tom could see it was already swelled up.

"Do you think you can walk?" asked Dixon a little anxiously.

Kemper helped Hall to his feet, but he promptly sat down again. "No, sir, I cain't." He rubbed the swelling. "Hit's sprung purty bad, I guess."

Dixon pondered. "Well, stay here and I'll take your place. We don't have much farther to go."

It didn't seem right just to go off and leave Hall, so Tom said, "Just stay here till th' regiment comes up, then get someone to help you down the road and get on one of the wagons."

Dixon looked at Tom like he had spoken out of turn. "Get back in line, you men," he said abruptly. "There's no time to talk."

They left Hall sitting on the grass with one shoe off and resumed the advance.

Beyond the farmstead the growth grew so dense it was almost one continuous thicket. The men had to force their way through it, and they made a lot of noise. When the regiment started forward again, it sounded like a herd of elephants crashing through the brush, and Tom didn't think it would be able to maintain much of a line.

Hall's men had much easier going. Tom was often out of sight of everyone on his left, even Billy, but he could always see Hall's men with Dixon following along behind.

The line of battle fell farther and farther behind and Tom expected Dixon to halt them until it got closer, but he didn't. Tom once saw the colonel appear in the growth behind them on horseback, but he just took a look and turned back.

As the advance went on, Tom became so preoccupied with fighting his way through the briers and brush that he forgot what it was all about until Billy suddenly shouted, "Hey! They's men b'hind that ol' rock wall up ahead! I kin see 'em!"

Kemper shouted, "Halt!" and what sounded like echoes ran up the slope as the men passed the order on. Hall's men stopped, too.

The growth was thinner ahead, and Tom could see a tumbledown rock wall about a hundred yards in front. Beyond it was a wood.

Captain Dixon ran up toward Kemper and Billy, who were standing together peering at the wall. The captain had trouble with his sword scabbard in the brush and briers. "What's the matter?" he called as soon as he was close enough. "Why have you men halted?" His voice was high and excited.

"Beely sees men oudt dere, behindt dot vall," replied Kemper. He pointed toward it.

Dixon joined him and they moved a little ahead of the line, then stopped and studied the wall intently. "I can't see anything," said Dixon after a while.

Tom couldn't either and started feeling ashamed for Billy. Dixon would be contemptuous and the men would tease him for "seeing things."

Billy was insistent. "See thar," he said shrilly, "whar hit looks like a piece uv th' wall has fell down! Them ain't rocks. Them's men squattin' thar!"

Tom looked closely. He could see the place Billy was talking about, but only stones seemed to fill the gap. Then he realized that tumbled stones wouldn't be as regular as these shapes, which gradually took on the appearance of heads and shoulders above a low section of the wall. They were uniformly dark toward the top and lighter farther down, about where a face would show under a hat or cap. "I see 'em!" he called. "There where Billy says!"

"Shoot then," said Dixon. "I still don't see anything."

Before Tom could raise his rifle, Billy fired. The explosion sounded unusually loud and violent. A man popped up behind the wall and fell over backward, his weapon flying up in the air.

Several spurts of smoke lanced with orange flame jetted from behind the wall, accompanied by sharp reports. Hissing sounds filled the air, and small objects tore through the growth.

Tom could see the Rebels plainly now as they bobbed up to fire. He fired at a man just as he ducked to load and missed him. Kemper fired also and there were several revolver shots. Evidently, nobody else could see anything to shoot at. Anyhow, none of them fired.

As he loaded his rifle, Tom saw Kemper plying his ramrod and Dixon firing his revolver from a kneeling position. He heard Billy fire again but could see nothing to aim at but a cloud of smoke. Suddenly he realized there was no more shooting from behind the wall.

Kemper waited, his rifle poised, but all was quiet. After a few moments, he advanced cautiously on the wall and Tom followed. Billy started to come along, but he waved him back.

When he reached Dixon, the captain was looking around in the briers and weeds at his feet. "Lose something, sir?" Tom asked as he started past.

Dixon looked up, his face pale and sweaty. "Yes, I dropped the empty cylinder for my revolver." He seemed shaky enough to drop the weapon, too.

Kemper reached the low place in the wall, stopped, and looked beyond. Suddenly he jumped over it and disappeared. By the time Tom reached the wall, Kemper was a little way into the woods, but he started back when he saw him.

"Are th' Rebels gone, Sergeant?" Tom asked.

*"Ja, Alle* budt dis vun." He pointed to one side.

Tom looked and saw a lean figure in brownish gray sprawled at full length behind the wall. The man had not been handsome in life, and in death he was horrible. His twisted features and staring eyes accentuated a long nose and a sharply pointed chin. At first sight he seemed to be wearing a tightly fitting red skullcap, but it was only because the top of his head had been almost shot off. The stones nearby were splattered with blood and brain tissue to which whitish splinters of bone and dark hair adhered. Tom felt sick.

"Beely keel dis *Mann,*" said Kemper. "De furst schoot."

Billy ran up. "Whar'd they go? Let's git atter 'em!"

Tom felt like bawling him out for leaving his place but instead pointed at the dead man. "Look there."

Billy's eyes bulged and his mouth fell open. "Is . . . is that a Rebel, one uv them we wuz shootin' at?"

"Yeah, it's th' one you got with your first shot."

Billy tried to speak but could only make a strangling sound. Finally he got his voice. "Y' mean . . . y' mean I shot that feller, blowed his head off like that?"

"We only saw one git hit, the one you shot first thing."

Billy's legs started trembling and he looked down, blinking rapidly. "Aw, Gawd," was all he could say.

Kemper spoke up. "Beely," he said softly, "dat iss vat de solchers doo; dey vight *und* dey keel de odder solcher, de enemy." He patted Billy on the back. "Eet iss var."

Billy looked up, his face twitching and eyes still blinking. "Yo're right, Sargint." He swallowed convulsively and shook his head. "I guess I never knowed what hit wuz really 'bout b'fore. I . . . I musta thought hit wuz jist a game er somethin'." His voice had gained strength, but his boyish chin still trembled.

"You saved several of us from gettin' shot, Billy," said Tom. "If you hadn't seen those fellows, we'd have walked right up on them." It made Billy feel better, and Tom was glad. A boy his age should never have to go through anything like this, though.

Kemper picked up the dead man's weapon. "Hah! Iss oldt musket, no rifle!"

"Th' range was just too long for those old smoothbores," said Tom. "That's why they didn't hit any of us." He turned to Billy. "They're as good as rifles up close, though, and it's a good thing you saw them when you did."

Billy was beginning to look normal again and managed a smile.

Kemper started them into the woods. The visibility was good because the trees were large and there was little undergrowth. Tom noticed Hall's platoon wasn't advancing and saw Kemper running down that way. He wondered what had happened to Dixon. Unless he showed up soon, Kemper was going to have a hard time of it, because the two platoons were strung out a great distance.

Tom went ahead of the line so he could watch the upper part of it and help Kemper, but the men were all keeping proper alignment and interval as far as he could see. Down where Hall's men were he heard Kemper shout several times.

The woods came to an end at a rail fence with a plowed field on the other side that hadn't been planted yet. It ran all the way up to the woods at the top of the slope but was only a few hundred yards wide. Beyond the plowed field was an open, grassy expanse behind another rail fence. About four hundred yards farther on, a line of trees and brush bordered what looked like a small stream running toward the valley below.

Suddenly an extended line of armed men came out of the growth along the stream directly toward Tom. There was movement behind them, and when he looked closely he made out a large formation of Rebel infantry facing him.

He dropped to a crouch behind the fence and cocked his rifle to fire and give the alarm. He took a rest on the top rail and aimed at an officer a little ahead of the advancing skirmishers. The figure danced about strangely in his sights, but he calmed himself, drew a fine bead, and squeezed the trigger.

At Tom's shot the officer tumbled to the ground. The advancing skirmishers fired back, raised a yell, and broke into a run. A bullet struck the fence so close the splinters stung his face. Shouts came from beyond the stream, and what looked like a line of battle started moving toward him.

As Tom loaded, Billy appeared at the fence, leveled his rifle, and fired. Shots sounded as others came up and followed his example, but none of the Rebels fell. They came on, reloading as they ran.

Tom had just capped his rifle when he heard Kemper shout from somewhere to his right. *"Zurück!* Back! *Rennen!* Run!"

Tom let the hammer of his rifle down and took up the shout. "Back! Fall back! Run! Run!"

They whirled and ran, Billy with his rifle in one hand and ramrod in the other. Bullets hissed past and smacked into tree trunks to speed their pace. They ran like the devil was after them. Tom saw Ab clear a fallen tree with a magnificent leap.

They were soon out of sight of the Rebels, but no one slowed down. Tom heard Kemper shouting, but this time he was so far away he couldn't understand him. The shout spread along the line, and he heard. "Th' wall! Th' wall! Stop at that first rock wall!"

The tumbledown wall appeared ahead through the trees. Tom was panting when he jumped across. Figures appeared along the fence as far as he could see in both directions, scrambling across and crouching on the other side. Hall's men had run back along with Kemper's, although no one was advancing on them.

"Hold here! Hold here at th' wall!" came another cry. Kemper was so far away Tom hadn't heard him.

He rested his rifle on the fence and saw Billy finish loading. Ab was beyond him, but Ben Noble, who should have been next to him, was nowhere in sight. "Ab!" Tom shouted. "Where's Ben?"

"I dunno!" was the reply. "I ain't seen him!"

Tom told Billy to move up to fill the gap and moved up a little himself. He came on the dead man and moved a little farther than he should have so he wouldn't be in sight of him.

He saw movement in the woods and shouted, "Here they come!" as he cocked his rifle.

The men behind the wall crouched and leveled their weapons. The movement came closer and Tom could see men darting among the trees. He took aim several times, only to have his target disappear before he could fire. These Rebel skirmishers were experienced and as quick as cats.

A spurt of smoke came from behind a tree, and a bullet ricocheted off a rock with a bansheelike howl close to Billy, who took quick aim and fired back. There was a thrashing in the leaves behind the tree, and Tom thought he saw flailing limbs.

The rebels stopped advancing. Each of them was behind a tree. There was no need for them to advance any farther. Behind them their line of battle could be heard grinding forward like a great machine. Periodically they sent bullets at the wall, but none of them was visible except for the briefest instant. Tom waited with leveled rifle, his eyes on a tree a shot had come from.

A head and upper body behind a rifle barrel leaned out from behind the trunk. Tom aimed quickly and fired. His target disappeared without firing, but there was no way of telling if Tom's shot had scored. No more shots came from behind that particular tree, though.

As he loaded behind the stones, he again heard the noise of the enemy advance. There was no sign of the brigade, and unless it appeared soon, they would have to fall back or be overrun. But who was going to give the order? Kemper was nowhere in sight. He simply had too much of a line to manage by himself.

He looked at his brother crouching behind the fence with his cheek cuddled to the stock of his rifle and made up his mind. When the last moment came, he would shout for Billy to run and stay himself.

He capped his rifle and raised his head carefully as several shots rang out along the wall. He was astonished to see the enemy skirmishers darting among the trees again, this time falling back. He fired at a fleeting form and missed, then suddenly realized that the sounds of the advance through the wood toward him were dying away. He was astonished and stood erect to load without being shot at, then got up on a heap of stones to see better.

There was a flash and a spurt of smoke from back in the woods and something tore at his left forearm, sending a shock all the way to his shoulder and numbing his arm. It threw him off balance, and he fell.

Billy shrieked in terror, "Tom, air ye hit?"

As Billy ran toward him, Tom got to his feet and brushed a little dirt off his rifle. "No, I'm not hit, not bad anyhow." he shouted, despite the numbness of his arm. The sleeve of his coat was torn, and blood had soaked through. "Get back!" he shouted at Billy. "And get down, or you'll get shot, too! It's just a scratch!"

Billy dropped to a crouch behind the wall. "Air ye shore hit ain't bad, Tom?" He looked like he had when he had first seen the dead man lying nearby.

"Sure! Sure!" Tom extended his arm, bent his elbow, and flexed his fingers, although it ended the numbness and brought pain. "See there? It just tore my coat and creased my arm. Get on back now, and keep down!" Blood started running down his hand when he brought his arm back, but Billy couldn't see it.

Billy still stayed. "Air ye shore yo're all right, Tom?" His eyes showed whitely in his smudgy face.

"Now listen, Billy. I'm all right, and you just go back where you belong." Tom spoke impatiently and was immediately sorry.

Billy went back in a crouching run, although there was no longer any need to, and kept looking back over his shoulder. Once he was far enough, Tom tore a piece of lining from his coat and stuffed it up his sleeve to keep the blood from running down, then stripped some leaves off a low limb and wiped the blood off his hand.

There was no sign of any Rebels in the woods any longer, and he wondered why they had started out like they had and then turned back.

A crashing in the growth from the rear indicated that the brigade was moving up, and Kemper came running up the wall. He saw Tom and slowed to a walk.

"Are we going on again, Sergeant?" Tom asked.

Kemper shook his head. *"Nein,"* he gasped. *"Wir bleiben hier."* He plopped down on a stone and took off his cap, then produced a handkerchief and mopped his face. He was soaked with sweat, and his face was beet red. *"Ich bin erschöpft,"* he sighed.

Tom nodded. "It's Dixon. He's gone and you had to handle the whole line by yourself. What happened to him anyhow?"

Kemper sighed again and shook his head. "I nodt know." Suddenly he noticed Tom's arm. *"Himmel! Du bist verwundet!"* He got up and came over. *"Zeih' den Rock ab, und wir schauen."*

Tom took off his coat. "Just a scratch," he said as he rolled up his blood-soaked sleeve and saw an ugly red gash just below his elbow. It was still bleeding, but only a little, and it hurt like the devil.

Kemper looked closely. "Hmm." He drew a piece of cloth and a small bottle filled with dark red fluid from a pocket, tore off a strip of the cloth and cleaned the wound with water from his canteen, then tore off another strip. He folded it and soaked it with the fluid from the bottle, then bound it on the wound with what was left of the cloth. It felt like a red-hot iron on the wound, but Tom didn't flinch.

Kemper stepped back and looked at his work, then nodded with satisfaction.

"Think it'll heal up right away, Sergeant?" asked Tom.

*"Ja ja.* Iss de goot *Medizin. Die Wunde will nicht angesteckt werden."*

Tom had learned enough German from being around Kemper to understand him pretty well. He noticed that his arm was stiff as he put his coat back on, but the pain was easing.

The crashing in the growth behind them was very close, so they turned to look. A skirmish line made up of a whole company was the first thing they saw. A tall, aristocratic-looking officer strode in front. He was Captain Harlow, not one of the most respected officers in the regiment. His men had thrown away a lot of equipment on the march a few days before, and the colonel had made him take them back and pick up every piece of it after they camped. It had taken them half the night to do it.

Harlow halted his men and approached Kemper. "Are you in charge of these pickets?" he demanded.

Kemper came to attention. *"Jawohl, Herr Hauptmann!"*

Harlow grimaced disgustedly. "Where's Captain Dixon?"

"I nodt know, *Herr Hauptmann!"*

"Was he wounded or captured or something?" Harlow's voice was sharp and his eyes hard.

Tom wanted to spare Kemper. He came to attention and said, "We last saw him out there a little ways, looking for a revolver cylinder he dropped." He pointed.

Harlow looked at Tom. "Nobody asked you anything, Soldier," he sneered.

"Yes, sir." Tom could feel his face burning.

Harlow turned back to Kemper as the rest of the regiment came up. "What can you tell me about the Rebels?" he asked with the air of a schoolmaster questioning a backward pupil.

Kemper took him to the wall, pointed into the woods, and began talking. Harlow couldn't follow him and kept making him repeat himself. Kemper's English was worse than usual, but Tom kept his mouth shut. He had had enough of Harlow. Billy and several others drifted down toward them.

Finally Harlow seemed to understand it all, but he wasn't done with Kemper. "I don't think anyone who's so stupid he can't even speak English has any business being a sergeant!" he snarled.

Kemper snapped to attention, his face rigid. *"Jawohl, Herr Hauptmann!"*

"Can't you even say, 'Yes, sir,' in English?" sneered Harlow.

Tom couldn't stand it any more. "That man has forgotten more about soldiering than you'll ever learn, Captain."

There was a dead silence. Harlow turned on Tom, his eyes narrowed and jaw set. "So it's you again, Soldier!" He advanced menacingly, his hand on his sword. "Do I have to teach you a lesson?"

Tom felt a reckless anger. "I'm ready for any lesson the captain wants to teach me," he said as he gripped his rifle.

A horseman approached, but all eyes were on Tom and Harlow.

Harlow stopped and his mouth fell open. "Why, you . . . you—"

A deep voice cut him off. "Captain Harlow! Aren't you supposed to be taking a skirmish line into those woods there, sir? And here I find you quarreling with soldiers like a sutler! You're delaying the advance of the brigade!" It was Colonel Rivers on his horse.

Harlow was startled. "Y-yes, sir, I am, but this man—"

"Well, go! In God's name, go!" boomed Rivers. "Those woods may be full of the enemy!"

"But, sir, I'd like to—"

"I don't care what you'd like, sir! Go, this very moment, if you want to keep your company!"

Harlow went without another word, his face red and twitching. The colonel wheeled his horse and was gone.

"Whew!" exclaimed Billy. "I thought you was a goner, Tom!"

There were several intakes of breath and sighs of relief.

"No *Mann* say noddings von dis," said Kemper. "Berhaps iss *vergessen.*" He looked the men over. *"Verstehen?"*

They all nodded. No one was to say anything about what had happened, and maybe it would be forgotten. Tom only got a sigh and an exasperated shake of the head, but he expected more later.

In the meantime the regiment had gone from line into column and started marching down along the wall toward the valley. Lieutenant Mertens, a tall, blond fellow in his late twenties, held his two platoons back until Hall's and Kemper's could enter the column.

Tom looked back and saw the rest of the brigade going on after Harlow's skirmish line, with the lead regiment deployed into line of battle and the others following in column. Maybe the regiment was going down to the road to cut the Rebels off or move up on their flank.

He asked Ab about Ben Noble again, but he got the same answer. "I wuz too busy runnin' t' pay 'tention, I guess." Ab shook his head. "I 'spect th' Rebels got him. Them balls wuz comin' awful close thar at first."

As they marched, Tom looked around in the platoon. Three other men were missing, but at the moment he couldn't think of who they were. "Who else isn't here?" he asked.

Harve Akers replied, "My three bes' frens, Jim Kendall, 'n' Herb Luckett 'n' Bill Byers."

"What happened to them, Harve?"

"We got b'hind up whar we wuz an' the Rebels liked t' ketched us," was the sober reply.

"Did they take them prisoner?"

"Naw, they shot 'em, all three uv 'em. Never tried t' s'render. Jist run."

"How come they didn't git you, too?" asked Ab.

"I dunno. Balls clipped my hair an' tore my clothes. An' I flew; I mean I flew." Harve shook his head. "Th' Lord spared me, I guess."

"Why'd th' Lord spare an ol' rounder like you?"

"I dunno. I cain't unnerstan' hit either." Harve blinked his eyes and hung his head. "No more, though," he vowed. "I've done seen th' light, I have, an' I'm gonna be a diff'runt feller frum now on."

Nobody believed him, but nobody said anything.

The regiment reached the road and turned left to march southwest again. Some of the men speculated about their movement. Most of them thought they were going to flank the Rebels while the rest of the brigade engaged them in front, but it didn't turn out that way. There were no sounds of any fighting from the way it had gone, and it wasn't long before all three regiments were seen moving down the ridge toward the road in a column. They reached the road ahead of the regiment, which put it last in the line of march.

"I jist cain't unnerstan' why them Rebels done what they done," confessed Billy, "comin' at us like that an' then cuttin an' runnin'."

"Me neither," said George. "Y'd a thought they wuz gonna wipe us frum th' face uv th' airth th' way they come at us." He sighed and shook his head. "I seen 'em crost that plowed field past them woods. Hit looked like they wuz thousan's uv 'em, an' I shore thought we wuz goners when I heered 'em comin' inta that woods b'hind them skirmishers."

"What d'you think uv hit, Corp'ril, why them Rebels done like they done?" asked Johnny.

"I expect they just wanted room to maneuver, to get us off their back so they could start southwest, too. They were probably afraid if they attacked us th' division'd catch up and maybe even th' corps before they could finish us off. Frémont's supposed to be only a little west of here, and I guess they thought th' whole works 'd be too much for 'em." It made Tom feel like he was teaching school again, but the men were always asking him about things.

To everyone's surprise, the regiment left the column a few hours later when it reached a junction with a road that came from the south out of the mountains. A few hours' march along that road was a gap through the mountains that the regiment was to watch in case Jackson doubled back that way. Tom guessed the rest of the brigade wouldn't go very far and that the division was close, since a single brigade wouldn't stand a ghost of a chance of stopping Jackson, much less a regiment.

They went into camp along a creek where there was plenty of wood and water and were happy to find their packs on the regimental wagons.

# 11

The men camped along the right bank of the creek. Although most of the others trusted to the shelter of the trees, Kemper had his men put up their two-man shelter tents. It was dark by the time they finished and had their supper. Everyone was too tired to sit around and talk like they usually did, and soon all were in their blankets. No one even bothered to gather up leaves and boughs to sleep on.

The next morning their first concern was the four men they had lost, but a regimental inspection came before anything else. Evidently the colonel wanted to make sure no more equipment had been thrown away on the march. None had, perhaps because of the example he had made of Captain Harlow and his men. Rivers wasn't done with them either. He sent Harlow's company to picket the gap while the others took their ease in camp.

Captain Dixon appeared with the colonel at the inspection. The story was that he had gotten lost in the woods following after the skirmish line. He had blundered onto the road and turned south because that was the direction of the advance. He reached the road before the regiment did, caught up with the brigade, and went up to the head of the column because he thought the regiment was still leading it. He hadn't learned where it was until after dark.

Most of his men thought it sounded pretty fishy. They couldn't understand how anyone could get lost like that in such a small wood, but Johnny Conrad said it was easy to do, especially if you weren't used to being out like that. He remembered how he had gotten lost once squirrel hunting and had to find Cane Creek with the water running the wrong way before he could figure out where he was.

After the inspection, Tom went to see Jake about the missing men. He said Harlow's men had found them, all dead like everyone expected, but hadn't been able to bring them in or anything. He would see the colonel about it as soon as he could and let them know.

It was nearly noon when Jake came around. "A detail frum Comp'ny A's awreddy buried 'em," he announced, "up thar by that ol' rock fence. They put rocks at th' head uv their graves, too."

The men were upset. "Hit ain't fitten t' do like that!" protested George Sanders. "They wuz our frens an' we oughta done hit, an' had a fun'ral, too!"

Harve was even more vehement. "Don't that ol' man keer 'nough 'bout his men t' have 'em buried proper 'stid uv like somethin' found in th' woods?"

"Now wait a minit, Akers!" said Jake with a hard look. "Th' colonel said he wuz sorry, but hit's awreddy done. When he sent that detail out, he still thought we might hafta go on marchin' fast and maybe fightin', an' they wouldn't git buried a'tall lessen hit wuz done right then."

Akers wasn't pacified. " 'Tain't right; 'tain't right a'tall!"

"Well, you wanta go dig 'em up an' do it all over again?" demanded Jake.

Harve hung his head. "Naw, I don't wanta do nothin' like that." He looked down, blinking and scuffing his feet. "I don't wanta look at 'em with dirt on their faces—" His voice broke, and he abruptly turned away.

After the noon meal, word came that there wouldn't be anything to do until evening muster. The men could rest or visit around as long as they stayed in camp. Tom thought of asking for permission to go look at the graves of Ben and the others, but no one else said anything about it and he decided not to bring it up. Maybe it would be better that way.

There was a good deal of visiting between the companies. Even the Germans in the Third and Fourth platoons had visitors, but only Germans scattered out in the other companies. They seemed to play cards more than anything else and soon had several games going, with a great chattering and gabbling.

Kemper's men were the object of much attention, because they were the only ones who had actually met the Rebels so far. Billy was a particular attraction as the only fellow who had actually killed one of them for sure, but he was pretty reticent about it and Tom could tell it still bothered him. Harlow's men had found three other dead ones, and the detail from Company A had buried them along with the others.

Tom could have claimed at least one of them, but he didn't say anything about it. It was an awful thing to kill a man, like that officer he had shot down from the rail fence, even if that was what you were supposed to do. He was glad he hadn't been able to see what the man looked like and didn't know who he was. He even submitted to gibes about the best shot in Dubois County being outdone by his little brother. When anyone noticed his torn and bloody sleeve, he dismissed it as only a nick. Toward evening he went to the creek and washed the blood out, then sewed up the rents in his coat and shirt sleeves with a needle and thread he carried in his pack.

That night the friends gathered in front of their tents. "Well, I don't guess you got t' see yore fren' Cap'n Harlow t'day, Tom," joshed Ab.

Tom laughed. "He's no friend of mine, an' th' less I see of him th' better."

Ab chuckled. "Aw, I don't think you needs t' bother 'bout keepin' outa his way. He's in 'nough trouble awreddy 'thout startin' up more with you."

"Yeah," George chimed in, "an' hit goes 'way back, long b'fore this bisness 'tween you an' him, er him lettin' his men throw 'way 'quipment on th' march." He spat on the ground. "Th' colonel shore don't think much uv him."

"No one else does either," added Johnny, " 'speshully his own men. They say he always treats 'em like he done Sargint Kemper."

George then brought up the subject of their dead friends. "Y' know, I kep' hopin' Ben mighta jist got lost or been took pris'ner till we heered 'bout him."

A hush settled over the group. "Shot in th' back, went right through his heart, they said," sighed Ab.

"That's why we didn't know what happened t' him," said Johnny. "Hit kilt him right then, an' he didn't even holler."

Suddenly the Germans nearby began singing a slow, sad tune and the men listened silently until it stopped. Tom thought nothing could have been more appropriate or better timed.

"I b'lieve they usta sing that song last winter in camp," reflected George.

"Yeah," agreed Ab, "an' hit's shore purty. I jist wish I could unnerstan' th' words."

"Could you understand it, Billy?" asked Tom. He had caught only a few words himself.

"Yeah, hit's a sad kinda song, 'bout sol'jers marchin' off t' war an' leavin' their gals an' folks b'hind."

"Germans is musical," affirmed Ab. "They're always singin' an' playin' and dancin'." He nodded. " I knows. I lived jist crost th' Padoky frum 'em all my life."

George changed the subject. "Say, Corp'ril," he asked, "how's yer arm whar y' got shot?"

"It's startin' t' heal up already," replied Tom. "It's not very sore an' beginnin' t' scab over."

"Did y' go t' th' surgeon with hit?"

"No, wasn't any need to. Sergeant Kemper put some medicine on it and bandaged it up."

"Y'know," said Johnny, "I guess that feller knows 'bout ever'thing they is t' know 'bout sol'jerin'. We wuz shore lucky we got him fer sargint."

No one disputed that.

"One thing's for sure," Tom went on. "I'm not standin' up on any fences anymore an' lettin' th' Rebels shoot at me."

There was general amazement.

"Is that what y' done?" asked George.

"It sure is," admitted Tom. "It was when they'd stopped shootin' an' were pullin' back. I wanted to see better."

"A feller'll do things like that if he don't watch hisself," mused George. "Y' git so skeered an' 'cited y' really don't know what yo're doin'." He laughed shortly. "I know I did."

"Me, too!" exclaimed Ab. "When I wuz runnin', hit wuz jist like I wuz flyin', like my laigs wuzn't workin' a'tall." He cackled. "They wuz, though. They wuz workin' real good."

"D'you remember jumpin' over that blowdown?" Tom asked him. "I'll bet you jumped twenty feet."

Ab shook his head. "Naw, I don't. I felt like I wuz flyin' all th' way, over blowdowns an' all."

Everybody laughed. "Yeah," confessed George, "with all them Rebels a-comin' an' all them balls a-flyin', a feller kin really run. I know I never run s' fast in my life."

"Say, Corp'ril," Ab began, "what's got th' matter with yore shootin' eye? Back home you wuz th' best shot in th' hull county, an' hyar Billy is a shootin' rings round ye."

Tom decided to let it go again. "Well, I'll tell you, Ab, what it was I shot at back home didn't shoot back. Now it does, and that makes a lot of difference."

There was uproarious laughter.

"Hit shore does!" whooped Ab. "Hit makes th' rifle sights jump 'round somethin' awful. I never hit nothin'. Never even come close, I 'spect." He turned to Billy. "Hit don't seem t' bother Billy none, though. How come?"

"I dunno. I jist ups and shoots. Lucky, I guess."

"You might be like ol' Uncle Charley Polson back home," speculated George. "I usta hunt with him a little when I wuz a young un."

"Is he as good as they say?" asked Johnny.

"He wuz," vowed George, "an' I guess he still is, only he don't hunt much enymore. Hit didn't look like he aimed a'tall. I've seen him knock turkey down on th' fly, an' with a rifle, too."

"Could he do hit reg'lar?" asked Billy.

"Most ever' shot. Seldom ever missed."

Ab joined in, "I've heard Pappy tell 'bout huntin' with Uncle Charley when he wuz young; Pappy wuz enyhow. Uncle Charley wuz awreddy old then, I guess. They wuz still deer then, an' even a few bears. Said ol' Uncle Charley never bothered t' make a stand or enything. He jist shot 'em on th' run an' got 'em nearly ever' time."

Burk hadn't said a word all evening. That was usual for him. His huge bulk was just a part of the background, like a tree or a big boulder. All at once he spoke up. "Well, you fellers kin go on talkin' all y' want, but I'm tard an' I'm gonna turn in." He got up and started for his tent.

Tom got out his watch. "Yeah, it's after nine o'clock, an' I expect we'd all better do th' same."

The group dispersed and everybody followed Burk's example.

The first chance he got, Kemper gave Tom a lecture about his brush with Captain Harlow. A soldier should never, never talk to an officer like Tom had, no matter what the reason. Kemper understood why Tom had done it, but nobody ever had to speak up for him. Anyhow, words never hurt anybody. Bullets would, and it might come to that if it ever happened again.

Tom knew Kemper was right and promised never to do it again. He didn't tell Kemper, but he realized he had been lucky it was Harlow instead of someone the colonel thought better of. But no one who had Rivers's good opinion would ever bully men like that.

To no one's surprise, Harve Akers soon backslid from his pledge of being a different fellow. He found some new friends in Hall's platoon, and one night they smuggled some brandy into camp. They got so noisy Kemper had to go quiet them, because Hall was still gone. Tom slept through it all, but he heard Kemper took their bottles away from them, and laid one of them flat on his back when he tried to stop Kemper from breaking them.

# 12

A few mornings later, the regiment was roused earlier than usual and put on the march for the gap to the south. Word circulated through the ranks that Jackson had doubled back and was approaching from the southwest on a road that paralleled the main one in the valley. He was as close to the gap as the rest of the brigade, if not closer, and might well be out to cut it off and put them all in the bag. Presumably the regiment was supposed to hold the gap until the rest of the brigade came up, and the brigade was to hold it until the division got there.

Tom thought the crafty Rebel commander had outfoxed them again. The division might be able to hold him at the gap, but there was little chance the brigade could, and the regiment wouldn't stand a ghost of a chance. Unless the division was close, it looked like they were gone up, and the men were unusually quiet on the march.

When the regiment reached the gap, it deployed facing south along the crest of a ridge that sloped west into the northern entrance. The road ran on south into the gap along the bank of a shallow, rocky creek with a wide bed. The west side of the entrance to the gap was a high, sheer cliff fringed by tall trees at its base. Beyond the cliff the ridge was so steep and unscalable on its southern slope that Rivers only picketed it with a platoon along the crest.

The company was on the end of the line that ran along the ridge east of the gap. The two German platoons were on the extreme left, and Kemper's platoon was next to them. Beyond the Germans to the east the ridge again became so steep no one would be able to climb it. In front of the line the ridge fell away in a gradual slope covered by a tangle of low scrub dotted with rocky outcroppings. A dense forest began about six hundred yards from the foot of the ridge and extended to the right so far that it left a clear space only a few hundred feet wider than the creek and the road. It clothed a ridge higher than the one the men were on a little farther south, so Jackson would be able to deploy for his attack unseen and very close.

Tom could find no fault with the deployment. Jackson wouldn't be able to get on their flanks unless he spent a lot more time at it than he could afford. He would have to attack frontally through the gap like the Persians at Thermopylae, but Rivers and his men wouldn't be able to do like Leonidas and his Trojans. If Jackson attacked, he would smash his way through like an avalanche.

The colonel sent a platoon south through the gap as skirmishers, then put his men to building a barricade of wood and stone along the crest of the ridge. Bedrock was only a few inches down, and they couldn't dig. When they were done, the men rested and waited. Many of them fidgeted nervously, but nobody said anything until a group of horsemen emerged from the gap at a rapid trot, looking back over their shoulders. "Thar's th' cav'lry that's been watchin' Jackson!" exclaimed Billy.

"Aw, that don't mean nothin!" replied Ab. "That cav'lry never lets th' Rebels git in sev'ril miles uv 'em!"

Nobody seemed much reassured, though, and when faint firing sounded south of the gap all hope was lost. The men looked at one another.

"Wal, there's Jackson," sighed George, "an' no sign uv even th' brigade yit."

The period of silence that followed was finally broken by a resigned voice from the line to the right. "Well, hit wuz a good reg'ment while hit lasted."

Tom looked at his brother and realized it had been a mistake for them to come in together.

Kemper didn't seem bothered and moved along in front of his men lecturing them about aiming low when the Rebels got close, because they would be shooting down on them and their bullets would go too high if they didn't.

Jake and Captain Dixon came up the line about the time he finished. "That's zackly what I wuz gonna say, Sargint," said Jake approvingly. He stopped and looked the men over. "You fellers reddy up hyar?" he asked briskly. He looked like he was, but Dixon didn't. He was so pale and drawn you would think he was sick.

*"Jawohl!"* replied Kemper grimly.

Jake nodded and put on a show of confidence. "I reckon we kin hold 'em all right till th' brigade gits up."

"How close is hit?" asked Johnny.

" 'Bout an hour's march, th' colonel 'lowed," replied Jake as he went on. Dixon followed like he had no will of his own, almost like he was walking in his sleep.

The men looked at each other. Several shook their heads and there was a sigh or two, but no one said anything. They all knew the brigade might as well be a whole day's march away.

Kemper was surveying the only tree along the ridge top. It was a little to his left, and so tall its roots must have found some fault in the bedrock or it would have been blown down long ago. Suddenly he ran over to where Jake was talking with Lieutenant Mertens while Dixon stood dumbly by. Kemper spoke to Mertens and pointed at the tree. The big blond lieutenant looked himself, then south at the next ridge. He nodded and shouted for someone named Grabner. A tall, lanky fellow came out of the ranks and started back with Kemper.

The skirmish firing was getting closer as the two stopped at the foot of the tree. Kemper pointed up and spoke so rapidly that Tom couldn't follow him, but Billy could. "He's gonna have him climb that tree 'fore th' Rebels git too close t' see what he kin frum up thar. They say that tall feller kin see awful fur. Grabner, his name is."

Tom nodded. "Maybe he'll be able to see over the next ridge down there."

Grabner took off his belt, laid it with his rifle at the foot of the tree, and shinnied expertly up the trunk. He caught the first limb, swung up on it, then went rapidly upward.

"He kin shore climb," remarked one of the men.

"Yeah," agreed Ab. "He'd be a good feller t' have 'long on a coon hunt."

Tom thought he had plenty of nerve, too. That skirmish firing was getting awfully close.

Grabner braced himself in a swaying fork near the top and began looking south. Kemper shouted to ask what he could see, but he took his time about replying. When he did, there was a prolonged exchange. Grabner seemed hesitant at first but was soon speaking confidently.

Tom understood that he could see the road where it turned back east after skirting the cliff to the right of the gap, but then it got too fast for him.

Billy volunteered a translation. "He kin see th' Rebels comin', an' he says they ain't many uv 'em, only 'bout a reg'ment with two guns."

Everybody's eyes widened. "Well, whadaya think uv that?" came an astonished exclamation.

Jake has been attracted by the calling back and forth and joined Kemper at the bottom of the tree. Dixon tagged along. Jake found it hard to believe when Kemper told him what Grabner had seen. "Is he shore?"

Kemper shouted to Grabner. The fellow was sure, absolutely sure. There was only one regiment with two guns. No cavalry. Skirmishers out in front. That was all. He could see the road for a long distance south, and there was nothing else on it, nothing at all.

When Kemper translated, Jake looked at him with pleased surprise and even Dixon began to show a little animation. "They reely ain't no more uv them than they is uv us!" marveled Jake.

Kemper nodded. *"Ja.* Iss so."

Suddenly Grabner started shouting again. Another prolonged exchange with Kemper followed. Tom understood it pretty well, but the others had to wait for Billy's translation. "He kin see over the next ridge down thar, 'way south whar this road comes off that un that goes on east. He says they's a lot of dust stringin' out on that road that this un comes off uv atter hit goes on, like a hull army's marchin' east on hit."

Jake was electrified. "That proves hit! Jackson's only sendin' a reg'ment agin us an' goin' on east with th' rest uv his army! Th' colonel's gotta know 'bout this!" He left at a run, Dixon trailing in his wake and beginning to look normal again.

Kemper started another exchange with Grabner. He wanted to make sure about that dust moving east. He was assured that it was, and that it was moving awfully fast considering the distance.

The men nodded smilingly at one another. That settled it. It was Jackson all right.

Rivers arrived along with his adjutant, Captain Owen, a small, neat-looking fellow, clean-shaven and with sandy hair. When Rivers confirmed what Jake had told him, he reacted explosively. "Damn that cavalry! They reported Jackson was coming at us with his whole army!"

Owen shook his head. "That's because they didn't stay close enough."

Rivers didn't seem to think that anyone could see so far with the naked eye. Anyhow, he sent Owen up the tree with his glasses. The captain wasn't much of a climber, and Grabner had to reach down and help him to the first limb. Once he was settled, he only confirmed what Grabner had said and marveled at his eyesight.

The skirmish firing had been getting closer all the time, and suddenly the skirmishers who had gone out appeared on the road hurrying back. Rivers called up the tree, "Come down, both of you, or they'll shoot you out of there like a couple of crows!"

They came down, Owen first and a lot less gracefully than Grabner. Rivers went up to Grabner and said, "I want to thank you. You've done the regiment a great service."

The fellow understood he was being thanked. He brought his heels together and snapped to attention. *"Danke schön, Herr Oberst!"* Tom noticed that Grabner's hawklike face was complemented by light blue eyes with very dark pupils, a lot like those of a bird of prey. When he went back to his comrades, they welcomed him as "Old Eagle Eyes," or *"Alte Adler Augen,"* as they put it.

Rivers turned to Kemper. "Well, I know exactly what those Rebels coming up the road are going to do now!" Kemper only nodded, so he went on. "They'll try to bluff us into surrendering. They'll run up those two guns they've got and claim Jackson's whole army is behind them." He laughed, showing his strong white teeth. "Oh, I'm on to their game, thanks to you for sending that sharp-eyed fellow up that tree!"

Kemper came to attention. *"Danke schön, Herr Oberst!"*

Rivers seemed to understand him. "Well, we've got nothing to worry about now," he said smilingly. "Jackson's after bigger game than our brigade. I guess he just thought he'd snap us up in passing if he could."

Tom had been keeping an eye on the gap, but it was Billy who saw the Rebel skirmishers first. "Thar they air! I kin see 'em pokin' their heads up 'bove th' crick bank!"

Then Tom saw several nondescript hats and caps showing above the bank ground a bend in the creek. He saw the gleam of weapons, too, and shouted, "Get down, everybody! They're gonna shoot!"

There was a scramble to get behind the barricade, Rivers and Owen scrambling with the others.

A ragged volley came from the creek. Bullets hissed overhead or thudded into the barricade, Captain Owen hadn't hunkered low enough, and his hat flew off. He retrieved it and fingered a rent in the crown.

"That was close, Captain," said Rivers.

Owen nodded as he put his hat back on. "Yes, sir, it was. A little lower and I wouldn't have any head."

"Fire at will!" shouted Rivers, and his men began to shoot back, but slowly, because the targets were so fleeting. Both sides were being careful about exposing themselves, and the fire of the Rebels was also sporadic. The only casualty so far had been Owen's hat.

The Rebels had brought their guns up down the creek out of rifle range. They swung them around, backed the teams up, then started letting them down into the shallow, rocky bed.

Rivers took a look. "There's the only thing that bothers me. They'll give us a beating with those guns even if they don't do anything else."

"Maybe we can move the men back over the crest when they open up," suggested Owen.

Rivers shook his head. "No, they could rush us then. Those guns will be able to fire over their infantry until they'd be on us."

"Yes, sir, I guess you're right. I just wish we had some guns."

"You go back down there where we were, Captain," directed Rivers. "I'm going to stay up here where I can see better, for a while anyhow."

"Yes, sir." Owen went down the back of the ridge and started toward the gap.

Kemper was crouching some distance away studying the cliff face on the other side of the entrance to the gap, looking sideways through a low place in the barricade. Suddenly he turned and called, *"Herr Oberst! Herr Oberst! Kommen sie hier, bitte!"*

Rivers went over, moving in a crouch. Kemper pointed at the cliff and started talking; then Rivers got out his field glasses and turned them on the cliff.

The shooting was still going on, but Tom hadn't fired a shot. Every time he had aimed, his target had disappeared before he could fire, and he was getting impatient. Suddenly a head under a wide-brimmed black hat appeared above the creek bank closer than the others. Tom took quick aim and fired but knew he was going to miss when he pulled the trigger. Several others fired at Black Hat, but he was undeterred and took careful aim despite the bullets kicking up the dirt around him. A blossom of smoke lanced with flame obscured him, and to the right in the next company a man collapsed soundlessly over the barricade, his rifle slipping from his nerveless hands to clatter down the slope in front.

While he was loading behind the barricade, Tom noticed that Kemper was studying the cliff with Rivers's glasses.

Tom capped his rifle and raised his head to look over the log. Before he could find a target, a man appeared at the edge of the wood waving a white cloth. "Flag o' truce! Flag o' truce!" he cried, his voice faint with distance. "Parley! Parley! Don't shoot!" He seemed to be an officer. Anyhow, his uniform was better than most, and he wore boots.

"Well, here's their bluff," said Rivers as he got to his feet. He got on top of the barricade and shouted, "Cease fire! Cease fire!" although the shooting had already stopped. He looked back at Kemper. "All right, Sergeant. Pick your men and go ahead. Good luck."

Tom had no idea what Rivers meant and was watching the enemy gunners manhandle their pieces into position in the creek bed opposite the cliff to the right when Kemper took his arm. *"Komm mit mir,"* he said. Johnny and George were with him.

Tom couldn't imagine where they were going, but Billy seemed to know. "Kin I go, too?"

"*Nein*. I nodt take de two *Brüder*."

Kemper led them down the back of the ridge. Tom noticed that Johnny and George had removed their bayonets, so he did the same. When they reached the bottom, Kemper headed for the road at a run, the others following. Tom was mystified until George told him what they were going to do as they ran.

Kemper had spied a shelf of rock that ran along the cliff face opposite where the Rebels were setting up their guns. He was going to cross the creek and the road around a bend where they wouldn't be seen, then climb the ridge along the cliff on the other side of the gap. If he could find a way to get down to the shelf, they were going to fire on those Rebel gunners. It sounded pretty risky, but Tom guessed Kemper had thought it out.

They went the whole distance at a run and scarcely slowed when they climbed the ridge on the other side of the gap. Although his men would have been glad of a rest, Kemper didn't stop except to tell the lieutenant in charge of the picket line along the crest what they were going to do and ask him if the Rebels had pickets on the other side. He said the only Rebels his men had seen over there had been a few horsemen who had ridden around awhile when they first came up and then gone back. He seemed surprised at what they were going to do and shook his head when they left. It was pretty obvious that he never expected to see them again.

The tops of the tall trees at the base of the cliff gave them good cover, and when Kemper reached the edge he turned right and led them along it. He kept looking down, and all at once stopped and motioned them to get down and stay where they were. He slung his rifle, dropped to his knees, and disappeared from sight. Tom guessed he had found what looked like a way down to the shelf and was testing it.

While they waited, Tom could hear the Rebel artillerymen talking and splashing about in the creek, but the foliage screened them from view. Johnny was closer and could evidently hear better. Anyhow, he suddenly put his hands over his ears just as a tremendous explosion smashed the air, followed so closely by another that they were almost one. The Rebel guns had opened fire.

All at once Kemper's head appeared above the edge of the cliff. He beckoned, so they slung their rifles and crawled toward him. He was standing on the face of the cliff with his feet in a crevice. About ten feet below, the shelf ran along the face of the cliff. It was really only a ledge, narrow and irregular, with frequent gaps. It slanted steeply downward before leveling out and getting wider.

Kemper let himself down to the ledge, and his men followed one by one. Tom was last, and couldn't help thinking how far he would fall if he slipped from one of the precarious footholds. The tops of the trees growing along the base of the cliff were only a few feet from the ledge, and their trunks fell away to the ground far below. Through the foliage he could occasionally see the creek and the road beside it. Men were moving about between the woods and the creek, and although he could hear the gunners as they worked their pieces, he couldn't see them yet. He reached the ledge and moved along behind the others.

"KA-WHOOM!" Both guns fired together and the blast seemed enough to blow them off the ledge. Tom had never imagined anything could be so loud. Smoke trapped by the cliff began to obscure their view as they went on down the ledge, occasionally negotiating a gap. He caught a glimpse of the tumbled rocks at the foot of the cliff through one of them. The rocks seemed to be hundreds of feet below, and he wondered how few of them were going to get away once the shooting started and the Rebels saw them.

As they went on, the ledge leveled out and grew wider. Soon it was so wide a wagon could have rolled along it, and it was a relief not to have to cling to the face of the cliff like a fly.

Kemper stopped, his eyes on the creek. He had evidently found the position he wanted, but Tom couldn't see anything because of the foliage. Then came another shattering explosion, but the blast wasn't nearly as bad this time, which meant they were close to the guns. Smoke boiled along the face of the cliff, and Tom had to choke back a cough. He swallowed convulsively, and his eyes watered.

Kemper stepped back and motioned for his men to file past him. Tom started to pass the others, but Kemper stopped him and they put their heads together.

Kemper gave his instructions in a stage whisper. They were to aim low, at the gunners' knees, because of the firing angle. The Rebels would probably spot them after they fired a few times, and he would lead them back the way they had come. They were to watch him and run when he did. If anyone fell or was shot, the others were to go on. There wouldn't be anything they could do, and the Rebels would get them all if they stopped.

Kemper looked at them searchingly. *"Verstehen?"*

They all nodded as the guns roared again. George and Johnny looked tense and excited, but Tom felt as calm as if he were out on a shooting range.

Kemper spread them out ten or fifteen feet apart. Tom was on the far right and couldn't see anything from where he was, so he moved on until he could see the guns through the foliage at a steep downward angle. The pieces stood in the creek while the gunners splashed about them in a foot or so of water.

They unslung their rifles, capped them, and got ready to fire. Tom aimed at the man most directly in front of him, who was sitting on the trail of the nearest gun manipulating the aiming mechanism, and lowered his sights to allow for the angle. When Kemper fired he pulled the trigger and his target was knocked off his seat into the water, his cap flying off, but Tom knew his shot had been too low to be fatal. Another man went down screaming unintelligibly, but Kemper's target collapsed without a sound.

Tom loaded quickly. When he raised his rifle, a young-looking officer ran into view from the right, where he had been standing behind the guns out of sight. He aimed at the man's boot tops and shot him down.

The gray-clad artillerymen milled around in shouting confusion. Tom reloaded and shot a man waving a rammer staff. He fell; then all at once the survivors broke and ran for the woods beyond, leaving the guns deserted except for the crumpled forms around them.

Infantry ran about between the guns and the woods looking wildly for the source of the fire that had cut down the gunners. Some threw up their rifles and fired at the top of the cliff. None of them even looked at its sheer, smoke-shrouded face.

While he loaded, Tom saw out of the corner of his eye that Kemper was staying for at least one more shot. There were still good targets out there, and they hadn't been seen yet.

Just as Tom raised his rifle, an infantryman clambered up out of the creekbed and stopped directly in front of him, his rifle poised and eyes searching the top of the cliff. It was the best target yet and he didn't miss. At his shot the fellow tumbled back into the creek, still gripping his rifle.

Kemper wasn't running yet, so Tom started loading. As he rammed down a cartridge, a tall officer in a fine uniform came rushing toward the creek shouting and brandishing a revolver, his eyes on the cliff face. Behind him a mob of riflemen came at a run.

Tom capped his rifle without taking his eyes off the tall officer, raised it, and took careful aim. He fired and the fellow stopped like he had struck an invisible wall. As he crumpled to the ground, his hat fell off to reveal a mane of iron gray hair.

When Tom finally looked to his left, all he could see was George's flying form heading away from him along the shelf. He started to follow, but when the foremost of the Rebels stopped and raised their rifles, he realized he had waited too long. As he stopped they fired and something plunged off the shelf to crash through the trees toward the ground below.

Tom whirled and started the other way. He had no idea how far the ledge went, but it was his only chance. Maybe it ran on to where he could jump down to the ground, or maybe he could find a tree limb he could reach farther along.

He saw none as he ran, and after a hundred feet or so the ledge suddenly broke off. The ground was at least a hundred feet below. No tree limbs were even in leaping distance. He was trapped, and the Rebels would shoot him off the cliff like a squirrel out of a tree.

They were raising a great hullabaloo to his left and moving toward him, undoubtedly looking along the ledge. He could expect no mercy when they saw him.

He loaded his rifle so he could take one of them with him and started toward them. The ledge was very wide, and he stayed close to the cliff face so he wouldn't be seen until he was close enough to be sure of his aim.

He knew he was going to die in a few moments, but it caused him no qualms. He had always heard that pictures of a man's whole life ran through his mind during his last moments, but only one came to him. "Good-bye, Sally," he said to himself.

Piles of dead leaves had collected in the angle between the ledge and the cliff, so he walked carefully to avoid the rustling and crackling that could give him away. Suddenly the hard rock was gone from under his feet and he sank into the leaves, to his waist until he caught himself. He had blundered into a big leaf-filled hole in the shelf and would have gone all the way through if he hadn't. Scarcely believing his good luck, he wedged himself against the sides of the hole and burrowed into the leaves until he was completely covered, rifle and all.

He waited in his leafy bed as still as a mouse. It smelled of mold and decay, but it was a pleasant smell. It was nice not to have to die after all.

The Rebels were moving closer, out from the foot of the cliff, so they could see up on the ledge. They were talking loudly and angrily. "They's boun' t' be more uv 'em up thar," insisted one of them stridently. "They's boun' t' be! They done 'nough shootin' fer a dozen men, an' we only seen three uv 'em!"

"Yeah," grumbled another, "an' two uv 'em got away." George had undoubtedly been the one who hadn't. He had been last.

The Rebels stopped immediately below. "Wal, that shelf uv rock runs out jist over thar. They ain't none uv 'em come down this way eny furder."

"Naw, nobody's up thar, er we'd a seen 'em."

"Aw, Bob, y' dern fool!" scoffed someone with a high-pitched voice. "We cain't see back on that shelf hardly a'tall! Fifty uv 'em could be layin' back agin that cliff up thar!"

Bob took umbrage. "Well, how air ye gonna git up thar an' see, Mr. Smart Alec? Ye got wings?"

"Naw, I ain't got no wings, but I kin climb trees, an' they's boun' t' be one 'long hyar I kin git up thar on."

They went back the way they had come, their voices fading. After a while they stopped, and could be heard well enough for Tom to tell that the fellow with the high voice was climbing. As he went higher, he and his comrades began to call back and forth loudly enough to be understood.

"Sim!" called someone on the ground. "Y' might not be eny good fer enything else, but y' kin shore climb trees!"

Guffaws sounded from below. "Yeah! Jist like a dang monkey!"

Gleeful hee-haws came from the ground. Tom couldn't help grinning. These fellows sounded just like the men in his regiment, and it was hard to realize they would kill him without hesitation if they saw him. There was little danger of that, though. Even if Sim managed to reach the ledge, he wasn't likely to go poking through all the leaves on it.

Sim's voice grew louder as he joshed back and forth with his friends. After a brief silence, he called out from very close, "I ain't gonna go trying' t' git off on that shelf an' maybe breakin' my neck. I kin see all 'long hit an' they ain't nobody thar!"

"Ye shore?" asked a voice from below.

" 'S shore as death an' taxes," vowed Sim. "Wal, I'm comin' back down. You fellers pick me up an' put me back t'gether agin if'n I fall."

"Oh, we will," laughed someone from below. "Jist like Humpity Dumpity!"

"Y' reckon them Yankees mighta had some uv them britchloaders, er maybe even repeatin' rifles?" speculated one of the men on the ground.

"That must be hit!" exclaimed Sim, his voice fainter now. "That's th' only way them sonsabitches coulda done s' much shootin'!"

The others seemed to agree, and the talk died away as Sim descended. After a while he seemed to reach the ground and the voices faded away.

Tom raised his head above the leaves. He could see nothing through the foliage but the tops of the taller trees at the edge of the wood across the creek, but that was all right. No one could see him either. Skirmish firing was still going on, and from what he could hear the Rebels were still pretty active. He decided to wait until it was nearly dark before slipping away, so he might as well stay where he was. He made himself more comfortable in his bed of leaves, lay back, and relaxed. He hadn't realized how tired he was until he did. He felt like he had done the hardest day's work in his life, although he hadn't done anything but run around and fire his rifle a few times. Suddenly a feeling of weakness overcame him and he began to tremble all over. He closed his eyes and hoped the fit would pass. It soon did, but he couldn't understand what had gotten wrong with him all of a sudden.

After a while Tom could tell that the guns were being limbered up, hauled up out of the creek, and taken away, by men who didn't know much about it to judge from the shouting.

Before that was done the dead and wounded were collected under the direction of someone with a deep bass voice. Some of them cried out and one screamed something about his leg. It sounded like they were being loaded into wagons to be taken away.

Sounds of digging and desultory talk close to the base of the cliff showed what was being done with the dead. After a long time they stopped, and a funeral service was conducted by the man with the deep bass voice. Tom could only hear it well enough to tell what it was and recognize the hymn sung afterward as "Rock of Ages." He realized he was lucky his funeral wasn't being preached, too, and wondered about the men he had killed. He was really sure of only three; the artillery lieutenant, the infantryman on the creek bank, and the tall officer with the iron gray hair. The faint singsong of the service made him wish he hadn't killed anybody.

He didn't wait until it was completely dark, because then the way would be too dangerous. When he got up out of the leaves and started back along the ledge, there hadn't been any shooting for quite a while, but he went slowly and kept a wary eye on the road and the strip of open ground across the creek. Where the foliage in front was thin, he would see the Rebels clustered around small fires or walking about. None of them ever looked his way.

It was nearly dark when he came to the place where they had come down on the ledge. It was going to be harder to get up than it had been to get down and he wondered how Kemper and Johnny had managed it with the Rebels shooting at them. He slung his rifle, found a handhold, and pulled himself up to the crevice where they had put their feet on the way down. He made another few feet by finding a grip higher in the crevice. Then, balancing precariously, he reached as high as he could and felt around until he found a rock projection that seemed strong enough. After that it was easy, and he soon found himself safely on the ridge top. He called softly until he attracted the attention of the nearest picket, then identified himself and came out into the open.

Three men were standing a little to his left. Suddenly one of them called, "Tom? Tom? Is that you?" It was Billy, and the two others were Kemper and the lieutenant in charge of the pickets.

"Yeah, it's me," replied Tom, and Billy came rushing toward him.

He dropped his rifle and leapt on his brother, hugging him and nearly bearing him to the ground. "Tom! Tom!" he cried. "I thought ye wuz a goner!"

Tom braced himself. "Well, I'm not," he replied through a strange constriction in his throat. "Here I am, safe an' sound." Billy still clung to him and was half-sobbing, so Tom said huskily, "Come on now, Billy, let's get straightened out here."

Kemper was as pleased as Billy, but he didn't hug Tom. When they started down the ridge, Billy insisted on keeping an arm around his brother's shoulders. "What happened, Tom? Sargint Kemper an' Johnny come in sayin' George'd been kilt an' they wuz afeard you, too."

*"Ja,"* interjected Kemper. "Me *und* Chonny, ve vaidt und vait, budt you nodt *komm*. Ve go back *und* Beely vant back again to *komm*, and ve doo."

Tom told his story as they went on, admitting that he had gotten so taken up with shooting the tall officer he hadn't seen the others run. They agreed that it was a good thing, though, because he would have gone the way George had if he had followed him. One of Johnny's shoe heels had been shot off, and both he and Kemper had been peppered with fragments of rock and bullets. Kemper shook his head and admitted it was his fault. He had just waited too long.

Billy told what had happened with the regiment. That Rebel emissary had tried to bluff the colonel into surrendering, like Rivers had expected. He hadn't let on that he knew it was only a bluff and had palavered with him a long time, even going back and pretending to have a council of his officers about it. When the Rebel got tired of it and demanded an answer, Rivers told him no, his men would die where they stood rather than surrender.

Then the Rebels had opened up with their guns. The barricade was demolished in several places and several men hurt when the firing from the cliff broke out and put a stop to it.

Then some of the infantry had run toward the cliff and opened fire. Billy hadn't seen anyone fall, but they agreed George was dead. Even if he hadn't been hit, the fall would have killed him.

It was long after dark when they got back to their platoon, but no one had turned in yet. Tom's friends were glad to see him. Burk almost crushed his hand and Ab insisted on fixing him some supper, but he had little appetite for hardtack and salt pork and didn't eat much.

Tom's sleep that night was restless. He kept shooting down Confederate officers in fine uniforms, but they would always get up and reproach him. He couldn't shoot them again because they were helpless and unoffending. He woke up several times trembling and sweating.

The men manned the ridge top before daybreak, but when the sun came up there was no sign of the enemy. Mertens was sent out with one of his platoons to scout.

Tom was tired and sore, but Billy kept bothering him, talking all the time. They sat in the barricade watching Mertens and his men scout around. After a while a detachment of cavalry started south through the gap, accompanied by hooting and catcalling from the infantry.

"I hope they don't run back hyar th' first Rebel they see," grumbled someone.

"Yeah," replied Ab. "Y' cain't cou't on them yallerlaigs fer nothin'. If'n they'd kept clost t' th' Rebels yestidy we wouldn't a been thinkin' Jackson's hull army wuz comin' at us." He shook his head. "Y' know, I shore thought our time had come thar fer a while."

Several others made similar confessions.

Mertens and his men finished and started back.

"Hey!" exclaimed Billy. "I b'lieve they've took a pris'ner!"

It did look like it. They were bringing somebody along who wore the kind of clothing the Rebels generally did. Mertens took his men back to their position and sent the prisoner on along the ridge in charge of one of his sergeants, a small dark fellow named Grim. The prisoner was a slim, pallid youth with dark, tousled hair.

Kemper stopped them and spoke with Grim in German. The pallid youth stood listlessly, looking blankly about. *"Ja,"* said Kemper. "He iss preesnor."

"Hey, Johnny!" called Ab. "How come ye t' git ketched?"

"Went t' sleep las' night in a thicket so nobody'd bother me, 'n' these fellers woke me up. Ever'body wuz gone, th' hull reg'ment, guns an' all."

He talked just like anyone else. A change of clothing would make him one of them. The men clustered around gaping.

"Y' musta slep' purty sound, Johnny," remarked someone.

"Ah wuz tard, real tard," explained the prisoner. "We been marchin' fer a week, twenty, thirty mile a day, an' I'm a city boy, frum

Petersburg. I jist cain't stand hit like them backwoods country jakes," he admitted. "We calls ourselfs Jackson's foot cav'lry, an' a feller 'bout needs a hoss t' keep up." He shook his head sadly.

There was general laughter. The men appreciated that.

The fellow spoke to Ab. "I thought you fellers wuz 'mericans even if ye wuz Yankees. How come y' got all these furriners? Them fellers that took me in that thicket couldn't speak no English a'tall, 'ceptin' their lootenant."

"Oh, they's 'mericans all right," replied Ab with a nod. "Jist ain't larnt t' talk English very good yet."

"Dutchmen, ain't ye?" the prisoner asked Kemper.

*"Nein.* Chermans," was the reply.

"All th' same, I guess," said the Rebel with a wan smile.

Grim put a stop to it and took the prisoner on. Others wanted to stop them and talk, but he wouldn't allow it.

Captain Owen came down the line and had Grabner climb the tree again. He reported that the only sign of any Rebels he could see was dust going south on that road that ran through the gap. There was none on that road that it came off of like there had been yesterday.

"Well, I guess th' Rebels is gone fer shore," said Billy.

There was no argument about that, and the men began to take their ease around their barricade.

After a while Tom asked Billy, "Why don't you go down t' Regiment and see Anders? Maybe you can find out what that prisoner had to say."

Kemper agreed, so Billy left.

As soon as Billy was seen on his way back an hour or so later, an audience began to collect, because he obviously had something to tell. "Well, what'd y' find out?" he was immediately asked.

"Aw, Fred said th' pris'ner jist talked an' talked, told th' colonel ever'thing he knowed. Fred, he heered hit all."

"Where'd he say his reg'ment went to?"

"He 'lowed hit had gone back t' jine up with Jackson. Wazn't no orders yit when he went off an' went t' sleep las' night, though, an' then this mornin' hit wuz jist gone."

"What made him think that?"

"Well, they wuz jist sent off at th' las' minit when they come t' this road yestidy, 'cause that feller that talked t' th' colonel an' tried t' git him t' s'render knowed we hadn't been in any fightin' yit 'n' thought he could skeer us inta surrenderin', er that we'd be easy t' beat if he couldn't."

The men laughed. “Well, we shore didn’t skeer!” crowed someone.

Billy went on. “He said Jackson give this feller a reg’ment an’ two guns t’ skeer us with ’n’ told him t’ parole us if we give up. ’Lowed he didn’t want a bunch uv pris’ners on his hands.”

“Then what?”

“Well, Jackson told this feller t’ hold th’ gap if he took hit an’ send him word, but if he couldn’t take hit right ’way, t’ give hit up ’n’ go back ’n’ ketch up.” Billy laughed. “This hyar pris’ner, he ’lowed he wuz glad in a way he wouldn’t be ’long when they wuz ketchin’ up.”

“Y’ mean he really wuzn’t gonna ’tack us?”

“Oh yeah, if we got skeered an’ hit looked like hit’d be easy. He had strict orders not t’ try hit if’n hit looked like hit’d be tough.”

“Well, I got a good idy what hit wuz that made him think hit’d be tough,” said Ab with a laugh. “Hit wuz that shootin’ frum that cliff.”

Billy grinned. “Yeah, that really shook ’em up.”

“How many men did they lose?” asked Johnny.

“This pris’ner, he didn’t ’zackly know ’bout th’ wounded, but he seen seven graves fer th’ dead ones.” Billy sobered. “One uv’ em wuz George’s. They found him all broke up on th’ rocks. Th’ pris’ner said they had a fun’ral an’ all; their chaplain done hit. He said th’ chaplain prayed fer all uv ’em, George, too.”

Billy looked down and the men fell silent. Tom knew he would miss George more than most of the others. They had been boys together and used to go to church early on Sunday mornings in the winter to build a fire and get the building warm before the other people came.

“They wuz two uv ’em they didn’t bury,” Billy went on, “their colonel an’ an artillery lootenant. They wuz gonna take their bodies home ’cause they wuz frum jist up th’ valley th’ way Jackson wuz goin’.”

Billy’s words hit Tom hard. He had killed both of them, and they weren’t just anonymous targets anymore. The colonel was the tall officer with the iron gray hair. His wife was a widow now and his children fatherless. The lieutenant was a fine-looking young fellow, maybe engaged to be married like he was. He looked away and scarcely heard what followed.

“Y’ say hit reely shook ’em up?” asked someone eagerly.

“Yeah, an’ that feller that talked Jackson inta lettin’ ’em come agin us ’lowed he musta been wrong ’bout us bein’ new an’ all. Said we fit like vet’rans.”

Tom went toward the fire as the talk went on. He started making some coffee, although he really didn’t want any.

After a while Kemper joined him. *"Was ist los,* Dom? *Bist du krank?"*

"No, Sergeant, I'm not sick or anything."

Kemper looked at him understandingly and shook his head. *"Es ist schwer, aber es ist der Krieg, und Mann muss seinem Schuldigkeit tun."*

"Yeah, it's war, and a man's got to do his duty," replied Tom wearily.

Kemper switched to his version of English. "You iss goot *Mann,* Dom. You nodt miss vun schodt, nodt vun."

"Yeah, I guess I'm a good man, when it comes to killin' people anyhow." The coffee was done. "Here, Sergeant, have some."

After Kemper took the coffee, they sat sipping and silently looking into the fire.

# 13

The other three regiments of the brigade came up early in the afternoon and went into camp along the road to the north. The regiment stayed where it was along the ridge, and the men put up their shelter tents on the shady side, as they were sweltering in an early spell of hot weather.

The first chance they had, Tom, Billy, and their friends went to the graves at the foot of the cliff that the prisoner had told them about. There were ten of them now, because the three other men killed the day before had been buried there. Their graves were marked with headboards, but the others weren't. There was no way of telling which was George's, so they gathered wildflowers and decorated them all. Tom felt better afterward and was able to sleep untroubled by wild dreams.

One evening after supper they were told to cook two days' rations and be ready to march the next morning. After the rations were cooked, there was much speculation about where they were going, and Billy was persuaded to go find out from Fred Anders, who would be sure to know.

It was well after dark when Billy returned, and some of the men had already turned in. "Well," he announced, "they've d'cided Jackson ain't int'rested in trappin' us, so we're gonna trap him." The men already in their tents crawled out and hurried over.

"How're we gonna trap Jackson?" Ab wanted to know.

"Make a forty-mile march t'morra 'n' take a crossroads that'll cut off his way outa th' valley."

"Whar is hit? T' th' north?"

"Yeah, an' Banks's hull army is comin' southwest, down th' valley."

"An' he'll be ketched 'tween us," mused Ab. Suddenly he had second thoughts. "Who's gonna help us? Jackson ain't gonna git trapped with no brigade. Banks might hold him, but we shore cain't."

"Th' d'vision is jist west uv hyar. Hit'll git thar right 'way atter we do, an' th' rest uv th' corps is close. But we're s'posed t' s'prise that d'vision uv Jackson's that's holdin' th' crossroads an' take hit first. If we cain't do that, hit's all gone up."

The men ruminated. "A forty-mile march," sighed Johnny, "an' in this heat. They say hit wuz 'bove ninety yestidy."

Ab had additional doubts. "Now, how's a brigade gonna take somethin' frum a d'vision? Hit all sounds kinda cockeyed t' me."

"Hit's a little un, only three brigades and none uv 'em up t' stren'th, an' we're s'posed t' s'prise 'em."

"How?"

"Y' see," Billy went on, "they'll know when we start 'n' 'spect us t' take at least two days t' git thar, an' they'll 'spect us t' wait on th' d'vision b'fore tryin' enything enyhow."

"Why, they'll know whar we air ever' minit! That cav'lry uv theirn—"

"Naw, hit's all pulled out. They reckon Jackson called hit up t' whar he is, furder up th' valley frum that crossroads."

"Yeah, I know we ain't seen none fer sev'ril days now, but you know they'll have pickets 'n' outposts 'n' all that."

"Our cav'lry's gonna take keer uv 'em. Hit's gonna go 'head an' take 'em all up."

"I wouldn't count on that dum cav'lry fer nuthin'! They'll sound like a herd uv el'fants goin' up that road, an' they're th' biggest bunch uv cowards they ever wuz!"

"Aw, this is a new bunch, an' th' colonel says they're a lot better'n them we had b'fore. They ain't reg'lar sol'jers. Fred called 'em partysins er sumthin' like that."

"Wal, I shore hope they air," sighed Ab. "Them Rebels'll be layin' fer us if'n they ain't no better'n cav'lry gen'ally is."

"Th' hull thing's th' colonel's idy," Billy went on. "Th' gin'ral wanted t' wait fer th' d'vision b'fore tryin' hit 'cause that's what's holdin' that crossroads fer Jackson, but th' colonel talked him inta trying' hit with jist our brigade, s'prisin' 'em like that."

Tom had a question. "Now, if it doesn't work, if they're ready for us, we'll just sit tight an' wait for th' division after we get there, maybe for th' corps. Right?"

"Right. That's what we're s'posed t' do, but th' colonel's countin' on s'prisin' 'em."

Tom was satisfied and his estimation of Colonel Rivers went up several notches.

"Now, when hit comes t' trappin' Jackson," Ab went on, "I'm afeared no one's gonna trap that feller 'lessen he wants t' git trapped, an' then look out!"

"I shore hope he's fur 'nough frum that crossroads fer th' corps t' git thar b'fore he kin come down on us with his hull army," said Johnny.

Tom decided to put an end to this before someone brought up what was going to be the biggest problem of all, assuming they took the crossroads. That would be holding it against an immediate counterattack by what would probably be double their numbers. "Well," he said, "if we've got to make a forty-mile march t'morrow, we'd better be turnin' in."

The regiment was first on the road the next morning, so it would lead the column, with a Massachusetts regiment next in line. Kemper bustled about making sure all canteens were full and packs properly adjusted. "Ve make de *lange, lange Marsch,"* he warned, *"und* nodt trink de *Wasser* gone so soon!"

"Hit's gonna be a hot un, too," lamented Harve, "hotter'n 'twuz yestidy, I'll bet."

"That's gonna be awful hot!" added someone farther back.

"These hyar May hot spells is bad," sighed Ab. "A feller ain't used t' th' heat yit."

"For'ard, *march!"* sounded from the front, and the column got under way with a scuffle of feet and a creak and rattle of equipment, like some great disjointed machine.

For a time there was the usual chatter among the men early in a march, but it died away soon after the sun showed its brazen disk above the horizon.

As the sun rose higher and the temperature went up, the men began to sweat through their clothes. They marched in a perpetual cloud of dust, which caked their sweaty faces and gradually turned their uniforms into a shade of yellowish gray. It irritated noses and throats and caused continual coughing and sneezing. Eyes watered and were generally kept open only enough to see. Thirst was an added torture, but under Kemper's watchful eyes canteens were used sparingly.

About the middle of the morning the colonel rode back along the column. He reined up at the head of the company and spoke briefly with Captain Dixon, who left the column and stood to the side as the company went by. He fell in with Lieutenant Mertens leading the last two platoons, exchanged a few words, then trotted back past the marching men. Caked and smeared with dust, he was hardly the dandy now.

Mertens halted the last platoon, deployed it across the width of the road, and had his men fix bayonets.

"What's all that fer?" wondered Ab as the Germans quickstepped to catch up.

*"Für den Nachzügler,"* replied Kemper.

"For th' stragglers," translated Tom promptly, although he hadn't heard the word before.

At that moment Mertens shouted a command and his men brought their rifles down in unison, bayonets outthrust.

"You fellers see that?" asked Ab as the Germans went back to shoulder arms.

"Yeah, I seen hit," replied Harve Akers, "an' here's one feller that ain't gonna straggle. Them Dutchmen 'd stick a feller shore 'nough."

While the men were still looking back, they saw a wagon come up behind Mertens's men, only its top showing dimly in the dust. "I guess that's t' haul them that cain't make hit," said Billy.

"Must be," replied Tom, "an' there'll be some that can't."

"Yeah," agreed Ab, "sunstroke an' sich like."

"Why don't they let us put our packs in that wagin?" wondered Johnny. "Hit'd shore be a big help." You could tell by the way he talked that his strength was rapidly ebbing.

"That wagin's gonna be full uv men that cain't march no more," Ab told him. "Ain't gonna be no room fer eny packs."

"I b'lieve reg'lations says one hour marchin' an' ten minits restin'," gasped Johnny after a while.

"That's jist when y' got th' time," Billy told him, "an' we hain't. We got t' make forty mile t'day."

"Oh, I could shore use a few minits," panted Johnny, "jist a few."

Tom was about to tell him he would do better if he didn't talk so much when Burk spoke up. "Hyar, Johnny, lemme take yer rifle." When Johnny didn't respond, the big fellow just reached over and took the weapon. Johnny mumbled his thanks.

Tom looked at his brother, who was swinging loosely along, his head down and covered with dust. He was bearing up splendidly, and Tom marveled. The boy had resources no one would have expected, least of all his big brother.

Johnny progressively assumed a peculiar gait. He seemed to be leaning forward, on the point of falling, just before he took each step, as though his dragging feet could be impelled only by the necessity of catching his falling body. After a while Burk spoke to Kemper. "I'm gonna hafta take his pack, too."

Kemper dropped back and between the two of them they got Johnny's pack off as they marched. Kemper took the extra rifle, and Burk slung the pack on his broad back beside his own, then fastened the straps to his belt. Johnny scarcely seemed to notice and lurched along as before.

When the sun reached its zenith, they halted and fell out along the banks of a small stream. Drinking, splashing, and washing had to wait until all canteens were filled, then commenced with abandon. Afterward the men hunted what shade they could find and sat or sprawled on the ground. A few munched their cold rations, Burk conspicuous among them. His big body needed more fuel than the others. Johnny lay next to him like a dead man. He had drunk, splashed a little water on his face, and then collapsed.

Johnny had been a sickly child and really never seemed to have grown out of it. Tom remembered how his parents had worried about him. He was their only child, and they had been middle-aged before he was born.

Burk looked at Tom and shook his head. "He's havin' a hard time, pore Johnny is."

Tom nodded. "We may have t' put him on that wagon back there."

Burk started taking off his shoes. "Ain't no need uv that. I'll take keer uv him. I'll carry him if'n I have to."

"D'you think you can?"

Burk tied the shoes to his pack. "Shore I kin. He's awful little an' light." He shook his head again. "That's his trouble. He ain't got no stren'th."

"Give me your rifle if you do."

Kemper was up and about as usual. Beyond ducking his whole head into the water and blowing like a whale, he made no concession to the heat. He came up to Johnny with water dripping from his hair and beard. "*Wie geht's,* Chonny?"

Johnny sat up and made a show of rejuvenation. "Oh, I feel lots better, Sargint." He grinned wanly. "This rest an' water was jist what I needed. I kin take my pack back now," he said to Burk.

Kemper shook his head. "*Nein*. Burk keep de pack."

"Fall in! Fall in!" sounded all too soon. The men got to their feet, slung their packs, and secured their equipment. Johnny struggled gamely to his feet and made for the road with the others.

After they formed up, the Massachusetts regiment went past to take the lead. "Eat our dust awhile!" called a sergeant whose hair showed redly through the dust.

“Yeah,” answered someone in the First Platoon. “You-uns been eatin’ ourn long ’nough!”

“You damned Indiana grease bags talk just like the Rebels do,” sneered one of the New Englanders.

There was a shocked silence.

“But we ain’t no nigger-lovin’ abolish like you dum Yankees is!” replied Ab hotly. Several voices seconded him.

The exchange of insults went on until the Massachusetts men had passed and gone on ahead. There had been friction before, but it had never gone this far. Even the officers got involved, and after the march resumed the men were so angry there was a good deal of talk for a while.

“They wouldn’t be no war an’ we’d still be home if hit wuzn’t fer them dam’ abolish!” fumed someone from the First Platoon.

“Yo’re right,” agreed a comrade. “They’re th’ very ones that skeered th’ Southerners outa th’ Union, agitatin’ an’ carryin’ on ’bout slav’ry all th’ time.”

“Y’know,” confided Ab, “I’d almost ruther fight them dum abolish than th’ Rebels.” Tom wasn’t surprised when several others voiced emphatic agreement.

The talk died away as the strain of the march made itself felt again. As the afternoon wore on, Tom came to think that this must be like the Purgatory of the Catholics, as they toiled along in the glow of the dust cloud under the burning sun. But it was worse than Purgatory. They had passed beyond it, through the brazen gates of Hell, and now went on seared by its fires and choked by its fumes.

Tom itched tormentingly where the sling of his rifle and the straps of his pack rubbed his coat. Like the others, he was seized periodically by fits of coughing and sneezing. They made his nose and eyes run, which added to the crust of dust and sweat on his face. Wiping only made it worse. Fatigue weighed him down and dragged at his limbs. His feet felt like wooden blocks and his legs like inflexible sticks. He looked at Billy, expecting to see his misery duplicated, but his brother still swung loosely along and seemed to be doing better than he was.

The ranks parted and flowed around a man lying motionless in the road, his face in the dust. He didn’t seem to be breathing, and Tom guessed he was dead. No one said a word as the column moved relentlessly on.

Johnny didn’t seem far from going down. He was reeling drunkenly, occasionally colliding with those around him. Burk turned to Tom, his eyes peering redly through the mask of dust and sweat that covered his face and clogged his eyebrows and beard. "I'm gonna hafta carry Johnny."

Tom took his rifle. The big man moved in front of Johnny and seized his arms, then stooped and drew them around his neck. He straightened and hoisted the thin little body on his back, lodging it between the two packs there. He did it all without breaking his stride or losing a foot of ground, and marched on with his great horny feet slapping the road. Johnny was too far gone to react. He lay on Burk's back with his head lolling and toes trailing in the dust.

Harve Akers seemed likely to go next. He kept falling back and Cole Burton behind him would shove him forward again. Burton was big and burly, a somewhat smaller version of Burk except for being black-haired and swarthy where Burk was blond and fair. Akers began to wobble on his feet, gasping convulsively and choking on the dust. Suddenly Cole called, "I'm gonna hafta take his pack, Sargint."

Kemper dropped back, took Harve's rifle, and handed it to Ab. Between the two of them, he and Cole took off Harve's pack and Burton slung it on his back as they marched. Akers slobbered his thanks.

The men moved on like automatons, ghastly with their dusty faces, like they had been a month in the grave. Only continual coughing, gasping, and sneezing betrayed their humanity. There was another parting of the ranks and another man lay in the dust, but he struggled to rise, his mouth open and eyes rolling wildly. He couldn't make it and sank back as the column went on.

Tom felt himself sinking into a mechanical apathy, his mind blank and his limbs moving automatically. It was almost like being asleep, and gradually the acuteness of his discomfort lessened.

The Massachusetts regiment ahead had been dribbling stragglers since soon after the noon halt. Some of them dragged and hobbled at a slow pace beside the column, rapidly falling behind, but most staggered to the roadside and sank to the ground. Suddenly the column halted and Tom almost ran into Burk and Johnny.

"Stay in ranks! Stay in ranks!" came a hoarse voice from farther up. It sounded like Jake.

Then Tom noticed that the regiment ahead of them was leaving the road and straggling in knots and groups into the fields on both sides. Colonel Rivers and the Massachusetts colonel, both on horseback, argued and gestured by the roadside. The Yankee colonel was a tall, thin fellow, older than Rivers.

Someone laughed hoarsely. "They're givin' hit up, th' dam' abolish!" The speaker fell into a fit of coughing.

"Cain't take hit!" shouted a high cracked voice. "Hey, you dam' Yankee abolish, ye givin' hit up?"

The regiment was rejuvenated by the spectacle. Hoots and jeers, interspersed with croaking and coughing, spread through its ranks.

"Hey, you Yankees!" shouted a stentorian voice. "Send home an' git yore wimmin! They could do better!"

"Yeah!" jeered another. "Git 'em 'way frum them big black bucks they're sleepin' with!"

Uproarious laughter followed. "Petticoats!" "Nigger lovers!" "Woolyheads!" and other epithets were showered on the Yankees. They paid no heed and huddled along the roadside or sprawled on the ground, officers and all.

Rivers finally gave up the argument with the Massachusetts colonel and reined away. The march resumed, and the recumbent Yankees were the targets of vociferous contempt until they were lost to sight. None of them said a word in reply, but hangdog expressions showed how they felt.

Except for the front ranks, the clear road ahead brought no lessening of the dust, which soon enveloped the column again in its choking, yellowish fog. Rivers rode along the column, looking at his men. He saw Burk carrying Johnny and reined up close. "Here, that man can have my horse." He started to dismount.

"Keep your horse, sir," said Burk. "I kin tote him all right."

"Can you keep it up, though?"

"Yes, sir. I'm prac'ly a horse m'self, sir. I kin tote him all day."

Rivers nodded and smiled through his dusty beard. "You're a good man, Burkhart."

"Yes, sir. Thank you, sir."

Rivers noticed the men with the extra packs and rifles. "That's it, men. Help one another out."

"We shore showed them dum' abolish, didn't we, sir?" asked someone in the First Platoon.

Rivers laughed as he reined away. "I guess we did."

The march went on through the murderous heat and the eternal cloud of dust. More men fell on the road and were left behind. Tom realized that not a man in his platoon had fallen out, and a strange feeling of exhilaration seized him, like once when he had been sick with lung fever. Pride swept over him, pride in himself, Billy, and the others. They were iron men, immune to heat, thirst, and dust. The man who had put the iron in them marched at their head, even if he looked like Father Christmas now with his burly body and beard frosted with dust. Tom unslung his canteen and took a few swallows.

The water had a bad effect. His exhilaration vanished and he clumped along with wooden legs and leaden feet as before. He gradually sank into a daze and began to feel like he had been condemned to eternal torture for some horrendous sin and would have to march on forever.

His mind began to wander. He heard distant bands playing sweet and wonderful tunes he had never heard before and heavenly choruses singing beautiful melodies he couldn't understand. Suddenly he was by the spring branch at home, where cold, clear water caressed by mint plants flowed through the leafy tunnel under the trees. His feet crushed some of the mint, and its sweet, tangy odor reached his nostrils. He bent over to pick up one of the crushed plants, lost his balance, and fell face first into the water.

He caught himself barely in time to keep from falling on the road, and it brought him to his senses. No one had noticed. Lurching and staggering were too common. He got a grip on himself and forced the daze from his mind.

As the hours passed, the glaring sun sank toward the horizon behind them. Tom had lost all sense of time and could tell it was getting late only by the lengthening shadows along the roadside.

All at once the road turned sharply to the left, but some of the men went straight on and blundered into a ditch. Then after a while the road turned back to the right and there seemed to be a large river to the left. Tom couldn't see the water for the dust, but he could hear the cool, delicious liquid gurgling over rocks in the bed. Suddenly thirst gripped his throat and convulsed his stomach, and he had to suppress a wild desire to rush out of the ranks and throw himself into the water.

Tom fumbled for his canteen. Tepid water flowed into his mouth, and he drank in great gulps before forcing himself to stop. Billy followed his example, his Adam's apple working up and down in his slender, grimy neck. Some of the water trickled out of the corners of his mouth and ran along his jaw, making brownish runnels. They smiled wordlessly at one another as they restored their canteens to their belts.

Strange figures on the back of a horse materialized in the dust alongside the column. The horse was the colonel's, but he was leading it. There were two men on its back, both slumping forward with chins on chests and bobbing loosely to the animal's gait.

Suddenly there was a commotion to the rear as Mertens's men broke for the roadside and began chasing some stumbling forms that were vague and indistinct in the dust. Some men from the forward companies had broken ranks and made for the water. There were shouts, scuffles, and a flashing of bayonets. Soon the stragglers were being herded back toward the column. Some of them complained vociferously and cursed the "damn Dutchmen" who stolidly prodded them on. A laggard received the point of a bayonet in the rump, which speeded up his pace remarkably and had a quieting effect on the others. The Germans put the delinquents at the rear of the column and marched directly behind them. Under the menace of the bayonets, they scrupulously kept up the pace.

The shadows grew longer, but the column marched on. Tom knew the heat was lessening, but he was past all feeling. He couldn't understand what kept them going. They were drained of strength; they were consumed by thirst; they suffered intolerable torment. Yet they plodded on, one foot before the other, then behind the other, their packs bearing them down, on and on and on. They were mechanical men, moved by a force beyond comprehension and essential to their integrity. If they ever stopped, it would leave them and they would collapse into jumbled pieces that would give no clue as to what they had been.

It was dusk when the column finally turned off the road toward the river, now a hundred yards or so away. Getting out of the dust brought no relief from it. It was in their mouths, throats, and lungs. It covered them from head to foot. It coated their bodies and rubbed grittily on their skin.

The head of the column reached the river and turned to parallel it. They marched until the entire regiment was strung out along the stream, but not a man fell out, although the cooling water was almost in arm's reach.

Finally they were halted and "Fall out!" sounded. The men stacked their rifles, then removed their packs and belts. Caps, coats, and in some cases trousers and shirts followed. Soon most of them were in the river, washing and drinking, all amid a strange quiet except for the splashing. The strictest silence had been enjoined, and no fires were permitted when they turned to their rations.

# 14

The regiment broke camp and was on the road before daybreak. The men were stiff and sore, but the marching soon took it out of them. Naturally the dust came back, but they had the satisfaction of knowing it wouldn't be for long.

There was the first talk about whether or not they would be able to hold the crossroads after they took it. Since those Yankees had fallen out, they would have only three regiments when they got there. But because no three regiments could expect to get the best of three brigades that were on their guard, the chief concern was still achieving surprise.

Soon after sunrise the column had to take the side of the road when thirty or so prisoners guarded by as many rough-looking horsemen went by going the other way. The prisoners were mostly fine-looking young fellows who were uncharacteristically subdued. When one of them was asked how they had been taken, he glanced apprehensively at the nearest horseman and said something in an undertone about sneaking guerrillas coming on them before daylight and catching them off guard.

Not only were the horsemen unkempt and uncouth; they weren't in uniform, although a few wore regulation coats and caps. Their weapons were clean and bright, though, and they obviously knew how to use them. A huge black-bearded fellow who looked even more like a brigand than the others seemed to be their leader. They looked so intimidating that no one said anything to any of them.

After they had gone by, Billy said Fred had told him they were a gang of cutthroats from the mountains far to the west who were supposed to be Unionists, although they were more bandits than anything else. They had joined up for only ninety days and everyone was glad when their time was up, because not only were they inveterate plunderers; they also had a habit of murdering prisoners.

They served their purpose, though. No regular cavalry could have taken up those Rebel outposts like they did.

The march lasted only a few hours before the column halted at the foot of a long, grassy ridge that ran on both sides of the road. It sloped off half a mile or so to the right but went on out of sight to the left, although it was covered with woods after a few hundred yards.

When the deployment began, the men knew the crossroads they were supposed to take was just over the ridge ahead of them. The regiment formed a line of battle in the grass to the right of the road, and one of the others did the same to the left. The third remained in a column on the road. After that, the men capped their rifles and fixed their bayonets. The commands were given in low tones, and it was all done very quietly.

Rivers rode out in front of the regiment and signaled for the advance. The two others moved forward at the same time. When he reached the top of the ridge, he shouted, "Quickstep, *march!*" and the line speeded up.

When they cleared the crest, the men saw first the church spire and then the outlying buildings of a small town across a wide valley running across their line of advance. On the other side of the valley was another ridge, but it didn't run nearly as far to the right as the one they were on and the town lay just beyond where it terminated. It was also forested about the same distance to their left. A tree-lined creek ran down the middle of the valley, and a road along its far bank crossed the one they had just left a short distance beyond a bridge.

There was nothing between the advancing line and the crossroads, but beyond the trees lining the creek toward town there was a great commotion. Men ran about singly and in small groups as bugles blew and drums rattled. Faint shouts of urgent command were borne on the breeze that blew in the men's faces. A body of horsemen seemed to be the only ones who were organized. They galloped toward the creek, and some of the men on foot had to scamper out of their way.

Suddenly reddish-orange flashes followed by puffs of smoke and seconds later by deep detonations came from high on the opposite ridge well to the left. A salvo of roundshot screamed across the valley and plunged into the column on the road. Shouts and screams went up, and the column writhed like a giant snake struck on the back, dribbling debris as it moved on.

Tom saw that farther down the slope they would be hidden from the guns by the tops of the trees along the creek. The guns fired a second salvo, this one of explosive shell aimed to the right of the road. Again they were dead on target, and the fuses were cut to a hair. Shattering explosions rent the regiment. Great gouts of dirt and smoke leapt up from bright orange flashes, and a hail of fragments mangled the line. Burk seemed to be the only man in the platoon who was hit.

The big fellow staggered and almost fell but kept to his feet and came on. The side of his head was bloody.

Another salvo came down, this one to the left of the road, and the explosions were muffled and the flashes hidden by men's bodies. The enemy guns were ranging along the line with uncanny accuracy, and Tom's scalp tingled strangely. His cap was all that was keeping his hair from standing on end.

A stone fence crossed the line of advance about halfway down the slope. The colonel jumped his horse across, but the men had to clamber over the barrier, then dress their ranks before going on. This threw the enemy gunners off, and the next salvo came down in front at a safe distance. Six vivid flashes blossomed precisely in a row and a curtain of dirt and smoke hid Rivers and his horse, but they emerged unscathed on the other side.

Before the guns could fire again, the line was screened by the tops of the trees along the creek, so they blasted the column on the road again, most of which was still in the open. The line wouldn't come back into view from where the guns were until it moved farther down the slope, below the tops and larger limbs of the trees that hid it now. Then there would be only about time for one more salvo before the line would be so far across the floor of the valley that the guns would no longer bear on it.

The body of horsemen had crossed the creek directly in front and were getting ready to charge. As soon as they formed up, they lunged forward at a gallop, brandishing weapons and screaming like demons.

Rivers reined up, spun his horse about, and shouted, "Halt!"

The line lurched to a stop as company officers repeated the shout and the men automatically dressed their ranks. Rivers reined into the interval between the two middle companies and shouted, "Front rank, *ready!*" As the echo of "Ready! Ready!" came down the line from the left, Tom cocked his rifle and brought it up with the others.

*"Aim!"*

The rifles leveled on the charging horsemen. They were now in good rifle range, thundering down on the line like an avalanche, and yelling more fiercely the closer they got. Their sabers flashed dangerously, but the line stood as steady as a rock.

*"Fire!"*

The volley crashed out as evenly as if it were a single charge fired from a monstrous cannon. The sheet of smoke that spurted out was immediately whipped away by the brisk breeze blowing from the east, to reveal a great tangle of horses and riders thrashing on the ground, but the others charged on.

"Front rank, *load!*" The men snatched cartridges from pouches, bit off the ends, and started them down barrels with thumbs and forefingers.

As they unshipped their ramrods, "Rear rank, *ready!*" brought the rifles up behind them. Rivers's voice sounded just like it did on the drill field.

*"Aim!"* came as Tom was ramming down his cartridge, and *"Fire!"* brought the volley from behind. Rifles exploding a few feet on each side of his head burned his ears and the back of his neck with powder particles and made his head ring. He saw horses and riders going down in heaps as he shipped his ramrod and reached for a cap.

"Rear rank, *load!*" was followed by rustling and tearing sounds from behind, shortly followed by the clank of ramrods.

By this time the horsemen still in their saddles were beginning to rein up and wheel to go back or turning aside to angle back toward the creek.

Tom was ready to fire well before he heard the command and took the chance to pick out an individual target rather than just aiming at the mass of them like he had before in order to get off his shot quickly.

At *"Aim!"* he drew a careful bead on the broad back of a big man flogging his horse directly away from him.

*"Fire!"* He squeezed the trigger at the same instant and the other rifles of the front rank blasted out and saw the man he had shot at being dragged with a foot caught in a stirrup, his arms flying up as he jounced over the ground. Riderless horses with flapping stirrups raced about, some wounded and neighing shrilly. A few cripples dragged along.

"Front rank, *load!*" sent Tom reaching for another cartridge and going on through the process of loading.

There was no second volley from the rear rank because too few targets were left, and Tom wondered why the Rebels had made such a suicidal charge. Maybe they thought the brigade would form a square, which was what infantry was supposed to do when charged by cavalry, and give their infantry time to come up. Maybe it was just desperation at being surprised.

As soon as the front rank finished loading, Rivers rode out in front again and shouted, "Forward! Forward!" Tom looked to his left and saw that the regiment on the other side of the road hadn't been charged by the cavalry, but it must have halted during the action because it was still in alignment. The other one was still in a column on the road.

The line slowed and became disordered when it reached the wreckage of the cavalry charge. There was a lot of shouting about alignment, but no halt, and the men ran on.

Men and horses lay all around. Some of the wounded tried to drag themselves out of the way, and a few put up imploring hands like they expected to be bayoneted. A horse paralyzed in its hindquarters flailed with its forefeet and screamed almost like a person. Tom had never imagined a horse could make such a sound. One of the officers shot the poor creature with his revolver, and the screaming stopped.

A strange odor lay upon the air that caused Tom's nostrils to flare and his hair to prickle anew. It was a mixture of burned powder, blood, and raw wounds, but there was more to it than that.

He came upon a man who sat leaning forward and groaning heavily, his hands clasped over his middle like he was holding his intestines in his abdomen. He looked up, his face indescribably twisted and the sweat of agony on his brow. "Kill me, Yankee!" he cried in an awful voice. "I'm gonna die anyhow! Put me outa my mis'ry!" He was a slight, fair fellow, nearing middle age and balding.

Tom couldn't bear the sight of him and looked away as he hurried by.

When the men reached the bottom of the slope, they could see through the scattered tree trunks along the creek. A large formation of infantry was marching to meet them, but they would reach the crossroads well before it would. A blast of grapeshot tore through the tree trunks as soon as they came in sight of the gunners high on the slope ahead. No one in the platoon was hit, although men fell on both sides. The colonel's horse went down, but he kicked free of the stirrups and landed on his feet. His horse lay shivering and kicking. Its neck looked like it had been torn by giant claws, and Rivers's uniform was splotched with great gouts of blood.

Before the guns could fire again, the line was too far across the valley for them to bear. There was no longer any danger from them, because if they moved down to where they could fire, they would be in rifle range.

Before the line reached the creek, Rivers ran up toward the road and Captain Owen took his place in front of the regiment. He halted the men on the near bank and told them to drop their packs, then to get down in the shallow water and take up firing position by the far bank. It was a smart move. Behind the shoulder-high bank, the men would have cover as good as any entrenchment, and the scattered tree trunks along the creek would offer no obstruction to their fire. To extend the line to the right so it wouldn't be overlapped, Owen formed it into a single rank.

The men stood with their rifles at the ready watching the enemy infantry advance. It was strangely like a parade. The serried gray ranks moved toward them at a steady pace under a forest of gleaming bayonets. Flags and banners of vivid hues waved above them at regular intervals. Tom expected them to wheel into a column to move down the creek and cross it so they would take the brigade in enfilade unless it left the creek to face them, but they didn't. They came steadily on, maintaining a front as straight as a string.

A glance up the creek beyond the bridge showed that the regiment up there had followed their example. It looked like Rivers was commanding the brigade. He was standing on the bridge looking at the advancing enemy with field glasses, and Owen had taken command of the regiment. The column on the road behind Rivers had been shortened so the guns on the opposite slope couldn't shoot it up. It was being held back as a reserve, to be rushed up to support any part of the line that needed it. After he looked it all over, Tom could find no fault with the deployment. He just hoped the Rebels kept on coming as they were.

"Hold yer fire! Hold yer fire!" came down the creek. Evidently some of the men were getting jumpy, because Tom saw several rifles come down from the aiming position along the line to the left. It sounded like Jake's voice, and Tom wondered what had happened to Dixon.

"Aw, Gawd!" exclaimed someone up that way. "They must be a millyun uv 'em!"

Although there were certainly a lot of them, Tom saw nothing to be afraid of as long as they kept coming like they were. Their front extended on both sides of the bridge only as far as the brigade's line went, and they were going to be shot to pieces unless they changed their tactics. He wondered why they were so determined on this head-to-head business when even he could see how it was bound to come out. Maybe it was panic at having been caught napping and losing the crossroads the very first thing.

When "Ready! Ready!" came down the creek from the left, Tom wondered if Rivers had gotten jumpy, too, because the range was much too long for aimed fire.

What came next showed he hadn't. "Aim! Aim high! Aim even with their flags! Even with their flags!" Rivers had calculated the range and was allowing for bullet drop. The volley would come down on the Rebels like the arrows of the English longbowmen on the French knights at Crécy and Agincourt back in the Middle Ages.

Tom aimed at a banner directly to his front, a bright red affair that seemed to have a blue cross on it.

"Fire!" brought the volley, fired so evenly that the men's shoulders jerked back together on recoil. The brisk breeze blowing in his face whipped the smoke away so quickly that he saw the gray ranks come on seemingly unharmed for long seconds.

"Load!" had sounded and he was biting off the end of a cartridge when tremors suddenly struck the enemy line and irregularities appeared, but it came steadily on.

Several more volleys were fired, aimed a little lower each time, and as the target drew closer the effects could be seen more plainly. Gaps would suddenly appear in the gray ranks, but they would close up and come on, neither slackening nor increasing their pace. Whatever else it was, it was a magnificent display of courage and discipline.

When the range had closed enough, Rivers gave up volleys and passed the order, "Fire at will!" The men began loading and firing as fast as they could, and a continuous roar of discharges built up, at times heavier and then lighter, in an uneven, unpredictable rhythm. Cartridges were snatched from pouches, the ends bitten off and rammed down barrels still smoking from the last discharge. Exploded caps were brushed from nipples and fresh ones put on with lightning speed; then hammers would fall like striking snakes. Most men just dropped their ramrods on the bank in front after using them, then snatched them up to ram the next cartridge home.

Although they were taking terrible punishment, the gray ranks came steadily on. The target was so large there was no need to waste much time aiming. The air stank of burned powder, but the breeze kept the smoke from building up. The brush in front was mown down and the tree trunks slashed by the storm of bullets.

The advancing line suddenly halted and stood for a few moments, convulsing under the hail of bullets. Concerted motions brought down the bayonets, and a tremendous flash and roar burst forth as the Rebels fired their first volley. Most of the bullets went too high, but several men went down, one of them just to Tom's left. Most of them were shot in the head and scarcely moved after they struck the inches-deep water, but a few flopped about like fish.

Instead of charging, the Rebels loaded for another volley, their ramrods pumping up and down. Tom threw his rifle to his shoulder and fired just as the gray ranks again spouted fire and smoke. Most of the men ducked instinctively, but he went on loading, although the missiles hissed past his ears or tore up the dirt in front.

Tom saw only one man go down this time, a tall, thin fellow from the First Platoon on his left. Hit in the head in the act of loading, the man kept his feet in an amazing display of tenacity. He reeled drunkenly, working his mouth and fumbling with his rifle. He dropped it and when he bent to pick it up, fell headlong into the water so close to

Tom that he was splashed. The man lay twitching and blowing up a bloody froth as Tom capped his rifle and turned to fire.

When he looked at the Rebels over his sights, Tom could tell they were wavering. After he fired, he could see a few backs moving away, and before he could load, more were going back. When he was ready to fire again, all he could see was gray backs moving away.

After he fired, Tom was suddenly seized by an overwhelming compulsion to go after the withdrawing enemy. He yelled exultantly and started up the bank along with several others, only to have Billy seize his belt and hold him back.

Tom turned angrily on his brother, but the fit passed as suddenly as it had come when he saw Billy's anxious face and heard him plead, "Stay back, Tom! Stay back! Don't go out thar!"

"All right, Billy," he managed to say, "you can let me go." Several other berserkers who hadn't had anyone to hold them had to be yelled back, and Tom wondered what had come over him to make him act like that. He was glad that no one but Billy seemed to have noticed.

The Rebels restored their formation as they retreated, but they didn't stop. The firing fell off and soon stopped entirely, although they were still in range for quite a while after it did. There was no command or anything. The men just stopped shooting, maybe because they began to hear the cries from out in front.

Soul-chilling groans and cries of deadly agony arose from the huddled heaps of brownish gray spread thickly where the line had stopped and thinning out only gradually as far back as the eye could see. Some stirred, some crawled, and a few tried to get to their feet, unsuccessfully except in a few cases, and most of them didn't get very far.

Suddenly Tom felt like the blood was draining from his body and he had to turn away. A deadly chill came over him. His teeth chattered and he had to struggle to keep from trembling all over.

"Y' all right, Tom?" he heard Billy ask anxiously. "Yo're awful pale. Y' shore y' didn't git hit or somethin'?"

Tom felt ashamed and got a grip on himself. "Oh, I'm all right, Billy," he said as casually as he could. "Just tired, I guess."

"Yeah, I guess we both air." Billy shook his head. "It's been a hard couple uv days."

Tom was glad to see he wasn't the only pale-faced fellow when he looked around. There were peaked countenances on all sides, and he thought he heard sobbing from down where the Germans were. When he looked that way, he saw Mertens and a slender youth standing by a still form propped against the creek bank. Mertens had an arm around the youth's heaving shoulders and was talking to him while the others looked on sympathetically. Billy said it was the sobbing youth's brother who lolled lifelessly against the bank, and Tom realized how lucky he was that his brother stood safe and sound beside him. With a sinking feeling he also realized he had paid absolutely no attention to Billy during the entire action and might not have noticed if he had been hit.

Kemper was busy with the wounded. By this time they had all been taken out of the water and placed on the far bank, but their wounds were mostly in the head and upper body and nothing could be done for most of them. The dead outnumbered them, but there really weren't many of either. The body of the tall, thin man from the First Platoon lay face down in the water close by. When he looked at him closely, Tom saw he was an older man, probably well past thirty. Pinkish brain tissue protruded through blood and bone splinters where part of his skull had been shot away. Although he knew most of the men in the First Platoon, he didn't know this fellow.

"I jist cain't see how he stayed on his feet s' long, with a piece uv his head shot off like that," said Billy. His voice sounded strange, like when it had started to change, and his eyes were very wide.

"Here," said Tom, "let's get him out of th' water. He's dead, but he shouldn't be left like this." This fellow hadn't, but he suspected some of the wounded had drowned with their faces in the water.

Tom took the arms and Billy the legs. The man was very tall and hard to handle. His hips dragged and it was difficult to move him along.

Suddenly a man ran down the creek and helped them hoist the body up on the far bank. "Pore ol' Bill," he said. "I couldn't 'magine whar he'd got to till I saw you-uns a carryin' him!"

"Bill who?" asked Tom. "Where's he from?"

"Bill McCall," was the reply, "frum a lil' west uv Celestine 'way back in th' woods. Had a lil' farm back thar but hunted an' fished mos'ly." He shook his head. "Quiet feller, Bill wuz. Didn't have eny fren's. I guess I'm 'bout th' only one that knowed him, an' that's jist 'cause he married my sister."

"Oh, he was married then," mused Tom. "Any family?"

"Yeah, a hull swad uv chillern, five uv 'em." He shook his head again. "I guess Paw'll take keer uv 'em. Bill didn't have no folks." He went back, still shaking his head.

Tom wondered why a man with such a large family would go off into the army. Before he turned away, he saw Charley Newton's body lying on the bank. Charley seemed to be the only man from the platoon who had been killed, but Tom had known him pretty well and didn't want to look at him any more closely.

When the surgeon finally showed up, Kemper came back to his men, although the fellow tried to get him to stay, maybe because he had one of his own to take care of. Burk had stuffed a rag under his cap on the side of his head, but blood was dripping down his jaw and his sleeve was smeared red from wiping it off.

Kemper had him take off his cap and get rid of the rag, then cleaned the wound with a piece of cloth. Next he applied the dark red fluid he had used on Tom's arm and put on a bandage that was so tight Burk could put his cap on over it.

"It'll scab over and heal up right away now," Tom told him. "That medicine's the same stuff he put on me that time when I got nicked."

Burk nodded and patted the bandage. "I'm much obliged t' ye, Sargint. Y' saved me from th' surgeon. He mighta cut my head off."

Everybody laughed. No one had any faith in army surgeons, least of all the one they had. Some of the men claimed he had only been a horse doctor.

Tom was sorry when it was done, because when he wasn't occupied he couldn't keep his attention from the wounded out in front. They still groaned and cried out, and several who could move dragged themselves away, like they were afraid the men along the creek would come out and hurt them.

To take his mind off them, Tom began thinking about what to expect next. Most of the men seemed to think the Rebels had had enough of it, but he knew better. Once they got their wits about them, they would undoubtedly do what they should have done the very first thing; form a line across the creek to the south and move up. Rivers would have to leave the creek and deploy to face them, and when he did his right would come under fire from those guns on the opposite slope. After it was shot to pieces, the Rebels would charge it, drive it back, and take his left in enfilade. That would be the end of his brigade.

It looked like Mertens and Kemper expected something like that. They were standing on the far bank near the end of the line on the right, looking south and talking earnestly.

Jake came splashing down the creek. "You fellers is gonna git yore feet wet standin' in this hyar water," he joked.

There was only a little halfhearted laughter, but the men who actually were standing in the water moved out of it.

Tom couldn't stand it any longer. "Sergeant, d'you reckon th' general knows what's comin' next?"

Jake looked surprised. "What's that?"

"Why, they'll deploy across th' creek down there and move up on us. Then we'll have to come out an' form a line to face 'em, and those guns up there will bear on our right."

Jake shook his head and sighed. "Th' gin'ral's dead. Th' colonel's senior an' he's took over th' brigade. I guess he'd think uv that."

"How'd th' gin'ral git kilt?" asked someone.

"Got hit by that artill'ry when we wuz comin' up, th' very first salvo they shot. Purty nigh took his leg off, they say, an' he bled t' death."

"Say, whar's Cap'n Dixon?" asked Cole. "Ain't seen him since we come over that ridge back thar." He snickered. "I don't reckon he got shot, too."

None of the men had any respect for Dixon anymore, but no one had ever shown it to Jake and some of the men expected him to put Cole down.

Jake only shook his head and looked away. "Sprung his ankle comin' down that ridge, when we crossed that rock fence. He'll be 'long atter a while, I guess."

Tom wasn't surprised when Jake changed the subject. "Hey thar, Burk! I didn't know y' got hit! How air ye?"

"Oh, hit don't 'mount t' nothin'," rumbled the big fellow. "Hit me in th' head, that artill'ry did."

Jake laughed. "Hit's a good thing hit wuz yore head! Mighta hurt ye if'n hit'd been enyplace else!"

Burk grinned ruefully as the men broke into laughter.

"Head harder'n a cannonball!" whooped someone, and the merriment reached new heights. It sounded a little hysterical, though, and really didn't seem all that funny.

Jake noticed Mertens and Kemper on the far bank still looking down the creek and talking. "See enything frum out thar, Lootenant?"

They turned and started toward Jake.

"Nothing yet," said Mertens, "but they'll be moving on us from down there pretty soon."

"Yes, sir. That's what Tom hyar 'lowed, but I 'spect it'll be a good while yet 'cause they's a flag o' truce comin'."

Tom was glad to hear that. Maybe Rivers would think of something before the truce ended.

"Oh, there's a truce?" asked Mertens.

"Yes, sir, er soon will be. That's why we ain't sent out no skirmishers er enything. We sent t' th' Rebels an' ast if'n they wanted one t' take keer uv their wounded, an' they said they did." Tom thought it was a smart move on Rivers's part. The Rebels couldn't very well refuse, and it would give him more time.

Mertens nodded. "I'm glad to hear that. Those poor fellows shouldn't be just left lying."

There was a chorus of agreement, and Tom was glad to learn he wasn't the only softhearted fellow around.

"Say, we shore s'prised these hyar Rebels, didn't we?" asked Billy, and Tom got the impression he wanted to change the subject.

Jake laughed. "We shore did. Hit wuz that marchin' yestidy, two days in one an' hit over ninety in th' shade. That an' them g'rilla fellers takin' up their outposts. They wuzn't 'spectin' us till t'morra, an' we snuck up on 'em." He paused and sighed. "Hit wuz awful hard, that marchin' yestidy, but hit's like I heered th' colonel say once; a bucket uv sweat ain't worth one drop uv blood."

"Wal, I kinda wisht hit'd been t'day 'stud uv yestidy," said Johnny. "Hit's clouded up an' turned a lot cooler."

"Gonna rain, I 'spect," said Ab with a look at the sky.

Captain Owen shouted that Jake, Kemper, and Mertens were wanted up at the bridge, so they left and those who weren't already up on the banks got up there to see what it was all about. They saw the three join Rivers, Owen, and Dixon. Dixon was leaning on a crude crutch.

"So Dixon's sprung his ankle, huh!" scoffed Ab.

The men snickered. "Yeah," sneered Cole, "th' last time he lost th' cylinder fer his revolver."

"Jist like a dang dog I usta have," snorted someone. "He'd run an' hide th' first shot he heered." Contemptuous laughter followed.

Rivers seemed to be doing most of the talking, and in a little while Dixon hobbled away with no handshakes or good-byes. The others just ignored him.

"Wal," drawled Ab, "I'll bet a hunert dollers we never sees that feller agin." He looked around. "Eny takers?"

"Nary a one," replied Cole. "They ain't no suckers in this bunch."

"I reckon Lootenant Mertens'll take over th' comp'ny now," opined Billy.

Tom noticed that Kemper and the colonel had fallen into an earnest conversation, and after a little while Kemper started up the creek toward the woods that covered both sides of the valley with what looked like a case for field glasses slung from his shoulder. He had a pretty good idea what Kemper was going to do.

Suddenly the enemy guns on the ridge ahead and to the left opened fire with a tremendous blast that sent most of the men jumping back into the creek before they realized they couldn't be the target, which was a four-gun battery going into position on top of the opposite slope. The gunners were unhitching their pieces from the limbers and wheeling them about when the first salvo struck. It was a bull's-eye, and the friendly guns never got off a shot. The men stood half in and half out of the creek and watched the slaughter. Shellbursts leapt up among the hurrying cannoneers and horses or spangled the air just above them. Not a round missed the target, and not a shell failed to explode.

A limber chest blew up with an awesome detonation, followed rapidly by another. Salvo after salvo thundered out with incredible speed. Soon there was nothing left but wreckage half-obscured by a cloud of dirt and smoke shot through with vivid flashes. A few survivors scampered back over the ridge, and some wounded horses dragged themselves about. Finally the guns fell silent.

"Aw, Gawd!" sounded an awed voice. It had been truly awesome. Tom didn't know much about artillery, but he doubted if he would ever see shooting like that again.

"Pore fellers!" sighed Johnny. "They never had a chance."

"I jist hate t' think uv what them guns is gonna do t' whoever has t' go up that ridge back thar when th' Rebels come up on us frum down th' crick like th corp'ril says they're gonna do," said Cole.

"Whoever 'tis'll git slaughtered," forecast Ab glumly. "I jist hope hit ain't us."

" 'Twon't make eny diff'runce," sighed Billy. "Them guns'll massacree our right, 'n' then their infantry'll flank th' rest uv us."

It was quite a while before the flag of truce came out the road from the direction of town. It was followed by a procession of wagons that looked like ordinary farm vehicles. Tom was dreading having to watch them go around picking up the wounded and was actually glad to see Kemper come running down the creek carrying a huge sledgehammer and obviously with something important on his mind.

"Whadaya doin' with that big ol' hammer, Sargint?" asked Ab.

Kemper ignored the question and handed the hammer to an astonished Burk. "Ve go *gegen die Kannonen* oop dere," he said as he pointed up toward the enemy guns.

"Like y' did back at that gap a few days ago?" asked Billy eagerly.

*"Ja."*

Tom wasn't surprised. He had been expecting something like that ever since he had seen Kemper and Rivers talking up by the bridge.

Kemper went on to tell them how they were going to do it. They were going up the creek into the woods and on to a ravine that ran down from the top of the ridge close to where the guns were. They would follow the ravine as far as they could, then leave it and creep up on the gunners. After they took the guns, Burk would break off their trunnions with the hammer.

"Why not jist spike 'em?" asked Ab. "That'd be quicker."

Although he could see Kemper was in a terrible hurry, Tom thought he ought to explain. "Oh, spikes can be drilled out pretty quick. Breakin' th' trunnions off'll ruin 'em for good. There'd be no way of holdin 'em on th' carriage anymore, an' Burk's strong 'nough t' do it."

Kemper nodded emphatically. "*Ja,* iss so."

Several of the men were pulling long faces and no one seemed enthusiastic except Billy, and that was mainly because he wasn't going to be left behind this time. They knew that guns always had infantry around close and couldn't see how a mere platoon could have any hope of even taking the guns, much less getting back.

Tom was sure Kemper had seen that the way was clear and decided to lend a hand. "There's no infantry up there with those guns, is there, Sergeant?"

*"Nein! Nein!* I haf *die Glässer, und* I look de *lange Zeit,* ef'revere I look, *und* iss no *Infanterie,* no *Infanterie!"*

Tom nodded. "Yeah, I can see why. Those guns are out in th' open up there, and they won't be expectin' anything like this, an' if we can sneak up on 'em, we can do it all right." Getting away would be another matter, but he didn't want to say anything about that. He only wished Billy wasn't going along.

The men seemed to think he was right and to feel better about it.

*"Komm!"* Kemper led them up the creek at a run.

They went straight on until they were well into the woods that covered both sides of the valley and reached a shallow ravine, then turned to follow it up the ridge toward where the guns were. Water had swept the ravine clear of dead leaves and branches, so their progress was quiet. The only time they were in the open was when they crossed the road that ran along the creek, and they saw no one then. Even after the woods disappeared on their right, the ravine was lined with enough growth on that side to hide them. When Tom could see through it in that direction, he saw a field of tall grass studded with overgrown outcroppings of rock. To their left the woods went on as dense as ever.

They had a long climb up the ridge until Kemper stopped them close to the top. He motioned for them to stay where they were, then went through the growth to the right, dropped to his knees, and disappeared into the tall grass.

It seemed a long time until he came back. When he did, he ostentatiously capped his rifle and fixed his bayonet, then waited until his men had done the same. After that he slung his rifle, signaled for his men to follow, and crept back the way he had come.

Tom was the last man in line, and when he crawled out into the grass he felt naked and exposed, although it was high enough to hide him from anyone who wasn't pretty close. A line of rumps moved ahead of him like a procession of turtles, and he soon found he had to hump along as fast as he could to keep up.

After an interminable crawl, the rumps up ahead stopped and Tom raised his head. He saw Kemper had reached one of the overgrown outcroppings that studded the field. He signaled his men to stay back, then got up and entered the growth. Shortly he reappeared and motioned for them to come on, before disappearing into the growth again.

Each man crawled until he reached the outcropping, then got up and entered the thicket. When Billy's turn came, Tom made up his mind to see to it that he was left behind if they ever did anything like this again.

They crawled on toward another outcropping several hundred yards beyond and farther up the ridge. Tom could see the taller bushes around it when a series of stunning concussions beat upon his ears. The enemy guns had opened fire, and they were very close.

Kemper leapt to his feet and broke into a run, unslinging his rifle. His men followed and when Tom got to his feet he saw a cloud of smoke boiling up beyond the outcropping ahead. In the distance on the other side of the valley was a thin blue line pummeled by shell bursts.

The men raced madly around the outcropping in single file behind their leader, who angled up the slope to go along just below the crest and bring them down on the guns from behind. The guns came into view just as they fired another salvo. The pieces hurled themselves back in recoil amid a haze of smoke and a tremendous blast of sound, and the gunners leapt to trails and wheels to run them back. There were six of them, close together on a level space a hundred yards below the top of the ridge. Limbers with open ammunition chests stood between them. The gunners were so busy they never looked up, and an officer with field glasses to his eyes stood in front with his back toward them. Carbines were stacked in neat little tepees well behind the guns.

Kemper led them on until his line was centered on the guns then turned and led them down the slope. The hurrying cannoneers still saw nothing.

Kemper stopped, raised his rifle, and roared, *"Hände hoch!* Gif oop!"

Tom was afraid the German might not be understood, so he shouted, "Hands up! S'rrender!"

The gunners were caught in the middle of loading. Rammer staffs were down barrels, thumbs on vents, and primers ready at hand. They looked up in blank surprise, mouths falling open and eyes staring incredulously.

The officer in front broke the spell. He shouted and ran toward the guns, drawing his revolver. His men dropped whatever they were doing and broke for their carbines, yelling with surprise and urgency.

*"Feuer!"* bellowed Kemper, and the volley blasted half the gunners off their feet. Some of the survivors shrieked in terror and bolted. One of them ran into the officer and knocked him down.

"Charch!" shouted Kemper as he hurled himself forward with bayonet outthrust. His men yelled exultantly and followed his example.

It was too much for the remaining gunners. They whirled and ran, although they had almost reached their carbines, heading south along the ridge. The officer regained his feet and stood his ground, cocking his revolver and facing the charging men. He took deliberate aim and fired, and someone in the middle of the onrushing line went down. The officer cocked his weapon, aimed carefully, and fired again. Another man went down, but Kemper was on him before he could fire another shot, moving catlike in a crouch with deceptive speed. The officer jumped aside as he cocked his revolver, but the bright bayonet leapt out and plunged into his throat. He was borne over backward and fell with a strange, gurgling cry, his revolver falling from his hand and a gush of blood reddening the front of his coat.

The men lunged after the fleeing gunners shouting wildly. "Halt!" roared Kemper. *"Laden und feuer!"*

They loaded hurriedly and sent a ragged volley after the flying men. Tom aimed at a short fellow in line with his position. At his shot the man's cap flew off to reveal a shiny bald pate and he tumbled into the grass. Several more of the fugitives fell, but two of them only staggered and went on. One soon went down, though.

Tom loaded in time to catch the last of the fleeing gunners just as he reached the growth around the closest outcropping. It was a long shot, but his bullet caught the man in midstride and threw him into the thicket, where his body rested momentarily on the bushes before sliding out of sight.

"Good shot, Tom!" called Billy as he rammed down a charge. His cap was gone and his hair awry above his smudgy, sweaty face. He looked for all the world like a boy fighting a brushfire as he wielded his ramrod.

Kemper shouted for Tom to put men out to watch and ran for the guns with Burk and his sledgehammer.

When the Rebels came, they would probably come from the south along the ridge, so Tom sent Billy and Ab in that direction and told them to go only as far as it took to get a good view. He told Harve and Cole to go on to the top of the ridge behind and watch the other side. Tom sent another man down the slope far enough to be able to see all the way to the creek where the regiment was and spread the others out in a line facing the direction Billy and Ab had gone. "Keep close watch, now," he cautioned them, "and sing out if you see anything."

"Yeah, they're gonna come bilin' up hyar 's mad 's hornets, an' purty soon," forecast Jim Polson. He was old Uncle Charley Polson's grandson and was red-haired, with plenty of freckles.

Two men were missing, shot by that officer. Johnny Conrad was one of them, but Tom couldn't think of who the other was. He was about to send someone to look about them when Cole shouted from the top of the ridge, "Hey! They's a bunch uv hosses on a picket rope jist over th' top hyar!"

They were the horses for the guns and really ought to be killed, but Tom didn't have the heart to do it. "Just cut th' rope an' chase 'em off!"

In the meantime heavy rifle fire had broken out in the valley below and the men were all looking that way. "Pay no 'tention t' that shootin'!" shouted Tom. "Jus' tend t' your own bus'ness an' keep good watch!"

He went down the slope to look himself, though. The thin blue line went almost all the way up the ridge on the other side of the valley, and what he could see of it on his side of the creek showed it went as far in the other direction. Smoke would spurt out sheetlike, and long seconds later the sounds of the volley would reach his ears. The Rebel line was harder to see because it blended into the background, but it was well south of the road and the range seemed pretty long. The Rebels were firing back but not in volleys. He doubted if they would press their attack with their guns out of action. In the distance it looked like a battle between toy soldiers.

He went back up the slope and on toward the guns to see how the wrecking was going. He saw two of them leaning drunkenly on their carriages and Burk swinging the hammer to bring it down on the breech of another. The big hammer looked small in the big fellow's hamlike hands, and he swung with tremendous force. The anvillike crash seemed enough to smash the gun itself.

Suddenly he found himself among the dead and wounded lying in front of the guns, and one man heaved himself up on his elbows. "Corp'ril, gimme a drink uv water, please, a drink uv water," he pleaded in a dry, rasping voice. He had a bad wound in the thigh, and his knee lay at an odd angle to his hip.

Tom unslung his canteen, removed the cap, and handed it to the fellow. He took it and said, "Thank ye, thank ye," before he drank.

Close by a man with a chest wound gasped his life away. Tom had to move on.

"Hey, don't ye want hit back?" asked the man with the shattered thigh.

Tom didn't want to stop, but he did. "Had 'nough?' " he asked as he reached for the canteen.

The wounded gunner nodded and said, "You fellers really fixed us, didn't ye?" He was a big man, dark-complected, and his eyes glittered feverishly. A sweeping black mustache accentuated an unnatural pallor.

Tom only nodded as he took the canteen, but before he could go on the fellow sighed, "That's th' last uv th' Blue Ridge Artill'ry, I reckon. We wuz th' best batt'ry in Jackson's hull army. He said so hisself." He looked at Tom reproachfully. It made him feel like a criminal.

"I've got no time t' talk," he said abruptly as he went on.

He didn't look at any of the others. Instead, he took another look across the valley. He could only see that part of the line that ran up the opposite slope over there, but the shooting had stopped and there was no sign of any Rebels.

He stepped on something and looked down to see a revolver lying in the grass. Without thinking he stooped to pick it up, and when he did his eyes fell on the officer Kemper had bayoneted. He was blond, square-jawed, and handsome. Blue eyes stared sightlessly at the sky, and a great red patch gleamed dully on the fine gray cloth of the coat. Tom stuck the revolver in his belt and went on wishing he had never seen it.

Kemper saw him as he and Burk hurried toward another gun. Only two still stood undamaged. *"Bringst die Männer zurück! Wir wollen bald gehen!"*

Tom ran back shouting, "Come in! Ever'body come in! We're 'bout ready t' go!" This time he was careful to skirt around the dead and wounded gunners.

The men took up the shout, and Cole and Harve soon came running down the ridge. The man down the slope was on his way, too.

"No sign uv Billy an' Ab, Corp'ril," said Jim.

"I'll go after 'em," Tom replied. "Th' rest o' you stay here."

He ran toward the overgrown outcropping Billy and Ab had gone beyond and started shouting for them at the top of his lungs.

He neither saw nor heard anything until he passed the outcropping. Then faint yelling punctuated by rifle shots came from straight ahead where the ridge became so brushy he couldn't see very far. Suddenly two running figures burst into view. "Th' Rebels is comin'! Rebels a-comin'!" shrieked one of them. It was Billy's voice. He and Ab had gone too far trying to get a good view.

Tom had never seen anyone run so fast. They seemed to fly over the ground and came closer with astonishing speed. A few hundred yards behind, gray-clad men dodged through the growth in pursuit, still yelling but no longer firing.

Tom whirled and ran with the two when they reached him. They were panting like steam engines, but at first he had a hard time keeping up. He wondered what Kemper would do now as they ran. Those Rebels back there were pretty close, and although there weren't more than a few dozen of them, a great many more were undoubtedly close behind.

When they came in sight of the wrecked guns, no one was to be seen, absolutely no one.

"Aw, Gawd!" gasped Ab. "They've gone off an' left us!" It looked like Kemper had made the logical decision to sacrifice three of his men so the others could get away.

Their pursuers were yelling about "murderin' Yankee sonsabitches!" and would show them no mercy. They would have their chance when the men they were chasing crossed the long open stretch between the guns and the closest outcropping toward the ravine they had come up in, and, in all probability, bullets would catch them before they could reach it.

They were almost on the guns before they saw the men lying in the grass with their rifles ready. Kemper rose on his elbows and gestured imperatively as they slowed to stop. "Nodt halt! *Fortgehen! Rennen! Rennen!*"

They obeyed instantly, running on. Kemper was going to ambush their foremost pursuers in hope the others would stop to deploy and let him get all his men away.

A heavy volley blasted out behind them, followed by screams and startled shouts. Kemper bellowed, "Charch!" and his men raised a great shout. Tom stopped with the other two and looked back to see the Rebels rapidly going the other way, those that were still on their feet.

Kemper and his men ran back, reloading as they came. As soon as Burk reached Tom, he gave him his rifle and just dropped the hammer, then went back to where a slight blue-clad form lay in the grass. It was Johnny. "I'm gonna carry th' pore lil' feller back," said Burk. There was a smear of blood just above the glassy eyes.

Another lay farther back, a much bigger man, and Tom recognized Hoss Bagarly by his blond thatch of hair.

Kemper looked back along the ridge and saw no sign of a renewed pursuit. *"Gut. Nun, wer tragt der Bagarlee?"*

"I'll take 'im, Sargint," said Cole as he handed his rifle to Cal Fairbanks. Next to Burk, Cole was the biggest man in the platoon, but Hoss was a lot bigger than Johnny and Cole was going to have a harder time.

"You help him if he needs it, Cal," Tom told Fairbanks, who was pretty husky himself.

Kemper picked up the sledgehammer and ran toward the ravine that would lead them to safety. *"Komm! Mach schnell!"*

Tom stayed back to take his place at the rear while the others ran by, then followed. There was still no sign of pursuit, and by the time he reached the ravine he knew they were going to get clean away.

They did, and afterward Tom gave Kemper the revolver that had belonged to that brave Rebel officer, both because he deserved it and to show his admiration for the way he had handled the whole affair.

Later Tom heard that Rivers called Kemper in, thanked him profusely, and said he was going to do his best to get him commissioned.

Tom could understand that. Rivers had stuck his neck out about that crossroads, at least about holding it after he took it, and Kemper had saved him from getting it cut off.

He felt he had learned a lot from Kemper's expedition against those guns, but there was one thing that worried him afterward. Killing men didn't bother him anymore, even those gunners he had shot down when they were only trying to get away. But when he thought about Mark Dixon leaving, something worse came to mind. Dixon would undoubtedly be going back home soon. He was interested in Sally, and her father owed his a lot of money.

# 15

That night most of the men fell asleep lying on the ground along the creek where they had fought. About an hour after dark it began to rain, lightly at first, then harder. Soon it was a veritable downpour. Tom and Billy put up their tent with the first drops and scarcely got damp, but many of the others waited too long and got pretty well soaked.

Billy promptly went to sleep, but Tom lay awake listening to the rain beat down on the canvas a few inches above his head. It wasn't blowing in the open ends of the tent, and he felt comfortably warm and dry. This was only until he heard Burk and Ab talking and splashing about. They were ditching their tents, something he had forgotten. It had to be done, or he and Billy would soon be lying in water. Tom raised himself on his elbows and shouted, "Let me know when you're done with the shovel!"

"Jist stay in thar, Tom," came a disembodied voice from outside. "I'll do yores, too." It was Burk.

"Oh no!" protested Tom. "You just let—"

Burk cut him off, "Jist stay in thar, Tom! I'm awreddy wet an' they ain't no use in you gittin' wet, too!"

Tom needed no persuasion. He was happy to stay under the canvas and listen to Burk ply the shovel. He wondered where it had come from. Ab had probably lifted it somewhere. He had a talent for that sort of thing. Billy had never woken up, and not long after the noise of the ditching stopped, he went to sleep himself.

He woke up a little after dawn and left the tent to see what his ears had already told him. The creek was bank-full and booming. A little more and they would have been flooded out. The rain had stopped, though, and the clouds were thinning, so there was no longer any danger.

Burk was already astir and had a fire going with wood he had kept dry with an extra tent half. The big fellow was still wet, and his clothing steamed as the fire grew hotter. Even the bandage about his head was still wet. "How's your head, Burk?" Tom asked him.

Burk was making coffee in a large bucket. "Hit's aw right, Tom. Never got nothin' but a lil' headache out uv hit."

"Is it very sore?"

"Jist a little."

"That stuff Sergeant Kemper put on it ought to heal it up right away. It shouldn't cause you any trouble."

Burk only nodded, like he had done all the talking he wanted to.

Tom wondered where Kemper was. He was generally the first one up in the morning.

The aroma of boiling coffee brought about a general resurrection, and soon most of the men of the platoon had gathered about the fire, drying themselves and drinking coffee.

"I'm hoongry," announced Ab as he rummaged in his pack, "an' I b'lieve I'll have a lil' brekfus'." He brought out a piece of meat wrapped in oilcloth and sniffed it suspiciously. "Spilt!" he exclaimed disgustedly, then hurled it into the creek.

The other men ran to their packs and made the same discovery. There was general lamentation. "Nothin' t' eat! What're we gonna do!"

"Eat hardtack and drink coffee," advised Tom. "That'll fill you up." He got out what was left of his ration and found it fit only for throwing away, too.

Those who had finished their rations the day before had the laugh on the others. "I dang shore ain't gonna keep no rashuns three days in hot weather enymore," grumbled Ab. "I'm gonna eat 'em up 'fore they spiles."

Most of the men weren't satisfied with coffee and hardtack for breakfast and were wondering what they would have for dinner and supper when a wagon turned off the road and came down the creek toward them. It didn't stop despite shouts from men farther up the stream. When they saw Kemper on the seat beside the driver, the men broke into smiles.

"Thar's our rashuns," jubilated Ab. "Sargint Kemper's bringin' 'em!"

"Bless his ol' Dutch heart!" sang out someone back in the group. Laughter and shouts of endorsement followed.

Kemper had something for his men beside ordinary rations. He had two clean new boxes filled with cuts of beef so fresh the blood still oozed from them, and the men fell upon them like wolves. They hadn't had fresh meat in a long time and showered blessings on their sergeant. The rest of the division had come up during the night, and the butcher was "anodder Dutchman," as Kemper put it, and a special friend of his. The rest of the regiment got only the usual salt pork.

The men only cared about the beef, but Tom was more interested in the news that the rest of the division had come up, and was glad to hear from Kemper that the whole corps was expected in a day or two. Jackson was supposed to be only a few days' march to the northeast and might well come down on them.

Most of the frying pans the men had were only canteen halves with stick handles. They were small, light, and easy to make. All you had to do was split a canteen along the soldered seam and whittle out a stick to fit, and you had a frying pan. Tallow was soon melting and before long the aroma of frying beef filled the air. Two more fires had to be built, which took all the dry wood there was. Either because they were too impatient or because they had no frying pans, some of the men just charred their beef on ramrods held over the fire and wolfed it down.

Ab had a regular skillet he had lifted somewhere, probably from the officers' mess, and gave his first steak to Kemper, because there wouldn't have been any at all if it hadn't been for him. Kemper took one of the boxes the beef had come in, cut his steak with his bayonet, and dined in style. Tom followed his example with the other box when his piece was ready.

Kemper had barely finished eating when someone shouted in German from across the creek. It was a man from one of the platoons out on picket. He had been sent in to report and wanted Kemper to go along because he was afraid his English wasn't good enough. The two shouted back and forth at some length; then Kemper got up and started up toward the bridge where Rivers's headquarters tent had been pitched.

The men immediately wanted to know what the two Germans had said, and Billy told them, "Th' feller said th' Rebels had skedaddled up th' valley an' left most uv their wounded b'hind, in town in people's houses."

There was a hubbub of excited comment. "Y' reckon hit's 'cause th' rest uv th' d'vision's come up, Corp'ril?" asked Cole.

Tom swallowed his last piece of beef. "I expect it's because they've found out th' rest of th' corps is comin' up."

"Whadaya reckon Jackson'll do now?" asked Billy.

"March on Washin'ton, maybe?" guessed someone.

"Whadaya you think, Corp'ril?" asked Cole. "Yo're always studyin' them milytary books an' readin' th' papers."

Tom had a ready answer. "Well, this is th' way I see it," he began. Everyone quieted to listen, and it made him feel like he was teaching school again. "I don't think Jackson'll move on Washington. I don't think he ever meant to."

The men were puzzled.

"Well, what's he doin' hyar in this Shenandoey Valley, then?" asked Jim Polson.

"Keepin' Lincoln scared so he won't send enough men to McClellan's army on that peninsula down there close to Richmond. If he would, McClellan would take Richmond, an' th' Rebels know it. That's why they sent Jackson up here in this valley, t' keep 'em so scared at Washington they'd hold all the men they could get their hands on back to protect it instead of sendin' 'em down to McClellan."

Polson nodded his red head. "Y' know, I 'spect yo're right. Th' way Jackson's been doin' wouldn't make no sense if'n he wun't up t' somethin' like that."

"How's that?" someone wanted to know.

"Jist marchin' hyar an' thar an' never really doin' enything."

Most of the men seemed to agree, but Harve Akers emphatically did not. "Aw, th' presydent knows what he's doin'! He ain't no dum' fool!"

"Well, what *is* he doin?" demanded Polson.

"Pertectin' Washin'ton, that's what he's doin," was the prompt reply. "If'n Jackson takes Washin'ton, we're gone up."

"Wal now," interjected Cole, "if'n McClellan takes Richmond, th' Rebels is gone up, ain't they? An' frum what I hear, Washin'ton's more'n pertected awreddy." He turned to Tom. "Ain't that right, Corp'ril?"

"I'd certainly think so. We've got three armies up here in this valley guardin' Washington. There's Banks's, Frémont's, and McDowell's, and then ther're all those forts around Washington. There's bound to be a lot of men in them."

"Why, I'll bet we've got three or four times 's many men 's Jackson's got, up hyar in this valley an' 'round Washin'ton!" exclaimed Cole.

"More'n that, I 'spect," sighed someone.

The men looked thoughtful.

Tom went on. "Lincoln could've sent everybody to McClellan except maybe Banks, pulled him back close to Washington, and then McClellan would've had a good chance of takin' Richmond. Th' way it is, I'll bet th' Rebels have got more men down there on that peninsula than he has."

"An' if McClellan took Richmond, th' war'd be over," mused Polson. He shook his head and sighed. "That Linkun's a dum' ol' fool, y' know that?"

Harve rose to the president's defense. "No, he ain't neither! Yo're agin him jist 'cause he's a Republican, that's all!"

"Well, yo're jist fer him 'cause he's a Republican," was the quick rejoinder. "Ever'body kin see how he's lettin' th' Rebels make a fool outa him."

Harve got sarcastic. "Well, Jim, you oughta go up thar t' Washin'ton an' tell him 'bout hit. I 'spect he'd make ye a gin'ral when he seen how smart ye wuz."

Polson began to get angry. "I don't claim t' be smart. I jist got a little common sense, that's all, an' that's somethin' that damn abolish Linkun ain't got."

Harve responded heatedly, "Linkun ain't no abolish! You know he ain't! Yo're jist a damn copperhead, that's all!"

Polson's face flamed and he went after Harve. "Yo're a damn abolish, too, y' lil' sneak, an' I'm gonna use ye up!"

Tom seized him. "Here! Here! We're not gonna have any of that!" He wrestled Polson back, and the redhead quieted, so he turned on Harve. "You'd better keep that dirty mouth of yours shut, Akers. I won't be around sometime and somebody'll put a big fist in it."

Harve threw up his hands. "Hit's awful hard bein' th' only loyal man in th' platoon; that's all I gotta say!"

That set Tom off. "What d'you mean, th' only loyal man in th' platoon? Loyal to what?" He advanced on Akers.

Harve's eyes widened and he backed off. "Now lissen, Corp'ril—"

"You listen to me, Akers; that's what you do. There's not a man in this whole regiment that's not loyal! Ever' last one of them volunteered t' fight for th' Union, an' a lot of 'em are gonna get killed doin' it!" He glared at Akers. "Just 'cause we don't fall down an' worship Lincoln an' criticize him once in a while don't make us Rebel sympathizers!"

"Well, hit's jist that hit don't sound very good—" began Harve lamely.

"You just don't let it bother you, no matter how it sounds, and keep your mouth shut. Hear now?"

Akers nodded and looked down.

Tom didn't want to be one-sided, so he turned to Polson. "And you, Jim, don't be so quick on th' trigger, hear?"

The redhead nodded and Tom suddenly noticed Kemper in the background. It looked like he had been there all the time, and he wondered why he hadn't said anything.

*"Wie geht es hier, Gefreiter?"* he asked with a smile and a wink.

Tom understood. Kemper had wanted to see if he could handle it. "Oh, everything's all right, Sergeant. Some of the boys just got a little worked up, that's all."

Kemper nodded and smiled again. Soon everything was back to normal, but Harve didn't stay around long. Somebody said he had gone to the First Platoon, where there were supposed to be a few Republicans.

Suddenly jeers and catcalls broke out from up toward the bridge, and the men looked to see a column crossing the bridge and going on toward the town. "Hit's that Yankee reg'ment," laughed Ab. "Th' boys up thar is givin' hit to 'em fer fallin' out on th' march day b'fore yestidy."

Men joined in all down the line. They did their best to contribute to the ragging, but most of them were too far away to be heard very well.

"Whada ye reckon they're gonna do, them Yankees?" wondered Billy.

*"Es ist der Aufklärungsmarsch,"* replied Kemper.

Nobody understood, not even Billy, but Tom knew what Kemper meant, although he had never heard the word before. "They're goin' out t' see what th' Rebels're doin', a reconnaissance, you know."

Once the Yankees had gone beyond the bridge, the jeering died away and the men began speculating about what was going on.

"Sargint," asked Billy, "kin I go up t' brigade headquarters fer a while?"

"*Ja.* Ve doos nodding dis day, I nodt tink." He looked at Billy inquiringly. "You sees *der Anders, nicht wahr?"*

"Yeah, that's why I'm goin'. Me an' Fred's good fren's, an' maybe I kin find out somethin'."

"He shore oughta know what's goin' on," remarked someone, "now that he's with th' colonel at Brigade."

Billy nodded. "Well, I'll go 'head, then," he said as he started up the creek.

The men loafed about the rest of the morning. When the Germans on picket came in, Kemper learned more about the Rebel withdrawal. They had pulled out bag and baggage, only leaving the wrecked cannon where they were and the worst of their wounded in care of the townspeople. They had marched northeast up the valley like they were going to join Jackson. The Massachusetts regiment was going only a few miles beyond the town to camp, and put out pickets.

"Wal," observed Cole, "we ain't gonna go chasin' after 'em, enyhow."

"I wunner what happened t' that trap we wuz gonna ketch Jackson in?" snorted Cal Fairbanks.

Ab laughed. "I 'spect th' gin'rals is like th' feller that had a tiger that got outa his cage. They jist d'cided t' let him go."

There was general laughter and the men seemed glad it had turned out like it had.

Billy didn't come back until almost suppertime, but he had little to add except that the colonel didn't expect Jackson to move on them now. In fact, he believed Jackson would take his army out of the valley and go down to join the main Rebel army fighting McClellan on the peninsula near Richmond.

Tom nodded. "That's about what I expected. He's done what he was supposed to up here, and they want everything they can get to throw against McClellan down there."

"Whadaya mean when y' say he's done all he wuz s'posed t' do up hyar, Corp'ril?" asked Zeke Kerns, who had just joined the group.

"He's thrown such a scare into 'em over at Washington that they'll keep every man they can get their hands on up here and not send McClellan anything."

Cole sighed. "With Jackson's army jinin' in agin' him, I guess McClellan won't have much uv a chance. He's outnumbered awreddy frum what you said b'fore."

"Yeah," agreed Zeke gloomily. "Th' Rebels'll shove him back an' th' dang' war'll jist go on an' on." Zeke was a little black-haired fellow, as quick and alert as they came. He was about the only rival Ab had as a wit, but he looked pretty gloomy now.

"Hit's politics!" exclaimed Ab. "They don't want McClellan t' beat th' Rebels an' win th' war 'cause he's a Dimmycrat an' they're skeered he'll run agin Linkun in two year an' beat him!"

That hit the men pretty hard, but what Sam Price had to say hit them even harder.

"What I'm skeered uv is that they're gonna keep foolin' 'round till th' radycals gits their way an' ol' Linkun 'bolishes slav'ry." Sam was older than most of the men and the father of two children. He was a quiet, serious fellow, and the men listened when he had anything to say.

Dan Howard flared up immediately. "By golly, they'd better not! Th' minit they does that, I'm throwin' down my rifle an' goin' home! I didn't jine up t' free no niggers 'n' have 'em all come up nawth!" Dan was another redhead, but bigger and older than Jim. He had the reputation of being a wild sort of fellow but had never caused Tom or Kemper any problems.

"Ever'body else'll do th' same!" exclaimed Jim. "They won't have no soljers enymore!"

There was a chorus of agreement, and Tom felt uneasy. He blamed himself for starting it, but all he had done was give an honest opinion. He was just glad Harve Akers hadn't been around.

With the Rebels gone, the colonel took the opportunity to hold a funeral for the men who had been killed in the fighting. All the regiments of the brigade except the one from New England were drawn up to take part. The Yankees were camped on the other side of town and hadn't lost anyone anyhow, because they hadn't come up until it was all over.

The chaplain of a Pennsylvania regiment conducted a short and solemn service. He preached only briefly, and a chorus from his regiment sang "Rock of Ages" very beautifully after he finished.

As far as Tom was concerned, it was mainly for the men from his platoon, particularly Johnny Conrad, but of course there were a good many others. He didn't count them, but someone said there were over fifty graves along the top of the ridge. Most of them were men from the regiment massacred by the Blue Ridge Artillery.

# 16

John Traylor sat and watched his wife wash the supper dishes. When she finished and started drying them, it seemed that she didn't straighten from her stoop. That was because she was getting bent. Also, gray had come to her hair, wrinkles to her face, and angular lines to her figure. Her old vivacity had disappeared. She was silent and withdrawn most of the time. Sometimes she couldn't sleep and paced the house in the darkness. She had aged twenty years since the boys had been gone. Again he felt pangs of guilt. He should have kept Billy at home. That would have helped.

While John ruminated, Sarah finished the dishes. There were so few of them that it never took long. "Go hitch up th' horses and get ready to' go, John," she said in a tired voice. "I'll be dressin' while you're doin' that."

He did not stir immediately. "I hate t' go," he said at length. "You know th' Conrads'll be takin' it awful hard, 'specially Annie. Johnny was the only child of theirs that lived."

Sarah sighed. "I feel just like you do, but we got to go. They're our neighbors, an' then Billy an' Johnny always used t' play together when they were younger." Her lips trembled.

John yearned to comfort her but could think of nothing to say that might not bring on the tears she was close to. He arose. "It won't take me very long," he said. "I'll drive up to th' porch."

When he reined up, she was waiting for him, thin and stooped in the gathering darkness. He got down from the buggy and helped her to her seat. "Bear up, now, Mother," he said softly. He took up the reins, and they began to move.

The trip promised to be a silent one. Nothing John could say ever lifted the gloom that had settled over Sarah, and he had almost quit trying. Not even letters from the boys cheered her. She would generally find something in them to cause additional worry. John worried about the boys himself, especially when their letters didn't come as expected, but it hadn't affected his behavior. Or had it? He pondered. They would pass the site where he and old Dan Martin were building Tom's house. They would stop, and maybe that would cheer her up.

Sarah said something under her breath.

"What is it, Mother?"

"First Ben Noble, then George Sanders, and now Johnny Conrad," she said despondently. "Who'll be next?"

John heaved a sigh. "We'll just have t' bear up an' endure, Mother. There's nothin' else we can do."

She remained silent for a time. "Then Tom's been wounded, and Burk and Mark Dixon, too," she said gloomily.

"Oh, Tom was just scratched," he replied. "He didn't even mention it. Billy did when he wrote." He paused briefly. "Then you know what else Billy said. Dixon wasn't wounded at all, like his old daddy was tellin' ever'body. He just sprung his ankle."

"Well, they were fightin' when it happened, which makes it about the same thing."

"Oh no, not at all, an' Billy said th' men thought he didn't 'actly spring his ankle. Th' enemy was shootin' at 'em with some big guns, an' he just got scared an' d'cided t' quit."

"He's comin' home now, they say."

John snorted. "Yeah, he went up there t' Boston where he went t' school an' got that big doctor t' put plaster on his leg an' give out that he'd never walk without a crutch or cane again. Didn't any army surgeon say that." He snorted again. "You don't get crippled for life by just springin' your ankle." He flapped the reins and shouted at the horses. "Get up!"

They went on silently for a time. The moon had come up, and as the buggy crested a hill John stopped the horses. "Well, there it is. We've got th' foundation down an' th' sills laid."

"Oh," replied Sarah. "Tom's house." She brightened. "It'll really be a nice one when you get it all finished."

John felt like a great load had been lifted from him. The outline of the house and some neat piles of beams and lumber could be seen in the moonlight. "And it's such a nice location, on a south slope lookin' over that valley out there." He turned to his wife. "And they'll have an orchard already. All th' apple 'n' plum 'n' pear trees need is a little trimmin', an' most of th' cherry 'n' peach trees is still alive. Old man Haskins always kept a good orchard, y'know."

They looked over the scene, lovelier in the soft light of the moon than at day. "It's close enough so we can visit back and forth a lot," John ventured. "T' see our gran'children," he added laughingly.

"Grandchildren," mused Sarah. Suddenly she threw her hands to her face and burst into tears. "Oh, John! There'll never be any grandchildren!" she sobbed. "Tom's not comin' back, or Billy either!"

A pall seemed to descend over the landscape. The moon took on a funeral glow, and the shadows grew deep and dark. What had looked like a house under construction suddenly seemed to be one that had been destroyed, and the trees loomed dismally. Sarah sobbed despairingly.

John fought off the fit of depression. "Yes, they will, Mother," he said as he leaned over and put his arms around her. "They'll be comin' back, both of them," he went on with artificial assurance. "There'll be gran'children all over th' place, runnin' 'round barefooted in th' summertime." He clasped her to him. "There, there, Mother; don't cry."

Sarah nestled her head on his shoulder. "John, John, there's no use foolin' ourselves," she said brokenly. "You might as well stop th' buildin'. They'll never come back." Her voice choked off and then resumed. "This war'll drag on and on till they're all killed. A lot of them are gone already, three of 'em neighbor boys we've known all their lives." She broke into weeping again.

John could only hold her in his arms and rock from side to side. He knew she was probably right and felt like crying himself. He followed the war closely in the papers, and had even subscribed to the state Republican paper because it seemed to cover the war more closely. The boys hadn't been in any real battles yet, only what were called skirmishes or minor engagements, but every sixth man from the township had been killed. What would it be like in a really big battle, like the ones on the peninsula near Richmond?

He regained control of himself with an effort and drove such thoughts from his mind.

"Come on, Mother. We've got t' go see th' Conrads, an' Annie's goin' t' be bad enough off without you comin' in cryin' an' all red-eyed." He shook Sarah gently and kissed her on the forehead.

She drew away, sat upright, and wiped her tears. "All right, John," she said in a quivering voice, "Let's go on."

He shook the reins and the buggy rolled on toward the long, deep shadows farther down the slope which yawned before them like the pit beyond the abyss. As they descended into the gloom of the forest, John realized he couldn't stop work on the house. If he did, they would never come out of the darkness.

# 17

The brigade stayed in camp by the creek even after everybody knew that Jackson had left the valley and marched south to join Johnston's army before Richmond. The men had little leisure, though. After a rigorous inspection, lost or damaged equipment was replaced and new uniforms issued. The uniforms were badly needed, because the old ones had seen over a year's hard service. After that, regimental drill occupied the mornings and brigade drill the afternoons. It looked like Rivers was going to be as exacting in command of the brigade as he had been of the regiment.

One morning Jake announced there would be no drill until the afternoon, and after breakfast the men loafed about speculating on what had interrupted the usual routine.

It wasn't long before they found out it was something unusual. Suddenly Lieutenant Mertens appeared and shouted, "Leave arms stacked and fall in by platoons!" He had a grin and purposeful air.

The men fell in. "Platoon sergeants, inspect for neatness of dress!" came next.

Kemper made a quick inspection and found everything in order. After that the company was assembled and marched up the creek to the road along with the others, where the regiment was formed into a column. When the two other regiments camped nearby joined the column, it moved across the bridge toward the town.

Lieutenant Mertens stood by the roadside resplendent in a tailored uniform of fine cloth, as his company marched by. He positively gleamed and glowed, but his mood was grim. "No talking in ranks!" he barked as the men went by. "Platoon sergeants will enforce absolute silence!" He repeated his orders in German to the last two platoons, then hurried back to the front of the company past the marching men.

The men looked apprehensively at one another, as silent as mutes, and an atmosphere of foreboding settled over the column.

They marched until they met the Yankee regiment that had come out from beyond the town, then were halted and faced left while it faced right.

Before them lay the battlefield of several weeks ago. A squad with rifles at the trail stood beside the road. Some distance behind were four men. One was the brigade provost, Major Pedigo. The others were another officer, a civilian in a black broadcloth suit, and a disconsolate-looking soldier with his hands tied behind his back. Behind the soldier was a freshly dug oblong hole in front of which was a long wooden box.

Colonel Rivers and another officer came from the direction of town and joined the group in the field. They conferred with the provost while the men stood mute and motionless facing the scene. It was strange not to hear even the shuffling of feet.

The colonel moved the column to form a three-sided rectangle enclosing the site on all but the side away from the road. Another armed squad appeared there and spread out in extended order across it.

Tom found himself on the road close to the corner of the rectangle nearest to town. After the deployment was carried out, an expectant hush settled over the ranks. He dreaded to watch and even thought of closing his eyes, but the others gazed at the scene with wide-eyed fascination.

Not far to the left, Rivers faced the ranks along the road. "Men," he began in his deep, resonant voice, "you are about to witness the execution of a man who has proved to be an unworthy comrade." He paused and unfolded the papers in his hand. It was so still you could hear them rustle. He identified the prisoner, read the charges against him, and gave the findings of the court-martial that had tried him. He was a member of the New York regiment who had fled during the battle of a few weeks ago and hidden in the woods until it was over. This was desertion in the face of the enemy, and the man was to be shot for it.

While Rivers was reading, a large dark bird appeared overhead and began circling. Tom wondered if it had some way of sensing what was going to happen.

When he finished, Rivers folded the papers and put them in his pocket. "Highest authority having refused appeal, and it being the appointed hour of the appointed day, the sentence will be carried out."

Rivers wheeled to face Major Pedigo and the others in the field. "Provost, parade the prisoner!"

Pedigo and a sergeant conducted the prisoner to the end of the rectangle on the right, then wheeled smartly and paced along the silent ranks. The fellow went docilely but kept his head down and looked at no one. When he passed, Tom saw he was a nice-looking young man.

His features were regular and clean-cut, and his light brown hair was neatly combed.

While the prisoner was paraded around the ranks, the large dark bird still circled overhead, but a flight of doves that had headed down from the woods toward the scene suddenly banked aside and swept over the creek out of sight.

After the prisoner and his escort had passed all around the ranks, they came back to the hole and the box and halted in front of them facing the road.

The civilian member of the group had stood aside while the prisoner was being paraded. Now he came up and began talking to him. Tom guessed he was a minister. The condemned man did not speak in reply. He only nodded his head a few times. In the meantime, the squad spread out across the open end of the rectangle divided and joined the farthest extension of the ranks on each side, then stood with rifles at the ready.

After a short time, the civilian walked away from the prisoner with his head down and his hands folded behind his back. As soon as he was out of the way, Rivers called, "Provost, do your duty!"

Major Pedigo drew a black cloth from his pocket and deftly bound it over the prisoner's eyes. Tom thought he took a last despairing look at the blue sky and the fresh greenery of early summer just before the cloth went over his eyes. He permitted himself to be led forward a few paces and halted facing the road. His grave yawned behind him, and Tom wondered at his passivity.

Major Pedigo was a medium-sized man with an olive complexion and a trim black mustache. "Squad, *attention!*" he barked, and the men of the firing squad snapped erect at trail arms.

"Shoulder *arms!*" The rifles came up to rest on shoulders in three snappy coordinated movements.

"Forward, *march!*" The squad marched toward the road in precise step and alignment.

"Halt! Right about, *face!*" The squad stopped and wheeled to face the prisoner. Pedigo took position to the right of the squad, several paces from the man on the end.

Blank-faced and eyes forward, the men of the squad stood facing the prisoner. Tom thought they were from the condemned man's own regiment until he recognized one of them, who for some reason had looked like a stranger until now. He was a fellow named Barker from the Gibson County Company in his regiment.

The men in the ranks around the scene stood awestruck and silent. Only their eyes moved, flickering back and forth between the squad and the prisoner. He stood in front of his coffin and his grave with his head hanging down. Tom wondered what he was thinking of, his last moments on earth.

"Support, *arms!"* The rifles of the firing squad snapped over at an angle, sinewy brown hands gripping stocks and forearms.

"Ready!" Left feet took one step forward as bodies faced right and braced. Thumbs brought hammers back to full cock, and it was so still you could hear the clicks.

"Aim!" The rifles snapped up to align on the man standing in front. Weathered young faces squinted as eyes sighted along the dull blue barrels. A puff of wind ruffled the condemned man's hair above the black cloth.

"Fire!" The rifles spurted flame and smoke as the volley blasted out like a thunderclap in the stillness, echoing and echoing up toward the woods.

The prisoner was knocked over backward by the impact of the bullets like someone had hit him with a club. His hair flew up and his mouth opened as if in startled surprise. He struck the ground beside his coffin, and his limbs moved convulsively for a few moments.

"Order *arms!"* The rifles came down in sharp, mechanical movements and butts thumped the ground as the smoke wafted away. The big dark bird had disappeared.

The officer with Pedigo moved toward the body, which was lying completely still by the time he reached it. He bent over the body, took one of the limp arms, and held it briefly. He let it fall, leaned over to touch the face, then straightened and nodded to Pedigo. The provost spoke to his sergeant, who called the firing squad to attention and marched it toward the open end of the rectangle.

Pedigo and the other officer came together, then paced up to the colonel. They halted and saluted. "Sir, the sentence has been executed!" reported Pedigo.

Rivers returned the salute, then faced about and began shouting commands that transformed the brigade back into a column on the road and marched it toward town until its rear was even with the execution scene. Then it was halted, faced about, and marched off the road toward the dead man.

Major Pedigo stood by the corpse studying the men's faces as they went by. Tom only pretended to look at the dead man and when Pedigo's sharp black eyes rested on him was suddenly afraid he would be called out of the ranks. He felt relieved when the provost shifted his eyes to someone else.

After the men filed past the body, they turned back to the road and marched back toward camp. There was no talking, even after they were halted beyond the bridge and put at rest in place.

The companies were detached and marched back to their camps one by one. Only after Tom's company fell out was there any talking, and then it was not about what the men had just seen. A military execution is an awesome thing.

# 18

The company had been detached from the regiment and put on picket duty at a ford across a river. Lieutenant Mertens had laid out entrenchments the very first day and the men had dug them, but they were occupied by only one platoon at a time. Each had a six-hour stint, and the ones not on duty spent their time at their camp a hundred yards back in the woods from the north bank.

The Rebels had pickets on the south bank, and an informal truce reigned from the beginning. As one of them put it, "If you'uns won't bother us, we won't bother you." A certain wariness between the two sides continued, however, and there had been no fraternization.

There were a lot of fish in the river, and Mertens got hooks and line so the men could have something to eat besides their rations. Only the Second Platoon took much interest in fishing, mainly because of Ab's enthusiasm and Burk's appetite. Ab not only loved to fish; he was the champion fisherman in the platoon. The others said it was just luck, but he claimed it was because he had been born and raised on the Patoka River and could think like a fish.

One day while one of the German platoons was on duty, Ab, Billy, and Tom were fishing while Burk lounged on the bank. Ab was throwing fish out one after another. Tom caught one occasionally, but Billy had no luck at all. "Th' durn fish jist won't bite for me, that's all," he complained.

"Yo're too impashunt," counseled Ab. "Y' gotta leave yer hook in jist one place. You skeer th' fish movin' hit 'round all th' time."

"Well, I cain't stand jist settin' an' fishin' when I don't git no bites," rejoined Billy.

"Y' gotta wait an' be pashunt like I say," replied Ab.

Billy went downstream a little and looked around. "Aw right now, this is a good-lookin' place hyar, deep water at th' end uv this riffle." He plunked his bait in the water and stuck his pole in the bank. "I'm gonna stay hyar till I ketch somethin'. I ain't gonna move no more."

Ab threw out a nice bass. "Hey, hyar's 'nother one, Burk!"

"Lookit, that," grumbled Billy. "Them fish jist cain't stay 'way frum that feller."

Burk detached the fish and baited Ab's hook anew. The giant pulled up the stringer, dripping with water and wriggling with fish, and put the latest addition on it. "Gonna have a nice mess fer supper," he rumbled.

Three Rebels had come down the opposite bank out of the bushes, where they squatted and watched, looking hungrily at the fish.

Tom had never seen any of them closely before. But for the color and raggedness of their clothing, they looked just like the men on the other bank. One of them was a tall, lanky fellow who could almost pass for Ab, and another was a slender youth like Billy. When Burk put the stringer of fish back in the water, their eyes followed it.

Billy stood by his pole and looked at the men on the other bank. Suddenly the line shot out into the river and the pole bent and came out of the bank. "Hey!" he shouted as he made a vain grab for the pole, which moved rapidly and mysteriously through the water toward the middle of the river.

"Git him!" shouted Ab. "He's a big un! Jump in atter him!"

While Billy hesitated, the slender youth on the other bank dived into the water and swam rapidly toward the moving pole. It disappeared into the water, but he came up with it and detached the line while treading water, then deftly tied it to his belt and swam toward Billy.

Everybody was on his feet shouting. The Germans in the entrenchments caught the excitement and added to the din. Kemper came running from the camp. Jake was on detached service, and he had taken his place as sergeant major.

Billy reached for the swimmer's hand and helped him up the bank. He trailed a huge catfish. Everybody gathered around as he untied the line from his belt and hefted the burden. It was all he could do to lift its head and upper body clear of the ground.

"Lookit that fish!" marveled someone. "I'll bet he weighs fifty pounds!"

Ab pressed in close. "I never seen a fish that big but wunst in m' life an' hit wuz caught outa th' Ohio River at Rockport."

Billy took the line, but it slipped out of his hand and the fish flopped on the ground.

"Grab him!" shrieked Ab. "He'll git back in th' water!"

Billy caught the line and hauled the fish farther up the bank. "You ain't gittin' 'way frum me, mister fish!" he gloated.

Kemper horned in. "Who iss dis *Mann?*" He jabbed a finger at the young Rebel.

The fellow blanched. "M-me? I-I'm frum crost th' river," he stammered. "I jist caught this fish fer this feller. He'd pulled th' pole outa th' bank an' got 'way, but I ketched him and brung him over." He swallowed nervously as he stood there in his dripping clothes.

Kemper looked at him menacingly. "You iss de enemie!"

"Now, Sargint," Billy broke in. "Ye shorely ain't gonna take him pris'ner. He ketched this fish fer me 'n' brung hit over. Hit'd a got 'way if'n he hadn't."

Kemper broke into a smile. "You iss de goot boy. You katch *der fisch für* Beeley." He patted the dripping man on the shoulder. "I nodt make you de preesoner."

The youthful Rebel was greatly relieved, and everybody laughed like it was a joke.

By now the opposite bank was lined with gray-clad men, most of them with rifles. A few held them at the ready. The Germans in the trenches watched with leveled weapons.

The wet boy shouted to his comrades. "Hit's all right! They ain't gonna take me!"

The men in gray relaxed, and their rifles came down. "Ask 'em 'bout havin' a fish fry!" shouted one of them.

Ab's eyes had been only for the fish. He squatted admiringly beside it talking to himself, but at the words "fish fry" he got up. "Good idy!" he called. "This hyar fish'll be 'nough fer fifty men!"

"Yeah!" shouted Billy. "Come on over!"

Tom felt he had to speak up. "Now, wait a minute! There's a war on, you know!"

Kemper didn't understand. "Vat you means, Ab, de *fisch* fry?"

"Fry up fish an' eat 'em, a hull bunch t'gether," was the reply. " 'Twon't do no harm."

Billy was all for it. "Let's do! What 'bout hit, Sargint?"

Kemper pondered. "I nodt know. *Der Herr Leutnant,* he must say."

At that moment, because of the commotion, Mertens came up. He and Kemper talked in German and looked at the big fish.

In the meantime an officer had appeared on the other bank. His men were talking excitedly and pressing him about something. Finally he came down to the edge of the water. "Hello over there!" he called.

Mertens walked down the bank. He stopped short of the mud, always careful of his bandbox appearance. "Yes, sir?" he shouted.

"What do you think of it?" came from across the river.

"You mean this affair of having a fish fry?"

"Yes."

"I have no objections, but we will have to decide a few things first."

"What do you suggest?"

"Well, there isn't enough fish for everybody. I'd say there's only enough for thirty men or so."

Billy spoke up before the reply could come from across the river. "Lootenant, sir, they's a big sandbar out in th' river down 'bout a hunert yards round that bend. That'd be a good place t' have hit!"

"Did you hear that?" Mertens called.

"Yes, it sounds like a good place for it. We've got a skiff, so no one need swim. There's deep water on your side of it."

Mertens talked briefly with Kemper, then turned and shouted, "What do you think of this? Fifteen men from the platoon of the men who brought the fish over and fifteen from the platoon of the men who caught it meet on the sandbar and have the fry."

The man on the other bank laughed. "Agreed, the two men who caught the fish choosing who goes."

Mertens signaled approval and the men seconded him enthusiastically, then began making preparations.

Harve eliminated himself immediately. "I ain't gonna eat with any Rebels," he swore. "I'm not gonna set down with th' enemies uv my country."

"That's fine!" replied Billy hotly. "I wuzn't gonna ask you enyhow. I knowed no dang black Republican wuz fit fer decent comp'ny!"

Harve caught Kemper's stern eye and only walked away with his hands in his pockets.

The frying seemed like it was going to be a problem until the Rebels said they had found a big, long pan for making sorghum molasses in an old barn on their side. They would scour it clean with sand and bring it to the sandbar. Mertens helped by appointing his orderly as cook. The fellow was an expert, but he couldn't speak a word of English. Billy could do what translating was needed, though, and either Tom or Kemper could help.

Billy soon made his choices, but those who were left out didn't seem to mind, maybe because they were a little scared by the idea.

The Rebels ran a ferry service with their skiff and, after the chosen ones had gathered on the sandbar, were much impressed by the big fish. " 'Nough fer forty men," vouchsafed one of them as they surveyed it hungrily.

"Maybe we oughta bring more fellers out hyar," suggested Billy.

The Rebel sergeant shook his head. "No, we done made our 'greement, an' I don't want t' git th' cap'n thinkin' 'bout hit agin." He nodded wisely. "You knows officers. He might change his mind."

"Yeah," interjected one of his men, " 'speshully if'n he gits t' thinkin' 'bout what ol' Buck'll do if'n he finds out."

The sergeant explained. "Ol' Buck's our colonel, an' he hates Yankees like pizen." The Northern men looked embarrassed, so he added hastily, "He's kinda tetched, ol' Buck is."

" 'Bout Yankees enyhow," added one of his men.

"But he's all right 'ceptin' fer that," said another. "He ain't crazy er nothin', even if he's got n' awful high temper."

"He's a holy terror when he gits mad, ol' Buck is," said another, and his comrades all but shuddered.

The cook had taken charge and generally managed to make himself understood. He was a big, ruddy fellow, reddish-haired and well into middle age. Some of the men helped him construct a rude tripod and hang the fish from it. Others put the big pan on rocks and built fires under it. The cook had brought fat pork, which he put several men to cutting into small pieces into the pan and removing them when they were fried out. The Northern men just threw it into the water until they saw that the Southerners were eating what they took out. Tom even saw some of them left behind on the bank fishing pieces from the water and eating them.

By this time the big fish was gutted and skinned, and the chef was expertly cutting off fillets. He refused importunities to start frying immediately, evidently because he wanted the pan filled first, so the men on the sandbar sat and waited.

Kemper undertook to converse with his Confederate counterpart. "*Der fisch,* he iss de gut *Essen.*" He sniffed the air and smiled.

"Yeah, hit's shore a purty day," was the reply. Billy couldn't suppress a smile, and the sergeant looked puzzled.

Kemper tried again. "Your boys, dey haf plenty of de foodt?"

This time the Southerner did better. "Nope, I'm sorry t' say." He shook his head. "We ain't got nothin' much but parched corn."

"Parched corn!" exclaimed Jim Polson while Kemper looked puzzled in his turn. "How d'ye manage hit?"

"We jist chaws hit," replied an older man. "Hit's kinda hard on yer teeth, though." He thoughtfully tested one of his molars with a thumb and forefinger, and Kemper nodded in comprehension.

The Northern men looked at one another in surprise. "I ain't complainin' 'bout salt horse no more," vowed Ab.

One of the Rebels came over and sat down beside Tom. "How come y' got s' many uv them Dutchmen, like yore sargint an' that cook?" he asked in a low voice. He was a clean-cut young fellow with a friendly air, and Tom liked him immediately.

"Oh, there's just a lot of them that live in th' country where our company was raised," he replied.

"Y' mean they ain't Hessians, hired sol'jers like th' Britishers had in th' Revolution?"

"Oh no, they're not mercenaries. They're Americans. They just came from Germany and settled there, or maybe their folks did."

"They live all t'gether like that?"

"Yep, they talk German an' think German an' make beer an' sauerkraut an' all that, just like in Germany, I guess."

The fellow smiled. "We thought ye wuz all Dutchmen fer a while, er Germans I guess I oughta say."

Tom laughed. "Yeah, th' German platoons went on picket b'fore th' rest of us. I heard you had a hard time makin' 'em understand that you didn't want any shootin' or anything."

"Yeah, yore lootenant had t' straighten 'em out 'bout hit." He looked inquiringly at Tom. "Is he a German, too?"

"Yep."

"I kinda thought so, but he kin talk English real good, a little too good t' be a 'merican, I guess."

"Yeah, he's an educated fellow. He was an officer over there, in Germany."

"What 'bout yore sargint?"

"Fifteen years in th' Prussian army, and a sergeant too."

The man whistled. "I 'spect he really knows his bisness."

"He sure does—" Tom cut himself off. He had started to tell about when they had wiped out the Blue Ridge Artillery before it occurred to him that it might not go over very well with someone on the other side.

The fellow waited for Tom to go on and, when he didn't, looked away. Tom felt embarrassed, and their conversation ended.

"Where's y'all frum?" asked the boy who had caught Billy's fish.

"Injianny," replied Cal Fairbanks, "Dubois County, down in th' Pocket. That's in th' southern part uv th' state," he added when the Rebels looked puzzled.

"We're frum No'th C'lina," announced the youth, "frum th' piney woods, all but me."

"How come yo're in with fellers frum someplace else?"

"I wuz workin' fer th' railroad an' wound up there." He sighed. "Th' railroads's liable t' take a feller enywheres."

"Whar air you frum, then?" asked Billy.

"Th' Banks, 'long th' coast, where th' ocean is."

"So that's why y' kin swim s' good, 'n' handle big fish like y' done."

The boy smiled. "Yep, I've done a lot uv that, heap bigger fish than you ketched."

Billy admired him. "Whales 'n' sich?"

"Naw, no whales; sharks sometimes, though."

"They'll eat a feller up, won't they?"

"You bet, jist like they'll eat enything else. A feller's jist somethin' t' eat t' a dang shark."

Billy was impressed. "I shore wouldn't wanta be roun' them things."

The aroma of frying fish filled the air. Covert glances showed that the first fry was nearly done. The Rebels looked ravenous, and Tom noticed that there wasn't a spare ounce of flesh on any of them. Bones and tendons showed through rents in their clothing. Hollow eyes, sunken cheeks, and skinny necks made it seem that their existence was something like a permanent famine.

Burk was moved to speak. "Smell that? They ain't nothin' better'n fish cooked up 's soon 's y' ketch 'em, right outa th' water."

"He's th' champuyn eater uv th' hull army," remarked Ab. "Hit's 'cause he's s' big."

Burk did his best to grin pleasantly as the Rebels regarded him. "I ain't never seen enyone 's big 's he is," said one of them. The others nodded agreement.

*"Es ist fertig!"* called the chef. *"Komm!"*

Even the Carolinians understood and rushed for the fish.

Kemper held his men back. "Vaidt," he whispered. "De Rebels, dey haf de *gross* hoonger. Dey haf onlee de hardt *Korn*. You haf *die gute Rationen."*

The men in gray had it all to themselves, but they were too busy to notice. They snatched pieces of fish directly from the pan and ate them ravenously. This upset the cook, who wanted to serve them in proper fashion, but they couldn't understand his remonstrances. Kemper caught his eye, so he gave up and silently began replacing the pieces taken out as fast as he could.

Finally the Confederate sergeant noticed the one-sidedness of the feast. "Hyar, you dang pigs! Stan' back an' let these fellers have some! Yo're hoggin' hit all!"

His men were embarrassed and hastily stepped back, still eating. "Sorry," mumbled one of them, "but we-uns is s' dang hoongry all th' time."

Kemper let his men take only one fillet apiece except for Burk. He allowed him two, then motioned them back to let the Southerners get to the pan again. Some of them tried to take pieces not yet fully cooked, but the chef stopped them by stabbing at their hands with his huge fork. "Nein! Nein!" he shouted. They understood him and waited on his nod.

The fish was perfectly cooked and delicious. Tom thought it was the best he had ever eaten. The others felt the same. "Boy!" exclaimed Ab. "I ain't never et no fish this good!"

When Kemper translated for the cook, he beamed and nodded.

The Confederate sergeant again shood his men away from the pan. "Hyar, you fellers," he said to the others. "Have 'nother piece 'fore these razorbacks eat hit all up."

The Northern men had another helping while the Southerners watched hungrily. "Hey!" exclaimed Billy through a mouthful. "Th' fish is 'bout all gone!" It was true. Not much was left of the big catfish.

Ab got an idea. "Billy, why don't you an' yore fren' take th' skiff 'n' go git that string uv fish we awreddy had 'fore you ketched this big un?"

"Let's do!" urged the lad from the Banks.

"Let's go!" shouted Billy as he got to his feet and started for the skiff. "Last one t' th' boat's a bad Injun!" He won because he had a head start, so the Carolina youth was the bad Injun. Tom watched them row away laughing and skylarking like boys. Come to think of it, that was what they were.

Although they had eaten most of the fish, the Rebels were still hungry. "How many fish did you-uns have 'fore ye quit?" asked one of them.

"About enough for another servin'," replied Tom.

"I wish they wuz more," sighed the speaker.

Ab took something from his pocket and tossed it at the man's feet. It was a short stick wrapped with fishing lines and hooks. "I didn't lose nothin' on this hyar sandbar," he said significantly.

The fellow picked it up and put it in his pocket. He tried to speak but couldn't, then tried again with more success. "You-uns is shore . . . shore fine fellers," he said huskily. He looked at his feet and shook his head. "Hit's jist too bad we gotta fight—fight 'n' maybe kill one 'nother."

Everybody seemed embarrassed. The men fidgeted uneasily and looked down or cast their eyes across the river.

"Hit's th' dang war," said Ab with a sigh.

"That's th' way hit is," replied the Rebel sergeant. He looked gloomily at his feet. "They's no help fer hit."

"Hit's jist that we're frum diff'runt parts uv th' country," said Jim Polson.

"Yeah," sighed the older man who had feared for his teeth. "A man cain't pull up his roots, no more'n a tree can."

No one had anything more to say. Suddenly Billy and his companion appeared in the skiff. They were glum and silent. Tom found himself hoping they hadn't quarreled or something.

The boat grounded on the bar. The young Rebel was white-lipped and furious. "Stole 'em, them dang fellers did!"

"Who stole what?" asked one of his comrades.

"Th' fish, an' our fellers stole 'em," was the clipped reply.

"How d'ye know our fellers done hit?"

"Them Germans seen 'em."

There were expressions of anger and disgust from the men in gray.

"Why'd they let 'em do it, th' Germans, I mean?" asked Tom.

"They didn't know hit till 'twuz done."

"How's that?"

"Some uv our fellers went in swimmin' crost frum 'em. They stayed on their side uv th' river, but atter a while one uv them Germans seen one uv 'em goin' outa th' water with a string uv fish, up th' river b'hind some bushes, but they seen 'im. Guessed he swum under th' water 'n' got th' fish."

"Is that what they said, Billy?" asked Tom.

Billy nodded glumly. "Yeah, that's what they said. They made 'em git outa th' water 'n' keep t' their own side then, but 'twuz too late."

"I knows who done hit, too," announced his companion.

"Who?" demanded his sergeant.

"Billy said them Germans said 'twuz a little dark feller that went outa th' water with th' fish."

"Peachy!" exclaimed one of the Carolinians. "That thievin' little houn'!" Despite his words, he didn't sound angry.

"Who's Peachy?" asked Ab.

"He's an Eyetalian," explained one of the Rebels. "Cain't nobody pernounce his name, an' hit sounds somethin' like Peachy, so that's what we call him. He kin scrounge up somethin' t' eat 'most enywhere. I alus liked him till now." The fellow sounded like he still did.

"Yeah, me, too," said another. "He kin play eny kind uv a music instermint they is, 'n' he's always laughin' 'n' jokin'." The speaker shook his head. "He's a sight, Peachy is," he added admiringly.

"How come y' got a feller frum Italy?" Ab wanted to know.

"Dang if I know," replied the sergeant. "He wuz a kind uv trav'lin' player, goin' 'round over th' country playin' at fairs an' dances an' sich like. He had a couple uv Niggers that could play real good on th' banjer 'n' fiddle, 'n' he could play enything hisself. He jist happened t' be 'round when we raised our comp'ny 'n' 'jined hit. Sold his niggers 'n' jined up."

"Yeah," laughed one of the others. "When he went t' sign up, th' cap'n ast him how come, him bein' a furriner 'n' all. Ol' Peachy 'lowed he wuzn't no furriner. He wuz a Southerner, 'n' he wuz gonna fight fer his country."

"Hit mighta been on 'count uv his gal thar in Lumberton," opined another.

"Naw, that couldn't uv been th' reason!" exclaimed the older man. "He's got gals all over th' country! We ain't been no place where they wuz people 'round that he didn't have a gal, er git one right away." He laughed shortly. "An' they's no keepin' him in camp."

"Yeah, th' wimmin really goes fer him," added another fellow. "Hit's that han'sum face 'n' white teeth 'n' dark eyes." He chuckled. "An' not jist single ones either. You fellers rec'lect that lawyer's wife when we wuz camped close t' Richmond?"

Several laughed gleefully.

"He found out 'bout hit, that lawyer did," explained the young lad, "an' come lookin' fer Peachy. Whooo-ee!" he shouted, slapping his leg. "Well, Peachy'd heered he wuz comin' 'n' got a big ol' horse pistol 'n' laid fer him." He had to stop to laugh again. "That lawyer, he took one look down th' barr'l uv that big ol' horse pistol 'n' turned 'round 'n' left!"

The young fellow stopped and did his best to get angry again. "I'm gonna beat th' daylights outa him 's soon's we gits back, though," he added unconvincingly.

"Oh, don't try that," advised Tom. "I expect any of th' rest of us would do th' same if we were half-starved and saw fish like that, if we had th' nerve anyhow."

"Well, I'm shore gonna tell 'im what I thinks 'bout hit, th' thievin' little skunk." He grinned in spite of himself. "Cain't nobody stay mad at Peachy," he explained.

"Say, you men!" It was the Confederate captain from the south bank.

"Yes, sir?" replied the sergeant as he and his men got to their feet.

"You'd better get back over here. The colonel's headed up this way."

The Carolinians were galvanized. They rushed to the boat and those who couldn't get in took to the water, shallow enough to wade on their side. "He'll take th' hide offa all uv us if'n he finds out what we been doin'," bleated one of them.

"Yeah," agreed another as he sloshed through the water. "He'd prob'ly have th' cap'n shot!"

The Northern men watched the stampede open-mouthed.

"That colonel uv thurn must be a turrible feller," said Ab.

"I'm durn' glad he ain't ourn," sighed Jim. "Them fellers is skeered t' death uv him."

"Well, hit looks like we're gonna have t' swim fer hit," observed Ab as the Rebels scrambled up the opposite bank and into the trees. "They took th' boat."

Suddenly one of the fleeing men turned back. He was the boy who had saved Billy's fish. He slid down the bank, seized the skiff, and rushed out into the water with it. He came about halfway, then gave it a shove. He was pale and wide-eyed. "Sorry fellers. We wuz s' skeered we fergot. You kin jist keep th' durn skiff," he added as he turned and started floundering toward the far bank.

Billy took a pole and caught the boat. His Rebel friend suddenly stopped in midcareer up the bank and turned to shout, "Hey, you fellers!"

"Yeah?" replied Billy as he pulled the boat in.

"We'd shore 'preciate hit if'n you'uns'd knock all that stuff down, 'n' throw sand over hit, thar wyar we et."

Billy laughed. "We shore will," he promised as the lad took off again. When he disappeared into the trees, there was no longer any sign of the men on the other side. It was almost as though they had never been there.

The men wiped out all traces of their feast, even burying the big molasses pan in the sand, then rowed themselves to their side of the river and hid the boat in some bushes.

The next morning, it was the turn of Tom's platoon on picket. He was in charge because Kemper was taking Jake's place. Their feast companions of yesterday were nowhere in evidence, and neither were their comrades. Several remarked about it.

"I 'spect that colonel uv thurn et 'em all up," joked Ab.

It wasn't long before a voice called from the other bank, though. "Hey, you fellers!"

"Yeah?" shouted Billy.

A figure emerged from the bushes at the edge of the trees. It was Billy's companion of yesterday. "Howdy!" he called as he walked toward the water's edge.

"Well," drawled Ab, "I see one uv 'em didn't git et up enyhow." He raised his voice. "Did that colonel uv yourn find out 'bout our fish fry?"

"Naw. Didn't nobody tell him nothin'. They knowed better."

"What 'bout yore clothes bein' all wet?"

"Told him we'd been scoutin' 'crost th' river. He didn't know 'bout th' boat, an' hit tickled him. He's always tellin' us t' do stuff like that." The lad laughed a little nervously.

"Well, maybe we kin git t'gether agin sometime," said Billy hopefully.

"Naw, we cain't. That's what I come t' tell ye 'bout." He paused and looked sad. "We're leavin', an' a South C'lina comp'ny's comin' t' watch th' ford. Ye better be keerful with them 'cause they're a rough bunch."

"Many thanks!" called Tom.

"Shore, shore," was the reply. "Well, I gotta go now. Th' other fellers told me t' wish you-uns good luck." He had started to turn when a small, dark fellow appeared beside him. The men on the other bank could see the flash of white teeth as he smiled and waved.

"Peachy!" shouted Ab. "We heered all 'bout you, y' dang rascal!"

Everybody laughed.

Peachy made an elaborate bow. "T'ank you, Yankees, for de feesh!" he called. His companion took a playful punch at him, and the two disappeared laughing into the bushes.

# 19

The company was back with the regiment in camp near an important road and a sizable town in the Shenandoah Valley. The other three regiments of the brigade were supposed to be close enough to get them all together quickly, but the division was all scattered out and no one had any idea where the rest of the corps was.

For the first few days the camp had a transient air. No one expected to be there long, and it wasn't until the first rain that many shelter tents were put up. After that they all were and the men settled down for a stay.

Ab and his friends constructed a rude stone fireplace near their tents, then used poles and extra tent halves to put a roof over it for rainy days. The place soon became the favorite resort of Kemper's entire platoon, and the men spent most of their waking hours there, because there was no drill and only morning and evening muster. The colonel had gone back to Indiana on military business, and Captain Owen commanded the regiment in his absence. Relatives from Indiana were visiting Owen. They had brought his fiancée along, and he spent most of his time in town.

This was perfectly all right with the men. They could get passes and go to town, too, but the people weren't very friendly and no one had any money to speak of, because they hadn't been paid in months. This also kept them away from the sutler's tent. They generally loafed about camp, Kemper's men around the fireplace drinking coffee, smoking, and talking when they weren't cooking their rations and eating.

One afternoon Billy brought up a favorite topic. "I wunner how long we're gonna be hyar."

"Th' Lord knows," replied Cole Burton. "Y' ain't complainin', air ye?"

Billy laughed. "Not a'tall. This is th' easiest time we've had uv hit since last winter, an' I ain't chompin' at th' bit like I wuz then."

Several of the men laughingly agreed. "Well," drawled Ab, "th' colonel an' them went back t' Injianny last week, y' know. I guess that means we'll be hyar quite a spell."

"Nobody knows what we're gonna do," said Jim Polson grumpily, "but somethin's bound t' happen sooner er later."

"What we'll do depends on what th' Rebels do," said Tom, "and I don't think it'll be long till they do something. They've got the initiative now that Lincoln's givin' up and takin' McClellan's army off th' peninsula down there by Richmond. I read in th' papers where he's movin' it back up where it started out from."

"What's th' 'nitiative?" asked Charley Evans, a dark, skinny fellow who couldn't read or write. Some of the men looked down on him, but he was really as intelligent as they were.

"It means th' Rebels can do just about anything they want to and we can't do anything about it, until after they've started with it anyhow." Tom thought that was a pretty good spur-of-the-moment definition, even if he had made it himself.

Evans nodded. "That's 'bout th' way hit is, I reckon."

Tom hadn't intended to start anything, but he had. "Well," snorted Cole, "hit's Linkun's fault. If he hadn't let Jackson skeer him like he did in May an' June, an' he'd let McDowell go down on Richmond frum th' north while McClellan wuz movin' on hit frum th' east, they'd of beat Johnston an' took hit."

"An' th' war'd be over by now, I 'spect," added Cal Fairbanks.

The men ruminated gloomily.

"Now they's no tellin' when hit'll be over," sighed Jim Polson. "An' thar last spring we thought we'd be back home in time fer plantin' next spring."

"Yeah, I guess we're in fer hit now," said Cole. "Th' dang Rebels might even win, y'know that?"

"Hit'd be a blamed shame if they did," interjected Billy. "We've got more'n three times 's many people 's they've got, an' then we've got lots more factories 'n' railroads 'n' ships 'n' all that."

"Well, what we needs is a good man t' run th' gov'ment," said Ab emphatically, "an' that's somethin' we ain't got." He shook his head. "That Linkun's th' poorest excuse fer a presydent they ever wuz."

"Aw, he ain't that bad," rejoined Charley. "Hit's jist that he cain't git things organized right. Hit's them radycals. They're always messin' things up."

"How's that?" demanded Cole. "Wuz they th' ones that helt th' men back from McClellan when he wuz down thar close t' Richmond 'n' kep' ever'body else back t' pertect Washin'ton when they wuzn't eny Rebels in a hunert miles uv th' place?"

Evans shifted his ground. "Well, he's gittin' up 'nother army under that new gin'ral—Polk er whatever his name is—an' he's gonna do better."

"It's Pope," interjected Tom, "like the one in Rome." He felt like predicting that the Rebels would concentrate and move on Pope before McClellan's army could be brought back up the Chesapeake to join him and give him a chance of standing them off, but thought the better of it.

Charley's complacency irritated Jim Polson. "You jist wait an' see what happens t' yore Gin'ral Pope. Th' Rebels'll massacree him. He's not nigh 's good 's McClellan."

Charley grinned slyly. "That wouldn't be 'cause Pope's a Republican an' McClellan a Dimmycrat, would hit, Jim?"

He got a quick reply. "Naw, but that's why ol' Linkun's takin' McClellan's army 'way frum him an' givin' hit t' Pope." Jim gloated at Charley. "Ain't that right, now?"

Charley grinned and shook his head. "I wouldn't be s'prised if'n that didn't have somethin' t' do with hit," he admitted.

Tom was glad Harve Akers wasn't around to rise to the president's defense and start another big argument.

Suddenly Cole changed the subject. "Wal, I shore wisht I wuz Jake Bower, back home thar."

"Yeah, we ain't been seein' much uv Sargint Bower lately," said Fairbanks. "He no more'n gits back frum that d'tached sarvis that they sends him home."

"Well, he's back thar on bisness," said Billy, "recruitin'."

"We shore needs more men," sighed Jim. "We're short six men in this platoon, an' some uv th' others is worse off than us."

"Yeah, they's a platoon in Comp'ny D that ain't got but eight men in hit," said Charley. " 'Twuz hit bad by them guns when we fit th' Rebels in th' crick that time."

Billy took the subject on. "Well, men frum ever' comp'ny wuz sent back t' recruit. They oughta git 'nough men t' bring us all up t' stren'th agin."

"How'd they pick th' men that went back t' recruit, Billy?" asked Burk. "Y' know?" The big fellow so seldom had anything to say that it seemed strange to hear him speak up. His bandage had been off for a good while now, and only a little bald spot high on his temple showed where he had been wounded.

"Well, th' colonel went hisself, y' know, but mostly t' see th' gov'nor, I think. At least that's what Fred Anders says, 'n' he says 'bout th' others that th' colonel tried t' pick th' men that had been 'round th' most an' knowed th' most people."

"That's what y' git fer bein' sich an' ol' hermit, Burk," joked Ab, "livin' back thar in th' woods on Cane Crick an' never comin' out an' visitin' 'round."

"Oh, I didn't keer 'bout goin' myself," rejoined Burk. "I wuz jist curious. They ain't nobody back thar int'risted in seein' me, an' I don't know nobody I'd keer much 'bout seein' neither."

Burk wasn't really a hermit, although he did live far back in the hills and never got around much. His father had been killed in Mexico and his mother died a few years later, when he was twelve or fourteen years old, and he had lived by himself ever since. He had no relatives that anyone knew of.

"Y' oughta have a gal back thar, Burk," joshed Jim, "like our corp'ril's got." He grinned at Tom. "He's got th' purtiest gal in th' country, Sally Napier."

"Th' gals wuz always skeered uv me," sighed Burk. "I'm jist too big an' ugly, I guess."

"Yo're jist too big, Burk," Jim assured him. "What y' gotta do is find a gal that's big 'nough fer ye."

Burk only shook his head and resumed his habitual silence.

Tom could tell that the mention of Sally made the men think of Mark Dixon, but only Charley Evans said anything about him, and he made no connection. "Well, Mark Dixon's back thar t' home now I hear, a takin' hit easy."

"Yeah, th' damn' coward!" spat Ab. "Raised a comp'ny 'n' dressed up in a fine uniform 'n' went 'round showin' off with sword 'n' pistol 'n' all, then run out on th' men he'd brung in!" He snorted contemptuously. "They ain't nothin' more wrong with his laig than they is with mine, an' they let him resign 'n' go home!"

"Aw, his ol' daddy fixed all that up," said Cole. "He's a big Republican, y'know."

"Hit's s'posed t' be Dixon's ankle, Ab, not his laig," snickered Billy. "Pa wrote that he goes 'round with a cane all th' time atter they took that plaster off." He laughed. "I'd like t' see a bull git atter him. I'll bet he'd throw 'way that cane an' take out runnin' like a deer!"

Ab guffawed. "Somebody oughta write 'n' have some uv 'em do jist that back thar. Hit could be 'ranged. They's a real mean bull Paw usta have, only he ain't 'round enymore."

Tom wanted to get off the subject of Mark Dixon and saw an opportunity. "Is that th' bull that run you into th' Patoka that time, Ab?"

Ab nodded and grinned. "That's him. He wuz th' meanest critter they ever wuz."

Tom kept the new subject alive. "How'd it happen? I never really knew."

Ab filled his pipe and stuck a twig in the fire. Everybody knew a story was coming, and Ab was the best storyteller in the regiment. The men grinned at one another expectantly as he lit his pipe.

"Well, I tell ye," he began, "hit wuz my own fault." He stopped to puff vigorously, then went on. "I wuz workin' in th' barn an' went out through th' pen at th' back whar Paw kep th' bull 'n' lef' th' bars down goin' inta th' barn frum th' pen." He took his pipe out of his mouth. "Paw had him out t' cover a cow Si Blanchard had brung over an' didn't notice th' bars goin' inta th' barn bein' down when he put him back in th' pen."

Ab put his pipe back in his mouth and puffed a few times. "I wuz hoein' corn in that field by th' river jist b'low th' barn, a workin' away, when I heered somethin' comin' down frum th' barn. I didn't look up fer a little bit 'cause I figgered one uv th' cows had got out an' I didn't wanta quit 'n' chase her 'round fer a while. Fin'ly I d'cided I'd have to 'cause th' corn wuz jist 'bout knee-high an' she'd slaugher hit 'n' git foundered, too. So I looked up an' seen him. He'd come 'round through th' barn outa his pen, an' he seen me 'bout th' same time I seen him."

Ab's pipe had gone out, and he had to light it again. It occurred to Tom that tantalizing his audience was one of Ab's storytelling techniques.

"Well, go on, Ab, dang hit!" demanded Fairbanks.

Ab puffed a few times and savored the suspense. "Well, he come right at me, them horns stickin' out an' gruntin' an' bellerin' somethin' awful." He puffed some more. "He looked 's big 's a railroad locymotive, I'm tellin' ye."

Ab shifted his seat and puffed some more. "*Well*, I thinks, *I'm gonna larn ye a lesson, mister bull, even if'n hit kills ye.* I wuz awful tard uv dodgin' 'round th' dang' critter all th' time when he wuz out." Ab took his pipe out of his mouth. "So, I stood my ground. I had a good, stout, long han'le hoe, an' when he wuz close 'nough, I stepped t' one side an' swung that hoe, th' top uv hit, not th' blade, 's hard 's I could, an' hit him right 'tween th' eyes." He stopped and puffed his pipe.

Fairbanks couldn't wait. "Well?"

"Dang pipe's gone out," said Ab disgustedly. "I never could keep a pipe goin' while I wuz talkin'."

"Well, blame hit, quit tryin'!" exploded Charley.

Ab knocked his pipe out and put it in his pocket with great deliberation. "Oh, whar wuz I?"

"You'd jist hit th' bull 'tween th' eyes!" shouted Fairbanks angrily.

Tom had to hide a grin. Ab was a master of suspense.

"Yeah, right 'tween th' eyes," said Ab reflectively. "Well, he went down like a fallin' tree, an' I thinks, *Oh Lordy, I've kilt th' critter! What'll Paw say?*"

"But he got up and run ye inta th' river!" exclaimed Polson.

"Well, he wallered 'round a little, tearin' up th' corn somethin' awful, then he got up, an' I wuz reel thankful." Ab laughed. "He wobbled 'round a little, then he seen me, an' you know what? Th' dang critter come at me again!"

"An run y' in th' river!" shouted Cole.

"Naw, not yit," drawled Ab. "Yore gittin' 'head uv th' story."

"Well, how 'bout you gittin' 'head uv hit!" exclaimed Cole disgustedly. "Yore th' dangedest feller I ever seen fer draggin' things out!"

Ab laughed. "Well, I'll git on with hit, then." He shifted his lanky frame a little. "Now, I'd broke th' hoe han'le 'bout ha'fway when I hit him, but I still had th' rest uv hit, so I took 'nother clout at him. Then I heered Paw comin', hollerin' fer me not t' hurt th' bull!"

There was an outbreak of whoops and laughter. "He wuz worried 'bout th' bull!" exclaimed Fairbanks.

"Yeah, an' I hollered right back fer him t' tell th' bull not t' hurt me!"

The laughter broke out afresh.

Charley laughed so hard he cried. "Yo're a sight, Ab," he said as he wiped his eyes.

"Well, did y' do eny good with that second lick?" asked Fairbanks impatiently.

"Naw, he didn't even go down th' secon' time," said Ab with a shake of his head. "Hit addled him some, an' he staggered 'round a little; then he shook his head an' come at me agin, bellerin' an' snortin' like a steam injine!"

"Then y' took t' th' river!" anticipated Polson.

"They wasn't nothin' else t' do! That hoe han'le wuzn't 'nough t' fight him with. I seen that." He whooped and laughed. "I hit that river a-runnin' 's fast 's I could 'n' took a flyin' leap out inta th' water. That critter wuz right on my heels."

"Did he come in atter ye?" Billy wanted to know.

"Naw. I went out t' whar I had t' swim jist t' be safe, but he didn't come in atter me. He jist paced up an down th' bank snortin' an' gruntin' till Paw got thar."

"Did he go atter yer paw?" asked Cole.

"Naw, he didn't! Paw come up 'n' commenced talkin' t' him 'n' holdin' his hands out. He had a piece uv rope, an' wouldn't ye know, that critter let Paw put that rope on him an' lead him back t' th' pen jist like he wuz a calf!"

There were exclamations of disbelief. "I shore cain't unnerstan' that," remarked Cole.

"Me neither," sighed Ab, "but hit's th' Gawd's truth. He shore done hit."

"Maybe they's men that can charm th' critters," speculated Charley. "Ol' Lige Anderson kin charm bees. I seen him do hit once. A bunch uv us went t' a bee tree out by th' Wininger church once, 'n' th' bees stung us s' bad we had t' run off. But ol' Lige, they didn't bother him a'tall. He jist stayed thar takin' out honey by th' bucketful."

"Well," Ab went on, "Paw said hit wuz 'cause th' bull knowed he wuzn't 'fraid uv him, but knowed I wuz."

"How?" wondered Billy. "Ye didn't run frum him er enything."

"Maybe it's th' smell," speculated Tom. "Maybe we smell different when we're scared. Animals do, anyhow. They can tell it on one another, like a couple of dogs meetin'."

"Well, I wuz shore skeered," admitted Ab with a laugh. "I'll bet I jumped twenty foot out inta th' Padoky!"

The picture of Ab's lanky frame flying through the air brought more whoops and laughter.

Fairbanks wiped his eyes and cleared his throat. "Y' didn't hurt th' bull much, then?"

"Naw. Aw, he got a big knot er two on his head, sorta 'tween th' eyes, but hit didn't hurt him. He got meaner'n ever. Paw got rid uv him, though. Sold him t' a German 'crosst th' river."

"How come?" asked Billy.

"Hit wuz Ma. She like t' had a fit. She really got up in th' air 'bout hit. Said I coulda been kilt er crippled, an' she wuz always skeered t' death 'bout th' gals, 'specially th' little ones, and she wuzn't gonna put up with hit no more." Ab cackled gleefully. "She said they wuzn't room fer her an' her chillern on that farm an' that bull, too, an' Paw could have his choice, her er th' bull. He couldn't have 'em both." Ab stopped to whoop and laugh. "Well, Paw kept her an' sold th' bull!"

There was another outbreak of whoops and laughter.

"Her er th' bull!" cried Billy.

A din of mirthful guffaws followed. Some of the men rolled on the ground.

"What did that German want with sich a critter?" asked Charley when it began to die down.

"Aw, he'd been wantin' t' buy him fer a long time. He wuz a purebred somethin' er other, 'n' you knows how them Germans is 'bout livestock, always tryin' t' breed 'em up bigger 'n' better." Ab nodded. "I guess he done all right with th' critter. Never heered uv nothin' 'bout eny trouble enyhow. Course Paw took him t' this feller's farm 'n' made shore he knowed how mean 'n' dang'rous he wuz."

"He wuzn't th' feller that had a lil' girl kilt by a bull, wuz he?" asked Jim.

"Naw! Naw!" exclaimed Ab. "Hit wuzn't th' same feller, but when we heered 'bout hit, that wuz th' first thing we thought uv. Ma 'n' all my sisters started cryin' 'n' hollerin' that we oughta kilt th' beast 'stid uv sellin' him, but 'twuzn't him. Hit wuz th' bull uv 'nother German that lived over 'round Kellerville."

"You knowed him, didn't ye, Burk?" asked Cole significantly.

"Yeah, I knowed that feller," rumbled Burk. "He wuz with my daddy in Mexico." He shook his head. "I never had enything t' sorrow me s' much in my life. I cried when I heered 'bout hit. She wuz th' purtiest 'n' nicest lil' gal y' ever seen, yaller hair 'n' blue eyes." He bowed his head. "They figgered she wuz pickin' flowers 'n' got over in th' field whar th' bull wuz. They wuz flowers scattered all 'round when they found her."

The men were astounded. No one had ever heard Burk talk about himself or how he felt about anything before. In fact, no one could remember him ever saying more than a few words at a time.

Cole finally spoke up. "That bull wuz found dead a little while atter that, wuzn't he, Burk?"

Burk nodded silently and looked away.

"Ye wouldn't know enything 'bout that, would ye, Burk?" asked Cole pointedly.

Burk shifted uneasily and didn't answer for a few moments. "Well, I guess hit won't hurt t' tell," he said reluctantly. "I never 'spect t' git back home 'live enyhow."

Tom was shocked. None of the men had ever said anything like that before. "Now, Burk—" he began.

The giant cut him off. " 'Bout that bull," he began. "Well, th' lil' gal's daddy wuz jist gonna keep him. Wuzn't even gonna sell him. I found that out when I went t' th' fun'ral." He shifted his position as the men waited expectantly. "Didn't say nothin' t' enybody 'bout how I felt, but I'd made up my mind that that bull wuzn't gonna live after killin' th' only child that ever seemed t' think that I wuzn't somethin' t' run frum."

The men sat in wonder. It was amazing to hear the big man talk like this.

It was a little while before Burk resumed, and Tom could tell it wasn't easy for him. "I usta visit her daddy," he went on, " 'cause he wuz with my daddy in Mexico an' took an int'rust in me after my mother died 'n' helped me out a lot gittin' th' property deeds fixed up an' all t' our farm, then with th' managin' an' farmin' till I got big 'nough t' han'le hit all by myself."

That was a long speech for anyone, and the men were even more astounded.

"Enyhow," Burk went on, "when she'd see me comin, lil' Gretchen'd come runnin' an' put her lil' arms 'round my neck 'n' call me Uncle Burk." He paused and bowed his head. You could have heard a pin drop before he resumed. "Well, one day a couple uv weeks after lil' Gretchen's fun'ral when they wuz gonna be a moonlight night, I walked over thar, keepin' t' th' woods so nobody'd see me. I knowed whar th' feller kept th' bull, an' after hit got dark 'n' th' moon come up good 'n' bright, I got in th' field with that bull an' kilt him with my bare hands."

There were gasps of astonishment and incredulity. "How in th' world did ye do hit?" asked Cole.

"Hit wuz easy. I jist 'roused him up an' let him come at me while I went at him. I grabbed his horns 'n' twisted his neck an' broke hit. Hit wuz easy."

The men looked at the giant in awe and wonder. It was incredible, but it was the God's truth and they knew it.

No one said anything for a while; then Cole broke the silence. "I kinda 'spected somethin' like that 'cause I knowed how much y' thought uv lil' Gretchen. I'd seen ye buyin' candy 'n' ribbons 'n' stuff fer her in Pappy's store." He shook his head. "Course I didn't breathe a word uv hit t' enybody 'cause I thought uv doin' somethin' myself. I knowed lil' Gretchen, too. She usta come t' th' store with her folks, an' when she'd come in th' buildin' hit wuz like th' sun comin' out on a cloudy day." He sighed. "I thought uv shootin' th' beast, but I couldn't git up 'nough nerve t' do hit." He shook his head again. "I couldn't figger out how 'twuz done, though. That critter weighed fifteen hunert if'n he weighed a pound, an' they wuzn't a mark on his carcass."

"What did th' feller that owned him think?" asked Polson.

"He didn't know what t' think," replied Cole. "Some folks thought lightnin' had struck th' beast, but they wuzn't no storm. Lil' Gretchen's mother said th' Lord had done hit 'cause her man wuz s' stingy 'n hard-hearted he wouldn't do hit hisself."

There was a long pause. The men were silent and thoughtful. Tom thought the story was pitiful in a way, and not just because of little Gretchen.

# 20

The men were having their first coffee at the fireplace beside their shelter tents. Word had reached them already that the colonel and the men sent back home to recruit had arrived earlier that morning. Plenty of recruits and also some promotions were supposed to have come with them.

"What d'ye think, Sargint?" Ab asked Kemper. "Y' reckon yo're one uv th' men that's gonna be an officer?"

Kemper grunted and shook his head. "Nodt Kemper."

"Well, why shouldn't y' be?" demanded Billy. "Yo're th' best sargint in th' reg'ment, an' th' colonel said he wuz gonna do his best t' git ye one."

Kemper grunted again. "Dey nodt gif de *Kommission* to dumm Dutchmen dot nodt got no politeeks."

"Aw, that ain't so! Lookit Lootenant Mertens, not that he's dumm er enything, er you either."

"He vas *Offizier* in Chermany. He haf *die Ausbildung und kann* goot de Eengleesh speek."

Billy's reply was cut off by the shout, "Hey! Hyar come th' recroots!"

The men looked up to see Jake leading a group of men in new uniforms toward them. They would have been marked as recruits even if they had worn old ones because of the way they acted.

"Fresh fish!" came the standard greeting.

"Whar'd they git you lil' fellers? Ol' Jackson'll eat ye up, hide, hair, an' all!"

"Whoever got you-uns wuz robbin' th' cradle!"

"Yeah, er th' jailhouse!"

So it went, but the recruits only grinned. Jake had told them what to expect.

Suddenly Ab noticed the shoulder straps on Jake's new coat. "Hey! Sargint Bower ain't no sargint no more! He's an officer!"

Tom noticed that Jake's bars were silver. He had jumped a grade and was a first lieutenant. He was headed for Kemper's platoon but stopped and consulted a list. He pointed toward the First Platoon and sent three of the recruits to it, then came on with the others trailing him.

*"Achtung!"* barked Kemper as they approached. The men who were sitting jumped to their feet, and all snapped to attention.

Jake stopped and looked at them uncertainly. Kemper saluted smartly. *"Zu befehl, Herr Leutnant!"*

Jake lost his uncertain look and returned the salute. "At rest. I dunno what that means, Sargint, but hit sounds all right."

"It means we're at your orders, Lieutenant," said Tom.

Jake nodded. "I thank you fellers. I didn't quite know how hit'd be, bein' an officer, but you-uns showed me." He looked at Kemper. "I got news fer you, Sargint. Yo're comp'ny sargint major in my place now." He didn't notice that the recruits were wandering away.

*"Danke schön, Herr Leutnant!"*

Everybody seemed pleased but Billy. "Aw, he oughta been made an officer!"

Jake nodded. "I 'gree, but frum what I hear, hit couldn't be done." Tom took that to mean that the colonel had done his best but hadn't been able to get the governor's consent.

"Who's gonna be our platoon sargint now?" asked Jim Polson.

Jake looked at Tom. "Yore ol' corp'ril, Tom Traylor."

Tom felt thrilled but wondered how he could ever fill Kemper's shoes. He could manage a platoon all right, but not like Kemper had.

Kemper grinned and came over to take his hand. *"Gratulieren, Herr Unteroffizier!"*

*"Danke schön, Herr Feldwebel!"* Tom replied as they shook hands.

They all laughed and seemed happy about it, particularly Billy, who beamed with brotherly pride.

"Oh, you kin d'cide who's gonna be corp'ril in yore place, Tom," said Jake. "Jist lemme know right 'way."

Tom rose to the occasion. "I'll let you know right now."

"Who?"

"Cole Burton."

Cole grinned hugely as the men shouted their approval of Tom's choice.

Ab pretended hurt feelings. "Been passed over fer sargint 'n' corp'ril 'n' ever'thing else! An' hyar I am th' smartest man in th' reg'ment!"

Laughter swept the platoon. "You got th' biggest mouth in th' reg'ment, that's what you got, Ab!" guffawed Cole.

"Right! Abs'lutely right!" whooped Fairbanks.

Cole pounded Ab on the back, and everybody laughed again, Ab the loudest of all.

"Say," asked Billy, "what 'bout Lootenant Mertens?"

"He ain't no lootenant no more," replied Jake. "He's Cap'n Mertens now."

The men cheered and Billy ran to tell the two German platoons, where the news set off a noisy celebration.

"Did we get any more officers?" asked Tom.

"Naw. We're still only gonna have two in th' hull comp'ny, me an' Cap'n Mertens," replied Jake with a shake of his head.

"Aw, that's plenty!" exclaimed Jim. "We got good sargints, an' that's all we need." He grinned at Tom, which made him feel better about taking Kemper's place.

"Yeah," agreed Charley Evans. "Hit saves a hull lot uv salutin' 'n' carryin' on."

"Now, I got good news fer ever'body," Jake went on.

"What?" The men were all eyes and ears.

"Yore gonna git paid t'morra. Th' paymaster's already on his way."

"Money!" shouted Fairbanks. "I ain't seen none in s' long I've done forgot what hit looks like!"

There was noisy and prolonged rejoicing.

Billy had returned in time to hear. "Oh boy! I'm shore goin' t' town t'morra!"

"Now, what're you goin' t' do in town?" asked Tom.

Billy grinned bashfully. "Somebody I want t' see is gonna be thar."

Jake broke in and saved Billy from further questioning. "Now, I got news that ain't s' good." He looked pretty gloomy.

The men suddenly quieted, and he went on. "Th' colonel couldn't git confirmed brig'deer gin'ral an' has come back t' th' reg'ment."

"Aw, that's a shame!" cried someone, and everybody seemed to agree.

"Who's gittin' th' brigade, then?" Cole wanted to know.

"Stamford, th' colonel uv that Massychoosits reg'ment," replied Jake. "He's brig'deer gin'ral now." He shook his head in resignation.

There were indignant shouts. "How come!" demanded Ab. "He ain't ha'f 's good 's Rivers! He couldn't even keep his reg'ment on th' march that day, while back!"

Jack shrugged. "That's th' way hit is, though."

Jim Polson exploded. "Th' damn' abolish! Hit's jist 'cause th' colonel's a Dimmycrat an' that Stamford's a damn' black Republican! I'm tellin' ye—"

Jake cut him off. "You better hesh up, Polson. A brig'deer gin'ral ain't t' be fooled with, y' know that?" He nodded grimly. "He kin have ye shot."

Polson blanched, his freckles showing up more plainly. "I don't keer—"

"Y' don't keer if'n ye git shot?" demanded Jake.

"Naw, I didn't mean—"

Jake cut him off again. "Y' better keep yer mouth shut 'bout hit, then," he warned. He looked around at the rest of the men. "Th' same goes fer th' rest uv you fellers, too."

The men looked impressed and that was the end of it.

Jake looked around. "Hey, whar is them recroots?" He saw they had all wandered over to the First Platoon, where he had sent the first three. "Hey, you fellers, you recroots!" He beckoned imperatively. "Git back over hyar!"

They all started toward him.

"Naw, not all uv ye! Th' ones fer th' First Platoon stays thar!"

They stopped and looked uncertainly around as the old hands guffawed. Finally three of them turned back.

When the others reached him, Jake separated some from the others. "Sargint Kemper, you take these Germans t' th' Third an' Fourth platoons. You kin han'le 'em better'n me. They ain't none uv 'em that knows hardly eny English." He gave Kemper a piece of paper. "Hyar's th' list."

Kemper took the list and spoke in German. Faces broke into smiles at the sound of their own language. One boy heaved a sigh and said something. Kemper laughed and slapped him on the back, then led them away gabbling happily.

"Hyar's yore men, Sargint Traylor." Jake indicated the remaining seven. They weren't really men, thought Tom. They were only boys, but then most of the veterans were little older. He knew most of the recruits. They shifted uneasily on their feet and looked at him apprehensively.

"Jack an' Sammy Kellerman!" exclaimed Billy, singling out two of them. "What air you doin' hyar? Ye ain't—"

Tom headed him off. "I'm glad to see all of you fellows," he said as he gave Billy a hard look. He went up to them, shook hands with everybody, and learned the names of the ones he didn't know. This put them more at ease, and they relaxed even more when some of the older men followed his example and began asking about things back home.

Tom caught the eyes of the Kellerman boys and beckoned them aside. He was glad no one seemed to notice, even when Billy joined them. He knew them both. They lived in a remote part of the country back home, but Tom had an uncle who lived near them. He couldn't understand why their father had let them go unless he was afraid they would run off and join a strange regiment like a lot of boys had done. Jack was the older, but he was only seventeen. Both were big for their age and well grown, but they were too young for war.

"How'd you two get in?" Tom asked bluntly.

They looked enough alike almost to be twins, and Sammy was nearly as big as Jack. Both were tall and blond and would make fine-looking men some day.

Jack looked Tom in the eye. "They took us, Sargint, an' Pa let us go."

"How old are you, Jack?"

"We're both over eighteen," was the reply.

Tom snorted. "Now, that's not so. Neither of you is eighteen. Sammy, I doubt if you're even sixteen yet. I know you and I know your folks."

Sammy looked down, but Jack didn't. "We're both over eighteen," he said again.

Tom sighed. "Well, you both ought t' be sent back home, but you're here, and if you do get sent back, you'll probably run off and join th' first regiment that'll take you." He looked at them sadly. "I'll bet that's why your father let you go."

Jack only looked at him wordlessly, but Sammy nodded and said confidingly, "He knowed you, Tom, an' 'lowed you'd look atter us."

Tom looked at them and sighed again. They had china blue eyes and fair, almost girlish, faces a razor had never touched. "Well, if it's that way, I guess you can stay. I won't say anything, anyhow, and Billy won't either. You'll be with a good bunch of men here, and it's hard telling what kind of fellows you'd wind up with in another regiment."

Both of them were greatly relieved. "Thank ye, Tom—er, Sargint, I mean," mumbled Jack. "We'll be good sol'jers, won't we, Sammy?"

Sammy nodded. "We shore will. We kin march 'n' shoot 'most 's good 's enyone, an' we'll larn sol'jerin'."

Their eyes were mirrors of innocence, and Tom almost felt like changing his mind.

"Shore y' will," Billy said confidently. "Hit ain't hard. Hit jist takes a little time. That's th' way hit wuz with me."

Both of the boys smiled and nodded.

"Well," sighed Tom, "like I said, I won't say anything, and Billy won't either. I don't guess anyone else knows or they wouldn't have taken you." He started away. "Come on; we'll get back with the rest of them."

Ab was regaling the other five recruits and Tom didn't want to spoil the show, so he motioned Billy and the other two to stop.

"Now, hit's thisaway," Ab pontificated. "Th' army's an awful hard life, an' sometimes th' men has t' be drove like cattle." He nodded emphatically. "Ain't that right, Corp'ril?"

"Hit shore is," replied Cole solemnly, "jist like cattle." He shook his head. "Hit's awful sometimes."

"An th' officers," Ab went on, "is too busy t' pay much 'tention t' th' men. They jist turns 'em over t' th' sargints an' corp'rils."

"Yeah," agreed Cole, "th' officers got too much else t' do."

The recruits stood open-mouthed, taking it all in.

"Now," Ab went on, "d'ye have eny idy how they picks th' sargints 'n' corp'rils?"

They didn't. It was all strange to them.

"Well, I'll tell ye." Ab pretended to look around. "Hit's somethin' y' oughta know, so y' kin kinda pertect yoreselfs." He lowered his voice. "Now, don't let that handshakin' uv Sargint Traylor fool ye. He jist done that t' keep y' long 'nough t' git ye all roped in hyar." Ab pretended to look around again, then sidled up closer and spoke in a stage whisper. "Now, I'll tell ye how they does hit. They pick th' meanest man in th' platoon fer sargint an' th' next meanest fer corp'ril!"

The recruits looked terrified. Cole had to turn aside to hide a grin, and Billy suppressed a giggle.

"But," Ab went on, "they got hit back'ards in our platoon. They thought they wuz pickin' th' meanest man fer sargint, but he didn't turn out t' be nigh 's mean 's Corp'ril Burton hyar." Ab thrust his face forward and widened his eyes. "He's s' mean they ain't no tellin' what he'll do t' ye! Horsewhippin's th' least he's li'ble t' do!" Ab pulled his head back and nodded emphatically. "Now, Corp'ril, ain't I right? We gotta be honest with these new men."

Burton looked fierce. His swarthy complexion and big bulk made it easy. "That's right," he admitted. "I'll 'fess up. I'm th' meanest man in th' hull platoon. That's how I got t' be corp'ril, an I'm gittin' meaner all th' time. I'm lookin' t' be sargint someday." He put a hand on Ab's shoulder. "Now, take Ab hyar. He's th' smartest man in th hull reg'ment, but they ain't made him a corp'ril er a sargint er enything." His voice went down to a hoarse whisper. "Y' know why?" He met only timid, apprehensive looks. "He ain't nigh mean 'nough!" said the big fellow explosively, and the recruits rolled their eyes like frightened horses. They looked like they were ready to run, so Tom decided it had gone far enough.

"Now there's something I want to tell you new men," he began. They almost jumped out of their shoes at the sound of his voice, and he couldn't help laughing. "You new men," he went on, "don't want to believe a thing these old hands tell you! They're th' biggest liars on th' face of th' earth!"

The veterans roared with laughter at the looks of blank astonishment that came over the faces of the recruits. Ab and Cole whooped and stomped. They had to hold onto one another to keep from falling down laughing.

When the uproar died down a little, Tom went on. "No, they're really not that bad. Just learn to tell th' joshin' from th' truth and you'll learn a lot." He pointed at Ab. "But never believe a thing this fellow here tells you. He never does anything but josh."

Everybody had another laugh, the recruits included.

After a while Kemper came back to get his tent and gear. Tom went with him. "I'd like to talk with you a minute, Sergeant," he said after they had struck the tent.

Kemper began rolling up the canvas. "*Ja*, ve talk."

"Do you have any advice for me, now that I'm takin' your place?"

Kemper tied the roll, then replied with a grin, "*Nein*. You nodt need de a-aviss. You be de bedder sargeent dann Kemper."

Tom laughed. "Now, that's not so—"

Kemper cut him off. "*Ja*. You be de *Offizier* soon." He stepped back, arms akimbo, and nodded. "You be de goot sargent, *und* also de goot *Offizier*, too."

Tom could scarcely believe his ears. "Now, Sergeant, that's going too far, 'way too far."

"*Nein, es geht so*." He grinned and nodded. "Kemper knows. He iss solcher *für* de *lange* time. He iss solcher *für* de *fünfzehn Jahren*."

Tom could only shake his head as Kemper gathered up his gear and started off. "*Komm*. I say to de boys de *auf wiedersehen*."

Tom followed, wondering what had given Kemper such a high opinion of him.

# 21

When Billy came back from another visit with Fred Anders, he seized the first opportunity to beckon Tom aside, then led him away from the others with a conspiratorial air.

"Now, what's all this about, Billy?" he asked when they stopped.

"Tom, y' gotta help me talk Burk inta goin' t' town t'morra," Billy said earnestly.

"What in th' world for? He won't want t' go, you know that."

"Hit's Anders. His folks is hyar t' see him an' they brung a gal 'long, a cousin uv his, an' Burk's got t' meet her."

"You know Burk's not goin' t' town to see a gal as well as I do, Billy."

"He's jist got t' see this'n. Anders says she's 'most 's big 's he is."

Tom shook his head. "I'm afraid that won't make any—" He cut himself off. "As big as he is?"

"Yeah. Anders says she's more'n six foot tall an' good-lookin', too, with a nice figger." Billy nodded. "An' she kin talk English real good, too."

Tom pondered. "I see what you mean. He says gals are always scared of him 'cause he's so big." He looked at Billy. "It's a good idea. Burk's a mighty lonesome man, you know."

"Yeah. Hit wuz my idy. I thought uv hit jist 'bout 's soon 's Anders told me 'bout her. I told him 'bout Burk bein' s' bashful 'n' all 'cause he's s' big, an' he said this cousin uv his'n 'd be jist th' gal fer him. She cain't find no man big 'nough fer her."

"How old is she?"

" 'Bout twenty-five, Anders 'lowed."

"Pretty old for a gal not t' be married." Tom laughed. "She gets her eyes on Burk, and he'll be a goner. They'll be about th' same age."

"You'll help me, then?"

"Sure I will. I'll get some of the other men to help. We'll work on him."

"Now he cain't be told why we wants him t' go, er y' couldn't drag him 'way frum camp with a team uv horses," warned Billy.

"I know. We'll think of something else to tell him."

They began on Burk just after they got paid, but he wasn't the least bit interested. "I don't know nobody thar, an' they're all Rebels enyhow."

"Naw, they ain't," insisted Billy. "They's Union men 'round hyar."

Burk only shook his head negatively, so Ab took it up. "Don't y' wanta spend some uv that money y' jist got?" he asked.

"What fer? I don't need nothin'."

Cole tried next. "They got good beer at a place in thar, German beer. Wouldn't y' like t' drink some uv hit?"

Burk showed his first interest. "German beer?" He shook his head. "Naw, they couldn't be. They ain't no Germans 'round hyar."

"Yes, they is," insisted Cole. "They calls 'em Amishers er somethin' like that, an' they makes beer fer this place." He nodded. "I knows, 'cause I drunk some once b'fore I run outa money."

"Wuz hit 's good 's that they brung up frum Jasper that time when we wuz still at Injinap'lis?" Burk was wavering.

"You bet," replied Cole. He smacked his lips. "Hit wuz shore good."

Burk was persuaded. "All right, I'll go." He nodded thoughtfully. "No tellin' when a feller'd git 'nother chance t' drink beer like that."

Tom thought it had all been pretty obvious, but Burk didn't seem to suspect anything. "Now, don't you fellows go guzzlin' it all up," he said laughingly. "Save some for th' rest of us."

Billy looked surprised. "Ain't you goin'?"

"No. Only half th' platoon can go, th' captain says. They don't want th' town overrun, an' I don't care 'bout goin' myself."

"Well, how we gonna d'cide who gits t' go?" queried Billy anxiously. "I jist got to."

Tom wasn't going to show any favoritism. "Who wants t' go?" he asked.

"Ain't all th' men hyar," Ab reminded him.

"That's right," replied Tom as he ran his eyes over the group. "None of th' recruits can go. They've got to drill." He paused and counted. "Let's see, there's eight . . . twelve . . . sixteen men here. Only twelve can go, so that means four'll have t' wait till tomorrow with those that aren't here. I guess we can draw straws to see who has to wait."

Billy was scared half to death he would get one of the short straws, but he needn't have been, because only twelve men wanted to go. Tom was surprised, particularly because the others weren't all married men.

"Now, you fellows who are going have got t' pass th' captain's inspection," he reminded them, "so get out th' brushes and currycombs or he won't let you go."

There was a flurry of activity. Burk decided to wear the new uniform that had been specially made for him. It had come only recently; he had always worn one that had been cobbled together out of two others by a tailor back in Indianapolis.

When those who were going to town had left, Tom decided to go watch Kemper drill the recruits. He wanted to see how it went and didn't care to be around when the absentees came back and began complaining about having been left out. When he reached the drill field, Kemper put him to drilling the inevitable awkward squad, and he spent the rest of the day at it.

He went to sleep before the men who had gone to town came back. The next morning he dimly remembered their return, but it hadn't really woken him up. There wasn't any morning muster and it was Sergeant Hall's turn with the awkward squad, so he idled away the time after he got up until the revelers began to put in an appearance.

Cole was the first to come to the fire for coffee. "Well, how'd it go?" Tom asked him.

"Fer who?" asked Cole sleepily as he poured a cup.

"Burk."

Cole grinned. "Burk? He's a goner. That big gal's got her hooks inta him." He laughed. "Y' oughta seen hit."

"Yeah? Tell me all about it."

Cole shook his head, still grinning. "Well, we got inta town an' went t' that s'loon whar they had that beer. They didn't have none 'n' Burk wuz reddy t' go back t' camp when Anders come in." He looked at Tom wisely. "Him'n Billy had hit all fixed up, y' know."

"Yeah, I know." He grinned with anticipation.

"Anders, he says he thought they had some uv that beer over at th' hotel whar his folks wuz stayin' an' we got Burk t' go over thar with us." Cole laughed. "Course they didn't have none, but wunst we got over thar, that's all they wuz to hit."

"What d'you mean?" asked Tom as Billy joined them.

"Well, they wuz stayin' in this fancy hotel 'n' wuz all in th' parlor room, Anders' folks, I mean, settin' an' talkin'. We went in th' door an' Burk seen that big gal."

"She's real purty," interjected Billy, "but she's s'dern' big."

"Well, Burk saw that gal. Then what?"

"Well, I watched him close, an' he couldn't git his eyes offa her. Anders, he interduced us t' his folks, his ma, pa, sister, 'n' this cousin uv his. They all got up 'n' bowed 'n' his pa shook hands with us."

"They're real nice folks," Billy added. "Fred's pa's a doctor."

Cole grinned hugely. "They's 'nother feller that got hooked, too!"

"Who?"

"Yore brother, that's who!" Cole laughed gleefully. "He wuz 's bad 's Burk when he seen that purty lil' yeller-headed sister uv Fred's!"

Billy blushed and spilled some of the coffee he was pouring. "I knowed you fellers'd guy me t'day," he said ruefully.

"I want to hear about Burk first," Tom said.

Cole laughed. "Well, they wuz all this bowin' an' han'shakin', an' then we got t' talkin' with 'em thar in that parlor room. They could all talk English real good 'ceptin' Fred's ma, an' she cain't speak a word uv hit." He looked slyly at Billy. "That didn't hold yer brother back, though." He shook his head and laughed. "Ye'd a thought he wuz a shore-'nough Dutchman. I had no idy he'd larned t' talk German s' good."

Tom laughed. "How about Burk?"

"Well," Cole went on, "th' first thing I knowed Burk an' Katy—"

"Who's Katy?"

"That's Katarina," interjected Billy, "Fred's cousin, this big gal."

"Aw, I cain't pernounce hit," replied Cole, "so I'll jist call her Katy."

Tom was getting impatient. "Well, go ahead, for goodness' sake, before Burk gets up."

"Well, like I wuz sayin'," Cole went on, "th' first thing I knowed Burk 'n' Katy wuz settin' off by theirselfs actin' like they wuz ol' fren's. Katy wuz laffin' 'n' carryin' on 'n' ol' Burk wuz, too." He laughed and shook his head. "Hit wuzn't like Burk a'tall. Y'd a thought 'twuz 'nother feller. Y' oughta seen hit." He shook his head again. "I couldn't hardly b'lieve my eyes fer a while."

"Well, go ahead."

"Th' next thing, they got up an' went out on th' verandy uv th' hotel, Burk an' Katy did. I couldn't tell whose idy hit wuz, but I 'spect hit wuz her'n." Cole grinned and shook his head. "They're a pair, them two. I don't think Burk's more'n five er six inches taller'n she is. Y' see 'em t'gether an' hit makes ever'body else look like midgets."

"She's nice-lookin', though," said Billy. "She ain't fat er big 'round er enything."

"Yeah," agreed Cole. "She's got a real nice figger, little waist 'n' big bosom." He laughed a little. "I 'spect I'd a tried t' cut in on Burk if'n we hadn't all 'greed she wuz fer him."

"So they went out on th' veranda," said Tom.

"Oh, yeah," Cole went on. "They walked back'ards an' for'ards on hit fer a while. We could see 'em, an' Miz Anders, she kept an eye on 'em." He nudged Tom. "Then somebody else went out thar, an' I seen 'em holdin' hands walkin' 'round on th' verandy!"

Billy blushed redder than ever.

"It was Billy and Fred's sister!" laughed Tom.

"Shore wuz!" Cole laughed gleefully. "Walkin' back an' forth, 'n' once they fergot t' let their hands go when they come in front uv th' door an' I seen 'em!"

Tom laughed along with Cole. "Well, Billy, she's th' first gal you ever had."

Billy grinned bashfully. "Yeah, I never seen much in gals b'fore."

"Well, what about Burk, Billy?" asked Tom. "You must've seen more'n Cole did."

"Yeah," said Cole. "I didn't see much uv 'em when they wuz out thar on th' verandy. Cap'n Mertens, he come in, an' they wuz 'nother round uv bowin' 'n han'shakin'. Me'n Ab, we thought we oughtn't t' be 'round an officer 'n' started to leave, but Doctor Anders, he wouldn't have hit, an' took us inta th' bar 'n' started buyin' drinks. He'd buy one, then we'd buy one, then th' cap'n would, one atter 'nother." Cole shook his head. "Th' firs' thing I knowed, hit wuz nigh dark, an' they wuz bound we stay fer supper." He grinned. "I didn't see nothin' more uv th' lovebirds till then."

Billy saw his chance. "Yeah, 'n' Cole an' Ab wuz 'bout ha'f-drunk when they come in th' dinin' room! They wuz red 's beets 'n' their eyes wuz buggin' out! An' Cole run inta a cheer 'n' knocked hit over!"

"Aw, I jist didn't see th' blamed thing," replied Cole lamely. "But we did have too much t' drink, me'n Ab did." He sighed. "We tried t' keep up with them two Germans, th' cap'n 'n' Dr. Anders. Wouldn't git one drink down till they'd order up 'nother one."

Ab joined them in time to elaborate. "Yeah, th' doctor, he said 'twuz wonnerful t' see officers 'n' men drinkin' t'gether an' all, an' t' have ever'body equil 'n' 'lectin' their own gov'ment, 'n' not bein' ruled by kings 'n' princes 'n' sich like. He said that wuz th' reason he come t' this country."

"I think th' doctor may be carryin' it a little too far on 'count of bein' a foreigner," said Tom. "Not many officers drink with their men, and high-class people generally keep to themselves over here just like anyplace else."

"Yeah," agreed Ab, "I think so, too." He lowered his voice. "Y' know, he said he thought th' slaves oughta be free, th' doctor did."

Tom was astonished. "Is he abolish?"

"Naw, nothin' like that," Cole assured him. "He jist don't know nothin' 'bout niggers, an' th' cap'n told him he didn't in a perlite kinda way. He said niggers wuz'nt jist white folks with black skins like people that didn't know 'em thought they wuz, an' hit'd cause all kinds uv trouble if'n they wuz jist turned loose. He 'lowed he'd been 'round 'nough t' know that."

"Yeah," said Ab. "Now, th' doctor's a nice man, but he don't know nothin' 'bout niggers an' that kinda thing." He looked in the coffee can. "Hey! You fellers didn't leave me no coffee!"

"Well, make some more," Cole told him. "You knows how."

Ab started with it. "I needs coffee. Got 'n awful taste in my mouth."

Everybody laughed. "You're a reg'lar old boozer, Ab," laughed Tom.

Ab shook his head ruefully. "Me 'n' Cole, we tried t' keep up with two fellers that could carry hit a lot better'n we could." He sighed. "I ain't gonna try nothin' like that no more, an' I don't 'spect Cole will either. I like t' got drunk, I did."

"Me, too," confessed Cole, "but y'know, th' cap'n an' Dr. Anders, they didn't turn a hair!" He shook his head. "I wuz glad when suppertime come an' I could git outa that barroom 'thout havin' t' be carried out."

"I'm not interested in you fellows eatin' and drinkin'," said Tom. "I want to hear about these lovebirds."

Ab put the coffee on to boil. "Has Cole told ye 'bout hit?"

"Some. He got to the supper table, I think."

"Well, I dunno what went on while we-uns wuz in th' bar," said Ab with a sly grin. "Ye'll have t' git Billy t' tell ye 'bout that."

"Aw, he didn't see nothin' er nobody but Gerty!" scoffed Cole. "He couldn't tell y' nothin'! I'll bet he didn't even know when hit got dark!"

"Is that her name, Billy?"

"Naw, hit's Gerda. None uv these idjits kin pernounce German."

"Oh no, not nigh 's good 's Billy kin, 'speshully gals' names!" laughed Ab. "Y' oughta heered him a-talkin' German with Gerty's ma! I'll swear, he could talk hit 's good 's she could!"

"Well, what did you do while these fellows were boozin'?" Tom asked.

Billy blushed again. "Aw, we jist set 'round 'n' talked 'n' walked on th' verandy, then done 'bout th' same atter supper till we come back t' camp."

Burk came out of his tent. "Ain't no use puttin' hit off eny longer," he said with a grin. "I been layin' thar lissenin' t' you fellers fer a long time."

"Lovebirds!" whooped Cole. "You an' Billy!"

"He don't look like no lovebird t' me," said Ab. "More like a love buzzard."

The teasing went on for a good while. Burk took it in good spirit and really didn't seem bothered much. Billy didn't do so well.

"Well, are you fellows goin' back t'day?" asked Tom when it died down. "As far as I know, you can. A good many of th' men don't care about goin', or are willin' t' settle for goin' once."

"I'm goin'," replied Burk, and Billy indicated he was going, too. Ab and Cole thought they had had enough of it, though.

"Well, I'm gonna shave my beard off," said Burk, "so I guess—"

Uproarious laughter cut him off.

"Katy don't like beards!" roared Cole.

"Aw, I been gonna do hit enyhow," said Burk unconvincingly.

This led to renewed teasing, which went on until Burk took a pot of hot water away and went to work on his beard.

"Y'know," said Ab seriously, "I larned a lot frum talkin' with th' cap'n 'n' Dr. Anders thar yestidy."

"What?" asked Tom.

" 'Bout what th' war's 'bout an' how importint hit is." He shook his head. "I didn't have no idy why th' Germans is all fer th' war b'fore, even if Sargint Kemper did say somethin' a time er two."

"Yeah? Let's hear."

"Well, y'know, they've been busted up inta a bunch uv lil' bitty countries over thar in Germany fer hunerts uv years an' hit's been awful hard fer 'em."

"Yeah, I know," replied Tom. "They haven't had a government over all of Germany since th' Middle Ages. Each little country goes its own way an' looks out for itself."

Ab nodded. "Yeah, an' th' other countries, th' big uns, always been invadin' 'em, comin' in on 'em 'n' burnin' their houses 'n' barns 'n' takin' ever'thing they had."

"Mostly France," added Tom. "Germany's been nothin' but a doormat for them, th' French."

"An' they wuzn't nothin' them Germans could do 'bout hit," interjected Cole, "on 'count uv bein' all busted up like that. Them lil' countries could never git t'gether 'n' fight 'em off, them French."

"It'd be th' same way with us if th' Union's busted up," mused Tom. "If th' Rebels win, it won't stop with that. Th' states'll all start goin' their own way an' we'll wind up in th' same shape Germany's in."

"Yeah, that's 'zackly what they said," Ab went on. "Said we'd always be a quarrelin' an' fightin' with one 'nother, an' th' big, strong countries'd jist play 'round with us 'n' swap us 'round 'mongst one 'nother an' that kinda stuff."

The men were impressed and a period of thoughtful silence followed. Billy finally broke it. "Yeah, an' they wuz somethin' else. Miz Anders said she wanted t' come over hyar 'cause she didn't think we'd ever have wars 'ceptin' maybe with Injuns, an' her boy wouldn't hafta fight 'n' maybe git kilt like they wuz always havin' t' do over thar." He shook his head. "Then a lil' while after they come, we had a war." He sighed. "Hit wuz kinda sad."

"Well, when we get this one over with, there shouldn't be any more," said Tom, "among ourselves anyhow. Nobody's ever goin' t' try secession again."

"Oh, we won't have eny wars a'tall, 'mongst ourselves er with other countries," said Cole confidently. "We'll be s' big an' strong once we git this Union back t'gether that no other country's ever gonna mess with us."

Tom thought that was going too far, but he didn't say anything.

When Burk came back from shaving, all eyes turned to him.

"Hey, yo're nekkid!" shouted Ab.

Burk looked strange, deeply tanned and weathered except on the lower part of his face. "I feel kinda funny 'thout my beard," he said ruefully.

"Yeah, an' y' look funny, too!" exclaimed Cole. "Grow hit back! That phiz uv yourn skeers me!"

The giant only grinned and went on as the men broke into whoops and guffaws. "Y'know," said Ab aside, "he really looks a lot better, don't he?"

"Yeah," agreed Cole, "Burk really hain't a bad-lookin' feller." He whooped and slapped his leg. "Katy'll really go fer him now!"

"Y'know," began Ab confidentially, "they's somethin' changed 'bout Burk 'sides his looks." He bobbed his head emphatically. "He never usta joke 'n' laff with us b'fore. He'd always jist set thar an never say nothin'."

"Yeah," said Cole thoughtfully. "Hit's kinda like he come outa a shell er somethin'."

No one connected it with Katarina, but Tom knew that was what it was.

"Y'know," began Billy in a low voice, "Fred says she's purty well off, Katarina, I mean."

"Yeah?"

"He says her folks is dead an' she wuz th' only child. She's got a big farm down 'round Jasper someplace 'n' has t' hire fellers t' work hit. Brung some over frum Germany, but she cain't never git enybody t' stay long."

"Well, I hope Burk gets her," said Tom. "It'll be good for both of them. He'll manage that big farm of hers."

"Him git her!" exclaimed Ab. "Hit's gonna be her that'll git him!" His tone became confidential. "Y'know, y' kin tell when a gal really falls fer a feller, an' she's fell."

"You don't reckon th' captain will try t' cut Burk out, do you?" asked Tom. "He's almost as tall as Burk, and he's an officer."

"Aw, he'd never do enything like that," replied Cole. "He's got a wife in Germany but no chillern, I don't b'lieve. "He wuz talkin' 'bout her last night."

"How come she's over thar an' he's over hyar?" asked someone.

"Well, frum what I could tell, she'd gone back t' visit er somethin' 'n' th' war broke out, an' they d'cided she oughta stay over thar with her folks atter he jined th' army."

"Say, yo're goin' with us t'day, ain't y'?" asked Billy.

"You bet," replied Tom. "I want t' see these gals that have got you an' Burk roped in."

He didn't get to go, though. Before they could start, Kemper came for him to drill the recruits. He had other things to do, and Sargeant Hall was going to be busy with the awkward squad. Tom could go the next day.

There were Grim and Schaeffer, the sergeants of the two German platoons, but Tom guessed Kemper didn't want to turn the recruits over to them because they didn't know enough English. He didn't even ask about them, though, because he really didn't mind waiting another day. Anyhow, the more he drilled others, the better he learned drill himself.

No one got to go to town the next day, though. At morning muster the men were told to dismantle the camp and get ready to march in an hour's time. Rumor had it that the Rebels had made their long-expected move, and Tom believed this was one rumor that would turn out to be true. Burk took his disappointment better than Billy, but neither of them said anything.

Everyone was in such a hurry that nothing was said about the usual inspection before a march, but Tom hurried his men and had time for a quick one. He found everything in order, which made him realize how much he owed to Kemper. He just hoped he could do as well with the men.

The line of march passed through the town, right by the hotel where most of the visitors were staying, because the street it was on was also the main road that ran northeast. The company was last in the column, so everybody was out watching by the time it passed the hotel. This was undoubtedly why the colonel had called the regiment to attention and put the men in step as soon as they reached town.

The hotel veranda was packed with people, but Tom had no trouble picking out the Anderses' because Katarina towered above almost everyone. The best he could tell, Gerda was slender, blond, and rather delicate, and Katarina was a lot like her, although on such a larger scale that delicacy wouldn't describe her. Dr. Anders was a portly, dignified man, but his wife had her face buried in a hankerchief and Tom couldn't tell much about her.

Gerda and Katarina called and waved their hankerchiefs when they saw Burk and Billy, but of course they couldn't respond. Both of the women were weeping.

As the column marched by the hotel, the pounding rhythm of a thousand feet striking the ground together drowned out almost everything but the cries of the women on the veranda.

# 22

The regiment joined the brigade soon after the march began, and a few days later the brigade joined the division. They marched through gently rolling country with few woods, and for the first time Tom could catch glimpses of the whole column. He had never realized how large the division was before. Companies and platoons seemed to count for nothing in such an immensity, and individuals were totally lost. He couldn't understand how a mortal man could command it.

When the division joined the corps a few days later Tom learned what immensity really was. The corps was so huge you could never see it all, and surely only God could command it. The division led the column, which undulated for miles back over the rolling ridges completely out of sight. It was interspersed with guns and wagons at regular intervals, and mounted officers were spotted at the heads of regiments, brigades, and divisions.

The corps didn't seem to stay together after the march entered more rugged country with frequent woods and stretches of overgrown abandoned fields, but after that you really couldn't tell, because even the brigade was seldom visible in its entirety.

One afternoon brought a strange, muted thunder in the distance to the southeast, like a giant summer storm far away over the horizon. The men knew what it was although they had never heard anything like it before. A great battle was raging, and the thunder was massed batteries of artillery firing very rapidly. Sometimes it would die away and then come again, but it was so distant they couldn't tell if it actually was doing that or if it was only changes in the wind.

The rest of the day seemed to bring it no nearer, but darkness after they camped put an end to it. Everyone expected to reach it the next day, and the camp was unusually quiet that night.

After the march began the next day, the morning hours went much like the day before except that the thunder didn't die away and then return as often. Also, it seemed to be coming much more directly from the south.

In the afternoon the thunder grew louder and definitely came directly from the south. Tom began to think he could feel the concussions of the constant discharges as well as hear them. Rather suddenly, lighter, sharper sounds broke in, something like the spatter of a summer shower on new shingles.

"That's rifles," said Ab. "I reckon we're fin'ly gittin' close."

"Let's hope we win this one," sighed Billy. "We ain't won one yit."

None of the others had anything to say. Their eyes kept straying toward the sounds of battle, although they were much too distant for anything to be seen. The two Kellermans looked almost rapt, like it was something they were looking forward to, and Tom began to have qualms about having let them stay. They had done very well so far, though. They had learned drill quickly and stood up well on the march. Their size together with their uniforms and equipment disguised their youth unless you saw those rosy, girlish faces.

The sounds of battle grew steadily louder as the march went on. The rifle fire in an irregular drumming roar split with occasional volleys became much louder, and the concussions of the artillery could definitely be felt, almost like giant fans were rustling the air. Tom thought he heard faint cheering a time or two.

By this time they seemed to be moving past the battle on their right, and this was definitely the case late in the afternoon when the brigade suddenly wheeled by the right flank, went from column into line, and left the road heading directly south. It halted just off the road, and while the men dropped their packs, fixed their bayonets, and capped their rifles Tom saw the brigade that had been ahead of them going on east along the road. He looked to his right and saw the one behind them double-timing to close up and fill the gap in the column.

That seemed to mean that the brigade was going into battle by itself, which would be pretty small stuff in the kind of thing that was going on in the direction it was facing. There the roar of battle convulsed the heavens and Tom thought he could see a haze in the distance, powder smoke, if it was really there. The regiment was on the right of the brigade's line and the company was on the right of the regiment's, where the two German platoons made up the very end. Because of that, Tom expected the company to be sent out as skirmishers, but it didn't happen. The regiment on the far left sent them out.

While the skirmishers were running out and stringing themselves along the front, the men waited. They were generally rather pale and wide-eyed, and when they talked their voices were higher than normal. The two Kellermans were exceptions. They watched the deployment of the skirmishers eagerly and seemingly impatiently, like they could scarcely wait to get started. Ab was another. He chewed casually on a grass stem that dangled from his mouth and looked like he always did.

"Jist lissen t' that racket!" he exclaimed as the firing rose to new heights, mostly rifles now. His long face split into a grin. "Somebody's gonna git hurt if'n they don't stop that!" He drew only a little half-hearted laughter.

"Ab, you'd laff at yore own fun'ral if'n ye could," sighed Cole.

Ab's reply was cut off by the order to advance, and the line moved into one of the interminable overgrown fields this part of the country abounded in. The growth consisted mostly of low bushes, with few thickets or brier patches, though, so the going wasn't so bad and alignment was easily held. The skirmishers ahead made their way forward with rifles at the ready like men on a massive quail hunt.

The men were still at shoulder arms, and the long bayonets gleamed in the sun as they moved toward the sounds of battle. Burk stood out like a rock among pebbles as he always did, and his huge bulk seemed to move along like it was on rollers. Tom didn't believe Burk had said a half-dozen words since they had left camp, but he had a different look in his eyes, like a man whose life had been changed.

As the line moved on, Tom realized that the battle was coming nearer a good deal faster than they were advancing, and his heart sank, because that meant the Rebels were gaining ground.

All at once the roar of the firing fell off and a shrill, insistent kind of yelling took its place. It gave a horrifying impression of masses of men of demonic ferocity sweeping irresistibly forward, killing and destroying everything in their path. Only the Rebels could be yelling like that, and it sounded like they were carrying everything before them. The men tensed and became even more wide-eyed, like they had been suddenly shocked by a galvanic battery or some such device.

Suddenly the brigade wheeled left, went from line into column, and broke into a run, moving like an enormous millipede on its thousands of legs. It acted like some gigantic organism struck by a sudden panic transmitted instantly to its thousands of parts. Only after it was done did Tom realize it had been the result of commands he had heard and obeyed along with everyone else. The skirmish line conformed to the movement and raced along to the right as flankers.

They ran on east, but for a time the horrifying yelling and minor sounds of battle kept pace with them. Then, almost imperceptibly, they began to fall away to the west. The men ran as fast as they could, driven more by some appalling urgency they felt than by the shouts of officers and noncoms.

A group of officers on horseback appeared ahead, bobbing on nervous steeds to the right of the column. Tom was astonished to see an old man with snow white hair and beard among them who looked almost like Father Christmas. He waved his hat and shouted, "On, boys, on! Keep it up! Keep going!" His voice boomed above the scuffle of feet, the slapping of the brush, and the creak and rattle of equipment. A man his age should be at home with his grandchildren, telling them stories in the morning and napping in the afternoon with his snowy beard fluttering on his chest.

He was the center of a group of much younger officers with a profusion of gold braid and gleaming shoulder straps. Suddenly Tom knew who he was. He was General Stanfield, the corps commander and a Virginian who hadn't gone with his state. His was the God-like mind that controlled the corps, and if he had looked sterner he would look like what Tom had always imagined God would look.

A horseman raced toward the group from the south. He was hatless and his long black hair streamed from his head. One of the officers around Stanfield pointed at the approaching rider and called the general's attention to him just before they passed out of view behind.

The men had run so long that some of them were panting like dogs and rolling their eyes wildly. They began to stumble as they tired, and a few fell, to be trampled by those behind them, who sometimes also fell. Bayonets flashed dangerously and a rifle discharged close to the ground with a muffled roar. A scream pierced the air, and someone shouted unintelligibly.

Suddenly the column turned right and headed directly south. General Stanfield and his staff galloped furiously across the angle, drawing rapidly ahead of the column. He rode magnificently, like a man half his age, on a big bay whose flanks gleamed wetly.

Men still occasionally stumbled and fell, but they no longer stayed in ranks when they started to go down. They threw themselves to one side like men jumping off a speeding vehicle, then scrambled to their feet and ran alongside in frantic attempts to catch up. Some of them did and a man or two even got back in his place, but most of them settled for only keeping up.

The pace began to slow and most of those who had fallen out were able to regain their places. Those who didn't do so quickly were harried back by officers and noncoms. Tom never had to bother because no one in his platoon ever fell out.

All at once the column halted, leading to much overrunning, many collisions, and much shouting about interval and alignment before it transformed itself into a line facing west. To the left the ground sloped gradually upward, the growth thinned, and a stretch of open ground covered with wheat stubble began. The open ground went on several hundred yards to a thin, scrubby forest that covered both sides of a narrow valley and went on out of sight to the south. There seemed to be a road running east–west some distance into the forest, as dust rose in a line perpendicular to that of the brigade. The valley widened back from the woods, and the brigade's line ran along the bottom, just short of the dry bed of a small stream.

The regiment was still in the growth along with the one on its left, but the other two were out in the wheat field. The sounds of battle came from over the ridge to the west and had changed greatly. Instead of much yelling and little firing, there was much firing and little yelling.

Rivers put his men at rest in place and went out in front on foot. It was so noisy that few had heard the command and most just followed the example of those who had. General Stanfield rode up from the right with two aides and joined Rivers; then General Stamford, the new brigade commander, came through the line from the rear and rode toward them, bobbing uncertainly on his horse.

Stanfield dismounted and Stamford followed his example, nearly falling when a foot stuck in a stirrup. He was older than Rivers and looked just like a Yankee abolitionist was supposed to, tall and thin, with a long nose that almost touched his protruding chin. Tom despised him. He couldn't even ride a horse.

Rivers did most of the talking, although it was more like shouting with all the noise. He pointed over the ridge to the west and then toward the woods to the south. Suddenly he turned back and beckoned to someone in the ranks up toward the head of the regiment.

Fred Anders broke out of the ranks and ran after Rivers as he went back toward Stanfield and Stamford, the wooden case he always carried in the field on his back like a pack. Tom had always wondered what it was. It seemed to be a map case. Anyhow, Fred unslung it, took out what looked like a map, and gave it to Rivers.

It was a map, and Stanfield moved over close to Rivers as he unfolded it. Stamford came up when they bent together to look at it, but they paid him no heed. Rivers put a finger on the map and spoke earnestly to Stanfield, who bobbed his head occasionally while Stamford looked on.

The men waited, their eyes on the three officers in front. No one said anything because there was so much noise they would have to shout. One long, concerted roar of rifle fire came from over the ridge ahead, and Tom knew they would soon be moving toward it. His eyes sought out his brother, who stood gripping his rifle with whitened knuckles and still looking much like the boy he had been when they left home. *God, God,* he prayed silently, *let him come to no harm.*

Movement in front drew his attention, and he saw Fred running back toward the ranks while Stanfield and his aides rode off to the right. Stamford was coming back leading his horse, probably because he was afraid to try to mount in front of everyone. As Tom's eyes followed Stamford through the line, he saw that the brigade was still alone and wondered where the rest of the division was. With Stanfield around, the whole corps should be someplace close. Before he turned back, he saw the Kellermans in their place just behind him. They no longer looked rapt and eager. In fact, they looked for all the world like children about to be punished for something they hadn't done.

Suddenly Captain Mertens came running down the line from the left. He brought up sharply in front of his company, drew his sword and revolver, and shouted, "Company, attention! Forward, *march!*"

Tom and the men toward the middle of the company could hear him despite the uproar in front, but the men toward the ends couldn't and lagged behind when the company moved forward out of the line. Since none of the others moved out, the men knew they were going out as skirmishers and deployed smoothly into line at the proper intervals, although most of them couldn't hear the commands.

Mertens ran on ahead and his men advanced across the dry stream bed through the growth and on up the ridge. The growth wasn't thick and their wide intervals made for unimpeded progress. Since they only covered the front of the regiment, Tom guessed they were going out more as scouts than skirmishers, in the growth where the Rebels might not see them. Jake went out to the left of Mertens, running to catch up.

Just before Mertens reached the top of the ridge, a short line of men in gray rose from the growth with leveled rifles. They fired almost together and Mertens went down, but no one else was hit, probably because the Rebels hadn't allowed for the downward angle and their bullets went too high.

The men in gray disappeared as soon as they fired, and there was no chance to shoot back. Mertens tried to get to his feet but couldn't and sank back, shouting at Jake and motioning for him to take the line on. It seemed to Tom that he had been shot in the leg.

The line moved on, going faster as Jake shouted and motioned. When the men reached the top of the ridge, he shouted, "Halt!" and they lurched to an uneven stop.

A wide valley spread out before them with the woods about where they were on the other side on the downward slope, but they were bounded by a grassy pasture instead of the wheat field. A flimsy rail fence separated the pasture from the growth and the wheat field a short distance down the slope, and the pasture went on to a sizable creek that ran down the middle of the valley. On the opposite slope the woods replaced the pasture and covered the entire western side of the valley, but they didn't seem any thicker and the trees were still small.

The skirmishers who had shot Mertens were running on across the pasture and had almost reached the creek. They had covered a lot of ground in a hurry and were hard to see, because smoke had moved down the valley from the left.

That was where the action was, but at first glance only confused, indistinguishable masses of men half-obscured by sheets of smoke could be seen in the woods there. A closer look showed they were separated into two irregular lines, a blue one on the near side of the creek and a gray one beginning to cross from the other. They were very close together and were exchanging fire at a terrific rate. The noise was much more overpowering than it had been over the ridge to the east. It looked like the two lines ran south far into the woods, maybe even beyond the road on in that direction.

The blue line was giving ground steadily, and the reason was not hard to see. A gray column flowed down the slope through the straggly woods on the other side of the valley. It would soon reach the creek and not long after it crossed would go from a column into a line facing south and take the friendly troops in the woods to the left in enfilade. Its direction of advance would place it a hundred yards or so out in the pasture north of the woods, a perfect position. The commander of the blue line down there wasn't going to be able to withdraw fast enough to escape the enfilade because he was too hard pressed in front. Tom saw instantly that the only way to save him was to bring the brigade over the ridge from where it was deployed and compel that Rebel column to give up its move and form a line to face it or be taken in enfilade itself.

Jake only stood and gaped, obviously not knowing what to do. Mertens was the only one who did, but he was lying back there disabled and there was no time to go ask him.

Tom ran up to Jake and shouted in his ear, "We've gotta go back an' tell 'em what's goin' on over here! Th' brigade's gotta get up here quick an' stop that flankin' column!"

Jake clenched his teeth and grimaced. "Well, I dunno what they told th' cap'n t' do—" he began.

"There's no time t' find out! I'll go myself an' tell 'em! They've gotta know!"

Kemper had come up in time to hear. *"Ja! Ja! Gehen! Sofort!"* He understood the situation.

Jake couldn't make up his mind, so Tom shouted, "Well, I'm goin'!" and started back.

Kemper gave him a push and shouted, *"Mach schnell!"* after him.

He went over the crest and started down the slope on the other side in great leaping strides, thankful that the growth wasn't dense enough to slow him down. He passed close by Mertens, who was sitting on the ground with his left boot off and trouser leg cut away to show a bloody knee, which he was trying to bandage. He looked up in surprise and shouted after Tom after he went by, but he ran on.

The brigade was drawn up in line of battle just as Tom had left it. He was very glad to see Rivers standing in front, although Stamford sat on his horse beside him.

They looked at him in astonishment as he angled to his right and rushed toward them yelling, "Move up! Move up! Move th' brigade up!"

Stamford only looked more astonished, but Rivers ran to meet him. "What's that? Did you say, 'Move up'? Did Captain Mertens send you?"

Tom brought up panting so badly he could hardly speak. "No, sir—he's shot! But . . . we've gotta move up! Th' Rebels . . . 've thrown out a . . . flankin' column . . . an' it's gonna . . . take our line . . . down there . . . in enfilade . . . 'less'n we move up—"

Stamford had ridden up and chose this time to horn in. "What d'you mean running back like that?" he demanded. "Don't you know—"

Rivers cut him off. "A flanking column? Enfilade?" His eyes were so searching it was almost frightening.

"Yes, sir!" Tom had regained a little breath. "By now it'll be moving' 'long these woods here . . . over th' ridge . . . 'bout a hundred yards out . . . straight t'ward us . . . on th' right flank of our line over there!"

Stamford tried to speak again, but Rivers headed him off. "Have we got enough time?" He had analyzed the situation instantly and hit upon the critical factor.

"Yes, sir—if we move up right now . . . an' fast enough!"

"Where are your officers?" demanded Stamford "Where's—"

Rivers seized his horse's bridle and jerked him aside, then began expostulating earnestly with him.

Tom didn't think he was supposed to hear and moved away. He looked up the slope and saw that Jake was bringing the company back, but he wasn't hurrying. Two men were helping Mertens along behind. They were almost carrying him as he hobbled along on one leg with his arms around their shoulders.

Suddenly, "For'ard, *march*! Double-quick, *march*!" came from the left and the line began to move in jerky, uncordinated fashion toward him. There was no way of telling whether the command had originated with Rivers or Stamford.

Tom kept ahead of it and, when Jake started putting the company in formation to tack it on the end of the line when it came up, ran over to join his platoon. The men with Mertens put him down carefully and ran to take their places, probably because he told them to. He just sat on the ground, and the ranks parted to go around him. He didn't seem to be bleeding much, but he was awfully pale.

Just before the line reached the top of the ridge, a heavy volley crashed out on the other side. When he cleared the crest, Tom saw what the volley had led him to expect. The flanking column he had seen moving down the other side of the valley was now a line at a right angle to the hard-pressed blue line in the woods. The blue line was much closer than when he had last seen it, and whoever was in command was trying to refuse his flank to meet the enfilade. The movement wasn't going very well, and a line of blue-clad bodies dotted the edge of the woods. All this could be made out despite the fog of smoke building up in the valley.

The Rebel line along the edge of the woods was loading for another volley when the brigade came over the crest and started down the other slope. "Halt! Halt!" came down the line from the left, and the men lurched to an uneven stop, then dressed their line automatically.

Although their line was somewhat to the left of the center of the brigade, the Rebels were now in much the same position relative to it as the blue line in the woods was to them. When "Ready! Ready!" came down from the left, Tom could see surprise and alarm sweep along the gray line and it fell into momentary confusion.

"Aim! Aim low! Low! Low!" somehow made itself heard, and Tom shouted it on. Rivers wasn't making the same mistake those Rebel skirmishers had when they had shot Mertens and missed everybody else.

The Rebels reacted almost immediately. Their line had already fallen back and faced about to pivot on its right and swing around to face the brigade when "Fire!" brought the volley, irregular because no command could be heard all along the line and many just fired after others had. There was so much smoke that all Tom could see was what looked like a giant snake suddenly get its head cut off as the near end of the gray line was almost blown away.

No one waited for any command to load. As Tom reached for a cartridge, he could tell that what was now the left of the gray line since it had faced about was racing out into the pasture to begin the wheel to face the brigade.

The center was beginning to move and the whole line was starting to pivot on the remnant of its right by the time he was ready to fire again. There had been no command to fire at will, maybe because none was needed.

His was among the first of a scattering of shots that swelled instantly to a ragged fusillade as slower loaders finished. The smoke was so bad by now that Tom couldn't see what effect the shooting was having. More smoke from the south seemed to be moving north from where the major fighting was and combining with what was being generated in front to create a swirling gray curtain that obscured the Rebels almost entirely.

Tom fired at where the enemy line seemed to be and while he loaded saw a two-gun section of artillery had set itself up about halfway up the opposite slope, where the smoke was thinner. The sun hovering just above the ridge top was in his eyes, but he could tell they were being loaded.

Suddenly irregular pinpoints of flame broke out along a line down in the valley, which meant the Rebels had completed their wheel and had started firing. Most of the bullets went overhead or tore up the ground in front, which showed that visibility was even worse from down there.

Suddenly two deeper, heavier blasts rose above the continual roar of rifle fire and Tom saw two solid shot from those guns on the opposite slope strike short, then come bounding up the ridge directly toward his platoon. "Outa th' way!" he shouted as the dull black balls skipped closer with fearful speed. They looked strangely distorted, as though they shattered the air they passed through. As the men around him saw their danger and leapt one way or the other in a tangle of bodies and rifles, he threw himself forward and to his left, shoving Billy ahead of him so that they both fell.

The dread missiles passed just to Tom's right with a thumping, whistling noise, one so close he felt the hot breath of its passage. There was a horrible smashing noise, behind him, and choked, explosive cries went up.

As he started to get to his feet, he looked back and saw only quivering heaps of mangled flesh compounded with whitish splinters of bone and shreds of dark cloth where the Kellerman boys had been. When he was fully erect, he saw that they were intact only from their waists upward. Their faces were dead white and contorted out of all recognition.

He stood transfixed with guilt as much as horror until that shrill, yipping yell he had heard earlier from a distance made itself heard in front. The Rebel infantry deployed against the brigade was charging up the slope, maybe because they couldn't see well enough to shoot.

He remembered he hadn't capped his rifle, and while he was doing that the charging Rebels began to emerge from the heavier smoke along the valley floor. They ran crouched forward in uneven, widely spaced ranks, screeching like devils behind flashing bayonets, becoming plainer as they left the denser smoke behind.

He cocked his rifle and fired at one of them. His target fell, but they were falling all along their line and the rifles around him were firing steadily.

The Rebels weren't to be stopped. They rushed on through the thinning smoke, drawing nearer by leaps and bounds, and yelling more fiercely the closer they got.

By the time he was ready to fire again, Tom knew it would be his last shot. He aimed at a looming figure behind a viciously gleaming bayonet and pulled the trigger. The man was so close that the impact of the bullet overcame his momentum and hurled him over backward.

"Charge bayonets! Charge! Charge!" stopped the shooting and sent the men rushing down the slope to meet their foes. They crashed through the flimsy rail fence separating the growth from the pasture and charged on. They were no longer in any linear formation. Some had heard the command sooner and were quicker to obey. Others were slower, but Tom was among the foremost. A great exultation seized him, like he had lived all his life for this moment.

A big man in a floppy hat rushed to meet Tom. He held his rifle low and back, ready to either thrust or parry and to use either butt or bayonet like Kemper had taught them. His enemy yelled and thrust as they closed. Tom knocked the bayonet aside with his rifle barrel and drove the butt into the side of the man's head with all his strength as he went by. He felt the skull cave in under the blow, then whipped his rifle back around and charged on.

The two lines struck with an audible impact, like a big tree falling to the ground, but the blue one had the momentum of a downhill charge and bore the other back. The Rebels fell into confusion as their ranks were driven in on one another. They gave up their charge and tried only to hold their ground.

Tom thrust with his bayonet, parried with the barrel, and occasionally used the butt as they plowed into the increasingly disorganized enemy. They were rapidly losing all organization themselves, but there was no attempt to restore any because the price would have been loss of momentum.

Once when he wasn't occupied for the moment, Tom saw Burk rushing along beside him like a locomotive gone off the track. His bayonet was missing and he swung his rifle by the muzzle as a club, knocking men down like ninepins. A Rebel officer backtracked rapidly to keep beyond reach and aimed his revolver at the giant. He was a young fellow, about Billy's age, and his slitted eyes gleamed coldly as he took careful aim.

Tom made for him, his bayonet outthrust, yelling to distract him. He paid no heed and a stab of flame leapt from his revolver muzzle; then he spun nimbly about and Tom found himself looking into the barrel backed by the hard young face. The bullet almost burned his cheek as he dodged aside, only to trip over an inert form and fall. He expected a bullet at any moment while he was scrambling to his feet, but none came, and when he could look again the young officer was nowhere to be seen. Neither was Burk.

Tom rushed toward an older man, lean and rangy, with a stubble of gray on his jaw, who had just jerked his bayonet from Jim Polson's prostrate form. The lean man stood his ground as his comrades fell back around him. He was fast and thrust with lightning speed as Tom closed with him. He could only parry and collide with the fellow, rifle on rifle with a clash of wood and iron. He exerted all his strength in a driving push that forced his enemy back and caused him to fall. He sprawled helplessly, his eyes starting and mouth gaping as the bayonet lanced down on him, and a strangled cry burst forth as the blade plunged into his chest. Tom wrenched his weapon free and rushed on.

Although he didn't know it, he soon became the apex of a lopsided wedge of blue that drove deeper and deeper into the disintegrating gray ranks. Suddenly they began to fall back to the shouts of officers and noncoms. It wasn't so much a retreat as an attempt to get room to reorganize, but it was a mistake. The pressure was too great. What order still remained was lost, and soon the Rebels were streaming back in headlong flight.

Tom and those behind him were yelling exultantly in pursuit when he heard "Halt! Halt!" above the uproar. It sounded like Rivers, so he brought up short and, once he glanced to his left, saw the reason for the command. They were on the flank of an enemy line facing east. It looked like the Rebels had only closed with the regiment on the end of the original line and those facing the rest of the brigade had held back at the last moment.

The countercharge had put the regiment in a position to enfilade the Rebels that hadn't closed. The ones who had been driven back were streaming across the creek, splashing through the shallow water, so there was no danger they could reorganize in time to return to the fray. Rivers, Owen, and a few other officers were trying to halt the men and form a line facing south, but the onrush first had to be stopped.

Tom was glad he was in front of everyone. He whirled to face the men rushing on behind him and held his rifle horizonally over his head with both hands. "Halt! Halt!" he shouted at the top of his lungs. "Halt! Stop! Hold up!"

Most of the men obeyed, but a group led by redhead Dan Howard paid no heed and charged on. Dan's face was almost the color of his hair. His greenish eyes glared fiercely, and his mouth was open in a screeching yowl. His bayonet was thrust out, and Tom had to leap aside or be impaled.

Tom slung his rifle and seized Dan's belt after he went by. "Halt! Halt! Stop!" he shouted as Dan dragged him on. He dug in his heels, and the berserker was halted. The glare went out of his eyes and was replaced by a sheepish look as Tom spun him around and shoved him back.

Those following Dan stopped, too, and as other oficers and noncoms joined those who had already gotten the idea a line facing south began to take form. Tom did his part. None of them paid any attention to platoons and companies; they just lined the men up as fast as they could, and what had been a confused, jostling mass shook itself out and took the form of a line.

The Rebels facing the rest of the brigade were quick to see their danger and were hotfooting it back toward the creek well before the line on their flank took form. By the time it did, there was little shooting because they were pretty well out of the field of fire.

The fighting in the woods had died down in the meantime, and the best Tom could tell the Rebels had pulled back there also. He was utterly astonished to realize that it was almost dark. It seemed only a few minutes ago that the sun had been well above the ridge to the west. Now it was gone and shadows had moved all the way across the valley.

The regiment reorganized rapidly, and once the platoon was back together, Tom noticed his brother for the first time since the fighting had begun. Billy was safe and sound, and Tom was deeply ashamed that he had paid absolutely no attention to him, just like the last time. "Y' all right, Billy?" he asked before he realized how foolish it would sound.

Billy nodded and sighed. "Yeah, I kinda got b'hind you fellers in front an' didn't do much."

Tom shuddered to think of what one of those murderous bayonets could have done to him and was glad. He made up his mind he wasn't going to lose sight of Billy the next time.

The platoon seemed awfully small, so Tom began counting. There were only eleven of the twenty men he had started with. Something like panic swept over him, and he was dizzy for a moment. Burk was missing. So was Jim Polson. Then there were the two Kellermans. Other names were running through his mind when the regiment faced left, went into column, and headed north across the pasture. Jake and Kemper were in their places, but the rest of the company seemed as much reduced as his platoon.

He knew Jim Polson and the two Kellermans were dead, and he didn't remember seeing Burk after that youthful Rebel officer had fired at him. "Does anyone know anything about Burk?" he asked.

"Dead, shot in th' head 'bout like Johnny wuz," replied Ab. "I seen hit happen. A Rebel officer shot him with a revolver."

Tom found it hard to believe. How could a little revolver bullet fell such a giant?

"He ain't th' only one," said Harve heavily. "They ain't much more'n haf uv us left." His normally loose-lipped mouth was tight and his protruding eyes bloodshot.

"Who's dead and who's wounded, I wonder?" asked Tom.

There was no immediate answer. "Cap'n Mertens is th' only one I know uv fer shore that wuz jist wounded," said Cole. "I guess we'll jist hafta wait an' see."

"Wal, th' cap'n ain't gonna be with us no more," interjected Zeke Kerns. "I seen whar he wuz hit, in th' knee. Even if'n he keeps his laig, he'll never march agin."

"Thar's Cal Fairbanks," added Billy. "He wuz bay'netted in th' shoulder an' looked like he wuz bleedin' purty bad."

That brought the mention of a few others, but no one was sure about them. Tom didn't expect many wounded, though. Bayonets at close quarters were generally fatal.

The column turned right and moved up toward the wrecked fence and the beginning of the growth near the top of the ridge. The move north had evidently been only to skirt the late battlefield. As the column moved up the slope, Tom saw that the whole regiment was only about half as large as it had been before the fight.

The farther up they went, the better the light was, and he could see the bodies dotting the slope where they had fought. One of them was so much larger than the others that it could only be Burk's. Tom was glad in a way that he wouldn't be able to go look at him, and he stopped looking before he could see what was left of the Kellerman boys.

Someone came running out calling for Kemper to come help with the wounded. "Go 'head," Jake told him. "Maybe you kin save some uv 'em. I ain't got 'nough men enymore t' reely need eny sargint major," he sighed.

The only signs of the Rebels in the woods where they had been so thick were lights bobbing about like fireflies in the darkness under the slope to the west. They were looking for their wounded, Tom guessed, and he was glad to see men carrying stretchers rolled up over their shoulders moving over the ridge top to the right and starting down the slope. They would be taking care of the enemy wounded, too, because the Rebels had abandoned the field on that side of the valley.

The regiment halted soon after dark and went into camp along a small stream Tom didn't remember crossing on the way up. It really wouldn't be a camp, because the men had nothing to camp with. Their packs were still back where they had first deployed off the road, so there were neither tents, blankets, nor anything to eat. Nobody said anything about being hungry, though, and the night was so warm that tents and blankets wouldn't be missed unless it rained.

Probably out of force of habit, some of the men built a small fire and what was left of the platoon huddled around it. No one seemed to feel like talking, not even Ab. It was the first time Tom had ever seen him downcast. They all acted like men under sentences of death, and it gave him a sinking feeling to realize they actually were. Over half of them were already gone, and the way the war was going, it was only a matter of time for the rest of them. They all knew this.

Tom thought of Sally, of his mother and father and his farm, all in the same vein. He would never see any of them again, and neither would Billy. Tom could see his brother's sad, boyish face in the light of the fire and hoped with all his heart that his time would come first.

A little farther along the stream the remnants of the two German platoons also huddled around a fire. Suddenly they began to sing a slow, dirgelike song, indescribably sad and melancholy.

"Ich hat' ein' Kameraden
Ein' besseres findest du nicht
Ein' Kugel kam geflogen—"

Tom understood the first three verses, but then he lost it. The words meant nothing to anyone else but Billy, but they all recognized the song as a lament for fallen comrades, sung by men who expected to follow them sooner or later.

After the last haunting notes had died away, the only surviving recruit in the platoon suddenly buried his face in his hands and burst into tears. There was a general round of coughing, throat clearing, and covert eye wiping. The recruit choked back his tears and raised his head. He was Ed Howe, an eighteen-year-old who looked sixteen, and he was deeply ashamed.

" 'S all right, Ed," said Ab huskily. "You cried fer all uv us." He bowed his head. "I'd cry, too, if'n I could."

"A-man!" exclaimed Charley Evans. "That singin' 'd make a dang rock cry!" He sniffed and wiped his eyes.

They sat silently until someone stretched out on the ground, then all began following suit. Tom lay beside Billy, who soon went to sleep, but Tom lay awake a long time. The others dropped off sooner or later, but most of them slept restlessly. They tossed about and some made convulsive movements along with strangling sounds, like they were trying to cry out.

The next morning the brigade formed a column and moved northeast across the country. There were no sounds of fighting, and the movement looked like a retreat.

Jake dropped back and fell in step beside Tom. "Hey," he said, "you heered what th' colonel said 'bout you?" he asked.

Tom was surprised. "No, what?"

"He said you oughta be 'n officer. 'Lowed you wuz th' feller that seen what t' do back thar las' ev'nin' when th' Rebels wuz flankin' our men down in them woods. He ast me first if'n I sent you back t' tell him what y' told him atter we went out 's skirmishers 'n' Cap'n Mertens got shot. When I said I didn't, he wanted t' know if'n th' cap'n had. I said I knowed he hadn't 'cause he got shot 'n' couldn't go on up t' whar we seen what wuz goin' on." Jake nodded significantly. "That's when he said that 'bout you bein' 'n officer."

Tom hadn't thought about it at all. "Well, it seemed pretty plain what we had t' do, an' we had t' do it in a hurry."

"Wal, I didn't see hit till atter you wuz gone," Jake confided, "an' I prob'ly wouldn't of seen hit then if'n you hadn't." He nodded and smiled. "I think th' colonel's right, but then I thought that frum th' beginnin'."

Something much more important was on Tom's mind. "Did he have anything to say about how we came out back there, our side, I mean?"

"Yeah, we done lost 'nother battle. All that fightin' we heered when we wuz comin' up thar yestidy wuz th' Rebels a-winnin'. They drove back th' hull army that wuz agin 'em. We jist got in on th' tail end uv hit."

"Oh, so everbody's retreatin' now?"

"I reckon," was the gloomy reply. "We done our part, though. We drove them Rebels that charged us back down that ridge an' clean crost that crick, then flanked them others an' made 'em skedaddle, too."

Tom shook his head. "We sure paid for it, though. It looks like we lost half our men."

"Yep, nigh onta fifty percent, th' colonel said, an' hit don't look like t' me that th' rest uv th' brigade lost enyone hardly. You'n Grim's th' only sargints left in th' comp'ny b'sides Kemper."

"You mean Hall and Schaeffer were killed?"

"Yeah, both uv 'em. Well, I gotta git back up thar whar I b'long. I'll see y' later." Jake broke into a trot back up the column.

The brigade soon reached a narrow rutted road running north and took it. Where it went up a long slope ahead, Tom could see it was filled with marching columns interspersed with guns and wagons, which made it seem that the division had come together again. No one was behind the brigade, though.

Soon after they took the road the men heard a faint popping fusilade far ahead that sounded like a minor cavalry engagement. The fusilade soon tapered off and after a few isolated pops stopped altogether.

They marched a few hours before leaving the rough, brushy country and entering an area made up mostly of cultivated ground or pasture. Farmsteads began to appear, but they were generally well away from the road, with long lanes leading to them. No one was ever in evidence around them.

Now that they were in more open country, the men occasionally saw parties of gray-clad horsemen paralleling the column to the west, well out of rifle range. The Rebel troopers seemed in no hurry, and no one ever saw any friendly cavalry despite the engagement they had heard earlier.

A little before noon the columns ahead left the road and moved along the eastern slope of a wide valley running north–south. The brigade followed, and when it was off the road all of them halted and faced west.

Across the valley nearly a mile away a long column of infantry with guns and wagons at regular intervals moved north along what seemed to be another road. They were Rebels, as a segment of the column had detached itself and was moving toward them. A line of horsemen occupied part of the valley floor, and farther to the west others moved between them and the column.

It looked like there was going to be an engagement until the infantry that had left the distant column halted and formed a line behind the horsemen. Then a dozen or so guns that had followed the infantry swung into line back of it but didn't go about unlimbering. All this meant the Rebels were going to leave them alone if they were left alone, and it looked like that was going to be the case. Back on the road the long column moved on, closing up to fill the gap left in it and stretching out of sight on both sides.

General Stanfield and a group of officers rode along the line from the right and stopped directly in front of Tom and his men. Colonel Rivers and General Stamford rode out to join them.

Stanfield and General Carter, who commanded the division, dismounted and turned field glasses on the Rebels to the west. Carter was a diminutive fellow who seemed almost too small for his shoulder straps and never wore a sword because it would drag the ground. A mustachioed aide took their horses and moved back out of their way.

Stanfield's bay and Carter's black were close enough to be admired, and that was what Tom was doing when the aide holding them looked at him and shouted, "Sergeant, send someone out here to hold these horses!"

Tom hadn't been around horses since he had left home, so he gave his rifle to Billy and said, "I'll just go myself. Holler if I'm needed." He began to have second thoughts when he took the reins and saw how close to Stanfield and the others he would be. It made him nervous to be around so much high rank, but none of them seemed to notice him. He moved out of sight between the horses to make sure they didn't. Just about as soon as the mustachioed aide who had conscripted Tom got rid of the horses, he was sent with a message to someone named Haynes.

The smell of the horses reminded Tom of bringing in a team from a day's work in the fields at home. He rubbed their noses and tickled their ears. They seemed to enjoy it. Both were well groomed except for some burrs in the mane of Carter's black. He started removing them but was careful to pull no hair out.

"Well," he heard Stanfield say, "I guess those people over there don't have any interest in us."

"Yes, sir," replied someone. "They're just leaving a couple of brigades and a few guns to watch us and going on north there."

"Are you thinking of attacking them, sir?" asked Carter eagerly. He had a surprisingly deep voice for such a small man.

"No, I've got strict orders to stand on the defensive. I'm about all that's between them and Washington if they move from this direction."

"Oh, they're not going to do that," said Carter. "They're headed north."

"Don't get your dander up, Carter," cautioned Stanfield. "I know it's tempting, catching them on the move like that, but I can't let you attack."

"It'd be easy meat," was the disappointed reply. "They couldn't get anything out that could stop me before I'd be on them."

"I'm surprised they aren't moving on us," interjected Rivers. "I can't see them laying themselves open like that with a corps as close as ours."

"Perhaps they know we won't move on them," said Stamford significantly. "Perhaps they're privy to our intentions."

His tone was challenging, and Carter looked at him angrily before looking expectantly at Stanfield, but the general paid no attention and the little man only shrugged his shoulders.

Tom moved to where he could see across the valley just as a party of horsemen appeared in front of the infantry deployed against them. They seemed to be using field glasses, too.

All attention shifted to the horsemen. Tom couldn't tell anything about them, but Stanfield could. "I believe that's Roger Wentworth over there," he said.

"Really!" exclaimed Carter. "How can you tell?"

"By the way he sits on his horse. I was his colonel in the Fifth Infantry during those troubles out in Kansas back five years ago." Stanfield paused briefly. "I believe the rascal's grown a beard, though," he chuckled. "Hiding his handsome face to keep the ladies off him, I guess."

Carter cackled gleefully. "Oh, he's a ladies' man all right, always was. He was a class ahead of me at the Point and used to slay the belles up along the Hudson." He cackled again. "It's him all right. I can tell now."

Stamford didn't say anything, but his disapproval was pretty obvious.

"I believe it was one of Wentworth's brigades that tried to flank Grigsby in those woods back there yesterday," said Stanfield.

"What made you think that, sir?" asked Rivers.

"By the way they attacked your brigade. That's one of his favorite tricks. He'll move up on your whole front, then attack the regiment or brigade or whatever it is on one end of your line with whatever he's got opposite it. He won't close with the rest of your line, but he'll get close enough to stop any interference. He'll drive in one end of your line, then wheel and enfilade the rest of it before you know what's going on."

"I see, sir," said Rivers thoughtfully. "There'd be no way you could maneuver to meet it because he'd be too close to the rest of your line. It wouldn't be like a regular flank attack with troops that weren't engaged."

Tom was very interested. That explained what had puzzled him about the action yesterday.

"Yes," said Stanfield emphatically. "You haven't got a chance unless whatever unit's on the end of your line holds him. If it breaks, he'll wheel and roll up the rest of it like a carpet." He looked at Stamford. "You owe a lot to Rivers' boys, General. If they hadn't held, he'd have wiped you out, then gone ahead and finished Grigsby off in those woods." He sighed. "God knows what would have happened then. With Grigsby out of the way, he might have cut that road and put half the army in the bag before it got too dark."

"And about the only half that had any fight left in it," interjected Carter. "Then the road to Washington would've been open."

Tom was astonished. The whole thing had been a great deal more important than he had ever thought.

"General Stanfield," said Rivers,"my boys didn't just hold. They charged and drove back that bunch that attacked them helter-skelter. Then I wheeled them to enfilade the rest of their line, the part that hadn't closed, but I wasn't fast enough and they got away. They had to pull back off Grigsby's flank, anyhow."

"I didn't know that!" exclaimed Stanfield. "Whose idea was it to countercharge instead of just trying to hold them?"

Rivers looked significantly at Stamford. The Yankee general took his time about replying. "It was Rivers' idea," he said with obvious reluctance.

"Well," said Rivers, "we had a downhill charge and I thought we could get up enough momentum to drive into them and make them fall back." He sighed. "My men got too disorganized, though, and I couldn't pull off that enfilade before they got back out of the way."

Stanfield nodded. "That was quick thinking. They weren't expecting anything like that and got disorganized. They tried to pull back to get themselves together again, but you were pressing them too hard and they couldn't do it. Finally, they just ran for it."

Tom marveled. It sounded like Stanfield had actually seen the action, but of course he hadn't. Tom guessed that was why he commanded a corps.

"That's exactly how it happened," Rivers replied. "I just wish—"

Stanfield interrupted, "Oh, don't feel bad about not getting that enfilade on them. If you'd kept your men in order, they couldn't have driven into them like they did. You've got to be unorthodox at times like that."

Tom's interest was intense. He was sure learning a lot.

"I guess you're right, sir," admitted Rivers. "We got into a kind of wedge shape and sliced into them like butter. One of my platoon sergeants was right at the tip. He was slaying Rebels right and left, but he caught on right away when I was trying to halt my men and managed to stop the ones up there with him. If he hadn't done that, I don't think they could have been stopped." He laughed shortly. "They had the bit in their teeth and acted like they were headed for Richmond, Virginia."

Tom pricked up his ears. Rivers was talking about him.

"That same fellow—" Rivers began, but Carter cut him off.

"Well, there they go," said the little general with his glasses to his eyes. "I guess they got their fill of us."

Tom looked to see the horsemen in front of the enemy infantry riding back toward the column, the end of which was now in sight.

"That rascally Wentworth!" chuckled Stanfield as he watched them go away through his glasses. "He didn't even wave, and I know he recognized me."

"You know, sir," said Carter reflectively, "I wish we could've gotten him to stay with us like you and Thomas did."

Stanfield brought his glasses down and sighed. "That's a terrible choice to make, your government or your people." He shook his head. "I know. I had to make it."

"Do you mean you considered resigning and going with the Rebels?" demanded Stamford sharply.

Everyone looked at him incredulously.

"You wouldn't understand anything about that, Stamford," replied Stanfield angrily. "Things were a lot simpler for you Yankees, and you're too damned narrow-minded to appreciate how they might seem to anyone else."

Stamford only put his nose in the air and didn't seem to notice the covert grins at the put-down. He was soon called aside by an officer on foot and went away with him.

"That fellow!" spat Carter. "I can't stand him! Did you catch that aspersion he made a while ago about the Rebels knowing we weren't going to move on them?"

Stanfield nodded and sighed. "As a Virginian, I'm used to that sort of thing. My head goes on the block every day, I guess, and the ax is bound to fall sometime."

There was a period of silence until Rivers spoke up. "What do you think Lee's up to now, General Stanfield?"

"He's moving his whole army northeast, with Wentworth's division bringing up the rear. I expect he'll cross the Potomac and move on Washington from the northwest. They haven't got the fortifications up that way very far along yet." He paused and looked around. "I wouldn't say it if Stamford was here, but I don't see how we can stop him. Pope's beaten. He's in no shape to stop anything, and Lee would run rings around him anyhow."

Gloom settled over the group.

"That's what comes of politicians meddling with the army," sighed Carter. "They called off McClellan's campaign down there on the peninsula by Richmond and started transferring his army up here to Pope." He spat disgustedly. "I guess they thought Lee would just sit and watch until they got it done."

"And it's all because McClellan's a Democrat and Pope's a Republican," said Rivers. "Let's hope they give the army back to McClellan now. He's the only one who can save us."

"Be careful who hears you say things like that, Rivers," warned Stanfield. "Those politicians will break you like a dry stick if you aren't careful."

"That's right," agreed Carter. "Look what they're doing to Charley Stone. It was Baker's own fault that he got trapped like he did there at Ball's Bluff and got himself killed, but they're punishing Stone for it." He snorted angrily. "Baker had no business out in the field. He was just a politician."

Tom expected Stanfield to give Carter some advice, too, but he spoke to Rivers. "Do you know why you didn't get to keep your brigade, Colonel?"

"Because Stamford wanted it and he's got powerful friends."

"That's only part of it. I did my best for you, and so did Carter." He lowered his voice. "You're politically objectionable. Morton put them on to you. That's why you're back with your regiment. They'll have their eyes on you now, and you'd better be careful or you won't even get to keep it."

"Well, I owe a lot to the noble governor of Indiana," spat Rivers. "Just because I won't change my politics, he's—"

Carter broke in on him. "Here comes Stamford!" he hissed and everybody fell silent.

Stanfield stowed his glasses and called, "Bring me my horse! I can't stand around here gabbing all day. I've got a million things to do."

Tom brought both horses over. "Here's your horse, sir, and yours, too, General Carter."

Stanfield looked at him sharply as he took the reins. "I didn't know you were around, Sergeant." The Father Christmas face was gone, and his eyes were hard. "You heard a good many things I wouldn't want passed around."

Tom noticed that Carter was eyeing him too, but he wasn't afraid. "I didn't hear a thing, sir. All that shootin' yesterday made me deaf as a post until just now."

The hard look left Stanfield's eyes, and Father Christmas returned. "I like you Indiana boys. You are from Indiana, aren't you?"

Rivers spoke up before Tom could reply. "Yes, sir, and he's the very fellow I was telling you about—"

Stanfield interrupted, "He's the one who was leading that charge yesterday and then stopped the men?" He beamed at Tom and everyone else was looking at him. He could only stand at attention and wish he were someplace else.

"Yes, sir," Rivers went on, "and that's not all—"

Stanfield interrupted again. He jabbed a finger at Tom. "What's your name, son?"

"Traylor, sir."

"I want you to apply for a commission." The white head nodded vigorously. "I'll see that you get it myself."

"Yes, sir." Tom really didn't mean it, but there was nothing else to say.

"Oh, he'll apply!" promised Rivers. "I'd already made up my mind about that." He laughed shortly. "I'll put him in the guardhouse if he doesn't."

Everybody rode away laughing and Tom was glad of the chance to hurry back to his platoon. Kemper had come back and was talking to Billy and some of the others. He had news of the wounded, and the dead, too. Cal Fairbanks had nearly bled to death before the bleeding could be stopped and was injured in the upper arm, but he ought to live anyhow. Captain Mertens's knee was smashed and he would never march again. A total of six were dead, including Burk, Jim Polson, and the two Kellermans. That left two unaccounted for, but Kemper sighed and said he had been too busy to look around very much. Anyhow, all the dead were being buried and the wounded taken to hospitals. The Rebels had been there, too, but there was a truce and they had worked together until the field was cleared.

This brought it all back to Tom, and for a moment he thought he was going to do like Ed Howe the night before. He grieved for all of them, but with the Kellerman boys it was worse than grief. He wished with all his heart he had sent them back when they joined the platoon.

By this time the Rebels were all gone but a few cavalry, and the division marched back to the road it had left to deploy. The march went north until a faint and rarely used track branched off to the east; then it turned right and took it.

The regiment brought up the rear of the brigade like some sort of an appendage, as it was scarcely half the size of the others. Rivers riding in front was so close it looked like he was only leading a battalion, half a regiment.

Burk came to Tom's mind as they marched. "Billy," he said, "you'll be writing to Gerda, won't you?"

"Ever' chance I git."

"Tell her about Burk, how he was killed and all. She can tell Katarina."

Billy shook his head and sighed. "She's gonna take hit awful hard."

Tom couldn't understand it. He and Sally had been sweethearts ever since they were little more than children. "How could they get so serious about each other so soon?"

"Hit's like I heered you tell Burk once. They's a lid fer ever' kittle, you said, an' he'd find his someday." Billy paused and bowed his head. "They both knowed she wuz his, an' that they ain't never but one."

"How about you and Gerda, Billy?"

"Hit's th' same."

"But you're both so young, and you've only been together a couple of times."

"Aw, we wrote lotsa letters b'fore that, an' then things move fast in time uv war. People grow up real fast."

The track ran into a well-traveled road that curved off to the northeast, and the column turned to take it. After a while a group of mounted officers came into view, sitting on their horses to the right of the road. General Stanfield was among them, but they evidently expected no recognition. Anyhow, they had received none so far, and the regiment was last in the line of march. Their coats were dusty, which showed they had been there quite a while, and Tom wondered if Stanfield had been waiting for the regiment.

Suddenly Rivers's voice boomed out. "Regiment, *'tenshun!*"

The men snapped erect and fell into step as company officers chanted, "One, *two;* one, *two;* one, *two!*"

"Eyes *right*!" turned all faces toward the group at the roadside as Rivers came to the salute.

General Stanfield looked surprised and the others astonished. They quickly recovered and returned the salute, which was to be expected, but he doffed his hat and bowed his head, which was not. His face between the whiteness of his hair and beard seemed to be puckered, as though he was weeping, but his eyes were averted and Tom couldn't tell for sure. Maybe that was why the general had chosen that method of returning the salute.

# 23

It began to rain soon after the column passed General Stanfield and his escort, a cold, dismal drizzle, which gradually soaked the men to the skin. As they trudged through the mud, there was some transfer of rifles from the more- to the less-wearied. Hunger was taking its toll. It had been nearly three days since the men had eaten, and they began to complain. They were headed for the packs they had left by the roadside before they had gone into battle, but that offered no relief. They all knew the cooked rations they had been carrying could not have survived three days of summer heat except for the hardtack, but hardtack was better than nothing.

They reached their packs early in the afternoon only to find them plundered. Just about everyone found his shelter half and groundsheet missing, along with anything of value that had been in his pack. Their rations were lying spoiled in the mud, but there was enough salvageable hardtack and coffee to give everyone a skimpy meal when enough dry wood was found to build a few fires. They stood in the rain munching hardtack and cursing the thieves who had robbed them.

"By golly," vowed Ab, "I got all my stuff marked, an' th' minit I sees a feller with eny uv hit, I'm gittin' hit back an' he's gittin' a beatin'!"

"Marked yore stuff, huh," replied Charley. "Well, that's jist 'cause yo're sich a thief yourself. Nobody that wuzn't 'd ever think uv enything like that."

The laughter that followed was the first there had been in a long time. It was strange that none of the packs of the other regiments had been disturbed.

The colonel was incensed and rode ahead to see about the thievery when the march was resumed. When he returned, he said there didn't seem to be any way of finding out who had plundered the packs, but that General Carter had promised that all the stolen equipment would be replaced when they reached a quartermaster depot on the line of march the next day, and that there would be a square meal for everyone, too.

The men still faced a night without shelter on the soaked ground in the rain, but they camped beside a wood and managed to find enough dry wood for fires and to keep them burning long enough to make a little coffee. Most got brush or something to sit on and slept fitfully hunkered up in the rain with water streaming down their backs under their soggy coats. Ab found a discarded horse blanket, which he put up on sticks so it would shed at least some of the water and offered to share with Tom, but he told Billy to take it and spent a miserable night leaning against a tree with his face protected by the only waterproof article he had: the bill of his cap.

When they reached the depot the next day, it was still raining, but General Carter was as good as his word. He said he would always take care of his Indiana boys and saw to it that all missing equipment was replaced. There was also an issue of rations and an empty warehouse to cook them in with scrap lumber, old boxes, and empty packing crates for fires on the dirt floor.

After it was all over, Rivers said the building was large enough for what was left of his regiment, and that the men could spend the night in it. It was too late to catch up with the rest of the brigade anyhow, and they could do it the next day by marching a little faster.

This made the men very happy, and some of them immediately stripped and began trying to dry their clothing by the fires, displaying great ingenuity in the construction of racks if they couldn't hang their clothes up on the walls or rafters. Tom didn't bother. He didn't think anyone could get his clothes dry in time to get much sleep, and with all the fires it was so warm in the warehouse that sleeping in wet clothes would be no great hardship.

A little while before dark, Jake came around to see him and led him outside under the eaves. "Well," he began, "I guess I'm gonna be comp'ny commander now."

"Yeah, an' you'll soon be a captain, too," Tom replied.

"Well, I'd ruther not git permoted if'n hit's got t' come like hit did," sighed Jake. He paused and looked out into the rain, which was coming down harder now and running off the eaves like a waterfall.

"I'm sure glad we get t' sleep in this buildin' t'night," said Tom. "Shelter tents wouldn't be much good in that."

Jake got down to business. "What I come t' see y' 'bout wuz 'plyin' fer a commission."

Tom didn't know about it. "Well, I've got my doubts—"

Jake interrupted, "Th' colonel's got his heart set on hit an' told me not t' take no fer an answer."

Tom hesitated, so Jake went on. "Well, lookit me. Ifn I kin be an officer, you shorely kin. You've got an edycation an' yo're always studyin' them military books. All I kin do is read an' write, an' I ain't too good at either one."

"Oh, I've thought about it ever since you talked me into joinin' up when I was plowin' that day, but I just don't know if I'm ready. If I'm goin' t' be an officer, I want t' be a good one." He laughed shortly. "I've seen too many that aren't."

"Aw, you ain't got nothin' t' worry 'bout. Yo're th' best sargint in th' company 'ceptin' maybe Kemper. Men jist natcherly does what you tells 'em."

"Well, I haven't got much competition now that Hall and Schaeffer are dead."

"Oh, you wuz better'n either one uv them, 'speshully Hall, pore feller."

"What about Kemper, and Grim, too? Kemper'd make twice the officer I would, and Grim was in the army in Germany, too."

"They ain't no use even tryin' fer 'em," sighed Jake. He produced some cigars wrapped in oilcloth and gave Tom one, then took one himself, and they went to the nearest fire to light up.

"What about Grim and Kemper?" asked Tom as they walked back. "Maybe Grim can't speak enough English, but Kemper can."

"Yo're right 'bout Grim. He don't know no English hardly a'tall." Jake puffed on his cigar until the coal glowed red in the gathering darkness. "Now, 'bout Kemper, hit's a long story. Y' 'member when we went back home t' recruit an' th' colonel went t' see th' gov'nor? He's got hit fixed so they won't commission enybody in th' Injianny reg'ments lessen he 'grees t' hit, ol' Morton has."

Tom puffed his cigar before replying. "Yeah, he uses commissions in th' army t' help him in politics, just like appointments to state office."

"Well, th' colonel tried awful hard fer Kemper. Told ol' Morton that ifn he ever had t' turn th' reg'ment over t' enybody else, he'd ruther hit'd be Kemper'n eny officer he had."

"You know, I don't know but what I'd say th' same thing in his place."

"Hit didn't do no good, though."

"Why? That oughta be 'nough to get a commission for anybody, even from Morton."

"Well, y' know th' colonel's had a lot uv trouble with ol' Morton 'bout officers fer our reg'ment. Ol' Morton's always tryin' t' push Republicans off on him jist 'cause they're Republicans, an' he won't let him do hit, atter them first few enyhow." Jake laughed shortly. "An' he shore didn't keep them long."

"Yeah, but there must be somethin' else with Kemper."

"Oh, ol' Morton said hit wuz on 'count uv him not knowin' English good 'nough. Claimed th' men wouldn't be able t' unnerstan' him."

"Aw, pshaw!" scoffed Tom. "He can make himself understood all right!"

"Jist 'tween th' two uv us, I b'lieve hit's 'cause Morton wuz a Know-Nothin' back when they wuz big."

"He always denies it."

"They all do now. They's too many uv them furriners, an' they got too many votes. But back in '54 'n' '5, most uv them Republicans wuz Know-Nothin's. Ask yer pappy."

"Now, those Know-Nothings were against foreigners, especially Catholics, weren't they? Always hollerin' about th' pope an' all that. I was pretty young then."

"Yeah, they tried t' build up a new party outa that atter that ol' Whig party most uv 'em b'longed to went ker-flooey, that an' temp'rance." Jake laughed scoffingly. "But none uv that worked fer 'em, an' they took up this bis'niss 'bout slav'ry an' keepin' hit outa th' terrytories."

"Well, that sure worked for 'em. They built up their party all right, but they caused secession an' started this war. They cussed an' threatened th' South so much that th' people down there left th' Union after they took over th' government. They were simply scared t' stay."

Jake sighed. "Well, that's all over an' done with, so we might 's well fergit hit. Hit ain't no use beatin' a dead horse."

"Yeah, I guess you're right," replied Tom moodily. "But talkin' about politics, d'you reckon Morton will ever let me get a commission? Pa's about th' strongest Democrat you'll find, an' I'm not far behind him, you know."

"Well, ol' Morton cain't keep track uv ever'body. They's simply too many men gittin' commissions, an' then he ain't got much choice in our comp'ny." Jake chuckled. "'Lessen he tries t' shove someone off on th' colonel agin, he's gonna hafta swaller a Dimmycrat."

"Oh, there's Harve Akers," laughed Tom.

Jake laughed, too. "Well, he turned out better'n Mark Dixon, enyhow."

Tom shook his head. "I've been thinkin' about that fellow."

"On 'count uv him foolin' 'round with Sally Napier since he's been back home?"

Tom felt like a bayonet had pierced him. "Oh, is he doin' that?"

"Didn't y' know 'bout that?" Jake sounded surprised.

"No, I sure didn't." Tom felt like the bayonet was being twisted around inside him.

Jake sighed. "I figgered yer pa had wrote y' 'bout hit, er y' knowed frum somebody else, er I wouldn't of said nothin'."

Tom steeled himself. "Tell me about it, Jake."

"I hate to, Tom. Hit'll worry ye."

"I guess that's why Pa didn't tell me, or anybody else either." He looked down at the ground as a strange roaring came into his ears. "Go ahead, Jake. I might as well know now as later. I guess you found out about it when you were back home recruitin'."

"Yeah, that's when I heered 'bout hit." Jake paused, then went on reluctantly. "Yore pa's got hisself in trouble over hit, too. I guess I might 's well tell ye 'bout that while I'm at hit."

When it rained, it poured, thought Tom as the roaring began to subside. "Pa in trouble?"

"Yeah, ol' man Dixon had 'im put under bond."

"How's that?"

"Well, yore pa found out that Mark wuz seein' Sally an' waylaid him once 'long th' road when he wuz ridin' t' see her 'n' ast him real perlite t' leave her 'lone. Didn't think hit wuz fair, you bein' 'way in th' army an' all. Well, Mark jist laughed at him, then yore pa jerked him offa his horse 'n' grabbed him 'n' shook him 'n' told him if'n he didn't leave Sally 'lone he wuz gonna beat th' daylights outa him."

"Then Mark told his pa and th' old skinflint made Pa put up a peace bond?"

"That's 'zackly what happened."

"How'd Pa get th' money?"

"Mor'gaged his farm."

Tom bowed his head. He almost felt like he was drowning. "That's a pretty pickle," he heard himself say.

Jake coughed and spit on the ground. "I'm sorry, Tom. Me an' my big mouth. I never did have no sense 'bout things like that."

"That's all right, Jake. I had t' find out sooner or later, and I'm glad you told me."

"Y' know somethin' else ol' man Dixon done?"

"What?"

"He got pore ol' Burk's farm, sev'ril months ago."

Although his feelings were already deadened, Tom was shocked. "How'd he do that?"

"B'fore Burk jined up, ol' Dixon told him he'd pay th' taxes on his farm while he wuz gone an' Burk could pay him back atter he come back frum th' war."

"Then didn't pay th' taxes. That's just like him. But how did he get title to it?"

"At a tax sale nobody knowed nothin' 'bout. Fixed hit up with th' 'sessor, I guess, an' got hit fer prac'ly nothin'."

"That old son of a bitch." It was one of the few times in Tom's life he had ever said that. "How come Burk never said anything about it?"

"You knowed Burk. He never said nothin' 'bout nothin'."

"That's about the meanest, lowest thing I ever heard of."

"Yo're right, abs'lutely right, but hit's all legal, an' they ain't nothin' nobody kin do 'bout hit."

They fell silent and stared into the dismal darkness. "Well, Tom," said Jake after a while, "all I wanted t' talk t' ye 'bout wuz 'plyin' fer a commission."

Tom didn't reply. "Well, what 'bout hit?" asked Jake.

A consuming rage was burning in Tom. "What I oughta do is go right home an' kill Mark Dixon an' his old daddy, too."

Jake was frightened. "Naw, Tom, naw! Y' dasn't do that! Ye'd hafta desert, an' then ye'd really be in a pickle, facin' murder charges b'sides that! An' hit wouldn't help nothin', nothin' a'tall!"

"I've killed better men than both the Dixons put together, ten times better." Tom stared despondently at the ground. "I expect I've killed a dozen men, fine upstandin' fellows only fightin' for what they thought was right."

"I know that," replied Jake earnestly, "an' hit's a shame, but y' cain't go bustin' loose 'n' desertin' t' go kill th' Dixons."

"Oh, I won't do nothin' like that. Don't worry. It's hard, though, awful hard."

Jake sighed. "Life is gin'rally hard, Tom, only ye've gotta be hyar in this world thirty, forty year b'fore y' really knows hit."

"I'm finding it out," responded Tom. "I just never had anything like this happen t' me before." He found it all hard to believe. It was like a bad dream, only he knew there would be no waking up from it.

"Jist don't let hit tear y' up too bad 'bout Sally, Tom," advised Jake. "Some gals is like that. I had sev'ril myself, an' then when I found th' right one, she died."

Jake had married Zelda Persons soon after he got back from Mexico, but she died giving birth in less than a year. The child had died, too, and as far as anyone knew, Jake had never looked at another woman.

Suddenly Jake's sorrow was added to his own, and Tom burst out, "Th' world's a hell of a place, you know that, Jake? God sure does a poor job of managin' it. It's almost enough t' make a man think there isn't any God."

Jake was thunderstruck. "No God! Now, Tom, don't get t' feelin' like that! Ye'll go crazy er somethin'!"

"It just looks that way sometimes. Th' wicked get rewarded and th' righteous get punished. It's supposed t' be th' other way 'round." He laughed bitterly.

Jake was still scared. "Now, Tom—"

Tom headed him off. "Oh, don't get worried, Jake. I was just mouthin'. It all hit me pretty hard, all th' men that got killed, and then this about Sally and Pa." He spat on the ground. "No, I'm not going crazy, Jake. I'm just gonna expect th' worst from now on, and then I'll never be disappointed." He laughed cynically. "Nothin' goes right anymore. This war's torn everything up, everything." He ruminated despondently, scarcely hearing what Jake had to say. Without thinking, he rubbed out his cigar and threw it away, although it wasn't half-smoked.

Jake was urging him again to apply for a commission. "Let's go do hit right now. Fred's awreddy got th' papers, frum Gin'ral Carter. He's got hisself set up in th' end of th' buildin' back thar. He's made hisself a table outa a big ol' box."

Tom got up and they went to do it. After it was done, Jake had to leave, so he got some paper from Fred and wrote his father. It had to be done quickly because there was no telling when he would get another chance to write. He told his father to leave the Dixons strictly alone, because he didn't want a woman like Sally had turned out to be. He was glad he had found out what she was really like before he married her. He really didn't feel like that, but it should keep his father out of any more trouble.

He almost forgot to say anything about the battle of two days before. He wrote that he and Billy had come through it without a scratch, although the regiment had lost heavily. That shouldn't be a cause of worry, though. The regiment had just happened to get in a bad place, which wasn't likely to happen again.

Fred said he would send the letter out with the next mail, and Tom left. He could tell that Fred was a little hurt because he didn't stay to talk a while, but he didn't feel like it. In fact, he wished he could go off into the woods and be entirely alone, for a while at least.

He hoped everybody would be asleep when he went to his blankets, especially Billy, but he wasn't. It didn't make any difference, though. Jim Polson had told him about Sally and Dixon a week ago, but only after making him promise not to tell Tom. Poor Jim was dead now and

Billy couldn't have broken a promise to a dead man, so he was glad someone else had told his brother about it, because he ought to know. He just hoped Tom wouldn't let it bother him too much.

Tom told Billy the same lie about how he felt that he had told his father, although it was an even bigger one now. Billy seemed to believe it and said he was sure glad Tom was taking it that way.

Billy soon went to sleep, but Tom could not. He couldn't put Sally out of his mind. He couldn't bear the thought of her being with the dark, aquiline Dixon, maybe sitting with him on the couch where she had sat the last time he saw her. He tossed and turned as the vision ate into his soul.

After a long time, he made sure everyone else was asleep, then went outside, under the eaves, for the rain was still pouring down. He sat on a pile of lumber and looked out into the gloom, or rather from gloom to gloom. It seemed that there was no light anywhere in the world and never would be again.

Although he got only a few hours of restless sleep, Tom didn't feel bad the next morning. Maybe it was because he was kept so busy. Jake put the dead Sergeant Hall's platoon together with his, because both were not much larger than one ought to be, and the new men occupied his time. They were like careless children. Several items of missing equipment hadn' t been replaced, probably out of fear they would have to be paid for. Also, some of their rifles were still dirty and most of them were short on ammunition. Some of the cartridges they had were coming unwrapped and the powder spilling out. With Jake's help, he got everything they needed and made them clean and grease their rifles until they shone.

He was severe with the new men and could tell they thought he was a bad exchange for the easygoing Hall. It made him realize more than ever what Kemper had meant to his old platoon, and Tom made up his mind not to rest until he had brought the new men up to its standard.

Once the march was under way and he had time to think, Tom was surprised to find his mind clear of the torture of the night before. He felt strangely cool and purposeful. Suddenly he realized that he was a different man than he had been before. He was completely a soldier now, because there was nothing else left for him. It was almost as if he had been set up newly born but fully grown in the muddy blue ranks he marched among.

# 24

The regiment marched with the brigade in a northeasterly direction for several weeks, sometimes camping for a day or two at a time. Although the marching was leisurely, the weather generally good, and rations plentiful, the men always found something to complain about and showed a bitter and cynical attitude Tom had never noticed before.

It wasn't hard to understand. The army had lost another battle, and everyone knew the Rebels were going to carry the war to the North. The men knew it wasn't their fault. They had fought hard and well, and there was no reason to think that the men of the main army that had been beaten so badly hadn't done the same. The regiment had lost nearly half its strength, and from what they heard, it had been even worse for some of those who had been in that big battle they had come up too late to take part in.

It was all for nothing, though, because of meddling politicians and the blundering generals they favored. Both came in for constant and scathing criticism, particularly the president. The men were convinced that he had taken McClellan's army away from him and given it to Pope purely because of politics, and it was Pope who had put them in the fix they were in.

One day on the march cheering and whooping began to work its way along the column. The men picked up their ears and soon learned what it was about. "McClellan's back! Pope's been kicked out, an' McClellan's commandin' agin!"

The effect was almost miraculous. Rejoicing swept the column.

"Oh, we'll whup 'em now!" exulted Billy.

"He-e-ey, you Rebels!" sang Ab. "Little Mac's back an' he's gonna use ye up! We're comin' at ye, an' ye'd better run!"

"Put yore tails 'tween yore laigs an' skedaddle!" whooped Charley.

It went on for a good while. The officers seemed to feel about the same, although they weren't so demonstrative. The celebration soon lost its exuberance, but the effects remained. There was no more of the pressimistic cynicism and endless complaining of the last few weeks. In camp that night there was much excited talk about moving to meet the Rebels, who had already crossed into Maryland and were threatening Washington. There were even predictions that McClellan would give them such a beating they might quit, and a few hopeful souls started talking about what they were going to do when they got back home. Tom wasn't one of them, and not just because he thought it was all too optimistic. There was nothing much back home for him anymore, and if it wasn't for his parents, he wouldn't care if he never got back.

The very next morning, the men were told to cook three days' rations before the march began, a pretty good sign they would soon see action. Tom's new men weren't going to bother about it. They claimed that old cooked meat wasn't fit to eat and that they could always build a little fire to cook with. He made them do it anyhow. Fires might not be allowed, and no one was going to eat his ration raw. Tom didn't bother about explanations, though. He had tried that about their water, and it hadn't done any good. They would empty their canteens the first few hours of the march despite his warnings, then want to fall out and fill them at every creek or water puddle they saw. It had taken several hot, dusty afternoons without a drop to drink to cure some of them of it. He never had such trouble with the men of his old platoon, which made him appreciate Kemper even more.

They marched all day, with only a halt at noon. During the afternoon, some of the lightly wounded who had rejoined the regiment over the past few days began to have a hard time of it. A wiry little fellow from Hall's old platoon by the name of Wells had managed to keep up so far despite a bayonet wound in the thigh that should have kept him in the hospital. His friends were carrying his rifle, his pack, and even his belt by late afternoon, and before they camped that evening they were half-carrying him. Tom overrode his protests and sent him to the surgeon. He wasn't surprised when Wells didn't come back, and learned later that there had been several such cases in the regiment.

The next morning, the regiment was roused earlier than usual and put on the march without even time for coffee. The men ate cold rations as they marched, and Tom soon learned that some of his new men had eaten so much of theirs the day before that they were finishing them up for breakfast. He bawled them out, told them that they were going to get pretty hungry before they got anything to eat, and added that he didn't want to hear any complaining.

It looked like he was going to have to watch them like children, so he moved back to the head of his old platoon so they would be in front of him and he could watch them better. He couldn't understand why they acted like there would be no tomorrow until it occurred to him that there might not be for many of them. Maybe that was why they behaved like that.

In the afternoon a long mountainous ridge running across the line of march came into view. It ran on out of sight on both sides, and as the men came closer they could hear the sounds of battle coming from it. The Rebels held all the passes over the mountain and had to be driven out before the army could go beyond, where the enemy's main force was supposed to be. The talk was that McClellan had caught Lee with his army all split up and that the Rebel general was trying to hold the passes until he could get it back together beyond the ridge near a town with the name of Sharpsburg.

As the road passed over a succession of gradual swells, Tom could see a lot more of the column. The regiment was last in the brigade, but the brigade seemed to be near the middle of the division, or maybe the whole corps. Anyhow, he thought he saw General Stanfield's white beard among some horsemen in the lead, but it was too far to be sure. There was no mistaking General Carter's diminutive figure farther back.

Once when the regiment crested a higher swell, Tom saw the entire column. It was so long it could only be the corps, and there seemed to be another one behind it. Canvas-topped wagons and batteries of artillery stood out at regular intervals. Couriers dashed back and forth, and detachments of cavalry cantered by. The troopers generally stayed off the road, perhaps to escape the vociferous taunting of the infantry, but more likely to keep out of the dust.

The sounds of battle grew louder as the march went on, and the time came when rifle fire could be heard along with the roar of artillery. Eventually the men could see the pass they were headed for, and some claimed they could tell where the line of battle was by the smoke. It wasn't long before everyone could see where it was and also tell that it wasn't moving farther up the mountain. The Rebels were holding and buying time for their army to get together.

A little while after the men were close enough to see it, a fresh brigade deployed two regiments on each side of the road and started up the mountain. A three-gun section of artillery went into battery on the road and added its fire to that of guns farther back along the side of the road. When the infantry attacked, a line of tiny dark-clad figures moved up the slope, some of them dropping to spot the open ground. The artillery blasted away, often obscuring the scene with smoke and sending heavy peals thundering down the mountainside. Everything was so far away that it looked like a battle of toy soldiers and it was hard to realize that men were fighting and dying up there.

The attack started well, as the smoke and noise moved rapidly up the slope and the artillery stopped firing because friendly troops were in the way. Well before the advance reached the top of the slope, it stalled, and almost before the observers realized it, the line started falling rapidly back. Tiny figures in lighter-colored clothing burst into view, running down the slope, and the guns opened fire again.

"Aw, Gawd!" exclaimed someone. "Th' Rebels is drivin' 'em back!" A chorus of similar expressions of disappointment went up from the marching column.

Another section of artillery squeezed itself on the road and combined its fire with that of the one already there. The guns farther back along the side of the road also opened up. The view was soon hidden by smoke, and thunder shook the heavens. When the guns slacked off and the smoke thinned enough, the men saw that the line was stabilized farther down the mountain than where it had started, and that many little gray dots spotted the open spaces along with the dark ones.

Soon afterward the column halted but stayed on the road. A clear mountain stream looped nearby and Kemper came down the column telling the platoon sergeants to let their men fall out and fill their canteens. They were hot, tired, and dusty, and all wanted to rush to the cool, splashing water at once, but Kemper would let them go only one platoon at a time and stood on the bank to see that they didn't stir up the water. Other companies went farther up the stream, where some of the men dropped on the ground and threw water on their faces. A few even jumped, laughing and splashing, into the stream.

Kemper promptly charged up the stream and routed them out in his mangled English. Men often sassed a sergeant who wasn't over them, but these fellows all obeyed meekly. Everyone in the regiment held "that Dutch sargint frum comp'ny K" in great awe because of his two expeditions against enemy artillery in the spring.

After a little while the men were told to fall out along the roadside. They stacked their rifles, took off their packs, and sat down or stretched out on the ground. A few even took off their shoes and wriggled their toes luxuriously. Some of the Germans, now all under Sergeant Grim, produced cards and started games with a great chatter. Tom's men looked at them askance. Most of them thought card playing was sinful and never played when they thought they would be in action soon, although they often played at other times. Some of them would even throw their cards away on the march to battle and then buy new decks from the sutler when it was over. At least the Germans were consistent about it.

A brigade marched up the road from the rear, the smallness of the regiments and the worn and faded uniforms showing it was a veteran unit. As it passed, a burly yellow-bearded sergeant in its ranks announced that it was being sent up to clear the pass because it was the best brigade in the whole damned army. Good-natured gibes exchanged with the men on the roadside revealed that it was a Pennsylvania brigade from the southwestern part of the state, down near the Virginia line, made up of "mountin men an' ridge runners," as one of them put it. Their brigadier general was a strange-looking fellow. He was tall and thin to the point of emaciation, and although his face looked young, his hair was as white as General Stanfield's.

The sun was well down on the horizon by the time the battle began to move up the mountain again. Presumably that Pennsylvania brigade had begun its attack. Tom watched the tiny dark-clad figures dart about and fall in the clearings as rifles rattled furiously and cannons roared.

Most of the men soon lost interest and began wanting to eat. Tom told them to go ahead, but to be sure they saved something for the next day. He took occasion to remind the ones who had nothing left why they were going hungry. They acted like children getting a scolding, but one they deserved. He wasn't very hungry and ate only a few mouthfuls himself.

Just before dark there was an outbreak of particularly heavy firing on the mountain and the fighting moved rapidly upward. It stopped just short of the crest, but the heavy firing went on. As the light dimmed, muzzle flashes winked like hundreds of fireflies and artillery discharges continually lighted up the scene with yellowish glares that revealed little but smoke. Darkness had fallen by the time the winking moved over the crest, dimly outlined against the northern sky. The artillery fell silent and after a little while no more rifle fire could be heard. The pass had been cleared and the Rebels weren't trying to hold on the other side.

Almost immediately the column formed on the road and took up the march again. While they labored up the mountain, the men knew when they came to where most of the fighting had been, although they could see nothing in the dark. The groans and cries of the wounded came from both sides of the road and got worse as the climb went on. They were particularly bad near the crest. Agonized voices cried for water and pleaded for help in tones that made Tom shudder. Someone with a deep bass voice cursed ceaselessly. He cursed God, Jeff Davis, Lincoln, and the men he could hear on the road who were leaving him to die. It sounded like the voice of the boastful yellow-bearded sergeant, but Tom couldn't be sure because he had heard it only once.

Tom was very glad when he passed over the crest and the dreadful sounds died away behind, particularly the cursing. He wondered how a man could die with curses on his lips until he realized he might do the same thing, considering the way he had been feeling ever since Jake had told him about Sally and Mark Dixon.

About halfway down the slope, a point of light appeared ahead. It turned out to be a candle someone was shielding with a coat while a man with an arm in a sling was trying to read a paper by the flickering light. A regiment-sized formation loomed in the darkness around the candle. The men stood silently, their rifles at the trail, the barrels of the nearer ones gleaming dully in the dim light. There was something about them that stifled the badinage that was usual when different units met. As he passed, Tom recognized the man reading as the Pennsylvania brigadier with the old man's hair and the young man's face. He had cleared the pass, but it looked like it had cost him half his brigade to do it.

They went into camp as soon as the ground leveled out and the next morning found themselves with the great ridge behind them. Everyone expected to take up the march again soon, but they idled by the roadside as the morning hours went by and watched other columns move past. The only thing accomplished was an issue of three days' rations and cooking them up to take along. It was nearly noon before they took up the march again.

After crossing a creek on a stone bridge just before dark, the column turned right off the road and marched parallel to the creek. It moved across a succession of fields covered with grass or wheat stubble through gaps broken in substantial wooden fences. It was well after dark before the column halted and the men were told to fall out and get some sleep. They stacked their rifles, took off their packs and belts, and spread their groundsheets on the dewy grass. No fires were permitted, so there was no coffee to go with their cold rations.

Tom and Billy covered themselves with their tent halves, because they wouldn't be wet by the dew, like blankets, then talked a little while.

"We're gonna have a big battle t'morra, Tom," said Billy.

"It sure looks like it. I guess the whole army'a comin' up."

"Yeah, y' kin even kinda hear hit."

It was true. There was little real noise, but neither was there silence. Continuous sounds of subdued movement came from everywhere, with only occasionally a distinct noise like a faint command, a rattle of equipment, or the rumble of wheels on the bridge far to the left. It was as though thousands of men were groping about in the dark, taking care not to rouse some dread sleeping monster they had to pass by.

"There's an awful lot of men out there," allowed Tom.

Billy didn't reply for a moment. "I jist wunner how many uv 'em 'll be 'live this time t'morra."

"A good many won't be," replied Tom indifferently.

There was silence for a little while.

"What're y' thinkin' 'bout, Tom?"

"Nothing. It's not good for a fellow to think at a time like this."

"I know, but I cain't help hit. I think 'bout Ma 'n' Pa, an' Gerda."

Tom couldn't hold it back. "Well, I don't have anyone like Gerda to think about anymore."

"Hit's a shame, a cryin' shame, 'bout Sally, I mean."

Tom didn't reply, so Billy went on. "Y'know, I wouldn't of knowed what y' felt like a month ago, Tom, but I do now."

"On account of Gerda?"

"Yeah." Billy sighed. "Hit's like a big empty place inside uv me that I didn't even know wuz thar has been filled up. I don't b'lieve I could stand hit if'n hit got empty agin."

"I never got to see her except on that hotel veranda when we marched past."

"She's wunnerful, Tom, jist wunnerful. I think 'bout her all th' time."

Tom looked up at the stars twinkling in the sky. He wished Billy had never seen anything of Gerda but her letters. Then it would be as easy for him as it was for his brother. He didn't want to talk anymore. "We'd better go to sleep for a while don't you think?"

Billy agreed and they fell silent, but neither went to sleep for a while.

Tom woke up just as dawn was breaking. Movement and noise to the right had broken his sleep. It wasn't subdued, like the night before, but was so far away it was muted into an unintelligible medley of sound. A party of horsemen, dim in the faint light, moved across the front in that direction at a walk. They were talking, but distance made their voices only an indistinct murmur.

As the light brightened, he saw a line of recumbent figures stretching away into the morning mist on both sides, looking just like dead men ready for burial. Two dim forms approached from the right. One of them soon stopped, but the other came on. Tom had just recognized

Kemper's burly form when an eruption of stunning thunderclaps from the right rear shattered the stillness and brought the long line of recumbent figures to their feet in instant resurrection. The men stumbled for their rifles standing in neat little tepees in front, seized them, and looked wildly about. Some started to put on their packs without blankets or groundsheets, but Kemper's bellow; "Leef de packs! Leef de packs!" stopped them.

Tom hadn't been startled and got up for his rifle only so it wouldn't be tumbled to the ground. He put on his belt, stowed his tent half and groundsheet in his pack, then saw to it that his men did the same. In the meantime, the initial thunderclaps had settled down into the steady, blasting roar of large numbers of cannon firing as rapidly as they could be worked. The mist swirled like it was stirred by giant fans and some of the men put their hands over their ears, although the guns were too far away for the noise to be that bad.

It seemed to go on for a long time, but suddenly it stopped, and the silence was almost painful. Then faint cheering by immense numbers of men came from the far right, but a rapid succession of deep, distant detonations farther to the front there soon drowned it out as enemy guns opened fire.

Someone couldn't resist coming out with the obvious. "Boy! They's shore a big 'tack goin' in over thar!"

The sun was now above the horizon and the mist was rapidly dissipating, but powder smoke replaced it so rapidly that visibility grew no better to the right where the action was.

Everyone was on his feet but Ab, who lay propped at ease on his pack.

"Git up, Ab!" called someone urgently. "Git up!"

Ab yawned. "What fer? I'm restin' while I kin." He grinned cheerfully at Tom. "That's th' right thing t' do, hain't hit, Sargint?"

Tom couldn't help laughing.

"Yo're th' laziest feller I ever seen!" accused Charley Evans. "You'd lay down an' sleep on Jedgment Day!"

"I wunner if'n Jedgment Day'll sound somethin' like this," was the casual reply. "I never heered such a racket in my life."

Ab's humor wasn't much appreciated. The men knew it *was* Judgment Day for many of them. The lanky fellow sighed and got up. "I never seen sich a sour bunch in my life. I might 's well git up an' be sour, too."

Rifle fire spattered faintly to the right, at first barely audible in the thunder of the enemy's guns. It built up quickly into a steady, rattling roar, like small instruments playing background for the larger pieces of some gigantic band.

To the front the view wasn't obscured, and Tom could see far away what looked like a field of corn fronting part of a long, low ridge that was heavily wooded toward both ends. There was movement along the ridge, but he couldn't tell what it was until the sun made a sparkling like dew on grass. Then he saw it was the glinting on the bayonets of masses of gray-clad men moving to the right, hard to make out because they blended with the background. They were reinforcing their left, which was under attack, and this would be the best time for the corps to attack. The only Rebels to the front were those moving to the right, and they would be taken in the flank unless they halted and changed front. If they did that, their left wouldn't be reinforced and maybe the attack going in over there would succeed. Tom smiled at himself. Here he was, a platoon sergeant making like a major general.

Farther back and to the left on the ridge was a small white building that looked like a church without a steeple. There was a great deal of movement along a road in front of it, but it seemed to be going in both directions and made up mostly of guns and wagons.

The sun rose higher as the battle to the right raged on. It was completely hidden by distance and smoke, but the noise told where it was. Forward movement had stopped and it seemed to be going back and forth, like the two sides were alternately attacking and then losing ground.

By now enough of the corps line was visible as it bent forward toward both ends to make it seem that the regiment was approximately in the middle of it. Movement to the right rear where the line was farther from the creek revealed what looked like a brigade of regulars deploying into a column behind it. Anyhow, they wore hats, as regulars generally did, instead of caps like volunteers.

Suddenly the guns to the right rear opened up again, which meant that the infantry had fallen back and that the attack on the enemy's left had failed. The smoke began to thin in that direction, but the distance was too great to see anything. Rebel guns were undoubtedly firing, too, but they couldn't be heard because of the friendly ones closer at hand.

Tom was still peering to the right in an attempt to make things out when guns directly to the rear that hadn't fired before opened up. They were firing to the right front, but it was overhead for the regiment and the sound was so tremendous that the hearing was overcome and perceived nothing. It was almost like silence except for the awful concussions that beat on the men like clubs.

Officers went out in front of the line, Jake in front of his company. His mouth opened in shouts, but the men couldn't hear him. He gestured violently and shouted more, but no one could tell what he wanted. Kemper ran out and held up his rifle, then pulled out his ramrod and started loading.

The men understood and began charging their rifles, then fixed their bayonets when Kemper did. For the life of him, Tom couldn't understand why they needed such a demonstration. Everyone should have known that you don't go into battle with empty rifles.

When Kemper started back to the ranks, Jake motioned him to stay and they spaced themselves in front of the company.

All at once the guns behind them stopped firing. There was no firing from the Rebel guns to the right front either, and the men awaited the order to advance amid a strange silence.

Toy riders on toy horses pulling toy guns left the road in front of the little white church and headed directly toward the brigade. Soon the men were watching a six-gun battery of artillery take up firing position along the ridge in front. The horses were taken back while the gunners loaded their pieces. It was hard to realize that such tiny objects worked by those pygmy figures were capable of wreaking slaughter at a great distance, and Tom wondered why the guns behind them didn't go into action.

The men watched with horrified fascination as the enemy gunners laid their pieces and the tiny barrels lined up on them. When they flashed together and disappeared in bursts of smoke, some of the men jumped in fright and a few cried out, but the dread missiles shrieked overhead toward the guns behind them. The lack of following explosions showed that solid shot was being used.

The guns in the rear belatedly took up the challenge, and the enemy battery came under heavy fire. The men cowered under the blasts, which seemed almost enough to sweep them off their feet. Some even slung their rifles and clapped their hands over their ears with grimaces of pain.

The friendly guns were much heavier, to judge by their shell bursts, which were the largest Tom had ever seen. They were also rapidly served and accurately laid. A limber chest exploded among the enemy guns with a flash and roar heard even above the din. The Rebel gunners stood to their pieces, but the contest was unequal and in a little while the horses were brought back to take them away. Men and horses kept going down among the shell bursts, but the Rebels somehow managed it and got all their guns away, leaving only dead men and animals behind. Distance and smoke made it impossible to tell how far they went.

The guns in the rear stopped firing only briefly. When they opened up again, Tom saw they had a new target. Masses of men in earth-colored clothing were flowing down the side of the ridge in front, along its entire length, the best he could tell. The guns didn't have time to punish them long. When they reached the foot of the ridge, they could no longer be fired at because of the infantry in front.

Another hush descended on the field. General Stanfield rode alone from the left and reined up directly in front of the regiment, his eyes on the enemy.

The men looked at one another in surprise.

"He'd better git t' th' rear!" called someone. "We're gonna charge any minit!"

"I'll bet he's gonna lead hit!" shouted Billy.

"Shorely not!" came a reply, but it looked like Billy was right. The general sat on his big bay facing the enemy, like he was waiting for the final order, and he was alone.

Colonel Rivers and several other officers went out to the general. They seemed to remonstrate with him. One of them seized his horse's bridle and tried to turn the animal around, but Stanfield reined his steed back on its hindquarters and they jumped aside to escape its flailing forefeet. Stanfield drew his sword and waved them back, his beard showing whitely against his coat as he shouted at them. They gave up and came back, all but Rivers. He stopped halfway, looking indecisively back and forth between his men and the general.

Tom was sure Rivers was thinking about calling on his men to restrain Stanfield, so he ran forward calling, "Come on! Come on! We can't let him do it!"

Billy followed, together with Ab, Cole, and Charley. They passed Jake and Kemper, who looked at them in astonishment but said nothing.

Tom ran up to Rivers. "Do you want us t' try t' bring him back, sir?"

Rivers looked relieved. "Yes, Sergeant, by all means. Maybe he'll listen to you men."

The general's eyes were on the enemy, and he didn't see the five men until his horse tried to shy away when Tom grabbed the bridle. The Father Christmas face stared down at him in surprise. "We're not gonna let you get killed, General!" he shouted. "We're gonna take you back!"

The Father Christmas face disappeared. Stanfield's mouth tightened and he tried to rear his horse, but Billy seized the bridle on the other side and together with Tom prevented the animal from rising. "Come t' th' rear! Please, sir, go back! We're your Indiana boys! Remember me? I held your horse!"

Stanfield's anger disappeared. He smiled sadly and his eyes grew misty. "Yes, son, I remember you. Your name is Traylor. I know because I just approved your commission. You'll get it pretty soon now."

"Please, Gin'ral, come back!" pleaded Ab. "We don't want y' t' git kilt! That's jist fer us common sol'jers!"

The others chorused agreement as Tom and Billy pulled on the bridle to wheel the horse around. Stanfield turned his eyes on the brothers. "Let the horse go, my boys," he said so compellingly that they obeyed.

Tom started to protest, but the general headed him off. "I call you my boys because you're all I have. I have no sons, and I'm thankful for it, because if I did, they'd be over there." He pointed toward the enemy. "The way it is, it's too much to bear. The husband of one of my daughters commands a brigade over there, and another a regiment. My grandsons are in the ranks, and two of them are dead." He choked and looked down, then went on. "Maybe my own men killed them at my orders." His body shook and he had to stop.

"Yes, sir," was all Tom could say. The others stood spellbound.

Stanfield looked up and Tom could see tears in his eyes. "Last week my wife passed away. She had been dying a little each day of this horrible war the politicians brought on us. We had been married nearly fifty years." He had to stop and bow his head again. "I can't bear to be without her, and I can't endure this torture any longer."

Stanfield recovered and looked at them earnestly. "This is my chance to die honorably in battle rather than by my own hand." He studied their faces. "Now do you understand?"

"Yes, sir." Again only Tom spoke.

Stanfield raised his hands over them. "Now go," he said, "and may God protect you, and see you safely back to your homes in Indiana." It was like a benediction, and one from God Himself.

They turned back silent and subdued. "Hit's awful, this war," sighed Cole after a few steps. Nothing could have expressed Tom's feeling better.

When they reached Rivers, Tom said, "There's no stopping him, sir, and I can't say that I blame him."

Rivers shook his head sadly. "We did all we could, and I thank you men for what you did."

"Yes, sir."

They were scarcely back in their place when a courier dashed up to Stanfield and was almost immediately waved away, although he seemed hesitant about leaving.

Stanfield wheeled his horse to face his men. He drew his sword, flourished it over his head, and shouted, "For'ard, *march*!"

The line began to move after the white-haired horseman as the command was taken up and passed along. In a little while Tom could make out the enemy waiting in dense ranks all along the foot of the ridge ahead. The gleam of arms in the cornfield to the left showed he was there, too.

Another battery of artillery drew up on the ridge directly ahead and rapidly went into firing position. Tom expected a massacre with grape and canister, because the line was too far forward to permit counter battery fire from the guns in the rear.

He was wrong. Whoever commanded those guns back there was willing to take chances and they opened fire, but it was a near thing. The shells passed so close overhead that the men ducked and went on stooped like ancient graybeards. Tom could feel the hot breath of the missiles' passage and hoped none of the gunners got off their aim.

The first salvo was high, but the next one was dead on target and caught the Rebels before they could get off a shot. Tom expected they would all be put out of action, but when the smoke of the bursts lifted he saw most of them were still loading. Only two of their guns fired at first, but they were well aimed and blasted the line on both sides. A gun bearing directly on the company fired next, but it was aimed too low and the men were only showered with dirt as ricochets howled overhead. Tom blinked and ducked automatically and, when he looked up, saw that General Stanfield had gotten his wish. Both he and his horse were down, evidently caught in the center of the blast. The horse's body moved convulsively and its legs jerked, but the general lay still, his hat off and his white hair showing plainly against the ground.

The enemy guns were taking a beating from heavier metal but managed to get off a few rounds. One of them tore a hole in the regiment to the left, and another blasted the Martin County company just to the right. The survivors reeled about like they had been almost blown off their feet, but the "Close up! Close up!" of their captain put them back in order and took them on.

Suddenly the enemy gunners still on their feet began to limber up and withdraw. Enough men and horses survived to get four of the six guns away, but several of the horses were wounded and hard to manage. One of the guns left behind leaned drunkenly on a smashed carriage, but the other seemed undamaged.

The last shells of the guns in the rear passed so close overhead that Tom felt his cap lift. The men were going along with their heads drawn in like turtles, and some of them went on that way for a while after the shells stopped shrieking overhead.

The enemy's line of battle, already dim in the dust and smoke, suddenly stirred. "Halt!" brought the advance to a stop.

"Ready! Aim! Fire!" came in such quick succession that the volley was ragged, but it caught the Rebels before they could fire and thinned their ranks perceptibly. Then they steadied and fired in their turn. Their front broke out in innumerable pinpoints of flame followed immediately by a veritable sheet of smoke that almost instantly transformed itself into a cloud. It joined the one rolling toward it and obscured the ranks of the enemy. A storm of bullets lashed the blue line, bowling men over by the score. Some managed to keep their feet briefly only to collapse after reeling and stumbling about. Miraculously, not a man in the platoon was hit.

The two lines stood face to face and shot it out. The smoke was so bad almost from the beginning that the men could only aim at the muzzle flashes winking at them through the swirling gray curtain. While he worked his rifle, Tom kept an eye on his men. A fellow named Springer from Hall's old platoon tried to fire without capping his rifle, then started to put in another cartridge.

Tom had his ramrod out and reached to strike him with it. "Cap your rifle! It's already loaded!" he shouted at the top of his lungs.

Springer looked at him in surprise, holding a cartridge with the end clenched in his teeth. Just as the light of comprehension dawned in his eyes, a bullet struck him squarely in the chest with an explosive thump and knocked him into the rank behind. The cartridge end tore off as he flung his arms out, and a black stream of powder marked his fall.

"Get him outa th' way!" Tom shouted at the men behind him. Two of them slung their rifles and dragged the dying man aside like a sack of grain.

Tom's platoon wasn't being shot up as badly as the others, though. The Rebels in front of it tended to fire too high, and most of their bullets hissed overhead. He thought it was just poor shooting until a swirl in the smoke showed that General Stanfield and his horse lay almost straight ahead of him. The bay was a very large animal and looming before the Rebels in the smoke might look like an elevation or a barrier of some sort. Maybe the dead general was protecting his Indiana boys even in death.

Kemper had joined the German platoon on the left and was plying his ramrod at a terrific rate. Jake was nowhere to be seen until a puff of wind billowed the smoke upward from where it was thickest close to the ground. A dumpy figure in an officer's uniform was briefly revealed, lying motionless near Stanfield's body. It was Jake.

Another man in the platoon was hit, this time in the arm. He was a thin, sallow fellow named Harris, who had dropped his rifle and stood holding his arm, white with shock. It looked like his forearm was broken near the elbow because it went out at an odd angle there, but it was hard to tell because of the torn and bloody coat sleeve. "Go back!" Tom shouted at him. "Fall out and go back!"

Harris just stood there, holding his shattered arm and swaying unsteadily on his feet, so Tom shouted again.

This time Harris nodded dumbly and stooped to pick up his rifle but nearly toppled and fell.

"Leave it!" Tom shouted. "Leave it! Go ahead!"

Harris recovered his balance, nodded, and started back, cradling his wounded arm in his good one.

Harris was scarcely out of the way when another man fell and lay clutching his thigh where pinkish bone showed through torn cloth and mangled flesh. He was Jack Anderson, from Knoxville, near home. Tom slung his rifle and seized him under the arms. Jack looked at him reproachfully, like he was the cause of his injury.

"I can't help you, Jack," Tom gasped, "but I'll put you someplace safe." He dragged him to shelter behind Stanfield's horse.

"Tom, Sargint, don't leave me!" pleaded Jack. "I'm hurt awful bad—"

"I've got to, Jack, but we'll be back t' see 'bout you!" He only hoped they could.

He tore loose from Jack's grasp and ran back, unslinging his rifle as he did so. Something caused him to look up, and he saw a blackened rifle muzzle staring him in the face. He ducked just before the discharge blasted his ears and tore at his cap. The bill of his cap was all that saved him from being blinded by the powder particles that burned his lower face and neck. Charley Evans's grimy face gaped at him in horror as the rifle came down.

"Watch out where you're shootin'!" Tom shouted at him as he took his place in the ranks. Charley grimaced apologetically and reached for another cartridge.

While he loaded, Tom ran his eyes over his men. With their blackened faces, disordered clothing, and air of frantic haste, they looked like fiends doing the devil's work amid the fires and fumes of Hell.

Suddenly a cluster of flashes winked much closer to the left and a dense Rebel column plunged forward out of the smoke. The enemy was converting his line into a column and charging to try to break the blue line, rush through, and take it in enfilade. If he did, the battle on this part of the field was his.

The men had barely shifted their fire to the column when Colonel Rivers appeared in front, sword in one hand and revolver in the other. His hat was gone, his coat torn open at the collar, and he was as grimy as his men. "File left! File left!" he shouted. There must be a gap in the line there that the Rebels had spotted, and Rivers was trying to fill it before they struck.

The men turned left in jerky, uncoordinated fashion and began to run, but the move was too late and ahead of them the gray column struck the line with a burst of wild yelling and a flash of bayonets. The line recoiled rapidly at the point of impact, too rapidly for the rest of it, which began to look like a huge bow, although the regiments on each side had faced about and were racing back madly to escape the enfilade.

Then the Rebel commander made a mistake that saved his enemies. He halted his column and began converting it into a line again, probably because the speed and order of the withdrawal made him afraid that he would get enfiladed himself. The result was that the two lines soon found themselves facing one another just as before, only much farther back from the ridge and also farther apart.

Before they could begin firing in earnest again, an uproar of firing and yelling broke out on the far right and the Rebels began a precipitate retreat that carried them all the way back to the foot of the ridge. It looked like an attack had been made on their left flank that threatened to roll up their line, probably by those regulars who had deployed behind the line before the advance had begun.

There was no order to advance, and the men stood wondering why. "Let's go! Let's go atter 'em!" yelled Dan Howard. His greenish eyes had that glare again.

"You jist go 'head if'n y' wants to, Dan," said Ab. "I've had 'nough uv hit myself."

Several others voiced agreement, and it began to look like they would get their way. The noise of the fighting to the right had died away and there was only sporadic shooting from in front, because the range was too long for aimed fire.

Owen appeared in front and began walking back and forth, occasionally looking at the Rebels. He still had his hat and his coat was buttoned, but he didn't look nearly as neat and self-possessed as he usually did. He paid no attention to the occasional bullets that came his way as individual Rebels tried their hand at indirect fire. Suddenly one bullet tore through the platoon head-high and smacked into the ground behind.

Charley Evans dropped his rifle and clapped his hands to his face. "Oh, Lordy!" he quavered. "That wuz close!"

Tom ran over. "Are you hit?"

Charley emerged white and shaking from behind his hands. An ugly bluish-red streak showed high on his smudgy cheek. He tried to reply but couldn't. His Adam's apple just worked soundlessly in his skinny neck.

Tom looked at the bullet burn. "You're lucky, Charley, real lucky. A bullet couldn't come any closer without hittin' a man. You know that?"

Charley got his voice back. "Whew! I come in a whisker uv gittin' my head blowed off!" His voice still quavered and Tom had never seen eyes wider than his.

Ab picked up Charley's rifle and handed it back. "Aw, don't be skeered, Charley! No bullet's ever gonna kill you! You wuz born t' be hung. Ain't I always told ye that?"

Everybody laughed but Charley, who only fingered his cheek and shook his head. The laughter sounded strained, though, like the men were trying too hard.

A thunderous cannonade suddenly broke out far to the left, and soon afterward the Rebels along the foot of the ridge faced about and started up the slope, leaving a skirmish line at the top. How far back they went couldn't be made out. Some said they halted back of their skirmishers, but there was still too much smoke to tell for sure.

The thunder of the guns on the left abruptly fell off, and the drumming of massed rifle fire could be heard. That meant that another attack was being made down there, probably by another corps. You could tell that the Rebels weren't attacking because their artillery was still firing.

Tom couldn't understand it. Why were they making these isolated attacks that the Rebels could concentrate against? Why didn't the corps move up, at least to find out if there was anything behind that skirmish line in front and, if there wasn't, wheel to take those Rebels being attacked in the flank? He shook his head. Here he was, playing major general again. There might be good reasons why the corps wasn't moving up. General Stanfield was dead and maybe whoever had taken his place hadn't gotten hold of the reins yet. Maybe the generals thought the corps was too used up and disorganized to be battle worthy any more. Considering all the frantic maneuvering and the narrow escape from being enfiladed, that might actually be the case, and then losses had been pretty heavy.

"Y' reckon we're gonna go at 'em agin, Sargint?" Dan Howard asked eagerly, his greenish eyes gleaming from his smudgy face.

"I doubt it," replied Tom with a shake of his head. "We'd have gone in before now if we were. Maybe they think we got cut up too bad."

"Well, we wuzn't drove back er enything," maintained Dan. "Hit wuz th' Rebels that give hit up an' pulled back." He nodded so vigorously that the cap perched on his mop of red hair nearly fell off, and Tom wondered how he had kept it on all the while.

"Hit wuz close, though," allowed Cole. "I thought we wuz goners when that column come at us."

"Yeah, me, too," averred Zeke Kerns. "I shore wuz glad when hit stopped an' went back inta line agin."

Tom's forecast that they wouldn't go in again was eventually borne out. They stayed where they were until it began to sound like the attack on the left had failed, then formed a column and marched east. They went well back of where the fighting had been, and Tom was glad of it. That was where the wounded were. Of course, the dead lay there, too, but they made no noise.

The regiment was also west of where it had been at first, for it was some time before Tom saw General Stanfield's dead horse off to the left. The general's body was gone, though, and so was Jake's. Jack Anderson was no longer there either. Tom guessed the Rebels had gathered them up while they held that part of the field, probably because they knew who Stanfield was and had just picked the others up along with him. They could be counted on to bury Jake and send Stanfield's body back through the lines. He just hoped they would take care of Jack. Poor Jack. If he ever got back to Dubois County, it would be on only one leg.

After a while the column turned south and marched until it reached the creek, then paralleled it until the men came to the packs they had left behind. Tom noticed that Colonel Rivers was leading the brigade, which explained why Owen had suddenly taken over the regiment. Something must have happened to General Stamford. If it had, he wouldn't be missed much.

Before very long, it began to seem that the day's fighting was over. There had been only a little skirmish firing and occasional artillery duels for a good while, and it would soon be dark. No one knew but that the fighting would resume the next morning, but nobody seemed to think it would, and after they fell out some of the men began to speculate about what the battle they had fought would be called. Most thought it would be named after the nearby town of Sharpsburg, but some disagreed. They pointed out that the one they had fought the last of August was being called the Second Battle of Bull Run. Like the first one, it was named after a creek, and there was this creek that wound around the battlefield they were on. No one knew what it was called, but they found out later that it was known as Antietam Creek.

# 25

The morning after the battle Tom found out that his platoon had been lucky compared to the others in the company, and in the regiment, too, the best he could tell. Only Lloyd Springer of Hall's old platoon had been killed. Of course there was Jack Anderson, who would lose a leg at the least, but the Rebels had him. He hoped they would take care of him. They generally did the best they could with wounded prisoners, but that best wasn't very good. Beyond that only Paul Harris had been wounded. He was in a hospital someplace and would presumably be heard from, but probably only after his arm had been taken off. When the surgeons had a lot of wounded to deal with, amputation of a shattered arm like Harris had was only to be expected.

None of the packs had been pillaged this time, and everybody had cold rations for breakfast with hot coffee to wash them down. After he had eaten, Tom noticed Kemper and Captain Owen talking out in front of the company and went to ask Owen how the regiment had made out.

When he asked, Owen said, "We lost nearly a hundred men, ninety-seven to be exact, with thirty-three dead."

"Not so bad as the last time, then," replied Tom. "But bad enough, I guess."

Owen sighed and looked off into the distance.

"Do you think this battle's over, sir?" Tom asked.

"It must be. I haven't heard any artillery so far, and only a little rifle fire off there once." He pointed to their left.

"I tink he vas de *Kavallerie,*" interjected Kemper.

"It doesn't look like anybody won, then," said Tom.

Kemper and Owen nodded agreement.

"A standoff, I guess," allowed Owen. "We weren't beaten, anyhow."

"Captain, are you commanding the regiment now?"

"Yes, now that Colonel Rivers has taken over the brigade again."

"What happened to General Stamford?"

"Oh, he's all right. He isn't wounded or anything."

"How come he's not commanding the brigade then?"

Owen shuffled his feet and looked at the ground. He was so slow to answer that Tom wished he hadn't asked. "Well," Owen finally said, "there was a lot of confusion in our brigade yesterday, and General Carter blamed him for it."

"Yes, sir?"

Owen took his time about going on. "General Stamford's old regiment got confused, and he felt he had to take direct command of it."

"Then what?" Tom's curiosity was aroused and he wasn't going to be put off by Owen's reticence.

The captain sighed and looked off into the distance. "Well, General Stamford felt that he had to take his old regiment out of the line to get it back in order."

Tom had the bit in his teeth and went on. "Did it have anything to do with that Rebel column attacking?" He couldn't understand Owen's reluctance. Everybody would know all about it before the day was over, but the captain was a standoffish fellow.

"General Carter said that it did. He accused General Stamford of nearly getting the corps defeated and destroyed." Owen was being very careful to keep his own opinion to himself, and Kemper was keeping his mouth shut, but then he always did when officers were concerned.

Tom didn't let himself be held back. "Yes, sir, I can see how. The Rebels saw that gap in the line when Stamford took his regiment out and threw that column at it." He shook his head. "If they'd just kept coming, they'd have broken our line and cut us to pieces, it seems to me."

Owen was noncommittal. "Anyhow, General Carter put Stamford under arrest and is going to court-martial him." Owen sighed and looked away. "That's why Colonel Rivers is commanding the brigade." He had finally come out with it all.

Tom almost broke out about the politicians who had given the brigade to Stamford instead of letting Rivers keep it, but he swallowed his indignation and kept his mouth shut.

Owen changed the subject. "Say, you ought to know what Sergeant Kemper and I were just talking about. He's going to leave you and become regimental sergeant major. Sergeant Wilkinson was killed back there several weeks ago, you know."

Tom knew, but he suspected it wasn't just to replace Sergeant Wilkinson. Owen was going to need somebody to lean on, and Kemper was obviously the best prop he could find. "We'll sure miss you in the company," he said to Kemper.

Kemper grinned and slapped him on the back. *"Ja, du bist Kommandeur der Kompagnie!"*

Tom had forgotten all about what General Stanfield had said the day before. "Yes, I guess I will be."

*"Ja.* Grim iss nodt so goot *mit* de Eengleesh efen as me, und iss no serjents more."

Tom suddenly felt humble. "I just hope I can do it."

Owen smiled. "Well, if I can command a regiment, you can command a company, don't you think?"

Tom was astonished by the sudden familiarity. "Yes, sir, I suppose so."

"Your commission as first lieutenant is on its way."

That explained the familiarity. "First lieutenant? I wasn't expecting that. I thought a fellow started out as just lieutenant."

"Well, Lieutenant Jacobs was going to be promoted to captain, and you would have been the only other officer in the company. Then Colonel Rivers recommended it, and I guess General Carter did, too."

"Yes, sir." Tom shook his head sadly. "Poor Jake, he never lived to get it."

Kemper gave him another whack on the back. *"Jawohl! Herr Oberleutnant! Bald Herr Hauptmann!"*

Tom scoffed. "Oh it'll take a long time for me to make captain!"

"Oh, maybe not," said Owen. "If you do well, you'll soon be promoted. Companies are supposed to be commanded by captains, you know."

"Well, what about you, Captain? Regiments are supposed to be commanded by colonels."

"Oh, that would be too big of a jump," laughed Owen, "but my commission as major is coming along with yours. That's why I know so much about it."

Tom shook his head and looked at the ground. "I just hope I can be a good officer."

"You will be," Owen assured him. "You got excellent recommendations, even from General Stanfield, I understand."

Tom started to say something about the general getting killed, but Kemper preempted him. "Kemper tall you dat you be goot *Offizier, nicht wahr?*"

"Well, Sergeant, I'd rather have your good opinion than anyone else's I know of. You made me whatever I am, in the army anyhow."

Kemper nodded and looked serious. *"Es ist leicht, einen guter Soldat aus ein guter Mann zu machen."*

Owen broke in, "I don't understand German, Sergeant."

"Oh, he's just joshing, Captain. He says it's easy to make a good soldier out of a good man."

Kemper wasn't joshing, but he only grinned.

Owen laughed. "I agree. You know, I've never understood why you weren't commissioned to begin with. You've got a few years on most of the men, and then you're well educated."

"I didn't want to be. I was a total ignoramus on anything military. I was afraid I'd get my men killed out of ignorance."

Owen snorted. "Well, that sure didn't stop most of our officers, including myself."

"Oh, I thought the captain was in the state guard for a good while."

Owen laughed. "Just playing soldier! We generally just had picnics or something on muster day after a little drilling, and then marched in parades once in a while." He shook his head. "What drill we learned helped some, but not much."

"Well, I had nothing, absolutely nothing."

Owen looked at him quizzically. "And I understand you're quite a scholar. The men say you've studied every military book you could get your hands on."

Tom laughed deprecatingly. "Oh, it's just that I like to read, I guess. There've been a few military books around, and there's nothing else to do a lot of the time."

Someone cut it all off by calling for Owen, and he had to go.

Tom and Kemper started back to the company. Kemper had to get his equipment and move again, this time from the company to the regiment. When the men found it out, they clustered around and exchanged boisterous farewells, but Tom could tell that underneath they hated to see him go, particularly the Germans. It made him realize he had some big shoes to fill.

# 26

The brigade marched south along the east bank of the Potomac the day after the battle, forded the river the second day, and then went on southwest at such a rapid rate that some of the men thought they might be trying to cut off the Rebel retreat down in Virginia. Tom didn't think so. The brigade was all alone and certainly wasn't going to try anything like that by itself. In fact, they saw no other troops, hostile or friendly, either during the march or after it was over, and Tom never found out what kept them going from dawn until dark with halts only at noon. They evidently outran everything and everybody, because it was several days after the march ended before they got any news of what had happened since the battle.

The last part of the march was almost due west and ended near a sizable town in the Shenandoah Valley where there was an important road junction. The Massachusetts regiment left the column about a mile and a half from town and the Indiana men about a mile closer. The other two regiments went on to go through the town and camp south of it.

It was a long, hard march, but the men were in good spirits. Maybe they hadn't beaten the Rebels and driven them from the field, but they had stopped them and made them go back to Virginia. That was almost a miracle, considering the way things had looked a week or so before when the Rebels had started north. Then there hadn't been anything between them and Washington but a beaten army that was threatening to come apart under a general nobody had any faith in. McClellan had been put back in command just before the battle, and the men believed he had saved the capital and probably the whole country. Some of them had so much confidence in "Little Mac" that they were talking about beating the Rebels before winter set in and being home in time for spring planting.

The regiment had a good campsite. It was along a side road made by timber cutters maybe a year ago, which crossed a creek and ran up a gradual slope into a large woods after a few hundred yards. At the top of the slope, the road turned sharply to the left and went down the other side parallel to the main road. It was supposed to go on through the woods to where the New Englanders were camped half a mile away.

The loggers had left tops and limbs for plenty of seasoned firewood, and there was the creek for water. The camp was strung out from where Tom's company was at the foot of the slope near the creek to the top, where the headquarters tent and the officers' mess and sleeping tents were. All the companies pitched their two-man shelter tents along paths cleared out to the right of the road, because the growth was too heavy on the other side. There was enough clear space next to the road to give each company a place to assemble.

The camp was barely established and the wagons unloaded when they came down the road from the headquarters tent to pick up all the rifle ammunition. The story was that what the men had was too old and that a new issue would be made in a few days. Tom got no boxes to put his in like the other companies did and, when he went to see about it, was told that Owen wanted one company ready in case Rebel cavalry came around. After the wagons left, Tom wondered why the whole regiment couldn't have waited for the new issue like his company was.

Ab and some of the others took all this as indicating they could count on staying where they were for a good while and went about building a stone fireplace for cooking and coffee making sheltered by extra tent halves put up on poles like they had once before. Except for the Germans, who always kept to themselves, the company was again ready to spend its spare time around the fireplace talking, drinking coffee, and smoking.

Early the second day in camp, official mail caught up and Tom got his commission. He was called to the headquarters tent along with several other sergeants who were also to get commissions and expected Owen to make a big thing of it, but he didn't. All he did was give them their commissions and a perfunctory handshake. He looked worried and preoccupied, but Tom thought nothing of it at the time. After all, commanding a regiment was a big job, and Owen was new at it. He even forgot to give them the oath they were supposed to take.

Tom never felt that the commission was what really made him an officer. He always believed that Karl Hauser had much more to do with it. It began soon after some of the Germans came to join the celebration around the fireplace when the news spread to them. The rest of the men acted much like they had before toward him, but the Germans showed a marked change of attitude. When he spoke to one of them, the fellow would snap to attention, assume a blankly alert expression, and address him as *Herr Leutnant*. Both their sergeants,

Grim and the dead Schaeffer, had seen military service in the old country.

One of the Germans called Billy aside and engaged him in earnest conversation. He was Mertens's ex-orderly, who had cooked at the fish fry with the North Carolina men. He was well into middle age and undoubtedly the oldest man in the company.

After a while they approached Tom.

"This is Karl Hauser," Billy began. "He usta be Cap'n Mertens' orderly an' says th' cap'n left a uniform with him that he didn't want no more. He says he kin fix hit up fer you."

Hauser came ponderously to attention and smiled ingratiatingly. He was a big, fleshy man with reddish hair and a very fair complexion.

"Oh, it'll be too big!" Tom replied. "Captain Mertens was a big man, a lot bigger'n me."

Billy talked with Hauser, then turned back to Tom. "He says hit wuz 'way too little fer th' cap'n. That's why he left hit. He ordered hit ready-made an' they wouldn't take hit back when hit turned out t' be too little. Karl's shore hit won't be much too big fer you. He kin fix hit easy. He usta be a tailor an' has th' stuff t' do hit with. He wants y' t' come 'long so he kin git started with hit. He b'lieves he kin have hit done by mornin' when y' go t' officers' call if'n he kin git started with hit right 'way."

Tom had gotten the drift of it before Billy's translation, but still he hesitated. It would be nice to be in proper uniform when he went to officers' call the first time, but Hauser might want too much money for it, and it would be a hand-me-down tailored in a hurry. He might look better in his own coat after he took the stripes off and sewed on some shoulder straps he could get at the quartermaster's. "Well, I don't know—" he began.

Billy wouldn't let him finish. "Aw, c'mon—Lootenant, sir!" He itched to see his brother in an officer's uniform.

Tom gave in. "Oh, all right. We'll take a look at it anyhow."

Hauser had a coat, two pairs of trousers, and a hat with a flattened crown. Nothing looked like it had ever been worn, even the hat, and all were made of excellent material. The hat was only a little too large, but the coat was a good deal more. So were the trousers when he went into the bushes to try them on.

Hauser wasn't bothered. A strip of cloth inside the sweatband was all the hat needed, and it would be easy to restore the crown to perfect shape. As for the coat and trousers, Tom found himself being used as a clotheshorse. There was much careful measuring, marking, and pinning with the contents of a compact tailoring kit. Hauser would have a uniform ready by morning. He would sit up all night and work by a fire if he had to. The *Herr Leutnant* could depend on it absolutely.

Before Tom could mention cost, a fine pair of boots and an officer's belt complete with sword and scabbard were produced. They hadn't been Mertens' because the boots fit perfectly and the belt buckled in a hole that had been used before.

The sword was a little larger and heavier and a good deal more ornate than any Tom had ever seen. He pulled it out of the scabbard and tested the blade. It was as sharp as a razor, and there wasn't a speck of rust on it. "Solingen" was engraved just below the hilt in German script.

Tom was amazed. The weapon was a jewel. Steel had been made in Solingen for centuries and was supposed to be the best in the world. It hadn't been Mertens's either, because no one would leave behind something worth a small fortune. Tom wondered how Hauser had gotten it and how he had managed to transport it and all the other stuff around. He was obviously a man of infinite resources.

Tom decided to buy everything but the sword, which was probably worth more money than he had ever seen, on condition that the tailoring was satisfactory. But when he mentioned price, Hauser didn't want a penny, not even for the sword. He would rather not be asked about it or the hat, belt, and boots, but they hadn't cost him anything. An old soldier would understand that.

When Tom insisted on paying, Hauser came out with what he had wanted all along. It was to be Tom's orderly like he had been Mertens's. Most of the officers lived in a big wall tent and ate at the officers' mess, but those who didn't had orderlies. Tom was going to stay with his men like Mertens had, but he had never thought about an orderly. It didn't seem right to take a man out of the ranks to do what he could do himself. "No," he said, "I don't want an orderly. I can take care of myself. But I'll pay for this stuff and the work that goes into it, a fair price anyhow." That would undoubtedly rule out the sword, and he was tempted.

Hauser pleaded. His blue eyes were earnestly beseeching, and the wrinkles and creases on his ruddy face showed plainly.

It was too fast for Tom to follow very well, and he was glad when Billy volunteered a translation. "He wants hit awful bad. He says hit ain't good fer a man his age bein' jist a common sol'jer. He wouldn't of jined up, but Cap'n Mertens knowed him an' promised he'd be his orderly. Then Mertens wuz wounded an' he had t' go inta th' ranks. Now he's found out th' cap'n's crippled an' won't ever be comin' back."

Tom felt himself weakening. Hauser had a good case, but he still didn't like the idea. "No, it just doesn't seem right—"

Hauser burst into a flood of German and cut him off. He seemed almost ready to weep. Billy finally had to interrupt him. "He claims t' be the best they is. He wuz an orderly fer officers in th' army in Germany; then he wuz cook in a fancy hotel an' worked fer a tailor b'fore he come over hyar." Billy sighed and Tom could tell whose side he was on. "He's got his heart set on hit. He'd jist talked Lootenant Jacobs inta takin' him when he got kilt." Billy looked at Tom significantly. "He don't know what he's gonna do if'n y' won't take him. He's too old t' be runnin' 'round in th' ranks enymore."

Tom had understood pretty well, but Billy's translation gave him time to think and he decided to give in. "Well, if he was promised that to get him to enlist and if it's all that hard on him in the ranks, I guess we'll do it."

Hauser was overjoyed. The *Herr Leutnant* would never be sorry. Hauser would make him the finest-looking officer in the regiment, just like he had the *Herr Hauptmann* Mertens.

Tom wanted to make sure Hauser appreciated the value of that sword he was giving away. He certainly did, but like he said, it hadn't cost him anything, and he was always afraid someone would steal it. After that Tom was almost ready to believe the fellow would sell his soul to get out of the ranks if he had to.

Hauser would bring his things and start at once. He asked Billy to help but was scandalized when Tom offered to lend a hand. He was given to understand that *Offizieren und Herren* just didn't do such things, from which Tom gathered that he was going to get lessons in proper etiquette along with everything else.

He got another lesson when Hauser proposed to pitch a tent apart from the others for the *Herr Leutnant* and fix it up for his exclusive use. Tom thought it would look too snobbish and put up an argument until the men themselves took sides against him.

"He's right, Lootenant," interjected Ab. "Officers cain't 'sociate too close with their men. Hit wouldn't be right."

"Yes, sir," agreed Cole. "Yo're an ol' fren' an' all that, but things has gotta be diff'runt now."

Tom saw their point. Ab and Cole were making it as easy for him as they could, and he was grateful.

Hauser cleared out a space on the other side of the road in a cedar brake that would enclose it on three sides and act as a windbreak. While he was doing this, he put some of the other Germans to carrying large, flat rocks from the creek and laying them along the path leading to the clearing. After this he pitched the tent, but it was no ordinary affair. It had waterproof groundsheets over ordinary tent canvas, which meant that it wouldn't leak like regular tents always did when they got very wet. It was twice as long as an ordinary shelter tent, and the ends could be closed with pieces of canvas cut to fit and laced to the roof. Instead of boughs and leaves to spread his blankets on, there was a large bag made of an old canvas wagon top filled with straw.

Tom marveled. Even Mertens hadn't had a tent like that. Hauser must have been planning ahead a good deal. When he expressed his appreciation, his orderly spoke deprecatingly and promised to improve his quarters beyond this primitive state at the first opportunity.

The next morning Hauser was waiting with hot water, shaving soap, and razor. Tom understood that shaving would be a daily order of business, in camp at least, and resigned himself to it. After the shaving, a scissors and comb were produced and Tom's hair was carefully trimmed. He gathered that *Offizieren und Herren* had to be very careful of their appearance. The men grinned covertly at Hauser's masterful behavior and their commander's docility. He couldn't help grinning himself when his orderly wasn't looking.

The coat and hat were finished, but the trousers weren't. The tailor was very apologetic. He had been able to work on only one pair, and they had been only lapped over at the waist although the legs were done. The coat would cover the top, though, and no one would notice. The other pair of trousers would be finished by noon, and the ones that would be worn soon afterward. He attached great importance to the *Herr Leutnant's* putting in a good appearance at his first officers' call.

He certainly would. The coat fit perfectly and was pressed to perfection. For all anyone could tell, the trousers were the same, and the hat looked like it had just come from the shop window. The boots and belt were polished to a sheen. One of the men remarked that Tom looked like he had just stepped out of a bandbox, and they all took great pride in his appearance, Billy most of all.

Tom was the smartest-looking fellow present when he went to officers' call. Even Owen looked dowdy beside him, despite the gold major's leaves that gleamed on his shoulder straps. The other ex-sergeants still wore their old uniforms with the stripes removed and shoulder straps sewed on. It showed where the stripes had been, and the sewing was crude. They acted self-conscious and out of place while Tom felt completely at ease and thanked his lucky stars for Hauser.

Tom was glad Owen undertook no introductions because there was at least one of the old officers he wouldn't want to shake hands with. The fellow ignored him and he took pains to show he was glad of it.

Of course there were some more or less spontaneous handshakes and congratulations, and he got a few. He also got some envious looks and heard someone mutter something about "rolling in money" but pretended not to hear.

He got to talking with Lt. Marcus Allen of the Posey County company while they were standing around waiting for Owen to begin. Allen was engaged to Colonel Rivers's daughter, Carolyn, who had made the flag presentation back at Indianapolis when the regiment left for the field. Before he got to know him, Tom had expected Allen to be a handsome, debonair fellow, but he wasn't. He was thin and serious-looking, and the only stylish thing about him was a trim black mustache.

Major Owen finally got down to business. He said he was going to tell them what they would be doing, for a few weeks anyhow, if the Rebels left them alone. Beginning in two days, all four regiments of the brigade were going to rotate companies on picket for twenty-four hours, beginning at noon each day, on one of the four main roads leading into town. Theirs was the road from the east, and the guard point was the first bridge out of town. Company A would go out first, and the others would take their turn in alphabetical order. Unless the new issue came out before it went out, Company A would report to the headquarters tent for an issue of ammunition when the time came and turn it over to the company that relieved it. Until the picketing started, there would be only ordinary camp duties.

Tom was glad the companies would go out in alphabetical order, because his would be last and he would have plenty of time to find out how it was done. He wouldn't have to bother about ammunition either, but unless the new issue came soon, the others would, and he again wondered why Owen hadn't kept it all until then. It would avoid all this trouble about handing ammunition from one company to another and getting a lot of cartridges broken or unwrapped by being handled every day.

Owen went on to say that companies on picket were to let no citizens out of town unless they had passes from Major Pedigo, the brigade provost. There shouldn't be any trouble about that, because they all knew they had to have the passes. All persons coming in were to be screened for Rebel spies and couriers. Anyone who looked suspicious was to be sent to Major Pedigo under guard, and he would decide what to do with them.

Someone wanted to know why a whole company when it looked like a squad would do. Owen had a ready answer. A squad could be gobbled up easily by one of those roving bands of Rebel cavalry that infested the country. A company could fight them off.

Someone else asked how they could tell if a person was suspicious. Owen replied a little curtly that night travelers would naturally be suspect, and that he hoped they had enough common sense to tell about the others.

After the picketing started, the companies that weren't out would stay in camp and only have musters morning and evening. Sergeant Kemper had already set up the camp guard out of men that had delinquencies to make up.

This was greeted by smiles and murmurs of approval, because it meant that Owen was going to carry on like Rivers had about guarding the camp. There would be no daily guard mounting ceremonies and half the regiment wouldn't be kept out on picket to guard the other half from stray livestock and wandering Negroes, as was common in other regiments.

Owen hadn't said anything about drill, and that was something else to be pleased about. Rivers had never drilled the men just to keep them busy, and Owen wasn't going to either. It had been a hard campaign, and they needed a rest anyhow.

The best news of all came last. Six men from each company could have passes to town every day when they weren't out on picket. Officers wouldn't need any, but Owen would rather they all stayed in camp the first few days. There were immediate objections to this, so he added that if anyone really wanted to go, it would be all right as long as one officer from each company stayed in camp. When someone pointed out that several companies had only one officer, Owen sighed and said that they could go, too, as long as they let him know.

Someone asked about pass blanks. Owen replied that company commanders should send to the headquarters tent for them and give them out however they pleased. He added that they'd better make sure that the men who got them put in a good appearance and behaved themselves. The brigade provost kept a guard in town and would pick up those that didn't or who had no passes. Anyone who got picked up would be turned over for company punishment, and Owen didn't want to hear of anyone just being bawled out and let off. If they made examples of the first few, it would save a lot of trouble later. He sounded pretty abrupt, like he was trying to make up for having backed down about officers going to town.

Tom didn't care about going to town, but he knew most of the men would, even if they had no money, just to get away from camp for a while.

After Owen dismissed them, Tom asked him about a sergeant and a corporal for his company. Owen told him just to send the names of whoever he wanted to Corporal Stevens, the regimental clerk, and that he would see to it that they got their warrants. There would be another two when the company got up to full strength again, and he could do the same with them. That was more good news. Rivers had always let company commanders pick their own noncoms, and Owen was going to do the same.

Tom wanted to ask about having Hauser for his orderly and staying with his company instead of moving into the officers' quarters, but someone else got Owen's attention and he had to leave or run a risk of being late for his first morning muster and inspection as company commander.

On his way back to his company, Tom decided just to go ahead with it. After all, Mertens had used Hauser and stayed with his men, and he guessed Owen would let him know if he didn't want him to do the same. Anyhow, he wanted plenty of privacy for study now that he was an officer, and there would be little of that in the officers' quarters. The only problem would be finding something to study. He had already gone through everything he could lay his hands on. Maybe if he asked around among the officers, he could find something.

By the time Tom reached his company, Cole and Grim had already called the men out and had them drawn up and waiting. Cole called the roll and had a little trouble with some of the German names, but they were always answered to, even by Donhauer when he was called Donahue. Looking at Cole from the back always reminded Tom of Burk. Although Burk had been a lot bigger, Cole was built just like him and could give fifty pounds to most men and still outweigh them. Of course from the front there was little resemblance. Cole was dark-haired and swarthy where Burk had been blond and fair.

Tom and Grim did the inspection. Grim was a small, bustling fellow, darker than most of the Germans. The only fault they found was a rifle with a little dirt on the breech, probably because it had been dropped in the hurry of turning out. Tom wasn't going to say anything, but Grim pointed it out to the owner and managed to make clear that it hadn't better happen again, although he was from Hall's old platoon and understood no German.

By now Tom was sure that Cole and Grim were about the best noncoms an officer could have and that he could pretty well leave the men to them. He already knew this was the right thing to do, because the worst companies were usually commanded by officers who either did nothing or tried to do everything themselves, and one was as bad as the other. Also, the men always lost respect for an officer who was either lazy or a busybody.

After the inspection, Tom went back to his place in front of the company. When he did, "Tenshun!" rang out. The men snapped erect, their rifles at the trail.

"Present *arms*!" came next and the men brought their rifles up to the proper position in snappy simultaneous movements and aligned them as perfectly as pickets in a fence.

Tom returned the salute and gave his first command: "Order *arms*!" After the rifle butts thumped all together on the ground, he gave his second: "In place, *rest*!"

The men thrust their rifle barrels forward at a slight angle, put their left hands behind their backs, and moved their feet apart, all exactly together.

Tom hadn't stood before the whole company and watched it follow his commands often enough not to be strongly affected by it. These men would obey any command he gave like so many automatons. If he ordered them to load their rifles and shoot someone, they would do it in the same precise, mechanical fashion. His head swam at the thought.

Tom began by repeating what Major Owen had said about what they would be doing after a few days. His voice sounded casual and matter-of-fact, almost like someone else's. After that he told them that morning muster would be just like it had been today, but that in the evening there would only be roll call and no inspection. Every Saturday morning there would be an inspection in full marching order, except for not having shelter tent halves in the packs.

He ended by telling the men about the passes. He was going to leave it up to the platoon leaders as to how to give them out, but they would have to come to him for the pass, and he wasn't going to give one to anybody who didn't put in a good appearance. He also told them about the provost guard in town and cautioned them to behave themselves.

Before Tom finished, his eyes fell on Billy, who positively glowed with brotherly pride, and it caused him to hesitate a little before giving the command to stack arms and dismiss.

Afterward Tom joined the men sitting on logs and stumps around the fireplace. Cole presented him with a cup of coffee, and he stood sipping it and talking. He waited until there was a pause in the chatter to get down to business. "Say, Cole, I'd like you to be platoon sergeant in my place. What about it?"

Cole grinned hugely. "Yes, sir. I'd shore like t' be sargint, so I guess we've come to a 'greement."

"He likes t' have power over other fellers, Cole does," said Charley with a sly grin.

Cole admitted it freely. "I shore do! I jist love t' order other fellers 'round an' see 'em do what I tells 'em!" He laughed and slapped his chest.

Everybody laughed along with him. "Lootenant, sir, who's gonna be corp'ril now in place uv Cole?" asked Ab with pretended eagerness.

Tom knew what to expect when he said, "That's up to Cole."

Ab got up, cleared his throat portentously, and paraded his lanky frame before Cole. "Howdy, ol' fren'," he said with exaggerated courtesy.

Grins flashed across every face in the group.

"Not you, y' dang' ol' ridge runner!" scoffed Cole. "You ain't fitten t' be nothin', not even a privit!"

Ab pretended to be deeply hurt, and everybody roared with laughter. "Passed over agin, an' by me bes' fren'!" He sighed and rolled his eyes upward. "Oh, Lard, what've I done t' desarve—"

Uproarious laughter drowned him out. Everybody knew Ab wouldn't take stripes if they were made of gold. "An me th' smartest man in th' reg'ment!" he wailed.

The men fell into convulsions of mirth. Some from Hall's old platoon rolled on the ground. Ab was strong medicine for the uninitiated.

After the uproar subsided, Billy started it anew by crying, "Ab, yo're a case!"

Ab broke down and confessed, "I jist cain't help hit! I likes t' make fellers laff jist like Cole likes t' order 'em 'round."

Cole got up for more coffee from the can on the fire. "Well, hit takes all kinds uv fellers t' make th' world. Ab makes 'em laff an' I makes 'em cry." It wasn't so, because no one cried. They all laughed as hard as ever.

"This is shore a good bunch we're in with now," affirmed Tom Pinnick as he wiped tears of mirth from his eyes. He was a dark, sharp-featured fellow from Hall's old platoon. "We never had fun like this b'fore, did we, boys?"

The boys agreed heartily.

"Well, you-uns didn't have no Ab," Charley told them. "Jist wait till he tells one uv them stories uv his'n, like that un 'bout th' bull chasin' him inta th' Padoky." He hee-hawed in remembrance.

Immediate demands were put on Ab, but Cole headed them off. "Wait a minit!" he bellowed. "I gotta d'cide who's gonna be corp'ril, an' that's ser'rous bisness!"

"Well, who?" asked Charley. "Git hit over with."

Cole looked at Tom. "I b'lieve hit oughta be somebody outa Hall's men. They lost their corp'ril, too, Curtis, y'know."

Tom nodded his agreement.

"I b'lieve Tom Pinnick hyar 'd make us a good corp'ril," said Cole. "What d'you think 'bout hit, Lootenant?"

Tom nodded again. "Pinnick it is, then." Cole had made a good choice. Hall's men deserved a noncom, and Pinnick was a steady, dependable fellow the men respected.

The men shouted their approval and started pounding Pinnick on the back. He grinned his appreciation but had to fend off his congratulators or get a sore back.

"Where's Hauser?" asked Tom after a look around. "I'll get him to take th' stripes off my old coat and sew 'em on Cole's; then he can put Cole's on Tom's."

Someone said Kemper had sent for Hauser, so it would have to wait. Soon after Ab finished his tale and everyone was done laughing, Hauser came back. He had a revolver in a fine black leather holster, a book, and a small leather pouch with heavy objects in it. He presented them to Tom.

"Where'd you get these things, now?" wondered Tom.

Hauser said they were from Sergeant Kemper, who was too busy to bring them himself. The book was new to Tom. It was on company tactics and had Jake's name on the inside cover. "This was Jake's," he mused. "I guess Sergeant Kemper passed it on."

Hauser went on to say the revolver was the one Tom had given Kemper last spring, the one that had belonged to that Rebel artillery captain he had killed.

The men couldn't understand and Tom had to translate. He was reluctant to take the revolver. "I hate to be an Indian giver."

It was Hauser's turn not to understand, and Billy had to explain. He replied volubly. Kemper had no use for it. He couldn't wear it because he wasn't an officer. Now Tom needed a revolver, and Kemper wanted him to have this one.

"Well, all right," replied Tom. "I'll thank the sergeant when I see him, especially for this pouch and holster. I didn't give them to him." The pouch could be put on his belt like the holster and contained two extra cylinders for the revolver and a small bullet mold with folding handles. They would be nice to have. He could mold his own bullets out of minie´balls, and because each chamber of the cylinders had to be loaded separately with powder and ball, extra ones already loaded were a necessity.

Tom drew the revolver from the holster to see if it was loaded. It was, except for caps on the nipples. He thought of the brave Rebel captain and said, "I just wish I was as good a man as the fellow who first had this."

"Yeah," said Ab reflectively. "Stood up an' fit a hull platoon uv us." He shook his head. "Hit's a shame fer a feller like him t' git kilt."

Harve suddenly spoke up. "Aw now! He wuz a damn Rebel! Desarved hit, he did!"

The men looked at him in startled anger. "Sometimes I wunner 'bout you, Akers, whether yo're human er not," said Ab bitingly.

Dan Howard's dander was up. "Why, he wuz jist fightin' fer what he thought wuz right, jist like we air, fer our country an' our people!" He advanced on Akers. "Ab's right 'bout you. You ain't even human. Yo're a damn nigger-lovin' Republican!" He gave Harve a push and doubled his fists.

Tom let Cole take care of it. "Shet up an' set down, Howard!" growled the big dark fellow. "We ain't havin' no name-callin' an' fightin' 'round hyar!" When Dan turned away, Cole fixed Harve with a menacing eye. "You'd better larn t' keep that big, flappin' mouth uv yores shet, Akers, 'bout things like that, enyhow."

Harve looked down, made a long face, and shook his head. "I jist cain't unnerstan' hit, why ever'body's agin me."

Tom felt he had to say something. "You turn them against you by sayin' things like that! You should've known that before you said it!"

"He did know hit," muttered Dan Howard.

Tom thought something was behind Harve's outburst. He was about the only Republican in the company and hadn't joined in the celebration of Tom's commission. He didn't seem to think Democrats deserved promotion or anything else because they were always criticizing the president.

Harve looked thoroughly woebegone. "I guess they jist ain't eny place fer me in this comp'ny enymore."

Tom felt sorry for him. "Sure there is. You came in with us, and you've been with us all along. All you've got to do is keep from saying things you know will make someone mad."

"All my fren's is gone," mourned Harve, "ever' wun uv 'em."

The others were affected.

"Harve," began Ab earnestly, "we-uns ain't got nothin' agin ye. If'n ye wants t' be a Republican an' hate th' Rebels, that's all right. Jist try t' be reasonable 'bout hit."

Harve nodded and several others voiced similar feelings. He responded and before long it had all blown over.

In all the goings-on after Hauser had showed up with the presents from Kemper, Tom forgot about the exchange of stripes. He didn't remember until up in the afternoon, and sent Pinnick to Hauser with the coats.

Pinnick was back in a twinkling, still with the coats. "He won't do hit," was the terse explanation.

Tom was astonished. "Come along. We'll see about this."

Hauser was obdurate and Tom was beginning to get angry when Billy volunteered a translation. "He sez y' oughtn' t' ask him t' do work fer th' men. He wants y' t' unnerstan' he jist works fer you."

Tom had understood well enough, but Billy's translation gave him time to realize that Hauser was right. He would never ask him to do anything like this again, but this time had to be an exception. He couldn't let the fellow get away with such defiance in front of the men. "Tell him if he's going to work for me, he's going to have to do what I tell him to!" Tom could have told him himself, but the men wouldn't have understood.

Hauser got out his tailoring kit and went to work without another word. He had made his point, though, and everyone knew it. He wasn't an hour on the job, and the sewing was faultless.

Tom turned to the book Jake had left. He took a seat in his tent and started in on it but was soon disappointed. The book was too elementary and had little that he didn't already know. He was beginning to think that once a person learned the fundamentals, the rest of it was mostly just putting them into practice. He decided to go ahead with it anyhow, just for review and because he had nothing else to do.

It wasn't long before Cole and Pinnick came to say that the men were beginning to ask about passes, so Tom sent Pinnick to get the blanks from Corporal Stevens.

"What y' readin' thar, sir?" asked Cole.

"A book on company tactics poor old Jake left."

"Oh yeah, I 'member Hauser givin' hit t' ye."

"You want to study with me, or maybe you'll want it when I'm through?"

"Naw, sir. I ain't much fer readin' an' studyin'. Th' only book I ever tried like this is one a Rebel gin'ral writ, b'fore th' war, b'fore he wuz a Rebel. Hardy, I b'lieve his name is, but I didn't git fur with hit. They wuz really two uv 'em, little uns y' could put in yore pocket."

"Yeah, Hardee's *Tactics*. I've about worn mine out, and I guess I've gotten all I can out of 'em. I was hoping I'd find something new in this one, but it almost looks like it was copied from Hardee's book."

He looked significantly at Cole. "You know, you might come up for a commission someday like I did."

"Not me," sighed Cole. "I don't wanta be no officer, havin' t' dress fancy an' talk fancy an' all that. I'd lots ruther be jist a plain ol' sargint." He shook his head and laughed. "I jist couldn't do hit, ack like an officer's s'posed t' ack, I mean."

"Sure you could! Look at me! I'm a Dubois County clodhopper just like you!"

"Aw now!" scoffed Cole. "You went t' college an' you've teached school, an I 'spect you've read 'bout ever' book they is." He sighed again. "I jist went t' school long 'nough t' larn t' read an' write an' figger a little. Course I larnt figgerin' a lot better workin' fer Pappy when he wuz storekeepin' thar in th' Davis Crick settlement, atter I quit goin' t' school."

Pinnick came back with the passes, enough to last for a year, it seemed. Tom didn't know where to keep them until Hauser came up with a strong metal box that had storage spaces, slots for pens, and a container of ink that fitted in and had a top that screwed on. The top slid out and hinged down to write on, and it had straps for carrying. It was another inheritance from Mertens and was what army clerks used in the field in the old country. Tom was glad to get it and wondered why Jake hadn't used it. It would hold the company papers as well as the ammunition box they were in and would be much better to write on.

Tom set the affair up on a stump, readied pen and ink, and told Cole he was ready. Cole thought he would just give his out alphabetically, and Tom agreed that would be the best way to do it. After Cole left, he sent Billy to pass the word to Grim.

Six men soon showed up for passes, all spic-and-span and in high good humor. Harve was one of them and had recovered all his old ebullience, which led Tom to josh him about falling afoul of the provost guard. Harve laughed and averred that no provost guard would ever catch him.

Three of the six were Germans. Their names didn't run alphabetically, but that was Grim's business. One of them was a handsome blond fellow named Schlimmer, who seemed to have a reputation as a ladies' man. Anyhow, Hauser teased him about going after *die Rebellin,* rebel women. Tom was surprised to learn his orderly had a sense of humor.

It was all over in a few minutes, and Tom went back to his book. He hadn't been at it long when Hauser and two other Germans, Stutz and Hoepner, appeared carrying canvas, boards, and carpenter's tools. They only nodded to him and promptly went to work.

Before his amazed eyes, Tom's tent was raised so he would be able to stand erect and walk around in it and an awning installed so he could take his ease outside. Additional canvas took the sides and rear to the ground, and the awning came down to cover the front. A floor was laid so expertly it was as stable as the ground and perfectly level. Then came a hardtack box for a seat and an ammunition box to put the portable desk on, which made it enough higher than the seat to be worked at comfortably. A bed was made by putting together a rectangular frame of wide boards elevated several feet from the floor to contain the straw tick and blankets.

Tom's amazement was complete when it took less than two hours to do it all. When he thanked Hauser's helpers, they snapped to attention, saluted, then faced about smartly and marched away in perfect step. He was beginning to feel like Aladdin when the genie came out of the bottle. Where on earth Hauser had gotten the tools, lumber, and canvas Tom couldn't imagine. He just hoped the regiment would camp where it was long enough to make it all worthwhile.

Early the next afternoon Hauser came back from a visit with the other Germans with something urgent on his mind. Billy was with him. Hauser spoke so rapidly that about all Tom could understand was that it concerned clothing and a trip to town, until Billy intervened.

"He says yo're gonna have t' have two more uniforms, an' y' really oughta git three an' have four uv 'em. He cain't keep y' lookin' right with less than that, 'speshully on th' march."

"I guess he's right, about needing two more anyhow, but I'll just get them from the quartermaster."

Hauser was outraged. Regular issue uniform! Never! They weren't even fit for common soldiers. He couldn't bear the thought. In Germany, officers never wore such trash, even in the field.

When Tom asked where he was going to get anything better, Hauser had a prompt answer. There was a good tailor in town. Schlimmer had gotten acquainted with him and his daughter, naturally more with the daughter, it being Schlimmer. The tailor was a Jew, just like the one he used to work for in the old country. Hauser swore he could get the uniforms cheap, and they would be the very best. Jews were sharp fellows, but he knew how to deal with them, and they always had better cloth and did better work than anybody else.

Tom was won over. He sent word to Owen and started for town along with Billy and Hauser. When they reached the shop, they found the tailor alone. He was a small, dark, bearded man named Thiers who wore little rectangular spectacles and spoke good English. He and Hauser hit it off from the beginning and spoke German in such rapid-fire fashion that even Billy had trouble following them.

They were shown cloth that looked good to Tom, but except for one bolt, which he put aside after only a glance, Hauser would have none of it. Herr Thiers seemed to have a large stock. He brought out more and more, but Hauser was never satisfied. He would hold the cloth up to the light and run a fingernail across it or fold it and run a thumb along the crease, then turn it down. Finally a bolt of cloth was brought out that was so fine and glossy it looked like moleskin except for its color. In fact, that was what it was called. Hauser pounced on it. It was English *Maulwurfsfell,* the best in the world.

Hauser haggled about price. Herr Thiers figured with pencil and paper; then there was more haggling. The price they agreed on seemed astronomical, but Hauser insisted that it was cheap for the finest uniform cloth in the world, which he had never expected to find. Herr Thiers said he was offering such a low price only because it would help build up business with all these officers who were around now. The *Herr Leutnant* would be a walking advertisement for him.

Tom agreed and was measured with infinite care. While this was going on, a diminutive doll-like little beauty came in from the back, where the living quarters were. She was Herr Thiers's daughter, Rebecca, who looked to be a little short of twenty. She had big black eyes, an olive complexion, and tiny pearly teeth. Her voice was like the tinkling of little chimes, and Tom couldn't help gaping at her. She seemed too tiny and too pretty to be real. Billy was worse than he was, and it took an elbow in the ribs to get his eyes off her.

It looked like Schlimmer had lived up to his reputation, because she was interested in no one else. When she learned that Hauser knew him better, she gave him all her attention. Of course, it might have been because she assumed Tom and Billy couldn't speak German and her English was limited to a few words. Tom learned later that although her father and older brother had come from Germany five or six years ago, she and her mother had come only just before the war broke out. He guessed that Herr Thiers wanted to get settled in his business before bringing his womenfolk over. Rebecca's brother just seemed to have disappeared. No one ever saw him or could find out anything about him, even Schlimmer.

Tom thought that was strange. If he was in the Rebel army, that was nothing to hide. Most of the young men in town were, and none of their families seemed reticent about it. Maybe he had skipped out to the North or even back to the old country to escape the Rebel draft and his family was ashamed of him.

When they got down to business again, it was about *Felduniformen,* field uniforms. Tom was given to understand that he would need two of them or his orderly could not guarantee his appearance in the field. He objected. The uniform he had and the one he had just been measured for would be enough. Hauser strongly disagreed. Dress uniforms of fine cloth wouldn't stand the rough usage of field service. He picked up the bolt of cloth he had laid aside. It would wear like iron and look good enough for the field. They made field uniforms out of this kind of cloth in Germany. It was also English cloth. The English made the best in the world.

Tom shifted his ground. If he bought two field uniforms, he could get by with the one he had for dress.

Hauser was appalled. An officer simply couldn't appear in a camp-tailored hand-me down uniform on dress parades or at balls and social functions! It was unthinkable! The *Herr Leutnant* must consider his reputation!

Afraid there would be a scene if he argued further, Tom gave in, only to be faced with the necessity of an overcoat, another hat, and a pair of boots. He tried to draw the line on the boots and overcoat, only to be overwhelmed by argument. When even Billy took sides against him, he gave up. An overcoat for dress was essential, because issue overcoats were too uncouth for anything but field use. The boots he had were strictly for dress. He would need a heavy, durable pair for the field, or he would soon be reduced to wearing shoes like common soldiers. Hauser was horrified at the very thought. Tom could see the need for another hat and didn't argue about it. Weather and usage would make the one he had unfit for dress.

There was no haggling about the cost of the hat, coat, and field uniforms. Hauser was delighted at the figure quoted by Herr Thiers, who shook his head and said he wouldn't be making any money on this transaction. That was all right, though. Like he said, he was mainly interested in advertising, and the business the *Herr Leutnant's* appearance would bring him would more than make up for it. He went on to point out that it would be necessary to pay in advance. The *Herr Leutnant* would understand that it wouldn't be possible to sell uniforms tailored to his exact dimensions to anyone else in case something happened to him, and that was always possible in war. Tom was glad he had saved his money and had it all with him, because it took most of it.

After they had stopped at a boot shop and bought a pair of sturdy black boots, Tom was nearly bankrupt. He felt glum about squandering so much money, but Billy assured him that it was well spent. Tom would be so well outfitted he wouldn't have to spend another penny on clothes except maybe for boots and hats for years, if the war lasted that long. Billy offered his brother a loan if he ran short on money before they got paid again.

When Tom wondered about carrying all the stuff around, Hauser was quick with assurances. He would make a carrying case like officers used in the old country out of a wagon top he had salvaged, and one of the regimental teamsters was another German and a special friend of his.

# 27

Tom could tell something was wrong as soon as they came in sight of camp on their way back from town. The men were gathered in groups, and even from a distance he could tell they were worked up about something. As he came closer, he could hear angry shouting and see a few officers expostulating with them.

The first words Tom heard were delivered in an angry yell. "This is th' end uv hit fer me!" Other voices shouted approval.

"He lied t' us, th' ol' sunuvabitch! Hit's a dirty damn trick!" came another angry salvo.

"I'd never of gone if'n I'd knowed he wuz gonna do this!"

"Me neither, by God, an' I kin shore go back! I know th' way!"

So it went on, and Tom felt a sinking sensation. The regiment was pretty close to mutiny and a mass desertion. It could only be something about slavery. There had been rumors lately that it was going to be abolished, and nothing else could arouse the men like this. He sent Hauser to his tent with the boots and made a beeline for his company along with Billy.

Except for the Germans, Tom's men were all gathered about the fireplace and were almost as noisy as the others, but they quieted down as he approached. "What's all this carryin' on about?" he asked.

The men looked surprised.

"Don't y' know 'bout hit, Lootenant?" asked someone.

Tom noticed Harve Akers towards the back, but he seemed to be keeping his mouth shut, probably out of fear of getting beaten up.

"No, I just got back from town," he replied.

"Well, hit's th' proclamation th' president's put out, nigh onta a week 'go, they say," Cole told him. "Hit frees th' slaves," the big fellow spat. "He's give in t' th' radicals an' th' damn' abolish!" The black eyes blazed with anger. "He's tricked us, that's what he's done, th' dirty ol' bastard!"

"Yeah!" shouted someone toward the back of the group. "Promised they'd be no foolin' with slav'ry t' git us in th' damn army, an' now look what he's done!"

Tom was appalled. It wasn't just the excitable, less responsible fellows. Men like Cole had to be taken seriously. How could Lincoln be so stupid? Did he want half the army to quit? How was he going to beat the Rebels and put the Union back together with what would be left of it? Admittedly, slavery was an abstract wrong and ought to be done away with, but there were serious obstacles in the way, and this was one of them. He felt much like the men did, but he was an officer now and it was his duty to save what he could of the army.

"Are you men sure you're not going off half-cocked?" he asked as casually as he could. "There've been all kinds of rumors lately, and the president's always putting out proclamations." All he could do was play for time and hope to calm the men down.

"We-uns is goin' off frum full cock, Lootenant," said Charley emphatically. "Hit's in th' papers. Tom Pinnick hyar seen hit. It ain't jist somebody's tale."

"I shore did!" affirmed Pinnick promptly. "In black an' white." He shook his head. "Hit wuz a 'ficial proclamation, all done up in fancy words, his name to hit an' ever'thing." His normally friendly brown eyes were stony.

"Now, Lootenant," demanded battlefield berserker Dan Howard, "how kin he do somethin' like that? He ain't got no power t' 'bolish slav'ry. Not even congress kin do hit. Hit'd take a 'mendment t' th' Constitootion! I heered a feller say that 'while 'go, a feller that knowed what he wuz talkin' 'bout."

Ab spoke up before Tom could think of an answer to an unanswerable question. "He's makin' hisself a dictator; that's what he's doin'! He's been havin' people 'rested that's agin him, ain't he, 'thout warrant er enything?"

Tom felt it was almost hopeless. If he couldn't count on Ab, he couldn't count on anyone.

"I don't keer 'bout that!" exploded Zeke Kerns. "He kin make hisself a dictator all he wants to! I'm jist worried 'bout th' niggers! Now they're gonna be free, an you-all knows what they'll do. They'll pick up an' go north, an we'll reely be in fer hit!"

He spat on the ground. " 'Magine, havin' them filthy, thievin' black monkeys all 'round 'mongst ye!"

Several voiced loud agreement. Tom decided to be quiet for a while and let the men blow off steam. Maybe it would be easier to quiet them then.

"Yeah!" shouted Elmer Davis, a sallow, skinny fellow who needed a shave. "They'll be goin' t' school with our chillern 'n' mixin' with 'em. I got chillern already, an' you fellers'll have 'em, too, someday!" He thrust his face forward and snarled. "You fellers want yore chillern 'sociatin' with niggers 'n' gittin' t' like 'em? Maybe one uv yore darters'll marry one an' you'll have half-nigger gran'chillern! Lil' yaller uns!"

"An our wimmin," put in Sam Price, who was married and had children, too. "A big black buck'll risk his neck eny day fer a white woman! You know that! Yore wimmin won't be able t' go outa th' house 'thout takin' a chance uv gittin' raped!"

It was getting worse all the time, so Tom spoke up. "I think you men ought to quiet down a little and think about this thing. I want to read this proclamation before I go saying things like some of you have." He ran his eyes over his men. "Has anybody read it but Tom?" This seemed to have a quieting effect, and he was encouraged.

No one had read it but Pinnick.

"How much of it did you read?" Tom asked him.

"I read hit all, but kinda fast."

"Exactly what did it say?"

Pinnick furrowed his brow and scratched his head. "Well, I don't 'member a hull lot 'ceptin' that hit freed th' slaves, but . . . but they was places, er, states, whar hit didn't, an' hit didn't do hit right now."

"Well, hit don't make no diff'runce—" began Elmer.

Tom cut him off. "Go see if you can borrow that paper you saw it in, Tom, and let's see just what all this commotion's about." What Pinnick had said led him to believe the proclamation was qualified enough to give him some talking points and let him cool the men down. He knew any qualifications or exceptions wouldn't really make any difference, though. Even if it didn't free all the slaves right now, it meant that they were all going to be freed sooner or later. Otherwise it would never have been issued. He was going to have to try to deceive the men about it, and the thought almost gagged him.

Pinnick left to see if he could get the paper.

"Don't you men think that's what we ought to do?" Tom went on. "Read it and try to understand it and then talk about it sensible like?"

Some of the men were cooling down already. "Yes, sir, yo're right," said Cole. "I guess some uv us kinda flew offa th' handle."

Tom was beginning to feel even more encouraged when a man named Thompson from Hall's old platoon dashed his hopes. Normally, Thompson was a quiet, placid fellow. "Hit still frees th' niggers, I'll betcha! Ol' Linkun wouldn't've put hit out if'n hit didn't! Now, how kin enyone 'spect us t' stay in th' army 'n' fight t' free th' niggers? I didn't jine up t' do that! They told us hit wuz jist t' save th' Union, an' that they'd let slav'ry 'lone, didn't they?" He had hit the nail on the head, and Tom suddenly felt sick inside.

Dan Howard made Tom feel sicker. "Ain't we all got th' right t' pick up an' go home now 'cause uv that?"

Tom took the bull by the horns. "No, no one's got any right to desert. No one signed any contract that he could quit if this or that was done. Every man of you enlisted for three years, and that's a long time off yet."

"But hit ain't right!" protested Davis vehemently. "Hit jist ain't right! We all unnerstood, an' they unnerstood, that th' war wuz jist fer th' Union, an' they promised they'd be no meddlin' with slav'ry. Ol' Linkun hisself did!" He bobbed his head emphatically. "Ever' man uv us has got th' right t' quit an' go home, contract er not!"

Tom felt desperate and made a mistake. "If you quit and try to go home," he told Davis, "you'll be a deserter, and you know what they do with deserters, don't you? Remember that New York man last spring?"

Davis laughed harshly. "Y' gotta have men who'll do th' shootin' 'fore ye kin have a firin' squad, an' they won't be none if'n we all goes!"

That was the most dangerous statement yet, and Tom felt a thrill of panic, because he could see it affected the men strongly. Pinnick came to his rescue by arriving with a newspaper. "Hyar hit is!" he said as he extended it to Tom. "We gotta be keerful with hit, though, 'cause I gotta take hit back."

Tom unfolded the paper and searched the columns as a hush settled over the group. It only accentuated the uproar from the others, though. He found the proclamation and saw in its complex legal wording a source of new hope. He read it, putting the more difficult parts in plain language after reading them and throwing in comments as he went along. When he finished, he said. "See there, it really doesn't free any slaves at all! And here you fellows got all worked up about it."

"I cain't unnerstan' hit," mused Davis. "How kin hit 'clare th' slaves free an' then not really free eny uv 'em?"

"Well," Tom replied, "It's like this. It'll apply only to th' states that're still in rebellion January 1, and Lincoln won't have any authority in them." He snorted. "You don't think th' Rebels'll pay any attention to it, do you? They'll still be running things in those states. And it don't apply to states that've never joined th' Rebels, like Kentucky and Maryland, or parts of th' Rebel states we've conquered, like Louisiana."

"Well, what did he do hit fer, then? Why'd he wanta stir ever'body up like he's done 'bout hit an' then not really do hit?" Davis was more acute than Tom thought he was.

Billy gave him a hand. "Jist hittin' a lick at th' Rebels, maybe."

The men were still puzzling about it when Thompson carried on where Davis had left off. "All right, hit don't free eny uv 'em right now, but hit means all uv 'em is gonna be freed in time! We're gonna beat th' Rebels an' take over them states where hit does 'ply, an' their slaves'll be freed, an' them in them states that ain't jined th' Rebels'll be freed, too, then. They ain't gonna let them go on bein' slaves when all th' others is free, air they?" He snorted angrily. "You know they hain't!"

There was a chorus of agreement, and Tom saw he hadn't fooled anybody. He should have known better and decided to be honest from now on. "Well, what about th' Union if ever'body up and quits? It'll never be put back t'gether again."

"Th' Union'll be gone up, an' hit'll be their fault, that dum' ol Linkun an' his bunch!" spat Thompson.

"Won't that be cuttin' off your nose to spite your face?" asked Tom. "Th' Union'll be gone, and th' states'll go on breakin' up, maybe each one to itself." He saw he had scored and felt new hope. "Maybe that'll make you feel better, Thompson, if you can blame it on someone else when you're starvin' t' death in some little country cut off from ever'thing an' ever'body." The men were impressed, so he carried it on. "We'll be just like they are in Europe, you know. Maybe you'll be sendin' your boys off someday to fight Illinois or Kentucky."

Ab heaved a sigh. "Th' lootenant's right. They've got us. If we quits, hit'll be worse than if'n we don't. We'll git th' Union back t'gether agin enyhow, an' maybe they kin figger out somethin' t' do with th' niggers, like shippin' 'em all back t' Afriky."

Tom felt like a drowning man snatched out of the water. His lanky friend had come through after all.

There was a period of thoughtful silence broken only by the noise from the other companies, where things seemed to be worse than ever.

Finally Thompson spoke up. "Well, I guess yo're right, Ab," he admitted grudgingly, "but hit don't make me feel no better." He shook his head. "Th' dirty, lyin' ol' sunuvabitch! He ain't foolin' me no more, ol' Linkun ain't!" It all sounded strange, coming from a fellow no one had ever heard raise his voice before.

"Yeah!" agreed Davis angrily. "He's got us this time, but he hain't never gonna do hit t' me agin!" He shook his fist and raised his voice to a screech. "Jist wait till th' ol' rascal runs agin! Hyar's one vote he ain't gittin'!"

Grins and laughter followed. Everybody knew Davis hadn't voted for Lincoln two years before and never would because he was a Republican. The same could be said of almost everybody else here who had been old enough to vote then or would be by the time of the next election.

"You tell 'em, Elmer!" whooped somebody toward the back, and there was an outbreak of guffaws. The atmosphere had changed and Tom knew he had won. Of course, there were the Germans, but their innate discipline would keep them in line regardless of what they thought about Negroes and slavery, and he doubted if many of them thought about such things at all.

It was barely in time. Major Owen suddenly appeared wearing sword and revolver and looking very worried. He beckoned Tom aside and asked nervously, "Lieutenant, are your men reliable?"

Some of the men were joshing Davis about having voted for Lincoln two years ago and laughing at his vehement denials, so Tom could reply, "Yes, sir, you can count on them."

"To put down a mutiny?"

The uproar from the other companies gave Tom pause. "Is it that bad?"

Owen looked up the road that ran in front of the camp. It was full of shouting, angry men. "Well, it's pretty close to that in several of the companies, and all one of them has to do is break out. Then I'm afraid the others will follow." He shook his head and sighed. "We've been able to keep the companies pretty well separated so far. Thank God I didn't assemble the regiment like several of the officers suggested."

Before Tom could say anything, Owen went on. "Sergeant Kemper said you could be counted on to keep your men in hand back when I first heard about this proclamation and we got to talking about what might happen when the men found out about it."

"Oh, you saw this coming, then?"

Owen sighed again. "No, not exactly. I knew they'd be upset, but I hoped it wouldn't go this far." The uproar grew louder and he had to raise his voice. "Maybe I deceived myself. Maybe I should have called the men out when I first heard about it and told them about it and talked to them." He shook his head and grimaced. "I was afraid that . . . that making a big thing of it might cause something that wouldn't happen otherwise."

Owen was being unusually confiding. "Yes, sir, I understand," replied Tom.

"But I took some precautions. That's why I had the ammunition taken up. I didn't take yours because of what Sergeant Kemper said, not because I was afraid of Rebel cavalry." He shifted his feet nervously and looked at Tom, who saw fear in his eyes. "I hope I wasn't wrong, about your company, I mean."

Tom came to a decision. "Well, there's only one way to find out for sure." He went toward the men, Owen following.

When he got close, Tom stopped and shouted, "The major wants to know if he can count on us, boys! I told him he could! We're steady, aren't we?"

A chorus of agreement went up, and Tom could barely hide his relief. "We're 's stidy 's rocks!" bellowed Cole.

"We're frum Dubois County!" yelled Billy. "Ain't no unstidy men frum Dubois County, air they, boys?" The men endorsed him vociferously and Tom could have hugged his brother.

"Dubois County men air like big oak trees!" shouted Dan Howard. "Ain't nothin' that'll budge 'em!" Enthusiastic whoops seconded him.

Tom noticed Sergeant Grim come up and speak to Billy. He took the plunge. "We may be called on to put down a mutiny! Are we ready?"

"Ready! We're ready!" chorused the men.

Grim came toward Tom, stopped, and saluted. *"Wir Deutsch sind auch fertig, Herr Leutnant!"*

Tom had been counting on the Germans, but this was better than he had expected. He wanted to make sure that Grim understood the situation, though, so he risked his clumsy German. *"Ein Meuterei unterzudrucken?"*

*"Jawohl, Herr Leutnant!"*

Tom turned to Owen. "You heard the men, sir. They'll do it."

Owen couldn't restrain a sigh of relief. "Good. Sergeant Kemper was right." He looked up the road at the angry turmoil. "I've got to get back up that way. Get your men under arms and hold them ready." He squared his shoulders and started up the road.

Tom turned to his men. "Go get your rifles and belts and fall in here on the road!" He heard Grim shouting to his men as the others bolted for their equipment.

Hauser ran up with Tom's belt, sword, and revolver. He buckled them on and made sure there were caps on the cylinder of the revolver. By the time he had, the men were running back, and soon the whole company was drawn up under arms before him. Cole and Grim dressed the ranks; then everyone waited silently amid the din from the other companies.

"Hey! What d'you fellers think yo're doin'?" came an angry shout from up the road, and a knot of men started toward them.

Tom wheeled to face them. "Halt! Halt and go back to where you're supposed to be! We've got nothing to do with you!"

They stopped, looked at him uncertainly, then turned back, looking over their shoulders and muttering. None of Tom's men said a word or moved a muscle.

The uproar was unabated and after a while it occurred to Tom that having his men load their rifles in the most ceremonious and noisy fashion possible might make an impression.

"Company, *attention*!" he shouted.

The men snapped erect, rifles at the trail with their butts on the ground.

"Load in nine times! Sergeants, count the time!" He paused briefly, then shouted, "Load!"

Rifle muzzles shot forward from the vertical as Cole and Grim shouted, "One!"

"Handle cartridge!" At "One!" right hands went to belts and "Two!" brought cartridges to faces that were growing dim in the fading light.

"Tear cartridge!" At "One!" the men tore off the cartridge ends with their teeth.

"Charge cartridge!" Hands shot to rifle muzzles and started the cartridges down the barrels as "One!" sounded.

"Draw rammer!" The chant of "One, two, three!" brought the ramrods out of the pipes under the barrels and inserted them in the muzzles in three perfectly coordinated movements.

So it went through "Prime!" and "Fix bayonets!" After that, Tom shouted, "In place, *rest*!" and the men stood motionless and impassive, the firelight playing on their ranks and gleaming from the bayonets.

It had all been done with great precision and a maximum of noise. Tom had shouted each command at the top of his lungs. Cole and Grim had chanted the time as loudly as they could. The men had caught on and made all the noise they could, particularly when fixing their bayonets. The metallic clash and clang had rung out sharply. The clamor from the closer companies had abated considerably.

"What're you damn Dutchmen gonna do?" came a querulous call from someone who was trying to convince himself that only the Germans had turned out.

Tom didn't deign to hear, and an ominous silence was the only answer. It even seemed that the uproar farther up the road was beginning to fall off.

It was pretty plain that an impression had been made, but it wouldn't last long unless it was followed up promptly. Tom decided to march his men up and down the road in front of the camp. It would clear the road and make an even greater impression.

"Attention!" he shouted, "Right shoulder, *arms*! Right *face*!" He went around to the head of the column, drew his sword, and held it at the salute. "Forward, *march*!" After the men stepped off, he shouted, "Count time, *count*!"

The massed chorus roared out, *"One, two, three, four! One, two, three, four!"*

It was getting dark, but the road was illuminated by fires in the company areas and a big one at the top of the slope in front of the headquarters tent. The road was almost empty at first and the few men in it stepped aside, but more began to appear and show an increasing reluctance to get out of the way as the march went on.

*"One, two, three, four!"* came the massed shout behind Tom.

Some men in the road moved aside with sneers and snarls at only the last second. Suddenly one man braced himself in the middle of the road and tore his coat open to bare his chest. "Bay'net me! Shoot me! I dare ye, ye nigger-lovin' sonsabitches!"

Tom whipped his sword down from the vertical, its point only inches from the bared chest, and the fellow jumped hastily aside. "Why you . . . you big officer bastard!" he gasped. "You'd of stuck me!"

Tom snapped his sword back to the vertical and went on without breaking his stride and heard the defiant man's comrades break into guffaws at his discomfiture. That was a good sign.

*"One, two, three, four!"* chorused the company over and over again as the march went on, the stamp of feet punctuating the count. The men were shouting at the top of their lungs and bringing their feet down hard.

An angry group appeared beside the road. "Nigger lovers!" "Goddam abolish!" "Goddam Dutchmen!" and other insults showered the marching men, but they stared stonily straight ahead and drowned out the shouts with their roared chant, *"One, two, three, four!"*

Tom noticed that the group fell silent after the column passed. He expected more of it, but fewer men appeared along the road as the column progressed farther up the slope, and there were no more jeers or insults. When he reached the next to last company, no one was along the road. He heard Kemper's shouts and out of the corner of his eye saw him hustling men about and lining them up with the aid of Owen and some other officers, who seemed to be leaving the rough stuff to Kemper. Tom knew then that the last company would be standing quietly in ranks, and it was, all but one man sitting on the ground, groaning and holding his head.

The column reached the headquarters tent by the big fire, where the road turned sharply to the left, to go down a slope and be lost in the darkness of the woods. Here Tom halted his men, faced them about, and started back. There was much less disorder by now. Kemper had the second company in order and was starting on the third, which had suddenly become rather docile. Farther down the road, some of the other companies were still milling about and keeping up something of a clamor, but each was in its own area. Tom drowned them out by having the time counted again.

When the company reached its own area at the foot of the slope, Tom decided to march back to the headquarters tent for effect, then wait there until things quieted down enough to take his men to their tents and let them fall out. He soon saw it wouldn't be necessary to count the time. The uproar had almost died away.

Major Owen joined him before the halfway point was reached. "Capital idea, this march past!" he exclaimed. "It's helped a lot."

"I thought it would," replied Tom.

Owen looked like a new man. "And that loading in nine times! They heard it, or heard about it, and it really quieted them down. They thought your men would fire if it came to that, especially the Germans."

"Yes, sir, but I'm glad it didn't come to that."

The column reached the bend in the road where the big fire was by the headquarters tent. Tom halted the men, faced them about, and put them at rest in place.

Owen was staring around the bend in the road off into the darkness. "What in the world!" he suddenly exclaimed.

Tom moved away from the fire to where he could see better and saw what looked like the head of a column approaching out of the darkness with bayonets fixed. "Who's that?" he asked in astonishment. "Why are they coming like that?"

They moved farther from the fire. "Oh, my God!" gasped Owen. "It's that Yankee regiment! Keep your men turned the other way! If they see them, they'll attack them as sure as the devil!"

Owen was right. They hated the Yankees anyhow, and if they saw them coming at them like that, there would be no holding them.

Tom could see there was no danger unless the Yankees got a lot closer, though. Only the rear rank of his company was at the top of the slope where there was a view down the other side, and those men wouldn't be able to see much, because the fire was between them and the approaching column. They were Grim's men, too, and less likely to do anything.

Owen was heading down the road to meet the oncoming column, and Tom ran to catch up. There was enough light to see a tall, thin officer accompanied by a smaller one a considerable distance out in front. When they saw Tom and Owen dashing toward them, the tall fellow halted the column and the two came on to meet them.

"By whose orders are you here, sir, and what are you going to do?" asked Owen in an agitated voice.

There was no reply until the two men came up close and stopped. "I am here by no one's orders," announced the tall fellow, "and I am going to put down a mutiny among a bunch of Indiana copperheads!" Although they were at the bottom of the slope, there was enough light to see that he was a colonel with a long face and a beaklike nose and that his companion was a fresh-faced, boyish-looking major.

Owen was horrified. "No! No! That's the worst possible thing! My men will fight! There'll be bloodshed!"

The colonel's face twisted. "The glorious day has finally come, the day all loyal men have been waiting for! The slaves have been freed, and your men mutiny!" The high, nasal voice dripped with contempt.

"You don't understand my men," began Owen.

"Oh yes, I do! They're proslavery ruffians and copperheads, that's what they are! They're traitors, every one of them!" The man's eyes had the glare of a fanatic. "They must be punished!" he shrieked. Tom was glad the fellow was facing away from his men and that they were too far to hear him very well. Otherwise some of his officers might take it on themselves to join him.

"But there's no mutiny!" protested Owen, "So please—"

The colonel cut him off again. "Oh yes, there is! One of your own men came and told us there was, and we heard it before we were halfway here!"

Tom wouldn't have thought there was a man in the regiment who would do such a thing, but there was. He was undoubtedly some sneak who had been ostracized because of his radicalism and had seized a chance for revenge.

"That man lied!" insisted Owen. "there never was a mutiny! The men just got stirred up and noisy, but they're quiet now, so please go back, for God's sake, before there's trouble!"

The colonel advanced on Owen until Tom thought he would run into him. "I know better than that, Major! I heard it myself! There's a mutiny of disloyal men up there, and I'm going to put it down with my loyal sons of Massachusetts!" He thrust his hatchet face close to Owen's. "Now get out of the way, or I'll march my men right over you!"

Tom saw something had to be done. He stepped forward so the colonel would be between him and the waiting column, drew his revolver, and thrust the muzzle into the man's stomach. "Listen, Colonel," he grated. "You're going to tell this boy major of yours to go back, face your regiment about, and march it back to camp, or I'm going to kill you." He thrust his face up to the colonel's and fixed his eyes.

The Massachusetts man's mouth fell open, and his breath blew in Tom's face. It smelled sickeningly like medicine. The glaring eyes didn't waver, though. "Are you threatening my life, you dirty Indiana—"

Tom cocked his revolver and the click stopped him. "I'll take your life in a few more seconds, Colonel. I'll blow your guts out. I've already killed better men than you, men who'd be peacefully at home if it hadn't been for fellows like you." It wasn't only that. Fanatics like this had caused the war that had wrecked his life. His finger tightened on the trigger.

The colonel saw death in Tom's eyes, and his defiance abruptly evaporated with an involuntary shudder.

Tom knew he had won. "Just stand there like you are, Colonel. Don't make a move. Now, tell this boy major to go back and face those men about, just like nothing happened, and march them back to camp. Don't move a muscle, or I'll pull this trigger."

The colonel knew he would do it. "Very . . . very well. Major Lowell," he said shakily, "face the regiment about and march it back to camp, or this . . . this criminal will kill me."

"All the way back to camp!" barked Tom, giving the man a thrust with the muzzle of his revolver. "And fall them out when they get there!"

"All the way back to camp, and . . . and fall them out," gasped the colonel.

The boy major seemed paralyzed. "Why-why—" he stammered.

"Major, if you don't want to see me blow this man's guts out, you'll do as you're told!" snarled Tom. "And don't you say a word about this, or I'll come after you, too!"

"Yes-yes-yes, sir," stuttered the major. He turned and started back to the waiting regiment.

"In the meantime, Colonel, you just stay like you are," said Tom with cold menace.

The man started to say something, but a nudge of the revolver muzzle stopped him.

They heard commands in a shrill, shaky voice, and the Massachusetts men faced about and marched back the way they had come. As soon as they were far enough, Tom let down the hammer of his revolver and holstered the weapon. "I'm sorry I had to do that, Colonel," he said evenly.

The colonel regained his courage with a rush. "You'll be a lot sorrier when I get through with you, Lieutenant!" His voice rose to a screech. "Threatening a superior officer! Pushing the barrel of a cocked revolver into his chest!" His eyes were glaring again, and spittle dripped from the corners of his mouth. "I'll have you court-martialed! I'll have you shot!"

"I'm ready to take my medicine," replied Tom calmly, "but I had to do it." He looked the livid Yankee in the eye. "If it costs me my life, so be it. I saved our men and yours from killing each other, and God only knows what that would have led to."

Owen finally spoke up. "He's right, absolutely right! And he saved you from ruining yourself, Colonel. There would've been shooting if you'd gone fifty feet further." He pointed toward where the rear ranks of Tom's company could be seen by the fire at the top of the slope. "Those men there have their rifles loaded and their bayonets fixed. They wouldn't have gotten out of the way. No one could have made them get out of the way."

The colonel gave Owen a baleful look. "So you concur in the action of this criminal lieutenant of yours!"

"Absolutely! It had to be done. I regret it as much as anyone, but there was no other way to stop you. You must've been insane!"

"Very well," was the cold reply. "I shall prefer charges against you also, for aiding and encouraging an assault on a superior officer."

Tom saw that apologies and reasoning had no effect on this fellow. "Just wait a minute, Colonel!" he barked, and the man jumped like a revolver had been shoved into his stomach again. "How do you think this is going to sound to Colonel Rivers and General Carter? Who else is going to be court-martialed when they hear you tried to invade a camp in a hostile manner over the protests of its rightful commander and start a war among our own troops?" He snorted. "I'll be court-martialed, and maybe Major Owen, too, but yours will come right afterwards!"

The Massachusetts man was shaken but tried not to show it. "I don't care—" he began.

Owen broke in. "Just listen a minute, Colonel. You don't hear any noise from my camp, do you? Everything's quiet, isn't it? There never was a mutiny. Five hundred men will swear to that." He nodded grimly. "You'll get the same medicine we will, only a bigger dose of it. General Carter will see to that."

The man was beginning to see the light. "But I was only—"

Owen interrupted again. "You were only doing what you thought was right at the moment, Colonel. But you were wrong, dead wrong. You realize that now, don't you? The lieutenant here did the only thing that could be done to prevent a frightful tragedy. You had let yourself get so carried away that there was no other way to stop you."

"Colonel," said Tom evenly, "why don't we just forget it ever happened? I will, Major Owen will, and you can do the same. The only other person who knows what happened is Major Lowell, and you can see to it that he forgets it, too."

The Yankee colonel was weakening rapidly but hesitated to speak, and Owen preempted him. "If you go ahead and prefer charges against us, the whole thing will be aired out, and I really think you'll come out of it worse than the lieutenant or I will."

The Massachusetts man began pacing about in the light of the distant fire, head down and hands behind his back. He stopped and looked off the way his men had gone, then turned to face Tom and Owen. "Very well, that's the way it will be!" he snapped. "But if I ever see either of you again, it'll be once too much!" He glared at them, wheeled, and started back the way he had come.

They watched him disappear into the darkness. Suddenly Owen seized Tom's hand and began pumping it. "My God, Traylor! I thank you! I thank you! I'd never have done what you did! I just couldn't do such a thing!"

It was the first time Tom had ever heard Owen speak like that. "Yes, sir," said Tom with a sigh. "Let's just hope it all blows over now." Owen's complete shedding of his normal reserve surprised him.

Owen looked toward the fire at the top of the slope. "I don't think any of your men saw anything, and we're too far away for them to hear." He looked the way the Yankee colonel had gone. "I just hope that fellow's men didn't catch on either."

"I don't think they did, sir, or some of them would've done something, some of the officers anyhow. They probably think it was just an argument."

Owen nodded. "I sure hope you're right. If it gets out, the high rankers might feel they had to do something about it." He looked at Tom strangely. "But how could you do a thing like that, stick a revolver in a colonel's stomach? I can't understand how a man could do something like that."

"It was the only way I could think of to stop the damned fool," Tom replied, "and it had to be done."

Owen nodded. "Yes, yes, there'd have been a bloody battle if they'd gone on. Your men were the only ones who had ammunition, but the others all have bayonets, and they'd have used them on those Yankees."

Owen had let himself be sidetracked, and Tom was glad of it. A man whose past had been wiped out and who had no future could do anything, but you didn't talk about things like that. He went on before

Owen could get back on thc track. "I just can't understand a fellow like that Yankee colonel. You'd think he has no sense at all. Who is he, anyhow?"

"Winthrop's his name." Owen shook his head. "Oh, he's got plenty of sense all right. He's a professor at Harvard. I guess he just doesn't know how to use it."

"Well, I hope he uses it enough to keep his mouth shut about this."

"Oh, he will. He couldn't stand the humiliation, and then those New England fellows are scared to death of General Carter because of what he did to Stamford."

"What's that?"

"Well, Stamford's friends in high places can't do anything for him except arrange for him to resign. They can't save him from a court-martial if he doesn't, and they know he'd be convicted as sure as the devil. They say General Carter went to McClellan himself about it and got his full backing."

Tom laughed shortly. "That ought to take care of Colonel Winthrop, and I guess he'll keep that boy major quiet, too."

"Oh yes, we can count on that. Major Lowell was a student of his, and kind of a . . . a protegé, I guess. I've heard they're so . . . so fond of each other that women don't interest them."

Tom was so revolted he almost wished he had shot the loathsome creature. "Oh, God!" was all he could say.

Owen quickly changed the subject. "Well, I guess you can take your men back to their quarters and let them fall out. Everything seems to be quiet now."

It was. The road running in front of the camp was empty, the men were in their tents, and regular guards paced their lines. They met Kemper on the way, and he agreed that it was all over. He added his congratulations to Owen's, and they meant a great deal more to Tom. Kemper also said that Colonel Rivers was on his way to camp, which sent Owen hurrying to the headquarters tent. Tom knew he hadn't sent for the colonel, though, because he wouldn't want Rivers to think he couldn't handle his men by himself.

Tom didn't want to be around when Rivers arrived, so he dismissed his men and headed for his tent as soon as they reached their company area. Rivers might ask too many questions, and Owen was the fellow to answer them anyhow.

Before he could turn in, Billy came to see him. "Lootenant, sir, some uv Grim's men says that they was somethin' that went on 'tween you an' Major Owen an' some fellers that looked like they wuz headed fer camp, on down th' road frum whar they wuz up thar b'fore we come back hyar."

Tom felt a thrill of fear. "Yes?"

"Grim wanted me t' ast if'n you wanted enything said 'bout hit er eny questions ast. Hit ain't got b'yond him an' a few uv his men an' me yit, an' he says he'll stop hit right thar if'n you says to."

Tom blessed the dark little German. "Tell him I don't want another word said about it, Billy. It was just something those men imagined, if you know what I mean."

"Yes, sir, I'll tell him, an' he'll see to hit that they ain't."

Tom reached for his brother's hand. "Thanks, Billy, and thank Sergeant Grim for me."

Billy started back and Tom could finally bed down. The day was over.

# 28

A few days after the trouble about the president's proclamation, Tom was called to the headquarters tent. He was afraid the chickens had come home to roost, so he wore sword and revolver to make a good appearance.

General Carter and Colonel Rivers were there along with Major Owen, and the obvious good humor of the last two reassured him.

"Well, sir!" exclaimed Rivers, ignoring Tom's salute and extending his hand. "You've made a fine-looking officer, I see, and a very good one, from what I hear!"

"Thank you, sir," said Tom as they shook hands. He blessed Hauser for his appearance and Owen for his reputation. He expected General Carter to say something similar, but he didn't, and it brought back his worry. Rivers and Owen left to look over the camp, leaving him alone with Carter.

"Come inside a minute, Lieutenant," said Carter. He entered the tent and seated himself behind a small table. "Sit down," he said brusquely, indicating an ammunition box in front of the table. Corporal Stevens was nowhere in evidence, and Tom found himself wishing that he wasn't all alone with the general.

"I want to talk with you a little while," said Carter in the same abrupt fashion.

"Yes, sir." Tom began to get scared all over again, and it didn't help to tell himself that generals probably always acted like this.

"How do you feel about what happened the night of the big uproar, Lieutenant?" asked Carter.

Tom wondered how much he knew. "I'm glad it's all over, sir," was all he could say.

"You're wondering how much I know, aren't you?" The little face was hard and the eyes sharp.

Tom could only say, "Yes, sir," and feel a sinking sensation.

Carter looked at him silently for a moment. "I know it all, Lieutenant," he finally said. "I have ways of finding things out."

Tom felt like he would sink through the floor of the tent. "Well, I don't feel very good about what happened then." That wouldn't let him all the way in.

"What in particular don't you feel very good about?" came the sharp query.

"About what I had to do." He was being drawn in deeper.

"What *did* you have to do?"

He decided to make a clean breast of it. Carter knew everything anyhow, and he would at least go down with colors flying. "Drawing my revolver on Colonel Winthrop." He had done it, and could see himself before a court-martial with his commission and all the baubles that went with it gone.

Carter got up abruptly and walked about while the tent whirled around Tom. "That was a terrible thing. I've been in the army since I was a boy, and I've never heard of anything like it." He stopped and confronted Tom. "How do you really feel about it?" he demanded. "Aren't you really proud of it? Wouldn't you like to boast about it if you dared, doing a full colonel like you did?"

"No, sir. I feel terrible about it." He got up and faced Carter, whose hat brim only came up to his chin. "I'm ready to take my medicine, sir," he said evenly as he unbuckled his belt. He laid it and his weapons on the table. "I'm ready to go."

"You have it coming, don't you, Lieutenant?"

"Yes, sir, I do." He faced Carter and looked him unwaveringly in the eye. The general turned down the corners of his mouth and looked back at him. He could see the black muzzles of the firing squad staring him in the face, but the disgrace to Billy and his father would be worse.

Carter gestured imperatively. "Sit down, Lieutenant. I'm not done with you yet."

"I'm not going to sit down, sir. Call the guard and put me under arrest. I want to get it over with."

The general threw back his head. "So you defy me?"

"Sir, I see no reason to prolong this."

"Do you know what the penalty will be?"

"Yes, sir. I will be shot."

Carter let him stand there while he walked around again. "Tell me, Lieutenant, would you do it again?"

"Yes, sir, I would."

"And know you'd be shot for it?"

"I don't know. I can't say for sure, but I believe I would."

"Why?"

"I believe I'd rather lose my life than see our men killing one another."

Carter came up to him, cocked his head back, and looked him in the eye. "You're telling me the truth, aren't you? You really mean it."

"Yes, sir, I do." He looked steadfastly into the general's eyes. "If the general has had his fun, I'd like to go. Call the guard, please."

"So you think I'm doing this because I enjoy it?" came the angry query.

"I can see no other reason for the general putting me through this. He knows the facts of the case."

Carter thrust his face closer. "Don't you want to say anything about Major Owen? He was with you. Wasn't it his idea? Isn't he really to blame?"

"No, sir, it was entirely my idea."

"But he didn't try to stop you, and he's your superior officer. Doesn't that make him as guilty as you?"

"No, sir. I did it, and I am solely responsible for it." He looked Carter in the eye. "Please, sir, call the guard."

Carter underwent a sudden metamorphosis. He broke into a smile, seized Tom's hand, and pumped it enthusiastically. "You're a fine young man, Lieutenant Traylor," he said feelingly. "Nothing's going to happen to you. I just wanted to satisfy myself about you." He gestured toward the table. "Put your sword and revolver back on and sit down."

Tom could scarcely believe it. He felt numb and was surprised that he was able to put his belt back on without a fumble. He sat down not knowing what to think. It was like one of those nightmares you wake up from.

Carter sat across from him, his foxy face smiling. "Lieutenant, I want to apologize for putting you through what I did. You probably think I'm a cruel fellow, and I can't say that I blame you."

"The general no doubt had his reasons," said Tom as relief began to flood through him. He would get maudlin unless he was careful.

"Yes, I did. We've got a lot of officers that aren't fit for their commissions." He smiled at Tom. "I'm glad you aren't one of them. That's what I was trying to find out."

Tom could only think it was a little late for that and say, "Thank you, sir."

"Many men would have lied and denied the whole thing." He laughed. "I had no real proof of what happened. I just made an assumption from what I know did happen." Tom was astonished to hear this but decided to let the general confuse stupidity with honesty if he wanted to.

Carter went on. "Other men would have tried to justify what they did. More would have tried to blame Major Owen, or at least implicate him." He nodded. "You were honest and took it all on yourself. You knew you had committed a very serious breach of discipline and you were ready to suffer the penalty, although you still thought you'd done the right thing."

The general got up and started walking around again. "That shows you understand something that few men do, that discipline and subordination are the heart and soul of an army." He nodded thoughtfully. "That also shows that you understand something even fewer men do, that the army is more important than any man in it, and that it may be necessary to punish a man unjustly for the army's sake, maybe even to execute him."

"Yes, sir, but I couldn't say it as well as the general has."

Carter sat down opposite Tom. "Now we come to the real reason why I did what I did to you. Owen and Rivers want to make you a captain right off because of how you handled that disturbance about the proclamation the other night. Owen's convinced you prevented a mutiny."

"I'm obliged to them, sir, but I think the credit should go to my men."

"Don't be so modest!" scoffed Carter. "Your men are the same kind of fellows the others are, no better and no worse!" He nodded vigorously. "It's just that you kept them under control and the other officers couldn't. Major Owen says he believes they would have put down a mutiny if there had been one."

"Yes, sir, but we really don't know. It never actually came to that."

"Well, Owen credits you with the fact that it didn't. He told me about your having your men load by the numbers and then marching them up and down in front of the others counting the time. He says that really quieted things down."

"Yes, sir. I believe it helped."

"Well, back to this business of making you a captain. Owen and Rivers wanted to do it right off, but I wanted to size you up first." He laughed. "I was afraid you might be some pistol-wielding ruffian who had his men terrorized and jumped at the chance to buffalo a superior officer. I'm old-fashioned enough to think that an officer should be a gentleman." He smiled at Tom. "You qualify."

"Thank you, sir."

"So, I'm going to push your captain's commission. That means you'll get it in a few days. You'd have gotten it in time anyhow, so I don't think there'll be any trouble about it."

"Thank you, sir. I'll be much obliged to you."

Carter grinned. "I suppose you think you've more than earned it here today."

Tom sighed. "Yes, sir. I'd rather not be promoted again if it comes as hard as this."

Carter laughed and slapped the table. "Oh, I don't blame you, but after what you did to Winthrop, I felt I had to do what I did." He started laughing again and couldn't stop. "Oh, I'd give a thousand dollars if I could've seen it! He's such a pompous ass—" He had to stop and laugh some more. "Oh, oh," he cackled, "I can just see him, with his mouth hanging open and his eyes popping out!" He stopped and wiped his eyes."You'd have to know the fellow to appreciate it." Suddenly he sobered. "Imagine a man—a colonel—so stupid he'd start a war among our own troops!" He shook his head. "You have to understand, Lieutenant, that some of these fellows are just foisted on us, particularly these New Englanders. We don't have anything to say about it."

Tom nodded. "Yes, sir, I understand. It's politics."

Carter sighed. "Politics! It'll be the ruin of us, I'm afraid." He sighed again and shook his head with resignation. "There's nothing we can do about it, though. We've just got to put up with it and make out the best we can.

"Now," said Carter, "as I understand it, no one knows anything about what happened between you and Winthrop but you two, that major of his, and of course Major Owen and myself."

"Yes, sir, that's the way I understand it, too."

Carter nodded. "Yes, none of the men do, yours or his. His think it was just an argument, and I guess yours do, too." He looked at Tom sharply. "Now, we want to keep it that way. If it gets out, somebody might feel he has to do something about it. You understand that, don't you?"

"Yes, sir, I'll be as quiet as the grave; you can depend on that." He shuddered. "I hope I never hear a whisper about it."

"Well, you can depend on Winthrop keeping quiet, and that major of his, too. They know what would happen to Winthrop if it got out." He shook his head. "I ought to do something about that fellow, Winthrop I mean, but I can't or the whole thing would be brought out, and God knows what would come of it. I've been keeping my eye on him for a good while, though, and I'd already made up my mind to get rid of him the first chance I got. I'm just sorry I can't take advantage of this one."

Tom guessed that was because Carter knew what Owen did about Winthrop and his major.

The general smiled brightly. "Well, I guess I'm done with you, young man." They both got up, and Carter extended his hand. "I'm glad I got to know you, Lieutenant Traylor, but I doubt if you feel the same way about me," he said as they shook hands.

"I understand, sir. I harbor no ill feelings." Tom saluted and said, "Thank you very much, sir."

Carter looked at him smilingly. "For not having you shot or for the promotion?"

"For both, sir."

Carter laughed and waved him away. "That's all right, son. You got what you deserve."

Tom's legs were still shaky as he walked back to his company.

# 29

The people of Dubois County were having a meeting at Jasper to honor their war dead. Most of them were from the company the county had given to the regiment Congressman Baker had christened the Pride of the Pocket. The regiment had suffered heavy losses, mostly in the two recent battles of the Second Bull Run and Antietam, and the county had come in for its full share.

A few buggies and other vehicles made their way from the northeastern part of the county along the shortest route, which forded the Patoka and went on through Knoxville, crossing the river again when it reached Jasper, but this time on a bridge.

John Traylor had hired a surrey at French Lick, ostensibly to accommodate some neighbors making the trip, but really to avoid making it alone with his wife. In the backseat were Jim and Mary Polson and Jim's father, old Uncle Charley. Rob Sanders, whose son George had been killed in the spring, rode in the front seat with John and Sarah. They had started a little after daybreak and didn't expect to get back before dark.

Five of the six people in the surrey conversed in desultory fashion as John drove the horses over the rough and rutted road. "I'm sure glad it's a pretty day," remarked John. "I'd hate t' make this trip in bad weather, even if this thing's got a top on it." His wife said nothing. She sat silent and withdrawn like she always did anymore.

"Yeah, hit shore is a purty day," replied Rob Sanders. "Th' leaves has started t' turn an' fall, though." He sighed. "Bad weather'll be on us b'fore long."

"I see Herb Fairbanks has got a new buggy," observed John as a vehicle came out from a side road some distance ahead and turned in front of them. Herb didn't know the strange surrey behind him, or he would have stopped to let it catch up. Ordinarily John would have speeded up to overtake him and have company as they went on, but he didn't want to do it now with Sarah the way she was.

"Yes, his boy was spared," sighed Mary Polson from the backseat. "They say he'll be able t' go back with th' comp'ny right away now." She spoke in a resigned fashion that showed her own loss.

"John, you 'n' Sary has been awful lucky," ventured Rob. "Tom an' Billy has come through hit all 'thout a scratch."

"I know," replied John. "Th' Lord has protected 'em." Sarah stared unseeingly at the color-splashed woods along the road and said nothing.

"An' Tom gittin' t' be an officer, too," spoke up old Uncle Charley. "I'd like t' see him in his uniform, with sword an' all."

Sarah spoke in a dead voice. "I'll never see him again, him or Billy either." They were her first words, and John wished she hadn't spoken.

"Now, Mother," he sighed. "You mustn't lose hope an' talk like that. It just makes you feel bad, an' th' rest of us, too."

"You ought t' be happy they're still alive," sobbed Mary. "My Jim's dead an' far away, an' we'll never see him again." Her husband embraced her and old Uncle Charley bowed his head.

"There's no use bein' happy b'cause they're still alive when you know they're goin' t' get killed," said Sarah in the same leaden tones.

John didn't reply this time, and none of the others said anything either. He had learned a good while ago that there was no use trying to reason with his wife. People said she was "tetched," and they were right. His life had become a misery of loneliness and worry since she had gotten that way. Then that trouble with the Dixons had come to make it worse. He had had to mortgage his farm to put up that peace bond old Calvin had made him take out, but Sarah didn't know anything about it. He had kept it from her, and no one else had told her either.

Sarah's last remark all but killed further conversation, and scarcely anything was said the rest of the way to Jasper. When they arrived at the courthouse, where the people were gathering, John let everybody out and went back to the river they had just crossed to water the horses. The river was low and he got his boots muddy, so he had to take time to clean them. Afterward he drove back to the courthouse and was lucky enough to find someone just backing out of a place along the hitching rails near the square. He hoped he would find Sarah in one of the groups of women scattered about talking, but he should have known better. She stood alone near where she had alighted, her eyes fixed in a blank, unseeing stare. He took her arm and moved closer to the platform in front of the courthouse because the ceremonies were about to begin. He wished that Mary had stayed with her but could understand why she hadn't.

He saw men he knew standing around talking and would have liked to join them, but if he left Sarah she would be alone and attract attention by her silent, vacant manner. Men would catch his eye and nod but immediately look away. It hurt him because he knew they felt sorry for him. He just hoped they wouldn't meet any people who hadn't seen them since the war started. They might remark that they wouldn't have known Sarah if she hadn't been with him. It had happened because she had changed so much. Although she paid no more attention to such remarks than she did to anything else, they always pained him. Before the war men used to joke with him about being married to a woman who looked young enough to be his daughter. It wasn't that he looked old, but because she seemed so young and lively. They wouldn't do that anymore. She was getting to look more like his mother than his daughter. It wasn't just that her hair had whitened and she was getting wrinkles. She acted like an old woman and paid little attention to how she looked anymore.

A voice broke into his thoughts. "Mr. Traylor?"

He looked up to see a portly, well-dressed man he didn't know. "Yes, sir?" He took the man's extended hand, but Sarah paid no attention.

"My name is Anders," said the man as they shook hands. He had a friendly manner and looked sympathetically at Sarah.

"Oh yes, you're Gerda's father. Billy wrote us about you. You're a doctor, right?"

"Yes, I'm Gerda's father." He smiled. "It seems that our young people may be getting in the way of marriage." He spoke the correct, slightly accented English of an educated man who had learned it as a foreign language.

John laughed. "Yes, I guess they are, even if it's been mostly by mail. They've seen each other only a time or two."

The doctor nodded. "Our young people live only from day to day since the war began. They waste no time." He sighed and shook his head.

"Yes, I guess that's right." John turned to his wife. "Sarah, this is Dr. Anders, Gerda's father."

She didn't respond. "Mother, don't you want to meet Gerda's father that Billy wrote us about?" He had to nudge her to get her attention.

She looked around, dead-eyed and silent. With great embarrassment, John had to repeat himself. She turned indifferently, bowed jerkily, and looked away without saying a word. John didn't know what to say.

"Your wife, she is ill," murmured the doctor sympathetically.

"It's her mind, sir, worryin' about th' boys."

"Yes, I understand. It affects the ladies more than we men. They are mothers and have stronger feelings." He shook his head. "There is much of it because we have lost so many."

"Is that right? I thought she was prob'ly the only one."

Anders shook his head again. "In most cases it is not so apparent, but there are many mothers who suffer so. As a doctor, I know."

John glimpsed a ray of hope. "Do you think you could do anything for her, sir?"

"We will talk after the meeting. Wait, and I bring my wife and daughter. I cannot do it now because the ceremonies begin already." He went away through the crowd.

The Jasper *Männerchor,* made up of older men, opened the observance with a hymn. At least that was what John thought it was, because he couldn't understand German. It was beautiful, though, almost like the music of instruments.

John was too preoccupied to pay much attention to the early speakers, although he pretended to listen. Sarah didn't even do that. Two of them were clergymen, a Catholic priest and a Lutheran minister, both of whom spoke in German. There was a translator, a rotund white-haired fellow who put what they said into impeccable English, so impeccable it didn't sound natural.

Translations into German interrupted the main speaker, a member of the state legislature. He would speak a little while, then pause for the translator. John's attention would wander during the translation, and about the time he would begin to follow the speaker again another translation would commence. It seemed to be the kind of war speech he had already heard enough of, though, so he didn't feel he was missing much.

The only speaker who captured John's attention and held it was the last one. He was the Reverend Howard Stevens, a one-legged Mexican War veteran who had moved down from neighboring Orange County after taking the church where old Mr. Cowder had preached before he died over a year ago. This was the church John's family had always belonged to, but he and Sarah didn't attend anymore. He felt bad about it, but she never wanted to go, and when they did it was a trial for him, because she behaved the same way in church she did everywhere else.

After the introduction, Stevens stumped forward on his wooden leg, stopped, and looked out over the crowd for a few moments. He wore a black broadcloth suit, which heightened the arresting impression made by his tall, bony form and craggy features.

"We are gathered to commemorate our honored dead," he began in his deep, sepulchral voice, "the young men of this county who have given their lives that this Union might live." The translation didn't bother John at all this time.

"They went from us full of life, vigor, and manly courage," Stevens went on, "but they will never return." Several women began to weep softly, but Sarah only stared at the front of the courthouse with dull, uncomprehending eyes.

"The woods and fields which knew them will know them no more, and their feet will never again tread the paths they trod." This time Stevens bowed his head while the translator spoke, and John suddenly noticed that it had become almost dark. He looked up to see that a bank of clouds had moved over the sun. Of course, it seemed darker than it was because of the contrast with the previous sunny brilliance of the day.

"But they will live in our memory," Stevens went on, "and we will see their dear young faces as long as life lasts."

There was more weeping, and not only by women.

"Let us hope that future generations will cherish their memory, as we do, because it is for them the sacrifice has been made. These young men we mourn gave their lives that this country might once again be united, might enjoy peace and prosperity and rise to greatness among the nations of mankind."

Stevens raised his voice. "May we and our descendants be worthy of these splendid young men who gave their lives for us, and for them! May our leaders be worthy of them! May their minds be cleansed of politics and prejudice!" He threw up an arm. "May they choose generals who are wise and able, generals who *will not* throw away the lives of our sons by foolish mistake and stupid error!"

There were enough nods and knowing looks to show the reference was understood.

Stevens lowered his voice, but it carried a note of imperative urgency. "May the minds of our leaders be opened to thoughts of peace such as the Son of God urged upon us. May they seek a bloodless reconciliation with our erring brethren of the South. May this dreadful brothers' war be stopped and thousands of young lives saved, the lives of our sons and those of our kinsmen of the South."

Heads bobbed and signs of fervent agreement swept the crowd. The only ones showing signs of dissent were a few men from the nearby community of Ireland. They made angry grimaces and looked significantly at one another. John wondered if they would have enough sense to keep quiet. If they didn't, they would probably get beaten up before they left town.

Stevens bowed his head. "Let us pray," sounded hollowly, and every head bowed. "O God, we pray that Thou wilt take these, our sons who have fallen, to be with Thee in heaven, for they gave their lives for us, as did Thy Son upon the cross."

As on signal, the clouds passed and the gloom was suddenly transformed into bright sunlight, but a deep hush broken only by subdued sounds of weeping persisted for long moments after Stevens turned and stumped away.

The *Männerchor* sang to close the observance. It was a dirge so sad and beautiful that the weeping was no longer subdued. John caught only the recurring word *Kamerad* or *Kameraden* and gathered it was an old soldiers' lament. The Germans, even the men, were strongly affected, and several of them wept along with the women. It made John feel like weeping, too, all the more because Sarah gave no sign of even hearing it.

The ceremonies were over, but most stood motionless for a time, many wiping tears and stifling sobs. Even after people started moving about to disperse, Sarah still stood staring unseeingly before her until John took her arm.

Before they were able to move very far, Dr. Anders was back, this time with his wife and daughter. John bowed and said the appropriate things when the doctor introduced them, but Sarah only bobbed mechanically and continued her leaden stare.

The other two women murmured sympathetically in German and took Sarah apart. John thought Gerda was sure a pretty girl, and a nice one, too, but she was so young. She really wasn't much younger than Billy, though. Mrs. Anders didn't seem to be able to speak any English, but Gerda spoke it well. The mother was able to make her feelings clear anyhow, and both of them embraced Sarah.

"You must stay for dinner," insisted Anders, "and spend the night with us if you can."

"I'm sorry, sir, but we can't. I've brought four other people along, and I promised to take them back right after th' meetin'."

"I am also sorry. Perhaps you can come another time."

"Yes, sir, we'll sure try to." John straightened his shoulders and looked earnestly at Anders. "Like I asked you before, Doctor, do you think you can do anything for my wife? You see what shape she's in."

Anders nodded gravely. "Her sickness is of the mind, and I know little about such illnesses. I treat only those of the body."

"There's no hope, then?"

"No, I would not say that. There is hope. People may be cured of illnesses of the mind. It has been done."

"But you can't do it?"

The doctor sighed. "I do not know. I have never undertaken to treat an illness of the mind, but there are men who do."

"Where?"

"In Europe, in particular at Vienna, in Austria."

John shook his head. "I guess there is no hope, then. I can't take her all the way over there."

"That will not be necessary. I will do what I can, and I am not entirely without knowledge of such matters." He frowned thoughtfully and went on. "As a young man, I was interested in them. I wanted to study in the field of mental illness and went to Vienna, where there are men who say they understand the mind and can treat its illnesses like others treat those of the body." He shook his head. "After studying under these men for a time, I came to believe that it was not possible to do what they said they could and left them."

"But you've changed your mind since then?"

"Yes, I have. I was a young man then and too impatient. I returned to Germany and studied medicine. As I studied, I began to think that they might be right, those men who say it is possible to cure an illness of the mind. Now that I have practiced medicine for over twenty years, I am convinced that they are right." He paused and sighed. "A sick mind may be cured, but it is very difficult, because it is a science which is still in a primitive stage, like medicine a hundred years ago."

John felt a little hope. "Yes, sir," he said.

"The practice of medicine has taught me much more than I learned at Vienna, but yet—" He shrugged and failed to finish.

"Do you think you might be able to help my wife?"

"For the sake of our children, I will try."

John felt a rush of gratitude. "I'll be much obliged to you, Doctor, and I know our boys will be, too."

"You must bring her to me and leave her with me for a long time. I know enough to realize that it will take a long time, and even then we cannot be sure that she will be made well again."

"I'll take the chance!" exclaimed John fervently. "Any amount of time and any amount of money."

Anders put his hand on John's shoulder. "I will take no money, sir, not a penny. I will do it for our children, for our brave young sons who fight for the Union, and for my daughter, who loves your younger one." His eyes became misty. "Perhaps I do it for our grandchildren."

John impulsively seized his hand and shook it. "When should I bring her to you?"

"Could it be in a week, perhaps a week from today?"

"Sure," affirmed John as hope welled up within him. "Can you put her up without too much trouble?"

"Of course. I have a large house, and we can prepare a room for her. She will become one of the family. My wife and daughter will help me with her." He smiled. "Perhaps they will benefit her more than I."

John felt overwhelmed. "You've got no idea, Doctor, how much this means to me."

"I understand, sir, and I do it for you as well as our children. I only hope we can help her."

"I'm sorry, sir, but we've got folks waitin' for us, and I'm afraid we've got to go."

"Of course," replied Anders. "When you bring your wife, plan to spend the night with us at least."

"I will," John assured him as they went toward the women. John saw that Sarah was talking with them, at least with Gerda, and for once acting like she was aware of people and things. It raised his hopes even higher. "I'm sorry, Mother, but we've got to go. We've got people waitin' on us."

Sarah nodded and he thought she smiled.

"He will bring you back next week to stay with us for a while," Anders said pleasantly.

"Oh, I hope for a long time!" exclaimed Gerda. When she told her mother and her father added explanations, Mrs. Anders looked pleased. According to her daughter, she said they had just the room for Sarah and would have it all ready by the time she came.

Before they parted, Gerda and Mrs. Anders embraced Sarah, and she seemed to respond.

John took his wife to the surrey where Sanders and the Polsons waited. "I'm sorry, folks, for keepin' you waitin'."

"Oh, that's all right," replied Rob. "We've got plenty of time yet."

"We wuz entertained enyhow," cackled old Uncle Charley. "They had a fight over thar." He pointed up the street where a knot of men milled about talking loudly.

"Who was in it?" asked John as he helped Sarah to her seat.

"Oh, hit wuzn't really much," explained Jim. "Some fellers frum Ireland popped off 'bout what Preacher Stevens said 'bout makin' peace with th' Rebels. Said he wuz a traitor an' a Rebel sympathizer. Herb Fairbanks 'n' a couple uv others jumped on 'em and run 'em off." He laughed. "Wuzn't half a dozen licks hit."

"Yeah," said John as he unhitched the horses. "I saw some Ireland men lookin' like they didn't like what th' preacher said." He straightened the bridles and came back to take his seat. "I wondered if they'd have enough sense to keep their mouths shut." He laughed shortly as he took his seat and picked up the reins. "I figured they'd get beat up if they didn't."

"Oh, they didn't stay long 'nough t' git beat up," laughed Rob as their vehicle got under way. "They took right off!"

"They shore did!" whooped old Uncle Charley. "They wuz shore some tall runnin' done!"

Everybody laughed but Sarah, who had reverted to her withdrawn manner. John wasn't downcast, though, as he guided the horses around the square and out to the road.

The time they took to get out of town was taken up by Jim's remonstrances to his father about trying to get in that fight. He claimed he would have jumped out of the surrey and pitched in if it hadn't been for him.

"Now, Pa," he said,"you cain't go 'round mixin' up in ever' fight y' see like y' did when y' wuz young. Yo're too old, way too old, fer that kinda stuff."

Old Uncle Charley didn't deign to reply. He just wagged his beard and looked at the houses along the road.

"That was Dr. Anders you was talkin' to, wasn't it, John?" asked Mary after a while. He replied that she was right and told her about taking Sarah to stay with the Anderses while the doctor tried to help her.

"He's sure a good doctor, they say," replied Mary.

"I've heered Doc Bowes that I've knowed fer forty year say he wuz," interjected Uncle Charley. "He says they've got th' best schools fer doctors in Germany that they is in th' world."

"I sure hope he kin help ye, Sarah," said Mary, but Sarah gave no indication of hearing her.

"That's all right, Mary," said John. "Th' poor thing don't seem t' know what's goin' on, but I've got hope for her now." He did, and that was why he felt better than he had for months on the way back home. It made him feel light-headed to think of the chance that Sarah might get well again. He was so distracted he didn't join in when the other three men got to talking about how they agreed with what Preacher Stevens had said about peace, although he certainly felt the same way.

# 30

The night John came back from taking Sarah to stay with the Anderses, he went to bed feeling better than he had even since the meeting at Jasper. The doctor and his family had taken Sarah into a house where everything was nicer than she was used to and had been very hospitable about it. Although she seemed no better than usual at the time, her new surroundings and the company she would have gave John the idea that they alone might help. He believed the lonely life she had led since the boys had left might be a cause of her trouble.

John had been asleep for several hours when noise on the road in front woke him up. He could hear men talking and horses moving about. He reached for the revolver he kept hanging by the bed just as someone called his name. He hurriedly put on his clothes, left the house by the back door, and slipped around to the front, where he could look out from around a corner of the house. A man couldn't take chances in these troubled times. He could see men on horseback on the road in the dim light of the stars, and an occasional gleam showed they carried weapons.

"John! Hey, John Traylor!" came out again.

He thought he recognized the voice but had to make sure. "Who is it?"

"Hit's Ben Dickens an' some uv yore nabors!"

John thrust the revolver into his waistband and went toward the road. "What d'you want, Ben?"

"They've 'rested Preacher Howard an' we're gonna do somethin' 'bout hit," came another voice John recognized as Rob Sanders's.

"Preacher Howard Stevens? Who 'rested him? Why?" John asked as he came up to the horsemen.

"Soljers done hit, under that Tom Cartwright frum Paoli."

"Why? What's he done?"

"We dunno, 'lessen hit's 'cause of what he said at Jasper a week 'go." It was Ab Nickerson, who lived a few miles away.

"We're gonna take him 'way frum 'em," said Ben Dickens, "an' 'lowed you'd like t' be in on hit."

"Yeah, hit's 'gin th Constitootion t' 'rest a feller fer jist speakin' his mind, an' then soljers done hit, an' that's th' kind uv thing we cain't stand fer!" It was Ab again, and he was angry.

"Yeah, er we'll be jist like them pore folks 'crost th' waters that's got kings an' nobles an' ain't got no rights." It was Ollie Winger, and he was angry, too.

"I 'gree with you," replied John. "We can't let 'em treat us like this, or we won't have any rights a'tall b'fore long." It would be a good idea to find out more before rushing into it, though. "How'd you find out?"

"Miz Howard went t' lil' Johnny Tacker's, th' clostest house, jist atter hit happened. He says she wuz shore skeered."

"Yeah," elaborated Ollie, "said they jist rode up an' commenced poundin' on th' door, 'n' when th' preacher went an' opened hit, they jist grabbed him, six er eight uv 'em. Let him put on his clothes 'n' took him 'way right now."

Rob went further. "He ast who they wuz an' why they wuz 'restin' him, an' Cartwright jist laffed an' said they wuz United States soljers an' no traitor need t' ast why he wuz bein' 'rested."

Ollie gave more details. "Th' preacher said he wuz a free 'merican citizen an' couldn't be 'rested by no soljers 'thout eny warrant, but they jist laffed 'n' called him a damn copperhead traitor an' took him."

John felt as indignant as anybody but wanted to know something else. "Where're they goin' with him an' where are they now?"

Ben replied, "We figger they're takin' him through French Lick an' that they're prob'ly halfway thar by now. They'll go on t' Paoli an' then t' Orleans t' ketch th' train fer Injinap'lis, either that er put him in jail at Paoli 'n' go on t'morra."

"We've got t' catch 'em b'fore they get to Paoli, then," was John's opinion.

"Yeah," agreed Ab. "If'n we don't ketch 'em 'fore then, they'll prob'ly git 'way with hit."

"Let me get my rifle an' saddle my horse," said John as he started for the house. He was thankful Sarah was gone.

By the time he got back, old Uncle Charley Polson and his son Jim had joined the group. They were late because Uncle Charley had insisted on seeing little Johnny Tacker about following the soldiers and lighting fires along the road after them to show where they were.

Jim was still protesting that a man who was over seventy years old shouldn't go gallivanting around at night like this. Although his father was spryer than most men twenty years younger, Jim always acted like he shouldn't do anything but sit at home.

Uncle Charley was adamant and, as the only man with military experience, proceeded to take charge. He had been a sergeant under General Harrison fifty years ago.

Their ancient commander decided they should take a shortcut and come out on the road between French Lick and Paoli to head off Cartwright and his men. That would be a lot better than chasing them, and Uncle Charley had a place in mind where they could surprise them if they got there first and everybody kept quiet. That way maybe they could bluff Cartwright into giving the preacher up without a fight.

Ben Dickens didn't want to do it that way. "We oughta fight them fellers an' use a few of 'em up 'n' larn 'em free 'mericans won't stand fer what they're doin!"

Everybody else agreed with Uncle Charley, though, so Ben gave in. No one wanted to kill any soldiers, even if these weren't real ones, the kind that fought the Rebels.

Uncle Charley had lived in the country nearly fifty years and knew it like a book. He led his men north at a full gallop on an old road no one had used for years, occasionally taking shortcuts through the woods and fields. He wouldn't even slow up for the woods in spite of pleas that somebody was going to get hurt unless he did.

"Jist give yore hoss his head," he shouted, "an' watch out fer low limbs! Hosses kin see better'n men!"

They stopped at a spring a mile or so south of French Lick to blow their horses and let them have a little water, then galloped on until they neared the steep valley where the main road turned down to French Lick. They had to wait several minutes before they saw a faint glow spring up on the road where it started steeply downward.

"Lil' Johnny's doin' his work well 'nough!" exclaimed Rob as the glow grew into a fire. "I guess they're goin' through French Lick right now."

Uncle Charley led them on a wild gallop through the woods around the valley where French Lick was, a dangerous business, because it was too dark in the woods to see and rock cliffs abounded as well as other obstacles. He only slowed up enough to let Ollie Winger catch up after a low limb knocked him off his horse and skinned his forehead. The old warrior acted like he was out campaigning against the British and Indians again.

John rode close beside their leader. The old man was a superb rider and knew every rock and rill. He had always been a great hunter and had ranged over every foot of this country many times. John dodged several low limbs and once had to throw himself to one side and hang onto the saddle horn to escape one. He couldn't help worrying about rock cliffs, some of them fifty feet high, but Uncle Charley led the party unerringly around them, never slowing from a gallop except to climb ridges or slide down steep slopes.

They finally came out of the woods and faced a steep, brushy slope leading down to Lick Creek where the road to Paoli ran along the far bank. Emerging from the gloom of the woods made it seem much lighter than it really was. They slid down the slope in a flurry of loose earth and snapping brush, splashed across the creek, low at that time of year, and halted on the road.

"Now, here's what we're gonna do," began Uncle Charley in a voice that brooked no argument. "They's a place up th' road a little ways whar a thicket cuts 'crost hit. Hit's close on both sides. We kin d'ploy on both sides uv th' road thar outa sight." He paused and looked around at his men. "Le's see, they's eight, nine, ten uv us, ain't they?"

"Naw, twelve," said Ab.

A careful count was taken. There were eleven.

"All right," said Uncle Charley. "John, you take Ab, Ben, Sim, an' Charley on t'other side uv th' road when we gits t' that thicket. I'll stay on this side with th' others."

Somebody's horse snorted and stamped.

"Now, ye'll hafta keep yore hosses quiet!" enjoined the old man. "Snub 'em down with yer reins if'n they starts t' stomp er move, an' slap 'em on th' nose if'n they acks like they're gonna blow er neigh." He paused briefly. "Now, when we git t' that thicket, I want ye t' line up outa sight 'long both sides uv th' road like I said. When they comes up, I'll go out an' stop 'em. I'll ride out in th' road an' holler, 'Halt!' 'n' when I do all uv ye make a racket. Hit yore gun barr'ls with somethin' metal, 'nother gun er a knife er somethin'." He raised his voice. "Now don't ary one uv ye open his trap er let yerself be seen till I stops 'em!"

Jim objected immediately. "Now, Pa, yo're too old t' go out an' try t' stop them fellers! Ye oughta—"

"Hesh up," snapped his father. "I kin do hit 's well 's enyone, an' I don't want enybody t' be reck'nized but me."

"Why, they'll come atter ye jist like they would enyone else!" exclaimed Jim.

"They ain't gonna bother no seventy-year-old man that fit th' Britishers an' Injuns with Harrison," was the prompt reply. "Hit'd look too bad. Now, if they reck'nized eny uv you other fellers, they'd be back down atter ye 's soon 's they got t' Injinap'lis."

Everybody seemed to agree with that reasoning but Jim. "Now, Pa—" he began.

"Hesh up, Jim, like yore pappy says!" scolded the old man.

Jim shrugged his shoulders and gave up.

"Now, they'll be five uv ye on each side uv th' road," Uncle Charley went on, "an' I want ye t' keep back whar they cain't see ye, an' keep quiet, real quiet." He nodded for emphasis. "An' keep yore hosses quiet, too. They'll prob'ly have somebody ridin' out 'head t' see if'n hit's all clear. We'll jist let him go by 'lessen he finds out we're thar. If'n he does, I'll take keer uv him, but I don't think we gotta worry 'bout that 'cause they won't be 'spectin' enything this fur up th' road." He gave no time for questions before going on. "Now, they'll prob'ly have th' preacher back in th' bunch a little ways." He nodded again. "Enyhow, I'll d'cide when t' stop 'em. When I rides out t' do hit, all uv ye make a racket like I said." He paused and looked around again. "I want 'em t' think they's a hull bunch uv us."

Jim seized the opportunity to speak up. "What if'n they jist tries t' ride ye down?"

"Crowd up close 'n' start shootin', but watch out fer th' preacher. We don't wanta shoot him." He raised his voice again. "But let me fire th' first shot! Don't enybody shoot 'fore I do! Hear?"

Jim had another question. "What if they turn roun' an' run back?"

"We'll take out atter 'em, an' if'n they shoots, shoot back; only aim fer th' hosses." Uncle Charley laughed shortly. "They won't go back, though. They ain't got no fren's in that d'rection." He looked his men over. "Ever'body unnerstan' ever'thing?" Everybody seemed to, so he said, "Well, let's go," then led them up the road a short distance to where a dense but narrow belt of growth lay on both sides. "Now go t' whar I told ye, an' keep quiet, an' keep yore hosses quiet, er ye'll spile ever'thing."

The men moved to their assigned positions and waited silently in the dim light of the stars. Somebody on the other side of the road from where John was had trouble keeping his horse quiet, which drew a stern admonition from their veteran leader delivered in a stage whisper.

John felt a mounting excitement. The night might suddenly be illuminated by muzzle flashes, and men might die. The minutemen who turned out to meet the British back in '75 must have felt like this. He thought he knew how Tom and Billy felt just before a battle.

Time went by and John's excitement began to wane. Were they too late? Had Cartwright and his men already gone by? Had they taken another road? Maybe they had turned northwest toward Shoals Station instead of east toward Paoli after leaving French Lick. They could get to Indianapolis by rail in a roundabout way if they had, and they might have. Well, it was too late to do anything but wait where they were now.

The sound of horses' hooves came from down the road, but there seemed to be only one horse. It was probably the scout Uncle Charley expected to be sent ahead to see if all was clear. They waited, still as the grave and hidden by the brush. It was too dark to tell whether or not the lone rider was a soldier when he passed, but he gave no sign of seeing anything unusual if he was.

The lone rider was well out of hearing before horses' hooves sounded again, this time many of them. As they came closer, men's voices could be heard. One of them must have said something funny, since several of them laughed. They were making no effort to keep quiet.

John drew his revolver to strike his rifle barrel with, and those who were with him followed his example, except that most of them only had knives or something like that. John began to wonder how it would be to shoot down a man in uniform, like his own boys. These fellows weren't real soldiers, though, he told himself. They were cowardly stay-at-homes like Tom Cartwright, and undoubtedly Republicans like he was. He found himself breathing hard and fast but realized it was too late to have doubts and calmed himself.

The horsemen were almost abreast of the position when Uncle Charley reined out into the road and shouted, "Halt!" in a commanding voice. The clash of metal on metal rang out from the roadside, and horses moved in the brush.

The horsemen stopped abruptly. "Who . . . who's there?" came a startled voice. "What d'you want?" They looked apprehensively around at the shadowy figures along the roadside.

"Hit don't make no diff'runce who we air!" John could see Uncle Charley's big horse pistol leveled on the foremost horseman. "They's 'nough uv us t' wipe ye out! We want th' preacher!"

There was a murmur of talk among the men on the road. "He's under 'rest by United States soldiers!" came a reply. "You'd better not try anything!" The man's fear showed through his defiant words, though.

"He wuz 'rested 'thout eny warrant, an' sol'jers ain't got no right t' 'rest citizens! This is th' United States uv Ameriky, not Rooshey er someplace! Now give him up, er we're gonna wipe y' out!"

There was more talk among the horsemen, but none of them made a move. "I know who you are!" their spokesman shouted. "You're ol' Uncle Charley Polson!" The voice had gained a little courage.

"So I am! An' I know who you air, too, Tom Cartwright, ye sneakin' whelp! If ye wuz eny kind uv man, ye wouldn't be stayin' back hyar while th' good men has gone t' fight th' Rebels!" The old voice dripped with contempt.

"You better git outa th' way, ol' man!" threatened another of the horsemen. "We'll ride y' down if'n ye don't!"

"You try that an' nary a one uv ye'll live t' tell th' tale!" shouted Uncle Charley in a voice that cracked like a whip. "I wuz killin' Injuns an' Britishers 'fore eny uv ye wuz born, an' I'd as lief kill you!" He cocked his pistol with an audible click. "Now give us th' preacher, er I'm gonna git two er three uv ye with this load uv buckshot, an' them that's with me'll git th' rest!"

John cocked his rifle and leveled it at the group. A succession of metallic clicks sounded as the others cocked their weapons, and the horsemen seemed to shrink in their saddles.

"Brethren," came the unmistakable voice of Howard Stevens from back in the group, "I don't want blood shed on my account! Put down your guns!"

"Now lissen, Preacher," replied Uncle Charley. "we gotta stop this kinda thing, er hit'll git t' be whar a man dasn't open his mouth! Hit'll be jist like Rooshey 'n' other countries whar th' people ain't got no rights! They ain't got no right t' 'rest you!"

"I know they have no right to arrest me, and they know it, too, but this isn't the way to deal with it," replied Stevens calmly. "If you kill these men, there'll be no end to it."

"They oughta be kilt! Men that'd ack like that ol' Zar's p'lice, 'restin a free 'merican fer jist speakin' free like th' Constitootion says he kin, ain't fit t' live!"

"Please, Brother," protested Stevens, "please don't—"

Uncle Charley cut him off. "Come on now, Preacher! You give a leg fer yer country in Mexico, an' all you done was speak yore mind like—"

Stevens interrupted in his turn. "I won't go with you!" he insisted. "I won't go with you, so put down your guns and let us go ahead. I'm going with these men willingly."

The old warrior was stumped. While he was trying to think of something to say, one of the horsemen was emboldened to advance on him. He leveled his pistol. "Stop er yo're a dead man!" he snapped, and the fellow stopped. There was death in the sharp old voice. "Yo're a low, sneakin' scoundril, Tom Cartwright, an' yore ol' daddy's 'nother'n. They ain't nothin' I'd ruther do than kill you!"

John thought he saw Cartwright draw back in his saddle.

"You, y' sneakin coward," Uncle Charley went on, "layin' 'roun' up thar at Injinap'lis doin' this kinda dirty work, an' my gran'son Jim dead fightin' fer th' Union." You could tell by the old man's voice that he was on the point of pulling the trigger. "You goddamned sneakin', lyin' Republicans! Git us inter a war an' then won't go fight—"

Howard Stevens rushed in front of Cartwright. "Stop!" he shouted. "Don't shoot this man! Don't be a murderer!"

Uncle Charley lowered his pistol and let the hammer down. The thing was three feet long and gleamed in the starlight. "Thank ye, Preacher. Hit ain't that I ain't took human life b'fore, but y' saved me frum doin' hit agin. At least hit claims t' be human," he added bitingly.

There hadn't been a peep out of Cartwright. He had been a split second from death and knew it. The others seemed as scared as he was.

John uncocked his rifle also, and soft metallic sounds showed that the others were doing the same. It had been a close thing.

"I want you to go," said Stevens evenly. "I don't want to be taken from these men. Like it is, I'm the only one in trouble, and if this goes on, you'll all be." He was where he could see the looming forms in the thicket. "Do you hear me, men? Please go. Let them take me in. They'll be hurt a lot more that way."

Uncle Charley was loath to give up. "But hit's th' principle uv th' thing! We cain't let 'em—"

Stevens broke in again. "I won't go, old friend. I'll go on by myself if I have to."

"Wal, if'n ye won't be took 'way frum 'em, I guess we've done all we kin do," replied Uncle Charley reluctantly. "Hit's awful hard t' give hit up, though. Even King George uv England didn't do like ol' Linkun's doin', 'restin' free men fer jist speakin' their mind."

"They won't do anything to me," Stevens assured him, "and they won't keep me very long. Arresting a minister of the Gospel who lost a leg in Mexico won't sound very good when it's spread around. I don't think they thought this thing out beforehand very well." He came closer. "Old friend," he said earnestly, "I . . . I understand how you feel, and I appreciate what you want to do for me, but please put your pistol away and go."

Uncle Charley put his pistol in the big old holster at the front of his saddle. "All right, Preacher, we'll do like you say."

Stevens reached out and took his hand. "Thank you, old friend, thank you." They shook hands. Stevens raised his voice and addressed the men in the thicket. "Please go now. Go back to your homes and take God's blessing with you."

"All right, Preacher, we'll go," said Uncle Charley as he reined his horse aside. "You, Tom Cartwright!" he barked as the horsemen started past. They stopped and the old man went on. "Tell them abolish scoundrils that sent you out they'd better be no more uv this, er th' next time they won't be no preacher t' save yore skin! Y'hear?"

Cartwright didn't open his mouth, and the cavalcade started up again.

"Tell 'em somethin' else, too!" shouted Uncle Charley after them. "If'n they wants me, they know where t' find me, an' tell 'em t' come loaded fer bar, 'cause I ain't no preacher!"

There was no reply as the horsemen went on their way.

The ancient commander allowed his men no time to talk. "Let's git goin' now. Hit'll be daylight 'fore we kin all git home 'lessen we hurry, an' I don't want enybody t' be seen."

"Well," said his son as they started away, "they shore seen you."

"That's all right," was the confident reply. "Like I said, I don't think they'll bother me, but if they do, they cain't take many years 'cause I ain't got many left." He nodded emphatically. "Hit's diffrunt with th' rest uv ye, an' ye've all got families t' keer fur."

The party went back the way it had come, but at a somewhat slower pace, through the woods anyhow. Uncle Charley started another argument with his son when he told him he wasn't going to stay with him and Mary any longer because it might bring trouble on them. He was going to move back into the log cabin he had built when he first settled in the country. Jim objected strenuously and gave in only when his father promised to visit him every day he didn't come to see about him.

They were all back home before daylight, with a parting admonition from their veteran captain ringing in their ears. They weren't to tell anybody what they had done that didn't already know and were to see to it that their wives and families didn't tell anyone either. Of course John would have no trouble, but he doubted if the others could keep their womenfolk quiet.

The next week an article in the Indianapolis Republican paper John still took for war news attracted his attention:

> We learn that Lieutenant Cartwright of the post here returned from the darkest depths of the Pocket a few days since with an illiterate one-legged preacher who desecrated a memorial service for war dead with a treasonable harangue. The lieutenant told of an attempt by a body of rustic adherents of the copperhead messiah to bluff him into surrendering his prisoner, wooden leg and all. He relates that a prompt show

of weapons and a willingness to use them sent the would-be rescuers scattering into the woods and brush of their native habitat, where they yet roam as far as he knows.

Preacher Stevens's forecast was right. There was such an uproar about his arrest that he was back in his pulpit before two weeks were out.

# 31

At officers' call one morning Tom was told something he already knew, that it was his company's turn on picket at noon for twenty-four hours. When he asked Major Owen how to do it, he was told it was up to him, but to be sure that someone was awake all the time.

That didn't help much, so Tom decided to stay for coffee at the officers' mess and ask someone who had been out. He had stayed for coffee a time or two but didn't eat at the mess or sleep in the big tent where most of the officers stayed. He hadn't gotten very well acquainted with any of them yet, mainly because most of them seemed to want to keep their distance.

That was understandable in the case of Captain Harlow and his friends, but it went beyond them. At first Tom thought it was because he had come up from the ranks, but the way the other ex-sergeants were treated soon showed that wasn't the reason. Being promoted to captain after only a few weeks as a lieutenant caused some jealousy, but not that much. Maybe it was because of his dress. Thanks to Hauser, he outshone everybody, even Major Owen. Tom's boots were always glossy black, and his hat could have just come out of the box. His uniform wasn't issue and was always spotless and neatly pressed. Most of the others only wore shoes and a cap like the men did, and their uniforms had generally come from the quartermaster, were commonly rumpled, and often none too clean.

A few things happened that led Tom to believe that a good many of the other officers thought he was some kind of a desperate and dangerous character. There was nothing to cause that except what had happened the night of the big disturbance, though, and surely none of them knew about that. It frightened him to think that they might. Maybe it was jealousy, but not related to dress or promotion. It could be that it was because he had been able to control his men where they hadn't.

Whatever caused it, he didn't let the coolness in the mess tent bother him. He had never been much of a mixer, and if those fellows wanted to keep their distance it was all right with him. Anyhow, it would give him a lot more time and privacy for study if he could find something to study.

Lt. Marcus Allen of the Posey County company was one of the few he had gotten to know, and he had been out on picket, so Tom approached him. "How is it out there on picket, Marcus?"

Allen put down his coffee. "Oh, it's all right." He wiped the coffee off his mustache, which made Tom glad he was one of the few clean-shaven fellows among the officers. "The only problem is staying awake all night."

"Did you keep your men awake, too?"

Allen smiled. "I tried to, and the captain did, too, but it wound up with everybody asleep but us and a couple of sergeants." He shrugged. "It really doesn't make any difference as long as someone's awake when the provost comes around, and he's pretty regular, late evening and about nine in the morning."

"I guess you can do pretty well as you please, then." Tom put down his empty cup and got out pipe and tobacco. "I think I'll put half my men on picket each twelve hours and let the others sleep someplace." He filled his pipe and offered the tobacco to Allen.

"No thank you, I don't smoke." Allen frowned thoughtfully while Tom lit up and put the tobacco away. "I think that's what I'll suggest the next time we're on. There's a big tobacco barn close to the guard point the men can sleep in. There's even hay in it. Major Pedigo didn't like it when he found all of us in it when he came around in the morning."

"Oh yes, he's the brigade provost. Did he say anything?"

"Yes, he had a few words with the captain and me. He said the Rebels are always running couriers and spies through and we never catch any because we just watch that bridge where the guard point is and they slip around it. He said that's why they always know what we're doing."

"He wants a regular picket line thrown out then, on both sides of the road?"

"I guess so, but I don't know anybody that's done it." Allen laughed shortly. "We sure didn't."

Tom thought Owen must not take the business very seriously or he would have done something about it. "Well, I guess that spying and courier stuff is easy for the Rebels around here. From what I hear the people are all for them."

Allen nodded his agreement. "They sure are, especially the women. Of course," he added hastily, "that's just what I hear." He was engaged to the colonel's daughter, Carolyn, and didn't want to give the impression he knew firsthand.

Someone who would know firsthand joined them. He was Capt. Jack Arnold of the Spencer county company, reputedly the champion ladies' man in the regiment. He was everybody's friend, and Tom doubted if a more convivial soul ever lived. Jack was a dapper, handsome fellow with stylishly long brown hair and a mustache. "How about a game of euchre tonight, you fellows?"

Allen agreed, but Tom demurred. He had never played cards in his life, but not wanting to show his ignorance, he lied a little. "Thanks, but those are my study hours." Of course they really were, when he had something to study.

Arnold looked surprised. "Study hours? What do you study?"

"Military books, at least when I can find some I haven't been through already."

Jack lit a cigar from Tom's pipe and puffed vigorously. "I guess you take this business pretty seriously, Traylor."

Tom felt a little apologetic. "Well, it is a pretty serious business, Jack. It's life or death, you know."

Arnold shook his head and sighed. "It is, and that's about as serious as you can get." He puffed his cigar. "You know, I've got a half-dozen military books, and I've never even looked at a single one of them." He blew smoke and laughed. "I'm always finding something a lot more interesting to do."

Tom and Marcus laughed. They knew what he meant. "Say," said Tom, "let's go look at those books you've got. Maybe I can find some I haven't studied already."

"Come on," said Jack airily. "Maybe you're just the fellow who'll take them off my hands. See you later, Marcus," he added as he and Tom turned away.

They went to the tent where most of the officers slept. Jack went to the foot of a bunk and opened a big wooden trunk. He rummaged around in it and began taking out books, which he handed to Tom. "I'm making you a present of these things, Traylor."

"Oh no!" protested Tom. "I'll just borrow them."

Jack put on a mock scowl. "You'd better not bring these things back to me, or I'll throw them at you." He winked and grinned through the smoke of his cigar. "They spoil my leisure. I want to be lazy without my conscience bothering me."

It was easy to see why the ladies fell for Jack. He was a *bon vivant* if there ever was one, and Tom envied him with all his heart. Nothing ever bothered Jack. If he lost one sweetheart, he'd just grab another.

"Oh, all right," Tom replied, "if you put it that way." There were six books, and he was familiar with only one of them, Hardee's *Tactics*. Two had been translated from the French.

"Take them! Get them out of here!" laughed Jack. "You'll be doing me a favor. I really ought to pay you for taking 'em." He pretended to get confidential. "I'm not really being generous. They didn't cost me a cent. They're from an uncle of mine who has military ambitions for me." He laughed again as he closed the trunk. "I don't have any myself."

Tom decided to take Hardee's book along with the rest and pass it on to someone who would use it. "Well, I'm much obliged, Jack. These books will help pass the time."

Jack sat down on the bunk and looked at Tom quizzically. "Traylor, there are a lot more pleasant ways to pass the time." He puffed his cigar. "Take the ladies. They're a lot more interesting than books." He grinned and winked broadly.

"There aren't any around here who'd even look at us, though."

Arnold blew smoke. "Sure there are! Women are women, Rebels or not, and then they're always coming down here from Washington now that they've got the trains running again."

Tom nodded and tried to look interested, although he wasn't.

"I know a couple of them, from Washington, I mean." He looked at Tom appraisingly. "Want to try them out? All I've got to do is drop them a line."

Tom hesitated. He really didn't want to, but he didn't want to refuse outright. "Well, I don't know—"

Jack cut him off. "Oh, come on!" he laughed, his eyes gleaming raffishly through the smoke. "All work and no play—"

"Make Tom a dull boy!"

Jack nodded vigorously. "Right! What about it?"

He just couldn't refuse Jack. "Oh, all right, then."

"Great! I'll write them right away." He sized Tom up and laughed gleefully. "Oh, you'll slay them! A good-looking fellow like you, and the way you turn yourself out, they'll grovel at your feet!"

Tom shook his head. "I don't know about that. I'm no ladies' man, that's for sure." He wondered if Jack knew about Sally, but nothing he had said indicated he did, and as far as he knew no one outside of his old platoon, men from his neighborhood, knew about her.

A drum began to beat in frenzied fashion, and cries of "Fall out! Fall out!" resounded through the camp. It was morning muster for the companies, and they had to go.

"I'll let you know when they'll be here, those Washington ladies, I mean," said Jack as they parted.

When he took his company on picket at noon, Tom had Cole and Grim draw straws to see who went on first and got to sleep after midnight. Grim lost, but the Germans didn't seem to mind. It looked like it was going to start raining anytime, and whoever went on first would have to sleep in wet clothes. Tom sent Grim and his men to the barn Allen had told him about, which was only a short distance west toward town from the guard point on the bridge across a creek. He sent Billy with the Germans because he knew the language a lot better than his brother did, and Grim would need a translator if he stopped anybody on the road.

Tom had already made up his mind to do the thing right. He put Cole and two men on the bridge and spread the others out along a path that crossed the road and the creek that meandered along it a little east of the bridge. The path ran on through woods and up to the crests of the low ridges that enclosed the valley where the road and the creek were.

Major Pedigo was right about it. Anyone trying to sneak through would leave the road and take to the woods before he got to the bridge. Tom told the men to stay alert and that he was going to patrol the path to make sure they did.

It began to rain a little after dark, and the men immediately wanted to go to the barn. No rebel with any sense would be out on a cold, rainy night like this, they thought. Tom put a stop to that by asking what kind of a night they would pick if they were Rebel spies or couriers. They were soon thoroughly soaked and shivering, but their misery would keep them awake.

Tom stayed dry himself. Hauser had made a cape and a hat cover out of a waterproof groundsheet and brought them to him when it started raining. The cover fitted his hat like a glove, and the cape was well cut and neatly stitched at the seams. It came nearly to his knees, and Hauser had greased his new boots copiously to they would break in easily. He was glad he was wearing one of the two *Felduniformen* Herr Thiers had finished a few days before, because he was going to get pretty muddy despite the cape.

Not a soul came along the road after it started raining, but Tom kept up an irregular patrol along the path through the dark, dripping woods. The path became treacherous on the slopes, and he took several tumbles until he learned the places to avoid or found bushes and trees to hang onto. Once in a while he would stop at the bridge and have a pipe with Cole. The big, burly fellow envied his cape and said he was going to have one if he had to steal it. Tom laughed and said he would know where to look if his cape disappeared.

Major Pedigo came up from town about eleven o'clock, a lot later than Tom expected. He was very pleased when he learned that Tom had picketed the path up to the ridge tops. He said no one had ever done that before and that the men put on the bridge generally got under it and went to sleep if the creek was low. That was why they had never caught anyone although he was sure the Rebels regularly ran scouts, spies, and couriers through. He admired Tom's cape, although he had a cavalry slicker himself, and wondered where he could get a hat cover like Tom had. After a little while, he went back, saying he would be out again sometime in the morning.

At midnight Tom sent Cole to get Billy and the Germans. He waited on the bridge, listening to the water rushing along below. The creek was up, but it was too dark to see it or anything else. The rain beat down steadily, like it was going to keep it up all night.

Grim and his men came splashing up the road. Tom posted them like he had the others, keeping Grim and two men on the bridge. Before Cole started for the barn with his men, Tom told him he could build a fire in the wide entrance in the middle, but not to allow one anyplace else or the place might get burned down.

Billy obviously wasn't going to be needed at the bridge, so Tom took him along for company on his patrols back and forth along the path. It was slow going on the slippery slopes in the pitch darkness, and Billy took several tumbles until he learned the path better.

About two o'clock in the morning Tom and Billy had just started up the northern side of the valley when they heard a shout from the opposite slope. "Halt! Halt!" They whirled and ran back as a rifle fired with a dull detonation in the rain, followed by a commotion in the woods about halfway up the slope.

Tom drew his revolver and shouted for everyone to keep a sharp lookout as he ran. This might be just a diversion so someone could get through elsewhere along the line. They labored up the slope toward where the commotion was, slipping in the mud and grabbing trees and bushes for support. Someone came noisily toward the path from the north about the time they got even with him. Tom leveled his revolver and shouted, "Halt! Who's there?"

The reply was in German. It was Schlimmer and he had a prisoner, so Tom holstered his weapon. Schlimmer came toward them, hustling someone with him, to judge from the sound. Billy called to guide him, and Tom wondered how he had been able to see whomever he had, much less catch him.

Tom seized the captive and searched him. All he could tell was that he was a small, slender fellow with a lot of soaking wet clothes on. He had no weapon or anything else.

"Who are you and what's your business?" Tom asked roughly. He couldn't see the fellow's face in the dark and made the mistake of letting him go.

His reply was to dart nimbly away, but Billy tackled him and they fell thrashing in the mud. Schlimmer helped Billy bring the fellow to his feet, and they both kept hold of him.

"Yo're not gittin' 'way, feller," panted Billy.

Tom spoke to the captive, peering close in the vain hope of seeing his face. "All right, now, you tell me what I asked you."

The reply was in a soft, casual voice. "I live around here. I was only trying to get to town."

"Why didn't you use the road?" Tom demanded.

"I didn't want to get shot at. Too many of you fellows shoot first and ask questions afterwards." The fellow sounded like he didn't have a worry in the world. Whoever he was, he was a cool customer.

Tom thought he detected traces of an accent, probably German, so he had Schlimmer try to speak to the man. It did no good. The prisoner professed not to understand.

Tom pondered briefly. "Well, we can't tell anything about him in the dark. Take him to the barn and turn him over to Cole. Tell him to watch him close and we'll see what he looks like in the morning."

"Both uv us?" asked Billy. "I mean, y' want both of us t' take him?"

"Yeah, he's little, but he's slippery. Keep good hold of him and tell Cole to watch him real close."

"Y' wanta send fer th' provost?"

"No, he'll keep till morning."

They left with the prisoner and Tom shouted for Grim to send somebody up to take Schlimmer's place, then resumed his patrol. When Billy came back, they made it a twosome again, but nothing happened the rest of the night.

It was still raining at daylight when Tom went to the barn. He told Grim to yell for Billy if he needed him and let him come along. Everyone in the barn seemed to be asleep on the hay but Cole, who sat near the prisoner with his rifle ready. The fellow looked like he was asleep, but Tom felt he really wasn't.

"He cause you any trouble, Cole?"

"Naw, I kep' two uv th' men with me till a lil' while 'go, an' we watched him real close."

A big fire of the dry tobacco sticks piled about in the barn burned in the entranceway close by with the hay carefully scraped away around it. "Get Hauser up, Cole, and see if you can make some coffee. I'd like to have enough to take some up to Grim's men, but I don't guess we can."

"Aw, yes, sir, we kin. Th' men found two big ol' buckets an' cleaned 'em out real good. I think we got 'nough coffee, too."

"Good. Go ahead, then." Billy went along to help carry the water and naturally to get a cup of coffee as soon as he could.

The prisoner pretended to awaken and sat up. To Tom's astonishment he wore the uniform of a Confederate infantry lieutenant. It was wet but not muddy and seemed to be well tailored of fine cloth. He was a swarthy little fellow who looked to be in his midtwenties and had big black eyes that looked vaguely familiar.

"All right, now," said Tom. "Let's see about you."

The prisoner got up smiling. "Well, you've got me, that's all, and I guess you can see what you've got." He was as coolly casual as he had been the night before.

"Did you have that uniform on last night?"

"Of course I did. I would've had to, wouldn't I?"

Tom searched him again, but only to see if he felt like he had the night before. He didn't. He didn't have nearly as many clothes on. That was why his uniform wasn't muddy.

Tom stood back and studied the fellow. Suddenly he knew who he was. Those big black eyes were just like Rebecca Thiers's, and allowing for its masculinity, the man's face resembled hers remarkably. Then there was that trace of an accent, the dark complexion, and even the finely tailored uniform. Rebecca had an older brother, but no one knew anything about him. Here he was, and he would go before a firing squad if it came out that he had been wearing citizens' clothes over his uniform.

Billy, Cole, and Hauser were busy with the coffee and too far away to hear. Everyone else seemed to be asleep, but Tom took no chances. He beckoned the prisoner to follow and walked to the end of the barn where there was no hay or sleepers.

"What's your name, now, and what were you doing out slipping around in the woods last night?"

"I'm Alphonse La Rue, Sixteenth Louisiana. We were in camp here all last winter, and I, well, got acquainted with a young lady. I was coming to see her and got lost in the woods."

It sounded very plausible, all the more because of the way it was said. The big black eyes were unwavering and the voice casual and controlled.

"You didn't tell me that last night."

Thiers shrugged. "Well, you can't blame a fellow for trying to stay out of a prison camp."

The fellow was so convincing that it took an effort to disbelieve him. "Do you have any papers to prove who you are?"

"All I've got is a little money. I lost my furlough papers."

"Where are those clothes you had on over your uniform last night?"

The prisoner looked surprised. "What clothes? These are all I have, what I have on." This fellow had nerves of steel.

"I'm sure I'll find some wet citizens' clothes if I look around a little. I know you had clothes on over your uniform last night, and it wouldn't be another uniform." He looked Thiers in the eye. "Do you want me to start looking, or will you save me the trouble?"

The dark little fellow shrugged. "Go ahead and look," he said indifferently. "You won't find anything."

"You'd better tell me before the provost gets here and finds them himself. He'll see your uniform isn't muddy, and he'll know why."

The prisoner laughed. "I didn't have any, so neither of you will find anything, but why should I tell you if I did?" The big black eyes glowed humorously. "It wouldn't make any difference who found them, you or the provost."

"Oh yes, it would. He'll use them to put you before a firing squad. I'll get rid of them."

Thiers laughed again. "Why should you do that?" All Tom could see in his eyes was an honest puzzlement.

The aroma of boiling coffee was awakening the men. They began to sit up, complaining about being cold and wet and calling out to hurry up with the coffee. Some of them got up and started shivering for the fire, but nobody noticed Tom and the prisoner. They probably didn't know there was one yet and would undoubtedly be too busy warming themselves inside with the coffee and outside with the fire to take any interest when they did.

"You ask why I should get rid of the clothes," Tom went on. "It's because I know who you really are."

The little dark fellow smiled quizzically. "Who am I, then?"

"Your name is Thiers. You have a father who's a tailor here, and a lovely little dark-eyed sister. I know them both."

The black eyes flickered and Tom knew he was right. Nothing else would have broken that iron self-control, but it came back almost instantly. Thiers smiled again. "You couldn't be more wrong. I'm from Louisiana, and my father's a sugar planter. I don't even have a sister."

The act was so convincing that Tom half-believed the fellow, but he knew he couldn't be wrong, and he couldn't let Major Pedigo find the clothes. "You'd better own up and tell me where those clothes are," he said impatiently. "You're sentencing yourself to death if you don't."

Thiers looked him in the eye. "Why should I trust you?" The big black eyes were hard and searching now.

"Because I know your father and your sister, and I once saw a man shot by a firing squad." Tom looked back unwaveringly, although it was like looking into twin rifle muzzles. "Something else," he added. "The fellow who caught you is courting your sister."

That did it. "All right, I'm Ernst Thiers. I'll put my life in your hands. The clothes are up in the loft. The fire had gone out when we got here, and I managed to slip them off. Then I threw them up there when your sergeant wasn't looking." He looked at Tom strangely.

"It's a good thing you told me. The provost would have found them in a minute." He called Billy over. "Watch this fellow, Billy. I'm going to look around a little."

Billy had an extra cup of coffee and held out one. "Don't y' want this?"

Tom would have sold his soul for it any other time. He was tired and sleepy, and his mouth felt like it was full of cotton. "No, thanks. Just give it to this fellow."

Bill gave the cup to Thiers, was thanked for it, and sat down to drink with him.

Tom pretended to make a thorough search of the ground floor, looking grimly preoccupied to put off any questions. It was like he expected, though. The men had no interest in anything but coffee and the fire. The rain had stopped and some of them were trying to build another fire out in front of the entrance so more of them could dry out. Dan Howard ran afoul of Cole when he took too much from the old fire to start the new one, and there was shouting.

Tom went up into the loft on a notched log that reminded him of the cabin he and Billy had been born in, which had one just like it. He saw the clothes as soon as his head was high enough. They lay near a hole in the floor of the loft above where Thiers had been. There was a common jeans coat, a rough pair of pants, and a floppy hat, all soaking wet, muddy, and wrapped together in a bundle. He took them over to the side of the barn by the creek, found a loose board, and wedged it aside. No one was in sight and the creek rushed along almost directly below, out of its banks by the stone foundation of the barn. He tossed the bundle out. It dropped into the creek with a soft splash to join the other debris on the muddy water before it sank.

He stayed up in the loft until he had tramped all around. When he came down, Billy and Thiers were talking like old friends. To get rid of his brother, Tom told him to go help Hauser get the coffee ready for Grim's men. "Well," he said to Thiers, "you're clear as far as clothes are concerned."

"There's something else, if you don't mind," said Thiers softly.

"What?"

"There's a packet of papers wrapped in oilcloth near where I was caught, and a good colt forty-four which failed me only once." He looked at Tom significantly. "Just keep the revolver."

Tom saw there was more to the thing than he had thought, but he was in too deep to turn back even if he wanted to. "I'd better get up there. The provost will be here pretty soon, and he'll find that stuff if I don't." He started to go.

"Wait a minute, please." The big black eyes looked into his. "I don't know how I can thank you for this. You're a compassionate man." There was no effusion or sentimentality. It was just one gentleman thanking another for an important favor.

"I like to think so, and I thank you." He thought of something else. "Oh yes, I think you'd better tell them who you are, and that you were only trying to see your mother. They'll be easier on you that way."

Thiers demurred. "It might get my father into trouble, aiding and harboring, you know. I'll just be Lieutenant La Rue."

"Suit yourself. It's your funeral. Well, I've got to go before the provost gets here. If I don't see you again, good luck."

"Thank you again," said Thiers softly as Tom turned away.

Hauser had the coffee ready for Grim's men. That could have been a problem, but Tom turned it to account when Billy started to pick up one of the big buckets it was in. "Just stay here, Billy. I ought to be up there anyhow, so I'll just take one of them."

Hauser wouldn't let him do it and insisted on carrying both buckets himself. Tom half-expected a lecture on the things *Offizieren und Herren* shouldn't do once they were on the road, but Hauser didn't say anything. The fellow knew when he was well off. He had slept warm and dry in the hay all night while the others were cold and wet.

As soon as they were close enough, Hauser shouted, *"Kaffee! Kaffee! Heisse Kaffee für Kalten Deutschen Affen!"* Tom couldn't help laughing. Hot coffee for cold German monkeys! You'd never think the fellow had a sense of humor, but he sure did.

Hooting, laughter, and like insults came back from along the path. Grim and the two men at the bridge, shivering in their rain-soaked uniforms, grinned with delight at the sight of the coffee, and the pickets started gabbling happily. You would think every one of them was going to get his weight in gold. It was a lesson on what small comforts could mean to miserable men.

While Hauser prepared to ladle out the coffee, Tom told Grim to call his men in a few at a time to get their share. He then walked casually up the path, pacing himself to be close to Schlimmer when his turn came. When it did, Tom told the men on each side of him they could go, too. He would stay up there until they came back. They were delighted at not having to wait and took off down the path so rapidly that one of them slipped and went down the slope on the seat of his pants all the way to the bottom. The others roared with laughter and shouted to their comrades, then went on happily as guffaws broke out on the bridge and spread along the path on both sides.

Tom went into the woods where Thiers had been caught and began looking. It was hard to find anything in the thick, soggy leaves, and he was beginning to worry when he finally saw the gleam of metal. When he stooped to pick up the revolver, he saw the oilcloth packet nearby. It was nearly the color of the leaves, and he probably wouldn't have found it but for the weapon. He slipped it inside his coat and lodged it under his belt. The revolver was just like the one he had. A piece of twig wedged between the hammer and the breech showed why it had failed its owner and probably saved Schlimmer's life.

He cocked the hammer, dislodged the twig, then let it back down. He got out his handkerchief and ostentatiously wiped the weapon dry, then stuck it in his belt. He pretended to go on poking around until he saw Schlimmer and the two others starting up the path toward him, then headed for the barn through the woods. Traffic was starting on the road, but he saw Billy had joined Grim on the bridge, so there would be no language problem and they would send for him if he was needed.

Major Pedigo was there when he arrived. He looked a little like Thiers, but only because of his dark complexion. He was a lot bigger and had been an officer in the New York police before the war. He had a reputation of being tough and sharp, and Tom began to feel a little squeamish as he approached.

"Well, what can you tell me about this fellow?" asked Pedigo abruptly.

Tom told him about the capture, except for the extra clothes, including Thiers's story about being a Louisianan trying to see his girl.

The major's hard black eyes bore into him as he talked. "He was in uniform when you took him?"

"As far as I know. It was too dark to see when I searched him." Cole, Billy, and Schlimmer might know better, but Tom could count on them not to give him away if they did. Also, he saw that Thiers had smeared mud on his uniform, probably from his boots.

Pedigo nodded. "You could've told if he'd had clothes on over his uniform." Tom was glad it was a statement instead of a question, and that Pedigo took his eyes off him to look at the prisoner. When he looked back, his eyes didn't seem so hard. "Did you ask him his regiment?"

"Yes, Sixteenth Louisiana."

Pedigo nodded again. "That's what he told me." He sighed. "They're in Wheat's brigade, and were in camp here last winter, so I guess he's genuine."

Tom was impressed. Thiers sure knew his way around. "I guess one of the local belles caught him then," he said as humorously as he could.

Pedigo laughed. "Men will run any risk for women. They'll go through Hell fire for 'em. He's not the first Rebel we've caught like this."

"What'll happen to him?"

"Oh, he'll go to a prison camp someplace. He's in uniform and looks like he's what he says he is. You can spot these Louisiana Frenchmen a mile off."

Thiers was calmly sipping coffee and talking to some of the men like he didn't have a worry in the world.

Pedigo grinned slyly at Tom. "I do believe the fellow's glad he's out of it."

"Oh yes," said Tom. "I looked around in the woods where we caught him and just found this." He drew the revolver from his belt.

The hard black eyes were on him again. "Did you look well, for papers or anything like that?"

The packet inside his coat felt as big as a cotton bale, but Tom took heart from Thiers's equanimity and nodded affirmatively. "I'll just keep this if you don't mind," he said with an air of finality as he put the weapon back in his belt.

Pedigo nodded and smiled, the hardness gone from his eyes. "Go ahead. You ought to get something out of this. No one else would have kept his men out in the rain and tramped around all night keeping them alert like you did." He snorted. "They'd have holed up in this barn, and our Rebel friend would have seen his girl and gone."

The compliment eased Tom more than it pleased him. "Is that right?"

Pedigo produced two cigars and handed him one. "Absolutely. You can't get volunteer officers to take this sort of thing seriously, and the men are hopeless. They think all they ought to do is march and fight."

They went over to the fire, where Tom picked up a brand. They lit up and puffed.

"Thank you, sir. This is the best cigar I've smoked in a long time."

Pedigo smiled. "Havanas, the best. That's one thing I indulge myself with." He cocked an eye on Tom, cigar smoke curling about his head in the damp air. "I'll put in a good word with Colonel Rivers about how you handled this picketing," he said with a wink and a puff of smoke.

"Thank you, sir." Tom felt a great deal more at ease and wished his mouth wasn't so dry and cottony he could appreciate the cigar like Pedigo thought he did. "Have some coffee, Major?"

"No, thank you. I had a good breakfast before I came out, thanks to you."

"How's that?"

"You didn't call me out at two o'clock in the morning when you caught this fellow." he puffed and winked again. "I appreciate that." He laughed. "I'm getting used to civilized life again."

"Oh, I thought he'd keep."

Pedigo grew expansive. "You know, I think I'll try to get to stay here when the brigade leaves, probably next spring. They need a regular provost in a town this size." He nodded and emitted smoke. "I'll recommend they set one up, and I'll recommend myself for the job." He nodded vigorously. "I'm sure I can do it. I know the right people."

Tom smiled. "It'll beat being out in the field on campaign."

Pedigo suddenly pulled out his watch. "I've got to go. There's a pile of papers a foot high waiting on me." He pocketed his watch and stuck out his hand. "Good work, Captain. I'll be seeing you."

The major turned away and beckoned to Thiers. "Come along, monsieur," he said casually as he unbuttoned the flap of his holster and tucked it back over his belt so that his revolver showed. Thiers got up and Pedigo motioned him to go ahead. "I'll just ride a little behind you if you don't mind." He untied his horse's reins and mounted.

Thiers nodded glumly and started out without a word. Pedigo turned to wave at Tom and flash a smile behind his cigar; then they were gone.

Tom finally got some coffee and was glad to hunt his tent when his company was relieved. The first chance he got, he burned the packet of papers one by one and stirred the ashes. He tried to keep from looking at them but couldn't help seeing that some were tabulations of some sort, probably of troops and artillery, and that others were neatly drawn maps and what looked like diagrams of fortifications. One thing was sure. Ernst Thiers was no mere Rebel infantry lieutenant, and he didn't feel very good about the whole thing. It didn't salve his conscience much to tell himself that he was destroying information valuable to the enemy while he was burning the papers.

Tom got a bad scare a few days later when he got word that Pedigo wanted to see him at the headquarters tent. His legs felt like wooden stilts as he walked up the road, and there was an empty feeling inside him. He was glad Pedigo was alone and that his manner was as convivial as usual. He sat on a box smoking the inevitable cigar, and the first thing he did was give Tom one. "Say," he began, "do you know who our Rebel friend you caught the other night really was?"

Tom feigned surprise. "Wasn't he who he said he was?"

"No, and he got away the first night I had him. Pulled a revolver on the guard and made him go into the woods with him. Got him so lost he couldn't get back until morning." He shook his head disgustedly. "He got clean away."

Tom had managed to light his cigar without mishap. Now he felt relieved, and glad, too. "Who was he, then?"

"He goes under all sorts of names, and he's no mere infantry lieutenant. He's one of the best agents the Rebels have." Pedigo sighed. "I caught hell for it, believe me."

Tom wasn't really surprised. "Well, you had no way of knowing who he was."

Pedigo snorted angrily. "None at all. That's Baker for you. Keeps everything to himself and then expects men out in the field to know as much as he does."

"Who's Baker, sir?"

"Colonel, heads the secret service. I telegraphed a description of that fellow you caught as a matter of course, and the first thing I know, Baker sends three men down to get him, all armed to the teeth." The major heaved a long sigh. "It was too late. He was gone. If I'd had the slightest idea he was anything but a lovesick Louisiana lieutenant, I'd have put him in irons and allowed no one to see him, no one."

Tom was feeling better all the time. "You don't know who he is then, only what he is."

"He's a foreigner. Some say he's a German Jew. Others say he's a Frenchman, or a Louisianan. No one really knows, but I think he's a Frenchman, maybe from Louisiana like he said he was."

"Why's that?"

"I've got a Canuck corporal, and I tried him out. He spoke better French than the Canuck did. That convinced me, not that I really had any doubts." Pedigo got up and started to walk around. "Everything fitted together. His regiment camped here last winter. He looked French. He spoke French like a native." He smacked his fist into his palm. "He'd have fooled anybody, anybody!"

Pedigo wasn't the only one who had been fooled, thought Tom. Ernst Thiers was big game, altogether out of his class, and Pedigo's, too, for that matter. And Tom had thought he was only being merciful to a fellow like himself. He wondered if he would do it again, knowing what he did now.

"How did he get a revolver? He didn't have one on him. I searched him."

"I doubt if it was really a revolver; it was probably a derringer, but we searched him, too, and I know we didn't overlook anything. I even sent a man to search the barn and look in the woods, just in case you'd overlooked something." Pedigo snorted. "It was my fool sergeant. A girl must've given it to him. Came to see him. Said she was his girl. Cried and carried on. The idiot didn't even ask me about it, just let her see him and, when they started hugging and kissing, left them alone." Pedigo smacked his fist into his palm again. "I fixed him! He's on his way to a line regiment, and he's a private now!"

Tom hoped the sergeant would be the only victim of the affair. "Did you find out who the girl was?"

"The description I got would fit half the women under thirty you see on the street!" was the disgusted reply.

Tom was glad to hear it hadn't been Rebecca, which was what he had been afraid of. "That doesn't help much." They smoked in silence until Tom felt he had to say something. "You say he's one of the best agents the Rebels have?"

"That's what MacDonald said, and he ought to know. He was one of those fellows Baker sent down to get him." Pedigo shook his head. "They'd give their eyeteeth to get him, those people in Washington. They'd probably shoot him on the spot instead of waiting to hang him if they did."

Tom salved his conscience again by thinking the Rebels' best agent would go back empty-handed this time. Suddenly he learned why Pedigo had come to see him and the bottom dropped out of things.

"Baker's threatening to court-martial me for letting that fellow get away, and I want to use you as a witness if he does."

Tom felt like he had once a long time ago when he was wading in the Patoka and suddenly went in over his head. He managed to say, "Of course, sir." There wasn't anything else he could say."I don't think he can make much of a case against you, though," he added hopefully.

"Of course not! He never sent me a thing about this fellow!" Pedigo stamped his foot. "Lists of contrabrand runners and scouts, plenty of them, but never a thing about this fellow." He nodded significantly. "You'll testify the truth, that there was absolutely nothing about the fellow that would've led anyone to think he wasn't who he said he was, a lovesick Louisiana lieutenant seeing his girl."

Tom began to feel numb. He wouldn't be able to lie under oath to a court-martial like he could to Pedigo. He could see the stern faces of the judges and hear their harsh voices condemning him. "Let's hope it doesn't come to a court-martial," he managed to say.

"Well, that's what I'm going to try to stop." Pedigo drew a paper from his coat and came up to him. "This is a statement I'd like you to sign, after you've read it, of course."

Tom was afraid his hands would tremble as he read it, but they didn't. It was a summary of what he had told Pedigo about the capture and the captive and ended by saying there was absolutely nothing about him to indicate he wasn't what he said he was. "I'll sign it." He couldn't do anything else. While Pedigo looked for pen and ink, he wondered why things like this were always happening to him. This was worse than the affair of the Yankee colonel. He took the pen, signed with wooden fingers, and handed the paper back, acutely conscious that it made him a perjurer, maybe even a traitor. And he had always done his best to be honest and truthful.

Pedigo carefully refolded the paper and put it back in his coat. "I'm going straight to Rivers and show him this. He thinks a lot of you. I'll get him behind me, and General Carter, too. He'll help me with Corps. They always do anything Carter wants them to." Pedigo began walking around again, puffing smoke like a locomotive. "After I've been to Corps, I'm going to see Baker this very night. I'll drag him out of bed if I have to. I'll give him your statement to show what a poor case he'll have against me. I'll let him know I've got Brigade, Division, and Corps behind me." He stopped and stood there, hands behind his back and cigar clenched between his teeth.

"I sure hope it works," ventured Tom.

Pedigo emitted smoke and nodded confidently. "I believe it will. I know Colonel Baker. He'll slip a knife in your back if he can do it without any trouble, but he's got no stomach for a fight." He nodded emphatically. "When he sees he'll have the fight of his life on his hands and hasn't got any kind of a case against me either, I think he'll back off."

"I sure hope he does." Pedigo couldn't know how much Tom hoped.

"I'm not afraid of Baker. I've handled tougher characters than he's ever seen. If I have to, I'll threaten to file countercharges—dereliction of duty, failure to provide subordinates with information essential to the discharge of their duty." His teeth showed as he clamped down on his cigar. "I'll let him know I've got good friends in the War Department; right next to Stanton himself one of them is. He used to work for me in the New York police. That'll throw a scare into him."

Tom thought he sure wouldn't want to tangle with the major. Pedigo was a hard man, and if it came out that Tom was a perjurer and a fraud, he could expect no mercy from him. "Let's hope it doesn't go that far." He hoped his voice hadn't quavered.

Pedigo patted the pocket where the paper was. "I've got to go. I've got to see Rivers and Carter, then go to Corps. Then I'm going after Baker." He stuck out his hand. "I'm much obliged to you, Captain."

"Happy to be of any help, sir," said Tom as they shook hands. He hoped his hand wasn't as clammy as it felt.

Pedigo left, and on his way back to his company Tom saw him riding toward town at a gallop.

Tom had a pretty tense two days and didn't sleep very well at night, but it came out all right. The third day one of Pedigo's men rode out with a little package for him. Inside were a half-dozen Havanas and a note. It said: "He backed down like I thought he would. Many thanks, and drop in to see me sometime. Incidentally, while I was in Washington I got what I wanted and my own men to do it with, so you fellows won't have to do any more picketing around here."

Tom was glad of that. He dreaded going on picket and maybe catching someone like Thiers again. He fingered the cigars. He could put his pipe away for a day or two and would be able to sleep well at night.

The next day Schlimmer brought Tom word that his last uniform, the one for dress, was ready. He was glad it hadn't been a day earlier. He asked Schlimmer how things were going with Rebecca. The answer was: *"Schön, sehr schön!"* He had always heard that Jewish women were really women, and had found out it was true. He even thought his wandering days were over. As the handsome blond fellow walked away, Tom thought of what a strange couple they would make. He was twice her size and as fair as she was dark. Being alike didn't mean anything, though. Look at him and Sally. He glumly wished Schlimmer better luck.

When Tom went to get the uniform, he was afraid the Thierses would give themselves away, but he needn't have been. Ernst hadn't gotten his iron self-control from nowhere. The only evidence Tom saw was a moistness of the eyes and a slight quivering of the lips when Herr Thiers greeted him and a devastating smile from lovely little Rebecca when she came in from the back. Tom had to try on the uniform, though, so her father shooed her out, although there was a closet to change in.

The tailor put Tom before a big mirror and examined the fit meticulously while he admired himself. It was the first time he had seen himself in a dress uniform, and he was beginning to think he really cut a fine figure when Herr Thiers discovered a minute wrinkle. He attributed it to a button slightly out of line and blamed it on Rebecca. She had put the buttons on and here lately had gotten so she couldn't keep her mind on anything but Fritz, that soldier fellow she was seeing.

Tom couldn't see a vestige of a wrinkle, but he had to change uniforms again and wait. While he waited, Rebecca came back with her mother. Frau Thiers was a thin little woman, and Tom saw where her children got their big black eyes. When Rebecca introduced them, she bowed, then came up and clutched his hand with astonishing strength. She looked into his eyes with an expression just like his mother had when he and Billy had left for the army.

Tom found it a lot harder to talk with them than with the Germans in his company. They spoke a different kind of German and talked a lot faster, particularly Rebecca. The only reference to Ernst was a slip Rebecca made. She was telling how she and Fritz were going to get married and, after he got out of the army, her father was going to teach him tailoring and maybe they would move west where Fritz was from, because he said there were scarcely any tailors in the country out there. The slip came when she said her father hadn't wanted her to marry outside the faith but had given in because he had finally come to agree with what Ernst had always said, that if Jewish people over here kept apart from everybody else and married only among themselves like they did in Europe, they would be persecuted like they were there. Maybe they had no choice in Europe, but they did in America.

Frau Thiers frowned at her daughter when she finally stopped, and then Rebecca made it worse by putting her hand over her mouth and widening her eyes. Tom just pretended not to notice.

When Herr Thiers returned with the coat, he told Tom to be sure and go through the pockets before anyone else laid hands on it, but not now. When he started to leave, Rebecca indicated that she wanted to tell him something privately. When he bent over, she kissed him and then fled with a gale of tinkling laughter. Tom could only blush when her mother shook her head and Herr Thiers remarked that there was no telling what silly young girls would do nowadays.

A few doors up the street Tom found a little packet in one of the pockets and transferred it to the coat he had on without looking at it. Once he was alone in his tent, he took it out and opened it. It contained money and a note in a fine, regular hand. "Dear Friend," it read. "Please accept this uniform as a gift from one who owes you more than can ever be repaid." There was no signature, but Tom knew who had written it. The money came exactly to the price of the uniform. He put the money in his wallet and the note into the fire.

# 32

Tom's company was out with the regiment's Second Battalion as part of a reconnaissance force. Forty or so cavalry and a three-gun section of artillery made up the rest of it. The men understood they were to scout into a hilly, remote area readily accessible from the south where the Rebels were reported to be in winter quarters. They guessed they were supposed to find out if the report was true. No one saw much sense to it unless going into winter quarters themselves depended on it. One thing was for sure, it was high time they did. The weather was already too cold for shelter tents, and everybody believed the Rebels had been holed up someplace snug and warm since the first frost.

Three wagons went along, mainly to carry the infantry's packs so it could march faster. Three of the five companies were commanded by lieutenants, so Tom and Jack Arnold were the only captains. Jack presumably commanded the battalion because he was senior. A cavalry colonel named Davis commanded the whole force, though, so Jack wouldn't have much commanding to do. Davis had put the guns in the middle of the column, the wagons in the rear, and cavalry at both ends. He had the white canvas tops taken off the wagons because they were too conspicuous.

Soon after the march began, Tom got a map from Jack showing the route. It was well planned. The way out was roundabout, avoiding towns and well-traveled roads. The way back was direct, mostly on main roads. Davis didn't want to be seen on the way out and wanted to get back as fast as he could, because a small force like his could be gobbled up easily if the Rebels spotted it soon enough to concentrate against it.

The men were talking and joking like they usually did early in a march when the weather was good. Ab had a huge corncob pipe going full-blast.

"Ab," said Zeke Kerns, "y' oughta quit smokin' that big ol' pipe. Th' Rebels'll see hit a mile 'way."

"Aw, they'll jist think hit's a railroad locymotive," was the jocular reply.

Zeke shook his head. "I do b'lieve y' could fire a locymotive biler with that thing."

Everybody laughed.

"I'm shore glad th' weather's good," said Dan Howard. It was a clear November day, and the frost was rapidly disappearing in the sun.

"Yeah," replied Cole, "but y' cain't count on good weather lastin' long this time uv year."

"That's right," agreed Cal Fairbanks. "Hit's liable t' do enything th' next couple uv days, maybe even snow."

"How's your arm by now, Cal?" asked Tom.

"Hit's gittin' better all th' time, Cap'n. I kin do more with hit an' hit ain't s' numb enymore." Cal had recently returned from the hospital as part of a dribble of wounded going back several weeks. His left arm had been almost useless at first, and Tom didn't think it was that much better. Cal could have gone home with a discharge. There were others, like little Jimmy Wells, who still limped on the march, and Grim had a man who had been wounded in the head. The Germans said he wasn't right in his mind sometimes, and Grim had been doubtful about bringing him along, but he acted all right and wanted to go. Tom didn't have the heart to refuse such fellows, and they could be put in the wagons if they couldn't keep up.

Fairbanks was happy to be back. "Y' know," he said to no one in particular, "comin' back t' th' comp'ny's th' best medicine a feller kin git. I'm shore doin' lots better since I did."

"Gittin' back with this bunch uv buzzards ain't gonna help no one!" scoffed Ab. "Hit's jist yore 'magination, Cal."

"Lissen t' th' biggest buzzard in th' bunch speakin'," snickered Charley Evans.

Guffaws and hee-haws followed.

"Yes, sir. I'm th' head buzzard, I am," affirmed Ab, "an' this war's a good thing fer us buzzards, ain't hit, boys?"

Ab's joke didn't draw the usual laughter, for obvious reasons. He wasn't fazed. "Buzzard bait! Buzzard bait! That's what we air, ever' one uv us!"

"Aw, hesh up 'bout that!" scolded Charley. "Hit bothers a feller jist t' think uv hit."

"They ain't no need fer you t' be bothered, y' ol' cuss!" rejoined Ab. "You wuz born t' be hung, Charley, an' fellers that's hung don't git et by buzzards. They gits buried nice 'n' proper."

Charley chuckled. "Well, if'n I gits hung, that'll mean I gits back home safe an' sound. They don't hang ye in th' army. They shoots ye."

He cackled gleefully. "Home fer hangin'! I'm all ready t' go, jist 's long 's they gives me a little time first!"

Tom wondered what Charley had to go home for. His father was dirt poor, and all Charley had ever done was hire out for farm work. Come to think of it, though, Charley had as much back home as he did anymore except property, and that wasn't anything.

The first day's march was uneventful and leisurely. Tom was bothered by their slowness, which was mainly because of the cavalry. Detachments were always ranging around, exploring side roads and the like. To its disgust, the infantry often had to wait for the horsemen to get back from one of their expeditions. The men firmly believed all cavalry were cowards and took this as proof that they had been sent along to protect the troopers from the Rebel horsemen. A favorite gibe was the strident claim that no one had ever seen a dead cavalryman.

At first the artillerymen took a good deal of ribbing, too, mainly because they got to ride while the infantry had to hoof it. They were regulars under a hard-bitten sergeant named Knox, and gave as good as they got.

No fires were allowed and the men had a cold camp that night, but Tom found a brazier glowing in his tent. He remembered seeing Hauser burning wood banked with dirt to make the charcoal, but the brazier was a mystery. He settled down thinking it was nice to be spoiled.

The second day went much like the first until the column reached hilly, rugged country and there was one ridge after another to climb and descend. The wagons and guns slowed the pace going up and often slid most of the way down the other side with their wheels locked. The guns were frequently the objects of apprehensive over-the-shoulder looks from the men in front, but none of them ever got out of control. Knox's men managed them easily and nonchalantly.

Shortly after the noon halt, shooting broke out down a side road as the column passed. The infantry halted and turned to face the action, and Knox put one of his guns into battery. The regulars handled the ponderous piece with marvelous precision, and the men averred Knox had a voice you could hear a mile away.

After a spatter of shots, a squad of cavalry appeared galloping toward the column for all they were worth. A dozen or so gray-clad horsemen left the road behind them and rode along the column out of rifle range. They were swinging their hats and seemed to be yelling derisively.

With a whoop and a clatter, the cavalry detachment at the end of the column took off toward the Rebels. "Yay! Whoo-ee! Sic 'em!"

shouted the infantry as the Rebels fled and the blue-clad horsemen chased them, yelling and brandishing sabers. They disappeared over a swell in the ground, but not for long. Another, heavier spatter of shots sent them flying back toward the column.

Hoots and jeers broke out from the infantry. "Cowards! Yaller-laigs! Git back thar an' fight! That's what yo're paid fer!"

A sizable force of Rebel horsemen appeared behind the flying blue-coats but gave up the chase before it got in rifle range. An officer rode out in front and began studying the column with field glasses. Tom could see why the infantry claimed no one had ever seen a dead cavalryman. It seemed to be hit and run, mostly run.

Knox had his piece trained on the enemy, and the men urged him to let fly. The gun wouldn't have to be unloaded if he did, and he would save himself a lot of trouble. The veteran demurred. He didn't have any orders to fire, and artillery ammunition cost a lot.

After a few minutes, the column re-formed and took up the march again with the Rebels sitting on their horses watching. The cavalry at the rear kept much closer than before and was subjected to a heavy barrage of insults until it dropped back, either to get out of hearing or because the enemy didn't follow.

Colonel Davis rode back and began talking with Jack at the head of the infantry as the march went on. Davis was big, florid man of about forty. Tom knew he wouldn't get much help from Jack and ran up to join them.

Davis looked worried. "They've found us sooner than I thought they would. I was hoping we could get by today without being seen."

Tom put in his two cents' worth. "That cavalry of theirs is everywhere and knows the country like a book. It's pretty hard to get by those fellows."

Davis sighed. "How right you are!"

A captain rode up and joined them. Davis introduced him as Perine, commanding the cavalry. "I guess we can have a little council as we go along," Davis said.

"D'you think we ought to turn back, Colonel?" asked Perine. He was a tall, dark fellow with a full black beard.

"We may have to," replied Davis. "They might get us cornered." He sighed and shook his head. "They've got a lot of cavalry around here, and I'm tied to the infantry. They can run rings around me."

Tom got an idea. "Colonel, what would you think of an early camp and then a night march? We could leave fires burning, and it might throw them off our track?"

Davis looked interested. "Can your men stand it? They've been humping it for nearly two days now."

Before Tom could reply, Jack broke in. "Sure they can! They can march all night tonight and all day tomorrow if they have to. We did forty miles one day last spring when it was over ninety degrees."

Tom wished Jack hadn't been so effusive. The men could do it, but it would be awfully hard on them.

Davis was impressed. "I wouldn't want to do that with cavalry! It'd kill half the horses."

"I think Traylor's got a good idea, Colonel," interjected Perine. "We can go into camp about four o'clock like we're going to stay all night. Then when it's dark, we can leave a few men behind to keep fires going and march. I'll take a few men and go ahead and take up their pickets if they've got any." He grinned in his beard. "They'll see the fires and think we're still there; then the next day they'll have to look for us."

Davis frowned thoughtfully. "Well, we'll have to find a shortcut if we march after dark. The way it is, we can't get to where we're going before daylight, and they'll find us." He turned to Jack. "Where's that map I gave you?"

Tom gave it to him, and Davis went on. "If we can find a shortcut that'll get us to where we're going before daylight, we'll do it."

He studied the map. "Perine, you know this country. What about this road here? It'd save us two or three hours, and that's all we need."

Perine reined over and leaned to look where Davis had his finger as their horses ambled along. "That's no road, sir. It's just a path that turns off this road by a little white church on top of a steep ridge. It'd take a whole day to get the guns and wagons over it."

"Damn the guns and wagons!" exploded Davis. He was really worried. Tom thought he should have gotten worried sooner and marched faster.

Suddenly he got another idea. "How far is it along this path to where we're going?"

"About eight or ten miles," replied Perine.

Tom pondered. "Now, that's about six hours' marching there and back, without the guns and wagons. Can we get to where this path turns off before dark?"

"Oh yes," replied Perine, "several hours before dark."

"Would you want to leave the guns and wagons there and go ahead without the infantry?" Tom asked Davis.

"No!" was the emphatic reply. "They've got too much cavalry around here, and they might find me. I've only got forty men."

"Well, what about hiding the guns and wagons in the woods somewhere around that church and leaving one infantry company on guard, then going ahead with the rest of it after dark?"

Perine was enthusiastic. "Good idea! If they do find us, we can hold them off with the rest of the infantry."

Davis's horse slobbered and blew. Some of it got on Perine's beard, and he wiped it off with a disgusted look.

Davis frowned in concentration. "We can surely find a good place to hide the guns and wagons someplace around that church. It's pretty wild country." He made up his mind. "We'll do it. They'll think we're still camped there by that turnoff until daylight, and we ought to be able to get away with it."

"Whoever's left behind will have to lie low and keep quiet," warned Tom, "or they'll give the whole thing away."

Davis nodded. "You're absolutely right. You'll have to watch your men like hawks, and the gunners and teamsters, too."

"Me, sir?"

"Yes, I'll leave your company behind with the guns and wagons. You'll keep the lid on."

Tom thought Davis might be putting him down for talking too much, but he didn't act like it. "Yes, sir. I'll try to find someplace to emplace the guns and be ready to fight if the Rebels are on your heels when you get back."

Davis wasn't much impressed by the idea. "Oh, all right if you want to."

Jack laughed and slapped Tom on the back. "You can depend on Traylor! He always thinks of everything!"

"Always expect the worst," replied Tom. "That's my motto."

"I guess it takes a pessimist to be a good military man," sighed Jack. "Now take me; I'm an optimist."

Everybody laughed.

"I'll bet you enjoy life a lot more, though," chuckled Perine.

"Right! That's what it's for!" was the prompt reply.

Everybody laughed again but Tom, who only shook his head and thought how right Perine was. Davis and Perine went back up the column, and Tom took the side of the road to wait for his company.

A little before five o'clock the column reached the foot of the ridge where Perine said the little church and the turnoff were at the top. When he started up the slope, Tom noticed a good place to hide the guns and wagons. To the left a steep-sided hollow ending in a cul-de-sac up toward the ridge top paralleled the road. There was a precipitous dropoff from the road, and the hollow had a dense growth of bushes and small trees, mostly oaks with the dead leaves still on. They had just crossed a shallow creek with a rocky bed that went on at a right angle to the hollow, so it would be easy to get in and out of. He shouted to Jack to halt the column, then ran up to meet Davis as he rode back to see why they had stopped. Davis said it was all right and rode away with scarcely a look at the hollow. Tom took his company, the guns, and the wagons out of the column, and the rest of it went on. No one had seen any Rebels since the brush with them earlier in the day, so he felt safe about it.

After getting the guns and wagons along the creek bed and then up the hollow out of sight, Tom satisfied himself that they couldn't be seen from the road and had the marks at the turnoff erased. The road was so rocky on the slopes away from it there was no need to do any erasing on them.

After that, he got everyone together, told them they were going to stay there until Davis got back the next day, and impressed on them the necessity of lying low and keeping quiet. That made him think of the horses, who would be hard to keep quiet if anyone rode along the road, so he had the teamsters take them down the creek out of hearing and keep them there. He had Cole put a two-man picket on the road about half a mile back. They would have to keep well hidden and stay out all night to lessen the risk of discovery.

Tom told Grim to set up a guard on the camp, then started up the road to see Davis before he left. He hadn't gone far when he noticed where an old road overgrown with head-high brush came in from the right. It had been used a lot a long time ago, as it was cut down deeply. The angle of the junction made it seem that guns set up twenty or thirty yards out on the old road could sweep the newer one almost to the top of the ridge and the guns would be sunk almost to the level of the slope. The right bank of the newer road was too low to give much protection, and there was that steep dropoff on the other side.

When he went out on the old road, he saw he was right. The only obstructions in the field of fire were bushes and small trees the guns could cut down like matchsticks. Taking the horses and limbers farther along would put them out of hearing and sight and still permit getting the guns away quickly if it was all for nothing.

He went back to get Knox and see what he thought about it. It looked good to him. If the Rebels were chasing Davis in force when he got back, they would be coming down the road in columns and he could slaughter them. He looked around and allowed that with the guns down on that old road in all that brush, all the Rebels in Virginia could go by and never see them. The only digging he would have to do would be to sink the wheels so the guns would roll back after recoil. He always liked to do that because it speeded up the rate of fire so much.

Tom told him they would set up the guns the first thing in the morning and went on up the road. He made sure that the dropoff into the hollow to the left was so steep and abrupt all the way that there would be no danger from there. The infantry could be deployed in the woods to the right until Knox opened fire, then rushed up to hold the Rebels on the road. In case they smelled a rat, deployed off the road to the right at the top of the ridge, and came down on the guns through the woods there, the infantry could be wheeled to cover them until Knox got them away. Of course he would need all five companies to do all that, but he guessed Davis would go along with it if the need arose.

The cavalry and the rest of the infantry had gone into camp around the little church at the top of the ridge and built fires like they were going to stay all night. The building reminded Tom of the church back home. It had a fresh coat of whitewash, and "Midlow Church" was neatly lettered in black over the door. He wanted to tell Davis what he proposed to do if the Rebels were pressing him when he got back, but he never got the chance. Davis pointedly ignored him, so after standing around a while and talking with Jack, Tom started back. It nettled him, so he paid Davis back back in his own coin when he shouted after him to have everything ready to go when he got back.

On his way back, he saw things as the Rebels would see them if they were chasing Davis the next morning and was completely satisfied. By the time he ate and visited the pickets, it was dark, so he turned in. It was so warm that there was no need for the brazier, and Hauser hadn't set it up. It was also cloudy and very still, which might mean an early winter storm was coming. A disturbance among Grim's men during the night woke him up, but it was over before he could get his boots on, so he decided to wait until morning to find out about it. It was very strange to have anything like that among the quiet and well-disciplined Germans.

Tom went to see Grim the first thing in the morning. It had been the fellow with the old head wound. He wasn't right in his mind and had spells sometimes. He was tied hand and foot with a gag in his mouth. Tom didn't think that was necessary but found out differently when he had him untied. He snatched the gag out of his mouth and started shouting and carrying on, and had to be wrestled around until his hands were tied and it was put back on.

It was too bad that such a nice-looking young fellow had to be done like that, but it was a necessity. Grim thought he could be taken down to the wagons, where he could lie on the packs. The teamsters could watch him. Tom agreed and had Billy go along to make sure everything was understood.

Zeke Kerns and Sam Price had been picketing the road. When they were relieved and came in, they had a tale to tell. A Rebel cavalry scouting party had come up during the night and stopped right where they were. There had been three of them, and they had stayed until just before the relief came out and had been too close for anyone to come in and report.

To Tom's relief, the two agreed that the Rebels hadn't seen anything but the fires up by the church and had gone back the way they had come.

By this time Knox was hitched up and ready to go. Tom sent the teamsters word to stay where they were until they heard from him, then went up the road with the guns. He took his company with him and on the way told Cole and Grim to keep the men back in the woods out of sight. He had Grim send two men up to the church to keep watch from there, because whoever Davis had left to keep the fires going would probably be gone by now.

After the guns were set up, the only evidence Tom could see of them from the road was bark rubbed off some of the bushes and wheel marks leading in. Some dirt rubbed on the bushes, and a little work with pieces of brush took care of that.

After the horses had been taken away, Tom asked Knox if he had plenty of canister in his limber chests. The veteran said he did, but that grape would be better for the number-three gun because it would be firing at a range a little long for canister. Tom deferred to his superior knowledge. They joked a little about Davis ambling back right away with no one after him and all the trouble they had gone to being for nothing but agreed it was always better to be ready for the worst.

Tom went up the ridge through the woods where the infantry was and got Billy to take along as a messenger. When they reached the top of the ridge, Tom wasn't surprised to see Grabner roosting high in a tree. *Alte Adler Augen* had seen nothing yet of Davis or anyone else. Tom told him to stay up there but sent the other fellow back.

Tom and Billy were scarcely seated on the church steps when "Eagle Eye" called out that people were coming along the road toward them, mostly women and children. Tom leaped to his feet in panic. He couldn't imagine why women and children would be out traipsing around until Billy reminded him that it was Sunday and they were probably coming to church, even if it did seem a little early.

If any of these people saw anything, every Rebel in the country would soon know about it. The only thing to do was call Grabner down, warn everybody to lie low and keep quiet, then hide himself. He was so upset that he sent Grabner with the warning without thinking he might not be able to make himself understood to Knox and the teamsters, but Billy said Grim was always careful about things like that and would undoubtedly send someone on who could speak good English.

Tom knew that people would be coming the other way, too, and wasn't surprised when Dan Howard came panting up the road to tell him they were. Dan and Tom Pinnick were the pickets back on the road. Tom thought to ask if there were any dogs along, because there would be no hiding from them. Dan didn't think so. Anyhow, he hadn't seen any. Tom could only hope there wouldn't be any from the other way either. He sent Dan back to his post and told him to be careful to stay out of sight.

There was a clump of small cedars just across the road from the church, so Tom and Billy hid in it. When the people began to arrive, there were fewer from the way Davis had gone, but they got there first. Almost all were women and children, and everybody was on foot. Maybe they didn't have horses anymore, or they might be afraid to risk them out on the road.

The women and children went inside, but the few men that there were stood around and talked awhile before going in just like they did back home. They seemed awfully old, though. No dogs showed up and none of the people gave any indication they had seen anything.

Tom and Billy were so close they could hear the singing when it started. Tom couldn't understand the words, but the tunes were familiar. After the singing, someone prayed, and it sounded just like the prayers he had heard ever since he was old enough to remember. He prayed, too, although silently. He prayed that Davis wouldn't get back until the people were all gone and that there would be no fighting and killing around the church.

He saw movement in the distance on the path and realized his prayer wasn't going to be answered, part of it anyhow. He nudged Billy and pointed through the aromatic boughs.

Billy peered intently. "Somebody's comin'," he whispered.

Tom wished fervently he had a pair of field glasses. Without any, the sermon was well under way before he could be sure it was Davis instead of the Rebels. "Let's get out on this side, away from the church," he said, although he knew the people would soon see Davis. The windows were all on the sides.

He wondered what the people would do when they saw Davis and, after he and Billy emerged from the cedars, moved to where he could see the door. Suddenly it opened and they started coming out. They had to be kept inside, so he ran toward them. Without thinking, he drew his sword and waved it as he ran. They saw him and stood affrighted. "Get back inside there!" he shouted. "Back inside! Back inside!"

Everybody whisked back inside as he dashed for the church, Billy on his heels. Before they got there, a man came out, leaving the door open behind him. He seemed a lot younger than the other men and stood imperturbably in the doorway. Suddenly Tom realized he had drawn his sword and hastily put it back in the scabbard.

The man in the door was a small, pale fellow with an empty sleeve pinned to his coat. Tom could see frightened faces through the doorway. Children started wailing when they saw him, and a woman screamed. He felt like Attila the Hun.

"What do you mean by this?" demanded the one-armed man before Tom could say anything. "You're disturbing the house of the Lord!" He looked at Tom unwaveringly. His eyes were pale blue, so pale it was hard to see the pupils, and it looked like it hadn't been long since he lost his arm.

"I'm . . . I'm sorry, sir," stammered Tom, "but your service was over, wasn't it?"

"I ended it when I saw armed men coming," the pale fellow said coldly, "but you've frightened my people, and in a church of all places." He was the minister, then.

"I'm sorry, sir, but I must ask all of you to stay inside."

"Why's that?" The voice was hard and the pale eyes showed no fear.

"I guess you could say it's a military necessity, sir." Tom looked at the empty sleeve. "I expect you'd know about that."

"I gave my arm for the South, Captain," was the calm reply.

"I respect you for that, sir. You fought for what you think is right. So do I."

The pale eyes softened. "But only God knows who is really right." He extended his hand. "My name is Mason."

"Mine is Traylor, sir," said Tom as they shook hands. "I fancy myself a Christian, and I wish we'd met under more pleasant circumstances."

Mason nodded. "How long will you keep us?"

Tom pointed to the approaching column, now close at hand. "Until the colonel gets here; then he'll decide. I hope it won't be long," he added placatingly.

"Very well. I'll tell my people." Mason went back inside and closed the door.

"Stay here," Tom told Billy, "and don't let anyone leave."

He went to meet Davis, who was at the head of the column with most of the cavalry. There was still no sign of pursuit.

"Well, I'm glad to see you, Captain," said Davis in a tired voice. He seemed to be in a better mood than the night before.

"Yes, sir. Were you able to carry out your mission?"

Davis got off his horse and began to rub the seat of his pants. "Yes. there wasn't a Rebel camped in the whole area. Whoever said there was sure sent us on a wild-goose chase."

"Well, we know now that they aren't going into winter camp there, anyhow."

Davis began to walk around and stretch his legs. "Yes, and I guess that's something."

"Are there any Rebels after you, Colonel?"

Davis yawned and paid no attention. "Too long in the saddle," he said ruefully while he rubbed the seat of his pants again. "What did you say, Captain?"

Tom repeated his question.

"I guess we fooled them with that night march. There's only a little cavalry following us, about an hour's march back. There's a regiment of infantry with them, though, so we can't give the men more than a few minutes' rest, here anyhow. Maybe they'll give it up later, though, and we can camp someplace."

"Any guns, sir?"

"No, no guns." Davis yawned again.

"I wouldn't be much afraid of them, then."

"Oh, I'm not. It's just that I wanted to rest the men. They didn't get any last night." Davis stretched his legs again. "Do you have everything hitched up and ready to go?"

"No, sir. I have the guns set up down there to sweep the road, close to the bottom of the ridge, but—"

Davis cut him off angrily. "Now what did you do that for?"

Tom got angry, too. "I told the colonel what I was going to do yesterday," he said evenly, "and he said to go ahead with it. I wanted to be ready to fight a rear guard action if we had to." He looked Davis in the eye. "Anyhow, they're placed so they can be gotten out in a hurry."

Davis couldn't hold his eye. "Oh well, I don't guess it'll do any harm. I was going to let the men rest a little while anyhow. They sure need it."

"I'll go down and tell Sergeant Knox to limber up, then, and send word to the teamsters."

Davis seemed to think of something. "Wait, and I'll go with you." He beckoned Perine over and began talking with him.

The infantry had come up, Jack limping along at the head.

"How'd it go, Jack?" Tom asked.

Jack shook his head. "You lucky dog! You got out of it." He grimaced. "Oh, my poor feet!"

Tom laughed. "I guess you can fall out. The colonel said he's going to give you a little rest."

"Thank God!" Jack told the men they could fall out and sit down, then immediately sat down himself.

Davis was back on his horse and ready to go. Tom happened to think about the people in the church and asked him what to do about them.

"Just keep them in there awhile yet. They can always sing or something." Tom wondered why Davis wouldn't let them go but didn't want to ask. He told Billy about it and started down the road with Davis.

Davis had nothing to say until they were over halfway down the ridge. "Where is it you've got those guns set up, now?"

"They're there," Tom replied as he pointed toward them, "along an old road that joins this one in some bushes, but you can't see them anywhere along this road."

Davis looked. "You sure can't. You say you've got them sited so they can sweep this road all the way to the top?"

"Yes, sir, and Sergeant Knox has plenty of grape and canister. We'd have been ready for them if they'd been hot after you."

They went on. When they came to the junction, Tom pointed and said, "Well, here they are."

Davis peered into the bushes. "I still can't see them," he marveled. He looked at the road. "You can't even tell anything's been along here."

"Yes, sir. We covered up the tracks and wheel marks. We even rubbed dirt on where the bark had been skinned off the bushes."

"Uh-huh," mused Davis. He began forcing his horse through the bushes, and Tom followed.

Knox called his men to attention. Davis put them at rest and got off his horse. He sighted along the guns, nodding and talking to himself. He wanted to know where the horses and limbers were when he saw the limber chests beside the guns, so Tom showed him. "Can't see them either," said Davis to himself. "No one knows these guns are here?" he asked abruptly.

"No, sir. The only scout they sent along this road stopped half a mile back there, when they saw those fires up by the church, I guess."

Tom turned to Knox. "Did any of those people see anything when they went by here? Not that it makes any difference."

"No, sir. I hid up close an' watched 'em, an' none uv 'em seen a thing."

"Well, Sergeant, what do you think about this?" asked Davis.

"What does th' colonel mean?"

"About where you've got these guns. What could you do to a column strung out up along that road?"

"Hit's like I told Cap'n Traylor awhile 'go; I'd slaughter hit," was the confident reply.

Davis nodded thoughtfully. He looked at his watch, then went back to the new road. He stood there, gazing up and down the ridge, then came back. His horse started away, but one of the gunners caught it. "Where do you have those wagons, Captain?" he asked.

Tom told him, but he wanted to be shown, so they went back and Tom pointed toward where they were.

"I sure can't see them either," Davis remarked.

After they went back to the guns, Davis stood rubbing the stubble on his chin and pondering. "No one has the slightest idea these guns are here, and they won't see them until they open fire," said Davis half to himself. Suddenly he turned to Tom. "I just can't pass it up!" he exclaimed.

"Sir?" asked Tom.

"It's too good to waste, this artillery ambush. It's perfect! We can cut up that regiment that's following me and send those Rebels back with their tails between their legs. I just can't pass it up!" He laughed shortly. "Don't you agree, Captain?"

Tom had a sinking feeling. None of his prayer was going to be answered, and he wished he had left the guns in the hollow. "I don't know everything the colonel does, about what we'd have to contend with." Maybe Davis would have second thoughts.

He didn't, though. "Well, there's only about fifteen or twenty cavalry with that regiment that's following me, and they don't have any guns. There's nothing else close enough to bother us. I guess we really threw them off last night."

"But they found you this morning." Tom didn't want to give up yet.

"Yes, but too late to be able to do anything about it. We can shoot up this bunch and get away scot-free if we make good time going back." He slapped Tom on the shoulder. "We'll do it! I'm putting you in command of the infantry, Captain."

"But Captain Arnold's senior."

"Oh, he won't care! He's too tired anyhow!"

"I hope you're right, sir." Jack was one of the few friends he had among the officers.

Davis looked at his watch again. "Well, we've got to get busy. They'll be here in half an hour or so." He told Knox what they were going to do and said he would come back to the guns before anything happened.

Davis mounted his horse and they started back up the road. He hadn't said anything about the infantry, so Tom told him what he was going to do with it. Davis agreed and only cautioned him about keeping the men out of Knox's field of fire. By this time it was clear that Davis was going ahead with it, so Tom swallowed his qualms and made up his mind to do his duty.

Davis didn't think there was any chance the Rebels would get suspicious and scout the woods to the right of the road before they started down the slope or anything. "I've been running ever since they saw me, and they won't be expecting me to stop and fight. They probably don't know I've got any guns, either, this bunch anyhow."

Tom was thinking. "You know, sir, around that church would be a good place for that infantry to stop if they decide they can't catch us. They might just give up the chase there, and then catch us on the move when we try to leave." He shook his head. "We'd be in a bad fix then."

"That's right. I hadn't thought of that." Davis furrowed his brow. "Say, could I hide my cavalry in there where you've got the wagons?"

"Yes. You could hide them in that creek bed there, right on the road."

Davis laughed delightedly. "I've got it! I'll leave Perine up there by that church with a few of his men and put the rest of them in that creek bed at the bottom of this ridge. He'll make out like he's scared half out of his wits, and their cavalry will chase him. Then when they go by that creek, the rest of my cavalry will come out and pitch into them. That'll bring that infantry down the road sure enough!" He slapped his horse on the neck, which caused it to shy to the side. He reined the animal back and laughed again. "That'll do it!"

Tom was a little surprised to learn that Davis could have ideas of his own. "Yes, sir. That ought to bring them down the road."

When they reached the church and Tom saw Billy beside the door, he thought of the people inside. "I don't mean to prompt you, sir, but something's got to be done about those people in that church."

"Yes, we'll have to get them away from here, and I don't want them running to the Rebels about us." He detailed a corporal and two troopers to take the people out of the church and down the road as far as they could go before the action started.

Tom was careful to keep out of Mason's sight when he came out. He could hear the pale little fellow objecting and was glad he hadn't been given the job. The troopers herded Mason and his flock down the road out of sight while Davis talked with Perine. Billy wanted to go back to his company, so Tom let him.

Jack didn't mind at all when Tom told him Davis had put him in command of the infantry. "They're all yours, Traylor. You're all rested up, and you're a lot better at it anyhow."

When Davis was done with Perine, he told Tom to deploy the infantry and said he would be with Knox at the guns, then started down the road with most of the cavalry.

Tom took the infantry into the woods to the right of the road and deployed it in a line back in the woods where his company already was. After he gave the officers their instructions, he suddenly realized there was no plan to disengage and withdraw if the thing didn't work out and the Rebels were too much for them.

He hurried to the guns and found Davis idly talking with Knox. "Colonel," he began, "I believe we ought to do some thinking about getting away if things go wrong and they're too much for us. A half-strength battalion against a whole regiment is pretty heavy odds."

Davis obviously hadn't given it a thought. "What do you suggest, Captain?"

Tom thought fast. "We'll fall back and form a line on the guns while Sergeant Knox gets them away. We can hold them long enough for him to pull back and go into battery on top of that first ridge back there and support us while we fall back. Then we'll form another line there and hold them until he can find another place to support us from, and so on. They'll probably get enough of it before long and let us go. Perine can keep their cavalry off all right and even help us out if we need it. I think you ought to stay with the guns, though, so you can manage things." He had gone a good deal beyond making suggestions, but Davis didn't seem to mind.

The colonel turned to Knox. "What do you think of all that, Sergeant?"

"Sounds good t' me. Hit'll be makin' th' most outa th' only thing we got that they ain't, th' guns. I kin set up two guns enyplace 'long that road an' all three in most places. Th' leaves is off, an' we'll be able t' see good 'nough." He nodded thoughtfully and shifted his chew from one cheek to the other, then spat copiously. "Hit'd be 'bout th' only way we could git away if'n th' worst happens, an' a man's alus gotta figger hit might."

Davis nodded. "We'll do it that way, then, if we have to, but I don't think we will."

"I don't neither, Colonel," replied Knox, "but like I say, a man's alus gotta be ready fer th' worst." He nodded approvingly and smiled at Tom.

"All right, Captain," said Davis. "We've got everything planned out now, I guess."

"Here's hoping for luck," said Tom as he turned away, thinking it sure wasn't Davis's fault that everything was planned out. A man with his rank should do a lot more thinking than he ever did. If that was a crack regiment back there with some sharp colonel in command, they would be in for it.

Nothing was in sight yet when Tom reached the top of the ridge. Perine was using field glasses, and Tom was glad he was looking all around once in a while. No one had seen those Rebels back there for a long time, and they could be coming from almost any direction. Davis should have left a squad of cavalry behind to keep an eye on them.

Perine paid no attention to him as he sat on the church steps. The troopers were sprawled out on the ground with their horses tied to the church hitching rail. The time passed interminably, and Tom was getting restless when Perine suddenly called, "Here they come!" None of his men stirred, and Tom hoped they weren't really asleep.

"Are they still on the path?" asked Tom as he got up. "Are there any more of them?"

"No, they're all on the road. I guess they crossed over back there a little ways where it's close." He kept the glasses to his eyes.

Tom went toward him. "May I take a look?"

Perine gave him the glasses, and he turned them on the road. There were only fifteen or twenty cavalry. Their horses shambled along in front no faster than a man could walk. He picked up the infantry just as the column crested a slight rise, so he ignored Perine's impatience and took a good look. At first it seemed too small for a regiment, but he soon saw that was only because the column was so compact. The Rebels marched in regular ranks that were precisely aligned close together like they were on parade. That was very unusual; Rebel infantry on the march usually strung itself out all over the road and paid no attention to ranks or regularity.

Perine was fidgeting with impatience, so Tom gave the glasses back. "I'll be over here," he said, indicating the clump of cedars across the road.

Perine clapped the glasses to his eyes and paid no attention, then moved behind a corner of the church so the Rebels wouldn't see him.

Tom went down the road and into the woods. Jack came to meet him, so he told him that the enemy was in sight and to send someone down to the guns to tell Davis and on to the creek to tell the cavalry.

When he went back to the top of the ridge, Tom decided the clump of cedars was too small and too close to the road, so he looked around for another place to hide. A fringe of dense brush out in front of the woods a hundred yards from the road looked good, so he went there. The brush turned out to be so low he had to lie prone behind it, though, and it was so dense he could barely see through it. It was too late to look for a better place, and he would have to stay where he was. Although he wouldn't be able to see any details, he would always be able to tell where the Rebels were and what they were doing.

The horsemen came into view first, and Tom found that by moving his head from side to side he could see them a little better. Suddenly there was an outcry among Perine's men at the church, followed by confused rushing about and hasty mounting. One of them mounted so hurriedly that he nearly fell off before he could get firmly in the saddle and tear out after the others, who were fleeing down the road like the devil was after them.

The Rebel horsemen broke into exultant shouts and spurred to a gallop. They passed the church and thundered down the road, yelling and brandishing weapons. A few shots rang out, and then the hoofbeats faded away and the yells became fainter as they passed out of sight.

When the infantry came up, it halted with precision at a sharp command directly in front of Tom, where the density of the brush kept him from telling much about it. Then the command "At rest in place" told him there was no intention to deploy off the road or anything like that. The Rebels just stood there, shuffling their feet like men always do after a spell of hard marching. It certainly looked like they had gone as far as they were going to go.

Suddenly faint shouting and screeching punctuated by carbine and revolver shots broke out far down the road. The shuffling abruptly stopped and Tom felt it safe to move to his left, where he could see the head of the column plainly. He saw a large, portly man in ordinary clothing lumbering out ahead to look down the road. He took one look, then wheeled and shouted, "For'ard! For'ard! Double-quick!" The fellow pulled a big horse pistol from his belt and led the column down the road at a run.

As the Rebels streamed past the church, all Tom had to do was wait for Knox to open fire, then bring his men up to the road to keep the enemy from leaving it.

For the first time, he could see the Rebels plainly. They all seemed to be wearing ordinary citizens' clothing, which puzzled him. The Rebels generally wore anything they could get, but always enough of their own issue to make them recognizable. Also, these fellows seemed to be either very young or very old. Fresh-faced boys abounded and graybeards were common. Several oldsters brought up the rear, laboring stifly along in an attempt to keep up. One of them was even using his rifle like a cane.

Not until the last of them had gone out of sight down the road did he put it all together, the very young and the very old, the citizens' clothing, and the parade ground marching. They were home guards only trying to be soldiers, probably called out against Davis because no regular troops were close enough.

Tom cowered behind the brush overcome with horror. He had engineered a massacre of boys and grandfathers fresh from their homes and families. The enormity of it paralyzed him, and before he could get hold of himself Knox's guns opened up with a crash and a roar. Funneled up the ridge by the road, the sound was overwhelming. Startled cries and shrieks of agony went up as canister and grape tore into the column, only to be drowned out by another salvo and its fearful club of sound.

Tom got to his feet and rushed toward the road. Dirt and rock fragments flew up from its surface, and ricocheting grapeshot howled past the church as another salvo blasted out. His legs seemed to be working automatically, and he heard himself trying to shout above the uproar. The guns fired with dreadful rapidity, and their blasts seemed enough to uproot the very trees.

Tom's men took his action as a signal to attack the white-faced, shrieking figures scrambling out of the road toward them. They threw up their rifles and fired, then rushed on the fugitives with their bayonets. Tom shouted for them to stop, but his voice was only a whisper lost in the roar of another salvo. He shouted again, but they paid no heed and went on stabbing and clubbing, yelling like madmen.

He found himself at the road with the guns still firing, no longer in salvos, but one after the other. Grapeshot and canister whizzed past inches ahead. The road was filled with dust and flying pieces of rock, which partly hid the carnage. Bodies lay in the road like leaves on the ground, some in heaps that seemed to contort and expand as canister and grape lashed them. At his feet weaponless, white-faced figures hugged the low bank to escape the storm of death. Their eyes widened with horror as they saw him standing over them.

*Cease firing! Cease firing!* shouted a voice from within him. Although none of the gunners could have heard, the guns suddenly fell silent and his men brought up sharply on the edge of the road.

"We s'render! We s'render!" screeched the boys and old men couched against the bank or groveling amid the mangled bodies on the road. "Don't shoot no more! Please don't shoot no more!"

Similar cries went up all down the road, along with a horrible medley of every conceivable sound that could be made by men in mortal agony. Looking at the road was like taking the lid off hell.

Some strange force entered Tom's being. He was walking along the road among the shattered and mangled bodies in the grip of an icy calm, unaffected by what he saw or heard. He had the unwounded survivors assembled and sent to the church under guard. He did what he could for the wounded and had the dead moved aside. He noted dispassionately that the dead and dying outnumbered the wounded because of the concentrated fire of the guns.

He never willed a word he spoke or a thing he did. He functioned automatically, like a mechanism operated by a spring that never ran down. He saw mutilation and suffering beyond all imagination, but none of it affected him. He wondered if this was how it was to lose your mind.

Billy ran up to him, his eyes wide and frightened. "Tom! Tom! Air ye all right? Ye shore y' wuzn't hit by them guns? Yo're white as a sheet!"

"I'm all right, Billy," an unnaturally calm voice replied. "I'm not wounded or anything." Tom went on, but Billy stood watching him for a while with worry showing on his face.

The men were getting over their excitement and starting to react. Shock and horror spread over their faces, and a few got sick and retched on the ground. Tom was no more affected by that then he was by anything else. Once the road was clear enough, he had the men fall in and form a line, then put them at rest in place.

Davis rode up the road followed by several troopers. Their horses shied and snorted at they passed mangled bodies and trampled in pools of blood. "Well, Captain," said Davis, "it doesn't look like many of them got away." He didn't sound very happy about it.

Tom heard himself speak accusingly. "Do you know who they were, Colonel?"

Davis reined up and nodded. "Home guards. I didn't know that. They never got close enough." He shook his head and looked down.

"I should've seen what they were before it was too late, but I didn't. It was all there to see."

Davis looked at Tom strangely. "Don't feel too bad about it, Captain. It couldn't be helped." He sighed and ran his eyes over the carnage. "Those fellows shouldn't have gone out playing soldier when real ones were around." He looked at Tom again, his eyes showing concern. "Are you all right, Captain? You look awfully pale."

"I'm all right, sir." Tom was afraid he would be like that the rest of his life, as pale as death. It would be God's stamp of infamy for what he had done. Suddenly he desperately wanted to flee the scene of his crime. "Don't you think we ought to be getting out of here, sir?"

"Yes. I've sent for that preacher fellow and his people. These are their men, and they'll take care of them." He sighed. "God knows we can't."

"Shall we parole the prisoners or take them with us?" For the first time, it sounded like his own voice.

"Where are they?"

"I sent them to the church under guard." The voice was his again, and he began to feel like his spirit was returning to his body. "There aren't many of them."

"Just turn them loose. I don't want to be bothered with them, and they won't need any paroles." He laughed shortly. "No one's ever going to get those fellows out again."

"Well, I'll just send someone up there to tell the guard to let them go and get ready to march."

"Yes, the Rebels are going to get all riled up about this, and they'll be after us as soon as they can." Davis nodded. "I'll tell Knox to limber up and get out and send word to the teamsters."

After the guard returned from the church and the wagons came out on the road, Knox joined the column. The veteran didn't seem particularly cheerful, but his men were laughing and chatttering. They hadn't seen the results of their shooting. "Good shoot, wasn't it, Cap'n?" shouted a burly corporal riding one of the horses. Tom pretended not to hear him.

Before the column was ready, the people who had been in the church began to go by. Tom avoided looking at them and closed his ears to their anguish. Suddenly someone spoke at his elbow. It was Mason, the last person he wanted to see.

"You're an accomplished murderer, Captain," he said in a voice that throbbed with loathing. "I'm sorry I ever shook your hand."

Tom steeled himself and looked into the pale blue eyes. "Listen," he began earnestly, "I didn't know who those men were. No one did. We all thought—"

A cavalry trooper escorting the people broke in. "C'mon! C'mon! Keep goin'!" To Tom's great relief, Mason moved on, and nobody gave any sign of having heard him.

Soon after the march began, Tom realized that in all that had gone on he had forgotten about the deranged fellow who had been left in one of the wagons, but Grim said he was looking out for him. The man was riding in one of the wagons, and the teamster was watching him. He seemed all right now, and they had untied him.

Nothing was seen of the Rebels the first day of the march back, not even of their cavalry. Maybe it was because the column followed a different route back, or maybe the Rebels were busy someplace else. It might even be because the weather was threatening, but that was doubtful. Davis kept up a smart pace anyhow. There was no halt until dark, when he stopped at the edge of a woods to make camp.

As soon as they halted, Tom went up to Jack Arnold. "Everything's over now, Jack. Don't you think you ought to take over the infantry again?"

Jack didn't have a jealous bone in his body. He laughed and said, "Oh no, go ahead with it!"

"But you're senior," Tom insisted.

Jack drew him aside. "Listen, Tom. They made me a captain because I raised a company, back when they were turning men away. They made you one because you're a natural-born military man. The way you set up that action and handled it would've done credit to a general."

"I don't think there was any credit in that," replied Tom morosely. It was on the tip of his tongue to say it hadn't been anything but murder, but he held it back.

Jack saw how he felt and put a hand on his shoulder. "Buck up, fellow!" he said earnestly. "That's war, and nobody knew who those fellows were, did they?"

"No, but they were just boys and old men, home guards—" He felt himself slipping and couldn't finish.

Arnold shook his head. "You're a strange fellow, Traylor."

"I guess I am," replied Tom woodenly as Jack turned away. He hadn't said anything about Tom being pale, so he guessed his color had come back.

It was very warm and the men didn't want to bother about shelter tents, but Tom made them put them up anyhow. It looked to him like an early winter storm was coming, with rain probably changing to snow as the temperature fell. Davis didn't seem to concern himself about anything, so he had the wagon tops put back on, too. Before dark

Grim came to say that the fellow they had had in the wagon had come back to his platoon and seemed all right, but he would keep an eye on him and they would have to do something about him when they got back.

It did start raining during the night, and the march began the next morning in a steady, penetrating drizzle that promised to get heavier. Tom had the men drape themselves in their groundsheets, but it didn't help much because there was no way of fastening them. All they could do was become gradually soaked to the skin and envy the slickers of the cavalry. Tom marched warm and dry under his cape and hat cover.

The temperature fell as the morning wore on and added to the misery. Before noon, the rain changed to sleet and the column soon moved encased in ice except where movement kept it from sticking to the men and horses. Word came down the column that there would be no halt at noon, and both men and animals plodded on, one as patiently and stoically as the other.

Early in the afternoon the wind picked up and blew steadily from the northeast. The sleet changed to snow, and soon the column was enveloped in a driving snowstorm. Before dark, Perine rode back along the column saying there would be no halt until they reached camp, which wouldn't be for a long time. None of the men complained. They knew they wouldn't be able to build fires and that whatever shelter they could put up wouldn't keep their wet bodies from freezing.

As the snow got deeper, Tom took it on himself to halt the infantry and put the guns and wagons ahead to break the way. He also moved his company ahead of the others, because his men had slept all the night before and the others hadn't.

He walked along the column looking the men over. They lurched along, heads down against the driving snow that built up on their caps and shoulders. Those with beards looked like grandfathers. Billy swung along in his usual loose-jointed gait and seemed to be bearing up as well as any.

The last hour was the hardest. Two men collapsed and had to be put in the wagons. The others labored through an increasing depth of snow in the pitch darkness, scarcely able to see the backs of the men in front. Their leaden limbs seemed to move mechanically, propelling their exhausted and freezing bodies on and on.

When the cavalry and guns left the column, Tom knew they were close to the town south of camp. Davis led them off without a word and left the infantry to fend for itself. When the men passed through town, they could scarcely see the buildings along the streets because of the driving snow.

It was late at night when the column finally reached camp. Some didn't react to the order to halt and blundered into the men in front of them. Many swayed on their feet, like snow-covered cedars buffeted by the wind. When they got their packs out of the wagons, most of them were willing to settle for the first one they found, but Tom made them sort the packs until the officers reported that each man had his own.

Next Tom faced the problem of keeping the men on their feet until fires could be built and their shelter tents put up, but Rivers and Owen solved that problem. Rivers had taken over the officers' sleeping and mess tents in the whole brigade for the men to sleep in. He had known there would be no managing men in their condition and that some of them might just pile down in the snow and freeze to death. Tom's and Marcus Allen's companies got to stay with the regiment, but the others would have to go on to where one of the other three regiments was camped. The two of them could be accommodated because Owen had given up his headquarters tent, too. No one seemed to mind going a little farther for good shelter, even those who had to go back through town.

When Tom wondered where the officers who had been turned out had gone, Owen said Rivers had sent them to that big old cabin where he had his headquarters and told them that if anyone didn't like it there, he could put up at the hotel in town.

Tom told Marcus Allen to take half his men to the headquarters tent and said he would take the others to the officers' mess and sleeping tents along with his men. Allen's captain had been badly wounded at Antietam, and he was commanding the company. He was so far gone he could only sway on his feet and nod dumbly, but his sergeant major was a big, burly fellow who looked like he could take care of the men and Allen, too.

The officers' tents had wooden floors and stoves like the headquarters tent. The tables and benches were all piled outside in the snow, but the bunks and trunks were stacked up and covered with canvas.

The blankets the men had in their packs were pretty dry, so Tom told them to strip to the skin and roll up in their blankets on the floor. He sent for the orderlies who worked in the tents and told them to keep hot fires all night and dry out the clothes. Ropes run around the sides through the ties and between the poles in the middle would do to hang the clothes on, but there wouldn't be nearly enough room for all of them at once and they would have to be changed as they dried. If any of the men wanted food or coffee, the cook was to serve it up.

This brought the cook of the officers' mess into it, and he didn't like it at all. He was a squat, fat fellow gone soft on his easy job and used to getting his way. He wouldn't have to stay up all night, but the orderlies would, and he took their part. He said these fellows ought to be able to take care of themselves and he didn't think anyone ought to be kept up all night on their account.

Tom lost his temper. He called the cook a big fat loafer and said that losing a night's sleep was nothing to what these men had been through and maybe he ought to go along the next time there was anything like this and find out what it was like. He wound up by threatening to take the hide off him and the orderlies, too, if every article of clothing wasn't dry by morning or if he heard a single complaint about food and coffee.

After a little food and coffee for himself, Tom went to his tent. Hauser had the brazier glowing and Tom told him to go with the others. He was just as wet and would get just as sick if he didn't.

He couldn't go to sleep himself and got up several times to see that the orderlies were doing what he had told them to do. Toward morning he reached a semiconscious, relaxed condition, but he had to get up to see about the men. They were all still sleeping, wrapped in their blankets and heads pillowed on their packs. Both tents were good and warm, and the last batch of clothing was drying on the ropes.

Although he felt like he had just crawled out of his grave, he decided to stay up. He didn't want any breakfast. He just drank a little coffee and smoked his pipe. After the sun came up he was surprised to see that the snow was only about four inches deep. He had expected a foot, but it was heavy and compact. The day was going to be clear, but too cold to melt much of it. Snow never lasted long this time of year, though. After he washed, was shaved and barbered, and changed his uniform, he felt a little better.

During the morning, he brought his men back to their company area and told Cole and Grim to have them clear away the snow, put up their shelter tents, and get boughs from the nearby cedar brake to spread their blankets on. Their shoes hadn't dried, so enough fires would have to be built to dry them. They could be put up on sticks around the fires, and the men could sit around until they dried. After that, the shoes would have to be greased so they wouldn't start coming apart.

Tom was going to take a nap in the afternoon, but Billy and Grim came to see him before he could stretch out. Their shoes were already dried and greased, because Grim knew an old soldiers' trick of putting hot stones in them.

The first thing was about that fellow who kept going out of his mind. He was all right now, but there was no telling how long it would last. Tom promised to see the surgeon about him the first thing in the morning. He thought it could wait until then.

Then Grim said he would like to have Billy as his corporal. It was mainly because he had to have someone who could speak both English and German, and Schlimmer was about the only other man he had who knew English well enough. He had asked him a good while ago, though, but he had turned it down, and Grim was damned if he was going to ask him again. He guessed the fellow was afraid it would take too much time from chasing women, and they laughed about that. He had needed a corporal ever since Kapp had been killed back in August.

Tom knew about that but had been waiting for Grim to bring it up. He asked if he thought Billy would make a good corporal. There were other things about it than knowing English and German, and they would have to be careful because Billy was his brother.

Grim was sure Billy would make a good corporal. He was a smart boy. Look how he had learned German. He could speak it as well as men who had been born in Germany. Grim wished he could speak English half as well, but he had never been very good at things like that. Billy could handle men, too, and always stood up well on the march and in battle. Also, he knew drill like a book.

Billy had been a little embarrassed at first. "Well, Billy," Tom asked him, "do you think you can do it?"

Billy grinned confidently. "I b'lieve I can."

"Well, I'll see Major Owen about it. Grim's got to have a corporal, and we've got this language problem in our company. I'm sure the major will go along with it." He sighed. "I ought to know German better than I do myself."

"Aw, you do purty good with hit. You kin talk t' Sargint Grim hyar all right. Jist keep on with hit an' you'll larn hit jist like I did."

Tom laughed. "Not like you've done. You've got a mind like a sponge. You learn everything and never forget anything."

When Grim understood, he agreed emphatically. He had never seen anyone with a mind like Billy's. He could read a page out of a book, close it up, and tell you what it said almost word for word. He ought to go to a university and be a doctor or lawyer or something. It would be a shame to waste a mind like his just farming or working at something.

Tom had felt the same way ever since he had taught Billy in school, but his brother had never been interested. Tom thought he might feel differently now, so he asked, "What do you think about that, Billy?"

Billy nodded. "That's what I'm plannin' t' do. I'm goin' t' Germany an' study medicine when I git outa th' army. Hit'll be only 'bout a year an' a haf now, y'know."

"What gave you that idea?"

"Aw, Fred Anders is my bes' fren', an' I write t' Gerda all th' time. She's talked t' their pa 'bout hit. He went t' school over thar an' says he kin fix hit up fer me. We kin stay with some uv his folks right in th' town whar th' university is." He blushed and looked down. "Course Gerda 'n' me'll be married by then an' she'll be goin' 'long."

Tom was glad to hear it. "I think that's exactly what you ought to do. Dr. Anders can fix it up for you, and I've always heard they've got the best medical schools in the world in Germany." He didn't know about the rest of it, though. "You'll be pretty young to be getting married, Billy. Maybe you ought to wait until you get through medical school."

Billy shook his head. "Hit's like I told y' once. People grow up quick in time uv war."

Grim thought it was a good idea. Getting married settled a man down, and Billy wouldn't be out drinking and running around like a lot of students did.

Tom still didn't get his nap after Billy and Grim left. Quartermaster Sergeant Winters ran out of boot grease. After he said it might take several days to get any, Tom borrowed Owen's horse to take the requisition to the brigade quartermaster. He could have sent Winters or someone else, but he felt he had to keep himself occupied, that something bad would happen if he didn't. By the time he got back with the grease, it was too late to take a nap.

# 33

After his first good night's sleep, Tom found out what it was that had made him want to keep himself occupied. The second night, the slaughter of the home guards, those boys and old men innocent of war, began to haunt him. Ever since it had happened, he had either been too busy to think or so tired his conscience couldn't awaken his sluggish brain. Once he was rested and at leisure, it all came back to him and at night he tossed and turned sleeplessly. He heard the monstrous roar of the guns and the shrieks and groans of their victims. He saw the mangled bodies strewn in the road. The loathing in Mason's voice curdled his soul. He was a mass murderer. Hundreds of women and children mourned because of him. Sometimes he would writhe in agony and almost cry out.

It went on that way day after day and night after night. Tom slept only in fits and snatches if he slept at all. Often he would get up at night and walk aimlessly about the sleeping camp. Sometimes he would sit staring into the fire while the camp guard changed several times. He didn't drink coffee or even smoke anymore, and he didn't eat enough to keep a bird alive.

The few friends he had among the officers avoided him. Even his men regarded him askance. They always fell silent when he came around, and looked at him strangely. At first he thought it was because everybody felt about him like he felt about himself, but after he heard several remarks about the thing being an accident and something that couldn't have been avoided he knew that wasn't it. It was because of the way he acted, but he couldn't help that. Billy approached him several times, but Tom was always so short with him that he didn't say anything or found an excuse to send him away before he could. He did the same with Cole once when he obviously wanted to talk, and the big fellow never came back.

After a week of it, Tom sat down on a log before his tent one afternoon and tried to understand himself. It wasn't just the massacre. First there had been the affair of the Yankee colonel, then Ernst Thiers and Major Pedigo, and now this. What was wrong with him? Why did he go straight from one crisis to another? It was out of the frying pan, into the fire, and then back into the frying pan again. It was too much. It was making his life a torture and a misery.

Why wasn't he like everyone else, say, Jack Arnold? It wasn't one mess after another with him. He never got in any messes at all. Neither did anyone else Tom knew, at least not the kind he got into. What was wrong with him?

Suddenly it came to him. He was too forward. He was always taking something on himself. He didn't have to pull his revolver on that Yankee colonel. He could have let Pedigo take care of Thiers. No one had told him to set up that artillery ambush.

That was it! He made his trouble for himself, like some satanic force had him in its grip. It all went back to Sally and Mark Dixon. That had done worse things to him than he had ever realized.

Well, there wouldn't be any more of it. He was just going to sit back and let things take their course. No more pistol pulling or jumping in to save total strangers from firing squads. No more making like Napoleón with the artillery.

Tom began to feel better, but he couldn't stop with that. Suppose he had let that Yankee colonel start a bloody battle in camp that time? Suppose he had let Pedigo put Ernst Thiers before a firing squad? How would he feel about it? Then what about setting up Knox's guns the way he had? He had only been thinking of saving Davis's column if the Rebels had been on his heels. He wouldn't be a good officer if he didn't do things like that.

He was trapped. He was damned if he did and damned if he didn't. There was nothing he could do or stop doing, and the realization drove him from despondency to despair. His revolver hung in his tent. A bullet in the brain would end it all, but it would mean disgrace, too. General Stanfield had shown how it could be done, though, and Tom made up his mind not to survive the next engagement. If he couldn't blow his own brains out, he could let the Rebels do it for him.

Tears came to his eyes after he passed sentence on himself. It was all because of the war. If it hadn't been for the war, he would be happily married to Sally and probably a father by now. He remembered how he used to look forward to their children, to teaching them to walk and talk, to lisp his name, and to seeing their little faces crowded around the table at mealtime. He had loved Sally. He had counted on marrying her ever since he was old enough to think about it.

Now that would never be. Sally was lost, and he would soon be gone to that undiscovered country "from whose bourne no traveler returns." The war had wrecked his life, and now it would consume him entirely. An inexpressible sadness came over him.

Suddenly he heard someone speak his name and looked up to see Colonel Rivers standing before him. He leapt to his feet and saluted. "I'm sorry, sir. I—I didn't see you coming!" he stammered.

Rivers didn't return the salute. He just waved cheerily, sat down on the log, and indicated that Tom should sit down, too. "Well, how are you, Captain?"

"I'm fine, sir. How are you?" It was the biggest lie Tom had ever told. He felt like death and probably looked worse. Rivers wouldn't be fooled.

"Oh, I'm busy, always busy," replied Rivers with a laugh. "You'll find out if you ever command a brigade."

Tom only nodded dumbly, so Rivers went on. "Say, I hear the cook in the officers' mess is down on you, and the orderlies, too," he said with a broad grin.

Tom managed to grin himself. "Yes, sir, I guess they are. I made them stay up all night when we got back from that expedition last week."

"Well, you're the only company commander who doesn't have a bunch of sick men on his hands," said Rivers approvingly.

"I know I don't have any, but I didn't know about the others." He wished he hadn't said it because it gave him away.

Rivers didn't seem to make the connection. He gave Tom a cigar and stuck one into his own mouth. Hauser materialized like a genie with a burning stick, and they lit up. "All the others that went out with you have a lot of sick men. Several are in the hospital with lung fever. Lieutenant Allen's one of them."

Tom told a lie. "Yes, that's what I heard." Allen was engaged to Rivers's daughter, Carolyn. "How is the lieutenant?"

Rivers blew smoke and shook his head. "He's pretty bad off."

"Oh, I'm sorry to hear that. I must go to see him."

Rivers looked at him appraisingly. "You're a good officer, Captain. You took care of your men. They didn't sleep in wet clothes and have to dry them out on their backs the next day."

"Well, I wasn't nearly as tired as the others, and my men weren't either. Colonel Davis kept my company back from that night march, and we all got a good night's sleep before we started back."

"You'd have done it anyhow!" scoffed Rivers. "I hear you even made your men put their shoes up on sticks around fires the next day to dry *them* out, and grease them afterwards," he added laughingly.

Tom confessed, "Yes, sir, I did. I'm a regular busybody, I guess. I plague my men all the time."

They both had a good laugh, and Tom was beginning to feel better. "That's the way to do it, Captain. An officer's first responsibility is his men. He's got to take care of them before he even thinks about himself, regardless of what shape he's in."

"I just try to do my best, and I thank the colonel for the compliment." He was beginning to feel somewhat normal again.

Rivers suddenly changed the subject. "Say, have you seen Davis's report on your expedition?"

"No, sir, I haven't. I never interest myself in such things." It started to come back on him. "I'd just as soon forget it."

Rivers nodded reflectively and puffed his cigar. "That's unusual. Most men wouldn't only have found out about it; they'd be hopping mad about it."

Tom felt a sinking sensation. "He blamed me for it, then?" The abyss yawned before him. The world knew of his crime.

Rivers looked surprised. "By no means! He didn't even mention your name." He shook his head in puzzlement.

Tom felt relieved. "I'm sure glad to hear that."

Rivers looked at him strangely as he puffed his cigar. Finally he spoke. "Well, that report Davis turned in to me doesn't match up very well with what an old friend told me the other day."

Tom was frightened all over again. "Who was that?"

"Sergeant Knox. I knew him in the old army. He was a corporal under me back in '49 and '50, when he was in the infantry."

Tom decided that Rivers hadn't come to accuse him after all and felt a lot better. "He's a good man, Sergeant Knox is. He can really handle a section of artillery."

"He can handle a battery just as well. He'd have been an officer a long time ago if he didn't have just one bad habit. He gets on a spree every once in a while and just goes to the dogs. He's been broken back to private a half-dozen times, I expect."

"That's too bad."

"A good many old regulars are that way. Military life isn't natural for a lot of men, I guess, life as an enlisted man anyhow." He nodded sagely. "I guess that's what makes so many of them like that."

Tom was mildly interested. "Is that right?"

Rivers flourished his cigar. "Knox told me you placed the guns and planned the whole thing and Davis just fell in with it. He also said you figured out how to fight your way out if the Rebels were too much for you, leapfrogging back on his guns. Davis didn't know but what he was taking on the best the Rebels had at odds of two to one, and was just going to get out of it the best he could if it backfired on him."

"I guess that's about the way it was," said Tom mildly, "not that I want to fault Colonel Davis or anything." He nodded thoughtfully. "But the responsibility was his. If the thing had gone wrong, it would have been his neck, not mine."

Rivers looked at him strangely again. "Oh, that's right, but he should have given you due credit instead of hogging it all. It makes him look pretty small. Anyhow, I gave you the credit you deserve in my endorsement to General Carter, and I didn't spare Davis for trying to take it all. I even got a deposition from Knox and enclosed it." He laughed shortly. "I don't know how it will all come out for Davis, though. The Rebels are making a big thing out of it. They're calling it the 'Midlow Massacre' after that church there. They may declare him an outlaw like they did Butler."

Tom bowed his head and started to sink again. His crime even had a name. The Rebels might blame Davis for it, even if they knew better, but he wasn't the guilty one.

Rivers paid no heed. "I got another deposition from Captain Arnold and put it in with the report," he said suggestively. "I called him up to headquarters after I saw Knox so I could get a deposition from an officer if he'd be willing to give one." Rivers nodded. "He was more than willing."

"He's a fine fellow, Captain Arnold is," replied Tom. "Nothing ever gets him down," he added glumly.

Again Rivers paid no heed. "He backed Knox up and told me a few things besides. He said leaving the guns and wagons behind and making that night march from the church was your idea, and that you hid everybody and everything so well that those people that passed by on the road never saw a thing."

Tom got up and started walking around, his cigar cold in his hand. "I don't want any credit for that business." He turned and looked Rivers in the eye. "It wasn't anything but mass murder, sir, mass murder."

"Do you really feel like that, Captain?" asked Rivers earnestly.

"Sir, those were just boys and old men, right from their mothers and grandchildren. They weren't soldiers at all, not that it would have been much better." He spread his hands and looked at them. "I should have a spot, like Lady Macbeth."

Rivers sighed. "There aren't many men who'd feel like that, and confess it to a superior officer anyhow."

Tom had to tighten his lips to keep them from trembling. "I can't help it, sir. That's just the way I am."

"Don't you have military ambitions?" Rivers's voice sounded sharp.

Tom felt that he had gone too far to turn back. "Yes, sir, I guess I do, but I don't think I'm cut out for it. A real military man shouldn't feel like I do."

"Well now, you've done pretty well so far. You started out in the ranks, and now you're captain. There are plenty of men who started out as lieutenants and that's all they'll ever be."

"I've just been lucky, I guess."

"Captain," said Rivers earnestly, "you've earned every promotion you've got, and if someone asked me who the best company commander in the brigade is, I'd say it was you." He nodded emphatically. "I'd also say that you've shown the capacity for higher command, and that I wouldn't be surprised if you made major soon."

"I'm glad the colonel thinks so well of me," was all he could say.

"The regiment needs an adjutant. Owen can't make up his mind who. He thinks you're the best man, but he's worried about seniority, that the older captains won't like it."

"Yes, sir, I can understand that."

"I'm going to make up his mind for him. When he makes colonel, I'm going to see to it that you make major and adjutant. That way he can blame me if it makes anybody sore. When General Carter reads my recommendation and the report on the Davis expedition, he'll be all for it. He can get it done, too, just like that." Rivers snapped his fingers.

"That's fine, sir," said Tom with all the enthusiasm he could muster, "but what about politics? The War Department won't give commissions above captain to anyone Governor Morton doesn't approve of, and I know he won't approve of me. The colonel knows you won't find a stronger Democrat than my father, and it won't take him long to find out I'm just like him."

Rivers leaned close and spoke confidentially. "I have reason to believe that the noble governor of Indiana is under a misapprehension about your politics."

"How's that, sir?"

"Isn't there a man named Taylor in your part of the country who has a son about your age?"

"Yes, sir, that's Mr. Samuel Taylor, Esq. He lives within a few miles of where I do, and he's a strong Republican. His son's got the same name I have, but he's still at home." He snorted. "His health suddenly got delicate about the time the war broke out."

Rivers laughed. "That's it! Just take the *r* out of your name and you're him as far as a busy man like our governor would know." He got even more confidential. "We'll take care not to disabuse Mr. Morton, and you'll be all right."

"Oh, he's bound to find out sooner or later."

"Let's hope it's later." Rivers got very serious. "But you'll have to keep quiet about politics."

"That'll be awfully hard to do, sir." He shook his head. "The way these Republicans are playing politics with the army—"

Rivers cut him off "Just keep it to yourself, Captain. Whatever you'd say wouldn't make any difference, would it?"

"No, sir, I guess not. Nothing's going to change those fellows. They don't even learn from experience."

"We're stuck with them, Captain. We've got to beat the Rebels and restore the Union in spite of them." Rivers sat back and puffed his cigar. "You don't want to wind up like me. Here I am, commanding a brigade and about as likely to make brigadier general as I am to sprout wings and fly. I'm politically offensive. I was in politics, two terms in the state legislature, and I won't change."

"I admire the colonel for that. Plenty of lifelong Democrats have changed their politics for promotion." He snorted contemptuously. "Some of them would sell their souls if it took that. Look at Alvin P. Hovey, one of our own from the Pocket."

"Thank you, Captain. Some people think I'm just being a fool." He grew confidential again. "But you've got no brand on you, and Morton's under this misapprehension. Just keep quiet, and maybe when he does find out it won't make any difference."

Tom nodded. "I'll do my best, sir."

Rivers looked at him quizzically. "I must say, Captain, you don't exactly seem overjoyed about making major."

Tom got up all the enthusiasm he could. "I'll be much obliged to you, sir, and I thank you for all you've done for me."

Rivers suddenly got to his feet, and Tom did the same.

"Captain, I want to tell you something that happened to an artillery officer I knew."

Tom couldn't imagine why. "Yes, sir?"

"One foggy morning not so long ago he took a brigade under fire and it turned out to be one of ours. He shot up one regiment terribly."

"Oh, God! How awful!" That was worse than he had done.

"And that very night he blew his brains out with his revolver."

Tom heaved a sigh. "Poor fellow! I know how he felt."

Rivers sat down and slapped the log. "Sit down, Captain." After Tom complied, he went on. "No one blamed him for it. It was an accident. Everybody knew that. He knew it." Rivers put a hand on Tom's shoulder. "What he didn't know is that things like that happen in war. They happen all the time. They can't be helped."

A light began to dawn on Tom and a great weight rose from his heart. "I believe I see what the colonel means." He looked at Rivers searchingly. "That's the way it was with me, only I thought—"

Rivers wouldn't let him finish. "You thought you were the only fellow who ever had anything like that happen to him."

"Yes, sir."

Rivers sighed and flicked the ash from his cigar. "Son, war is confusion. The best you can say is that it's organized confusion. We can only try to understand what's going on and hope to master it. We're bound to make mistakes, and some of them have horrible results." He shook his head sadly. "No one's going to command in the field very long and not have something like that happen to him." He paused briefly and added, "I know. I speak from bitter experience."

"Yes, sir?"

"Once in Mexico, I had a company out after guerrillas. We spotted the bunch we were after about dark, going into camp in a little ravine. By the time I got my men in position, it was too dark to see well, but we opened fire and almost wiped them out." He looked at Tom sadly. "But they weren't the bunch we were after. They weren't guerrillas at all. They were just some people who were trying to keep out of the way under a priest, and a good many of them were women. Some were even children."

The light dawned fully on Tom, and the weight was gone from his heart. New life throbbed through him. His crime was only an accident. Even worse things had happened to other men, like to Rivers. "It all looks different now. I feel a lot better about it. I should have been able to figure it out for myself, but—"

Rivers threw his cigar away and cut him off. "I thought you needed a little help. That's why I came to see you." He got to his feet, and Tom did the same.

"Does the colonel mean he—"

"Yes. Owen told me he thought you were letting that thing get you down, and I didn't want to see someone suffer like I did back in '47."

Tom was so overcome he forgetfully stuck out his hand. Rivers took it.

"Colonel, I don't know how to thank you. I'm beginning to feel like Lazarus must have."

"Well," said Rivers smilingly, "I've spent my time well if I've done that."

"I'm sure obliged to the colonel. I feel like a new man."

Rivers regarded him earnestly. "Personally, I think the way you felt is a credit to you. Men with sensitivity and feeling like yours are hard to find in the middle of a war."

Tom could only say, "Yes, sir. Thank you, sir."

Rivers took his leave. "Carry on, Captain," he said as they exchanged salutes, then turned and walked briskly away.

That night Tom slept like a baby, and the next morning he felt like he had been reborn. When the men of his old platoon gathered around the fireplace to drink coffee, smoke, and talk as they usually did after morning muster, he joined them. They were obviously glad to see the change in him, and although none of them said anything, he knew they understood.

He accepted a cup of coffee, then smoked and talked with them just like he always had. Someone got Ab started with one of his tales, and men from close by hurried over to listen and laugh with the others. It was just like old times again.

That evening Tom and Jack Arnold went to see Marcus Allen in the hospital. Tom felt bad about it. If he had only looked out for Allen and his men in the nearby headquarters tent like he had those with him, it wouldn't have happened. He had seen what shape Allen was in, and it was only a few steps. Allen wasn't a very strong-looking fellow, and exhaustion followed by a night sleeping in wet clothes, probably without a fire, had put him where he was.

The hospital was in a tobacco warehouse. A ceiling had been put in, the walls tightly decked, and several large stoves set up. Colonel Rivers had established a good hospital for his brigade. Most of the others only had large wall tents that couldn't be kept warm in cold weather.

Allen was with other sick and wounded officers in a part of the building that had been partitioned off. He was out of his head with a raging fever and didn't know them. His lungs were badly congested and his breathing labored, but his emaciated body thrashed about on the cot and he babbled occasionally about "Carrie," as he called the colonel's daughter.

A civilian surgeon who came by said he doubted if Allen would live through the night, so Tom wrote a note to Rivers telling him this and arranged to have it delivered before he and Jack left the building.

On the way back to camp, Arnold said he had heard that Carolyn and her aunt had sat up with Allen the night before and that his parents were on their way to see him. They hoped his folks would get there in time but had little else to say to each other as they made their way back to camp through the gloom of the winter night.

The next afternoon Tom heard that Allen had died early that morning. His parents had arrived just before the end and, along with Carolyn and her aunt, had been with him when he died. They were going to take his body back home for burial.

# 34

Jack Arnold had never said anything more about those ladies from Washington and Tom had completely forgotten about them until his friend hunted him up early one afternoon. "They're coming today, Tom, so get your glad rags on and be ready to go about six o'clock."

"Who's coming?"

"Those two ladies from Washington." Arnold was exasperated. "Don't you remember?"

Tom did, but now that the time had come he was reluctant. He didn't like to meet strange people socially, particularly Easterners, and these were women. He had never taken a woman anywhere but to church or box suppers and such like, and that had always been Sally. He was afraid he would be backward, bashful, and make a fool of himself.

While he hesitated, Jack went on. "Look, Tom, you promised you'd go and I've promised you would. They're dying to meet you."

Tom couldn't break a promise, especially to Jack. "All right, I'll go."

"Great!" Jack elbowed Tom in the ribs and winked. "You won't regret it; I promise you that. It's a sure thing."

Tom didn't understand what he meant but didn't want to ask. He wondered what Jack had written them that made them so eager to meet him. He dreaded it, but there was no way out.

They met by Tom's tent and started for town. Tom was wearing his dress uniform for the first time, and Jack was much taken with it. "You look like a major general in that getup!" He cackled gleefully. "Oh, you'll slay them! You'll lay them low!"

Tom thanked him for the compliment and felt a little better about it.

"Where'd you get that uniform? How much did it cost?"

Tom told him but didn't add that he had gotten his money back.

Arnold shook his head. "I couldn't afford anything like that."

"Well, I've never spent any money for anything else."

"I guess that's what you've got to do," chuckled Arnold, "but I've got to have my fun, and that takes money."

They met the visitors at a hotel. It was a very sumptuous place, with both a bar and dining room. Jack looked around in the parlor room until he spotted two women and a slight, elderly man sitting on a couch by a large potted plant.

"There they are!" he exclaimed. The women weren't exactly young, but they weren't old either. Both were pretty brunettes dressed in the height of fashion. One was taller than the other and looked like she might be a little older.

The women saw them coming and got to their feet. "Jack!!" gushed the taller one. "You're just in time for dinner!"

They both looked appraisingly at Tom, which made him feel like a clothing store dummy. The taller one said something to the other that he couldn't hear except for the word "lucky."

Arnold made the introductions. The taller woman was Louise and the other Pamela. The old gentleman didn't get up until he had to. He was Mr. Pierce, Louise's uncle. Tom bowed to the women, shook hands with Mr. Pierce, and said the appropriate things. He wondered why the women didn't seem to have last names. They had eyes only for him, and it was very embarrassing.

Dinner was being served, and when they started for the dining room Pamela came up and took Tom's arm. It seemed pretty forward, but he didn't know how people like these acted and guessed it was the way they did. They didn't act like people from the Pocket. They had a glitter and an air of confident sophistication that was strange to him and made him feel ill at ease.

They had champagne while waiting for their order. It came in a bucket of ice on a little stand that had wheels on it. Tom thought it tasted like vinegar and would have much preferred beer but guessed beer was too common for people like these. His glass was still nearly full when the bottle was taken away empty and replaced by another.

Mr. Pierce seemed to love it. He gulped the stuff down and drank half the bottle himself. After the food came, he paid no attention to it and soon emptied the second bottle. Tom was surprised when Louise ordered another. The old gentleman seemed to have enough on board already, but he went after it with undiminished avidity.

Everybody talked volubly but Tom and Mr. Pierce. Tom couldn't think of anything to say, and Mr. Pierce was too busy drinking. Arnold and the ladies chattered merrily and laughed at everything, even Mr. Pierce's increasing inebriation. He paid no attention and drank on.

Tom spoke only when spoken to, but that was a lot. After she finished eating, Pamela turned her full attention to him, although he had only picked at his food and wasn't done with it. He tried to turn her away by pretending preoccupation with his plate, but it did no good and he finally put it aside. She wanted to know all about him, where he was from, what he had done before the war, and what he had done since. He tried to make his answers as short and final as he could, but she drew him out in spite of it. Eventually he found himself talking a lot more and feeling more comfortable about it. Somehow she kept getting nearer to him, and before long they were quite close. She was a pretty woman with a nice figure, and her perfume was like nothing he had ever imagined.

More champagne kept coming and Tom began to worry about Mr. Pierce. He was already so far gone that someone was going to have to look after him, and the way he was going, he wouldn't last much longer. None of the others paid any attention except to laugh at him and keep the champagne coming. Tom didn't think it was his place to say anything, though. He wondered why the old fellow didn't drink whiskey if all he wanted was to get drunk. Maybe he enjoyed it more when it took longer, like with champagne.

Arnold was in fine form. Everything was funny, even the war when it came up. Tom couldn't help falling in with him, and between them they kept the ladies in stitches. As he got the chance, he began to ask Pamela some of the things she had asked about him. She was evasive, and he grew impatient. After all, he had told her a lot about himself, including about going to college and teaching school.

She sensed his impatience and leaned closer, until her cheek was almost touching his. "I can't tell about myself like you can," she whispered. "Let's just forget about me and have a good time." Her perfume made his head swim, and her peachlike cheek and red lips were very close to him. He felt a strange stirring within him, like when he had gotten close to Sally. She was the only other woman he had ever been so close to beside his mother.

The dinner had long since been cleared away, but the champagne kept coming. It didn't taste so much like vinegar as it had at first. Mr. Pierce was about to go under. He hadn't eaten. He hadn't talked. He just gulped champagne in unbelievable quantities. Tom couldn't understand how such a slight old fellow could hold so much. The next time the waiter came, Louise talked briefly with him in undertones, then gave him some money and a key. The waiter got the old man to his feet and helped him away, all so discreetly that no one seemed to notice.

"Poor Uncle!" laughed Louise. "He sure didn't last long this time!"

The others laughed merrily and Tom thought it strange that they didn't seem embarrassed.

"Did you arrange to keep him supplied?" giggled Pamela.

Louise nodded. "He'll be taken care of all right." Everybody laughed again.

Tom didn't understand it all, but he laughed, too. Suddenly Pamela leaned to him, brushing his cheek with her lips and slipping her arm about his waist. Her perfume made him dizzy, and he submitted. "You're a splendid barbarian," she whispered.

Tom drew back and pretended that his feelings were hurt. "Now, I'm no barbarian!" he protested. "After all, I'm an officer, and that means I'm a gentleman, too."

She sighed and her eyes glowed. "Oh, I didn't mean that sort of barbarian," she murmured.

"What, then?" he asked challengingly.

She leaned close again. "You're so tall, so blond, and so . . . . so innocent, like those ancient Germans who came down on Rome from the north."

"Oh, you've been reading Tacitus too much."

She smiled and nodded, running her eyes over him and slipping her arm around his waist again. Suddenly he felt a slight jar and she pulled away. Louise had kicked her foot under the table and hissed smilingly, "We're still in public, Pam!"

Pamela giggled and bowed her head in mock contrition. Arnold grinned and winked broadly at Tom, who was beginning to feel like he was on a downhill slide and going faster all the time. Suddenly he wanted to get away, for a little while anyhow. "I'll have to ask you to excuse me," he said apologetically. He really had to go to the men's room, though.

"Wait for me!" exclaimed Jack. "I've got to go, too!" When the women exchanged knowing looks, he added laughingly, "It's the champagne."

They giggled.

"You wait until we come back, now," he cautioned waggishly, "or somebody'll get our table."

"We'll try!" giggled Pamela as they went away.

When Tom and Jack went to the men's room, they passed the doorway leading into the bar. Among a group of officers with their feet on the rail was a husky red-haired cavalry lieutenant who waved as they went by. He looked familiar, but Tom couldn't place him. "Who's that fellow?" he asked.

"Hansford. He's one of Davis's boys. He was on that scout with us."

Tom remembered. "I thought I'd seen him before."

"He's a real tiger," laughed Arnold. "I was out with him once with a couple of ladies."

When they got back to the women, they took their turn and left giggling.

"Say," asked Tom, "how much do you think our bill will come to?" Maybe it would be an excuse to beg off.

"You worried about money?"

"I'm no Croesus, that's for sure."

"Well, just forget about it," said Arnold with a wink. "Those two are loaded with it."

Tom was taken aback. "Why, I never heard of such a thing! I—"

Jack cut him off. "I've been out with them before. Their husbands are both in the Treasury Department, and they're making a fortune out of Rebel cotton. That's where they are now, down at New Orleans sniffing out more of it."

Tom had heard of cotton and corruption, but that wasn't what bothered him. "I didn't know they were married."

Arnold leered. "They're both married to older men, can't keep them happy anymore, I guess. Anyhow, they're always out after younger fellows every chance they get."

"But what about Mr. Pierce?"

Jack laughed. "They bring him along for appearance' sake, and he's glad to go. I guess they keep him snubbed up pretty close at home, and he grabs the chance to get drunk." He glanced apprehensively the way the women had gone. "Now for God's sake, don't let on that I told you anything, though."

Tom was so overwhelmed that he could only shake his head. He had only vaguely suspected there were women like these and had thought they would look like what they were.

"Cheer up, Tom!" exclaimed Arnold. "You're doing fine! Their mouths started watering the minute they saw you. You're a lady killer, you know that? I've had a hard time keeping Louise's attention."

"Oh, I never noticed," replied Tom apologetically.

Jack leaned over the table and leered again. "If I know her, she's going to want to swap before the night's over."

"Just like cows to the bull," said Tom half to himself.

Arnold laughed uproariously. "That's it! That's exactly it! Cows to the bull!" He couldn't get over it.

Tom had to act before the women got back. He pulled out his wallet, extracted a ten-dollar greenback, and put it on the table.

Jack looked at him in astonishment. "What's that for? I told you—"

Tom interrupted as he got to his feet. "I'm leaving, Jack. I'm sorry, but this is too much for me, and I want to pay my way."

Arnold was thunderstruck. "Why, why you can't just—"

Tom wouldn't let him finish. "I'll send Hansford in from the bar. If he's not there, I'll get someone else. One bull is as good as another when the cow's in heat. You can tell them I was suddenly called back to camp if you want to."

Tom left before Jack could recover enough to say anything. Hansford was still at the bar. He couldn't quite understand how it had come about but seemed agreeable. Tom just told him he had better get going if he didn't want to miss out on it. He watched him go through the door into the dining room, then went back to camp.

Arnold didn't show up at officers' call the next morning, so Tom assumed that things had worked out all right for him. When he appeared the next morning, he looked about like he had the morning after the expedition with Davis.

"You look tired, Jack," said Tom teasingly.

Arnold rolled his bloodshot eyes and sighed. "How right you are, friend."

After it was over, Tom started away, but Jack caught him. "I've got to give that money back." He got out his wallet.

"Oh no, I don't want it!" Tom protested.

Arnold pressed the greenback on him. "Take it! Take it! They paid for everything, just like I said they would."

Tom took the bill reluctantly. "Well, I hope nobody missed me."

Jack laughed weakly. "Oh, they were awfully disappointed, Louise as much as Pamela. Hansford and I made up a cock-and-bull story about an emergency at camp you had to see to, and they got over it."

"Well, I'm glad things went well for you."

"Oh, they went a little too well." Arnold shook his head and sighed heavily. "Two nights and a day—a whole day—are really too much for a fellow, though." He looked at Tom quizzically. "You know, Tom, I've never seen anything like it."

"Like what?"

"You turning down a pretty woman like that. I thought fellows like you went out when King Arthur did."

Tom laughed. "Well, I guess one bull was just as good as another and everything went on without me all right."

"No, not quite," replied Arnold. "Louise never wanted to swap."

With that Tom turned around and walked away.

In a few days he got a highly perfumed letter addressed in a fine feminine hand. It was postmarked: “Washington.” He threw it in the fire without opening it and in the course of the next several weeks did the same with three others. They stopped coming after that.

# 35

The only thing that really bothered Sally Napier when she realized she was going to have a baby was losing Tom once and for all. She thought that when she told Mark Dixon he would offer to marry her, because that was what honorable men did. But when she told him he just got up, walked out, and rode away on his horse without saying a word. He never came back, and when she heard that he had gone back to New England to school it was like the end of the world.

Sally finally got up enough nerve to tell her mother. She was sympathetic at first and they both had a good cry, but the next day she was cold and distant. She spoke to Sally only when she had to and was short about it then. Sally knew she told her father that very night, but he didn't say anything about it until she told him, too.

Mort Napier didn't get angry or anything. He questioned her closely and impersonally about when she and Mark had been alone together and marked the dates on a calendar. Then he made her write out what he called an affidavit telling where they had had relations as well as when, like the first time on the couch in the living room or other places like the hayloft in the barn and in Mark's buggy. It was awful and she wished God would strike her dead, but all her father did was pat her on the head when she would break down and cry. After that, he treated her just like her mother did.

Her father took her to old Squire Persons and made her sign the affidavit. Then the squire signed it and they went back home. The old squire had known her all her life and always called her his sunshine girl because of her bright yellow hair and pretty face. He wouldn't even look at her after he read the affidavit, though. He ignored her completely when they left, despite her anticipating smile, and she felt like someone had stuck a knife in her.

Mort Napier then took the affidavit to old Calvin Dixon, Mark's father. Sally never knew what they said, but Mort went to see him again in a few days and this time brought back a paper and what he called a cheque for her to sign. He wouldn't let her read the paper and folded it so she couldn't see what it said when she signed it. When she signed the cheque, she saw that it said to pay $5,000 to the bearer on demand, but she didn't understand what that meant or even know what a cheque was.

In the long hours before she would fall asleep at night, she would sometimes try to blame Tom for it. If he had gone ahead and married her like they planned before the war broke out, it wouldn't have happened. If he had taken her when she wanted him so badly the last time she saw him, it wouldn't have happened. If he had made her pregnant, she would have gone to him and he would have married her. He was that kind of a man. His trouble was that he didn't know women had feelings just like men did, and wanted men as badly as men wanted them. He seemed to think that women were pretty things, like flowers, who gave themselves to men just to please them.

She had saved all of Tom's letters and got into the habit of reading them and crying. She still loved him. She always had loved him, ever since she was a little girl and he was a boy. She hadn't cared anything for Mark Dixon. He had just been a man and she a woman who needed to be loved.

Once while looking through a book about King Arthur and his Knights of the Round Table Tom had given her a long time ago, she came across a picture she imagined looked like him. She cut it out and pinned it up in the little alcove where she always slept. It wasn't so much that the picture looked like him as it described him. It was a painting of Sir Galahad and showed him standing in armor with his helmet in his hand. Beneath it were these words: "His strength is as the strength of ten because his heart is pure." When she heard of Tom getting to be an officer and captain over all the Dubois County men, it seemed to describe him even better.

Sally hadn't wanted to see Mark Dixon after he left the army and came back home, especially after the men in his company started writing back about what a coward he was. Her father had forbidden her to turn him away, though, and she always obeyed her father like the Bible said to do. One day Mark came when her parents had gone to Jasper, but she let him in because of what her father had told her. They sat on the couch and talked. Somehow they got closer and closer together. The first thing she knew, they were embracing, and then she lost control of herself. After that, she was his any time he wanted her. She knew she was doing wrong, but she just couldn't resist him. She got weak and trembly every time he got close to her. She couldn't excuse herself by saying he had promised to marry her because he hadn't. Neither of them had ever said anything about it until she had when she told him she was going to have his baby.

She knew what happened to women who had babies when they weren't married. No decent man would have anything to do with them. Neither would any of the women. She was already being treated that way, mainly by her parents. They didn't want her around anymore. All a woman like her could do was live in a shack and be a neighborhood slut for dirty old men and ragamuffin boys. Either that or go to a city and become a prostitute. That meant being used by men like they used cigars and thrown away afterward. She couldn't bear the thought. She would rather be dead.

Finally she made up her mind. The day would come when whe would do away with herself. After this, she felt the first peace she had known since she learned she was going to have a baby. She would die and go to be with Jesus. He would forgive her and take her in like they said in church he did with sinners, and she hadn't sinned much. She cried when she thought of Tom. Maybe he would be killed like so many of the other men and come to be with her and Jesus. He would go to Heaven, because he had never done anything wrong in his whole life. They would be angels together, and he would love her again, like he said in those letters he wrote before he found out she was seeing Mark Dixon.

One clear November day when it was warm for that time of year, she walked in the orchard among the big old apple trees where the grass made a thick carpet that was still green. The orchard had been their favorite place when she and Tom had been younger, in the summer, when the trees would shade them from the sun. Now she would never see them in leaf again, and she cried when she thought of the happy hours she had spent under them with Tom. He always read a great deal and was very fond of books by a man named Scott. He was a Scotch lord or something, Sir Walter, she believed. She never liked to read but always enjoyed it when Tom read to her about the bold and honorable knights and how they fought for the honor of their ladies.

Once he picked up a stick for a sword and fought with one of the gnarled tree trunks, which was an evil knight who had stolen her away. He struck manful blows and vanquished the evil knight, then picked her up and carried her to his horse to spirit her safely away. The horse was a part of the rail fence around the orchard. She could almost hear herself shrieking in her girlish voice with his strong arms around her. He had been tall and strong even as a boy, but it was a sinewy strength that didn't come from bulging muscles and heavy bones.

She wished, oh, how she wished, that old Lincoln hadn't started this war like everyone said he had. She and Tom would be married, and the baby growing inside her would be his. Then there would be others, and they would be living in that fine house Tom's father was building, a house filled with rosy little faces and happy children's voices.

Oh, how she would like to see him once more, just once more, and be with him again! But she never would, even if she didn't do what she was going to do. His father didn't know her anymore. He had ridden past the house once when she had first started seeing Mark, just after old Calvin had made him put up that peace bond for threatening Mark. He had gone by stony-eyed, never looking at her, although she was on the front porch with a greeting in her throat.

If Tom could have seen her walking through the orchard, he would have remarked that she was more beautiful than ever. Nature was preparing her for motherhood. Her complexion was more the rose of June than the snow of January, and her figure had become fuller and more womanly. Even the trim ankles and little feet that showed under her skirts were lovelier, and the long blond hair shone with a brighter shade of gold.

Although it was no different from any other day, Sally knew when the last day of her life on earth had come. Her mother was busy with the housework she would never let her daughter help with anymore. Her father was out someplace on the farm.

She slipped out of the house and went to the barn where he kept the rat poison and went into the woods with it. She had seen a stray dog die in agonized fits after getting into the corncrib and eating some of it, and she didn't want anyone to hear her die. She knew she would die like the dog had, but that was why she had chosen the rat poison instead of her father's pistol. If she suffered like Jesus had on the cross, it would cleanse her of sin and God the Father wouldn't stop him when he wanted to let her in to be with him.

No one heard her when she died, but only because the windows in the house a hundred yards away were closed.

The face was no longer beautiful and the lovely feminine form was stiff and grotesquely contorted when they found her, but the yellow hair still gleamed like gold in the sunlight.

# 36

Tom knew something was wrong when he saw Billy coming toward him. He could tell by the way Billy looked and walked that he had something on his mind that bothered him. Billy was a fine-looking soldier, though, who looked like he deserved the corporal's stripes on his sleeve. He certainly wasn't the boy who had left home with his brother anymore.

Tom was sitting on the log beside his tent where Hauser always kept a fire working on some problems in tactics he had set up for himself. When Billy came up, he put the papers aside. "Sit down, Billy. I've been forgetting to ask you if Schulz's father got him back home all right, that fellow of Grim's who kept going out of his mind."

"Yeah, they made hit all right. Took th' train t' Shoals an' then went on t' Jasper. Someone wuz waitin' fer 'em at Shoals with a wagon, Schulz's uncle, I b'lieve."

"How's he doing now that he's back home?"

"They say he's all right. Started workin' on his pa's farm right off, buildin' fence."

"Maybe he'll be all right now that he's back home among his own people and all."

"Yeah, but hit's too early t' tell. They ain't been home more'n a few days, er hadn't when they wrote Grim enyhow."

"Sit down, Billy," said Tom. "Something on your mind?"

Billy finally sat on the log and looked uneasily at the fire. "Yeah, I jist got a letter frum Pa, an' he told me t' tell y' a few things that he didn't want y' t' jist read in a letter."

Tom was afraid it was about their mother. She had always written them until late in the spring, when their father had suddenly taken over the writing, and he had never explained it very well. "Is it about Ma, Billy?"

Billy looked like he was afraid something was about to blow up. "One uv 'em is."

"What about her?"

"She's been sick, 'bout t' lose her mind, Pa thought, but she's doin' heap better now."

"He should have told us." That couldn't be what was bothering Billy so much.

"He said he didn't want t' worry us. He figgered we had 'nough t' worry 'bout, fightin' 'n' all."

"Well, why's he telling us now?"

"I guess mainly 'cause she's doin' better, an' he figgered we'd find out enyhow." Billy sighed. "I've knowed hit fer a good while, though. Gerda wrote me 'bout hit but told me not t' tell enyone 'cause Pa didn't want us t' know."

"How did she know?"

"Ma's been stayin' with 'em, th' Anderses, an' Gerda's pa's been tryin' t' help her. Pa says he's done her a lot uv good, him an' th' wimminfolks. Says she's lots better."

"Is she back home yet?"

"Naw. Pa's 'fraid t' take her back yit. Him an' Dr. Anders thinks her stayin' out thar on th' farm with no one but Pa 'round an' bein' all 'lone when he's out workin' an' worryin' 'bout us all th' time is what got wrong with her."

"What's he going to do, then?"

"He's thinkin' 'bout sellin' th' farm an' buyin' one down thar close t' Jasper so Ma kin go t' town an' see people an' stuff like that."

"That's exactly what he ought t' do." Tom shook his head. "Poor Ma, lonesome and worryin' all th' time. I can see why she got sick."

"They's a problem 'bout that, though," said Billy, who then went on before Tom could say anything. "Th' only farm he kin find down thar close 'nough t' Jasper that's fer sale is a big un. Hit'll cost a heap more'n he'll ever be able t' git outa his'n, an' he don't wanta go in debt if'n he kin help hit." Billy looked at him strangely, which told Tom this wasn't what was bothering him either. "He wants t' know if'n he kin sell that forty acres he promised t' you but ain't never deeded over yit."

"Sure he can. He can sell my eighty acres, too. He can send me the deed, and I'll make it over to him." He looked gloomily into the fire. "I've got no use for it anymore, and he can deed me part of what he buys if he wants to."

Billy only nodded and looked at the ground. Tom felt the knife of fear. "What else is there, Billy?"

Billy began to blink rapidly, and his face contorted. "Hit's 'bout Sally," he blurted out. "She's dead."

It took Tom a moment to comprehend. "Sally? Dead? How? Why—"

"She kilt herself, Tom. Took rat poison."

Billy looked like he was holding an explosive shell with the fuse burning, but Tom no longer noticed. He couldn't believe it. It didn't seem possible. Was it on account of him? "Why did she do it, Billy?"

"She wuz going' t' have a baby, Mark Dixon's, an' he run off when he found out 'bout hit."

Tom involuntarily got to his feet and his hand went to his belt, although he wore no weapons. "That dirty son of a bitch!" burst from deep within him.

"Now, Tom! Now, Tom!" called Billy in fright. "Don't do nothin'! That's what Pa wuz skeered uv!" He got to his feet and put an imploring hand on his bother's arm.

Tom heard him as from a great distance. Rage seethed through his veins and made a great booming in his ears. If Mark Dixon had been in reach, he would have killed him on the spot.

"Tom! Tom!" shrieked Billy. "Y' look like yo're crazy!"

Tom saw the faces of his men about their fire swivel toward him, and it brought him to his senses. He was making a spectacle of himself in front of them, although they were too far to understand. He sat down. "Sit down, Billy. I'll be all right. It just hit me pretty hard."

Billy was greatly relieved. "Thank th' Lord! You skeered me, Tom. I ain't never seen nobody look like that."

Tom was frightened, too. He had never lost complete control of himself before, except maybe when he had tried to charge the Rebels out of the creek that time. "I'm all right, Billy."

"That's why Pa wanted me t' tell ye," said Billy with a sidelong look at the men about the fire. They were beginning to turn away now. "He wuz skeered you'd do somethin' turrible."

"It shouldn't affect me like that. I broke off with her as soon as I found out she was seeing Mark Dixon," he said heavily. "But I guess I still loved her." He looked at his brother and fought back the tears that were starting to his eyes. "I loved her ever since we were little—"

He was glad Billy interrupted him. "That ain't all uv hit, though."

"What else?" asked Tom dumbly.

"Hit's her ma an' pa. Folks is down on 'em an' is 'bout t' run 'em outa th' county."

"Why's that?"

"Aw, Pa says th' only reason she ever seen Mark wuz 'cause her pa made her, an' then atter hit happened all he seemed t' be int'risted in wuz gittin' money outa ol' Calvin. Says neither him er her ma seemed t' keer enything 'bout Sally, 'n'atter they got their money they acted like all they wanted t' do wuz jist git rid uv her."

Tom could only nod his head woodenly.

"He owed ol' Calvin a lot uv money, Mort did, an' Pa says he got him t' give hit up some way er 'nother, an' got a hull lot b'sides."

It was too much for Tom. He bowed his head and fought back the tears. Poor Sally, abandoned by everybody, even her own mother and father. Poor sweet, beautiful Sally. He forgave her. He forgave her everything. But it was too late. He wondered why she had chosen such an agonizing way to die. Maybe she was punishing herself.

He got to his feet. "I'll ask you to leave me alone a little while, Billy."

Billy got scared again. "Tom, y' ain't gonna do nothin', air ye?"

"I'm going to kill Mark Dixon if I ever see him again."

Billy looked relieved, then frightened again. "Y' ain't gonna go do hit now, air ye?"

"No, Billy, but if I ever see him again, I will. I'll do it with my bare hands if I have to."

Billy looked relieved again. "Well, I don't 'spect you'll ever see him agin. Pa says he told someone he wuzn't never comin' back t' that part uv th' country agin, that hit wuzn't fit fer human bein's t' live in. Said he wuz gonna live up thar close t' Boston, whar he's goin' t' school."

"I expect he's afraid somebody will kill him."

"Pa says he 'spects they's men that'd do hit, though they ain't nobody said nothin' 'bout doin' hit that he's heered uv."

Tom desperately wanted to be alone, but Billy gave no sign of leaving. "Billy, if you'll leave, you won't have anything to worry about."

"Y' promise, Tom?"

"I promise, Billy, and I wouldn't lie to you; you know that."

"All right," replied Billy. "I'll go, but I want y' t' call fer me if . . . if y' ever git t' feelin' like . . . like y' did when I first told ye." He started away, then stopped. "Y' will, won't ye, Tom?"

"I will, Billy."

After Billy left, Tom sat down on the log again and picked up his paper, but only for the benefit of his men. He looked at it, but he didn't see it. He saw Sally instead, as a little doll in pigtails, as a gangly girl in her early teens, and finally as the beautiful young woman he had left to go away to war. He finally had to go to his tent, where he wept for the first time since he was a boy.

One of the reasons he wept was because he blamed himself. If it hadn't been for his foolish notion that a man going off to war shouldn't be married, it wouldn't have happened. Sally's father couldn't have made her see Mark Dixon, because she would have been married. It had happened only because Dixon had gotten close to her and nature had taken its course. Nature wasn't interested in chasity or chivalry, only in reproduction.

During the long nights that followed, his torment led him to think about himself as he never had before. He came to realize he had been a latter-day Don Quixote, a chivalrous fool obsessed with antiquated notions and foolish illusions. He had tilted the windmill, and it had flung him to the ground, shattering his dreams and fancies. He would never be the same again.

No one knew what went on inside him during this time. An iron composure held him in its grip, and he went about his business as usual. Those who knew about Sally generally decided he wasn't much affected by what had happened to her.

# 37

Sally Napier had been dead five months and her parents gone to Iowa before Mark Dixon came back to see his father, and he came only because he was short of funds and couldn't pry anything out of the old man by mail. He wasn't nearly as generous as he had been before he had paid Mort Napier all that money, but Mark was sure he could get what he wanted face to face with him. After all, he had plenty of it. He was the richest man in the county.

Mark suspected it was a dangerous trip. No one had ever threatened him because of Sally that he had heard of, but he knew men had been killed in the Pocket for less. You could never tell about these surly, silent fellows. They had always hated his father and had never like him either. Violence was second nature to them, and revenge was sacred. It was because they could all be traced back to the South, that land of chains and brutality. He couldn't understand how he could be expected to marry a rustic girl from the Pocket anyhow, one he would be ashamed of in New England, where he was going to live. He wouldn't take any chances, though. No one but his father would ever see him in the locality.

He got off a night train at Shoals Station only after a careful look around showed no one who knew him. He knew where to get a horse from a man who would keep his mouth shut for a consideration. Mark got the horse and gave the consideration.

He would reach his father's house well before daylight, put the horse up in the barn where no one would see it, and stay in the house all day. Then late the next night he would ride back to Shoals, turn the horse loose, and catch the Saint Louis to Cincinnati train at three o'clock in the morning. The road between Shoals and his father's was only a forest track through wild, hilly, unsettled country most of the way. With any luck at all, none of the local primitives would ever see him.

None of them would have if one of little Johnny Tacker's children hadn't been sick. The child had the croup and kept his mother up well past midnight before finally going to sleep. Johnny's wife had fallen into an exhausted slumber when the coughing started again, so he got up to take care of the child. He gave him a drink of water and a piece of horehound candy to suck on in hopes it would stop the coughing. It did, and the child went back to sleep.

Johnny slipped on his shoes and went out to relieve himself before going back to bed. The moon was bright and the weather was going to be fine. He heard a horse on the road that ran in front of his house and wondered who would be out that time of night, so he went around the house, stood in the shadow of a tree, and watched the horseman go by. He recognized him immediately.

Little Johnny didn't go back to bed. He slipped into the bedroom, got his clothes, and put them on in the adjoining kitchen without awakening anybody. The sick child still slept. He left the house silently and ran through the woods and fields to where a friend of his lived who would be much interested in what he had seen. The friend swore Johnny to secrecy and told him to go back home and get back in bed without waking his wife up. Johnny was able to do it.

Late the next night, Mark Dixon rode back toward Shoals. Everything had gone fine. The old man had cried when he saw his son and he had gotten what he wanted. He was sure no one had seen the strange horse in the barn. His father had kept the hired men away and gone out to feed and water the animal himself.

The bright moonlight worried Mark a little, as it had the night before. He should have thought about that and come during a moonless period, but he doubted if he could have waited long enough. It wouldn't make any difference, though. The local yahoos always went to bed with the chickens. He was glad to be getting out of this benighted country, where the people talked like Rebels and weren't interested in anything but war, niggers, and the price of wheat. In New England the people were civilized and enlightened. They talked of natural rights and freedom, of idealism and pragmatism. They also understood that a man of sensitivity and intellect couldn't be expected to endure the rigors and brutalities of military service, which was beyond the comprehension of the denizens of the Pocket. He hoped he never had to come back.

Mark wasn't frightened by the play of the moonlight, the dark, looming woods, or the dismal hooting of the owls. In the absence of perceptible danger, he was quite a brave fellow.

Suddenly someone or something appeared in the track not fifty feet in front of him and his horse stopped. His heart leapt, then started pounding madly. He couldn't tell who or what it was, and a chilling fear ran through his veins. He didn't believe in supernatural visitations—no sensible, educated person did—but what was this? It seemed to have the shape of a man, but its head—its whole head—looked as white as snow and its arms seemed unnaturally long. He tried to speak, but his vocal cords were paralyzed. He felt the breath whistling through his mouth and his eyes starting from their sockets.

"Mark Dixon!" shrieked the creature.

"Y-yes, that's who I am," Mark heard himself say. It was a nightmare come to life, the worst nightmare anyone ever had.

"I'm Charley Polson!" came the laconic reply.

Mark didn't know whether to be relieved or not. Old Uncle Charley Polson wasn't some dread specter. With his hat off, his white hair and beard only made him look like one in the moonlight. Still, he had a reputation as a dangerous old rascal and he had a gun. That was what made his arms look so long in the shadows.

Mark recovered some courage. After all, you shouldn't be afraid of a man who was over seventy years old. "What do you want, old man?" he demanded in the best voice he could muster.

"Yer life, ye stinkin', low-down, nigger-lovin' abolish!" was the vicious reply. "I calc'late ye got a minit er two t' live, an' I jist wanted t' tell ye a few things 'fore ye die!"

Mark tried to fight back his panic. The murderous old villain was going to kill him. "No! No! I'll give you money! My father—"

"Money cain't buy me!" cracked like a whip. "All th' money I want offa you is 'nough t' buy Sally Napier a tombstone, an' I'll jist take hit offa yore carcass."

"Don't! Please don't—"

"Shet up!" The gun came up menacingly as Mark's horse moved. "I don't hafta tell ye why I'm gonna kill ye. Y' awreddy know that. I jist wanted t' tell ye why I don't want nobody else to do hit, an' they's a dozen that would." The gun came down.

"W-wh-why?" Even a few seconds became precious. If he could only shake off this deadening paralysis!

"Hit's 'cause I ain't got no chance with th' Lord. I've kilt too many. Once when I wuz out scoutin' fer Harrison, I come 'crost six Injuns, three bucks, a squaw, an' two little uns. Dead drunk they wuz, th' big uns enyhow." The terrible old voice cackled. "I axed 'em all, th' little uns, too!"

A thrill of horror shot through Mark's body. "Oh! Oh!" came forth involuntarily.

"Them wuzn't th' only ones, either! I've kilt white men, too. I don't want no man that's got a chance with th' Lord t' ruin hit by killin' you. I ain't got none t' ruin!"

"P-please don't!" faltered Dixon as the gun came up again.

"Think 'bout Sally Napier 'fore ye die, an' Tom Traylor a fightin' fer his country! Think uv what a low-down scoun'rel ye air an' how ye desarve t' die!" The gun came up and centered on Dixon's horror-filled eyes.

The world exploded in his face as the heavy charge of buckshot all but tore his head off.

People never knew what became of Mark Dixon. He just disappeared from the face of the earth. Around home only his father, little Johnny Tacker, and Uncle Charley Polson ever knew he had been back. After little Johnny's nighttime visit, neither of the last two ever said a word about Mark Dixon, even to each other. Mark's New England friends never knew he made the trip, and he had told them he was from Ohio anyhow, because he was ashamed of where he was from. The boardinghouse keeper where he stayed sold the clothing and what else he had left behind to make up his unpaid bill and disregarded all inquiries about Mark for fear there would be trouble about it. Mark's father thought he had gone back to New England, and since his son never wrote except to ask for money, he didn't get worried until six months had gone by. The man whose horse Mark had hired found the animal at his stable two days later and had been paid to keep his mouth shut, so he did.

When old Calvin Dixon did get worried, he couldn't find out anything except that Mark hadn't gone back to school and gave it up after a little while. Who would even know where to start? Mark had said something about going to California once, so that might be where he was. Maybe he would write someday.

No one found the skeletal remains in a thickly overgrown sinkhole in dense woods along the track to Shoals for many years. By that time weather, decay, and gnawing animals had made them unrecognizable as human to the squirrel hunter who happened on them. There had been little left of the skull to begin with.

Six months after her death, some anonymous benefactor had a wonderful marble tombstone put up over Sally Napier's unmarked grave. It really wasn't a tombstone, but a statue of a beautiful angel nearly life-sized, with the inscription on its base. The men who brought it said it came all the way from Italy. A woman who knew about such things said it was a work of art. People agreed that it must have cost a fortune and couldn't imagine who had paid for it.

Everybody knew Sally's parents hadn't. They were too heartless. Some thought Tom Traylor had, because he was a high officer in the army now and surely made a lot of money. He denied it, although he wrote his father that he wished he had.

A man visiting in the neighborhood thought that either old Calvin Dixon or Mark had done it after his conscience got to hurting, but local people laughed at the very idea. The old man was far too much of a skinflint, and neither one of them ever seemed to have a conscience. No one ever found out who paid for the tombstone statue, although curiosity made several try.

Mark Dixon was really the one who paid for it. His ancient assassin wasn't able to see well enough to count the money he took off the body and had taken it all. It worried him half to death until he remembered a magnificent tombstone he had seen as a boy back in old Virginia, which people said a rich planter had put up for his beautiful young wife who died in childbirth. He thought Mark's money would pay for one like it. What could be more "fitten' an' proper" for sweet, beautiful Sally, whom he had loved from afar with all his hardened old heart?

Giving out that he was going to visit folks in Kentucky, Uncle Charley went to Louisville and found the most exclusive monument dealer in town. He told him what he wanted and said he had the money to pay for it. It ought to be enough; it would buy a good farm. The dealer looked like he didn't much believe him, but he got out some catalogues and they looked through them until they found exactly what was wanted. The dealer then figured up the price. It cost so much because it would have to come from Italy, the only place you could get anything like it. To the man's obvious surprise, Uncle Charley said he had the money.

But he would buy it only on one condition. It had to be put up so no one could ever find out who paid for it or whom he had bought it from. The dealer said that could be done, but it would take some complicated arrangements and cost extra. The old man said he would pay the extra, although he knew it would take his own money to do it.

After the fellow took down the inscription and directions as to where to put the stone, they closed the deal. That was why no one could ever find out who paid for Sally Napier's tombstone. A few people noticed that old Uncle Charley Polson was often around the cemetery after it was put up, but no one thought anything of it. His wife was buried there under a stone he had chiseled out himself, with his own name and birth date on it, too. He was getting on to where he would soon be there himself, although the old fellow was so spry it was hard to realize it, and he had never been sick in his life that anyone knew of.

# 38

At long last the regiment was going into winter quarters where it was camped and it also received enough replacements to bring it up to full strength again. The men immediately began building their huts, but Tom had little to do in supervising his. Those who hadn't built good ones the year before had suffered for it all winter and could be depended on to do it right this time. He told Cole and Grim to distribute the new men among the veterans to make sure they had good huts to live in. The men seemed to enjoy the building. They worked like beavers and displayed great ingenuity in construction.

When Hauser built Tom's hut, he learned that the fellow numbered carpentry and masonry among his talents. He built a neat little log cabin with clay-daubed chinks and a real roof instead of just shelter halves stretched over the top. He rived shingles and fastened them down with stringers, then used shelter halves for a ceiling. The structure boasted a fireplace and chimney made of real brick from an abandoned house nearby and a floor of boards from the same source. There was a bed of rope stretched tightly over a frame fastened in one corner and a table for eating and writing made of a wide board hinged to one of the walls so it wouldn't be in the way when not in use. All that was lacking was windows, but Hauser said he had a good stock of candles. Of course it took longer to construct and the builder had to conscript some of his friends to help, but it was something of local marvel and the men would show it to visitors with proprietary pride. One of them once said it was a better house than a lot of people lived in, even if it was a little small.

Two-thirds of the replacements the company got were Germans. People said that men just couldn't be raised in the northern part of the county anymore because of the Proclamation and other things, but Tom thought it was partly because no one had been sent back to recruit like before. Anyhow, the other companies received enough replacements, and few of them were Germans.

Among the replacements was *Leutnant* Karl von Jagerhof, on leave from the Prussian army to get experience in actual warfare. Tom expected him to be an arrogant, overbearing sort of a fellow like

European noblemen were supposed to be, but he wasn't like that at all. He was only of average height and very slender, with blue eyes, yellow hair, and a very fair complexion. Instead of the big, blustering fellow Tom expected, he looked diffident and a little delicate, but his appearance was deceptive, as some of the men found out, and he had a voice like a bugle on the drill field. What was more, he spoke excellent English with scarcely a trace of an accent.

What Tom liked about him more than anything else was that he promised to be a fount of military knowledge. This was why he had Hauser build another bed and insisted that the *Leutnant* move in with him. Although he was younger than Tom, von Jagerhof had ten years of military training. Like most sons of the Prussian nobility, he had gone away to a military academy as a boy and had been continuously schooled until he was commissioned a few years ago. To top it off, he was a dedicated student of his profession and had a trunk full of military books. They were all in German, but Tom had no doubt he could study them and learn to read German at the same time.

He expected Hauser to kick up a row about having another officer to take care of, but he didn't. In fact, he seemed to welcome the addition, perhaps because his new charge was of such exalted social status that he furnished opportunities for much boasting to the other Germans.

Billy and Tom Pinnick got to be sergeants, and Sam Price, Schlimmer, Gus Buroker, and Sepp Hartman corporals. Tom guessed Schlimmer had made it up to Grim somehow to get his backing. Hartman would stay with Grim, but Tom put Schlimmer under Pinnick, because most of his men were now Germans. Buroker would be Billy's corporal.

Except for the Germans, who didn't seem to be any different, the replacements didn't measure up to the veterans very well. Several of them were pretty rough characters. The men said that two of them, Si Jones and Bob Ewing, had joined only to get out of going to jail for stealing. Tom put those two and others like them under Cole, who could be depended on to hammer them into shape. He started in early, as both Jones and Ewing showed up at morning muster pretty well beaten up the third day they were in camp. Tom didn't make it any of his business, but he learned later that Cole had taken them both on at once when they got smart with him and come out of it without a mark on him. That augured well for discipline in the Second Platoon, the only one where there likely to be any problems.

The replacements had to be drilled thoroughly, and Tom put von Jagerhof in charge of it. Like a good officer should, he left most of it to the sergeants. The first time Tom went to the drill field to see how it was going, he found Billy drilling a platoon and doing a first-class job of it. The commands rang out in his clear young voice, and the men marched, maneuvered, and faced about with great precision. It was a joy to see him put them through the manual of arms. When the time came for company drill, he couldn't tell the replacements from the veterans unless he looked at their faces. When Major Owen called the whole regiment out, Tom's company outshone any of the others. Some of them had men who acted like they still ought to be in the awkward squad. Most of the companies had to go back to drill, but Tom's never had to turn out unless the whole regiment did.

This gave him much time for study. He and von Jagerhof went at it together in the evening and, after they had no more company drill, during the day as well. Reading German was slow and laborious for Tom at first, but with von Jagerhof's help and frequent recourse to an excellent German-English dictionary the Prussian had, he improved steadily. The fact that he already knew the metric system helped a lot. For a while, von Jagerhof had to write out translations for Tom to study, but the time came when this was no longer necessary. He was afraid he was imposing on his lieutenant, but von Jagerhof insisted he wasn't. He claimed that even writing out the translations helped fix things in his mind, and after that was no longer necessary he said studying with someone who knew as much as he did was much better than going it alone. When Tom protested his ignorance as an amateur, the Prussian maintained that he had an instinctive grasp of basic tactics and principles that more than made up for his lack of formal training.

The German books were much more practical and less theoretical than the ones Tom was used to. They abounded in problems and exercises, which he enjoyed working out. They used a lot of paper, but von Jagerhof scoffed at Tom's offer to buy some. A lot of it went into making the topographical maps many of the exercises required but which hadn't come with the books. There were always small-scale examples to go by, though, and they both soon learned to make the maps quickly and accurately.

Tom would often sit up after von Jagerhof had turned in and work until late at night. The time came when he could solve any problem his fellow student could and work out an exercise quite as well. He eventually came to believe that von Jagerhof was right about his instincts, mainly because he could think of no other reason why the subject was so absorbing for him.

Billy and Pinnick borrowed some of Tom's old books and sometimes came to see him about problems they ran into. Von Jagerhof was amazed when he saw Billy could read a page, close the book, and recite it almost word for word. When he learned that Billy was going to study medicine in Germany, he thought it was an excellent idea. Billy would breeze through any medical school in the country once he got a good grounding in scientific subjects. That was something Billy hadn't thought of and he was taken a little aback, but von Jagerhof thought a year or so at a gymnasium, the German equivalent of an academy, was all Billy would need, particularly since he knew the language so well. He thought Billy might be able to pass an entrance examination by studying on his own if he could get the right books and put in enough time on them. That appealed to Billy and when he asked where he could find out what books to get, von Jagerhof said he had a cousin in the Prussian Ministry of Public Health and would write him about it. Billy was much pleased, and even more so when the cousin sent a big batch of books together with suggestions for study instead of only a letter in reply. The only trouble was they didn't come until just before the spring campaign began and he couldn't get very far with them.

In the meantime all the other companies passed muster at regimental drill. It was barely in time, for Colonel Rivers began a program of brigade exercises in the rough country to the southeast. It was a long march there and back, but he said they wouldn't be on any nice, flat drill field when it came to the real thing, and everybody saw the truth of it. They went whether it rained, snowed, or shined, and Rivers wouldn't be satisfied with anything short of perfection. Division maneuvers were coming up pretty soon, and he was going to be ready for them. It was pretty tiring, but Tom and von Jagerhof were never too exhausted to put in a few hours' study every evening.

After about a week of it, Owen told Tom on the march back to camp that he would command the regiment the next day. He couldn't imagine why he had been singled out and was afraid he would make a mess of it. When he unburdened himself to von Jagerhof that night, the Prussian scoffed at his fears. How often had they done it on paper? What possible maneuver could be ordered that the captain hadn't already carried out? Hadn't they decided that a regiment was handled in a brigade just like a company in a regiment? He remembered the captain saying himself that the only difference was in size and scale. It all bolstered Tom's confidence considerably, and he didn't stay awake worrying like he was afraid he would.

The next day he carried it off without a hitch. He was a little nervous at first but before long was handling the regiment with as much confidence and aplomb as if he had been doing it for years. He had already worked out on paper everything that was done, and it took only an instant to visualize the movement, transform the abstract into the concrete, and give the proper order. Having the best drilled regiment in the brigade helped a lot. Of course, he didn't have a horse like Owen did, but he was sound of wind and limb. He had no qualms about leaving his company in the capable hands of von Jagerhof.

Afterward Jack Arnold clapped him on the back and told him he was better than Major Owen at it, but Jack was always saying things like that. Tom's nervousness came back after it was all over and he got to thinking about all the things he could have done wrong but somehow hadn't, and attributed his performance to beginner's luck. Von Jagerhof was full of "I told you sos" that evening. They had a long discussion of the maneuvers they had gone through and wound up by putting them all on paper.

The last three days it was the whole division, and on the third day Tom was given the regiment again. He was careful to concentrate only on maneuvering with the brigade and not let himself be distracted by what the whole division was doing. It was so large and covered so much territory that it often couldn't be seen in its entirety, and when it could it was disconcerting and even a little intimidating to watch its movements. General Carter flitted about like a sprite on a horse, and Tom got the impression he was the object of the general's particular attention.

The regiment was on the extreme right of the division's line, and when Carter wanted a flank refused it was the right one more often than not. When it was, the regiment's wheel to move at a right angle to the line always seemed to go with agonizing slowness. The companies on the far end seemed to move at a snail's pace, although they would tear through the brush and briers like wild horses, while those adjoining the division front continually threatened to move too fast and get out of alignment. It would be the same thing all over again when Carter ordered the regiment back into line.

When Carter wanted skirmishers, he threw out a whole regiment rather than companies from each one like always before, and again it was usually Tom's. He would race out with his men, reach the proper distance in front, then order them to file left. The first company would run like mad across the division's whole front with the others stringing out behind like an unraveling ball of twine. Tom would run alongside, anxiously watching the interval and halting the companies one by one when they reached the right place. He had to do so much loud shouting that he sometimes felt he must be getting blue in the face. Once the skirmish line was established, he would order the men forward, swiveling his head like a weathercock on a gusty March day to be sure he was keeping the right distance in front of the division's line. All the while he had to run madly back and forth to make sure his men were keeping proper alignment and interval as they moved across flats, down in gullies, and up the hillsides, often through tangled thickets of brush and briers.

By the time it was over, Tom understood why regimental commanders were given horses to ride. He felt like he had made a thirty-mile march. He smarted from brier scratches on exposed parts of his body and felt bruised elsewhere. The worst part of it was that he couldn't understand why he had been singled out to handle the regiment when it had other captains senior to him.

When Owen came up to him on the march back to camp, he felt like asking him about it but decided not to. It might sound like he was resentful, and the major wasn't the kind of man you asked about things if you could help it.

Owen wanted to borrow Hauser for the evening. General Carter and Colonel Rivers were going to mess with the regiment. Since all the officers were going to be there, the cook was going to need some help. Tom readily agreed, although he suspected it wasn't help as much as better cooking that was wanted. Hauser would certainly fill the bill, and Owen might want to keep him in the officers' mess. It wouldn't be for long if he did, though, so Tom wasn't concerned. No one else would put up with the fellow very long.

The major was leading a horse, so Hauser could hurry on ahead of the column to camp. He grinned slyly as he mounted to the cheers and salutes of his comrades, then galloped past them so close he splashed them with mud and water. They changed their tune and he trotted on cackling gleefully, pursued by fist shaking and volleys of German cusswords. The others laughed about it and were soon joined by those who were splashed, who only vowed to give *der Hauser* the ducking of his life the first chance they got.

Even Owen laughed, one of the few times Tom had ever heard him do it. He went on to say that General Carter would have good news for the two of them after the meal and advised Tom to put in a good appearance. Tom knew what it would be because of what Rivers had told him and only hoped Carter wouldn't make a big thing out of it. It suddenly dawned on him that what he had gone through was probably a test Carter had put him to, and he was glad he was too slow-witted to figure it out at the time. If he had, he would have made a mess of it for sure.

While Tom and von Jagerhof were getting ready, the Prussian noticed Tom's scratches and produced some flesh-colored powder that hid them pretty well. They arrived at the mess tent a little early, and Tom wasn't surprised to see that Hauser had taken charge. He was bustling about in the adjoining cooking tent delivering instructions and admonitions loudly in German. Tom wondered how the cook and the orderlies could understand him, and also how long it would take them to rebel against such tyranny. Von Jagerhof smiled and shook his head. He knew Hauser, too.

The only ones already there were Colonel Rivers and General Carter, who were sitting by the stove smoking cigars. The general was so small he looked incongruously like a boy with a stolen stogie. Rivers called Tom and von Jagerhof over to introduce the Prussian to Carter.

"I'm very glad to meet you, Lieutenant," said the general after they shook hands. "All of us are going to benefit from having a man with your qualifications around. I believe the Prussian army turns out the best officers there are."

Von Jagerhof was suitably modest and said he hoped to see much action to round out his training. Rivers assured him that he would. Tom chimed in to tell how he had benefited already.

Rivers asked for particulars, then burst out laughing. "You got caught in your own trap, General!"

Carter ruefully admitted it. "It sure looks like it." He laughed and slapped Tom on the back. "You'll understand it later."

Tom thought he already understood, so he tried to look amused. The other officers were coming in, and there was soon a circle about Rivers and Carter. Several hadn't met von Jagerhof yet, and Tom was busy with introductions for a while. Most seemed to take the same attitude toward him that Carter did, and to look up to him like amateurs to a professional.

They took seats around the tables, and the food was served. It wasn't long before the regular patrons of the mess began to proclaim that it was the best that had ever been served there. Several knew why and dropped remarks about keeping that German fellow who was responsible for it. Tom felt no concern, because he knew if they did, there would soon be an uprising of the orderlies and probably the patrons, too, and he would get Hauser back.

After the meal Owen got to his feet, rapped on the table at the front where he was sitting with Rivers and Carter, and the talk died away. "We are honored to have General Carter and Colonel Rivers at mess with us this evening." He turned to smile at the two guests. "We hope they enjoyed the meal." Both of them nodded and smiled through the smoke of their cigars.

Owen looked around smilingly. "All of you hear from me often enough, so I won't take time from General Carter, who will speak to us for a while."

Carter rubbed out his cigar and put it in his pocket. Tom hoped he had rubbed well so it wouldn't burn a hole in his coat.

The general got up and looked his audience over, a half-smile on his face. "First, I want to congratulate you on having the best mess in the division. I haven't had food like this in a long time."

There was a general round of nodding, smiling, and expressions of agreement. "Second," Carter went on, "I want to congratulate you on being the best regiment in the best brigade I've got." He turned to Rivers. "How much of that you owe to your brigade commander I don't know, but I expect it's a great deal."

Rivers grinned in his beard, and everybody applauded. Carter indicated he should rise, so he did, but he only bowed and sat down again.

The general turned to Owen next. "I think the man who carried on where your old commander left off deserves some of the credit, too." Owen got up and bowed in his turn to another round of applause.

Carter went on. "As you know," he said with a smile, "I'm not a politician." Everybody laughed, because they knew he had no peer at politics of the military kind. He pretended to be embarrassed. "Well, I'm not a political politician anyhow," he insisted with mock contrition, and everybody laughed again. "What I wanted to say before I got into all this was that I won't make a long, windy speech like politicians do." There was more laughter and Carter waited smilingly until it died away. "I want to say that the performance of your brigade on division exercises was so good that I'm excusing you from further participation." There was much applause and a few shouts of approval. "The other brigades will be going at it out there in the weather until they get up to your standard." He looked grim. "That's going to take them a few weeks, and then we'll have division exercises again. Until then, your brigade will be inactive, and I guess you know what that means."

Everybody did. There was prolonged applause and more shouts of approval.

Jack Arnold looked at Tom and winked broadly. "Leave!" he gloated. Tom couldn't help laughing at him.

The general had seen it. "Certain of you doubtless have plans for your leisure," he said smilingly as he looked at Arnold, "and Colonel Rivers tells me you will be eligible for leaves of seventy-two hours, however Colonel Owen wants to give them." He addressed Jack, "Will that be enough, Captain Arnold?"

Jack got to his feet amid a roar of laughter. "Yes, sir," he replied, blushing beet red, then hurriedly sat down again.

Carter smiled indulgently. "I hope, sir, you are able to entertain whatever ladies you choose to entertain within that length of time." Everybody broke out laughing again while Arnold grinned sheepishly. The general seemed to know everything about everybody.

Carter got serious. "I suppose you thought I made a slip of the tongue when I referred to Owen here as colonel a while ago." He nodded solemnly. "Well, I didn't. I have his commission as colonel with me, and I'll give it to him now." He handed a paper to Owen, then shook hands with him while everybody got to their feet and applauded. Owen blushed proudly in spite of himself as he sat down again.

Tom guessed it was his turn next and had a sinking sensation. Everybody would be looking at him and Carter was sure to say something that would make them laugh. He surely wouldn't be expected to say anything himself, though. Owen hadn't.

Carter fixed his eyes on Tom, who could feel himself blushing already. "Next," began the general with a bright smile, "I have a few words to say about Captain Traylor." Eyes swiveled on him like rifle muzzles. Carter motioned for him to get to his feet, so he did.

"This young man is going to get a major's commission just as soon as it can be fixed up and sent down." He nodded and smiled. "I don't have it with me because I didn't think he was going to get it quite yet."

Tom felt like he was before a firing squad and took a chance on sitting down. To his relief, Carter only smiled and went on. "This young man has risen rapidly. Several of you were captains when he was only a private. Now he'll be a major in a few days and you'll still be captains." He looked at them knowingly. "You wouldn't be human if you didn't feel a little resentment, so I think I'd better tell you a few things about it." Everybody was still looking at Tom, but it wasn't so bad now that he was sitting down. He knew he was still blushing, though.

Carter began to walk back and forth behind his table. "We all like to say that we believe in Napoléon's maxim that every one of his soldiers carried a marshal's baton in his knapsack." He stopped and nodded. "But it rarely works out that way. Good privates get to be sergeants, and that's about as far as it goes."

Carter looked down and walked around a little. To Tom's relief, the men around the tables were beginning to take their eyes off him and look at the general again.

Carter looked up, stopped, and went on. "I had strong doubts about making Captain Traylor a major despite the earnest recommendations of Colonel Rivers and Colonel Owen." Eyes were turning back to Tom again. His scratches smarted and he wondered if it was because of blushing so long.

"I thought it was too soon," said Carter with a nod. "I didn't doubt that he would make major, but I thought he needed more seasoning." He paused and looked around. "So," he went on softly, "I decided to eliminate him for the time being." Tom began to get an idea of what he was leading up to.

"I told Colonel Rivers to let him handle the regiment a time or two during brigade exercises, and then I would try him out during division maneuvers. If he could do it, I would see to his promotion myself, and if he couldn't, he'd have to wait." Carter nodded thoughtfully. "I was sure he'd fall flat on his face, because I was really going to put him through the mill, and he wouldn't have a horse to ride around on. In the first place, I didn't think he could do it well enough, but if he somehow could, it wouldn't be for long." Carter shook his head and pursed his lips. "He'd lunge around in those thickets out there, tear his clothes half off, and wear himself out so he'd have to give it up."

Carter bulged his eyes and looked astonished. "But you know what he did? He handled the regiment like he'd been doing it all his life, and he kept it up all day without even tearing his clothes!" He smiled at Tom. "I guess that's because he had a uniform made out of good, strong cloth, because it looks like his hide didn't stand up so well."

Everybody laughed and Tom grinned ruefully.

"Well, I'd told Rivers and Owen that if he could do it, I'd see that he was made a major, and I'm a man of my word. Major Traylor will get his commission just as soon as it can be fixed up and sent down here."

Tom was hoping that was the last of it, but Carter went on. "Now I'll tell you all something. If anyone else wants to try to handle the regiment when you have division exercises again, and can do it on foot, I'll make him a major, too, even if I've got to jump him from lieutenant!" He raised his hand suggestively and looked around. "Any takers?" There were none, so Carter sat down.

Tom thought it was surely all over now and longed to get back to his cabin. He had never been so tired in his life, and this was the second ordeal Carter had put him through. The way it had been done ought to eliminate a good deal of jealousy about his promotion, though, and it made him feel that he had earned it.

Owen got up and said a few words, but Tom was so preoccupied he didn't hear. He smiled at Tom as he spoke, so he guessed it had been about him and managed to smile back. Then everybody began to crowd around, offering congratulations and shaking his hand, except for a few who left ostentatiously without even looking at him. He wasn't surprised to see Captain Harlow leading them. He hadn't forgotten his humiliation by Rivers last spring for quarreling with Tom when he was supposed to be leading a skirmish line.

Tom turned to von Jagerhof and said, "If it hadn't been for you and your books—"

The Prussian cut him off. "Oh, you'd have been able to do it anyhow!" When Tom started to argue, he put a finger to his lips. "Just let them think it's genius," he whispered with a wink of a big blue eye. "They won't be far wrong."

Arnold pounded him on the back. "The way you're going, you'll be a general before it's over!" he exclaimed. The fellow couldn't have been happier if it had been him.

Carter and Rivers came up. "I hope you don't think I was too hard on you," said Carter smilingly as they shook hands.

"Oh, no sir! We ridge runners from the Pocket are used to that sort of thing! We do it all the time at home."

Rivers shook his hand solemnly and spoke with a strangely sad look in his eyes. "I want to congratulate you, son," he said simply.

After it was over, Tom and von Jagerhof went toward their cabin. Something was going on there. All the company seemed to be around it, and the men raised a cheer when they saw Tom coming. He was touched. This meant more to him than the congratulations of fifty generals like Carter. He was touched even more when they started singing "For He's a Jolly Good Fellow." They made a mess of the song, mainly because the Germans tried to sing in English, but he appreciated it more than if it had been sung by an Italian opera company.

Tom knew he had to say something as the men gathered around and fell silent. He looked at faces that had been young and fresh not so long ago but were now weathered and worn, almost like those of men in middle age. He saw faces in the flickering firelight that were no longer there, Burk's, Johnny Conrad's, Jim Polson's, and others. It was a struggle for him to begin.

"I want you men to know something," he said. "Your respect and your affection mean more to me than any baubles they can pin on my shoulders." His voice began to tremble, and he had to pause. "I'll be leaving you pretty soon now," he went on, "and it'll be as hard as leaving home was. We came in together, you old hands, and we've been together ever since. We've been through a lot together—" He had to stop and look down. When he looked up, he realized he had run out of anything to say. "I'd rather shake your hands than General Carter's," he said huskily and turned away as the men raised another cheer.

He almost ran into Cole. "That wuz a right good speech, Major, sir, an' we're gonna miss you more'n you'll miss us."

Tom found he couldn't say anything and only shook the big dark fellow's hand.

It was appropriate for Kemper to show up, and he did. *"Gratulieren, Herr Major!"* he said with a broad grin.

Tom disregarded his salute and took his hand. "It's like I told you once. I owe most of it to you."

Kemper laughed deprecatingly, but Tom could tell he was strongly affected, too.

Some of the Germans set up a clamor to Kemper. "Dey vant de speech to unnerstan'," he explained. "Dey nodt unnerstan' de Eenglish."

Tom had settled down enough to be able to repeat what he had said in German. His audience listened raptly but took the business about handshaking literally and all insisted on shaking hands with him. Afterward they sang *"Hoch Soll Er Leben,"* their equivalent of "For He's a Jolly Good Fellow," and sang it beautifully.

While they were singing, the other men followed their example, and Tom wound up by shaking hands with every man in the company except Billy, who gave him a big hug instead.

Von Jagerhof was much impressed and afterward told Tom that any officer who could win the affection of his men like that deserved any promotion he got on those grounds alone. It was a lesson for him, he averred, another one of those things that couldn't be learned from books and schools.

A few days later, Tom heard that Hauser was boasting to the other Germans that he was such a good cook that Owen had wanted him to take charge of the officers' mess. He had turned it down, though, because if he left Tom and von Jagerhof it wouldn't be long before they wouldn't be looking like officers anymore.

Tom knew better than to believe the last part of it. Hauser had stayed with him because he knew very well that no one else would put up with his domineering ways very long.

# 39

When he became regimental adjutant, Tom was afraid he might have to move out of his cabin and live in the officers' tent, but he didn't. Owen didn't say anything about it, and of course Tom didn't either. He was also afraid of paperwork, but there wasn't much of it. Corporal Stevens, the regimental clerk, was an expert at it, and about all Tom and Owen had to do was sign papers once in a while. Supply was no problem either, because Quartermaster Sergeant Winters was as good in his department as Stevens was in his.

The best thing about it was that Tom got a horse. Hauser erected a crude but sturdy stable for the animal and cared for it with great solicitude, perhaps because he often got to exercise it. He delighted in riding about camp like a major general, gaped at by *Die Fusslatschern,* footsloggers, as he styled his late comrades.

The most serious problem Tom had was discipline among the replacements. Except for the Germans, the new men were a problem. They just didn't measure up to the veterans, although they came from the same places and sometimes even from the same families. They resented subordination and sassed their noncoms except for ones like Cole. Some of them even did it to officers. When they got passes and went to town, they often got to brawling and fell into the clutches of Major Pedigo. When they couldn't get passes, they would slip past the guard and go anyhow. They brought whiskey back and got drunk in camp.

All that had been done so far was to deal with the symptoms, and Regimental Sergeant Major Kemper had done most of that. Tom soon saw that it was up to him to attack the roots of the problem. He found out how serious it was the first two days he was adjutant. Six men were brought before him the first day and eight the next. None of them had done anything serious enough to get more than a good bawling out and warnings of dire consequences if they did whatever they had done again. Tom saw that if it went on like this, he would have time for nothing else and the regiment would go to rack and ruin, because some of the older men were beginning to act up, too.

That evening he got Owen's permission for what he was going to do. It would also be a good chance to establish to the officers that he was adjutant of the regiment. He knew very well that several of them resented his being jumped over them. Although none had shown it to his face yet, it wouldn't be long before one of them did. Tom heard that Captain Harlow was calling him "that copperhead farmer" behind his back, and Harlow had a friend named Samuels who had also been a captain from the beginning and seemed to share his feelings. Both men had been lawyers, and some said Harlow was a Republican.

Tom knew those two would jump at any chance to show him up. He was going to give it to them. At least they would think it was that.

The next morning after officers' call he assembled the company commanders in the mess tent even before the dishes were cleared away and told them their subordinates could take care of morning muster. Most of them sat around the tables looking like they thought he was wasting their time, especially Harlow and Samuels. They were ostentatiously indifferent. Only von Jagerhof looked very attentive, and the only smile Tom got was from Jack Arnold.

Tom stood before them a little surprised that he felt completely at ease. "Gentlemen," he began, "we're having entirely too many disciplinary problems, and the regiment's going to pot unless we do something about it." He paused and looked them over. "Too many of them are coming to me," he went on.

There was little appreciation in anyone's eyes. Several looked knowingly at one another. Tom didn't let it bother him.

"You know what the trouble is. It's these new men. They just don't measure up to the ones we started with. Sometimes it looks like they scraped the bottom of the barrel back home." Several nodded agreement, but there were no smiles or signs of cooperation except from von Jagerhof and Jack.

Tom saw that he had his work cut out for him, but it only made him more determined. "Now I'll tell you the way I see it. If you don't agree, just say so. I'm no know-it-all." Harlow positively sneered at him, then winked broadly at Samuels, who grinned slyly.

"You can talk to the old hands and reason with them. They're like soldiers have always been, I guess. They'll do things they shouldn't do and they'll talk back sometimes, but you can reason with them and, as likely as not, they'll see the error of their ways and straighten up. If they don't, some of the others will take them in hand."

There were a few nods and smiles, but none from Harlow or Samuels.

"This made it easy for us. Then we got these new men, and we've tried to do the same way with them." He paused and nodded significantly. "It just doesn't work."

The indifference had mostly disappeared except for Harlow and Samuels, who still kept up a show of it.

Tom set his trap. "Now, I'll tell you what these hard cases need." He raised a fist and shook it. "That's all a good many of them can understand. It's too bad, but that's the way it is."

Harlow walked right in. "Do you mean we officers ought to fist-fight with them?" His sneer was largely in his voice, and he looked about triumphantly.

Samuels snickered audibly, and all eyes were on Tom. The challenge was plain and they waited to see how he would react. Several seemed ready to join Harlow and Samuels.

Tom fixed Harlow with an icy stare. "I was speaking only in a figurative sense, but the captain doesn't seem to understand. I had assumed he had a certain amount of literary knowledge."

Several laughed outright and others grinned appreciatively. No one liked Harlow except Samuels and seemed to enjoy seeing him get some of the medicine he was always dishing out. Tom had been counting on that. Harlow flushed and stirred uneasily. Samuels looked at him expectantly, but he didn't say anything.

Samuels tried it next and Harlow perked up in anticipation that his friend would be able to do what he hadn't. Samuels was more subtle. "I don't think the major appreciates the problem," he began evenly. "Most of the new men he got in his company are Germans, and they never cause any trouble."

Tom knew what he was up to. He hoped he would draw a response like Harlow had, but he had raised a legitimate point that deserved an answer. If Tom fell into the trap, they would have him. Harlow's gloating smile would have been enough to give it away.

Tom nodded appreciatively and replied frankly, "You're right. They don't." He smiled calmly at Samuels and went on. "But I got some I'll compare with any of them, and to show you how I think it ought to be done, I'll tell you how the two worst ones were taken care of." Without naming anybody, he went on to tell them how Cole had tamed Jones and Ewing, and Samuels couldn't quite hide his disappointment at the way it had come out.

Almost everybody showed considerable interest. "I wish I had a sergeant like that," sighed Jack Arnold.

Tom jumped at the chance to make his point. "You probably do have, only they don't think they've got to do things like that. Or they might not be noncoms. Maybe they hadn't shown themselves yet when the stripes were passed out." He smiled appreciatively at Jack.

Arnold admitted it. "You're right. I just don't expect enough of my noncoms, I guess." He nodded reflectively. "And I've better men who aren't noncoms, I expect." He was honestly puzzled. "But what can I do about it?"

"Break those that won't do their job and put men that will in their places," replied Tom grimly. "Give them fair warning that you expect them to handle their men, and if they don't do it then, we'll break them back to private." He let it sink in. "Colonel Owen will approve any breaking we've got to do, and I'll see to it that the men you want get their warrants." He was really bluffing. He only hoped Owen would.

The men around the tables were impressed, and Tom pursued his opportunity. "Good noncoms are the secret of good discipline. They're the backbone of any army. It was that way with the Romans, and it's been true ever since." He nodded and walked about a little. "But we've got too many noncoms that won't carry their weight. They got their stripes when they first came in and think they inherited them, like property or something. Most of them are good men, and if they see they've got to do some unpleasant things to keep their stripes, they'll do them. I don't think we'll have to break many when it comes right down to it, but we'll break those we have to break."

Everybody was all eyes and ears, even Harlow and Samuels in spite of themselves. "Now in a little while I'm going to tell you what I think you ought to do. You don't have to do it my way, though. You're in command of your companies, and you're responsible for their discipline." He took another few steps around. "I'm not going to horn in unless you ask me to. It's not my place to. All I have any right to do is hold you responsible for discipline in your companies. How you do it is up to you as long as you stay in regulations."

He stopped and looked them over, nodding significantly. "I want you gentlemen to know you can't expect me to handle your disciplinary problems. You've got to handle them yourselves. I've got the same right to expect you to handle your men that you've got to expect your noncoms to handle theirs, and I'm going to exercise that right."

Most of them seemed to take it well.

"I'm not saying this just to make it easy on myself. I'm saying it because the regiment's going to the dogs unless our officers and noncoms get over the idea that someone else will solve their problems for them."

He let it sink in as he took another few steps about. "Of course it'll be easier on me." He stopped, faced them, and added emphatically,

"But it'll be easier on you, too. Some of you have been running yourselves ragged trying to run your companies single-handed. Maybe you could do it with your old men, even if it was pretty hard on you, but *you simply can't do it* with half your companies made up of these new men." He nodded grimly. "No man can keep close tabs on a hundred others all by himself. His company suffers if he tries to, because he won't have time for anything else." He paused for effect and saw that a light was dawning on several.

"You've all got corporals and sergeants, and most of you've got lieutenants. Use them. That's what they're for. Make it easier on yourself. You're going to work and worry yourself half to death if you go on the way you've been going, some of you, and you still won't be able to do it."

The light had fully dawned on a harassed and worried lieutenant named Caruthers who had a company that was too much for him. "You know," he marveled, "I never thought of it that way before!" He was embarrassed by his spontaneity, but no one seemed to notice.

"It'll sure make life a lot more pleasant," said Tom smilingly.

Most of them indicated agreement, and there were several appreciative looks. He felt like he had cleared the crest after a long, hard climb.

"Now I'll tell you what I think you ought to do. Call a meeting of your noncoms as soon as you can. Get them together away from the rest of the men and lay down the law." He put his hands behind his back and took a few paces. "Don't go blustering and threatening them. Just tell them that from now on you're going to expect the same thing out of them I've said I'm going to expect of you. You're going to expect them to handle their men and solve their own problems as far as they can. If they've got men they really can't do anything with, they can turn them over to you as a last resort." He paused for effect, then went on grimly. "If you can't do anything with them either, send them to me. I guarantee you I'll do it. I'll use any means in regulations, all of them if I have to, and they won't be problems anymore when I get done with them." Several eyes widened at this last statement.

He went on. "Tell your noncoms they've got to handle their men and, if they don't, you're going to put men in their places who will. Like I told you, any breaking you feel you've got to do will be approved, and the men you want will get their warrants. Give them a fair chance; then if they can't or won't do it, we'll see about breaking them. All you've got to do is show it's got to be done, and they'll be broken like that." He thrust out an arm and snapped his fingers.

"Now for your officers, do the same thing with them if you think it's necessary, only do it privately. We can't break them like we can noncoms, but I'm sure I can give them a proper appreciation of their responsibilities if you can't." He smiled thinly.

"All I've told you is what I think you ought to do. If you want to do it some other way, feel free to do so. But before you do, I want you to know that I want results, whether you do it my way or yours."

A thoughtful silence followed. Jack Arnold broke it. "Well," he said to no one in particular, "I'm telling you what I'm going to do. I'm calling my noncoms together just as soon as I can get back to my company." He looked around with an air of satisfaction. "I'm going to make things a lot easier for myself; that's what I'm going to do."

Tom could have hugged him, but he only nodded and smiled. "Well, gentlemen, that's all I've got to say to you. Thank you for your time."

The officers started getting up and leaving. Jack hurried out, throwing a friendly wave as he went through the flap. The atmosphere was certainly a lot different than it had been to start with.

Harlow and Samuels stayed behind, as Tom had half-expected. They were going to try to face him down alone. He went up to them smilingly. "Anything I can do for you gentlemen?" he asked calmly.

It wasn't starting off like they expected, and both were taken a little aback. Samuels was the first to recover. "Well," he huffed, "I just wanted to tell you something, Traylor." He paused to see what effect his deliberate use of Tom's name instead of his rank would have.

It had none. As far as Tom was concerned, it was man to man. "Yes, Captain?"

Samuels had to go on, although he looked like he wished he didn't. "I just think it's pretty presumptuous of someone who's commanded a company a few months to try to tell men who've had one nearly two years how to do it."

Tom looked him in the eyes and saw them flicker. "I'm sorry you feel like that, Captain," he replied evenly. He smiled coldly and Samuels dropped his eyes. "I've seen it from the bottom and the top, too. I thought it might benefit you gentlemen who've seen it only from the top."

Harlow had to say something, although he looked like he didn't want to either. "I've got something to say, too!" he blustered.

Tom turned his eyes on him. He despised the fellow and made no attempt to hide it. "Say it, Captain," he said challengingly.

"I don't appreciate being humiliated in front of my colleagues." The bluster was gone.

"You were ready to humiliate me, weren't you, Captain?" Tom asked bluntly.

Harlow's eyes dropped. "No, I was just trying to clear up—"

Tom cut him off. "You like to dish it out, don't you, Captain? But you can't take it—"

Harlow showed him he could interrupt, too. "Now listen!" he said angrily. "I won't be insulted!" He managed to look Tom in the eye.

Tom decided to put him down. "Does the captain want satisfaction?" he hissed.

Harlow's eyes flickered. "N-no," he stammered. "I didn't mean anything like that." He thought fast for a suitable answer. "I'm no slave-driving duelist," he sneered.

Tom was ready for it. "Be careful what you say, Captain, or people will think you are." Tom looked at him stonily. "Neither am I."

Harlow backed down. "Oh, all right," he sighed. "I just wanted to tell you I'd like to be treated with some respect, that's all." He met Tom's eyes briefly.

"I'll say the same, Captain," said Tom simply. He looked at both of them. "I guess we understand one another now, don't we, gentlemen?"

They were beaten. Samuels confessed it with a shrug and an attempt at a smile. "I suppose we do—better, anyhow."

Tom decided to finish them off. "I thank you for your time, gentlemen."

They turned and left without another word. Tom despised them both, although he didn't think Samuels would have gotten into it but for Harlow. As he left the tent, he saw the cook pretending to be busy in the adjoining cook tent and one of the orderlies waiting there to clean up the breakfast dishes. They had undoubtedly heard everything, which meant that every man in the regiment would soon know about it. None of the men liked either Harlow or Samuels, and what they would say would hurt the two a lot more than anything else.

A good while later Corporal Stevens told Tom that Harlow and Samuels had gone straight to Owen and claimed that he had challenged Harlow to a duel. Owen replied that such a thing was a serious matter and started asking them exactly what was said and having Stevens put it on paper. They seemed well satisfied until Owen remarked that he ought to get statements from disinterested third parties and was sure he could, since the cook and maybe the orderlies had undoubtedly heard it all.

At that Harlow and Samuels reconsidered and suddenly decided they wanted to think about it before going further. Maybe it wasn't so serious after all. They could have misunderstood the major.

That gave Owen a chance he had evidently been looking for. He told them it really might get serious when Major Traylor found out what they had tried to do, and he doubted if there would be much formality about it, like with a duel. He felt bound to tell the major about their accusation.

Owen went on to say it might be a good idea for them to take advantage of an opportunity that had recently come up. Officers were wanted for new regiments back home, and he had been asked if he could spare any. He could spare them. He certainly could, thought Tom when he heard about it. They were the worst two company commanders in the regiment and would have been gone long ago if they hadn't had good sergeants. Harlow and Samuels immediately decided to avail themselves of such an opportunity for advancement and were gone in a few days. They gave out that they had been asked for back in Indiana to head up new regiments, but it all got out and no one was fooled very long.

After this, Tom felt that his authority as adjutant was well established. In fact, a few of the officers behaved so obsequiously that he was afraid they thought he was a bully and a dangerous fellow. He believed he had seen the ones who acted like that going out of the mess tent with Harlow the night Carter had announced his promotion. He didn't hold it against them and tried to show he didn't by being friendly and polite with them. From what he heard, the men made a big thing of it, especially those who got out from under the two departed captains.

Discipline began to improve rapidly the next few days. Tom could tell because far fewer cases were brought before him. The time came when Owen remarked that it looked like the new men had finally been brought around, but Tom thought he sure hadn't had much to do with it and wondered what would have happened if he hadn't taken it on himself to deal with the problem. Only a few noncoms had to be broken, and Owen went along with it. The others got the message and disciplinary cases dropped off almost to zero, but not until Tom had attended to a few of the hardest cases. He had them bucked and gagged by their own sergeants. It wasn't very pleasant, but it was the only thing to do short of filing charges for court-martial. That would take it to Brigade and Division, and he didn't want Rivers and Carter thinking the regiment couldn't solve its own problems.

When a man was bucked and gagged, he was seated on the ground and a short, heavy stick run under his bent knees. Then his arms were drawn under the stick to his elbows and his wrists tied together in front. After his wrists were tied to the stick, his ankles bound, and the gag put in, he was let in his company street with only enough of a fire to keep him from freezing on cold nights. Tom limited it to twelve hours, although he was sometimes urged to make it longer by an irate sergeant.

There was always a good deal of teasing and baiting, but it didn't end with that in two cases. One fellow was half-covered with dirt when morning came, and the other claimed he had been urinated on. Tom thought that was why he had to do so little of it and never the same fellow twice.

After Tom left the company, von Jagerhof became its commander and another officer was needed. The two of them tried to talk Cole into applying for a commission, but they couldn't do it. The big fellow said he would rather just be a sergeant so he could knock the men around when they needed it. Von Jagerhof was able to persuade him to become company sergeant major, though, and gave his platoon to Sam Price. Neither Pinnick nor Grim was interested in a commission. Grim said he couldn't speak English well enough and was too old to learn. Pinnick just didn't want to become an officer and have to wear a fancy uniform, use fancy manners, and all that. Tom knew that was Cole's real reason, too.

Billy was the only other sergeant and didn't want to apply either. He pleaded all sorts of things and von Jagerhof gave up on him, but Tom didn't. He took Billy aside and found out what it really was. "Th' men jist won't look up t' me an' they'll give me all kinds uv trouble 'cause I'm younger'n most uv 'em, th' old ones enyhow." He looked at the ground and shuffled his feet.

"Well now," replied Tom, "you haven't had any trouble being a sergeant, have you?"

Billy looked up. "No, I ain't, but my men's all Germans, an' they ain't like th' other fellers. They're a hull lot easier t' handle."

"Who's going to be company sergeant major?"

"Cole is, but ever'body's skeered uv him; he's big an' tough." Billy looked down again and sighed. "I'm jist too little an' skinny—"

Tom cut him off, "What do you think Cole will do if somebody in the company acts up?"

"Beat th' daylights out uv 'em, an' they know hit." Suddenly Billy looked up and broke into a smile. "I see what y' mean, Major, sir. I guess I will 'ply atter all."

Tom clapped him on the shoulder. "Just don't depend on Cole or anybody else too much, though. Be your own man. You've seen a lot of action, and you're the best shot in the regiment." Billy's appreciation showed all over him. "Something else," Tom went on. "You've got more brains than any of them, and they know it. Just act like you expect them to obey you, and I don't think you'll ever need any help."

Tom thought he was done with that, but when Stevens came back from Division with the application, he said candidates for commissions now had to pass an examination on Hardee's *Tactics* before a board of officers General Carter had set up.

Billy was ready to back out, but this time von Jagerhof did the persuading. Billy had studied that book a lot, hadn't he, and didn't he remember everything he studied? In fact, he probably knew it better than the examiners would. This bolstered Billy's confidence, and from what Tom heard that was about the way the examination went.

As soon as they heard Billy's commission would go through, Tom urged him to go to Herr Thiers and get himself outfitted. Billy wanted to be ready when his commission came, so he went that very morning, although it was almost dinnertime.

Tom was surprised to see him back in camp early that afternoon and remarked on it. Billy grinned and said it had been fast work. A whole bunch of officers from a brigade that had just been paid were in the shop when he got there, and he was just waiting his turn when Rebecca saw him. She went outside and around to the front, beckoned him out, then took him in back of the shop where they lived and measured him herself. Billy laughed and said she acted like he was someone special, but it wasn't until she was done and had taken his order that he found out why. She gave him a big kiss and told him it was for his brother. He thought maybe Tom was cutting in on Schlimmer.

Tom laughed and said he wasn't. Young girls were just like that, he guessed. They loved to tease and flirt. He wouldn't cut in on Schlimmer even if he could, because he and Rebecca were going to get married.

There was something else. Before Billy left, Rebecca's father dropped his work and came to shake his hand, then her mother hugged him like he was her own son. He couldn't understand that at all, and of course Tom couldn't enlighten him.

# 40

When General McClellan was dismissed as commander of the army early in November, there was a good deal of dissatisfaction in the regiment, but not as much as in some of the others, from what Tom heard. He guessed the men had gotten it out of their system back at the time of the Proclamation, when they had nearly mutinied. Maybe they were just resigned to such things. The officers seemed to be put out more than the men. Several blamed it on politics, and none of them had any confidence in General Burnside, who had taken McClellan's place. A few of them predicted dire consequences, but Tom kept his mouth shut. He was adjutant now and had to set a good example.

When General Carter held division maneuvers again, he was satisfied after only two days. The men went back to camp thinking they would stay there until spring, but a few days later orders came early one morning to get ready to march by noon with three days' cooked rations.

Owen said he had to go to brigade headquarters and left immediately, so Tom had to do it all until he came back, and by then it was nearly time to march. The men didn't like leaving the huts they had spent so much time getting snug and warm, but they didn't show too much resentment. Maybe they thought they were headed for a battle that would decide something one way or the other, probably the other, because they had no more confidence in Burnside than the officers did.

Tom had a busy morning, but when Owen came back he could tell him the regiment was ready to take the road. Owen said there had been a postponement, though. They wouldn't march until the next morning. Tom didn't want the men to spend the night in roofless huts, so he sent Kemper around to tell them to take their shelter halves out of their packs and put them back on. It was a good thing he did, for they would spend two more nights in them, and the weather was cold.

The next morning the second postponement came early enough to catch the shelter halves still on the huts, so the men didn't fret much about it. They settled down for another day in camp and started carrying on as usual.

Hauser was grooming his horse, so Tom went to the baggage wagon to get what he needed. In the process, he came across the revolver Ernst Thiers had dropped in the woods. It was exactly like the one he had, and it occurred to him that two revolvers might come in handy if it came to close quarters. Capt. Herb Parker of the Martin County company had an extra holster, so he went to see about buying it.

Parker and his father kept a store and livery stable in Shoals, and Tom had bought a team of mules from them just before the war broke out. When Parker wouldn't take any money for the holster, Tom told him he was learning bad habits in the army and would have a hard time making a living when he got back home. Parker laughed and said the holster hadn't cost him anything, so he wasn't losing any money on the deal. He was unusually talkative as well as generous, so they talked about things back home for a while before Tom left.

Waiting was even more tedious the second day, so Tom went to visit his old platoon. The men were lounging around their outdoor fireplace where there was a roaring fire and started to get up, but he told them it was only a social visit and to stay like they were. They took up their talking and joking again, and it was soon just like old times when he was one of them. Cole gave him a cup of coffee and made a place for him on the log where he and Ab were sitting.

"Well, Major, you'll be ridin' that big bay on th' march, won't ye?" Cole meant the horse that had come with Tom's new rank.

"Yes, and I expect it'll be colder than marchin'," Tom replied. "I may be wishin' I was back on foot again."

"Now, Major, if'n hit gits too cold fer ye, jist turn him over t' me an' I'll ride him awhile," joked Ab.

Charley Evans snorted. "Ab, yo're th' laziest feller they ever wuz! 'Magine, a privit ridin' a hoss on th' march!"

"Naw, I ain't neither th' laziest feller they ever wuz!" denied Ab emphatically. "Now, you knowed Bill Summers back home, didn't ye?"

The lanky fellow laughed. "Bill's a heap lazier'n me, Bill is. Even his shadder's lazy."

"Well, come t' think uv hit, I b'lieve Bill does beat ye," admitted Charley. "They's no doubt 'bout him. He *is* th' laziest feller they ever wuz."

"Who's Bill Summers?" asked someone from another neighborhood.

That got Ab started and a crowd soon gathered. Even some of the Germans came over. They couldn't understand very well, and Billy had to do some translating, when he was able to stop laughing long enough.

First, Ab told how one of Bill's fields grew up into a woods because he couldn't keep the sprouts cut out of it. Then there was a tale about the time Bill tied a couple of big rocks to his plowshare so he could keep the point in the ground easier. It spooked his mules into running away and wrecking the plow. Then one spring Bill's wife had to fix the roof on their house because the fishing in the Patoka was so good.

An uproar of guffaws and mirthful whoops broke out again and again as it went on, and Tom laughed as much as anybody. It wasn't the stories themselves nearly as much as the way Ab told them. It certainly took the men's minds off whatever worries they had, and from that point of view Ab was the most valuable man in the company.

The fourth day, the order to march wasn't canceled. The regiment took the road south through town and joined the brigade on the other side of it. It was last in the column, but the dust wasn't bad enough to make much difference. The weather was clear and cold and Tom found himself wanting to dismount and go on foot for a while, but he never did. The men noticed he was wearing two revolvers and joked with him about being a two-gun man. At first there was a lot of cavalry around and the men visited their usual humorous contempt on the troopers. Colonel Davis rode by once on the other side of the column. He pretended not to notice Tom, which was all right with him.

The brigade joined the division the second day and brought up the rear as the march went on, which put the regiment at the end of the column. Late in the afternoon several days later, they reached a narrow but deep and swift-flowing river spanned by an unusual pontoon bridge, which seemed to be held in place by two cables running along its sides and tied to trees or large stakes driven into the ground on both ends. Tom guessed the current was too swift for the pontoons to be anchored or maybe the balks that normally held such a bridge together didn't fit right or something.

The brigade halted before following the rest of the column across, and Rivers came back to tell Owen that his regiment was to stay at the bridge to guard it. He said General Carter thought the Rebels might try to destroy it because it would be on an important supply route if the move the army was undertaking went as planned. Rivers thought both banks ought to be guarded, because it seemed to him that cutting those anchoring cables would let the current sweep the bridge away. A few cavalry with sharp sabers could swim to either bank somewhere out of sight and do it, so a close watch would have to be kept.

Owen thought the regiment should be divided and a battalion put on each bank and, when Rivers agreed, took the first battalion across the bridge and left Tom where he was with the second one. Owen didn't tell Tom how to deploy, which left him to his own devices.

It seemed to Tom they were likely to be there several days at least, so he decided to rotate the five companies on outpost at a cedar brake about a mile back every twenty-four hours, with orders to keep one platoon spread out in skirmish order on both sides of the road. The others could put up their shelter tents back along the road and sleep when not on duty but were to be ready to turn out at any time. He sent von Jagerhof's company out first.

Tom spread the other four companies out along the riverbank, two on each side of the bridge. They were to put up their tents and could build fires. Each company was to keep two men on guard day and night, and they would have to watch the river closely for anyone crossing away from the bridge.

It was a cold night and Hauser's brazier made his tent cozy, but Tom had Jack Arnold's company guard wake him each time it changed, because it was the closest, and always crawled out to look around. He made two patrols along the riverbank to make sure the guards were alert and once saddled his horse and rode out to where von Jagerhof's company was. He found all his men in their tents spaced out along the road except for Billy's platoon, which was spread out on both sides of the road as a picket line. Von Jagerhof said he was going to keep Billy's men out all night so there would be no noisy blundering around in the dark but had promised them the next day off so they could catch up on their sleep. Tom thought that was a good idea. With nobody moving around and no fires at the outpost, the Rebels wouldn't find out much if they scouted the bridge that night.

Before breakfast the next morning, Tom thought he heard a few rifle shots from out where Billy's platoon was posted. He called for his horse, then heard more shots. There was no doubt about it this time, but the shooting was so sporadic that Billy was probably only engaging a cavalry scout. Tom called the four companies close to the bridge out under arms anyhow and posted Jack's across the ramp with orders to stay there. He told the officers of the others to hold them ready, then galloped toward the firing.

An open grass-grown field ran back about halfway to the outpost on both sides of the road; then there was a cornfield with the shucked stalks still standing sere and brown in the winter sunlight, rustling and rattling when the wind blew. Beyond the cornfield, about three hundred yards short of the cedar brake, an area densely overgrown with brush and small trees began, and it ran on out of sight on both sides of the road, for at least a mile, as Tom remembered. The firing began to increase as he got closer.

Von Jagerhof was leading his men along the road at a run as Tom galloped by. Not far beyond, he met Billy's men falling back. "They're flankin' me!" his brother shouted, his face flushed and his eyes wide. "Look thar!" He pointed at a gray skirmish line advancing through the growth. It was in long rifle range and seemed to go on out of sight on both sides of the road. The advancing Rebels were firing steadily but moving slowly. Individuals would stop, aim, and fire, then load as they came on. Bullets whizzed about. Billy's men were shooting back in the same fashion as they withdrew.

Behind the advancing skirmishers was what seemed to be a line of battle, although the dense growth it moved through made it hard to tell. Tom began to think he might be up against several regiments, maybe a brigade, and he was glad he had put the outpost out as far as he had. It would give him time to find out what he was really up against before having to call the rest of the battalion up or maybe even ask Owen to come to his support.

Von Jagerhof's company came panting up, and Tom told him to deploy his men as skirmishers on both sides of Billy's and take charge of the action, because he wanted to scout around. The Prussian did it smoothly and quickly, and soon the rest of the company was firing and falling back along with Billy's men.

Tom rode along just behind the line studying the advancing Rebels. He made a good target and bullets hissed close by, but he ignored them. He soon saw that the enemy line overlapped von Jagerhof's by a great margin. The line of battle, if it was one, seemed to do the same, but he could see it only at intervals in the growth and the Rebels' grayish clothing made it hard to see even then.

Tom saw he was going to have to call up three more companies, only three because one would have to be left at the bridge in case all this was only a diversion. He had a horse and von Jagerhof was conducting the action as well as anyone could, so he decided to go himself. He told the Prussian to keep on like he was, firing and falling back as slowly as possible, and that he would be back with reinforcements as soon as he could.

Just then a man to the left of the road was hit and fell out of sight. A comrade ran over, took one look, then turned and shouted, *"Kopfschuss! Tot!"* Shot in the head. Dead. The line moved to fill the gap automatically.

Tom took a careful look farther along the road to see if the Rebels were bringing up more men or had some they hadn't deployed. The road was empty, so he spun his horse around and galloped for the bridge.

He expected to see Owen waiting when he came in sight of it, but there was no sign of him. Tom had time only to send a man to tell him what the situation was and asked him to be ready to come to his support if he was driven back too close to the bridge. He told Jack to deploy his company across the ramp in front of the bridge and led the others back toward the fighting at a run. On the way he decided to put von Jagerhof in charge of the action, because he wanted to be free to move around himself. Although it was the Prussian's first action and he was junior to Parker and Hutchinson, the other two captains, Tom had more confidence in him. They might resent it, but he would cross that bridge when he came to it.

He got impatient and galloped ahead. Von Jagerhof was still falling back because the enemy skirmish line overlapped his, but his men were keeping their faces to the front and firing steadily. Back in the heavy growth the Rebel line of battle looked as formidable as ever.

When the three companies came up, Tom told von Jagerhof to take charge and deploy them in extended order in line with his own men. He carried out the movement with a speed and precision that must have impressed the Rebels. The slender blond fellow was as cool as a cucumber, although the enemy came steadily on and bullets sang briskly about. Billy said two more men had been hit but had to be left behind and he didn't know how badly they were hurt.

When von Jagerhof had his line formed, Tom saw that the enemy's overlapped it only slightly and was on the point of telling him to halt his men and have them fix their bayonets when he did it himself.

The Rebels also halted. Their skirmishers were well out into the cornfield by this time, but their line of battle back in the thickets could be seen only where the growth was thinner.

Tom rode back and forth along the line to make sure no flanking move was under way and again looked back along the road to see if the Rebels had men they hadn't deployed. There was no flanking movement, and the road was still empty. He was once more a target for the Rebel skirmishers, and bullets whizzed close. One burned his horse's rump and nearly cost him his seat when the animal leapt.

He kept on despite the bullets, trying to figure out why the Rebel commander had stopped his advance. He was using most of a battalion as skirmishers, and from what could be seen of his line of battle, he had at least two regiments deployed back there.

Why didn't he come on? It didn't make sense for him to hold back in the face of only four companies. Did he really have several regiments back in the thickets or was he only filling open spaces in the growth so it would look like he had? If that was the case, what was he up to?

Suddenly it dawned on him. He had been drawn out and was being held, probably by only one regiment with half of it deployed in a skirmish line. There was only a battalion back there in the thickets, with the men carefully placed only where they could be seen. He had been drawn out so a dash could be made around one of his flanks, undoubtedly by cavalry, because infantry wouldn't be fast enough. It would be around his right flank, because a bend brought the river too close on his left to hide such a move.

Jack was at the bridge with his company, but it would be expecting too much of him to have his men back on the ramp and on guard against what was coming. They would want to see what was going on and would talk him into moving them so close to the action that horsemen would be able to sneak around behind them by keeping to the growth along the riverbank to their right. He should have left someone else.

The cables were going to be cut and the bridge wrecked. Unless Tom acted fast and was lucky, those golden major's leaves would soon be gone from his shoulders and he would be utterly disgraced. He would rather be dead. What was worse, he had been fooled by some crafty Rebel commander in his first independent command.

All this passed through his mind in a flash. He shouted to von Jagerhof to hold where he was as long as he could and tore back toward the bridge at a mad gallop. He met Kemper on the way but disregarded his questioning shout and raced on.

When he came in sight of the bridge, it was worse than he had expected. Jack hadn't even kept his men in line. Most of them were scattered out far in front of the bridge watching the action. Jack himself was close to the bridge, but he had only a few men with him and their eyes were on the action, too. The closest men merely stood and gaped at Tom as he thundered toward them until he was close enough to make himself heard, and even then they took their time about turning and going back.

A glance to his left revealed movement among the trees and brush lining the riverbank, and he made out a group of horsemen closer to the bridge than he was. There was only one thing to do, leave the road and charge them. It would warn Jack and might delay them long enough for him to get his men together and stand them off.

Tom headed off the road directly toward the Rebel troopers, drawing both revolvers and shouting at the top of his lungs. They reined up and stared at him as though they couldn't believe their eyes, then started milling about. The confusion didn't last long, though. An officer shouted, motioned, then headed to meet Tom with two of his men following while the others broke for the bridge. Jack was yelling to his men and getting them together, but the Rebel horsemen were bearing down on him at a gallop, waving their sabers and screeching like demons.

Tom and the three Rebels were on a collision course. He scorned the officer for bringing anyone with him. There should be only the two of them, galloping toward each other behind ornate shields with long lances thrust out.

The two troopers brought up their carbines and the officer brandished saber and revolver, but Tom was going to hold his fire until they were within fifty feet or so, then open up with both revolvers.

One of the troopers fired his carbine, but the shot went wild. He was a tall, rangy fellow who looked near middle age and who immediately drew his saber. The other was a younger man, good-looking and well built. He was more deliberate. It was marvelous the way he stood in his stirrups with flexing knees, remaining stationary while his horse rose and fell under him. He was an expert at shooting from horseback and took careful aim. When he fired, the bullet struck Tom's horse squarely in the chest. The stricken animal slowed and collapsed so quickly that Tom was barely able to kick free of the stirrups and avoid being pinned down. As it was, he found himself on his knees beside his dying horse with the enemy officer almost on him. He was a brawny black-haired man with a big square jaw that needed a shave. He whooped triumphantly and raised his saber to strike just before Tom's bullet struck him. His falling body bowled Tom over backwards, but it saved him from the rangy trooper's saber, which whizzed close by his head as he fell. Lying flat on his back, he shot the man out of his saddle as he reined about to come back.

The expert shot evidently preferred carbine to saber and had stopped to load not thirty feet away. He was amazingly fast and was capping his carbine when Tom rose to a sitting position and fired. The bullet tumbled the fellow from his saddle, but his horse bolted and a foot caught in a stirrup. He was dragged like a sack of grain until the leather broke and he flopped in the grass.

In the meantime a great uproar had broken out by the bridge as the rest of the Rebel cavalry charged Jack's men. Tom scrambled to his feet and ran toward a wild melee of plunging horses and fighting men as fast as he could go. Jack's men had no bayonets fixed and after they fired could only flail at the agile horsemen with empty rifles while trying to parry their sabers and dodge their carbines. The horses wouldn't actually run a man down. They always turned aside at the last second, which saved several from the sabers. Jack himself was in the middle of it, alternately appearing and disappearing as he wielded sword and revolver.

As Tom ran for the fight, heavy firing broke out back along the road, which probably meant the Rebel infantry was attacking von Jagerhof. Tom kept his eyes on the immediate danger and ran on, cursing his dragging feet, although he was running faster than he ever had in his life.

Suddenly Kemper was running beside him. He had his rifle ready, but neither of them could fire for fear of hitting Jack's men instead of the Rebels they were all mixed up with. Tom couldn't see Jack anymore, but his men were fighting desperately and so far had held their assailants back from the bridge.

They were still several hundred feet from the fighting when a roar of heavy trampling punctuated by shouts and whoops came from the bridge. Owen was finally rushing his men across, and Tom wondered if he had been caught napping like Jack had.

One of the enemy horsemen, a big red-haired fellow who had lost his hat, yelled something and broke away, the others rapidly following. They made off to the right, bending low in their saddles and going for all they were worth, heading for the shelter of the trees at the bend of the river where it came close to the road on the other side of the bridge. Kemper took a shot at them but didn't seem to hit anything. They were too far for a revolver, so Tom holstered his.

Almost simultaneously the heavy firing behind him began to taper off and Tom turned to see that although von Jagerhof had been compelled to give ground, his line was still intact and was beginning to move forward. The Rebels were giving it up there, too, so it looked like it was all over. Owen had deployed his battalion across the ramp of the bridge and stayed there.

Suddenly Kemper spoke. *"Bitte, Herr Major*, nodt to gedt angree *mit* de oldt *Freund,* budt nodt doo such a ting effer again." He showed his earnestness by trying to speak in English.

"What do you mean, Sergeant?" Tom was honestly puzzled.

The bright blue eyes under the grizzled brows looked earnestly at him. *"Der Herr Major* vas ferry, ferry follisch, for to vight *mit* tree enemie. He shouldt gedt killed."

Before Tom could think of a reply, a frantic voice from near the bridge called for Kemper to come and help a man who was bleeding to death, so he broke away and ran over.

Tom hadn't thought of it like that before. In fact, he hadn't thought about it at all. He had just done it. He guessed Kemper was right, though, and that he had been awfully lucky, but it was all over now and he had saved the bridge. That was what counted.

The firing back along the road had almost died away when Tom turned for another look. Von Jagerhof's line was well into the cornfield, and he had thrown out skirmishers who were just entering the growth on the other side. They seemed to be doing what little shooting there was. Not a Rebel was in sight.

Owen came up on his horse. "It looks like they've given it up, doesn't it, Major?"

"I believe so, sir, thanks to you. I believe they'd have had us over here if you hadn't come when you did. We couldn't have held off their infantry much longer." He sighed and shook his head. "I just wish you'd come a little sooner and helped us with that cavalry."

Owen didn't take it as a reproach. He laughed from high up in his saddle. "Oh, you fellows were doing a pretty good job of holding them off here, and I was afraid it was only a feint or something."

"Yes, sir." Tom noticed his hat lying out in the field. "Pardon me, sir; I've got to get my hat." He started toward it. "I don't want to have to buy another one."

Owen rode along with him. Tom wished he hadn't gone after the hat when he reached it, because it was close enough to two of the horsemen he had shot to see them, but he didn't look. He was glad Owen kept looking off toward the cornfield and the thickets beyond and didn't notice the recumbent gray forms. "I see your line's advancing out there." Tom looked just in time to see von Jagerhof's men disappear into the thickets on the other side of the cornfield. The shooting had stopped entirely.

"Whoever's in charge knows his business," Owen went on. "He's stood off what looked like a regiment with only four companies, then thrown out skirmishers as soon as the Rebels started falling back and followed them up." He paused momentarily. "Say, who is it?"

Tom halfway expected a reproof for not staying with his men. "Captain von Jagerhof, sir. I had to be free to move around, and I have complete confidence in him. He's a professional. The rest of us are just amateurs."

Owen nodded approvingly. "Yes, brought up to it since he was a boy, I hear." He nodded again. "Parker and Hutchins are senior to him, but I think you did right to put him in charge if you couldn't stay yourself." He looked at Tom quizzically. "You're likely to have trouble with them now that it's over, though."

"I'll take care of it myself if I do." Tom assured him.

Owen looked off toward the thickets again. "I just hope he won't go too far—Captain von Jagerhof, I mean."

"Oh, he'll stop when he gets to where I had my outpost."

Owen changed the subject. "Where's your horse, Major?"

Tom pointed to where he lay. "There he is. I guess I'll be walking for a while."

Suddenly Owen noticed the bodies lying near the horse. "It looks like you had a tussle out there. I see two no, three men lying out there. Are they Rebels?"

"Yes, sir. I went at them and they came at me. There wasn't anything to do but fight them."

"And you killed all three of them by yourself?" asked Owen incredulously.

Tom nodded affirmatively. It occurred to him that Owen couldn't know much about what had happened, so he told him all about it and didn't spare himself for getting fooled so badly. He didn't say anything about Jack's carelesness, though. Jack was his friend and he would take care of it himself.

Owen shook his head. "Well, it seems to me that whoever commanded those Rebels would have fooled anybody, myself included." He reined his horse around. "Well, I'd better be getting my men back across," he said. "You never know; they might try something over there."

As they started toward the bridge, Tom was glad Owen was satisfied with his explanation and hadn't reproved him like Kemper had for taking on those Rebel troopers or, what would have been worse, want to know why he thought he had to do it. That would have exposed Jack's failure and might have gotten him into trouble.

Tom was going to take care of that himself. Friend or no friend, Jack was going to get a good bawling out as soon as Owen left. If he had kept his company drawn up across the ramp and on the alert, those Rebel troopers would never have dared show themselves and there would have been no need for him to fight three of them.

There were so many men moving around until Owen started his men back across the bridge that Tom couldn't see Jack anywhere. He noticed that the column carefully skirted something near the ramp, and when it was out of the way he saw it was a body lying in a great pool of blood, the head at an odd angle to the torso. It was Jack. His head had almost been severed from his shoulders by a saber stroke.

Tom's anger evaporated. Poor Jack happy-go-lucky, easygoing Jack. Being a good fellow had cost him his life. He couldn't bear looking at him anymore and had to turn away. Jack's men were grief-stricken, and several wept openly.

They were now under a lieutenant named Johnson, a tall, earnest-looking fellow who had made up for his ex-captain's shortcomings in more ways than one. He said they had lost three men besides the captain. One of them had bled to death from a saber cut on the shoulder, a wound that neither Kemper nor the surgeon could stanch. They had saved another man with an arm half cut off, or rather Kemper had. He seemed to know more about such things than the surgeon did.

Two other men had been killed by carbine bullets at point-blank range. Lesser wounds were common. One man had lost an ear, cut off as clean as a whistle, and was otherwise unscathed. A fellow named Doaks who had lost two fingers and part of another protested loudly when told he would have to go with the other wounded. He claimed he could still shoot because it was his left hand and that he was bandaged up as well as they could do in any hospital. Tom admired his spirit, all the more because he undoubtedly knew he would be sent home from the hospital.

The Rebels had left three dead and one wounded near the bridge. The wounded man had a leg so badly mangled that it would have to come off. He had been shot at such close range that he was badly powder-burned, too. He was a slender dark-haired youth who sat clutching his shattered limb and absolutely would not speak, even in answer to questions.

Owen sent over two wagons to take the wounded away. Tom sent one of them on to his battalion because he knew it would be needed and one would carry all the wounded there were at the bridge.

There were picks and shovels in one of the wagons, so Tom told Johnson to have his men bury the dead and mark their graves if they could. Johnson said he would have headboards made out of some extra floorboards lying by the bridge and have the names burned on with ramrods heated in a fire. It was a good idea, because Tom knew Jack's people would send for his body and some of the others might do the same. Johnson went on to say that he had a man who had been a preacher at home and would have him conduct a funeral service, for the Rebels as well as his own friends.

Someone called from out in the field that there were three Rebels out there, two who were dead and one shot in the belly who soon would be. Tom had forgotten about them. He asked Johnson to take care of them, too, then told him to keep a close guard and started out the road to his battalion, although not a shot had been fired in half an hour and there was really no need to. He just didn't want to be around when those three troopers were brought in, particularly the one who was dying.

Tom hadn't gone very far when he suddenly began to tremble all over. He couldn't understand it and was glad nobody was around to see it. He kept on walking and the trembling stopped as suddenly as it had begun, but then he felt as weak as a kitten. He hoped he wasn't getting sick or something. To give himself something to do, he stopped and charged the empty cylinders of the revolver he had fired. He could have just snapped in one of the two loaded cylinders he always carried, but he was glad he hadn't because the weakness went away while he was doing it.

Tom was about halfway to his destination when someone on horseback came up from behind. It was Hauser. He had caught a fine-looking horse left by the Rebels and put Tom's saddle on it so the *Herr Major* wouldn't have to go around on foot like lesser officers. Tom was happy to be remounted so soon and thanked him for it. The horse was a dun gelding, as large as the bay had been, and he might even be as tractable as soon as he settled down.

He found von Jagerhof deployed across the road at the cedar brake with skirmishers so well beyond that only a few of them were visible in the growth, just like he would have himself. The dead and wounded were being put on the wagon he had sent out. Putting them together wasn't the best thing, but there was only one wagon. When he saw Billy, he realized that for all he knew, his brother could have been among them and made up his mind not to be so forgetful the next time.

There was one dead man from Billy's company, Schlusser, who had been shot in the head early in the fighting, and two from the others. The Rebels had evidently taken their dead and wounded back with them, since none were to be found.

Sam Price would soon join his dead comrades. He lay dying of a chest wound. Tom had known him well back home and knelt to try to talk to him. It was no use. Blood gurgled in his throat and ran from his mouth as he gasped convulsively. His eyes rolled blankly, and his face was already taking on the waxy pallor of death. Tom thought of the little cabin up near the Orange county line where buxom Bertha Price would now be a widow and two little children fatherless. Suddenly he choked up and had to turn away.

There were five wounded, but only two seriously, both from Billy's company. Bachman had a shattered arm and Cal Fairbanks another shoulder wound, this one from a bullet. Bachman would lose his arm and Tom didn't think Cal would be coming back to the company this time, although he was already talking about it. He claimed it was only a flesh wound, but his arm dangled uselessly and it looked like his shoulder joint was damaged. Billy had bandaged the wounded up the best he could and had contrived slings for Cal and Bachman.

By the time the others were on the wagon, Sam Price was dead, so his body was put on also. Tom sent Billy and his platoon back with the wagon so they could catch up on their sleep and told him to see to it that the dead were buried properly and the wounded sent on to the hospital by the surgeon.

Von Jagerhof wanted to send out scouts to see if the Rebels had really left and Tom thought it was a good idea, although Owen had said nothing about it. The Prussian sent Schlimmer and six men from Sam Price's old platoon. The top of Schlimmer's cap was half shot off, and Tom joked with him about how close Rebecca had come to being a widow. He grinned and said it hadn't gone that far yet but was about as close as that bullet had been to his head.

After Schlimmer and his men left, Tom rode along the line where the men were resting on their arms, ostensibly to look things over, but really to see if Hutchinson and Parker would say anything about von Jagerhof being put over them. Neither of them said a word about it or showed the slightest resentment. Tom wasn't going to make trouble for himself, so he said nothing about it either. Come to think of it, having to hold off a regiment with only four companies was something they might have been glad to get out of.

The skirmishers reported no sign of the Rebels, so Tom decided to let the men fall out and take their ease. If Schlimmer reported the same when he came back, Tom would leave one company on outpost and take the others back to the bridge.

No one had had any breakfast, so coffee making began immediately for those who had coffee with them. Those that didn't could be counted on to scrounge from those that did. When Tom was offered a cup, he accepted it, although he suspected the coffee was pretty well mixed with powder from loose cartridges, tobacco crumbs, or whatever else the men had in their pockets. It tasted all right, though, so he drank it.

Soon afterward Hauser showed up with pack and pot and announced he would provide breakfast, not just for his two charges, but for all the other *Offizieren*. Tom told him they would just settle for coffee because that was all the men had, and he soon had a pot ready.

When Hutchinson, Parker, and the other officers gathered with Tom and von Jagerhof to enjoy Hauser's largess, they all congratulated the Prussian on his handling of the action, which showed Tom that his surmise had been correct. Hutchinson was particularly complimentary to "von", as he called him, and he was the only one Tom had thought might be resentful. Parker was a quiet fellow who seldom had much to say, but Hutchinson was a short, thickset, florid man who was inclined to be rambunctious at times.

When the others left, Tom added his congratulations. Von Jagerhof thanked him for the compliment and more for the opportunity. He had never expected to command anything larger than a platoon, and now he was a company commander who had conducted a battalion action. It would look good on his record when he got back to Prussia.

Schlimmer came back in about two hours and reported the Rebels were all gone. The only sign of them he had seen was where they had turned off south on a little-used road about three miles to the west. There had been wagon tracks, but none of artillery. He had taken his men about half a mile along that road and then come back. Few men would have been as thorough, and Tom wasn't surprised when von Jagerhof gave him poor Sam's old platoon.

Tom then took the other three companies back to the bridge and left Hutchinson's on outpost with instructions to duplicate von Jagerhof's dispositions of the night before. Nothing happened during the night, but Tom rode out to see Hutchinson twice anyhow.

It was quiet all morning the next day, and early in the afternoon Billy came to see his brother. He wanted to walk out on the bridge and talk. They went about halfway across, then stood looking at the cold, dark water flowing around the pontoons and swaying the bridge under their feet.

"Tom," Billy began, "yo're my brother an' I want t' talk t' ye like one even if yo're my major, too."

Tom knew what was coming. "Go ahead, Billy."

"What's this I hear 'bout you takin' on three Rebel cav'lry single-handed?"

Kemper was behind it. Nobody else could have seen enough to know what happened. "I guess I did, Billy, but—"

His brother cut him off. "Now lissen, that wuz a dum fool thing t' do. You wuz lucky you wuzn't kilt. You know that as well as I do."

Billy was right, but Tom wanted to explain. Before he could begin, Billy went on. "An' ridin' 'long th' line on yore hoss with ever' Rebel in sight shootin' at ye, an' keepin' hit up! I seen that with my own eyes. You made a reg'lar target outa yoreself!"

Tom looked down into the dark, swirling water. "Billy, you don't understand how it was, being in command out there and responsible for everything."

Billy's voice rose a little. "Yo're gonna hafta quit that kind uv thing, Tom, or yo're gonna git kilt fer shore!"

"Billy, they'd have gotten to this bridge if I hadn't gone at that cavalry."

"What 'bout ridin' 'long that line an' lettin' th' Rebels shoot at ye?"

"Well, I had to try to see what we were up against," replied Tom lamely. "Maybe I sort of forgot myself, though."

"Y' sorta fergot yoreself when y' went at that cav'lry, too, only y' won't own up t' hit." He fixed Tom with an imploring look. "Now, Tom—"

Tom interrupted, "I can't say I agree with you about that, Billy," he said shortly. He had to look away, though, upstream where the water gleamed in the winter sunlight. Billy was making him think, and he didn't want to.

Billy sighed with exasperation. "Y' won't lissen t' me. I'm still jist yore little brother, an' y' think I don't know nothin'."

Tom was touched. "Billy, I'll always listen to you." He looked into his brother's eyes and saw the tears were about to start. He was thoroughly ashamed of himself. "Go ahead," he said softly.

Billy started blinking and had to look down at the rough boards under their feet. Suddenly he looked up. "Somethin's happened t' ye, Tom. Y' ack like y' jist don't keer 'bout yoreself enymore, like y' wanta git kilt. Is hit on 'count uv Sally?"

It was Tom's turn to look down. Billy was right, absolutely right. He had built his whole life around Sally, and now that she was gone, there was nothing left.

Billy went on. "I'm askin' that 'cause I know how I'd feel if somethin' like that happened t' Gerda, but I don't think I'd do like you been doin'."

Tom thought of something that might put Billy off the track. "Billy, there's honor, and duty. They're more important than life."

It didn't work, entirely, at least. "I guess hit's 'cause honor an' duty's all y' got left now that Sally's gone." Billy looked at him searchingly. "Ain't that right, Tom?"

Tom could only look down and say, "I really don't know. I don't understand it very well myself." There was some truth in that.

"I want y' t' promise me somethin', Tom," Billy implored.

Tom looked at him sadly. "What, Billy?"

"That y' won't never do nothin' like that agin. Hit'd ease my mind a hull lot if y' would."

Tom looked in Billy's eyes again. "I won't, Billy. I promise." He said it only because he didn't want to cause his brother worry.

Billy smiled. "Well, I guess we've been talkin' long 'nough, Major, sir."

"If you think so, Billy," replied Tom as they started back along the bridge.

The regiment stayed at the bridge for over a week, but no more Rebels were ever seen, not even a cavalry scout. It turned warmer and rained several times, but never enough to affect the roads for very long. It was always enough to wet the men, though, so Tom had some rude shelters of bark, brush, and extra boards from the bridge put up so they wouldn't have to stay in their tents when it rained. They kept fires burning in the shelters, and companies coming in from outposts always had a place to dry out if they got wet. Owen kept the rations coming, so they never ran short.

Everyone was surprised when the division came back to the regiment instead of the other way around, but they were glad, because it meant they would go back to their winter quarters and wouldn't have to build new ones someplace else.

On the march back the men learned where the rest of the brigade had been and most emphatically what it had seen. Although it had been held in reserve and hadn't taken part, it had seen a big battle across the river at Fredericksburg, only you really couldn't call it a battle. It had been butchery, just plain butchery, with the Rebels doing the butchering. Most of the army, including the rest of the division, had been taken across the river, through the town, and thrown against the strongly entrenched Rebels on the heights beyond, not just once, but several times. There had been no attempt to turn the enemy's flank or do any maneuvering at all. It looked like all Burnside wanted to do was kill off his men, and he had really done a good job of it. The Pennsylvania captain who told Tom all this shook his head and thanked the good Lord the brigade hadn't been thrown into the slaughter like the rest of the division had.

The men were gloomy and unusually quiet on the march and even in camp at night. Tom heard enough to know why. No one could understand why such a stupid fellow as Burnside had been put in command, and almost everybody believed that if McClellan had been kept on no such thing would have happened. What was worse, most of the men were convinced that it was all because Burnside was a Republican and McClellan a Democrat.

Tom agreed. Although he didn't think McClellan was the military genius most of the men did, he certainly would never have done anything like Burnside had at Fredericksburg. Rivers had hit the nail on the head when he said they would have to win the war in spite of the politicians at the top.

Often while riding along the column during the day or lying awake at night Tom pondered about what made the men go on in spite of the cynical political manipulation that had led them to bloody defeat both times McClellan had been replaced by someone else, Pope at the Second Bull Run and now Burnside at Fredericksburg. Although he couldn't be sure about men from other parts of the country, Tom finally decided on what it was and what it wasn't that made the men of his regiment go on in spite of it all. It wasn't belief in a cause, no longer, anyhow. Most of the men had gone to fight to save the Union like he had, but only on promises that things wouldn't be done that had been done. Although they wouldn't put it in those terms, he knew a great many of them thought those betrayals had freed them of any moral obligation to serve.

What about saving the Union? Once you got to thinking about it, you had to admit that it was doubtful if it could ever be done and getting more so all the time. The people wouldn't put up with this futile slaughter and sacrifice indefinitely. The time might come when Lincoln or whoever was in his place would have to make peace with the Rebels and let them go. Then all the dead, all the crippled and maimed, and all the suffering and sacrifice would be for nothing. No one wanted to be killed or crippled, but he liked to think that if he was, it would be for something.

Tom didn't count. Fellows with commissions and the fancy uniforms, pay, and privileges that went with them could stand it, but what about the men, who got nothing but bullets, bad weather, and eleven dollars a month? What made them go on, faithful to faithless leaders and a failing cause? He finally decided the answer was in the men themselves. It was their pride, the pride of strong men in their manhood and in the people they sprang from. Men who had pride in themselves and their people didn't quit. They would let stupid political generals throw their lives away before they would.

Congressman Baker had named the regiment better than he knew, and their pride would be the death of most of its members. But worse things would come of it. The girls they had left behind would go barren to their graves or turn to lesser men. They would never become fathers, much less ancestors. Their memory might last only a generation or two, but the people of the Pocket would show their loss forever. Future generations would never see their like again.

After the regiment settled in its winter quarters again, Tom learned that he was something of a celebrity. His passage about camp was heralded like that of a champion of the lists for a while. It was all because of tales about his fight with the Rebel cavalrymen near the bridge. Kemper was the only one who had really seen it all, and his reticence permitted imagination to run riot. The tamest tale had Major Traylor taking on three big Rebel troopers in hand-to-hand combat with sword and saber and killing them all.

It caused Tom a lot of embarrassment, because he knew he didn't deserve it. There was nothing he could do about it, though. There was no way of making men understand the difference between real courage and the things a man would do who had nothing to live for anymore.

# 41

Everybody had known for a long time that there was going to be a division ball at the big hotel in town New Year's Eve, but Tom had never considered going. He didn't know how to dance, and dancing was what went on at balls. The only dancing he had ever seen was when he dropped in on a ball when he was in school at Bloomington. He had done it only out of curiosity and hadn't stayed long. The dancing looked easy, but he knew there was a lot of difference between just watching and actually doing it.

Then, a few days before New Year's, the dance was announced at officers' call and it was added that General Carter expected every officer who wasn't on duty to be there. Tom wasn't going to be on duty and would have to go after all. His only attempt to get out of it didn't work. Billy was going to be officer of the day New Year's Eve, and Tom offered to substitute for him so he could go. Billy wouldn't hear of it, though, probably because he couldn't dance either.

Tom was going to make it quick and easy. He would only show his face, stand around a while, and then sneak out. Von Jagerhof was going with him, but he didn't think that would be a problem. He was such a polished aristocrat that the ladies would take quick possession of him and he would never notice when Tom left.

The day before the ball, Herb Parker came around to see him and told him to be sure to look him up at the ball. He didn't say why, but then he was such a laconic fellow that Tom thought nothing of it. It was probably to see his wife, Eliza, since most of the married men's wives seemed to be coming. Tom didn't think it would hold him up very long, though.

Hauser attached great importance to the occasion and spent many hours pressing, brushing, and polishing, so that his two charges looked like military fashion plates when they went. It was only the second time Tom had worn his dress uniform, and von Jagerhof was much taken with it. He immediately wanted to know where he could get one like it, and Tom told him.

There were a lot of officers in the division, and just about all of them seemed to have ladies. Von Jagerhof was a foreigner and wouldn't be expected to have one, but Tom had no such excuse and it stiffened his resolve to duck out as soon as he could. This wasn't to mention the daringly low-cut gowns many of the ladies wore, which embarrassed him even to look at. He would be petrified if he had to talk to one of them.

General Carter and his wife stood near the entrance greeting people as they came in. She was so much larger than he was that she almost looked like his mother. There were many people and they came so fast that the general had to hurry, so Tom was able to get by with only a brief handshake and a bow. Von Jagerhof was immediately seized upon by a German colonel and two ladies, and Tom was able to melt away into the crowd without their noticing. He headed for an unobtrusive exit he had spotted, but he didn't get very far.

Colonel Pater of the brigade's Pennsylvania regiment seized Tom as he tried to sneak by and insisted on introducing him to a circle of other colonels and their wives as the man who had taken on three Rebel troopers single-handed and laid them low. Tom would have rather have faced the whole Rebel cavalry under Jeb Stuart himself than these mature ladies in their low-cut gowns, but he was trapped. After the introductions, he stood with his sweaty hands clasped behind his back in an agony of embarrassment, trying vainly to keep his feet from shifting about. When the music started for the first dance, he expected them to leave him and take to the floor, but none of them did. He was rendered desperate by the fact that several of the ladies acted like they would be delighted to be asked to dance, husbands or not. He had to get away before the next dance, or one of them might take matters into her own hands.

A familiar voice in his ear offered salvation. "Major Traylor! I've been looking all over for you!" It was Parker, so Tom was able to excuse himself on grounds of a previous engagement he had completely forgotten, which was the absolute truth.

Eliza Parker was standing with a woman who looked much like her, only taller and a little younger. She was tall, slender, and shapely, with red hair and a very fair complexion. Her features were strong and regular, but not so much so that she wasn't pretty, and she had wide green eyes that acted like a magnet on Tom's. She was Miss Mary Worthington, Eliza's younger sister, and received his bow when Parker introduced them with a smile that thrilled Tom to the depths of his being.

"I've seen you before, Major," she said in a stirringly feminine voice, "but I've never met you."

"Well, I've never seen you, Miss Worthington, or I'd remember," he replied gallantly. These were home folks and he was at ease with them.

She laughed appreciatively. "I've been staying with Eliza at Shoals since Herbert's been gone, but before that I always lived just across the county line from the Davis Creek settlement with my mother and father."

"Oh, that's only a few miles from where I've always lived." Tom shook his head smilingly. "It's sure strange that I don't remember seeing you, because I surely have." It really wasn't strange at all, though. He had never had eyes for anyone but Sally.

Mary laughed again, her full bosom quaking under her gown, which wasn't nearly as low-cut as most of the others. "I remember seeing you once at church when I was visiting over close to where you live and once in the store at Shoals."

Tom was still pretending to marvel at not remembering seeing her when the next dance started and, to his dismay, she took his arm and started for the floor. He was terrified, but there was no way out of it. He would just have to do the best he could. It was worse than going into battle.

Before he knew it, he was dancing. He couldn't have been much more surprised if he had suddenly taken wing and gone flying around the hall like a bird. He guessed it was like swimming: you didn't know how and then all at once you were doing it with no awareness of having learned to.

He was so unstrung for a little while that he was only vaguely aware that his partner was talking to him. He tried to understand, but it was like listening to running water. Suddenly she exclaimed, "My, Major, you sure aren't much of a talker!"

She looked hurt and he felt utterly miserable. "I'm sorry, Miss . . . Miss Mary, but this . . . this dancing is a little strange to me."

A teasing light came into the green depths of her eyes. "Oh, I've always heard Dubois County men were all good dancers."

Tom managed a smile. "Oh, I guess it's because of the Germans. They're always having dances, but the rest of us never had any." He was glad he hadn't stammered again and began to feel a little less oafish.

She smiled back, and he was struck with her beauty. The combination of green eyes, milk white skin, and coppery hair was entrancing. The long, shapely arm seemed to tighten a little on his shoulder as she moved her head to one side and looked at him archly. "You know,

Herbert's told us a lot about you since we've been here, and he used to write about you, too."

Tom's equanimity returned with a rush, and he said smilingly, "I'll bet he told you I'm a terrible fellow, rough and rowdy and all that."

She laughed, throwing back her head to show the lovely white column of her throat. "Oh, no, nothing like that." The laughing green eyes were on him. "He told us some of the things you've done, like that mutiny, I believe he called it, that you put down, and then those three Rebels—"

He cut her off. "Military men are always telling tall tales!" he scoffed. "Believe half of what they tell you!"

She looked surprised. "Oh, Major, those weren't tall tales! I've heard it from others, too, since we've been here."

"Now, like I said, only believe half of it. It was just a ruckus, not a mutiny, and those three Rebels—"

A peal of silvery laughter broke in on him. "Were only one and a half!"

They were still laughing when the dance ended and they were making their way off the floor. There was an intrusion soon after they rejoined the Parkers. Blakey, Parker's lieutenant and an ex-sergeant like Tom, joined them. He was a tall, gangling fellow so ill at ease that his natural awkwardness was a great deal worse. He was all hands and feet and couldn't figure out what to do with them for the life of him. They were so much in motion that it almost looked like he was trying to dance. Tom could scarcely keep from laughing at him until he remembered he probably hadn't looked much better a little while ago.

He and the others did their best to put Blakey at ease, and he did come out of it enough to ask Mary for the next dance without stammering. When it began, she threw a "wait here" look at Tom as they started for the floor. Parker decided he wanted to dance, too, and swept Eliza to the floor, although she looked like she didn't want to go, and threw Tom the same kind of look Mary had.

This was his first chance to leave the place, but he no longer wanted to. He had discovered he could dance after all, but the main reason was Mary. He could see her tall, graceful form swirling about the clumsy Blakey, her eyes always coming back to him. The coppery hair tastefully piled on her head glinted in the lamplight, and she looked even more beautiful from a distance.

Someone came up beside him. It was Colonel Rivers. "Happy to see you here, Major!" he boomed.

"Yes, sir, I'm right happy to be here. This has turned out to be quite an affair."

"Would you like to meet my womenfolk, my daughter and my sister?" He sounded strangely like he was asking a favor.

"Oh yes, sir, I'll be very pleased to meet them." Tom lied because he wanted to wait for Mary. He remembered Rivers's daughter Carolyn from the flag presentation in Indianapolis when the regiment had left for the field. He was a little surprised to hear she had come, because Marcus Allen had died only about six weeks ago. Rivers was a widower and his maiden sister kept house for him.

Carolyn and her aunt sat on a bench next to the far wall. Carolyn looked pale and listless, and her pallor was accentuated by the conservative black gown she wore. She obviously wasn't dancing. Her aunt was a jolly, matronly lady who looked like anything but an old maid.

When Rivers introduced them, Tom bowed and expressed his pleasure, a little more sincerely in Carolyn's case because of the impression she had made on him the only other time he had seen her. He couldn't help comparing her with Mary. Carolyn wasn't nearly as tall and was really more delicately featured and pretty, but her blue eyes, pale skin, and black hair didn't have the magnetism of Mary's emerald green, milky white, and coppery red.

They made small talk and Tom was thinking of excusing himself to go back to Mary when it dawned on him why Rivers had searched him out. In all likelihood, it was because he thought Tom would take the chance no one else had and ask Carolyn to dance, probably in hope it would break her obvious depression. Well, he was the fellow for taking chances, he guessed, and Rivers knew it, so he stayed. When the music started and Carolyn looked a little wistfully at the couples thronging toward the floor, he took the plunge.

"Will you dance, Miss Rivers?"

"I haven't so far," she sighed. "It just doesn't seem right—"

Her aunt interrupted. "Go ahead, Carrie! Watch out or you'll be an old maid like me!" She laughed merrily.

"Go on, Carolyn," urged her father. "It'll be good for you. You've just *got* to start living again!" His words confirmed Tom's suspicion about what he was supposed to do.

Carolyn arose with a sad little smile and took Tom's arm. "I just don't feel right about it," she confessed. "I didn't want to come, but Father insisted, and Auntie did, too."

Tom undertook to reassure her. "I understand how you feel, Miss Carolyn, and I hope you'll forgive my boldness, but I'm like your father. I think a little dancing will be good for you."

She only sighed by way of reply. She was much smaller than Mary, and dancing with her was a lot different. The music seemed to have a different rhythm, too. The dancing wasn't going very well and Tom was trying to think of some excuse for his awkwardness without confessing the truth when Carolyn looked up at him and said ruefully, "I'm sorry I'm so clumsy, but I haven't danced in ages."

"Oh, it's my awkwardness, Miss Carolyn. Don't apologize. You're an excellent dancer."

"You're very kind, Major." She smiled fleetingly, and it was probably the first one in a long time. The dancing began to go better, and Tom guessed he had adjusted to whatever difference in rhythm there was.

"Did you know Marcus very well?" she asked sadly, her blue eyes wells of sorrow.

"Not very well. You see, I've been an officer for only about six months now."

Her eyes flickered to his shoulder straps, but she wasn't tall enough to see them. "Oh, I thought you were a major!" The delicately molded little face expressed surprise.

"Oh, I am. I've been lucky, I guess, and then some other men were unlucky."

She nodded and studied him searchingly, her lovely lips forming an unspoken question. After a while she said, "I believe I've heard Father talk about you, now that I think of it, and others have—"

Tom headed her off. "Oh, a person hears all kinds of talk. I'm not nearly as bad as they say," he added waggishly.

Her smile wasn't fleeting this time. "Oh, it wasn't bad. They said you were a remarkable fellow, but I thought of a different sort of a man."

"You thought I'd be some big, rough fellow who'd look like a pirate," he laughed, "and I've disappointed you."

Carolyn threw back her head and laughed, probably for the first time in weeks, and suddenly her pallor was gone. The laughter subsided into a captivating smile, and he heard again the voice he had thought would stir a dead man back at Indianapolis so long ago. "Oh no, I really didn't think you'd look like that, but I didn't think you'd be so . . . so well turned out."

He exploited her little stammer. "Are you sure you didn't start to say 'so young and handsome'?" he asked brightly. This brought another peal of silvery laughter, and he thought she squeezed him just a little.

Before she could recover from her mirth the dance ended, and all she could do was smile and shake her petite head at him as they made their way through the crowd leaving the floor.

Rivers beamed at Tom and so forgot himself as to embrace his daughter. He must have been really worried about her, and Tom was glad he had helped break the spell of her despondency. He only hoped it wouldn't be just temporary.

He was beginning to think he was quite a gallant when a fellow appeared who really was one. Several young officers had come up now that Tom had broken the ice, and Rivers introduced them to his wife and sister. Among them was Lieutenant Hayes of the Pike County company, a darkly handsome, dashing fellow who had taken poor Jack Arnold's place as the champion ladies' man in the regiment. After a sidelong look at Tom, he asked Carolyn for the next dance and she accepted.

Suddenly Tom saw Herb Parker frantically looking around in the crowd. He knew who he was looking for, and Hayes was monopolizing Carolyn's attention, so he made his excuses and broke away. Rivers seemed taken aback and Carolyn looked like she wanted to say something, but Hayes intruded and she didn't, so he went on.

Parker couldn't hide his relief when he saw Tom. "Here you are!" he exclaimed with an uncharacteristic grin. "A fair lady's got to be rescued from a dragon, she says, so come along." That didn't sound like him either. Somebody had been spurring him pretty hard, and Tom thought he knew who it had been.

He knew who the dragon was, too. It was Blakey. He was still hanging around, and Mary looked like she couldn't stand it much longer. Her eyes lighted up when she saw Tom. "Oh, Major Traylor! I thought you'd strayed away!"

"A stray hasn't got much of a chance around here," he laughed. He was glad Hayes had taken over, and when she came up and stood beside him he made bold to take her hand. She rewarded him with a melting smile and a gentle squeeze. She was much taller than Carolyn, not that Carolyn was undersized, but Mary was unusually tall for a woman. Her upswept hairdo made her nearly equal to his six feet. He was admiring how the symmetrical column of her neck blended into her inviting snowy shoulders when Blakey stammered out a request for the next dance, only to be met with the cold reply that it was promised to Major Traylor.

When the music started, he swept her grandly out on the floor. "Oh, how I'd like to get rid of that fellow!" she exclaimed as soon as they were out of hearing.

"You've got your work cut out for you," he warned laughingly. "He'll stick like a leech."

Mary sighed with exasperation. "He can't dance, either. He stepped all over my feet."

"We can go to another part of the hall after this dance, and maybe he'll leave. Herb and Eliza will understand."

"How about leaving the hall for a while?" She smiled enigmatically.

"We can go to the dining room for some refreshments."

"Champagne?" she asked smilingly. "I've always heard of it but I've never had any."

He laughed. "I doubt if you'll like it, but you'll be able to go back home and brag about drinking some."

She laughed throatily, and the long white arm gave him a squeeze. "Splendid! We'll do it!"

Blakey was still there when they went back to the Parkers. "The next dance, Miss Mary?" he asked eagerly.

"The major and I are going for some refreshments," Mary said as she exchanged significant looks with her sister.

Blakey was struck with the fidgets worse than ever. Parker started to say something, but Eliza's elbow in his ribs cut it off.

Tom and Mary went along the corridor that connected the ballroom to the parlor and the dining room. "This hotel's a nice place," she said. "I didn't expect they'd have anything like it down here."

He agreed. "Yes, the Rebels used to live pretty well down here before the war, but we've just about taken everything over now."

They came to a short corridor leading to a stairway going upward. "That's the way up to the rooms, I guess," he said casually.

Mary stopped and looked at him, a half-smile on her face and a glow in her eyes. "My room's just up there, Tom," she said softly.

The invitation was unmistakable. He was thunderstruck and stood gaping at her, unable to say anything. Her face fell and she bit her lip, then lowered her eyes and blushed deeply. She started to turn back, but he took her arm.

Finally he was able to speak. "Let's . . . let's go on," he said haltingly.

There was a strained silence between them the rest of the way. His mind was in such turmoil that he couldn't think of anything to say, and Mary was too crestfallen. She walked silently beside him, sucking her lip, and eyes on the floor.

It looked like the tables in the dining room were all full, but not with diners. Most of their occupants were young infantry officers with equally young women, and all the merrymakers seemed to have stayed behind in the ballroom. Everybody seemed sunk in the deepest gloom, and some of the women showed signs of weeping. Tom saw a few familiar faces, but they indicated only fleeting recognition.

They all seemed to be in the grip of some great sorrow. Suddenly he knew what it was. It was the last tryst for many of them, and they knew it. Most of these men had fought in three major battles since late in August. Casualties had averaged 50 percent in the division and had been higher for company officers. With the war going the way it was, the new year offered little but death and the weeds of bereavement.

Suddenly he wanted to take the beautiful woman beside him in his arms and learn of love while life still lasted. He looked at her in a new light, but she wouldn't meet his eyes and he cursed himself for a bumbling fool.

There seemed to be no empty tables and he was ready to turn away when a wizened little waiter with a pronounced limp bustled up. the peg of a wooden leg showed in place of one shoe. "Table for two, Major?"

"Yes, but you don't seem to have any."

"This way, sir." He led them around a corner to an alcove off the main room where there was an empty table. As they seated themselves, Tom noticed that the inmates of the alcove seemed even sadder than the others.

"What'll hit be, Major?" asked the little waiter briskly.

Tom looked at Mary questioningly, but she still refused to meet his eyes. He saw she had bitten her lip so badly it was bleeding. "Champagne," he said to the waiter, who bowed jerkily and stumped away. "That was what you wanted, wasn't it?" he asked.

Mary nodded wordlessly and gave him a fleeting glance that revealed a marked mistiness in her eyes. He desperately wanted to say something, but it was like a wall was between them. His frustration was agonizing.

They were silent until the iced bucket came. The little waiter popped the cork and poured in their glasses. "Will that be all, Major?"

Tom looked at the man's face and saw that what he had taken for the marks of age were those of suffering. Something moved him to ask, "Were you a soldier?"

The fellow nodded and a proud light came into his eyes. "Yes, sir. I wuz a sargint in th' Fifty-third Virginia."

Tom felt a great compassion for the man, shot to pieces on the battlefield and compelled to scrape out a living stumping around on his wooden leg serving his late enemies. "Wait," he said, taking out his wallet. He handed the fellow a five-dollar greenback. "This isn't charity. It's a token of respect for a brave man crippled fighting for what he believed in."

The little man took it reluctantly. "Thank you very much, sir." He sighed, the lines and creases in his face showing more plainly. "I lost this here laig, an' I'm all tore up inside, too. I cain't farm no more, an' hit's awful hard t' s'port a wife an' five chillern on what I make here." He put the greenback in his pocket. "Thank you agin, sir. Yo're a kind man, an' may God bless you an' yore lady." He bowed and stumped away.

Mary had taken it all in and looked like she wanted to say something, but when Tom turned to her she averted her eyes and took up her glass. They drank; then he broke the silence. "Well, how do you like champagne?"

She smiled wanly. "Well, it's like nothing I've ever drunk before."

He forced himself to be jocular. "Now you can go back to Martin County and say you've drunk champagne. That'll astonish the natives."

Mary's attempt at a smile was a complete failure. Tom struggled to think of something else to say, but he couldn't for the life of him. The atmosphere was becoming unbearably strained when Mary suddenly broke the silence. "I suppose you think I'm a . . . a bad woman," she said quaveringly.

Tom felt like something inside him was going to burst. "No, no, Mary, I don't think that, and I want to—"

She didn't let him finish. "Well, I'm not," she quavered. "It's just that—" She couldn't hold back her tears any longer and had to reach for her handkerchief.

Tom was devastated. "Please, Mary, don't cry; don't cry." He half-rose from his seat, horrified that people would be looking at them, but no one was. Tears were too common in the alcove.

Mary put aside her handkerchief and looked at him with tearful eyes and trembling lips. "You men, you just don't know how it is with us women—" She had to stop to fight back the tears.

"Mary, Mary," he pleaded, "I didn't . . . I didn't mean to—"

She interrupted a little stridently. "I want to explain!"

"Oh no, you needn't explain anything!" he interjected. "I'm the one who ought to—"

She ignored him and went on. "No, no, I must explain. Maybe you'll think better of me if I do." When he subsided, she went on. "It looks like there aren't going to be any men left with this war just going on and on. By the time it's over, most women my age won't be able to . . . to find a man, and we . . . we have feelings just like you men do."

"I know; I know," he began, but she cut him off again.

"It's terrible, just terrible," she sobbed, "to think that you'll shrink up and dry up into . . . into an old woman and never . . . never have a man."

He tried to speak, but she went on through her tears. "And you, from what Herb says and the others, too, you're going to get yourself killed for sure!"

He broke in on her. "Oh, don't pay any attention to those tales!" He knew he didn't sound very convincing.

Mary went on. "Oh, what they say! You take such terrible chances—like you're trying to throw your life away! You rode around the battlefield and let the Rebels shoot at you! You fought three of them all by yourself—" She broke off and looked at him with tear-filled eyes. "You're certain to get killed if you go on like that!"

How could he explain? "But, Mary, you don't understand—" he began, but she wouldn't let him go on.

"You'll get killed!" she said despairingly. "All the good men will get killed! What are left won't be worth having! Look at you! Such a splendid man, and you'll be dead, and no woman will ever have anything of you!" She bowed her head. "It'll be just like it was with Harold, and I . . . I can't stand to think of it." She broke down and cried as though her heart would break.

"Harold?" he asked when she began to recover. "Who was he?"

"Harold Howland," she said without raising her head. "He was Herb's lieutenant."

Tom remembered him, a big, bluff, hearty fellow who had been killed at Antietam. "You were . . . were engaged?"

She nodded dumbly and raised her tearstained face to his. In the cloudy depths of her eyes was an unspeakable sadness. "He wanted to . . . to have me, to make love, before he left, but I wouldn't, and after . . . after we heard he was dead, I swore, I swore that if ever . . . if ever I—" She bowed her head and broke down again.

He reached across the table and took her hand. "Please, Mary, don't cry anymore, and let me explain."

She recovered with an effort and headed him off. "Now . . . now do you understand?"

He nodded silently, still holding her hand. "Mary," he said firmly, "You've got to let me explain why . . . why I acted like I did and stop interrupting. All right?"

She nodded distractedly but didn't withdraw her hand. "Mary, I . . . I've never had a woman, and I was, well, I was startled and just didn't know what to say. I'm sorry, very sorry, that I hurt your feelings like I did."

She looked at him in a new light. He saw love in the emerald depths of her eyes; his heart swelled with love in return. "Oh, Tom," she breathed, "I didn't know! You're so nice-looking and so well dressed, and you're not a boy anymore."

"I don't know about that, but I . . . I never have, had a woman, I mean."

She squeezed his hand. "You're pure! You're innocent! I'm so glad, because . . . because I am, too." Her look simply melted him inside.

"And then there's another reason I . . . I acted like I did."

"What, Tom?" Her eyes were clearing now, and the tearstains were disappearing.

"There are your sister and Herb, and we've got to think of—"

She overrode him. "Oh, Eliza would understand. We talked a lot about . . . about men and women after I got over losing Harold. She said I should have given in to him, and that she'd feel just like I do if she'd never had a man, with so many of them getting killed. She was expecting us to . . . not to come back, and she'd have seen to it that Herb didn't say anything."

Tom was astounded. "Do you mean that . . . that you talked about me, about us, being together before you came out here?"

She blushed furiously and withdrew her hand. "Oh, now I've really let the cat out of the bag! What are you going to think of me?" She averted her face.

He took her hand again. "I think you're wonderful, Mary, dear Mary. We don't, we can't behave like we used to, when everybody expected to live out a full life, when there was no war with men getting killed all the time. I understand. I feel the same way, only I just didn't . . . didn't realize it."

She had looked up and a beautiful smile replaced her tears like the sun coming out from behind a dark cloud. "Oh, I might as well confess." She squeezed his hand. "We heard so much about you from what the men wrote back home, and from what Herb wrote." Shyness overcame her, and she looked down.

"Please go on, Mary. It'll only make me love you more."

She went on without looking up. "Well, I started thinking about what you'd looked like when I saw you, and Eliza and I got to talking about you, then Herb wrote us about coming out here." A blush returned to her face and her voice trailed off, then went on. "We didn't . . . didn't exactly plan it, but we made up our minds that I'd meet you, and I . . . we hoped . . . hoped something would happen—" She raised her eyes timidly to his.

A grand passion swept over him. He leaned toward her, pulling her a little closer at the same time. "Oh, I'm glad, so glad you did, Mary, that we found each other. I love you, Mary. I want to make love to you. Will you?"

They came close enough to brush their lips lightly, and she murmured, "Yes, oh yes, I want to—I love you, too, Tom." She pulled back just a little. "Tom, oh, Tom, now that we're going to be lovers, just promise me something." Her plea was projected by her eyes as much as her voice.

"What, darling?"

Suddenly she sat back and the tears came again. "Oh, how sweet that sounds—darling."

"Mary, darling Mary, don't cry anymore," he pleaded.

She raised her face, wiping her tears and looking indescribably beautiful. "I won't have any more claim on you than . . . than any other woman, but—"

"Oh, but you will!" he insisted. "I'll be yours and you'll be mine!"

She shook her head. "I don't want it to be that way, Tom. I don't want to marry you or even be engaged to you."

"Now, Mary darling! I want to—"

"No, Tom, no." She began to cry again. "It would be just like it was with . . . with Harold, and I couldn't . . . couldn't stand to go through with . . . with that again."

He sighed. "After the war, then?"

She nodded and dabbed her eyes. "If you . . . if you're still alive—" She could go no further, and the tears came again.

He waited, and she sobbed brokenly, "But you'll have to promise . . . promise me something—"

"What, darling?"

She looked up and stopped sobbing. "That you'll stop taking those awful chances, that you'll try—at least try—not to get killed. Will . . . will you?"

This was a promise he could make with absolute sincerity because he was going to have something to live for again. He leaned toward her as she inclined toward him and their lips brushed again, this time not so lightly. "I promise, darling Mary; I promise—" As they drew apart, he glanced around to see if they were attracting any attention. They weren't. Too much of the same thing was going on in the alcove, and in the dining room, too.

Tom thought of something. "Did you . . . do you know about Sally Napier and me?"

She nodded sorrowfully. "We heard all about it. It must have been as bad for you as . . . losing Harold was for me." She reached for his hand. "But I hope you understand that she, Sally, wasn't just being false to you by . . . by taking another man." She nodded wistfully. "She was just being a woman in times that . . . that have unsettled everything."

He thought of telling her how that had been at the root of his recklessness, but he didn't want to bring that up and start her weeping again. "I do, I understand," he said softly. "God rest her soul."

He wanted to get off the subject, so before she could say anything, he took up the champagne bottle. "Here's this stuff!" he exclaimed laughingly as he picked up his glass. "We don't want to waste it. It costs a lot even if it does taste like vinegar."

Mary responded to his change of mood and giggled. "Vinegar! It does taste like vinegar!" She sipped, then put her glass down.

"Do you want any more of it?"

"Not really, unless you do."

"I don't either. I'll go pay the bill. Just wait here." He touched her cheek with his lips as he got up. "Don't run off, now!"

"Oh, don't *you* run off," she laughed. "Here, I'm going with you to make sure you don't." She arose and kissed him on the cheek.

As they went along the corridor toward Mary's room, he felt he had never been so happy in his life. He told her, and she said she hadn't either.

He felt even happier afterward, although it had been painful for Mary at first and he had been awkward. After a while he thought they ought to put in another appearance at the ball, so they did.

Blakey was gone, but the ball was still going full-blast. When they found the Parkers, Mary and her sister embraced and cried a little, but Herb didn't say anything, although he undoubtedly knew everything that Eliza did.

As Tom and Mary danced the next number, they passed close to Carolyn, who was dancing with an artillery lieutenant. Tom guessed her father had given Hayes the gate. He wasn't interested in the slightest when Carolyn smiled in recognition, but he smiled back. He noticed that she sized Mary up at some length and then looked at him again, but he didn't respond.

Womanlike, Mary had noticed and had to know who Carolyn was and all about her. When he told her about Marcus Allen, she put her head on his shoulder and tightened her arm about him. "Do you see, Tom darling, why I won't get engaged, although I love you?"

He didn't, but then you could never understand women.

"You know," she whispered, nuzzling her nose under his chin, "I loved you before I even saw you—here, I mean."

He found that hard to believe but didn't want to say so, so he settled for endearments whispered in her ear.

During the next dance, they somehow found themselves close to the platform where the musicians were at the far end of the hall. One look at them explained the markedly German flavor of the music. It wasn't that they looked different or anything, but you could tell they were Germans. Maybe it was the way they handled their instruments. They were all in uniform, and their director was an elderly major who wore glasses.

Toward one of the corners a couple was dancing whose skill astounded onlookers and dancers alike. They were von Jagerhof and a blonde whose blue-eyed beauty reminded Tom of Sally. They were a wonder to behold, and Tom and Mary gaped with the others. Von Jagerhof's nimble feet performed the most intricate revolutions as he swept his partner about, and she was up to his standard. Tom guided Mary closer.

When the Prussian noticed them, he broke out into a big smile, his eyes widening as he took in Mary's tall and shapely form. "Major! Major!" he called as they came close. "I didn't know you had a lady for the evening, and look what a splendid bronze-haired goddess you have!"

Tom grinned and Mary smiled.

"You've got quite a beauty yourself!" Tom replied.

Von Jagerhof laughed. "Oh, I haven't got her! She's got me!"

They laughed as the blonde pretended to be angry. The music stopped and they talked.

After the introductions, Mary exclaimed, "My! Imagine meeting a German nobleman! I never dreamed I would, not in my whole life!"

"Oh," scoffed von Jagerhof, "it's nothing! Over here I'm just another Dutchman!"

Tom thought it was particularly funny, and they got a big laugh out of it.

The blonde was Klara Haverlee, daughter of the colonel of a New York regiment. Her English wasn't up to much participation in the conversation, so she mostly just smiled, looked beautiful, and hung onto von Jagerhof. He said the bandsmen had a big room off the end of the hall where they went for refreshments during intermissions.

The Germans of the division had just about taken it over, but the bandsmen were Germans, too, and had a good time with them. They had tables brought up and were having a great time eating and drinking when they weren't dancing. Von Jagerhof wanted Tom and Mary to join them there, but Tom could tell Mary didn't want to, so he refused with thanks, saying he wished they had known about it earlier, but it was too late now.

When the next dance began, Tom and Mary took their leave and danced toward the other end of the ballroom. The clock showed it was the last dance, and it was a sad, haunting tune Tom had heard the Germans in his old company sing. The beat throbbed like a great heart, and the muted horns carried the tender, touching melody.

There weren't many dancers on the floor, and most of them seemed to be young couples who had come up from the dining room for the last dance. Tom heard soft sobbing as a boyish infantry lieutenant glided past with a petite, brunette head buried on his chest. All couples were dancing very closely, and Tom hugged Mary to him so that their bodies moved in the closest intimacy. She snuggled her head on his shoulder and whispered words of love into his ear, and he returned them to hers.

When the dance was over, the Parkers had gone. Mary said it was so she and Tom could go back to her room without seeing them. Tom hadn't thought about spending the night with her but could see no reason why he shouldn't. There was no duty for anyone the next day except for a few who had already been told, and he wasn't one of them.

Mary and Eliza stayed a week, and Tom spent every night with Mary. After a few days, they didn't avoid the Parkers anymore and even got to eating with them. Tom was uneasy at first and could tell that Herb was, too, but they soon got over it, mainly because the women acted like it was the most natural thing in the world.

When they ate, Tom insisted on being served by the little waiter with the wooden leg. He always left a nice tip, and the first time Herb saw him do it, he looked surprised. When Mary told him why, he said he was going to do the same thing, and the little fellow always picked up something very much worth his while afterward. He never said anything until after breakfast the morning the women were leaving; he had heard them talking about it. When they were putting on their wraps and he was waiting to clear away the dishes, he said that if it had been left up to men like them, there never would have been any war. They all agreed, and Tom and Herb shook hands with him on it.

One night after they had made love, Tom asked Mary something that had been bothering him. "Mary, darling, what if you find out you're going to have a baby? You'll have to marry me then."

She snuggled up close to him. "No, darling, I won't have to marry you, but I hope I have your baby."

He sat up bolt upright in bed. "But . . . but what do you mean? It doesn't make sense!"

She rolled over on her back and looked up at him, her eyes glowing to their emerald depths and a beatific expression on her face. "I'll still have something of you . . . even if—" She suddenly sat up, threw her arms about him, and began weeping.

He clasped her to him and felt the wet tears on his chest. "What, darling? Even if what?"

"Even if . . . even if you're killed," she sobbed.

He couldn't give it up, so after she had quieted, he tried a different approach. "But, Mary, if you have a child, it'll be a bastard."

She pulled back and looked at him, smiling a little. "I'm going to have to tell you, I guess." She let him go and sat beside him, leaning her head on his shoulder. "I've told you everything else about Eliza and me, so I might as well tell this."

He bent over and gave her a peck on the cheek. "Tell me, darling."

"Well," she sighed, "Eliza and Herb can't have any children. Anyhow, they've been trying ever since they've been married and haven't had one yet."

"You mean they'd take ours?"

"Eliza's afraid Herb will get killed, and she's desperate for a child. If it turns out that we, that I'm going to have one, we'll go away together and not come back until after it's born and she'll claim it's hers."

Tom was astounded at this revelation of the wiles of women, and she went on before he could say anything. She hugged him tightly and nestled her head on his chest. "That way we'll both have what we want. I'll have something of you, and Eliza will have a baby."

He recovered and protested vehemently. "But it'll be mine, too, and I'll want to claim it, and you, too, and then there's money! You'll have to live—"

She cut him off. "Tom! Tom!" she pleaded, pressing him back on the bed. "Don't worry about money! Eliza's got plenty! She runs the store and the livery stable. Herb's father just manages the farm."

He rolled over and confronted her as she sank down beside him. "But the child will be mine as much as yours, and I'll want both of you! I'm not going to go along with this!" he added firmly.

She kissed him. "After the war, darling, after the war, if you're still . . . still alive—" She wrapped her arms about him and started weeping again.

He could see there was no use arguing with her, and her weeping like this simply tore him up inside. "Oh, I'll still be around, and the first thing I'm going to do is to claim you, and the child, too. Eliza hadn't better try to keep it, either."

Mary started laughing as suddenly as she had started crying, her voice muffled on his chest. The abrupt change from tears to mirth was beyond him. "What's so funny?" he asked irritably.

She pulled away a little and looked up at him. "Oh, Tom, we're talking like it's sure to happen, almost like it's already happened, and I may turn out to be barren like Eliza is."

"Oh, it's her instead of Herb?"

"The doctors think so. They went to one in Cincinnati who was supposed to be the best, and that's what he said." She put her head on his chest again and giggled. "If it wasn't for that, Eliza wants a child so bad I believe she'd . . . she'd go out and get another man, and let Herb think it was his."

Tom could only shake his head again and conclude that you could never understand women. A good while later it occurred to him that a baby for Eliza might have been behind the whole thing, but that didn't seem possible at the time.

They never talked about Mary having a child again. He tried to bring it up a few times but had to give it up because she would always relate it to his getting himself killed, start crying, and make him promise to change his ways. All he could get out of her was a promise to write.

The week he spent with Mary was heavenly. He was in love, but it was different than it had been with Sally, and not just because it had gone to where it had. With Sally, it had always been there. He had just grown up into it. With Mary it had been sudden and shattering, breaking on him unawares and sweeping away a lot of notions he hadn't quite gotten rid of.

Sometimes on his way to camp in the morning, he would wonder how he could ever put those shapely white arms he had just left out of his mind and concentrate on his duties. He always did, though, and was able to carry on like he always had. He and Herb never went back together, though. No one wanted to advertise the affair to men who might write home about it. Otherwise, it probably wouldn't get out, because there were so many wives, fiancées, and relatives in town that half the officers weren't staying in camp at night, and Tom was by no means the only single fellow among them.

When Mary and Eliza left, there was a tearful scene at the station and Tom came near contributing to it. Mary had come to mean so much to him that he felt like he was losing a part of himself. When they had their final embrace, she clung to him until she extracted the thousandth promise that he would change his ways and be careful. Eliza hugged Herb just as hard and cried, too, but didn't seem to need any such promises.

Tom and Herb went back to camp together for the first time. Although there was no uneasiness between them any longer, neither of them could find much to say.

# 42

About a week after Mary and Eliza left, Tom was called to brigade headquarters by a courier who didn't know either who wanted to see him or why. He felt a little apprehensive on his way there, although he couldn't think of any reason why he should.

Headquarters was in a big old log house that had taken a good deal of fixing up to make suitable. Rivers could have ejected the occupants and taken over the finest house in town. The fact that he hadn't showed what kind of a man he was.

When Tom went in, Anders said it was the colonel who wanted to see him, but he didn't know why. Rivers would be busy with his quartermaster for a few minutes yet, so Tom sat down and talked about things back home with Anders until the quartermaster came out and Rivers appeared in the doorway of his office. He invited Tom in and closed the door behind him.

Tom came to attention, saluted, and reported in the prescribed manner.

"Have a seat, Major," said Rivers casually. "I want to talk with you about some more or less personal matters, so we'll dispense with the formalities."

Tom sat down wondering what it was all about. "Thank you, sir."

Rivers sat on his desk. "Major, I've been hearing a good deal about your affair at the bridge last month." He looked at Tom benignly as though to reassure him.

"Yes, sir?"

"From what I hear you were lucky you didn't get yourself killed."

"Yes, sir, I guess I was." That was the God's truth, as he realized now.

"I just wanted to talk to you about it." Rivers got up and started to walk around. "I'd hate to lose one of my most promising young men."

Tom grinned ruefully. "Yes, sir, I'd hate for you to lose him, too, not that he's especially promising or anything." He undertook to explain why he had done what he had, but it didn't seem to impress Rivers. He asked some questions about how the enemy had deployed his infantry and how Tom had reacted. After that he sat down on his desk facing Tom and looked serious.

"Now this is the way I understand it. You felt your own stupidity had let the Rebels nearly get to the bridge, and that you had to stop them even if you died in the attempt. Is that right?" Rivers's dark eyes were searching.

"Yes, sir, but that's a lot better than the way I put it." He nodded. "That's exactly how I felt at the time."

Rivers nodded in his turn. "Well, let me tell you something. It wasn't stupidity. Anybody would have been fooled by the way that fellow deployed against you. Do you know who he was?"

"No, sir, but I sure would like to. He certainly knows his business."

Rivers smiled significantly. "Brigadier General William G. Maxey, C.S.A. I knew him in the old army, and he's as foxy a fellow as you're ever likely to meet. He used to fleece everybody at poker out in New Mexico." He shook his head. "We captured one of those troopers who went at the bridge a few days ago and he didn't mind talking about it, since it was all over. In fact, he started it. He wanted to know who that fellow was who charged them all by himself."

"Is that right? I'd sure like to talk to him. There are some things I'd like to find out."

"Oh, he's already on his way to prison camp, but I can pretty well tell you what he said."

"I wish the colonel would."

"Well, it was just a nuisance raid. The bridge wasn't all that important. I think the Rebels just wanted to scare Burnside, make him worry about his communications." Rivers folded his arms across his chest and nodded, then went on. "Well, there was Maxey, just out of the hospital and standing around with nothing to do, so they gave him a regiment and a few cavalry and sent him against that bridge. They didn't expect to find more than a company or two guarding it, and when Maxey saw we had a battalion on each bank he decided he'd draw you out. He'd use about half his men as skirmishers and deploy the others back in those thickets so it would look like he had a couple or three regiments, all told. He thought you'd pull everybody away from the bridge so you could hold him as far back as you could, then he'd sneak his cavalry around your flank and cut the cables."

"You know, sir," mused Tom, "that's exactly what I decided he was up to, only I was a little late about it."

Rivers nodded solemnly. "This trooper we captured said you'd left a company at the bridge, but the men were all scattered out watching the action. The cavalry was sneaking up along the bank in the trees and was almost on them when some damn fool on a horse came hell-bent back along the road and went at them all by himself. He raised such a ruckus that the men around the bridge saw what was coming in time to get together and stand them off long enough for the battalion on the other side to start crossing."

"Well, I was that damn fool on the horse, all right," admitted Tom.

Rivers laughed shortly. "This trooper allowed that fellow was either the biggest fool or the bravest man he'd ever seen, he didn't know which, but he was really a fighter, what ever else he was. Their captain and two of his best men went out against him, and as near as they could figure out, he did all three of them in."

"Well, it isn't often a man can find out what the enemy thinks."

Rivers frowned. "You know what I told that trooper?"

Tom sobered. "I can imagine."

"I told him I didn't know which you were either, but that I thought you were probably a little of both."

Tom felt chastened. "Mostly a fool, I guess."

Rivers got up and began walking around again. "I'd heard about it before, but that was straight from the horse's mouth, and I thought I'd better have a talk with you."

Tom guessed he was in for it. "Yes, sir."

"You know, Major, I've seen a good deal of fighting and I've known a good many fighting men in my time. I was with Scott in Mexico, and we had some hard battles down there, and now I've seen a good deal of it against the Rebels." He came back and sat on his desk again. "Do you know what always happens to men like you?"

Tom felt even more chastened. "Yes, sir. They get killed."

Rivers nodded emphatically. "You're exactly right." He looked at Tom sadly. "You're no fool. You're just one of those very few men I've known who don't know the meaning of fear. It's not exactly bravery. Bravery's the ability to overcome fear and go on. You just don't feel fear at all."

"Oh no, sir, you're wrong; I get scared—"

Rivers interrupted. "You just get excited, that's all, and you think it's fear because you really don't know what fear is. You wouldn't have charged that Rebel cavalry all by yourself if you did. You wouldn't have done other things you've done if you did." Rivers shook his head slowly. "Now don't misunderstand me. It's an admirable quality, but it always has the same result. A man's luck just doesn't go on and on, and luck is all that saves fellows like you."

Tom looked down. He was beginning to feel resentful, but he knew Rivers meant well.

Rivers seemed to sense how he felt. "Major Traylor, you're a fine young man. I lost my son in New Mexico over ten years ago along with my wife. Carolyn's all I've got now, and I wouldn't have her if she hadn't been staying with her mother's people in Kentucky when the cholera broke out." He bowed his head, then got up and walked around without speaking for a little while. Tom could tell he still grieved, and his resentment evaporated.

Rivers came back and sat on his desk facing Tom again. "My son would be about the same age you are if he had lived, and I like to think he'd have grown up to be a man like you." Sadness hooded his dark eyes.

"I'm glad the colonel thinks so well of me." That trite statement was all he could think of.

Rivers went on. "I can't help thinking of you as a . . . a son, which is really why I wanted to talk to you, I guess." He looked at the floor while Tom vainly tried to think of something to say.

Suddenly Rivers looked up and spoke earnestly. "You have a great future if you don't get yourself killed. You have a capacity for decisive action, and that's a rare quality. You can size a situation up, decide instantly what's got to be done, and then you have the courage—or maybe it's the lack of fear—to do it. Men like you don't get upset or rattled. Your mind works coldly and logically when other men's would be paralyzed by fear and excitement." The colonel sounded like he was talking about some imaginary fellow, maybe a character from one of Scott's novels.

"It's an inborn quality," Rivers went on. "No amount of training or education can give it to a man. Those who have it don't even know it. They think everybody's like they are. It would never have come out back in Dubois County because there wouldn't have been anything to bring it out." He looked at Tom searchingly. "Do you understand what I mean, son?"

Tom nodded. "I believe so, sir." He wanted to be honest and disabuse Rivers of his illusions, but he couldn't do it. How could he tell him about Sally, and that he had acted as he had only because he had nothing to live for until Mary came into his life? It would sound maudlin and foolish. Rivers would lose all respect for him.

"You've shown it several times, the first one when you reported back to me what to do, before we had that bayonet fight last August. You analyzed the situation, saw what had to be done and that it had to be done instantly, then ran back and told us, Stamford and me."

Suddenly Rivers's mood changed and he tried unsuccessfully to suppress a laugh. "Then . . . then there was what happened when the regiment nearly mutinied last fall."

Tom knew what he thought was funny, the same thing Carter had. He wondered how Rivers had found out about it and began to feel apprehensive despite his mirth.

Rivers read his mind. "I know all about that, son. General Carter took me into his confidence." He didn't try to suppress his laughter this time. "Oh, I'd like to have seen it, too!"

Tom didn't think it was funny, because it still scared him. Rivers slapped him on the shoulder, still laughing a little. "Now, don't let that bother you anymore. Winthrop and his boy major are long gone, and General Carter even arranged to have their old regiment transferred out of the corps last week."

Tom felt better. "I know I never saw them again, not that I wanted to or anything."

Rivers was only smiling now. "They both decided they were needed back at Harvard soon after that happened. I don't know whether it was because of that or because they thought it was safer to maintain abstract principles in the lecture hall than on the battlefield." He laughed again. "General Carter was glad to see them go, too."

"Well, I guess it was good riddance, from what I know about them."

Rivers warmed to his subject. "Now, that's the kind of thing I mean. Not one man in ten thousand would have done what you did. You sized the situation up. You knew what would happen if Winthrop marched his men into camp. You saw what was the only way to stop him, and you did it." He snorted. "Owen would never, never have done it, or anyone else I know of."

While Tom was trying to think of something to say, Rivers went on. "Like I say, it would be a shame for you to get yourself killed in some skirmish. You'll go far. You're going to take over the regiment when Owen's resignation is approved, and unless I'm badly mistaken, a brigade won't be long in coming."

Tom was astounded. "Why, I didn't know Colonel Owen had resigned! Why, might I ask?"

"It's business. His father's quite old and has fallen ill. They have a big wholesale house in Evansville. There are a lot of debts and uncollected accounts, and they'll be ruined unless he can get back there and straighten things out. He thought at first he could take a month's leave and do it, but he's found out it'll take a lot more time. He's had to resign."

Owen was sure a secretive fellow, thought Tom. He had been married a month before anyone knew about it. "Well, sir, I hope I'm up to commanding the regiment, but I have my doubts." He shook his head. "Last year at this time I was just a corporal, you know."

Rivers gave a short laugh. “It’s like I said a while ago. You have this inborn quality, then you study a lot, and you can put what you study into practice. There’s no gap between the abstract and the concrete for you. You showed that on division exercises.” He laughed again. “I believe you could have knocked General Carter’s eyes off with a stick a time or two.”

“I wish I could share the colonel’s confidence,” sighed Tom.

Rivers reached out and clapped him on the shoulder. “I have all the confidence in the world in you, son. You’ll be the best regimental commander I’ll have, just like you were the best company commander I had and the best adjutant I’ve got now.” He nodded emphatically. “Do you know that your regiment’s the only one in the brigade that hasn’t had men up for court-martial, and that Owen’s the only commander who isn’t always running to me about discipline with these replacements we got?” Rivers nodded again. “And I know who hammered those fellows into shape in your regiment. It wasn’t Owen.”

Tom hadn’t been paying much attention. He felt a little overwhelmed. “When is Colonel Owen leaving?”

“His resignation’s in the hands of Adjutant General Thomas now. I doubt if it’ll be a week. General Carter’s an old friend of Thomas’ and he’s seeing to it.”

“I wish he’d told me about it,” said Tom a little irritably. “I could have been getting ready.”

Rivers laughed deprecatingly. “You needn’t worry about that. You’ll just take up the reins and drive off with it, like you did when you got to be company commander and adjutant.” He thought of something. “Oh, say, who do you want for adjutant? I’ll leave it up to you.”

Tom didn’t hesitate. “Captain von Jagerhof.”

Rivers nodded. “He’s the best choice. He’s a professional, trained since boyhood.” He frowned and looked thoughtful. “It might cause you trouble with your senior captains, though. He’s junior, and then he’s a foreigner, too.”

“I’ll take care of it if it does,” replied Tom, “but I don’t expect any trouble about it.”

Rivers grinned in his beard. “I don’t expect you’ll have any either, come to think of it. I heard about Harlow and Samuels.”

“Yes, sir.” Tom wondered how Rivers found out about everything and hoped the colonel didn’t think he was some kind of a bully.

Rivers went back to his main subject. “Do you see now, son, why I wanted to talk with you? It’d be tragic if a young man with your prospects got himself killed. It’s not that there’s any way of avoiding danger in our business. There's always a chance of getting killed, but you can make it a certainty."

"Yes, sir," Tom said reflectively. "I'm not going to do anything like that again. I can promise the colonel that." He was glad Rivers didn't seem to know about his riding along the line and making a target out of himself.

"You'll have to watch yourself. You don't have the . . . the restraints most men have that hold them back. You'll break loose and do the same sort of thing again if you don't watch out."

Tom looked down and smoothed his hat. "I will, sir. I realize . . . I see things differently now. I needed a good talking to, I guess." How could he lie like that? He hadn't needed a talking to at all, not since he had met Mary. He would probably be a coward now.

Rivers looked at him appraisingly. "Well, aren't you going to ask about those eagles for your shoulder straps? You'll skip lieutenant colonel."

Tom sighed. "Well, sir, I doubt if General Carter will go along with it. He'll probably want me to stay a major for a while, and then won't want me to skip anything."

"Oh, you're thinking of the fuss he made about your last two promotions. Well, I had a long talk with him just after I found out Owen was going to resign. I told him you'd have been commissioned when you first came in if you'd applied, and that I felt it was my fault that you didn't. I knew you were better educated than most of the men who were commissioned and that, well, I'd sort of forgotten about it until there at the Second Bull Run when you spotted that column flanking Grigsby and showed you knew what to do about it."

"Sir, I'm glad I was an enlisted man. I think I'm a better officer for it, and then it put me under Sergeant Kemper." He nodded thoughtfully. "I've learned more from him than from all the studying I've done."

"He's a fine man, Kemper is," replied Rivers. "Now, about General Carter." He smiled knowingly. "He didn't know anything about your education and all that. I guess he thought you were one of those unlettered clodhoppers from our part of the country who'd somehow learned to talk properly and dress himself up."

"Well, sir," said Tom emphatically, "I'm proud of being one of those clodhoppers. There aren't any better men—"

Rivers interrupted. "Oh, of course, son. I didn't mean to be derogatory, but they do lack polish—"

It was Tom's turn to break in. "Polish!" he laughed. "Polish would ruin them! They wouldn't be half the men they are." He shook his head. "They're the best God ever made."

Rivers nodded his agreement. “You’re right, absolutely right. They’ll march faster and further in any kind of weather, and they’ll fight anyone, anytime, anyplace.” He shook his head sorrowfully. “They’re splendid, and it breaks my heart to think of how many we’ve lost.”

“And how many we’ll lose yet,” added Tom gloomily.

“Back to General Carter,” said Rivers. “He understands things a lot better now, and those eagles won’t be long in coming. He’s made up his mind you’ll get them, and what he wants he gets.”

Tom looked at Rivers significantly. “Everything but a brigadier general’s commission for the colonel.”

Rivers sighed. “Well, that’s out of his reach. He can’t do anything with the Senate, and it’s got to confirm generals’ commissions.”

“I guess Morton gets Lane to block you there,” speculated Tom.

“That’s the way I understand it.” Rivers sighed again. “Oh, it’s the substance that counts, not the baubles that go with it.”

“I don’t guess our noble governor’s learned the difference between Taylor and Traylor yet,” said Tom. “He’s bound to find out sometime, though, and that’ll be the end of it.”

Rivers chuckled. “As far as I know, he’s still in the dark about it, but when he does find out he’ll send someone to sound you out on politics and try to suborn you, like he did Hovey. He always does that.” He shook his head. “That man’s a politician to the core of his being.”

Tom was wondering how he would react if that actually happened when Rivers went on. “Of course, he’s got problems as far as your regiment’s concerned. He simply can’t find any Republicans fit to promote. You’ve noticed you’re always shortchanged on officers. Every company’s supposed to have a captain and two lieutenants, and you just don’t get them.” He nodded grimly. “He was always trying to push Republican officers on me, but I wouldn’t take them unless they were from the Pocket, and I wouldn’t keep those I took that weren’t any good.” He snorted. “This is his revenge. I’m a colonel commanding a brigade, and that’s all I’ll ever be.” He put a hand on Tom’s shoulder. “Son, you just keep quiet about politics like I told you before, and don’t get yourself identified with the opposition.”

“But, sir, he’ll try to foist Republicans off on me, and I won’t stand for it either.”

Rivers shook his head. “I don’t think so. He never bothered Owen, anyhow. I guess I fought the battle for you fellows.”

“I hope so, sir.” Tom felt he had taken enough of Rivers’s time, so he got up and extended his hand. “I’m very grateful for all the colonel has done for me,” he said feelingly.

Rivers took his hand. "I could say the same, son." When Tom looked puzzled, he went on a little diffidently. "I guess you know why I looked you up at the ball a few weeks ago."

Tom thought it best only to nod, so Rivers went on. "I was worried about Carolyn. She's all I've got, you know." He shook his head. "She took it awfully hard about Marcus. She lost her appetite and weight. She couldn't sleep. She'd just sit and brood, and she got to worrying that something would happen to me." He sighed. "Martha and I managed to persuade her to go to the ball, but she insisted on wearing black, and I guess the young men were all afraid to ask her to dance. She was wanting to leave and, well, I happened to think of you and your capacity for decisive action—"

Rivers was showing some embarrassment, so Tom broke in. " 'Capacity for *headlong* action' would be more accurate, sir!"

Rivers laughed, too. "Well, anyhow, you broke the ice. The others came flocking in, and she wound up having a good time." His eyes showed his gratitude. "She's been a lot better ever since. She's started living again. I could tell the difference on our way home that night."

"Well, dancing with a lovely young lady's the most pleasant way I ever earned a commendation," replied Tom laughingly. "I'll do it anytime."

The dark eyes brightened. "Oh, incidentally, she's been asking about you."

There was only one thing he could say. "Would she . . . she see me if I called?" He hoped he hadn't sounded too hesitant.

Rivers broke into a smile. "She certainly would." All at once his face fell with a suddenness that would have been comic in anyone else. "Oh, for God's sake, don't tell her I breathed a word about it!" He shuddered.

Tom couldn't help laughing. "I won't, sir, not a word!"

Rivers laughed himself. "Oh, God! She'd disown me if she ever found out!" He shook his head. "Women are such strange creatures."

"But wonderful ones, sir." He was surprised at his urbanity, or was it artfulness? "When shall I call?"

Rivers sighed. "Great liar that I am, I'll say you asked me and I suggested seven o'clock tomorrow evening. Is that all right?"

"That's fine, sir." He came to attention and started to salute, but Rivers seized his hand. "Let's just shake hands again; what do you say?" The way he looked showed he was thinking of his son again.

Rivers saw him out. "We'll be expecting you tomorrow at seven, then, unless you hear otherwise from me."

"Yes, sir. I'll be looking forward to it." His sincerity surprised him.

Anders was busy at his desk, so Tom only nodded and smiled at him as he went by. As he mounted his horse and rode away, he hardly knew what to think of himself.

A few blocks along, he met a buggy with a pretty young woman in gray seated beside an elderly gentleman. She was undoubtedly a local girl and thoroughly a Rebel, but she couldn't keep her eyes from straying to the Yankee major or hide the admiration on her face. Tom pretended not to notice so she wouldn't be embarrassed, but the episode banished all doubt about what he had gotten himself in for.

He had a mad impulse to spur his horse to a gallop and go whooping down the street, but of course he didn't.

# 43

The first time Tom called on Carolyn, she made a show of how her father had taken things out of her hands, but he could tell it was only that. After a little while, the colonel and his sister, Martha, left the young people in the parlor, where they sat on a couch. Tom was a little surprised that he felt no uneasiness at all, and if Carolyn did, she was too polished a young lady to show it.

Tom soon saw that if their conversation ran out, it would be his fault. She had left a first-class girls' school in Kentucky only two years ago and was well informed on what was going on in the country, and in Europe, too. He was glad he read the papers almost every day.

When they got to talking about each other, she couldn't understand why he had gone back to farming after going to college. He tried to explain how a farmer's life was the best there was, mainly because of its independence and closeness to nature, but he could tell she didn't understand and was only being polite in not saying so. She probably thought farming was only for men who couldn't do anything else, like most people did who weren't farmers themselves. He didn't tell her about Sally, or about Mary either, except to tell who she was when Carolyn asked because of having seen them together at the ball.

They enjoyed each other's company and talked easily and casually. Tom found her very attractive and thought she was also attracted to him. She was so much different from Mary, though. She seemed so small and delicate, but that was only because Mary was almost as tall as he was and everything else about her was in proportion. Carolyn was also prettier, but her black hair and blue eyes didn't have the dazzle of Mary's coppery red and emerald green.

After his first visit, Tom was such a frequent caller that the colonel and his sister were soon almost treating him like one of the family. Martha always retired early, so when the colonel was absent, as he often was, Tom and Carolyn had things pretty well to themselves. There were careful to keep their distance, though, and it wasn't until they were saying their goodnights after several visits that he dared take her hand. He thought she squeezed his a little, but it might have been his imagination.

The next time he called, the colonel was absent. Tom got to talking about the men of his old platoon, and Ab naturally came in for special attention. Tom undertook to repeat some of the tales Ab was always telling, even to imitating his mannerisms and nasal drawl. Of course it was nothing like the genuine article, but Carolyn's laughter was.

She asked about others, and he told her about Burk without thinking where it would lead. She was caught up and carried along with the story, and when he told her how the big fellow finally found Katarina her bosom heaved and her face glowed with satisfaction and sympathy. She wouldn't let him stop there, and he had to tell her how Burk had been killed only a little while later. Suddenly she looked away and he could tell she was fighting back the tears. She lost the fight and, before he knew it, had buried her face in her hands and was weeping.

Instinctively he took her in his arms. He could have let her go immediately, but she submitted to his embrace, rested her head on his chest, and sobbed, "Oh, how . . . how tragic! Just after he found somebody—"

The tender feminine body in his arms aroused him, and he clasped her tightly. "I know," he said, "I don't believe I've ever felt worse about anything in my life."

Suddenly she raised her tearstained face to his and said accusingly, "What they say about you! Why, Father says—"

The Cupid's bow of her lips was irresistible, and he cut her off with a kiss. She slipped her arms about him and responded, then suddenly pushed herself away. "Oh, Tom, we mustn't–we mustn't." The blue eyes were wide, and the delicate little nostrils quivered.

He took her hand. "Please forgive me, Carolyn," he said huskily. "When you started crying, I just couldn't help it, and then, well, I just couldn't resist, I'm sorry; I'm sorry." He really wasn't, though. Her momentary response had banished everything but desire.

She nodded her petite head. "It's all right, Tom. I shouldn't have started crying, but I . . . I just couldn't help it." She dabbed at her eyes with a handkerchief. "He was so big, and so lonesome, and couldn't find anybody, and then, just after he did—" She had to stop and fight back the tears again.

"Oh, it was my fault," he said apologetically. "I shouldn't have told you, but I didn't think of the ending when I started."

She blew her nose with a charming little snort, and his arm stole about her again. She didn't try to move it away. After she finished with her handkerchief, she leaned against him but reached out to hold off his other arm. "Now, what I started to say. Father and the others say you take the awfulest chances, that you just don't seem to care, or be afraid, ever." Her tone was still a little accusatory, but her lips were trembling.

He stirred uneasily. "Oh, I'm not that bad. It's just that I've been a little forgetful, or careless a few times."

She looked up at him, her lips only inches away, but the tragic light in her eyes held him back. "I wish . . . I wish I could believe you," she said, and the movement of her tender little lips overpowered him. He put his arms around her and kissed her again. She returned the kiss, not passionately, but languorously, and a wonderful ecstasy flooded over him.

When their lips parted, she made no move to pull away. "Tom, oh, Tom, we shouldn't be doing like this. I'm . . . I'm supposed to be a lady, and you're . . . you should be a gentleman."

It was his turn to sigh as he embraced her and felt the soft, inviting flesh in his arms. "I'm afraid I'm not a gentleman—anymore, anyhow."

She nodded the shapely little head cradled on his chest. "Nor I a lady, or I wouldn't be letting a man hold me in his arms that I'm not, that I barely know."

"Neither of us are what we used to be."

Their lips came together again, and this time the kiss was less languorous on her part. He felt the bones of her shoulder and back in his embrace, and she slipped her arms around him, hugging him tightly.

She drew back, but only to take her arms from around him. She still nestled against him with his arms around her. "It's the war," she mused. "You may be lying dead in a few days. I know it. You know it. That's why we're doing . . . like this."

"It's like we're standing on the edge of a sword and our feet are slipping." He thought he had never expressed himself so well.

She sighed and he saw a tear stealing down her cheek. "That's just the way I feel, too, Tom." She snuggled against him, picked up one of his hands, and caressed it, her own white and tiny compared to its sinewy size. "Eat, drink, and make love, for tomorrow you die," she said with a trace of bitterness.

"You're a philosopher," he whispered into her shell-like little ear. "That's almost original."

She heaved a great sigh, or perhaps it was a sob, then looked up at him, her eyes great pools of sadness. Suddenly she reached up, pulled his face down to hers, and kissed him passionately, making soft little murmuring sounds. He tightened his arms about her and felt her hard little breasts against his chest. They reclined, and he moved a hand down to her hips, pressing her tightly to him. She responded by moving her body against his. They were being rapidly swept away when she suddenly tore herself loose, swung about, and went back to a sitting position.

She was breathing hard and fast, and tiny droplets of perspiration showed between the Cupid's bow lips and the delicate little nose. He reached for her, but she blocked his hands. "Tom—oh, Tom." She sighed tremulously, her little bosom heaving. "You'd better . . . you'd better go—"

He started to protest. "Oh, Carolyn, we're so—"

She was regaining control and cut him off. "Yes, you'd better go. We've . . . we've gone off the track." She smiled appealingly. "Let's get back on, shall we?" She shrugged her trim little shoulders and straightened her dress.

"Are you sure it's not that we just got *on* the track?" He took one of her hands.

She nodded. "It may be, but it's the wrong track, Tom. We've got to get off before we . . . we go too far."

He started to take her in his arms again, but she blocked him a second time. "Please, Tom. Please go now." The rosy little mouth was open, and the tips of her pearly teeth showed.

Her eyes belied her words, but he got up to go. He felt that he had somehow been suddenly brought back from a distant and wondrous place just as he was about to enter. She got his hat and coat while he straightened his uniform, then saw him to the door.

He took her hand. "When?" he asked simply.

She looked at him silently for what seemed like a long time, a strangely hesitant look on her face. They were being drawn together again when she suddenly put a hand on his chest to hold them apart. "I'll write . . . a note," she finally whispered.

He nodded. "I'll be waiting for it."

"Good-bye, Tom," she said tremulously.

He was startled. "Is it good-bye, or only good night?"

She shook her head, anguish showing in her eyes. "I don't know; I just don't know."

He sighed. "The choice is yours. I won't try to force myself on you."

She only shook her head slowly and repeated, "I don't know; I just don't know."

"Well, write the note, anyhow, will you?"

She nodded and started to say something but turned abruptly and went back into the house.

Two days later, before any note came, the regiment marched.

# 44

They made no show of it when Owen left and Tom took command of the regiment. Owen had always slept in the tent where most of the officers did, but Tom didn't want to give up his privacy. He was thinking of partitioning off a corner of the headquarters tent and setting up a bunk there when von Jagerhof announced that was what he was going to do. Tom protested that he was the one who ought to be there all the time, but the Prussian said that in his army it was the adjutant who stayed at headquarters and took care of whatever came up at odd hours. If the major didn't mind, that was what he wanted to do. Tom didn't mind. His cabin was much more private and comfortable than the headquarters tent would be. After von Jagerhof got Hauser to fix it up and a long piece of canvas was hung, his bunk set up, and his camp cabinet moved in, it made a cozy corner and didn't take up much room.

After von Jagerhof moved out of the cabin, Hauser and two other Germans came with a big wooden wardrobe that had been foraged God knew where. Tom didn't much want it and told him they couldn't get it in the cabin anyhow. Hauser gave him to understand that they could and insisted he had to have it if he was to keep the *Herr Major's* uniforms looking like they should. The *Herr Major* should consider such things more now than when he was a mere adjutant. There was no arguing with the fellow, so Tom told him to go ahead. The door frame and part of the front of the cabin had to be taken out, but they got the wardrobe in and soon had everything back like it had been.

When Tom pointed out that the thing was much larger than needed for his uniforms, Hauser said he was going to keep von Jagerhof's in it, too. The *Herr Hauptmann* had an orderly of his own now, but the fellow wasn't to be trusted with uniforms, not yet anyhow.

His orderly laid another obligation on Tom after he became commander of the regiment. He had to wear a clean shirt every day. When he protested that was carrying it too far, all he got was a snort of exasperation and he wound up buying four new shirts so it could be done. He also wore a different uniform every day, which had been scrupulously cleaned, brushed, and pressed. His boots as well as his other leatherwork were shined to a mirror finish because Hauser now disdained grease for the boots and used the best polish money could buy. The fellow was a worse tyrant than ever, but Tom guessed he was worth putting up with. He even outshone General Carter when he came around.

Tom made a few changes in the way Owen had run things. One of them was to turn Kemper loose. As regimental sergeant major, he was supposed to have authority over every noncom in the regiment. Owen had never let him use it, probably because he was afraid the company officers wouldn't like it. Tom wasn't concerned about that, and Kemper was soon patrolling the camp every day. Nothing escaped his sharp eyes, and the noncom who was responsible for any deficiency was promptly called to account. It wasn't long before the camp was in apple-pie order and no one saw men with ragged uniforms or broken shoes like had been too common before. He also saw to it that the huts were neat and clean as well as warm and dry, and was not above turning the occupants out to make a thorough inspection.

Tom began inspecting one company each day in full marching order except for shelter halves, which most of the men used to roof their huts. He staggered the order of the companies and occasionally inspected one twice in a row, so none of them knew when their turn would come and they had to be ready every day. Dirty rifles, missing equipment, and untidy packs soon became things of the past. In the unlikely event of an order to march, he would be ready. Owen had never held inspections except on the eve of a march and then of the whole regiment. Tom remembered how that had been.

One day he saw some men from another brigade with ponchos, new items of equipment. They were only waterproof groundsheets with holes for the head and buttons for the back, but they would keep men dry in the worst weather, and he remembered the march back from Davis's expedition. He pestered the brigade quartermaster until he got a complete issue of ponchos for his men. They remembered, too, and were glad to get them.

Von Jagerhof said he wanted to do what regimental adjutants in Prussia did, and Tom came to believe they must do almost everything. Of course there was Corporal Stevens to do the paperwork and Sergeant Winters to handle supply, but von Jagerhof did almost everything else, and what he didn't do Kemper did. As a result, Tom had a lot of time on his hands, but he put it to good use. He spent most of each day in the headquarters tent with von Jagerhof's books, the supply of which was always growing with new ones from Prussia. The later ones concerned artillery, which the adjutant explained by saying that

Prussian officers were expected to master all arms regardless of their speciality. Tom had already learned the metric system and had always liked mathematics, physics, and geometry, so he attacked the subject vigorously. His German was good enough by now to enable him to get along without much help. There was a big table to work on and a plentiful supply of paper for exercises and diagrams. He would sometimes get so absorbed that Hauser would have to bring him his dinner, and he still had sessions with von Jagerhof almost every night.

Tom was working at the table one day when his adjutant came in with a package that turned out to be a set of books with fine leather binding and gold lettering. "A present for you, sir," he said with a smile as he set them on the table, "and they're in English, too."

Tom took the first volume and saw the set was on brigade infantry and artillery tactics translated from the German. "Well, Captain," he said, "I surely do thank you, but there's no need for any present, and they look like they cost a lot."

"Oh, not too much. The translation is just out. I happened to learn of it, and thought you'd like something in your own language. It's the best. The faculty at our Potsdam War College wrote it."

"Well, you can just keep them and I'll use them like the others. You don't owe me anything."

"Oh, I beg to differ with you, sir. I owe you very much."

Tom started to scoff, but the Prussian headed him off. "I came a stranger and a foreigner, and you took me in. Here I am, a regimental adjutant soon to be a major." He nodded significantly. "I know whom I owe it to."

"Oh, Captain, you don't owe me a thing! You were the only officer left after I left the company, and then, well, you were just the best man for adjutant, and Colonel Rivers agreed with me." Tom got up and slapped him on the back.

It was von Jagerhof's turn to scoff. "Oh, but, Major! A foreigner can always expect prejudice. It's only human nature. You'd meet with it in Prussia, or anyplace else, for that matter. There's some among the officers of this regiment. Some of them didn't like it when I became adjutant, although nobody dared say anything to you. And then there's your American prejudice against nobility."

Tom laughed. "I won't pretend it was just my good nature. I expected to learn a lot from you, and I haven't been disappointed. I owe you a lot more than you owe me. If it hadn't been for you and your books, I'd have made a mess of it when General Carter put me through the mill at division exercises."

"The books probably helped, but that dictionary of mine would have done anything I did."

Tom didn't agree, but von Jagerhof cut off argument by taking his leave. "Excuse me, sir, but I must see Sergeant Kemper about something."

"Well, I'm much obliged to you for these books, anyhow," said Tom as he took up the first volume again. "They'll entertain me for a long time."

The Prussian was going out of the tent when he heard it. He stopped like he had run into a brick wall and looked at Tom incredulously. "Entertainment!" he exclaimed, then went on.

That was what it really amounted to, though. Tom found the new books a sheer pleasure. The problems and exercises they contained were a challenge that left a glow of satisfaction when he worked them out, especially the ones on artillery, which was still new to him. He worked on them hour after hour, and Hauser would have been bringing him his supper as well as his dinner if he hadn't drawn the line and insisted that the *Herr Major* come to his quarters for it.

One day when he was alone in the tent and in the middle of a particularly absorbing exercise on artillery deployment, Tom looked up to see General Carter standing before him. He jumped to his feet, scattering papers in all directions, and came to attention. "I-I'm sorry, sir," he stammered. "I just didn't notice the general come in!" He had never been so mortified in his life, standing there with his coat unbuttoned, shirttail half out, and papers scattered all over the place.

The general looked amused. "It looks like I caught you buried in paperwork."

"Yes, sir. I just wasn't paying attention."

Carter began to look at some of the papers. "Hmm. What's this you're doing, Major?"

"Oh, just some exercises from some books Captain von Jagerhof gave me." Tom laughed apologetically. "He's such a good adjutant that I have a lot of time on my hands—" It sounded so lame he cut himself off.

"Humph. You're the first regimental commander I ever heard say that." He picked up the book Tom was using, scrutinized the open pages, then put a finger in the place, turned to the title page, and looked at it. To Tom's relief, this gave him enough time to tuck his shirttail in and button his coat.

Carter put the book down and looked at the lettering on the others. Suddenly he looked up. "Let's see what you were doing when I came in."

He came around the table as Tom began a hurried search for the right paper, a topographical map he had drawn himself. He couldn't find it for the life of him and mumbled apologies. Finally he found it on the floor. "Here we are, sir."

Carter took the map. "Let's see now," he said, frowning as he looked at it. Tom showed him the exercise in the book, a complicated one involving the displacement of a battery of guns across rugged country to support advancing infantry and going into firing position at specific intervals. It was difficult to place the guns so the gunners could communicate and still have an adequate field of fire, particularly with grape and canister, and he had done a lot of erasing and redrawing. The paper looked like it had been used to wipe the floor or something, and he was heartily ashamed of it.

It didn't seem to bother Carter. He studied it at length, referring back to the book from time to time. Suddenly he gave it back. "You're almost done with it, so finish and I'll just watch."

Tom was still flustered, but once he got to work he settled down and finished it, thankful that he didn't have to do any more erasing. "Here you are, sir," he said as he gave the map back to Carter.

The general looked at the map, frowning and tracing the moves with his finger as he looked back and forth between it and the book. Suddenly he put it down, grinned, and exclaimed, "Good work, Major! I'd have had trouble with that one!"

"Oh, the general's just not used to doing things like that on paper. He'd have no trouble with it in the field."

The grin stayed on the foxy little face. "You know, Major, exercises like this are nearest a man can come to the real thing, and they sure save wear and tear on the troops and equipment." He looked at Tom quizzically. "But why are you studying brigade tactics, and artillery at that?"

"Oh, I've finished everything I could get hold of on regimental infantry tactics, and, well, Captain von Jagerhof gave me these books, and . . . I . . . didn't have anything else to do." He was afraid Carter would think he was overly ambitious.

The general looked at him strangely. "This is the way you spend your spare time, Major?"

"Yes, sir. It keeps me occupied, and . . . and I sort of enjoy it." He laughed to try to hide his embarrassment.

Carter nodded thoughtfully. "I guess Rivers is right about you," he said half to himself.

Tom wasn't sure he heard it correctly. "Beg pardon, sir?"

The general disregarded his question. "Let's go out and look around your camp."

"Yes, sir. Of course, sir."

Tom got his hat and they went out. As they walked around the camp, Carter looked everything over and even stopped to talk with some of the men. He never said anything, but Tom saw a thousand things wrong. Men were going around with their coats unbuttoned and caps awry. The huts looked uneven and weatherworn. Their chimneys were crooked, and to top it off, one of the kegs the men often put at the top to give better draft caught fire. The inmates turned out with a great clamor to push it off to the ground with a long forked pole one of them ran and got. Everybody was jubilant when it was all over and the hut saved. Carter chuckled about it and said it was a good thing they got it off so quickly, because the whole shebang might have burned down.

When they got back to the headquarters tent, Tom was surprised when Carter said, "You've got the best camp I've seen so far, Major."

"Thank you, sir, but I'm afraid I can't claim much credit. I've got the best adjutant and sergeant major in the whole army, I'll bet." He nodded emphatically. "Like that forked pole business. It was Sergeant Kemper's idea that each company have one leaning against the first hut on the right in every company street." He chuckled. "If they don't put that one back, he'll take the hide off them."

"He's a gem, Kemper is, and von Jagerhof, too," agreed Carter.

Tom pointed to the books and papers. "That's why I'm able to spend so much time with that sort of thing." He picked up one of the books. "This set is in English and it's a lot easier."

"Oh, you read German?"

"Pretty well, but I have to ask Captain von Jagerhof or Sergeant Kemper about something every once in a while."

Carter nodded. "Well, I wish all my officers spent their spare time like you do. A lot of them drink too much commissary whiskey, or chase women all night and sleep half the day."

They laughed.

"Well, I never cared for whiskey, and I'm not much of a woman chaser either," said Tom.

Carter pretended to give a confidence. "Don't chase them, and maybe they'll chase you," he said in a stage whisper. They had another laugh; then Carter said, "Well, I've got to go, Major."

"Thank you for visiting us, sir," said Tom as they went outside.

Carter's orderly came up with his horse, and the general mounted. Tom saluted and Carter returned it airily. "We'll be seeing you, Major," he said as he wheeled to ride away.

Tom went back in the tent and went to work on another exercise. He never knew if Carter's visit had anything to do with it, but about a week later Rivers called him and Billy to brigade headquarters, where he gave them new commissions. Tom was now a colonel and Billy a captain. After the handshakes and congratulations, they left and, on the way back to camp, stopped in a saloon and had some beer to celebrate.

When von Jagerhof came to Tom's cabin that night for their regular study session, he had something beside handshakes and congratulations. It was another present, a pair of the largest field glasses Tom had ever seen, in a fine leather case.

Tom wasn't going to take them. "Oh, no, Captain! This is too much! Those books and now these!" He shook his head emphatically. "And I've never given you anything."

"Oh, I beg to differ with you, sir! But for your generosity, I'd still be—"

Tom cut him off with feigned severity. "Now, let's not go through with that again! It's like I told you—"

The Prussian interrupted in his turn and thrust the glasses on Tom. "Please, sir! Take them! I have no use for them. I've never taken them out of my baggage until now."

Tom was sorely tempted. Ever since the expedition with Davis, he had been held back from buying a pair only by their astronomical cost. He took the glasses and found them surprisingly light. "Well, I'll tell you, Captain; I'll take them on loan. They'll still be yours."

"Fine, sir!" laughed von Jagerhof. "That's the way we'll do it, only just don't ever try to give them back!"

Tom was bemused. "Oh, I don't know about that." He took the glasses out of their case. They were finely made and finished in dull gray so they wouldn't gleam in the sun.

"They're the finest glasses in the world," said von Jagerhof. "They're made by Zeiss of Jena, in Thuringia."

"I'll bet they cost a lot," ventured Tom.

"About three months' pay, I'd say," was the casual reply.

Tom promptly put the glasses back in their case and thrust them back. "No, sir! It's out of the question! That's too much—too, too much. It's like jewelry or something!"

Von Jagerhof stepped back and wouldn't take them. "Oh, that's just what they'd cost you over here, if you could ever find any. They wouldn't cost nearly that much in Prussia, and they didn't cost me anything."

Tom still held the glasses out, but a little doubtfully. "How's that?"

"Oh, my family's well connected in the military. The glasses were a departure present from the head of the Zeiss firm himself, at a little party we had in Berlin before I left. That's one way he makes sure of army contracts."

Tom laughed. "Well, I guess you do things over there about the way we do here." He doubted if anybody in the whole army had glasses like these and was weakening rapidly. He withdrew them unconsciously.

Von Jagerhof pressed his advantage. "Take them, sir! Please take them! They'll just be wasted going around in my luggage, and somebody's likely to steal them sooner or later."

"But suppose you need them sometime? You may be—"

"Oh, if I ever do, I'll just write a letter and get another pair just like I got these."

Tom surrendered. "Oh, all right then," he laughed. "But," he went on as he pretended to fix his adjutant with a baleful look, "You've got to agree to take them back if you ever need any in a hurry!" He couldn't help smiling.

The Prussian laughed. "Agreed! Only don't ever expect such a pressing need to arise!"

They made a ceremony of shaking hands on it, and Tom hung the glasses on the wall. He noticed that there was another strap around the case, probably for fastening it to the belt so it would hold tightly against a man's chest.

After that they got out books and went to work as usual, but Tom couldn't keep his eyes from straying to the glasses on the wall. He had never imagined he would ever have any like them and itched to try them out.

The very next morning Tom rode to the top of the highest hill there was near camp. A squadron of cavalry was exercising in a field so far away he could hardly tell there were men on the horses. He had a little trouble focusing the glasses, but once he did, it was like the horsemen were within a hundred yards and he should be able to hear the hoofbeats. He could even tell they were armed with the new repeating carbines by the shortness of the barrel and the thickness of the breech.

He was like a boy with a new toy and stayed out observing the animate and inanimate until it occurred to him that Hauser wouldn't like it if he was late for his dinner.

It wasn't long before von Jagerhof's commission as major came through, and when it did the fellow demonstrated his largess was unlimited. He wanted to get some beer for the men so they could celebrate, too. Tom told him to go ahead and was astonished when a big wagon came out from town one afternoon with four barrels of beer that surely held a hundred gallons each. The provider said it was imported from Munich, in Bavaria, where they made the best beer in the world. Tom remarked that it must have cost a lot and offered to help pay for it.

Von Jagerhof wouldn't hear of it. "A small thing, Colonel, a small thing. I'm not dependent on my own resources, you know."

Tom gathered he meant his family had a lot of money, which was the way it was supposed to be with the nobility. Sergeant Grim and the Germans from Billy's company took charge of the preparations. They set the barrels up on the drill field, knocked together some crude benches, and gathered wood for fires.

Late in the afternoon the festivities began. When suppertime came there was another surprise; a wagon loaded with barrels of sausages and loaves of fresh white bread. The sausages were small and delicious. The Germans called them "bratwurst," and von Jagerhof said he had ordered both them and the beer from Baltimore, where there were a lot of Germans. The men put the sausages on sticks and roasted them over the fires, then ate them with the bread and washed it all down with the beer. Tom wondered what it all had cost and guessed money didn't mean anything to his adjutant.

The men had a roaring good time. They proclaimed they had never eaten such delicious sausage or drunk such good beer. They toasted Major von Jagerhof as the best adjutant in the whole army and hoped it wouldn't be long before he got another promotion and gave them another such celebration.

Tom wished he had thought of something like this for his last promotion, even if it had only been a few kegs of cheap beer. God only knew how many of these poor fellows would be alive a few months from now, after the spring campaign got well under way. He felt sad as he watched them celebrate and couldn't join in until Sergeant Kemper got him in with Ab, Cole, and the other survivors of his old platoon.

# 45

Early one evening late in January a courier arrived with orders for the regiment to get ready to march in twelve hours, which would be early the following morning. It was understood to be a part of a general movement by the whole army and had been rumored for several days, but no one had believed it.

They hadn't because even the lowliest private in the regiment knew what shape the roads were in this time of year and that, if it rained, the army wouldn't get a few miles before it would be mired in the mud. And rain it almost certainly would. That was about all it did in Virginia during the winter. Of course it snowed sometimes and the ground frequently froze, but thaws almost always restored its normally waterlogged condition in a few days.

Tom knew supplying the men would be impossible if they got more than a few miles. Even the infantry would have hard going, and the wagons wouldn't be able to go except at a snail's pace, not to mention the artillery. Because of this he had rations instead of the reserve ammunition supply loaded on the regiment's wagons, so his men wouldn't have to go hungry once the three days' cooked rations they were carrying ran out. The men could be depended on to keep these wagons going because they knew they would go hungry if they didn't.

Leaving the ammunition was risky and he would be in for it if he was found out, but he wasn't going to see his men suffer. Any fool could see they wouldn't get far enough to see any Rebels except maybe a few cavalry scouts. He had the ammunition put in huts like his own that had permanent roofs, because no one would expect to find it there. He took the added risk of leaving a platoon out of Herb Parker's Martin County company to guard the camp and told the men to lie low unless someone with plunder on his mind came around.

Although it wasn't really necessary, Tom inspected the companies one by one during the evening, mainly to stop the cursing and complaining for a while. The men didn't think much of General Burnside to begin with, and this topped it off. It would have been a lot worse if they had expected to get far enough to be gone very long.

Just after dawn the next morning, Tom assembled the companies on the drill field near camp and went before the whole regiment for the first time as its commander. It was a strange feeling to stand before nearly a thousand men and know they would obey any command he gave them. There was his old company, with Billy's slender form at its head and Ab's lanky frame towering above the others. Berserker Dan Howard, with his cap perched on his mop of red hair, looked so much like Jim Polson from a distance that Tom thought of Burk, Johnny, and others who were gone.

A deep hush settled over the ranks, and the men looked at Tom expectantly. Suddenly a sharp, decisive voice barked commands and broke the silence. It was his own, and the men made precise, concerted movements like puppets worked by the same string.

The skies were threatening, so he sent the wagons to the front where they were less likely to get mired, then deployed the regiment in a column so wide it took up the whole road. That way the men do less trampling in one another's tracks and the mud wouldn't be quite so bad. The couriers and other horsemen that would be moving along the column could take to the woods and fields along the road. When everything was ready, Tom took his horse from Hauser, rode to the head of the column, and began the march.

The going wasn't so bad at first because the rain held off and the road was better near town. After the regiment marched south through town and assembled with the rest of the brigade, the road got worse and it began to rain. While the men were getting out their ponchos and putting them on, Tom rode up to the head of the column and asked Rivers what he thought of the move. All he got was a snort of disgust and query if he had something besides ammunition in his wagons. None of the other regimental commanders did, and Rivers hoped he had one who had some sense. When Tom replied that he guessed he had some sense, Rivers laughed and said he could always count on him.

The rain continued and what everybody expected happened. The brigade, minus its wagons and guns, managed to reach the place where the division was to assemble, but it was the only one that did. After waiting two days, during which it rained most of the time and the men huddled fireless and miserable in their little tents, Rivers got word to give it up and go back to camp. Because the brigade's wagons were still back there someplace, along with its artillery, Rivers had to come around and tell Tom to have Sergeant Winters issue rations to the other three regiments and promised to have them made up.

On the march back, the men saw why none of the other brigades made it. Except for its infantry, the brigade following was completely mired down. Tom had never heard such profanity, most of it directed at General Burnside and whoever had put him in command. Many of the infantrymen were carrying their shoes and going barefoot in the freezing mud because they couldn't keep them on. Some of the men joked about seeing a team of mules sunk so deeply in the mud that only their ears showed. Tom never saw anything like that, but it was bad enough.

While they stood waiting in the cold, sleeting rain, Tom noticed that only his men had ponchos. Not even the other regiments of the brigade had any, and there would be no fires at night hot enough to dry the men out. Rivers's guns and wagons were stuck along with the rest. After a while, he took his infantry off the road to get around the jam and told the artillerymen and teamsters to get back the best they could. They immediately protested they would never make it, so he told Tom and Colonel Pater of the Pennsylvania regiment to leave a company behind to help.

Tom chose Billy's company because it brought up the rear. He didn't think the men would like it, but they seemed to take it as a lark and were left behind laughing and joking about how they would get to sleep in the wagons at night and ride in them, too, if the ground froze, which it probably would. Tom knew all of them couldn't get in the wagons even if the brigade quartermaster would allow it, which was highly doubtful, and that a freeze hard enough to let them ride was highly unlikely, but he didn't say anything.

Von Jagerhof remarked about this and confessed himself unable to understand why Billy's men were taking it like they were, because they surely knew the same things. Tom said he couldn't understand it either, unless it was getting out of the monotony of the march. Neither of them could see how digging and heaving guns and wagons out of the mud could be preferred to marching. Herb Parker had joined them in the meantime, and when he said understanding the men was about like understanding women they got a big laugh out of it. Tom gave him a broad wink before he went on to let him know he understood whom he meant.

After his men had toiled through the mud for a while, Tom asked Rivers if he could take them off the road and go cross country. He had loaded them with enough rations to last until the wagons got back. The colonel said to go ahead if he thought it would be easier. It wasn't easier, but it was shorter, and Tom's men were back in camp half a day before the others, but it took so long for them to clean up that they had little idle time until dark. The Martin County men who had guarded the camp said no one had come near the place while the regiment was gone.

Billy came in with his men two days later. They were bedraggled and plastered with mud, but strangely exhilarated. Tom couldn't understand it until Billy confided that the brigade quartermaster had been so grateful for their good work that when they reached his depot he had given Billy enough whiskey to provide each of his men with a stiff drink if he wanted one. He had promptly doled it out and made them drink it before they started away, and the tipplers always said commissary whiskey was potent stuff. Some of the Germans said it wasn't as strong as good schnapps or Steinhager, though.

The day after the regiment returned to camp, Tom got a note from Carolyn inviting him to call that evening. When he arrived she greeted him a little wanly, but her words were cheery. "I'm glad you got stuck in the mud!"

Tom laughed. "So am I. I guess the Rebels didn't even try to come out. No one saw anything of them, anyhow."

"They had too much sense," chimed in Martha. "You'd think your general—whoever he is now—would have known better, too."

"It's General Burnside, Auntie," said Carolyn.

"Oh, they change so fast I can't keep track of them!" replied Martha with a laugh.

Martha soon retired and Tom sat on the couch with Carolyn. "Will your father be home this evening?" he asked.

Carolyn shook her head. "No. He sent word not to expect him."

"I wanted to talk to him about our 'mud march,' but I can't honestly say I'm sorry he'll be gone." He reached for her hand, but she evaded him without seeming to.

"Tell me about it," she said with transparent gaiety.

He told her a few of the most humorous episodes. She seemed to enjoy them, but her laughter didn't ring true. He reached for her hand again, and this time there was no doubt about her evasion. "What's the matter, Carolyn?" he asked.

She shook her head. "Nothing, Tom. It's just that we found out last time where that sort of thing leads to."

"I'm sorry about that, Carolyn. I guess I just got carried away."

"And I did, too." She looked at him sadly. "You know, Tom, we're dangerous for one another."

"Oh, I wouldn't say dangerous," he replied jocularly.

"Maybe not for you. It's not that kind of danger." She looked at him searchingly. "Tell me, Tom, are you engaged or anything?"

He was taken aback and didn't know what to say for a moment. "Well, no, not exactly—"

She interrupted. "You are, or you'd just have said no."

"No, Carolyn, I'm not, but I do have an understanding—"

She broke in again. "With the red-haired woman?"

Her astuteness startled him. "Yes, if I'm still around after the war, I'm supposed to look her up, and then, well, maybe. But we aren't engaged."

She sighed. "Do you love her, Tom?"

He was trapped and his agony was acute. "Well, when she was here, I . . . I did, but since I've been seeing you—"

She cut him off again, her eyes glowing. "Do you love me, Tom?"

He leaned toward her. "Yes, darling, I do." He tried to kiss her, but she held him off.

"You're just saying that because you're with me. If you were with her, you'd tell her that."

Her tone was accusatory and it nettled him. "I don't believe I'm as fickle as all that," he said shortly. "Men can change their minds just like women, you know." He saw a tear stealing down her cheek and was emboldened to take a shot in the dark. "Do you love me, Carolyn?"

Her lips trembled. "Yes, I'm afraid I do, and that's why I'm leaving."

He was astonished. "Leaving? Because you love me?"

She nodded sadly. "I've written Uncle Ted to come for me. He was Mother's brother. I'll go back to Kentucky with him and stay . . . until the war's over, I guess."

"But, Carolyn! It doesn't make sense! You leave me because you love me!"

She was on the point of tears and he was able to slip an arm around her, but she wouldn't submit to his embrace. "It's the only thing to do," she sobbed.

He let her go and sat back. "Please explain it to me, Carolyn. I can't understand it."

"Oh, Tom! If I stay here, I'll just become your doxy! I won't be able to help myself." She wiped her eyes. "I found that out the last time you were here."

"But, darling, if we love one another—"

She interrupted. "We're not sure. It might turn out to be lust—just lust."

"We can be married. Will you—"

She interrupted again. "Oh no! If it *is* love, and if we were married, it'd be like it was with Marcus, only worse, much worse."

"Worse? How?"

She had to sob a little. "Because . . . because he wasn't like you. He was careful."

Tom tried to speak, but she headed him off. "I found that out when you marched this last time. I couldn't sleep. I could just see you lying all bloody and dead somewhere." She stopped and cried, "Oh, it was terrible! I'd get up and walk the floor—"

"But, Carolyn, it's not that bad! It's not suicide or anything!"

It was a little while before she spoke again. "Oh, I didn't tell you." She sat erect and regained some of her composure. "Auntie and I go to the hospital almost every day. The day after you were here last we visited a man with a bad saber cut who was at that bridge where you were not so long ago, when the Rebels nearly got to it and you fought them." She sighed and looked at him almost accusingly. "We got to talking about how he had been wounded, and, oh, what he told us about what you did, and some of the other men spoke up—"

Tom cut her off. "Oh, those are just soldiers' tales—"

She shook her head. "No, no, I'd heard it before, things Father said—and others, about times before that."

Tom took her hand and she let him. "Darling, I'll stop doing things like that if you stay. I'll have reason to be . . . be more careful."

She let him kiss her on the cheek. Then she shook her head. "No, you wouldn't," she said sorrowfully. "You couldn't. You're just that sort of man. Everybody says you are." She looked at him sadly. "They say you just aren't afraid of anything, that . . . that it's almost like you're trying to throw your life away."

"Oh, Carolyn!" he scoffed. "I'm not that bad! You should know how it is. A fellow's a little careless a time or two, and he gets a reputation—"

"No . . . no, Tom, it's not that; you *know* it isn't!"

This was the time to tell her why he had been so reckless, but if he told her about Sally, then Mary, she would think he was a featherhead. Before he could say anything, she got to her feet. "You'd better go, Tom. We'd better not see each other again."

He pleaded, "Please, Carolyn, don't leave." He reached out and took both her hands. "Reconsider, please."

She stepped back when he got up from the couch but didn't withdraw her hands. "No, Tom, no—I've made up my mind. I'm leaving. Uncle Ted has a big plantation. It's wonderful there, peaceful and quiet. I won't have my heart torn out by the roots like here, every time you march—and Father, too. Uncle Ted keeps my horse for me, the one he gave me when I was a girl. I'll ride around the woods and fields, and maybe I'll find peace."

Tom was hurt and angry. "You want to forget all about me, don't you?"

She shook her head. "No, I don't want to forget you. I'll always think of you." Her eyes were great wells of grief.

He tried to embrace her, but she fended him off and went on. "I just don't want to be around when . . . when they bring you in dead—" She snatched her hands away, buried her face in her handkerchief, and sobbed her anguish.

He could do nothing but stand and wait for her to stop. "After . . . after the war?" he finally asked.

She stopped weeping and looked up, dabbing her eyes. Their ethereal blue was nearly obscured by redness and swelling. "For you, Tom, there won't be any 'after the war,' " she said tragically.

He managed to scoff. "Oh, I'm going to surprise a lot of people! I'll still be here!"

She slowly shook her head. "No, if you survive this one, there'll be another one somewhere, and you'll go."

He snorted indignantly. "I guess you've got a crystal ball someplace! You must, because you didn't read my palm."

"Tom—oh, Tom—you won't be able to help it! It's your nature! You were made for it!"

"How much of this did your father tell you?" He demanded.

"I asked him, Tom, and he told me," she said tremulously.

"I must remember to thank him for it!" he said bitterly.

"Don't get angry at Father, Tom. He didn't say anything . . . anything bad about you. He admires you. He likes you, and I had to drag it out of him. After what those men at the hospital said, I had to know."

He gave up. "There's no point in arguing with a seeress, I guess." He started for his hat and coat. "You want me to go, so that's what I'll do."

She stood watching him while he put on his coat, looking like she desperately wanted to say something but couldn't. When he was buttoning up, she heaved a great, sobbing sigh. "Oh, it's awful . . . awful, but it's better this way."

He nodded as he buttoned. "You're right. It'll all be over, and you'd best forget me as soon as you can." He finished and took his hat. "Good-bye, Carolyn. I won't expect to hear from you, or see you, ever again."

She only stood there gazing at him as if she was trying to impress his image on her memory, looking indescribably sad and beautiful. She was still there when he went out the door. He thought he heard her gasp his name, but he didn't turn back.

# 46

When Tom got his next letter from Mary, he was glad he still had her, but the first few lines gave him a scare, because she had found out about him and Carolyn. She went on to say that although she was awfully hurt at first and pretty angry for a while, she had soon gotten over it. She knew how it was with him and really didn't mind sharing him with another woman as long as she could have him when she wanted, and hoped it was like that. After all, she didn't have any claim on him, and that was the way she had wanted it. She still loved him and proceeded to express herself in such explicit terms that he decided this was another letter of hers he would have to burn.

He knew better than to deny he had been seeing another woman, so he wrote back that what she had heard hadn't amounted to anything and was all over anyhow. Without actually saying so, he made out that it had never been anything but social and implied that military etiquette had been behind it. Whoever had written back about it wouldn't know any better than that. His conscience bothered him, but only a little. He guessed it was a lot more flexible than it used to be, and then everything was supposed to be fair in love and war.

He wondered who had tattled on him. It probably hadn't been Herb Parker. He wasn't that sort of a fellow, and knew he would be the first suspect. Blakey was more likely, but then almost anyone in the Martin County company could have done it, or even someone from an adjoining county. It might have been told in confidence and then talked around until Mary heard it.

The weeks went by with no more letters from Mary. He wasn't much worried at first and went on writing as usual. After a time his letters became more urgent and inquiring. Thinking his affair with Carolyn might be at the bottom of it after all, he finally wrote a letter going through the whole thing again, but he really wasn't any more honest about it than he had been before. Still he got no reply.

He finally went to Herb Parker about it. The fellow wasn't much of a talker any time, and this time he was no talker at all. Tom was sure he knew something, but he couldn't get it out of him. He tried everything but physical violence, and all he accomplished was to make

Parker mad. It wasn't that he said or did anything, but he got pale and abrupt and wouldn't look at Tom when he talked. Tom saw he had gone too far and apologized, excusing himself on grounds that he was afraid Mary might be in trouble because of him. Parker knew he meant she might be pregnant and came around a little. He said there wasn't anything to worry about. Mary was still at Shoals with Eliza, and he would do what he could to get her to write.

It was the middle of April and the spring campaign was about to begin before Tom finally got a letter from Mary. He was in the headquarters tent when it came and started reading it there. She began by saying she hadn't been able to get up enough nerve to write him, although she should have done it a long time ago. The reason she was finally writing was because she was getting married in a week.

After he read that, Tom had to leave the headquarters tent and go to his cabin. He never remembered anything about going there. He just found himself sitting on his bunk with the letter in his hand.

Mary went on to say that it wasn't because she was pregnant. She was marrying the man Eliza had gotten to manage the store and livery stable back last December when they left to see him and Herb. He was such a good man and did so well at it that Eliza had just about turned everything over to him, because a man could do such things a lot better than any woman ever could.

His name was John Stillwell and he was from Terre Haute. He had tried to enlist but had been turned down because he had lost the sight of one eye in a boyhood accident. He had clerked in stores ever since he was old enough to work, which was why he could manage Eliza's business so well.

Mary went on to say that a woman had to look out for herself, which was why she was marrying John. He was a good, sober, hard-working man, the kind a woman could always depend on, and would undoubtedly do well in business. She didn't know whether she still loved Tom or not but was afraid she did. She would be all right, though, as long as she never saw him again, and she hoped for the sake of both of them that she wouldn't. She went on to tell him what a fine fellow he was, and how she had enjoyed being with him when she and Eliza had been there.

She concluded by saying that she had truly loved him, but that a woman had to think of something beside that. Women couldn't get along by themselves like men could, and she hoped he would understand.

Tom understood all right. John Stillwell would be around when the war was over, but she didn't think Tom Traylor would. He let the letter fall and stared unseeingly at the floor.

A great bitterness came over him. She was probably right, and he really didn't care anymore if she was. He was back to nothing again.

# 47

It was a warm May morning and the spring campaign was well under way. Late in April, the army had taken the offensive under a new general who liked to be called "Fighting Joe" Hooker. It had moved southwest, then marched and maneuvered for several days before taking up what was supposed to be an advantageous position.

The Rebels had done nothing but put up a show of resistance until the evening before, when a surprise attack on the right flank led by the Rebel general Jackson had destroyed an entire corps. Jackson had attacked late in the day, and probably only the fall of darkness had saved the rest of the army. During the night there had been much moving around and the corps had formed a new line facing north. The men had slept on their arms if they slept at all.

General Carter's division held the extreme left of the new line, and he had sent Rivers's brigade out as a flank guard, so it was isolated from the rest of the division. Tom's regiment was on the brigade's left, and the nature of the country made its position very dangerous. The entire corps was in a wilderness of brush, briers, thickets, and stunted trees, with a few patches of forest scattered about. Some places were almost impenetrable, and visibility was generally only a few yards. The men knew that a mass of yelling Rebels could burst on them at any time, like had happened to that corps the evening before, and because they had to depend on their ears more than their eyes, they were unusually quiet.

Although he was on horseback, Tom could see little more than the men. Listening was really more important than looking, so he didn't ride around much except to visit his pickets once in a while. They were all within a hundred yards, because sending them any farther would put them completely out of sight and maybe even get them lost.

Everything was quiet, but a threat hung in the air. The enemy had the initiative and could be counted on to make the most of it. What bothered Tom more than anything else was that the game of blindman's buff they were playing was one-sided. The Rebels had men born and raised in this part of the country who knew its interminable waste of thickets and brush traversed by long-unused roads like a book. Their surprise flank attack of the evening before had showed that.

During one of his visits to his pickets, Tom rode out in front of the line and saw a hillock with some sizable trees on it. One of them was unusually tall, and he should be able to see a good distance from near its top and put those Zeiss glasses to use. He didn't have to worry about leaving the regiment. He wouldn't be far and von Jagerhof could handle it as well as he could anyhow. He told the nearest picket what he was going to do and asked him to pass the word along, then rode out to the hillock.

He tied the reins to the tallest tree, stood in the saddle, and caught a limb. He pulled himself up, then climbed from limb to limb, being careful to stay close to the trunk in case the Rebels had scouts out there in the brush.

Before he was very high, Tom saw he wouldn't be able to see very far to the north because the gradual slope that ran up from the south ended with a short, steep ridge a few hundred yards in that direction. The line faced north, though, so there was little danger the Rebels would come from there, and less chance they would surprise anyone if they did. Rivers might move the brigade north and deploy along that ridge when he learned it was there.

The view to the south was excellent from where he first stopped, so he decided to make the most of it, although a flanking move from the west was the greater danger. The naked eye showed little beyond the brigade's line, which showed up as splotches of dingy blue in the growth, so he unslung his glasses and began to search beyond it.

He could see no movement despite a careful search. A few companies could be hiding out there, but only if they weren't moving. About half a mile directly south, a winding creek ran to the west at the bottom of the slope that came down from the ridge behind him. It aroused his suspicion, so he studied it carefully. The near bank was low and only fringed by growth, but the far one rose steeply as a bluff fronting a densely overgrown plateau, which extended for about five hundred yards between two horseshoe bends. There were no men in the creek unless they were hunkered down, and they wouldn't be doing that. The plateau was so heavily overgrown that all he could tell was that there was no movement on it. A wide, dry ravine bisected the plateau from the south, but it was empty, too. There was no immediate threat to the brigade's rear.

As he brought his glasses down, he thought he saw movement in the brush close behind the line and tried to focus on it. He couldn't see any, but he saw something else. A road paralleled the brigade's rear by only a few hundred feet. It was pretty wide but hadn't been used in so long it was easy to overlook. No maps he had seen showed it, and probably only the Rebels knew it was there. If the Rebels came, it would be along that road.

Foliage blocked his view to the west, so he moved about in the tree until he could see in that direction. He found the road and discovered he could follow it easily because it angled south after a short distance and he was always able to pick it up again if he lost it in the growth. He followed it to the southwest and found it empty until it reached a patch of taller trees a great distance away. There he saw something. He focused carefully and made out the advance of a dense gray column emerging from the patch of trees.

He had to know its length, so he followed it back beyond the trees, where he could really see it better, because the road angled more to the south and went up a gradual incline in plain view. The column ended before the road disappeared over the rise, and he judged it was only a division. If it was the advance of something larger, another column would be close behind. He studied the road behind it as long as he dared but saw nothing.

It wasn't hard to understand. The Rebels wouldn't send out a division by itself unless it was only a feint for a big attack someplace else, probably to the north where the rest of the army was. A division was enough to destroy the brigade, though, unless it fell back on Carter's division and he wheeled to face west. The way it was, they would both be caught in the flank, and although Carter might get off without too much harm, the brigade would be wiped out. What was worse, it would be certain to draw attention from where the big attack would come in and might result in a major defeat for the whole army.

Whoever commanded that Rebel division was undoubtedly scouting the brigade's exact position, if he hadn't done so already, and Tom knew precisely how he would move when he learned what it was. He would stay on the road as long as he could. When he deployed to attack, he would advance guiding his center on the road and his right on that creek to the south as the only way to keep control in country like this.

Rivers had to be warned of what was coming and word sent to Carter as soon as possible. Tom stowed his glasses and started down the tree. He had just reached the next limb when a single rifle shot cracked out to the left front, about where the center of the brigade was, followed by a hurried command to face about and a burst of firing.

Tom couldn't see in that direction until he worked his way around the tree directly over his horse, and by that time the shooting had stopped. All he could see was smoke hovering above the brigade's line about where the center was, but as he looked, he saw half a dozen men in butternut gray dash across the road and into the growth on the other side. No one on the ground could have seen them. Those who had fired had only aimed at the smoke of the single shot, if at anything. Once across the road, the Rebels turned and raced west through the growth parallel to it. As soon as they were out of sight, they would go back to the road and hotfoot it back to the column they were scouting for now that the Yankees would be on the lookout for them.

Tom was in such a hurry that he jumped for the saddle while ten feet above it. He landed astride, but his horse was so startled that it tore the reins loose and stampeded. He nearly lost his seat before he could get his feet in the stirrups and bring the animal under control. In the meantime, the pickets were called in and the regiments faced about, but it was done unevenly, like each was acting on its own.

When he came close to the brigade's center, Tom saw men and horses clustered about someone lying on the ground. It was Rivers, and there was a great dark stain on his chest. A man on horseback made such a good target in the growth that one of those Rebel scouts hadn't been able to pass it up.

Anders was bending over Rivers, and two of the regimental commanders, Pater and Hartley, were talking excitedly with Major Cunningham, commander of the brigade artillery. A few others stood around, all as excited as they were. They almost jumped out of their boots when someone shouted in German from the far right and there was another burst of firing. Some of Billy's men must have caught sight of those Rebel scouts.

"Colonel, sir!" shouted Tom as he flung himself off his horse. "You've been shot!"

Rivers looked up. The pallor of death was stealing over his face, but his eyes still showed understanding.

Tom went on. "A Rebel division's moving on our right flank, along an old road down there! It'll be here in . . . in half an hour! We've got to do something!"

The group acted like a bolt of lightning had struck.

"Oh, my God!" gasped someone.

Rivers forced himself up on his elbows. "Are you sure? How do you know?" he asked weakly. Blood ran from the corners of his mouth to stain his beard and streak his neck.

"Yes, sir, I'm sure! I climbed a tree back there and saw them coming with my glasses!"

Rivers's head swayed uncertainly and he had trouble keeping his eyes focused. "Just one . . . one division?!" was the broken query.

"Yes, sir, I made sure of that. It's only a feint, but it'll wipe us out unless we do something!"

Another bolt of lightning struck the group as Rivers fell back, gasping and gurgling in his throat. He coughed blood, then said faintly, "I'm done for . . . son." His eyes welled tears, and his face twisted. "Oh, who . . . who'll take care of my little Carrie?"

Tom felt like it was his father. He knelt and took Rivers's hand. "I'll take care of her, sir! I'll marry her if she'll have me!" There was no time for this sort of thing, so he regained control of himself and asked, "But what are we going to do? We're going to be taken in the flank unless—"

Rivers interrupted. "You . . . you take command . . . son," he faltered as more blood ran from his mouth and his eyes dimmed. His hand tightened convulsively on Tom's and then relaxed.

"Why . . . why, I can't!" he protested, although he knew Rivers no longer heard. "I'm junior to everybody! Colonel Pater's senior! He's the one who should take it!"

Pater spoke up. He was a rather fat, balding fellow who was almost as pale as Rivers. "My God! I can't do it! I don't even know where the division is, and there's no time! I'd just get lost in this . . . wilderness!" His voice had risen almost to a falsetto.

Hartley spoke next. "Don't call on me!" He was a small man, neat and sandy-haired. "Not in this country! Now if it was open and a man could see—" He spread shaky hands and left the rest unsaid.

Tom got up and faced them. He looked at Cunningham, a tall, lanky fellow with a red mustache. He was a regular officer, but he shook his head and looked down.

"You heard Colonel Rivers!" said Pater frantically. "He told you to take command, Traylor, and you've got to do it!"

"Yes, yes!" seconded Hartley hastily. "We all heard him!"

Tom was shocked. Both men were nearly old enough to be his father. "Where's Colonel Simkins? Maybe he'll—"

Pater wouldn't let him finish. "Oh, he won't take it either, and he's not here anyhow!"

It couldn't be put off any longer, and suddenly Tom wanted it. He knew exactly what he was going to do, like he had thought it all out beforehand. "All right!" he said explosively, "I'll take it! Somebody's got to."

Pater and Hartley exchanged looks of relief. "We're at your orders, Colonel," said Hartley. Cunningham looked down and shuffled his feet.

There was one thing Tom had to be sure of. "Are those Rebels that started that shooting all gone?"

"God only knows!" sighed Hartley. "There could be hundreds of them out there, and you'd never know it."

"If there was just a squad of them, they're gone," said a scholarly-looking lieutenant named Hamilton, the only one of Rivers's aides who seemed to be around.

"How do you know?" asked Tom.

"Your brother sent some men out in front there on the far right, and they saw about half a dozen Rebels running west along an old road down there. They shot at them and hit one fellow, but the others picked him up and went into the brush. Then someone climbed a tree and saw them come back to the road and go on, still carrying the one that was hit. They were out of range by then, though."

The tree climber would have been Grabner, so there was no doubt those scouts were gone for good.

Tom looked at his watch, sent for von Jagerhof and Kemper, then turned to Hamilton. "Take a message to General Carter, Lieutenant."

Hamilton produced pad and pencil. "Yes, sir?"

Tom gave Carter the particulars of the situation and asked him to notify Corps. After waiting for Hamilton to catch up, Tom came out with it: "I think the enemy will advance guiding his center on the road he's moving up on and his right on a creek that runs parallel to it about half a mile south of where we are. I'm going to move the brigade south to the creek, hide in it, and take him in enfilade when he comes by."

There were gasps from the group, but everyone seemed too shocked to say anything.

Tom let Hamilton write until he caught up, but still no one said anything. "The enemy will wheel to face me when I open fire. That will set him up for you to strike his left flank and wipe him out."

Cunningham and the two colonels stood open-mouthed, looking at Tom in mixed awe and consternation.

Tom went on. "You'll have to move fast, though, or he'll make short work of us."

There were jerky nods of agreement and a sigh or two.

"I'm going to send a scout out before I move to that creek to make sure the enemy isn't advancing with flankers on his right or his skirmish line extended that way. If he is, or if he shows any signs of knowing where we are and moving against us, I'll give it up and go east along the creek until I meet you."

Everyone looked a little relieved while Hamilton scribbled. He caught up and asked, "Is that all, sir?"

Hartley started to speak, but Tom preempted him. "Now, read it back to me." He wanted to make sure Hamilton had it right. He did. "Go now, and hurry," said Tom as Hamilton made for his horse.

Hartley took his chance. "Colonel Traylor, you're taking an awful risk—"

Tom cut him off. "You had your chance to take command, sir."

Hartley shook his head and looked down.

Cunningham was next. "What about my guns? It's going to be hard getting them through all that growth. Maybe I ought to go east along that road and get out of the way."

"No, Major, I'm going to need you, and you can make it through the brush all right. I've got a good position for you when we get down there."

Cunningham only nodded, so Tom asked, "Where's Colonel Simkins?"

"He's supposed to be on his way here," replied Pater doubtfully.

"Well, we can't wait for him. If he doesn't show up in a minute or two, I'll go to his regiment and start us off from there. Just start south for that creek when he does. Don't worry about alignment or anything. Just keep the men going as fast as they can go. We can sort them out after we get there."

Anders stood at Tom's elbow. *"Der Herr Oberst ist . . . tot,"* he said brokenly. In his grief he had reverted to German. *"Wenn sie mir sparen kann—"*

Tom didn't wait for him to finish. "Go ahead. Take his body and go find an undertaker. There's always plenty of them around where there's fighting. I guess you know where to send it."

*"Ja. Er hat mir die Anrede gegeben, lange her."*

"Just use his horse. Sling the body across it and go. Take as much time as you need."

The slender blond youth nodded dumbly and turned away.

Kemper and von Jagerhof had come up in the meantime, so Tom turned to them. He filled them in on the situation, including how he expected the Rebels to advance. He told Kemper to scout them and report back immediately if they were doing otherwise. If they were advancing as he expected, Kemper was to stay with them as long as he could and only wave his cap when he came in. If he wanted a horse, he could have one.

The veteran said he would rather go on foot and would only take Grabner with him, to lessen the chances of being seen, then left at a run.

Von Jagerhof started back to his regiment, and Tom headed for Simkins's but met him on the way. Pater and Hartley had evidently told him what to expect, because he didn't seem surprised when Tom told him what they were going to do. He was a sleek, dark-haired fellow several years Tom's senior, but he had no objections and didn't say a word about taking over the brigade himself.

Cunningham's guns were waiting in a column where Simkins's regiment joined Hartley's, so Tom started everybody out. It was a mad rush to the creek, and by the time they arrived the companies were all mixed up, although the regiments had stayed together pretty well. While the company officers were sorting their men out, Tom told the regimental commanders to form a line along the creek between the two horseshoe bends and went about the only thing that had him worried. That was getting Cunningham's guns across the creek, up the ravine that ran into it from the south, and out on that overgrown plateau above where the infantry would be.

Tom needn't have worried. Cunningham knew his business and, once he knew what to do, put his men to work digging ramps down into the creek and up the ravine, one on each side so the guns could leave it and go out on the plateau. He told the major to hide his guns back in the growth, load with canister, and have his firing positions picked out so he could run up and open fire as soon as the infantry did.

When Tom got back to the infantry, he had all the officers' horses brought up and taken back with the ones from the guns. When he gave his to Hauser, he told him to take charge of all the animals and make sure they were all hidden back in the brush. His field glasses would only be in the way, so he sent them with his horse.

The creek was dry except for isolated pools, three to four feet deep and twelve feet or so wide, about like Tom had expected. To make sure the right of the Rebel line wouldn't get close enough to see the men in the creek too soon, he moved the line a little to the west before putting the men down in the creek. That way it began just below the first horseshoe bend, which jutted to the north and was so thickly lined with brush and briers that the files on the right would undoubtedly bear away from it as the Rebel line moved across in front. He wanted concentrated fire, so he shortened the line from the east until the men were so crowded they would barely have enough room to work their rifles.

A horseman came through the brush from the east. It was Hamilton. "General Carter's coming with the rest of the division. His advance should be here in twenty minutes or so."

Tom looked at his watch. If he had the timing right, it would be close. "He'll have to hurry."

"Yes, sir. The general says if you're sure of the enemy's disposition, do like you said. Take him in enfilade, and when he wheels to face you the general will strike him in the flank. If you're not sure, he wants you to move east along his creek until you meet him."

"I'll soon know if I'm right about the enemy's disposition, and if I'm not, the general will be seeing me soon. Sergeant Kemper's scouting his advance."

Hamilton nodded and reached in his pocket. "Something else, sir. He confirms you in temporary command of the brigade." He extended a note.

As Tom put it in his pocket, it suddenly occurred to him that he had been taking a lot for granted, but Carter was showing complete confidence in him and maybe he hadn't been so presumptuous after all.

Hamilton produced a rough, sketchy map and said Carter wanted the brigade's exact position marked on it. About all the map showed was where the creeks ran, and it was easy to find the one they were on because of the two horseshoe bends. Before Hamilton left, Tom had one more thing to tell him: "If the general gets here early, I hope he'll hold back until the enemy's engaged and makes his wheel to expose his flank." He didn't want to sound like he was giving Carter orders.

Hamilton smiled as he reined away. "I'll pass on your suggestion, sir."

While he was waiting on word from Cunningham that he was ready, Tom called the regimental commanders together for their final instructions. They all looked grave, even von Jagerhof.

Tom impressed on them that everything depended on surprise and that they were to make sure their men lay low and kept quiet. They weren't even to cock their rifles until they heard the order to fire, because someone's thumb might slip. The Rebels would be passing along out there in front for a good while before they got in enfilade, and some excitable fellow might up and let fly too soon unless they watched their men carefully.

As soon as he finished, Pater spoke up. "Colonel Traylor, may I ask something?" He was pale, and his voice sounded a little uncertain.

Tom saw that Pater was the spokesman for the other two colonels and that he had a crisis to deal with. "Of course, sir," he replied calmly.

"Suppose the Rebels see us before they get in enfilade?" Pater's voice had lost some of its uncertainty.

"I'll be watching them, and we'll open fire the instant they do, if they do. They can't possibly be far from where we want them by then, though, so it's nothing to worry about."

Pater had another question. "Are you sure you'll know in plenty of time if they're on to us and move against us here in this creek?"

"Yes. We can count on Sergeant Kemper letting us know in plenty of time if they've caught on to what we're going to do. The same if they're advancing with flankers or skirmishers out our way who'll see us before we're ready. General Carter's moving our way, so it won't take long to reach him."

Pater wasn't finished. "But what if General Carter's late in getting here? It's going to be a brigade against a division and, if he is, we'll all wind up dead or in Libby Prison."

"Well, General Carter sent word a little while ago that he was on his way, and you know what I sent back?" He laughed shortly. "I asked him to be careful not to get too close until the enemy makes his wheel to face us and exposes his flank." He nodded and smiled confidently. "I guess that shows you what I'm worried about the most."

It turned out to be a happy inspiration. The doubters seemed reassured, and Tom wished he could let it go at that, but he couldn't. He had to provide for the worst.

"Now, I don't think General Carter *will be* late, but if he is and I see the enemy's going to close with us, I'll lead a countercharge."

Eyes widened, even von Jagerhof's, but Tom went on before anyone could speak up. "Now, that won't be as hopeless as it sounds. The enemy's going to try to flank us on the right, to get *us* in enfilade and cut us off from the division. He'll see how short our line is, and he'll throw a column down on our right after he wheels to face us. He won't be expecting us to charge, so he won't hesitate to weaken his center to do that, and that's where we'll strike him. We might be able to cut him in two. Anyhow, that'll be the only way we can hold him any longer."

It would also be the only way to keep from being cut down like cattle in the creek. They would be cut down in the open instead, but he couldn't tell them that. These men weren't like him. They had families and futures.

The three colonels seemed awestruck, but von Jagerhof nodded and smiled to himself.

Tom went on. "Now, I don't think it'll come to that, but we've got to be ready for the worst." He paused briefly and acknowledged a signal from Cunningham at the top of the bluff behind them that he was all ready, then went on. "If it does come to that, just have your men fix bayonets, get them up out of the creek, and see that they follow me.

I'll lead them. Don't try to organize them or anything. We'll just go at them as we are. That's all we'll have time for." He folded his arms across his chest and stepped back a little. "That's all I have to say, gentlemen, so go back to your regiments and pass on everything I've told you."

There were grave looks and shakes of the head among the three colonels as they left, but they seemed resigned to going through with it. Anyhow, they all gathered their officers about them as soon as they got back and began passing on their instructions. From time to time company officers would turn and look at Tom much like the three colonels had when he told them they might have to make a counter-charge, but there were never any signs of objection or protest.

After the officers started back to their companies, Tom walked up the slope through the brush to see if he had interpreted Cunningham's signal correctly. He guessed he had, because he could see no sign of the guns, horses, or anything else except an officer who was obviously an observer posted to watch for the Rebel advance.

As Tom made his way back to the creek, he saw that the company officers had assembled their noncoms, so he could be satisfied that his instructions would be passed all the way down.

According to his watch, the Rebels should arrive in a matter of minutes, but there was no sign of Kemper yet. Tom guessed it was taking more time that he had allowed for. A division was hard to handle in country like this. Deployment from column into line would be slow in all that brush, and the advance would be slower than normal, because the Rebels would be as quiet about it as they could.

He began to stroll casually along the creek toward the west so as to be closer to where Kemper should appear, stopping to look around once in a while like he didn't have a worry in the world. He had to set a good example. These men in the creek knew by now that they were taking as long a chance as men could take, and he didn't want them to get the idea that he was jumpy and nervous. They sat or hunkered down in the creek bed as quiet as mice and looked up at him as he went by like children about to try some difficult and dangerous game under his direction.

The waiting was harder than anything else, and Tom began to worry in spite of himself. Any one of a thousand things could go wrong. Maybe the Rebel division coming his way was an advance force and he would find himself facing the whole Army of Northern Virginia. The Rebels might have other scouts out in the brush. They might have caught Kemper and Grabner. They might be stalking him now, closing in to shoot the men in the creek like fish in a barrel. Well, it was too late to do anything but go through with it now, and he wouldn't be around to face the consequences if the worst did happen. In that case, Mary Worthington could congratulate herself on her foresight, he thought bitterly.

When Tom got as far up the creek as he wanted to go, he stopped again and looked up the slope to the north. It was a beautiful day under the warm May sun. The sky was a clear blue, and the air still had the balminess of spring. The leaves of the brush and thickets were still freshly green, and colorful birds flitted among them, their songs floating cheerily on the air. If he were back in Dubois County, he would be putting in the second planting while the tender green shoots of the first one pushed their way through the soil. He shrugged and sighed to himself. There was nothing back home for him anymore, and it was foolish to think like that.

He saw movement up the creek and made out Kemper's burly form coming through the growth with the lanky Grabner close behind. When they saw him, both of them took off their caps and waved them ostentatiously. When he waved back, they disappeared into the creek where his old regiment was. All his worrying had been for nothing, and he felt greatly relieved. The Rebels were advancing unsuspecting and unprepared.

He passed the word and took a last look around. As the news spread in low tones and whispers, he could see it sweep away on both sides. The men clutched their rifles and sank even lower in the creek. He fought back an impulse to race down the creek and jump in. He walked at only a moderate pace and let himself down in the creek when he reached an isolated bush about halfway along the line.

As the men made room for him, he nodded and smiled at them. A yellow-bearded corporal smiled back and whispered, "We're really gonna use them Rebels up, ain't we, Colonel?"

Tom inclined his head, still smiling. "You bet we are."

The corporal grinned and nudged the man next to him, which led to a general round of nodding and smiling in his platoon. Fellows like him were worth their weight in gold.

At the first sound of the enemy's advance, Tom took off his hat and crouched behind the bush. He looked to his left up the slope in time to see a file of men in gray cross a slight elevation in the open, closely followed by another and another until he lost count. The advancing line was almost dense enough to be a column, but a division advancing on a narrow front would look like that. Farther up the slope, movement in the growth showed that the line stopped well short of the top of the slope, which would put it all in range. He had been counting on that.

Also, the right seemed to be bearing away from the horseshoe bend to Tom's left, something else he had counted on. As the advance came closer, he could mark its entire length by the waving tops of scrub trees and taller bushes where he couldn't actually see it. The Rebels moved with surprising speed and made a good deal less noise than he had expected. It was marvelous the way the files separated to go around denser parts of the growth and flowed back together, all without audible commands. These were veteran troops commanded by men who knew their business. Suddenly the skirmish line passed directly in front, the gray forms slipping easily and silently through the growth, eyes front and moving fast to draw farther ahead of the main body. Some overconfident Rebel commander was in for a rude shock, whatever else he got.

When the rear finally came into view, Tom saw that his line was going to overlap the enemy's by only fifty yards or so, less than he had hoped for, but still enough. His men were so quiet he involuntarily looked out of the corners of his eyes to make sure they were still there. They were, and were crouching so low it almost looked like they were lying down piled upon one another.

The Rebels continued passing in front. They weren't bothering about restoring their right after passing that overgrown bend to Tom's left. They were in too much of a hurry, and the files that had been closest to the creek merely blended in with the others.

As soon as the advance and the rear of the line going by in front were roughly equidistant, Tom ducked below the bank, put on his hat, and drew both revolvers. He rose to a crouch, and the men closer to him did the same, their thumbs on the hammers of their rifles. The movement spread away on both sides toward the ends of the line. As he stepped from behind the bush and went up to his full height, the men followed suit with leveled rifles. Some of the Rebels closest to the creek saw them, shouted in alarm, and spun about to raise their weapons.

Tom shouted, "Fire! Fire!" at the top of his lungs and shot down a man who already had his rifle up to his shoulder, then another who was actually aiming at him. Just as he fired his second shot, every rifle in the creek blasted flame and smoke in a nearly simultaneous volley. The sound was hurled back by the bluff behind and seemed enough to flatten the growth in front.

The men in gray went down by the score, and a great tumult of shouting, screaming, and crashing in the growth followed. The tops of the bushes and small trees danced wildly in every direction almost all the way up the slope, which showed the entire line was under fire. The men weren't just shooting at the plainest targets.

Tom screamed, "Fire at will!" as he fired again, this time at a more distant target, because the closer ones had all been mown down by the volley. Repeats of his cry were punctuated by a scattering of shots, mainly from revolvers; then an uneven blasting roar built up as slower loaders followed faster ones.

Tom had emptied one revolver before peremptory shouts and loud commands faintly audible above the uproar in front began the enemy's reaction. A rapid succession of stunning concussions drowned out everything else as Cunningham's guns opened up from the top of the bluff behind. Their blasts bent the men in the creek like treetops in the wind and deluged them with smoke and fiery debris from wads. Canister lashed the brush and cut the Rebels down in heaps.

Still, the movements in the open and the commotion in the growth began to assume definite form and Tom could see that the enemy was changing front to face him, all but the files closer to the creek. They were moving to his right, undoubtedly to form a column and come down on his flank there, as he had foreseen.

All the while the brigade kept up a rapid fire, the uneven, undulating roar of the rifles punctuated regularly by the blasts of Cunningham's guns. Smoke was beginning to build up in front by the time Tom's second revolver was empty, but he could still follow the enemy's movements as he replaced the empty cylinders. The files in front were turning right into column when they reached a point beyond the end of the line and starting down the slope. The men in gray went down steadily before the fearful fire, sometimes in groups, but others took their places and kept on in an awesome display of courage and discipline.

By the time Tom had emptied another revolver, the gray column on the right was making progress down the slope toward the creek. Suddenly the Rebels remaining in front raised their usual yell and charged down the slope with fixed bayonets. Unless Carter struck in a few moments, the brigade was going to be enfiladed on the right, charged in front, and the men slaughtered like sheep in the creek.

The charging files in front began to halt and fire one after the other, each rushing on down the slope after firing to clear the target for the one behind. Such precision seemed impossible in such growth and under such fire, but there it was. In view of what Tom was going to do, it was a mistake. The Rebels were spreading their files well apart, and a dense mass of men would be able to bowl them over one by one and drive in deep enough to escape the enfilade on the right. It could go only so far, though, and unless Carter attacked by then, the brigade would be enveloped in a fight to the death.

One storm of bullets after another tore into the creek bed as each enemy file fired in its turn. Only the first one did much damage, though, because most of the men ducked the others. Tom had to keep his eyes on the game, so he stood upright as the successive swarms of bullets hissed and howled by. He was unhit, but the yellow-bearded corporal next to him on the left wasn't so lucky. He was hit in the head by the third volley, and Tom was so spattered by blood and brains that he had to paw his face to clear his eyes.

Time was running out. The column coming down on Tom's right would soon reach the creek and cross it, then face right and rake his line with fire while the files in front closed with the bayonet, The last one had fired and the first one was so close that the bayonets gleamed in the smoke and individuals could be singled out.

Tom could wait no longer. He shouted, "Fix bayonets!" and vaulted up on the creek bank as the sharp steel came forth and snapped on the muzzles. Cunningham's guns abruptly fell silent. Tom drew his sword, flourished it over his head, and shouted, "Forward! Forward! Charge! Charge!"

It was like throwing a pebble into water, only the movement spread along a line rather than in a circle. The men began scrambling up out of the creek and running toward him as he backstepped, holding their bayoneted rifles before them and yelling madly.

Tom whirled and made for the enemy. Carter wasn't going to save them, and this was the end. There was a dull, pulsing roar in his ears, and wild visions whirled through his mind. He saw Sally as plainly as in life and knew he would soon be with her in death. The thought raised a shriek of joy in his throat and gave his driving legs the strength of steel.

He kept an empty revolver in his left hand, gripped his sword with his right, and hurled himself on the enemy coming at him. He didn't look back, but his men were on his heels and the charging mass he led had assumed a wedgelike shape, with him at the apex.

They struck the onrushing files of men in gray and bowled them over one after the other. Tom saw only fleeting faces and forms that he stabbed and slashed with his sword while fending and bludgeoning with his revolver. He burst through file after file, leaping and dodging with tigerish agility and striking with maniacal strength. He screamed and yelled like a madman. His men caught the contagion. They yowled with primeval ferocity as they smashed their way forward. The Rebels halted their rush and vainly tried to stand their ground. Bayonets flashed and clashed or thrust into struggling bodies with dull, meaty sounds. Rifle butts swung through the air and thudded on heads or shoulders. A few muffled shots sounded amid shrieks of rage and pain as the wedge of men in blue drove on.

The enemy ranks began to compact, and the drive slowed. The Rebels on the flanks began to assail the sides as it lost momentum. Finally it stalled. All Tom's slashing, stabbing, and clubbing couldn't clear his way. He cut down one man only to have another take his place. He couldn't dodge or leap aside any longer to avoid bayonets. The Rebels were too crowded to use their weapons effectively, or he wouldn't have lasted a few seconds. That wouldn't last, though, and he knew it. He screamed his defiance and gave himself to death.

Suddenly there were panicky shouts and urgent commands among the Rebels, and they began to try to disengage. Their foes yelled triumphantly and regained their momentum, Tom in the forefront. This ruined the attempted disengagement and wrecked what organization the Rebels had left. Individuals began to turn and run, then groups, and soon there was nothing left in front but a disorganized fleeing mass. Tom and his men were yelling exultantly in pursuit when he was checked by a sudden burst of heavy firing to his right, followed by the massed cheering and shouting of charging men. Carter had struck the Rebels' flank, and they were finished.

Most of the men realized what was happening and stopped, then headed back for the creek. Some didn't, and Carter's men would sweep them up along with the Rebels unless they got out of the way. Tom began shouting for them to halt and go back. Others took up the cry, and soon everyone was in full flight for the creek, even the berserkers who had charged on at first.

Hauser dashed up on Tom's horse. He must have ridden down across the creek and followed close behind the attack. He leapt off and flung the reins, but the horse reared and he barely caught them. He seized the halter and brutally jerked the animal's head down, then vaulted into the saddle before it could recover. The thick, sweetish smell of blood on the air combined with all the noise and confusion to make the creature almost unmanageable, but he got it under control and galloped for the laggards in the race for the creek.

"Hurry! Hurry! Get back! Get out of the way!" he shouted as he cut behind them and began harrying them like cattle. They ran faster, crashing through the brush and thickets in their haste and looking fearfully to their left. Cunningham's guns opened up as soon as their field of fire was cleared, and the men ran even faster. Tom looked to his left and saw that Carter's men had smashed through the enemy column that had tried to enfilade him, and soon his men were passing through its fleeing remnants. Strangely, the enemies paid no attention to one another except to dodge or evade when their paths crossed.

As soon as the men had all reached the creek, Tom faced them about so they could open fire on the fleeing Rebels, although they were so crowded and mixed up that many of them couldn't do it. Their fire added to that of the artillery on the bluff above to wreak fearful execution on the hapless Rebels, run as they might. Some of them dropped their rifles and cowered on the ground to escape the storm of death. When Carter's men swept in from the right, the shooting stopped. The Rebels still on their feet fled wildly in every direction, some throwing away their rifles to run the faster. Many of them were overrun, and those that escaped the bayonets stopped and raised their hands in surrender. Carter's men paid them no heed and crashed on, past the horseshoe bend on the left and on out of sight.

While the companies and regiments were being put back together, some of the surviving enemy soldiers out in front began coming in to surrender, but most of them stayed out in the brush milling aimlessly around. The ones who came in acted dazed and bewildered. A few still had their rifles and looked astonished when faced with demands to give them up. It was hard to believe they were the same men who had been so full of fight a few minutes ago.

Tom told Simkins to take charge of the prisoners they already had and go out and round up those still out in the brush before they began to recover their wits and get away. Tom was going to join the division as soon as he could, and if he was gone when Simkins finished he was to follow with the prisoners.

The black-haired fellow left a company to guard the prisoners who had come in and crashed off through the growth with the others, his men shouting like they were herding cattle.

During the period of relative quiet that followed, the wounded out in the brush began to make themselves heard. Their cries and entreaties sent cold chills through Tom and made him afraid he would get to feeling like he had after the Midlow Massacre last winter. He sent a message to Cunningham to limber up and rejoin the brigade. That would take quite a while, and in the meantime Tom could only endure.

The surgeons and their assistants had already begun to gather up the wounded and take them to a grassy clearing near the creek to the right. Men in Confederate uniforms were with them. Tom guessed they were surgeons, too, but he certainly wasn't going out there to find out. He was very glad to see the first of the guns come out of the ravine and start across the creek. He could count on Cunningham to follow, so Tom faced the brigade left and took up the march. Simkins soon caught up and said that Carter's provost had showed up with two regiments to take charge of the prisoners and comb the brush for the Rebels still out there. Tom told him to fall in at the rear of the column and went on.

He stayed close to the creek to avoid the dead and wounded until he passed the battlefield, then turned a little north to where Carter had passed. From there on the going was much easier, because a lot of the brush and even some of the thickets were flattened like a herd of elephants had stampeded over them.

The column met a train of ambulances following the route Carter's men had broken, and Tom turned it a little to the right to avoid them. A lieutenant with a beardless baby face rode ahead and reined over toward him, so Tom told Pater to take the column on and rode to meet the fellow.

When the lieutenant got a good look at Tom, his mouth fell open and an expression of horror spread over his face. It made Tom realize he must be an awful sight, spattered with blood and brains and looking like he had been dragged by his horse. Baby Face only wanted to know where the wounded were being gathered so he could take the ambulances there, and when Tom told him he acted like he was being addressed by a ghost. After that, Tom headed for a pool in the creek to clean himself up a little. He only leaned in the saddle, wetted his handkerchief, then reined back into the brush and began wiping himself as he rode. When he got to his hands, he first became aware that the left one was bruised and painful, but the right one bothered him much more. It was crusted with dried blood, and so was his sword. Blood had even run down the outside of the scabbard. He shuddered as he wiped his hand and suddenly felt weak and shaky. What had he done? How many men had he killed? Suddenly he remembered how he had rushed on the enemy screaming like a maniac, convinced he was going to die and welcoming it. What kind of a man was he to behave like that? He shuddered again and bowed his head.

A familiar voice jolted him back to awareness. He felt like he had been asleep, and it frightened him. The voice was Ab Inman's. Tom had caught up with his old company. There were Billy, Cole, Charley, and the others. Oh, God! He hadn't given a thought to any of them, not even his own brother! Billy could have been lying dead back there along the creek for all he knew, and the others with him.

"What'd you say, Ab?" Tom croaked as he reined back.

"I jist hollered out, 'How're ye doin', Gin'ral?' " was the jocular reply.

Tom managed a hollow laugh. "Oh, you've got me all wrong, Ab. I'm just a plain old colonel." His voice sounded normal and he started feeling a little like himself again.

" 'Twon't be fer long, I'll bet!" chimed in Charley. "Hit takes gin'rals t' command brigades, ye know!"

"Yeah!" jubilated Dan Howard. "Ye shore used them Rebels up, Colonel sir, a hull d'vision uv 'em!" He brandished his rifle and whooped, "Gin'ral! Gin'ral Traylor!" Others took it up, and soon the whole regiment seemed to follow suit. It was all so artless and sincere that Tom found himself laughing with the others and almost feeling normal again.

Billy hadn't joined in, though, and it bothered Tom, so he spoke to his brother. "How was it with you fellows down there on the end of the line?"

"We got off easy. Them volleys they fired didn't seem t' reach down thar whar we wuz very much. They got pore ol' Harve Akers, though, an' then Schutz an' Rotenweiler got bay'neted an' died right 'way. Three er four others got cut up some, but none too bad." Billy looked like he wanted to say something else, but he didn't.

Tom shook his head. "Too bad about Harve, and Colonel Rivers, too." He sighed. "I was with the colonel when he died, Billy, and it was almost like it was Pa."

Billy nodded. "I know. I felt 'bout th' same way when I heered 'bout hit. He shore wuz a fine man." He still looked like he had something else on his mind.

"Well," said Tom, "I'd better get on up there where I belong." He waved to acknowledge the noisy farewells and rode on worrying about Billy's troubled looks. The only time he had acted like that before was when they had talked on the pontoon bridge last winter. Tom hoped it wouldn't come to that again, because he had a lot to answer for.

Von Jagerhof reined out to join him as he passed the advance of the regiment. "Congratulations, sir!" he beamed. "You handled that action splendidly! We destroyed a whole enemy division!"

Tom laughed ruefully. "Thank you, Major, but it was pretty close. It's a good thing General Carter pitched in when he did, or—"

The Prussian interrupted smilingly. "Oh, nothing ventured, nothing gained, as you Americans say." He dropped back with a little wave, still smiling.

The rest of the division had halted, and the brigade soon caught up. Pater had halted the men and put them at rest in place by the time

Tom reached him. The men drank from their canteens, then got out pipes and tobacco. While they smoked or chewed, they exulted about how they had given the Rebels a dose of their own medicine.

The brigade adjutant, Major Dodson, and two aides, lieutenants Dickens and Marter, came riding up. They looked apprehensive and nervous, obviously expecting a bawling out for being absent during the action. They had it coming, so Tom gave it to them. "Where have you fellows been?" he demanded. "I sure could have used some help back there."

The major was a dark-haired fellow who acted like he half-expected Tom to draw his sword and attack him. "I'm sorry, sir, but I was . . . was, well, detained. Colonel Rivers had sent me to General Carter, and you'd moved when I got back. I couldn't find you, so I—"

Tom cut him off. "Humph," he said grumpily. "Be sure you stay around and don't stray off again, all three of you."

Dickens and Marter looked like schoolboys despite uniforms, weapons, and carefully cultivated mustaches. He didn't have the heart to single them out.

"Yes, sir," replied Dodson, nervously fidgeting with his reins. "We'll always be here when the colonel needs us."

Tom changed the subject. "Do you know if Sergeant Anders got back to the main road with the colonel's body all right?"

"Yes, sir," replied Dickens. "When General Carter sent me to Corps, I saw him there. He said an undertaker was on his way and was going to send the body back to Kentucky, where the colonel's people live, like he wanted."

Tom nodded. "I'm glad to hear that, and I told Sergeant Anders to take all the time he needed." He went on to commiserate with them about Rivers's death, and they seemed relieved to learn he wasn't some kind of a wild man who didn't care about anybody or anything.

Anyhow, Dodson said something that had probably been on his mind all along. He pointed toward the creek and ventured, "There seem to be several pools of water down there. If the colonel would like to clean up a little, I can take care of things until he gets back."

Tom couldn't help smiling. "Thank you, Major. I sure need it. It scares people to look at me."

They all laughed and he could see they were beginning to think he might not be such a bad fellow after all. Instead of going to the creek himself, though, he sent Hauser to get some water. He didn't have anything to get it in, but Tom knew he would find something.

Hauser had only left when Lieutenant Hamilton came back along the column to tell him that General Carter wanted to see him, so the cleaning up would have to wait. He left Dodson in charge and answered the summons.

Carter and the other brigade commanders were gathered around a big blond man with a flowing mustache who wore a Confederate uniform. He could only be a prisoner, but the others were talking with him like old friends.

When Carter saw Tom, his eyes widened. "Are you hurt, Colonel?"

An orderly took Tom's horse as he dismounted. "No, sir. A man close to me was shot in the head, and I haven't had a chance to clean up yet."

Carter noticed the bloody scabbard. "It looks like you pitched into that hand-to-hand fighting, too," he said disapprovingly.

Tom was nettled. "With all due respect, sir, how could anyone get a brigade to attack a division unless he led it himself? And there wasn't time to organize or anything like that."

The others looked surprised at such plain talk, but Carter only smiled and turned to the Confederate officer. "General, I want you to meet Colonel Traylor. He's the fellow who sort of ambushed you. Colonel, meet General Ramsdell. He was a classmate of mine at the Point."

Ramsdell stepped forward and extended his hand. "I'm pleased to make your acquaintance, sir," he said in a deep bass voice. If he was taken aback at Tom's appearance, he didn't show it, and his manner was so open and frank that Tom liked him immediately.

"I'm pleased to meet the commander of such a fine division," he said as they shook hands.

Ramsdell shook his head. "There's not much left of it now."

"Bad luck, sir. If General Carter hadn't come in when he did, it would be me instead of you."

"Thank you, Colonel. You're very kind. I might say I've never seen men fight like yours did."

Carter spoke up. "Colonel Traylor's one of our best young men, but he just can't resist jumping into a fight himself." He laughed to show he wasn't being critical.

Ramsdell looked at Tom ruefully. "Well, you really caught me going along blind, no flankers out or anything. My scouts said you gave no sign of moving, and I thought I could get away with it, in country like this anyhow." He sighed and shrugged. "Then none of your people ever tried anything like you did. They always played it safe, and I thought that even if you did find out I was moving on you, you'd just fall back on your division."

Carter laughed. "Colonel Traylor's no fellow to play it safe. He'll take any chance there is." He didn't sound altogether approving, and there was a round of head shaking and grave looks among the others. They were all stern bearded men who looked twice Tom's age and probably thought he was some harebrained jackanapes who had just been lucky. Maybe they were right, but he didn't let it bother him.

Ramsdell went on. "That charge you made is what really did me in. You drove in so deep I couldn't get on your flank with that column I threw down. If I'd been able to do that, maybe I could've mopped you up before General Carter got there, and then stood him off."

"Yes, sir. Your mistake was having your men in front halt and fire by file. That spread them out so they couldn't hold me when I charged."

"Well, I wasn't expecting you to charge. Whoever heard of a brigade charging a division?" He looked around a little plaintively.

Carter replied. "Well, you just never ran into a fellow like Colonel Traylor before." Again, he didn't sound like he approved of it.

Everybody was looking at Tom like he was a circus curiosity, so he replied a little testily, "Well, it's like a friend of mine said a little while ago: 'Nothing ventured, nothing gained.' "

The stern, bearded faces looked back at him. Suddenly one of them spoke. "Well, I'll tell you one thing: anybody who'd do something like that's got plenty of nerve." It was General Canfield, who commanded a New Jersey brigade. He stepped forward and extended his hand. "I'd like to congratulate you, Colonel."

The others thawed just as suddenly and crowded around to shake hands and offer their congratulations. Tom was beginning to feel embarrassed when he saw Hauser some distance away trying to get his attention. He held a bucket and signaled imperatively.

"I think your orderly wants you, Colonel," said Carter dryly.

Tom replied humorously, "Yes, sir, and I'll be in trouble if I keep him waiting."

There was a general outbreak of laughter. Canfield seemed to think it was particularly funny. His bearded face split into a wide grin. "Yes, sir! It looks like the fellow's got you pretty well tamed, Traylor!" He guffawed and slapped his leg.

Tom laughed with the others, then turned to Ramsdell. "Well, sir, I've got to go. I wish you luck and a speedy exchange."

The big blond man stuck out his hand. "Thank you, Colonel," he said as they shook hands. "If we ever meet again, I hope it'll be under different circumstances."

Carter broke in. "What he means is he hopes it'll be under *opposite* circumstances!" He slapped Ramsdell on the back and cackled gleefully.

Tom took his leave amid the merriment that followed. The generals were whooping and laughing just like the men did and called cheery farewells after him.

Hauser was scandalized because Tom had let himself be seen in such condition by all those high officers. What kind of an orderly would they think he had? It was disgraceful. He had never been so mortified in his life.

It went on and on as he cleaned Tom's face and hands. Finally he got enough of it and said peremptorily, *"Halt's Maul!"*

Hauser shook his head sourly, but he did as he was told and kept his mouth shut while he worked on the uniform. Tom's sore hand was turning black and blue. That had come of fending off bayonet thrusts with his revolver. He was lucky the cylinder hadn't been knocked out of line.

The division faced about and started moving north before the cleaning was done, but Tom found his horse tied to a sapling and quickly caught up, as his brigade was last in the column.

The first thing he did was send Dodson and his aides around to get casualty reports from the regiments, and it was a good while before they returned with the figures and added up the total. In the meantime, the division had reached the road Ramsdell had come up on and turned west.

"We lost 526 men, sir, dead or disabled," announced Dodson, "with 183 dead."

Tom was appalled. "Oh, God! I had no idea it was that bad!"

"You had a hard fight, sir. You fought a whole division there for quite a while, I understand, and it was one of their best."

Dickens spoke up. "Yes, and I understand General Carter was very complimentary about the way you handled the action."

Tom grunted. "Well, he didn't say anything like that to me. About all I got from him was a remark about pitching into the fighting myself."

They all took that as indicating Tom was in a bad humor, and the talk died away. Tom was glad of it. He didn't feel like talking anymore after he learned how many men he had lost.

The column marched west until it reached the main north–south road, then turned north and began to ascend a gradual slope leading to what looked like a sizable wood at the top. As they went on, the view began to improve, because of thinning growth and greater elevation. Tom could see both the road they were on and the one Ramsdell had used for a considerable distance. Both were empty, and he began to wonder what had happened to the ubiquitous Rebel cavalry. No one had seen even a single horseman for several days, which was very strange.

It was nearly a mile from the crossroads to the woods at the top of the slope, and when the column was about halfway there a few guns fired far away beyond them, and the first few discharges rapidly grew into a full-scale cannonade. It looked like the big attack he had been expecting ever since he had first seen Ramsdell's division was coming in. He hoped Carter had passed the word and that whoever was up there was ready for it.

Suddenly the regiment ahead of his broke into a run, and his men followed suit. As they ran, the roar of the guns came steadily closer and rifle fire became audible, sounding at first like a fire in dry weeds, but rapidly becoming louder and more continuous. Carter wanted his artillery toward the front, and, "Make way! Make way!" heralded the passage of Cunningham's part of it. The guns went tearing by in a cloud of dust, the gunners bending low over the horses' necks or clinging to their seats on the limbers as they bounced and careened over the rutted road.

When the column reached the edge of the woods at the top of the slope, Tom was told to halt and deploy as a flank guard while the rest of the division went on. While the battle raged with undiminished fury farther on, he deployed his brigade across the road facing south, far enough back under the trees to be out of sight. He sent flankers out to the left and right but decided he could do without pickets in front because the view to the south was so good.

Carter obviously expected a flanking move from the south, so Tom sent for Grabner to serve as a lookout and Kemper to interpret what he saw. Tom gave the lanky, hawk-faced fellow his glasses and sent him up the tallest tree they could find at the edge of the woods. Once he got settled, Grabner reported that these were sure good glasses the *Herr Oberst* had. He could see for a great distance and follow both roads easily, because he could see over the brush and thickets from up where he was.

In the meantime the battle to the north seemed to have passed its climax. Rifle fire was falling off rapidly, and although the artillery kept up its blasting for a time, after a while only desultory discharges were to be heard. It looked like the Rebels had given it up when they saw they weren't getting anywhere.

Billy's company was nearby, and he came over to talk. Tom was afraid of what his brother wanted to say, so he got off a nod and a smile to von Jagerhof in hopes he would join them. He did, and the danger was averted for the time being.

Both of them agreed with Tom's evaluation of what had happened to the north, and Billy was glad that for once they had been ready for the Rebels when they attacked. While they were talking, Cunningham came back with the guns. That probably meant that Carter thought they would be needed here, but Grabner had seen nothing yet and the flankers reported no movement on either flank.

Tom told Cunningham to stay in column on the road and be ready to run up to support the infantry. If the Rebels came from the south like Carter seemed to expect, he would move the infantry out from under the trees and far enough down the slope so the guns could be set up behind and fire overhead.

Cunningham said he would be ready. He was always ready for anything. He had water tanks on his limbers and always kept them full. He carried plenty of feed for his horses, too, so he never had to send them off to be fed and watered like some fellows were always having to do. Tom was astonished to realize that it was an attempt to impress him, and by a man who was older than he was and a regular besides. He hadn't realized what a big man a brigade commander must look like, to others anyhow.

About an hour before dark, Grabner suddenly called out that an enemy column was coming east on that old road down there. All he could see yet was the advance, and there were no scouts or skirmishers out ahead. There wasn't any cavalry either.

Carter had left a courier, and before sending him back Tom told him to be sure to report that there was no cavalry and that he thought it was a new enemy force, because no one who knew what was going on would be moving along like that with no scouts out ahead.

Carter himself soon showed up with a retinue of aides and couriers. He wanted particulars, but all Grabner could report was that he couldn't see the end of the column yet. All he could tell was that it had a long train of guns, over thirty of them.

When Tom translated, Carter whistled. "That means it's more than a division." He reined over and asked in an undertone, "How reliable is that fellow up there?"

"Absolutely reliable, and he's got the best eyes a man ever had." Tom pointed to Kemper, who was calling back and forth with Grabner. "Sergeant Kemper there will understand anything he doesn't."

Carter seemed satisfied.

Tom brought up something he had been wondering about all along. "Where's the cavalry, sir? We shouldn't have to be climbing around in trees like monkeys to find out what's going on."

"There's no cavalry in the whole corps, not a bit," replied Carter glumly. "I don't guess the others have any either. Hooker took it all to send out a big cavalry raid in the enemy's rear. It won't amount to a damned thing, and here we've got to play blindman's bluff with the Rebels. They must be in the same fix, though, probably because they had to use theirs to stop ours. Ramsdell had to use men on foot to scout you, you know." He shook his head. "Of course, they know the country a lot better than we do, like that road they're coming up on. Nobody had any idea it was there until you reported Ramsdell was moving up on it."

"How would you like to have some mounted scouts, say, six or eight?"

"Just fine, but where am I going to get any?"

"I can give you the men if you can get the horses."

"Who? You don't have anybody who's trained for scouting or anything."

"Yes, I do." He pointed to Kemper. "That man's the best scout you'll find. Just let him pick his men, give them horses, and you'll have your own cavalry."

"Oh yes, yes! Why didn't I think of something like that? I've heard all about Sergeant Kemper, and you Indiana boys can all ride!" He laughed and slapped his leg, then sobered abruptly. "But what about horses? I can't get any, not right now, anyhow."

"What about dismounting the adjutants in a couple of brigades? They're all young fellows and can hoof it with the men."

"Sure! That'll give me eight horses!" He jabbed a finger at Tom. "Go get yours, and I'll send up to Kersey for his. We can have them in a few minutes."

Only three horses were forthcoming, because von Jagerhof had no adjutant. When Tom got back, Carter was talking with Kemper and solved the shortage by dismounting one of his junior aides. Carter then went back to Kemper, who stood stiffly at attention until the general kicked aside some leaves on the road and began to scratch out a map with a stick. Then Kemper had to hunker down with Carter to study it. Tom had Hamilton copy it so Kemper could take it with him.

Kemper wanted revolvers and rations for his men if he could get them. He might be out a long time and was bound to run into enemy cavalry sooner or later. Tom immediately gave him one of his. Carter disarmed his aides and got five more, confiscated Dodson's, and donated his own. He sent for packs from a light artillery battery and rations from his quartermaster. Kemper wanted to take his men from Billy's company because he knew them all. Billy went along to have a voice in the matter.

Before Kemper returned, Grabner shouted that the column had ended, but another one was close behind, probably another division. Carter thought it all might be the same one, but Grabner was sure of himself and provided convincing details.

The advance of the first column could now be seen from the ground. It was getting close to the crossroads, and if it turned north, there would be big doings pretty soon. Tom didn't think it would. It would soon be dark, and the crossroads was a good place to camp.

Carter took no chances. He sent a courier to Corps about the new sighting and another to tell the rest of his division to move up with the artillery in front. He expected another division, maybe two more, because the Rebels generally operated three or four together as a corps. He was glad they had no cavalry and that Tom had kept his men back under the trees out of sight.

Kemper came back with seven men, all small fellows and good riders. They were all Germans but Zeke Kerns and Charley Evans. Tom expected Kemper to take Grabner, but he didn't, maybe because he thought Carter needed him worse. Anyhow, Carter gave Kemper his own field glasses, saying he could always borrow a pair if he needed them. Four more horses, packs, and rations had arrived, so Kemper put his men to adjusting stirrups, filling packs, and strapping them on.

In the meantime, Kemper talked with Carter. His men finished before he did and had time for badinage with their late comrades, now scorned as "dum foot soljers." The raillery went on with predictions that they would turn out to be cowards like all the cavalry and do nothing but run from the Rebels. Kemper put an end to it by leading them off through the woods to the west.

Carter wanted to know how it was that Rivers had been killed before there was any fighting. When Tom told him, he sighed and shook his head. "That's the way it is around here. Some sharpshooter could be out there in that brush right now, just waiting for someone to show himself." He shook his head again. "I've lost the best brigade commander I had. I hope that governor of yours is glad he died a colonel."

Grabner called down from the tree that the first Rebel column was going on east past the road junction and that the advance elements seemed to have halted and started building fires. A little later he was sure of it, and said it looked like the whole column was going to do the same.

Carter wanted to be sure that no scouts had been sent north toward them, and when he was assured none had, he exclaimed, "Well, what do you know about that! They must think there isn't anybody in miles of them!"

"Well, this is a new bunch for sure," said Tom, "and I don't guess their communications are working very well."

Carter laughed. "Oh, they have their troubles just like we do, I guess, although you wouldn't think so sometimes."

"I'm going to make sure they don't see anything up here," Tom assured him. "I'll go on keeping my men out of sight and won't allow any fires. I'll wait until after dark to send an outpost down that road just in case they send someone up this way."

Carter nodded. "I don't think they will. It's already getting dark in the woods here." He called for his horse and mounted. "Well, I've got to go to Corps about all this. I expect that Second Division will go into camp down there, too. If it doesn't or if anything happens, let me know."

"Yes, sir," said Tom as the general reined away.

He went around himself with orders to let the men fall out and bed down, but to keep everyone back in the woods and allow no fires. As soon as it was completely dark, he sent a platoon out to set up an outpost about halfway to the crossroads, with instructions to be back under the trees well before daylight.

Tom's wanderings took him past Billy's company, and to his consternation, his brother came out to talk to him. He could tell by the fires springing up around the crossroads that the second Rebel column was going into camp down there, too, so there was no escape this time. "I ain't had th' chance t' tell ye how proud I am uv ye, commandin' th' brigade an all," said Billy warmly.

Tom told him how it had happened and added that he didn't expect it to last long, because of seniority and politics.

Billy snorted. "Well, hit danged well ought to! Them other fellers wuz too skeered t' take hit back thar when things looked bad, atter Colonel Rivers got shot, an' none uv 'em oughta git hit now, politics er sen'ority er what. An' th' way you handled hit! Wipin' out a hull Rebel d'vision!"

"Oh, General Carter did that. I just sort of set it up for him."

It was going better than Tom expected when his brother came out with what he had been dreading. "They's jist one thing that bothers me. Did you hafta lead that charge like y' did?"

"Yes, Billy. There wasn't time to do it any other way. They'd have been on us in a few minutes, butchering us like hogs in that creek.

And then no one's going to get a brigade to charge a division unless he leads it himself."

To Tom's relief, Billy seemed satisfied. "I guess yo're right 'bout th' time, an' I know that when th' men seen you wuz gonna lead 'em, they wuzn't no holdin' back." He didn't stop at that, though. "I wuz skeered hit mighta been woman trouble agin. I heered 'bout that woman frum Martin County gittin' married after sparkin' with you when she wuz hyar over New Year's. Worthington, I think her name wuz, an' I know you'd been writin' back an' forth with her."

"No, it was like I told you, Billy." He hoped he sounded more convincing that he felt and wondered how much Billy knew about him and Mary.

"Well, enyhow, I hope y' won't never do enything like that agin," said Billy severely. "Men commandin' brigades cain't go jumpin' inta hand-t'-hand fightin', y'know."

Tom was glad it was over and laughed a little. "Well, General Carter made that pretty plain to me."

Just after they parted, someone said that Kemper had sent in his first messenger, so Tom waited on the road until the man came back. He was a German named Hoffman who spoke some English, and he confirmed what everyone was thinking. The Rebels had all gone into camp around the crossroads like there wasn't an enemy in a hundred miles.

The Germans of Billy's company seemed to be having a good time about something. They were hooting like owls and hee-hawing gleefully. Tom couldn't understand why until he heard rich Teutonic oaths descending from above. Poor Grabner was still up in the tree, and his comrades were ribbing him about it. Tom called him down and apologized for forgetting him. He returned Tom's glasses and said the Rebels must have a thousand fires going down there. His friends welcomed him back with more hooting and hee-hawing and began calling him *die Eule* instead of *Alte Adler Augen*. "Old Eagle Eyes" would now be known as only an owl.

By this time most of the men were sleeping on their arms under the trees and those who hadn't bedded down already were preparing to. Hauser had some cold rations and a bed of boughs ready for Tom, and after his horse was taken away for feed and water he ate his supper. He hadn't realized how hungry he was until he started eating or how tired he was until he sat down to do it. Before he turned in, he told Dodson, Dickens, and Marter to stand watches one at a time and wake him up before daylight, unless something came up before then.

He only took off his boots, belt, and hat before stretching out. He was so tired he thought he would drop right off, but he didn't. He started thinking about Carolyn Rivers. Poor Carolyn. First she had lost her mother and brother, then the man she was to marry, and now her father. She had no one now, and he wondered how she would bear up under it. He was deeply ashamed when he thought of how he had tried to seduce her. A great sorrow welled up within him, and he suddenly realized he loved her. She loved him, too, but she had left to get away from him. Once she knew he loved her, too, she would marry him and he could keep his promise to her father. She would know it the moment she saw him, just like she had known it had only been lust before.

He would write her the first chance he got. He would confess how it had been before and assure her it was true love now. Maybe he could get leave when the campaign was over and go see her. Maybe she could come to see him if he couldn't. Maybe the uncle she was staying with could bring her. He remembered her saying that her uncle sometimes had business with the government that took him to Washington, and the army would never be very far from there. He would write her uncle if he had to.

Tom was just drifting off to sleep when he heard a party of horsemen come down the road from the rear and stop nearby. Someone started calling for him, so he sat up, put on his boots and hat, and went toward him. As he came closer, he could hear someone talking in a loud, scolding voice. It was General Hobson, who had replaced Stanfield in command of the corps, and he always talked like that. He was a heavy, jowly fellow, one of the political generals there were too many of. People said he treated his subordinates like dogs, except for Carter, who wouldn't stand for it. Tom hoped Hobson didn't start in on him like that, because he wouldn't stand for it either. Good men like Stanfield and Rivers were killed while Hobson lived on. It was almost too much to bear.

The horsemen were only darker shadows in the gloom under the trees and Tom couldn't identify any of them, so he faced the center of the group, came to attention, and saluted. "Colonel Traylor reporting, sir."

Hobson seemed to be in the middle of the group. "Now, you're the fellow who took over Rivers' brigade, aren't you?" he demanded peremptorily.

"Yes, sir," replied Tom simply.

"I want to know just how it was that the junior colonel in a brigade presumed to take it over," said Hobson testily.

"Perhaps the general should ask the division commander," suggested Tom evenly.

"I already have," was the sneering reply. "I want to hear it from you."

Tom kept his temper with an effort. "Pater and Hartley wouldn't take it and put it on me. Simkins wasn't there and Colonel Rivers told me to take it before he died. Somebody had to take it, so I did."

"Humph. Why didn't Pater and Hartley want it, and why didn't Simkins take it later?" demanded Hobson accusingly.

"They said the country was too difficult. They wouldn't be able to see and didn't think we had enough time to do anything. The enemy was moving on us. Simkins never said anything about taking command, and I'd already made my plans by the time I saw him, so I didn't either. I guess he felt like the others did."

Hobson snorted. "I've never heard of such a thing, the junior colonel taking over a brigade just before an action. It all sounds pretty fishy to me."

Tom couldn't take it anymore. Hobson was only bullying him anyhow. "Well, Colonel Rivers is dead, but the others are still around. The general can ask them if he questions my word."

"I'll question your word if I want to, Colonel," growled Hobson.

"Yes, and the general can browbeat me, too, if he wants to," replied Tom coldly. "That's his privilege."

There was a sharp intake of breath by someone in the group.

"Well!" exploded Hobson. "You don't seem to care about keeping the brigade!"

"That's up to the general," replied Tom indifferently. He wasn't going to lick anyone's boots to keep it, Hobson's least of all.

"I just wonder how such a smart-alec fellow as you ever got to be a colonel!" flared Hobson.

"I can tell the general one thing," snapped Tom. "I didn't get my rank by politics." With that he turned and walked away in a deliberate show of contempt. He expected angry shouts and calls for the guard, but there was only a shocked silence, and before he was back in his blankets the horsemen moved away. He thought anger would keep him awake, but it didn't, and he soon fell asleep.

Dickens had the last watch and woke Tom up before dawn. Hauser had a cold breakfast ready and a bucket of water to wash in, but before anything else Tom made sure the platoon on outpost had come in. The sergeant said they hadn't been bothered all night, so the Rebels still didn't know if anyone was in the woods above them.

Shortly after daylight, Carter came riding down the road alone. The first thing he wanted to do was get that sharp-eyed fellow back up in the tree. When he did, Grabner said the Rebels weren't stirring yet and their guns were still standing limbered up on the road down there.

After Carter sent Marter back with the information, Tom said, "Well, they haven't found out we're up here yet, or they'd be doing something. Do you think Hobson's going to attack them?"

Carter sighed and ignored the question. "You've gotten yourself in a mess, Colonel," he said as he got off his horse.

"Yes, sir, I expect I have," replied Tom as they moved apart, Carter leading his horse.

Carter sighed again. "Rivers was right about you. You aren't afraid of anybody or anything."

"Well, sir, I don't know about that, but General Hobson had no right to browbeat me like he did. I gave him no reason to."

"He wasn't picking on *you*. He's that way with everybody."

"I know, General, but nobody can treat me that way and make me like it. All I did was show him I didn't like it."

Carter only nodded and didn't reply for a few moments. "Can I rely on your confidence, Colonel?" he asked suddenly.

"Absolutely, sir."

"Well, I'm going to tell you a few things about Hobson. He's one of these political fellows, as you already know, but there are other things you probably don't."

"Yes, sir."

"He's a big man in politics. He was one of the founders of the Republican party and about the first fellow outside of Illinois to back Lincoln for nomination for president. He got elected to Congress in '60 but got beaten for reelection last fall. He's been wanting in the army ever since but wouldn't settle for anything less then a corps. He's one of those fellows who think they can do like Jackson and Taylor did, win a big military reputation and get elected president. Well, they didn't put anyone in General Stanfield's place for a while, and he managed to get it when they did." Carter sighed and looked off into the trees. "That's the sort of thing we've got to put up with. It's politics, politics, politics. We'd have beaten the Rebels by now if it wasn't for politics."

"Yes, sir, I know."

"Now, these political fellows always make a bad blunder sooner or later. None of them know anything about the military, and advice from men who do can only carry a man so far. Hobson's the worst I've seen, and he won't listen to professional advice like most of them will. He'll make his blunder sooner than most and there'll be a big uproar and they'll have to get rid of him. Of course, he won't be dismissed or anything like that. He'll resign to take a diplomatic appointment or something, like they always do." Carter looked down and shook his head. "It'll probably cost a lot of good men their lives, but there's no help for it." He looked up at Tom suddenly. "Anyhow, General Hobson won't be with us long."

Tom couldn't see what Carter was driving at. "What's that got to do with me, sir?"

"Well, if you keep your brigade, you'll have it when Hobson's gone. If you don't, somebody else will get it and you'll be stuck where you are. If you get through this all right, you'll get to keep it. You might even make brigadier general. You were never in politics like Rivers was."

"What do I have to do to keep it, though?"

Carter didn't answer directly. "Well, Hobson's all rattled. You humiliated him in front of his staff and two division commanders. One of them told me about it before I heard from Hobson." Carter couldn't help laughing a little. "This fellow said that when you told Hobson you hadn't got to be a colonel by politics, it hit him so hard he couldn't say anything. He didn't know what to do. He couldn't have you arrested, because you hadn't said anything he could charge you with and too many men who wouldn't lie for him had heard it all. He'd found out what browbeating you led to. He couldn't do anything, and it really got him. I guess this is the first time anyone ever turned the tables on him like that." Carter laughed again. "He doesn't look like he slept well last night."

Tom started to speak, but Carter headed him off. "The first thing this morning, he called me up to see him and said you had to go. I argued with him. I tried everything. I told him how you set up Ramsdell for me. I said I'd never seen such nerve. Anyone else would have run back to Division. You got men twice your age to go along with something that must have scared them half to death. You got a whole brigade of men to follow you in a charge that must've looked like suicide." Carter looked at Tom earnestly. "I can't understand how you did that. You must be the one in a million that men will follow into anything."

Tom hadn't thought of it like that and was so bemused he couldn't think of anything to say until Carter went on.

"I even told Hobson that all I did was follow your suggestions, that you handled the whole thing a lot more than I did and that was what

I was going to say in my report when it's all over." Carter nodded and smiled. "You know, you've got natural talent. I know you study a lot, but books and training don't give a man what you've got. That's the kind of thing you're born with."

Tom finally thought of something to say. "I appreciate the general's compliments." He ought to be honest and tell Carter what it really was, instead of nerve and talent, but he couldn't do it.

"That's why I want you to keep your brigade. I'd move heaven and earth to do it, but you've got to do it yourself."

"What do I have to do, sir?"

"Go to Hobson and apologize. I think he might change his mind if you'd do that."

"I can't do it, sir. I've got nothing to apologize for."

"You could just say you're sorry it happened. That really wouldn't be apologizing for anything."

Tom shook his head. "He wouldn't be satisfied with that. He'd want to make me crawl, and I might not be able to hold my temper this time. I despise men like him."

"Well, you'll lose the brigade then. You see, you weren't put in command formally. I can't do that. Hobson can't either, but Stanton jumps when he snaps his fingers, so it's the same as if he had the authority. The way it is, you've got to have Hobson's recommendation to get officially confirmed. All he's got to do is to refuse it, and out you go."

"I guess I'll just have to go," said Tom resignedly.

Carter looked at him keenly. "I know men who'd sell their souls for a brigade, Colonel."

"I'm sorry, sir, but I'm not one of them."

Carter sighed. "Well, I respect you for it, all the more because I can't say I wouldn't do it."

"Well, sir, it's your line of business. I might feel differently if it was mine."

Carter looked at him quizzically. "You ought to make it yours, Colonel. You were made for it."

That was about the same thing Carolyn had said. Tom knew better, but there was no way he could tell Carter. "Thank you, sir. I've never thought about it, but I don't think I'd like the army in peacetime, and this war won't last forever."

"You're right. We'll just wear the Rebels down, if things go on like they have been anyhow. There just aren't enough of them and they've got no industry to speak of, or much else for that matter. Then the fellows out in Tennessee and Mississippi are doing a lot better than we are here in the East." He laughed bitterly. "They're too far from Washington for the politicians to mess around with them like they do us."

Carter started to mount. "Well, I've got to go. When Bixby comes to take over your brigade, just go back to your regiment."

"Bixby? Who's he?"

"One of Hobson's staff."

"Pater's senior. It ought to be him."

"No, it'll be Bixby. Hobson's already promised him the first brigade that comes up."

"Is he one of those political fellows?"

Carter nodded affirmatively. "He's commanded a regiment, though, so he's bound to know something. He's not senior to Pater, but that won't make any difference. Stanton will confirm him." He eyed Tom speculatively. "Does that make any difference to you, Bixby being a political fellow?"

"No, sir. He'll be under you, and you'll see to it that he does a good job."

"I don't know about that," said Carter. "Bixby and Hobson are as close as two peas in a pod, and I may have trouble with them." He mounted his horse easily, which always astonished Tom, because the stirrups looked almost as high as he was. "Before I go," he went on, "I want to see what those Rebels down there are doing by this time."

Tom followed the general to the tree Grabner was in. He said the Rebels weren't doing anything but building a lot of fires, to have breakfast, he guessed.

"Whoever's in command down there must not be very energetic," remarked Tom. "We could have our whole army up here for all he knows." Carter only laughed, so Tom asked, "Hobson's surely going to attack them, isn't he?"

"Yes. We would've been moving on them now if Hobson hadn't got the corps spread out from hell to breakfast and the trains and guns all mixed up. I hope he gets everything straightened out before they find out we're here. It's just too good a chance to miss. We've got them outnumbered two to one, and we'll catch them off guard."

"Are we sure that's all they have, two divisions?"

"Yes. Sergeant Kemper's spotted every Rebel in twenty miles in that direction and even told me what kind of guns they've got down there, all brass Napoléons. He's worth a squadron of cavalry, that fellow." Carter mounted. "Well, I've got to go. Hobson should have things straightened out by now. Bixby will probably come soon, so just go back to your regiment when he does."

"Yes, sir, and I thank the general for all he tried to do for me."

Carter reined about and rode off, only waving in reply to Tom's salute.

It wasn't long before a strange colonel on horseback came down the road. He was a tall, slender fellow with an elaborate mustache and long black hair nearly down to his shoulders, a dandy if there ever was one. Two other officers trailed him some distance back but stopped when he did.

"Colonel Traylor?"

"Yes. You're Colonel Bixby, I guess."

Bixby nodded. "I've come to assume command of this brigade by order of General Hobson." He affected calm, but his flickering eyes gave him away.

Tom was nettled because Bixby hadn't dismounted or offered his hand but suspected it part of an attempt to provoke him and didn't show it. "Yes, General Carter said you'd be coming," he replied casually. "It's all yours." If the fellow wanted anything out of him, he was going to have to ask for it.

Bixby obviously didn't want to do it, but he had to. "What are your dispositions, Colonel?"

"The brigade's deployed across the road here at the edge of the woods, two regiments on each side. The artillery's unhitched on the road, but the horses are there with the guns."

"I understand you're in contact with the enemy. What can you tell me about him?" He fidgeted with his reins and his horse moved nervously.

Tom was astonished at the man's ignorance. "I'm not actually in contact, but I've got him under observation."

"Do you mean you can see the enemy but don't have skirmishers in contact?" Bixby asked haughtily.

Tom was more shocked than angered. "No, you see, the enemy doesn't know we're here, and—"

Bixby broke in on him, "Well, he's soon going to find out!"

Tom was horrified. "If you're going to send skirmishers out or anything, you'd better ask General Carter about it first!"

"Humph. I can command a brigade without running to the division commander about every little thing," sneered Bixby.

Those two officers who had come with Bixby gave it away. They pretended not to be listening, but they hadn't come for nothing. Hobson and Bixby were out to goad Tom into insubordination and had brought witnesses along. No one else was in hearing and Tom knew he should shut up, but there were the men to think of. They would pay whatever price was exacted from putting the Rebels on guard. "Listen, Colonel," he said earnestly, "you'd better take my advice and tell General Carter before you do anything."

"Are you trying to tell me how to command my brigade?" demanded Bixby.

Suddenly it dawned on Tom that it was all a bluff. Bixby had no intention of actually doing what he made out. Tom had nearly fallen into the trap Hobson had set for him. "No, sir, I would never presume to do that with such a distinguished soldier as the colonel is," he said mockingly as he turned away.

Von Jagerhof was surprised at his return and even more so when he learned why. "It's incredible! Who's this Bixby that he thinks he can take your place?"

Tom had to tell him about Hobson and Bixby and what had passed between him and them, but he enjoined the strictest secrecy and had made sure no one else heard. "I wouldn't tell you, but I've been thinking. They may actually order skirmishers out, and if they do, it'll be us."

"But when you start to obey, they'll call you back."

"I hope so, but don't count on it. We'll just have to wait and see."

They didn't have to wait long. A strange officer rode up through the trees, a headquarters type if there ever was one. He was a big, flabby, black-bearded major whose fish white skin had never been exposed to the elements. He extended a small piece of paper and, when Tom took it, wheeled away without a word.

It was an order to take the regiment out at once and establish a skirmish line in contact with the enemy. Bixby's signature was at the bottom.

Tom thought of going back for one last attempt to persuade Bixby, but he smelled a rat. Written orders were rarely given in the field, and a protest could be twisted into a refusal to obey with the right witnesses around.

He looked around for Carter, but he was nowhere in sight. Hobson had probably arranged to keep him away. Tom saw the flabby, fish-skinned major and several ruffianly-looking soldiers on the road behind him. They had their eyes on him and probably had orders to intercept any messenger he might send to Carter.

"May I ask if that is what you are expecting?" von Jagerhof asked.

"It is."

"What are you going to do?"

"I'm going to obey," replied Tom grimly. "It'll never be said of me that I disobeyed an order."

"Oh, I still believe they'll stop you before you actually do," said von Jagerhof hopefully.

"We'll soon see," replied Tom. "Call Grabner down and we'll get started."

Although he took his time about it, there was no attempt to stop Tom while he took his men out of the line, formed them into a column, and led them out from under the trees. He was well down the slope when he heard angry shouting back on the road. He looked back to see General Carter shoving his way through the fish-skinned major and his plug-ugly escort. The general had the advantage of being on horseback and broke through despite their efforts to block him. He spurred toward Tom shouting, "Halt! Halt there, Colonel Traylor! Come back! Come back here right now!"

Tom halted the column and turned to face Carter as he dashed up. "What's the meaning of this?" he demanded. "Why have you come out here and why did those men try to stop me back there? Have all of you gone crazy?"

Tom took Bixby's order from his pocket and handed it to Carter without a word.

Carter glanced at it; then straightened in his saddle and read it carefully. "I'll be damned!" he said incredulously. "I'll be goddamned!"

Tom said nothing as Carter folded the order and put it in his pocket. "I'll keep this, Colonel, if you don't mind."

"Be careful with it, sir. It might save my neck."

"I will. I'll be *very* careful with it, Colonel." The little general's eyes glittered like twin daggers. "You needn't worry about your neck, Colonel," he added ominously, "but I know a fellow who'd better worry about his." He nodded grimly. "Now, I'm going to be pretty busy for a while, so you just take your regiment back where it was and stay there."

"Yes, sir," said Tom as Carter reined away and headed back toward the fish-skinned major and his ruffians. By the time Tom had his men back in place, Carter had disarmed the major and his men and called a platoon out of Hartley's regiment to keep them under guard.

Hobson and Bixby rode up while this was going on, but Carter disregarded Hobson's attempts to interfere. After it was done, he took the two out of hearing, but they were still in sight, and it looked like the little general laid down the law. Anyhow, he did most of the talking, and after a little bluster by Hobson both he and Bixby took it quietly. After a while they left, looking pretty subdued. They took the fish-skinned major with them, but his men were marched away under guard.

After they were gone, Carter came back to Tom. "Let's get that German fellow back up this tree here."

When Grabner got settled in his tree, he reported that the Rebels were running around like mad. They had brought horses and were hitching up their guns. It looked like their infantry was forming a line of battle, or maybe a column. He couldn't tell yet.

When Tom translated, Carter said explosively, "Oh, Lord! They saw you! I was hoping they hadn't!"

"Yes, sir, I'm afraid they did."

Carter nodded grimly. "Our attack's ruined, absolutely ruined, and I know who's going to pay for it."

Tom knew who he meant, but he didn't say anything.

A horseman came through the woods from the right calling, "Gin'ral Carter! Gin'ral Carter!" He was Zeke Kerns.

"Over here!" shouted Carter, and Zeke headed toward them.

"I'm frum Sargint Kemper, sir," said Zeke as soon as he reined up, "an' he says t' tell th' gin'ral that they's two more Rebel d'visions comin' east 'long that ol' road down thar tords them two that's already there."

"How far away?" barked Carter.

" 'Bout two hours' march, th' sargint 'lowed."

A courier came galloping down the road, reined up in a shower of dead leaves and dirt, and called the general aside. Whatever he told him was evidently supposed to be secret.

Carter was galvanized. "That's it! That's the end of it! We're getting out of here!" He beckoned to Zeke as he wheeled away. "Come along, soldier," he said and led him toward the road. They turned north and broke into a gallop as soon as they reached it.

It looked like Carter was headed for another showdown with Hobson, but Tom wondered why he thought they had to run like that with only a corps to contend with. He guessed something must have gone wrong somewhere else, and was confirmed in this by what happened next.

A courier arrived in a few minutes, and Tom wasn't really surprised when he went to Pater instead of him. He knew what to expect when Pater called him over after reading the message.

The Pennsylvanian handed it to Tom with a shake of the head. "You'd better read this, Colonel."

As Tom expected, it put Pater in command of the brigade, but it also ordered him to march east across country immediately, leaving the guns and wagons behind and making all possible speed. Something bad must have gone wrong to the north, something very bad.

He gave the message back to Pater and said, "That's fine, sir. I'll be happy to serve under you."

Pater looked relieved. "Thank you, Colonel; thank you very much." He folded the message and put it in his pocket. "I can't imagine why they've done this, put me in your place and ordered us to march like this." He sighed and shook his head. "It seems to be an urgent matter, though, so I guess we'd better get started."

"By all means, sir. Do you want me to bring up the rear like I always have?"

"Yes, we'll carry on like we always have," replied Pater. "I'll come back and talk with you later if I get the chance."

"Yes, sir. I'll see you then," replied Tom as Pater wheeled away.

The brigade formed a column on the road, then turned east and took off through the brush and thickets at a mad pace, leaving the guns and wagons behind. Tom guessed the rest of the corps was doing the same. The gunners and teamsters threw off all harness and rode their horses, most of them bareback. They could dodge around and avoid the thicker parts of the growth, but the infantry couldn't do that and it looked like the men were going to tear their clothing half off their bodies before it was over.

The going was incredibly difficult. Not only were there the brush and thickets to push through, but the drainage pattern changed and soon the men had to climb one razorback ridge after another. Rushing and sliding down the other sides was almost as bad as clambering up the near ones. There were creeks, invariably lined with the thickest briers and brush, to splash across. After an hour or so, the men in the regiments farther up the column began to throw their packs away, and to judge by the number as time went on, almost all of them did. Although it was still pretty hard, Tom's men had it much easier than the others, because the way was partly broken for them and he saw to it that none of them threw away their packs.

Tom and von Jagerhof rode ahead. They had it a lot better than the men on foot but were still so busy keeping their seats on the steep slopes and sparing their horses the briers that they had no chance to talk until the column reached a wider valley and turned south. Here the going wasn't so bad and the ground was level, which was probably why they had changed direction.

Von Jagerhof took the chance to tell what he thought about Tom's losing the brigade. "It's a shame, sir, a shame, and I'm not just saying that because I won't have the regiment anymore."

"Well, I don't like pushing you out," confided Tom, "but I'd really rather be back with my old regiment than have the brigade."

"I understand, sir, and I'm happy to have you back," was the sincere reply, "but I still can't understand how they could do it after all you accomplished."

"That's the kind of thing that comes from mixing politics up with the war."

They reached an even wider valley running east and turned to follow it. The going was even easier, because there was more room to dodge the worst parts of the growth, and it occurred to Tom that the Rebels would find it the same way if they were following. He told von Jagerhof to take the regiment on and reined aside. Billy's company was last in the line of march, and when it came up Tom told him to drop back and act as a rear guard. He was to stay as far back as he could without losing sight of the regiment and send word if he saw any sign of pursuit. Tom cautioned him to close up immediately if he saw anything larger than a bunch of scouts he could drive off.

Shortly after that, Pater dropped back to tell Tom to do what he had just done. He still acted bothered and uneasy, so Tom insisted on shaking his hand and congratulating him on getting in the way of making brigadier general.

The Pennsylvanian smiled and nodded. "I'm glad you don't have any hard feelings, because I don't feel very good about taking over the brigade myself."

"That's all right, sir. They gave it to you, and you had to take it. You're senior to the rest of us, you know."

Pater sighed. "Well, you know why I feel the way I do. I turned it down back there yesterday when things looked bad and threw it on you. I think they should have let you keep it. I can't understand why—"

Pater didn't seem to know about Bixby and Tom didn't want to go into that, so he cut him off an humorous note. "Well, sir, nobody but a damned fool would have taken it then."

They laughed together; then Pater said ruefully, "Well, if we ever get in a tight spot like that again, I'll probably be calling on that same damned fool to help get us out of it."

"Just let him know and he'll do what he can," replied Tom laughingly.

"I'm much obliged to you, Colonel, believe me," said Pater as he speeded his horse to draw away. Whatever his shortcomings, he was certainly a big improvement over Bixby. There was nothing devious or dishonest about him.

The column followed the valley along the north bank of a sizable stream until about an hour before dark, when it reached a good road running north–south and turned left to take it. The bridge to the right was burning furiously, and some men were there to see that it burned down, probably left by Carter to block pursuit from the south.

Once the column was on the road and no longer making so much noise breaking through brush and briers, the sounds of battle were faintly borne by the wind from far to the northwest, but it was someone else's fight. The corps had no artillery or supplies of any sort and only what ammunition the men had in their belts. The sounds died away after a while, but maybe only because the wind died down as darkness approached.

The column halted just before dark and orders came to let the men fall out to eat, but to allow no fires and be quick about it. It would be very quick for most of them, because they had thrown away their packs and their rations with them. Tom had already sent word to Billy to close up, and when he did he said there was no sign the Rebels were after them.

Tom expected they would take up the march again as soon as the men who had rations bolted them, but they didn't, and he guessed it had something to do with Zeke Kerns galloping past while his men were still eating.

When Zeke came back, Tom stopped him. "What's the news?" he asked.

"Oh, th' Rebels ain't chasin' you-uns a'tall. Them that wuz awreddy down thar by that crossroads come up t' whar you-uns had been an' th' t'others jined 'em, them that come frum th' east." Zeke stopped to laugh. "They got to plunderin' th' wagins, whoopin' and hollerin' an' gittin' stuff out t' eat an' wear. They got inta some uv th' sutlers' wagins an' y' oughta heered 'em carryin' on 'bout canned peaches an' stuff like that. I guess they're still thar er Sargint Kemper'd a sent somebody atter me."

"Well, it's almost dark now, so I guess we're safe, for the time being anyhow." Tom laughed shortly. "How do you know about some of those things, like the canned peaches?"

Zeke laughed in his turn. "Aw, Sargint Kemper'n me hid in some bresh 'long that road leadin' nawth, whar most uv th' wagins wuz, up real close. I wuz skeered t' death they'd see us, but they wuz s' took up with what wuz in them wagins they didn't see us come er go."

"Well, they sure got a big haul. Say, Zeke, how do you like the cavalry?"

"Jist fine, sir. Hit shore beats marchin', even if hits kinda skeerey sometimes." He fidgeted in his saddle. "Colonel, sir, I gotta go, er Sargint Kemper'll take th' hide offa me."

"Sure, Zeke. Give the boys my best when you get back."

"Yes, sir." Zeke went on, and when he passed his old company he was recognized in spite of the darkness. "Hey thar, yallerlaig! Jine th' infantry an' do some fightin'!"

Zeke disdained to stop. He had no time for "dum foot soljers" and disappeared into the gloom followed by good-natured hoots and jeers.

The men marched the next morning but halted early in the afternoon and went into camp near a creek, still in the junglelike brush country they had been in so long. It wasn't much of a camp, though, because no one had anything to eat and only Tom's men still had all their packs. In fact, it looked like everyone had lost everything except what he had on him, and Tom was resigned to the loss of his baggage, fancy uniforms and all, when he got a pleasant surprise.

He hadn't seen Hauser since before the march began and thought he had lost him, too, when the fellow showed up astride a horse bareback with Tom's and von Jagerhof's valises and uniform cases tied together across the animal's back like a pack. He never undertook to explain why he had been gone so long, but Tom was so glad to get his baggage back that he asked no questions.

When he thanked him for it, Hauser grinned and said that a good friend of his who was a teamster never let him down. He had to take the horse back, though, so the *Herr Oberst* and the *Herr Major* would have to carry their baggage on their own horses from then on.

Neither of them minded in the least.

The hungry spell went on through the next day's march, but when the column halted to go into camp, wagons with rations came back. The men were famished and immediately got busy building fires and cooking. Hauser cooked a fine meal despite his lack of implements, and Tom enjoyed it along with his adjutant.

He was about to bed down for the night when General Carter rode out of the gathering darkness and got off his horse. He tied the reins to a sapling, and they walked apart.

"Well," began Carter, "I guess it's all over for us, and everybody else, too, it looks like."

"You mean the whole campaign, sir?"

"Yes, the whole business. I guess Hooker's given it up. Anyhow, he's disengaging and pulling back as fast as he can." The general sighed sadly. "We've lost another one, and I'm afraid we're really in for it now."

"Do you think Lee will cross the Potomac and move north like he did after he beat Pope last August?"

"Undoubtedly, and Hooker can't handle him. He's just showed that."

"Maybe Lincoln will call McClellan back like he did when Lee moved north last August."

"Not a chance. The radicals hate McClellan, and they've got Lincoln under their thumb. They'd rather lose the war than see McClellan come back."

"Who'll take Hooker's place then? Surely they won't keep him now."

"Oh no, he'll go, but God only knows who'll take his place. I just hope he's a lucky fellow, whoever he is. Luck is about all that can save us now."

They meditated gloomily for a moment; then Carter changed the subject. "I'm sorry you didn't get to keep the brigade, Colonel."

"Oh, I'd really rather stay with my old regiment, so I can't say I have any regrets."

"Well, I'd a lot rather have you than Pater, or any of the others for that matter, and I'd have tried to do something about it, but Hobson sort of slipped it over on me. In all the confusion back there after I stopped you from going out, I forgot about it, and the first thing I knew, Hobson had issued orders putting Pater in command. Of course, Stanton will confirm it and he'll keep it."

Tom was hoping Carter would go on about Hobson and Bixby, but he changed the subject again. "Say," he said suddenly, "Sergeant Kemper's going to be leaving you for good, and his men, too. I'm going to make them my headquarters guard. I've never had any because I didn't feel I needed one, but of course I won't really use them for that. I'm going to have my own scouts from now on. A man just can't count on having any cavalry anymore, and that Kemper's worth a whole squadron of it anyhow."

"Well, sir, I hate to lose him. He's the best sergeant major anyone ever had, and those men he took are the best. They'll do us all a lot more good scouting for you, though."

"I'm going to get him a commission, too, regular army. That way that governor of yours won't have anything to say about it."

"I'm sure glad to hear that. He should have been an officer a long time ago."

There was a pause; then Carter finally got down to it. "Now, what I came to see you about was Hobson and Bixby. I guess you know I fired Bixby and that Hobson had to give in to it." He lowered his voice and looked around. "They're both going to resign, so I've been told, but

I haven't talked to either of them since we had that big ruckus back there."

"Is that right, sir? I can't say I'm sorry to hear it."

"It's not because of what I might do. About all I could do would be to cause Hobson some embarrassment by filing charges against Bixby for sending you out without my authorization and waking those Rebels up back there. Hooker's after him."

"Why's that, sir?"

"Well, you've probably been wondering why we had to take off into that jungle back there and leave all the guns and wagons behind."

"Yes, sir, I have."

"It's like this. When Hobson started concentrating for his attack on those Rebels down there around that crossroads, he broke contact with the rest of the army to the north and didn't tell Hooker or anyone else about it. The Rebels found the gap and slipped a corps into it, and you could count on them moving against us from both sides as soon as they found out what a fix they had us in. It didn't take them long to find out either, and we got out just in time. That's why Hooker's after Hobson. He'll appoint a court of inquiry, and a court-martial's certain to follow."

"Won't Stanton put a stop to it?"

Carter laughed bitterly. "No. It's losing all the guns, wagons, and supplies for a whole army corps. If he'd only got a few thousand men killed, Stanton wouldn't mind, but he won't stand for *that*."

"Yes, sir, I see." Tom saw a chance to ask some things he had been wondering about. "You know, sir, there are several things about what happened back there day before yesterday that I don't understand. For example, why did Bixby give me a written order to go out and establish contact?"

"So they'd have the goods on you if you refused to obey."

"But then you hadn't endorsed it and that would've hurt their case against me, not to mention Bixby laying himself open to charges by acting without authorization."

"Oh, Hobson knew Stanton would back him up and thought he could just push me out of the way. You'd have refused to obey a written order, and it wouldn't make any difference if I'd countersigned it or not."

"Then, here's something else. If all they wanted to do was goad me into insubordination, why didn't Bixby stop me when he saw I actually was going out?"

Carter took his time about replying. "Well, I don't know. All we can do is guess about that, and my guess is that they were counting on your getting killed."

Tom hadn't taken it that far and was too shocked to say anything, so Carter went on. "I think you could count on the Rebels setting up an ambush in that brush out there just as soon as they saw you coming. Hobson and Bixby figured on that, and they knew you would see it the same way and go out in front of your men, probably on horseback so you could see better. That's the only way it makes sense. That would dispose of that written order and save them any trouble that might have come out of it. They could just say you went out on your own. You'd be dead, and dead men tell no tales. They thought they couldn't lose. If they couldn't goad you into insubordination, they'd get you killed."

Tom knew that Carter had guessed right because that was the only way it did make sense. He had underestimated Hobson and Bixby, or overestimated them rather. They knew him better than he knew them. Such depravity was almost beyond understanding, though, and he couldn't help saying, "That's hard to believe."

Carter went on, his voice rising a little. "But that's not the worst part of it. Hobson had issued his orders to attack before he sent Bixby to you. That shows he was willing to put the Rebels on their guard and get a lot more of his men killed just to get you."

Tom drew a shuddering sigh. "Oh, God! To throw away men's lives like that—"

Carter cut him off. "What do fellows like Hobson care about human life? They're the ones who drove the South out of the Union and caused this war, and they knew what they were doing all the while. Get votes and win elections, that's all they cared about. So what if it cost a few hundred thousand men their lives and devastated half the country? That wouldn't faze those fellows."

Tom could only shake his head at the enormity of it all.

Carter went on. "Well, we're rid of Hobson and Bixby, though, both of them. Hobson hasn't got any choice now, and Bixby will go with him. He knows I'll file charges if he doesn't resign, and without Hobson to protect him, he'd be a goner."

"Yes," said Tom, "I guess some good will come out of it after all." He shook his head sadly. "I just hope we don't get a couple more like them."

"Well," said Carter, "I've got to be going, but there's one thing I want to ask of you before I do."

"Yes, sir?"

"Help Pater if you ever think he needs it. He's a fine fellow, but he's slow and timid. He'll need you if he gets in a tight spot."

"Yes, sir, he's already told me that."

"Good. I'm glad to hear that," said Carter as they walked toward his horse. He untied the reins and mounted. "We'll be seeing you, Colonel," was his reply to Tom's salute as he reined away into the darkness.

# 48

The brigade had been in camp for several weeks a little northwest of Washington, but it was an uneasy time. Everyone knew the Rebels would follow up their victory at Chancellorsville with an invasion of the North and there would be a great battle. It was only a matter of time, and the men lived in momentary expectation of an order to march.

It was about noon when Tom received Carolyn's reply to the letter he had written just after Chancellorsville. He had told her how her father had been killed and of his promise to take care of her, sacred because it had been made to a dying man whose last thoughts had been for her. Tom wanted to fulfill his pledge by marrying her. He loved her and was now completely free of the red-haired woman. He hoped Carolyn felt differently than when he had last seen her and would have him.

The reply was disappointingly short at first glance, but what it said more than made up for that. She felt differently than when she had seen him last. She hadn't realized how much she loved him and wanted to be with him until after her father's funeral, when she had received Tom's letter. She had been almost out of her mind with grief, and her realization of their love was about all that had saved her.

Her Uncle Ted was coming to Washington on business, and she was going along on the chance she would get to see Tom. She had heard that his brigade was camped nearby and hoped to God it would still be there. This was a heaven-sent opportunity, because the papers said the Rebels were going to cross the Potomac and that there would be a great battle. She hoped and prayed she could get there before it all started. She and her uncle were taking a roundabout northern route to Washington in case the Rebels cut the more direct line.

The letter was nearly too late. She would arrive that very afternoon at four o'clock, which gave Tom barely time to meet the train, if he could get away in the next hour. That was the rub. The brigade was on one hour's notice to march and no one could expect to get a pass, but he had to have one. Like Carolyn said, it was a heaven-sent opportunity. The only thing was to see Pater about it.

Pater produced a pass blank even before Tom finished his story. "I was young once, and I can tell myself I'm doing this for Rivers."

"I'll be much obliged to you, sir. I just hope it won't cause you any difficulty."

"Oh, it won't. I'm sure General Carter will feel the same way about it. You can just turn your regiment over to Major von Jagerhof. I'm sure he'll be able to handle it."

Tom felt elated. "Better than I can, I expect."

Pater left the termination date blank. "Just put whatever you want in that. There's just one thing. I'll have to know where you'll be. We may march any time. I'll send your orderly for you if we do."

Tom gave Pater the address of the hotel where Carolyn would be staying. He guessed he could get a room there and, if he couldn't, she would know where to find him.

Pater waved him away. "You'd better hurry, Colonel."

"Yes, sir. Thank you very much, sir." He left in such a fever of impatience that he forgot he was wearing his sword and revolver.

Von Jagerhof saw him off. Tom had forgotten to tell Billy, so he asked the Prussian to do it. "Of course, sir. I hope you have a happy time. Give the young lady my best regards."

Washington was less than three hours' ride, but Tom knew nothing about the town. All he had was the name of the station where the train would come in and the address of the hotel where Carolyn and her uncle would stay. It would take too long to find the station, so he decided to go to the hotel.

Luck was with him and he got to meet the train after all. He overtook a courier going back after delivering dispatches. The fellow had been there for two years and knew the town like a book. He had plenty of time, so he took Tom straight to the station.

They barely made it in time. Tom had scarcely thanked the fellow and hitched his horse when the train came in. He dashed for the platform and placed himself about the middle of the train. A lot of people got off and he nearly twisted his neck trying to see them all before Carolyn and a distinguished-looking silver-haired man got off the next coach down.

She saw him at once and ran to meet him, leaving her escort looking after her in astonishment. She was as beautiful as ever, but her face seemed drawn and there was an air of tension and anxiety about her. They rushed into each other's arms.

"Tom! Oh, Tom!" She exclaimed as she clasped him with a strength he had never suspected she had. "I'm glad, so glad, you haven't marched yet! I was so afraid—"

There was an embarrassed cough from her escort, so she unclasped Tom and turned to him. "Oh, Tom—this is my uncle, Theodore Ridge." She was flustered and her face charmingly flushed. "Uncle Ted, this is Colonel Traylor. He was with my father when he was . . . was killed. He was very close to him."

"Well, I can see he's very close to you, too, Carrie," laughed Ridge as he extended his hand. "I've heard a lot about you, Colonel, and I'm very pleased to meet you," he said as they shook hands.

"The same for me," replied Tom, "and I hope what you've heard about me was as good as what I've heard about you."

"Oh, it was good, very good. I had no idea Carrie was such a demonstrative young lady, though," he said with a wink.

She looked even more flustered but didn't withdraw the arm she had kept about Tom's waist. "Oh, I'm sorry, Uncle Ted," she faltered, "but I was afraid he'd be gone, and he'd . . . I'd never see him again. If only you knew—" She had to stop and use her handkerchief.

"I understand, darling Carrie," replied Ridge sympathetically. "You've lost so much, and there's a big battle coming."

She sobbed into her handkerchief. "Oh," she cried, "if you only knew how it is with Tom, the things he does, you'd understand even better."

Ridge nodded, but Tom could see it was lost on him and moved quickly to keep it that way. "You're looking well, darling," he said to Carolyn. "You're more beautiful than ever." It was true. Her features seemed even more finely cut and her eyes a deeper blue.

She put aside her handkerchief and gazed into his eyes, a beatific smile overspreading her face. "Thank you, darling," she whispered. "So are you."

Uncle Ted coughed again. "Well, we'd better get to our hotel. They won't keep rooms for you very long around here."

They saw about the baggage and got a cab. Ridge insisted on riding Tom's horse, claiming he had had enough of coaches and cabs. A sly wink showed his reason, and they laughed about it.

Tom and Carolyn were scarcely in the cab before they were in each other's arms. "Tom, oh, Tom," she murmured between kisses, "I'm so glad we got here in time, and went that roundabout way through Columbus and on east. On the train we heard that Lee has crossed into Pennsylvania."

Tom sat bolt upright. "Lee's in Pennsylvania! I didn't know that! I'd better get back!"

She seized his arm, her hands like little vises. "No! No! Please don't go, Tom, not until morning, anyhow!"

He relaxed a little. "Who told you about where Lee was?"

She put her arms around him. "A fellow who got on our car about half an hour back. He was telling everybody."

"Who was he?"

"Just an ordinary-looking man, no soldier. He was probably just talking." She hugged him tightly. "Don't go, Tom; please don't go," she pleaded. "Wait . . . wait until morning anyhow, so we can . . . can be together tonight."

He relaxed some more. "It's probably just a rumor. I've heard much the same thing every day for the past week, I believe." Anyhow, Pater would send for him if they marched.

They embraced. "I love you, Carolyn, I love you," he murmured.

"I love you, too, darling. I love you so much it hurts. I never knew how much until they started talking about the Rebels coming north." She sighed tumultuously. "They've done it now, and you'll march, and there'll be a big battle, and the way you do—" Her voice trailed off into sobs.

He tried to kiss the tears away. "Don't worry, darling. I've changed my ways. I don't do like I used to."

She gave a sigh that was half a sob, her bosom heaving against his chest. "I'm glad, so glad, and I hope you'll be even more careful now."

"I will, darling." He hoped God she never found out some of the things he had done at Chancellorsville. "Carolyn, you say we . . . we'll be together tonight?"

"Yes . . . yes . . . we'll sleep together, all night!" She kissed him passionately.

A deep thrill went through him. "But what about your uncle?"

"He won't know," she whispered as she snuggled even closer. "Our rooms are on different floors. I saw to that. I knew we'd be lucky to have just one night together."

"But how . . . how can we manage it so he won't find out?"

"You say all you could get was a few hours to come and see me and you've got to go. You pretend to leave and I'll plead a headache. Come back in a little while. I'll be in Room Fourteen, on the first floor. I'll be waiting for you."

The cab stopped and the driver announced they were at the hotel. Tom had just paid him when a familiar voice called, *"Herr Oberst! Herr Oberst!"* It was Hauser, and his heart fell. They wouldn't have to lie to Uncle Ted now.

Hauser extended a note. Tom took it, wondering why Pater had bothered to write. Carolyn gave a little shriek and clutched his arm. "Oh, God!" she breathed, "Please, please—"

The note began like Tom expected, but it didn't end that way. The brigade had marched a few hours after he left, but he wasn't told to come back. All Pater did was give him the route of march for the first two days and tell him where he expected to camp at night. Tom blessed the good old Pennsylvanian who remembered how it was to be young and in love. He would take only one night, though. Two would be too risky for everybody concerned, although Pater was willing.

Carolyn's face was white and her lips trembled. "What . . . what is it, darling?" she whispered.

Uncle Ted was busy with the luggage, so Tom told her. She tightened her grip on his arm. "Oh, God, thank You, thank You—" She stopped and wiped her eyes, then regained control with an effort that made her tremble. "We'll do it now," she whispered. "We'll pretend you've been called back, and you leave. Then come to me. Wait long enough, but . . . but not too long."

Tom told Hauser to take his horse and wait by the hitching rail. He and Carolyn put on their act for Uncle Ted, who said he was very sorry, mainly for Carrie, but also for himself. He had looked forward to getting to know Tom and talking about the war.

After a tearful farewell in which Carolyn could have fooled him, Tom took his leave. He and Hauser mounted their horses and started down the street. Once they were out of sight, Tom told him he really wasn't going back, not now, anyhow. It probably wouldn't be until morning.

Hauser understood. There was a livery stable a few blocks farther along where he had stopped to ask directions. It was run by a German. He would take the horses there and wait. He would sleep on the hay and send out for anything he needed so he would be ready any time the *Herr Oberst* wanted to go.

After they reined over to the curb and Tom dismounted, he thrust a five-dollar greenback on Hauser for food and refreshment. He accepted delightedly. It would buy a lot of sausages and beer, also fine cigars, naturally to be enjoyed out of doors at a livery stable. He departed in high glee, leading Tom's horse and riding his own.

Tom idled about for a while, then went back to the hotel. Carolyn's door was unlocked almost before he finished knocking.

After their first lovemaking, they lay in each other's arms. She fondled his body, feeling the bones and muscles of his arms and shoulders. Suddenly she began to sob. "Oh, so beautiful, so strong and manly—"

"Why do you cry, darling?"

She couldn't answer for a moment, and when she did, he wished she hadn't. "Because you may be dead . . . dead like Father in a day or two—" She broke into a weeping the likes of which he had never heard. It came not from the heart, but from the soul.

He tried to comfort her. "Don't worry, sweetheart. I'll be careful, very careful."

It didn't seem to help. "Maybe there won't be a battle after all, at least not a big one," he added unconvincingly.

"Oh yes, there'll be a battle, and a big one. They're coming and you'll try to stop them and drive them back." She had to stop weeping to say it, and to his great relief, she didn't start again.

"I'll be careful," he promised earnestly. "I won't take any chances or anything."

She hugged him, again with a strength that astonished him. "Please do, darling, be very careful; please do. Don't get carried away. Always think of me and how I love you," she added with a note of desperation.

"I will, sweetheart, I'll always think of you, and I'll be careful." He ran his hand over her back, feeling the delicate flesh and bones, then went down to the gentle swell of her hips.

She moved against him and before long they made love again. Afterwards they dozed in each other's arms for what seemed like only a little while, but when he pulled away and looked at his watch by the window where a light shone in, it was midnight. Just as he got back in bed, the light went out and a dank, chill puff of air blew into the room.

He didn't like darkness and was thinking of getting up to light the candle when an eerie sound intruded gradually into the room through the window. It was the sound of marching men, many of them, but it was uncanny. They were in step and their footfalls beat a precise muted thunder that swelled until it filled the room like something physical and tangible. It was uncanny, because they marched in what was otherwise an ocean of silence. There were no commands, no talking, no creak and rattle of equipment.

Carolyn cowered in his arms, and his hair rose on his head. It was midnight and the light had gone out. Was what he heard the march of an army of phantoms, of men who had fallen on the bloody fields all around Washington? Were Burk, Jim Polson, and Sam Price in its ranks, still stained with their life's blood? Did Carolyn's father ride along the column on a spectral horse? Would Tom be with them soon, marching on and on, through all eternity?

He couldn't get a grip on himself until the sound faded and died away, and he shuddered when the light outside the window came back.

Carolyn hugged him tightly. "Were those . . . men?" she whispered. "It sounded so strange, like they were . . . ghosts or something."

Tom did his best to sound casual. "Oh, that was just a regiment, or maybe a small brigade, taking a shortcut through town."

"But . . . but it sounded so strange—"

"Oh, that was because we couldn't see them and the buildings along the street down there caught the noise of the marching and . . . and sort of made it sound so loud it drowned out everything else, something like an echo, you know." He didn't believe it, although it sounded logical, and moved his body to hide another shudder at the thought of what he might have seen if he had gone to the window.

Carolyn seemed reassured and went to sleep in his arms. He couldn't sleep, though, and disentangled himself so he could move about in the bed. Several times he thought he heard the ghostly marchers again, but the initial sounds either faded away or turned out to be something else.

He was so restless he sat on the edge of the bed. Carolyn slept on, so he got up and walked around the room. In the dim light he could make out his uniform draped on a chair with his belt, sword, and revolver.

Carolyn still slept. Parting from her in the morning would be worse than dying. Should he leave now? If he did, it would spare them both. There was paper, pen, and ink on the small table in the corner by the window where there would be enough light to write a note of explanation. She would understand.

He wrote the note and put it on the bedstand where she would be sure to see it, then slipped noiselessly into his uniform and eased out of the room in his stocking feet. In the hall he put on his boots and belt, then paused before the door. He heard nothing from within but the deep and regular breathing of the sleep that follows love. He had to tear himself away and blinked back the tears as he went down the hall. Only when he was outside did he remember that he had forgotten to lock the door to Carolyn's room behind him. He couldn't go back, though, or he would stay.

He had no trouble finding the livery stable, but it didn't sound like one. It sounded like a dance hall. Lively German music came from within, blended with the rhythmical stamping of feet and sounds of merrymaking.

Although the large doors in front were open, he could see no light. After a moment's hesitation, he went inside. The music and the noise came from around a corner where he could see light. He made his way toward it past a pile of hay, then, carefully keeping in the shadows, looked around.

He saw a well-illuminated room with a board floor through an open door, probably a sleeping room for occasional use, although there was no bed in it. It was crowded with people, but only because it was small. There didn't seem to be more than a half-dozen of them. A man sat on a bench against the far wall playing a concertina, and next to him was a keg surrounded by beer mugs. The others were dancing.

Tom could scarcely believe his eyes when he saw Hauser cavorting among them like a youngster. He was dancing with a buxom blond woman who looked to be about his age. They pranced about to the music, bobbing and bowing, then seized one another and whirled at a mad pace before separating and commencing the prancing again.

Hauser was having a wonderful time. He wore a perpetual grin and occasionally broke into laughter and joyful whoops. The others behaved much the same, creating the merry din that could be heard at the outside door. Hauser was a fast worker. He had doubtless gotten up the party and found himself a *Fräulein,* too.

Tom turned away and left the barn. Hauser was going the same place he was, and he wasn't going to deny him his fun. It might be the last he would ever have.

He went back to the hotel and was able to enter and undress without waking Carolyn. He didn't forget to put the note in his coat pocket. Only when he got back into bed did she rouse, but only muttered sleepily and turned over. He went straight to sleep.

She woke him stirring about in bed. Light through the window showed the sun was coming up. He was loggy and sleepy, but she wasn't. She wanted to make love again and soon roused his ardor. She was more passionate than Mary had been, probably because of what loomed before him now.

Afterward as they lay in each other's arms, the sound of marching men again came through the window, but it was not the macabre tramping of the night before. These men weren't in step, and there was talking along with the creak and rattle of equipment. He wondered about what he had heard last night, but Carolyn seemed to have forgotten it. Had he only been dreaming? He thought of asking her but was afraid she might not remember.

The marching reminded him of his duty. "I've got to go, my love, and Uncle Ted will be coming by for breakfast pretty soon." He shrank inwardly, expecting her to break into that heartrending, soulful weeping again, but she didn't.

"Not one more night, darling?"

"I'm afraid not. Pater went out on a limb to give me even one, and we couldn't dodge Uncle Ted all day." He kissed her forehead. "You understand, don't you, darling?"

She sighed. "Yes, I guess you're right." Then to his dismay she started weeping, but only softly.

He held her close and tried to console her. "But I'll be back, sweetheart. I'll be careful like I promised, and nothing will happen to me."

She stopped weeping and he felt her head moving against his chest. "Yes," she whispered, "I have faith. I have faith now. Nothing will happen to you. You'll be safe. I know it."

He was enormously relieved and very glad he hadn't left the night before. "We'll be married as soon as we can, and always be together like this."

She nodded again. "Always, always together."

"I'll try to get leave as soon as this campaign's over, if we hold them off anyhow. If I can't, you have Uncle Ted or somebody bring you wherever I'll be."

She spoke with determination, almost with desperation. "I don't want to wait until you can get leave. Just as soon as you get located after this is over, write me, and I'll come, by myself if I have to."

"Yes, darling, and I'll write as often as I can. You be sure to answer quickly."

"Oh, let's just write as often as we can, without waiting for answers. All right?"

"Yes, yes, we will, only I'll get a lot more letters than you will for a while."

More men were marching by, and he couldn't wait any longer. "I've got to get up and go, sweetheart."

They embraced and her slender white arms squeezed him like bands of steel. Then she let him go, and watched while he washed his face and dressed.

When he put on his belt with sword and revolver, it was like a great dark shadow came over her face. He was choking with emotion, but he put a finger to his lips and said softly, "Please, darling, let me remember you smiling."

A tremor passed across her face, and the shadow was gone. She smiled that beatific smile again. "I have faith. You'll be safe. I know it. I just know it."

He knelt for one last kiss, then went to the door. He opened it, then turned to her. *"Auf Wiedersehen, mein Liebling."*

Her puzzled look made him realize he had spoken in German. "That means 'until we meet again, my darling.' "

She smiled gloriously, looking like the most beautiful angel in all of Heaven. "How wonderful! 'Good-bye' sounds so . . . final, like it might be forever." Her eyes glowed as her lips moved to whisper, *"Auf Wiedersehen."*

He went out the door.

# 49

Tom and Hauser rode hard and overtook the division late in the afternoon. The brigade was leading it instead of going last like always before, probably because it had gotten on the road first. After stopping for a few words with von Jagerhof as he rode by, Tom went on up to where Pater was. He only exchanged a smile and a wave with Billy for fear of being asked embarrassing questions.

Pater, riding at the head of the column, greeted Tom with a smile.

"Colonel, sir, I'm reporting back, and I can't tell you how much obliged I am."

"Oh, think nothing of it," scoffed Pater. "I'm glad I could do it. Nobody missed you."

Tom laughed. "Well, I guess that shows how unimportant I am."

Pater filled him in on the military situation. The Rebels were deep into Pennsylvania, but nobody could make out what they were up to. Lee had divided his army into corps and even divisions that seemed to be all over the south central part of the state. Hooker was gone, and Meade had taken his place as commander of the army. Pater had heard that Lincoln and Stanton had offered it to John Reynolds, but that he wouldn't take it unless they promised not to interfere with his handling of the army, which they wouldn't do. It looked like Meade hadn't insisted on any such pledges and was willing to put up with the same kind of meddling that had ruined McClellan's peninsular campaign down near Richmond the year before.

"Well," remarked Tom, "that makes Reynolds look pretty good, but I can't say the same about Meade."

Pater sighed. "I guess all we can do is hope for the best. Maybe he'll be lucky and Lee will make some mistakes."

"I wouldn't count on it." Tom didn't want to go any further, because Pater was supposed to be a Republican, so he changed the subject. "Say, what part of Pennsylvania are you from, sir?"

"I'm from near a little town by the name of Gettysburg. It's only a few days' march if we keep on the way we're going.

"Well, sir, if we can run into the Rebels around there, you'll know the country. That'll be a big help."

"Yes, if that's where we meet them." Pater sighed again, and Tom could tell he had something on his mind. "I'd like to ask you a favor," he said after a little while.

"Yes, sir. After what you did for me, I'll be happy to oblige."

Pater hesitated a little. "Dodson's left to take over a regiment, and I'd like you to take his place as adjutant of the brigade."

Tom would rather stay where he was, but he had committed himself. "Certainly, sir, as long as I can leave my regiment to Major von Jagerhof."

"Oh, of course. That's understood. I've already talked to General Carter about it, and he doesn't doubt that General Browning will approve."

"Oh, General Browning's commanding the corps now?"

When Pater nodded, Tom went on. "Well, he's a professional. Maybe the politicians learned a lesson with Hobson."

Pater only nodded again and Tom could tell he didn't want to talk about it.

After the brigade went into camp that evening, Tom went to tell von Jagerhof and make his farewell to his old friends. "I'm sorry to see you go, sir," replied the major, "and I'm grateful that you made sure I'd get the regiment, very grateful."

"Oh, there was never any question of that. They'd have given it to you anyhow,"

Von Jagerhof smiled. "Not if you had nominated someone else." He wanted to shake hands. "I appreciate all you've done for me, sir. It will benefit me greatly when I go back to Prussia. Most men my age over there aren't even commanding companies, and here I've got a regiment."

Tom slapped him on the back as they shook hands. "Oh, you've mainly done it for yourself, Major, and you're getting the best regiment there is."

"Yes, I agree with that. I'd compare it with any regiment anywhere, even in Prussia."

Tom was intrigued. "How do our men compare with Prussians?"

Von Jagerhof had to think a little. "They're very different. They're much more independent, individualistic, you could say. They wouldn't take to the rigid type of discipline we have in Prussia. They aren't as good at drill and what you call 'spit and polish.' They're inclined to be careless about things they don't think important." He shook his head. "But when it comes to marching and fighting, they'll compare very favorably."

"I expected they would."

"Now of course, that applies only to regiments like ours. Your Eastern men, particularly those from the cities, aren't in the same class."

Billy joined them. To head off embarrassing questions, Tom immediately told him about leaving the regiment. "I'm sure going to miss you, and the others, too," he added. "We've been together just about all our lives, some of us."

Billy shook his head. "We're gonna miss you, too. Th' men has all kinds uv faith in you, but they'll be glad th' major is gonna take over th' regiment if you gotta go." He turned away. "Let's go tell 'em."

Ab, Cole, and the half-dozen survivors of Tom's old platoon came first. "Aw, yo're not goin' fur, sir," said Ab lightly. "If we-uns wants our nose wiped er somethin', we won't have fur t' go." He made as if to wipe his beaklike proboscis, and everybody laughed.

Serious business intervened. Von Jagerhof wanted Cole to take Kemper's place as regimental sergeant major. When Cole promptly agreed, there was the problem of filling his place as company sergeant major. When Grim pleaded his bad English and refused, Schlimmer agreed to do it. The fellow sure had changed a lot, undoubtedly because of Rebecca.

Ab put on another show about being passed over again, even for corporal, but it had the same effect as before. The men never tired of his brand of humor. It was just like old times, and Tom stayed so long he didn't have time for anyone else.

He found Pater sitting by a fire with a map. It showed south central Pennsylvania, which they would be entering soon, and was on such a large scale that Pater could point out the landmarks around Gettysburg. The two of them went on to trace their likely route of march and tried to locate the Rebels with the aid of a Harrisburg newspaper that was full of reports of their whereabouts.

"You know, sir," said Tom, "if we're right about where the Rebels are, Gettysburg looks like a good place for them to concentrate when they find out we're moving on them."

Pater studied the map. "I see what you mean. It looks like every road in that part of the country goes through it." He pursed his lips and nodded. "General Carter says he heard the Rebels don't have any cavalry hardly. Stuart's gone off with it on some big ride-around like he did against McClellan a year ago last spring."

"Good! Now maybe they'll be in the same fix we've always been in. We never could count on our cavalry."

"Yes, if Carter's right, they'll be going blind." He paused thoughtfully. "Maybe Meade will be able to catch Lee at a disadvantage."

"I sure hope so. Luck is about all that can save us now."

"Well, the Rebels have had their share of it. Maybe it's our turn now."

Tom thought there had been a good deal more to it than luck, but he didn't say so.

Pater turned in before long, but Tom sat by the fire studying the map for a long time. Although it showed a lot of country, the area around Gettysburg attracted his attention. He marked the names of the landmarks Pater had shown him on the map, and noticed the unusual arrangement of hills and ridges just southeast of the town. There were two separate hills called Round Top and Little Round Top. Just north of Little Round Top a long ridge began; Cemetery Ridge it was named. Its northern end was so much higher than the rest of it that it was called Cemetery Hill. Just to the east of it was a large horseshoe-shaped eminence called Culp's Hill. The open end faced east, and south of it was a smaller hill called Powers'. The whole complex resembled a giant fishhook, with the round tops its eye, Cemetery Ridge and Cemetery Hill its shank, and Culp's and Powers' hills its barb. Much of it seemed high and rugged, and it would make a good defensive position for whoever got there first.

When he caught himself nodding, Tom put the map aside and stretched out on the blankets and groundsheet Hauser had ready. He only took off his boots and coat. As he lay there, his mind went back to Carolyn and he reveled in memories of the night before. He went to sleep still thinking about her and wishing they could always be together like that.

The march went on for several more days at an average pace, then one afternoon it speeded up and the men went without their hourly rest halts. No one was surprised when artillery fire became audible from the north, the direction they were heading, and rifle fire awhile later. They weren't far from Gettysburg, and Tom began to think he had guessed right about meeting the enemy there.

General Carter and several aides galloped past and went ahead of the column, then began stopping to look toward the action with field glasses, talking excitedly all the while. Tom tried his, but he couldn't see anything.

The firing grew louder as the march went on, and it began to sound like the fighting was moving toward them. When the column went to the double-quick, Tom knew it was. That meant the Rebels were driving south, and he just hoped they didn't break through to that hill and ridge complex beginning to come into view. If they did, there would be no getting them out and Meade would only throw away his men, like Burnside at Fredericksburg last winter, if he tried.

The firing moved closer all the while, and Tom could see the smoke by the time he was abreast of Little Round Top. He thought he could hear the Rebels yelling like they always did on the attack. About an hour before sundown, when the brigade was well along Cemetery Ridge, the noise of battle flared up and suddenly moved a good deal closer. There was no doubt about the yelling this time, but it all soon stopped. Evidently the Rebels had made a big push and decided to call it a day, although it didn't sound like they had reached Cemetery Hill, almost directly ahead.

Soon afterward a courier came galloping from the north. He stopped and gave something to Carter, then spurred on along the column in a cloud of dust and a clatter of hooves. Tom couldn't stand the suspense any longer and asked Pater if he could go up and find out what was going on.

Pater said all right, so Tom went to join the group around Carter. The news wasn't good. Reynolds, commanding the army's advance, had been killed in the fighting northwest of the town, and both his troops and those of Howard's corps, which had held the right, had been driven back through the town to Cemetery Hill. The Rebels hadn't followed up, and what was left of Reynolds's and Howard's men were still there. General Meade was miles to the rear but had sent Hancock ahead to take command. He had evidently decided to concentrate the army on the hill-ridge complex as it came up, which meant he knew what would happen if the Rebels got it.

All the corps but Carter's division was to turn west off the road a little farther along and report to Hancock on Cemetery Ridge. Carter was to go on north until he was just south of Cemetery Hill, then cut east across country and go into camp just short of the Baltimore Pike, which ran southeast. That would put the division directly south of Culp's Hill and west of Powers'. Since both hills were already occupied, it looked like Carter was going to be held in reserve in case he was needed on either of them.

It was after dark when the division went into camp. There was a creek fringed with brush and trees a little farther east, so there was plenty of water and wood. Fires were soon twinkling as the men began making coffee to go with their cold rations. Hauser got Tom's supper and spread out his blankets on a groundsheet. Once everyone settled down, the noise of movement around Cemetery Ridge could be heard, but it was so constant and regular that it didn't seem to bother anybody. Anyhow, Tom soon went to sleep.

The next morning was quiet, so Tom asked Pater if he could go up between Culp's and Powers' hills to look things over. Pater said all right, but always to keep in sight, which kept him from getting a good look at either one. Culp's Hill was enormous, but it seemed to be strongly held. Entrenchments showing newly shoveled earth and barricades of earth and logs encircled what he could see of the eastern slopes, and his glasses showed they were filled with men. He could also see guns emplaced above and behind them.

Powers' Hill was another matter. At first it didn't seem to be occupied, but he risked an out-of-sight canter farther east and saw what seemed to be a brigade strung out along its eastern foot. There were no entrenchments or guns; the men wore uniforms so dark blue they had to be new.

Tom couldn't stay out of sight long enough to take a really good look, but he saw enough to worry him. Carter was talking with Pater when he got back, so he told him what he had seen on the two hills. He was worried because if the Rebels sent a force south and then east that was large enough, it could pin down the men on Culp's Hill, take Powers' Hill easily, and get in position to take Cemetery Ridge in the rear.

Carter said it would be just like Lee to try something like that and that there ought to be a division on Powers' Hill, but he had strict orders to stay where he was. Hancock was short of troops and was already robbing Peter to pay Paul. He was convinced the Rebels were going to make their big attack from the west on Cemetery Ridge and was putting everyone he could get his hands on there. Carter was surprised to hear there were so many men still on Culp's Hill, and didn't expect Hancock to leave many of them there very long. They were Slocum's corps, and he hoped they would stay. Tom was right about Powers' Hill. Only a brigade of hundred days' men just called up had been put there, but they ought to have enough sense to entrench and make themselves look as formidable as they could. If it wasn't for his orders, he would move up and occupy it himself, artillery and all. He could stretch them and move closer, though, and when he did Pater's brigade was in half a mile of its western side.

Early in the afternoon Tom saw a column moving west from Culp's Hill and guessed Carter had been right about Slocum not being left there very long. He watched it with his glasses as it went on to Cemetery Ridge and noticed that it seemed short on artillery. That probably meant most of the guns had been left behind, with maybe a brigade of infantry as support.

Suddenly heavy fire broke out farther south about where the

Round Tops were. The Rebels seemed to be making a big attack there, which probably explained why Slocum had been called over. The battle was so far away it was hard to tell much about it, though. It sounded like little artillery was involved, but the rifle fire was terrific.

Tom wasn't surprised when he saw a courier gallop up to Carter. He expected the whole division to go the way Slocum had, but it didn't. One of Carter's aides dashed up and said that Pater's brigade was to stay where it was when the other three left. To Tom's surprise, Carter left his artillery still strung out along the growth bordering the creek, with the gunners taking their ease in the shade.

Although the battle to the southwest raged with undiminished fury, Carter marched directly west to Cemetery Ridge, probably to replace a division Hancock had sent south into the fighting.

Pater was left alone with his brigade, and it bothered him. He rode around aimlessly or fidgeted in his saddle. Tom knew it was because Carter was gone and Pater was afraid he wold have to act on his own. Tom started a conversation to try to settle him down, but it did no good. Pater understood what he was trying to do and made an excuse for himself. "I didn't sleep well last night," he sighed. "In fact, I scarcely slept at all, and it's hard on a man my age to lose a night's sleep."

Tom nodded understandingly. "I imagine it is. I slept well myself."

"That's the way it is," said Pater plaintively. "When you're young and can go without it, you always sleep. Then when you're older and can't, you don't sleep."

Tom got out the map they had used yesterday in hopes it would help. "Let's have another look at this, sir."

As they studied it, they agreed that it looked like Lee's strategy was to attack the hills and ridges where the army was concentrating.

"He's going at it the wrong way," said Tom. "He ought to try to get out in the open where he can do what he's best at, fight a battle of rapid maneuver."

Pater nodded. "Yes, he's pretty good at that sort of thing. That's the way he beat us at the Second Bull Run and Chancellorsville."

"Now look here," Tom went on as he pointed out the places on the map. "If he'd go around Cemetery Hill and Culp's Hill, Meade would have to come out and fight, or he could go on to Washington or Baltimore, maybe even Harrisburg." He shook his head. "From what I've heard about Meade, he's too slow and cautious to stand a chance against Lee in open country. He'd get cut to pieces."

"Yes, and Meade's been in command only a few days. He really hasn't had a chance to learn how to handle the army yet."

"The way I see it, our best chance is for Lee to keep up the way he's started. If he does, all Meade's got to do is fight a purely defensive battle. He can reinforce where Lee attacks with men from places that aren't threatened and stand him off every time."

"You sound like a general," mused Pater.

"Oh, it's just common sense, sir," rejoined Tom. He took another close look at the map. "The only way I see any danger the way it's going is for Lee to throw a corps or two south around Culp's Hill and take Powers' Hill. Slocum's mostly gone from Culp's, but the Rebels probably don't know it and it looks like he left enough guns behind to make them think he's still there with his whole corps." He put his finger on Powers' Hill. "This one's open for the taking; those hundred days' men won't stand up against anything, and the Rebels will see they've got no guns or entrenchments if they come that way."

"Oh, Lord!" exclaimed Pater. "I hope they don't do that! Then they'd take Cemetery Ridge in the front and rear at the same time, and it'd be the end of us!"

"You're right." Tom pointed at the division's artillery still by the creek. "We ought to move up there and take those guns along."

"Oh, we can't do anything like that, and I don't have any authority over those guns!"

"I guess you're right," admitted Tom glumly. "It's out of our hands."

After a while the noise of battle to the southwest began to fall off. It had done that several times before but had always revived. This time it didn't, and it seemed the Rebels had given it up.

After supper Tom took the map he and Pater had been using back to Anders, then sat on a boulder and talked with him. Tom hadn't heard from home for several weeks, but Anders had gotten a letter from his father only a few days ago. He said Tom and Billy's mother had gone back home several weeks ago and seemed to be doing fine. She and their father spent every weekend with the Anderses. Tom suggested that was why his father had bought that team of trotters he had written about in his last letter. It was too bad he hadn't been able to sell his farm yet so he could buy that one near Jasper. Dr. Anders was afraid someone else was going to buy it before he could.

Billy joined them after a while. He got a dreamy look on his face when Gerda was mentioned. His innocence made Tom feel uneasy when he thought of that night with Carolyn, and then that whole week with Mary last winter. He guessed he was getting to be a regular rounder, even if it was true love with Carolyn. But then he had thought it was the same with Mary, too, and that made him feel even more uneasy.

It was beginning to get dark when the artillery on Culp's Hill opened fire with a succession of sharp blasts. Tom was shouting for the men to fall in when Pater came galloping up.

"What is it, Colonel?" he asked apprehensively.

"I don't know, but those guns are shooting at something, and I think we ought to form a line of battle and get ready to move up."

Pater agreed and they went about it. The line was scarcely formed when a rattle of rifle fire broke out from Powers' Hill directly in front. "Are the Rebels attacking that hill there?" asked Pater nervously.

"They must be, sir. Artillery from Culp's Hill and rifles from Powers' means they've come down from the north, skirted Culp's, and moved on Powers'."

"What should we do?" asked Pater frantically. "General Carter's not here—"

Tom broke in. "I'd move on Powers' right now!"

"But shouldn't we have orders?"

Tom could scarcely contain himself. "There's no one around to give orders!"

Pater looked at him helplessly. Even his horse seemed to be affected and began to toss its head and paw the ground. "Well, I don't know—"

Tom was desperate. "Well, I'll ride up there and see what's going on! Have the line ready to move!"

Pater was relieved not to have to make a decision yet. "All right. Go ahead."

As Tom rode east he saw that the division's artillery wasn't ready to move. The guns were unhitched, and the gunners were just standing around. A colonel by the name of Wheeler commanded it, and he seemed to be another fellow who had to have orders to do anything.

The eastern slope of Culp's Hill came into view first and about that time the guns there stopped firing, but an irregular rattle of rifle still came from Powers'. No rifles had ever fired from Culp's, so it wasn't being attacked, too. When Tom reached the fringe of brush and trees around the smaller hill, a heavy outbreak of rifle fire came from the other side, shortly followed by the screeching yelling of a Rebel attack.

Suddenly men in new dark blue uniforms came tearing around both sides of the hill toward Tom. There were only a few at first, but their numbers rapidly increased and he was faced by an onrush of a mass of pale, wide-eyed men, mostly without rifles and fleeing for all they were worth. "Git outa here!" bellowed a stentorian voice toward their rear. "We're overrun!"

"Yeah!" shrieked another. "Th' colonel's daid! Th' colonel's daid!"

Tom reined up and drew his sword. "Halt! Halt, you men! Hold here! Form on me!"

They paid no attention, either to him or to a few of their officers and noncoms who were also trying to stop them. Tom tried to block them with his horse, but they dodged around it. He struck them with the flat of his sword, but they only suffered his blows and ran on.

The triumphant yelling of the Rebels drew closer, and suddenly men in butternut gray burst into view back among the trees. The forerunners spotted Tom and several rifles threw wicked tongues of flame at him. He saw that he was only going to get himself shot if he kept up, so he wheeled his horse and started back, angling to his left to get a look at the eastern side of the hill. He dodged through the last of the fugitives while bullets hissed past and the yelling fell off.

From what he could see of the eastern face of the hill, there were no Rebels there, nor were any coming across the fields to the north and east. They were all on the western side and seemed to be forming a line at the edge of the trees where the bushes began. It looked like there was no more than a brigade of them, but he got out his glasses to make sure, although some of them started shooting at him again. A bullet that came so close it almost burned his cheek sent him on his way.

Pater sat in front of the line of battle with Dickens and Marter beside him. "Colonel," shouted Tom as he reined up, "there's only a brigade of them now, but they'll send for more. We've got to attack and drive them off right now, before they get settled!"

Pater shook his head. "No, let's wait for—"

"But we've got to!" Tom broke in. "If they get a couple of divisions up here, they'll take that ridge over there in the rear the first thing in the morning! Then we're gone up!"

"No, like I started to say—"

Tom couldn't help breaking in again. "We can't wait! We can't wait! It's up to us, and we've got to do it!"

When Pater shook his head again, Tom couldn't stand it any longer. He jumped off his horse, drew his weapons, and shouted, "I'll lead! I'll lead the charge! Just give the word!"

"Let's go! Let's go git 'em!" came from among the men, but Pater only shook his head again and said sharply, "Calm yourself, Colonel, and let me say something, if you please!"

Tom brought himself up short. "Yes, sir."

"Sergeant Kemper just got here, and he says General Carter should be here in a few minutes."

"With the rest of the division?"

"No, he's by himself, but he'll know what to do."

That didn't change anything and Tom felt himself boiling up again, but he stowed his weapons and got back on his horse. Unless Carter arrived in a few minutes, it was going to be too dark to do anything, but he had done all he could.

Suddenly he thought of something and looked around for Kemper. "Sergeant Kemper!" he called as soon as he saw him. "Come over here, please!"

Kemper had his scouts with him. He reined over. *"Zu befehl, Herr Oberst!"*

"Do you think you could go out there and keep those Rebels from getting any couriers back?" It might be too late already, but it was the only chance left.

*"Jawohl, Herr Oberst!"* was the prompt reply. Kemper understood the situation.

Pater tried to speak, but Tom overrode him. "Go, then, as quick as you can!"

Kemper wheeled away. *"Komm! Komm mit!"* he shouted as he led his men off between the two hills and into the gathering darkness.

It was completely dark by the time Carter arrived. The first thing he wanted to know when he found out what had happened was where Kemper was. When Tom told him, he replied, "That's exactly what I was going to have him do. It's about our only chance." He sighed. "They sent out that brigade that took this hill just to see what was up for grabs back here. They saw they could grab this hill, so they did. Now, if we can keep them from getting word to Lee that the back door's open, maybe we can do something about it before he sends a corps down here."

Carter took Pater aside and began talking with him. After a while, Pater left and rode toward his men while Carter came to Tom and took him aside. "Do you think Kemper can do it, keep those Rebels on that hill cut off?"

"Yes, sir, I believe he can, unless they sent someone back before he got to where he could catch him."

"I doubt if they did. They were pretty busy for a while after they took that hill, and they'd probably wait until it was good and dark anyhow." Carter sighed. "If Kemper does keep them from getting word back, I'll see that he's made a captain, I swear I will. If they get anybody back, Lee'll have a corps down here in no time. Then come daylight, he'll hit Hancock over there on that ridge from both sides."

"Well, if anybody can do it, Kemper can. He's a regular Indian. Come daylight, the Rebels will think the Shawnees have been around."

"I sure hope you're right, but I don't know if it'll do any more than delay things an hour or two tomorrow. Kemper won't be able to catch their couriers after daylight. He doesn't have enough men for that. They'll see him and dodge him." Carter heaved a heavy sigh. "Hancock won't send anything over here anyhow. I couldn't even pry my other three brigades out of him before the Rebels took this hill here, and it won't make any difference when he finds out they have. He'll insist on waiting to see what he's up against from the west in the morning, and then it'll be too late."

"I don't guess we can expect any help from those fellows on that other hill over there," said Tom.

"No. There's only Greene's brigade left there. Hancock pulled the rest of Slocum's corps out and sent them over to that ridge, and Meade's let him keep them. Greene's got a lot of guns, though, so maybe he can scare them from trying him out."

Carter wanted to know why Pater hadn't moved against those Rebels who had taken the hill as soon as he found out they were coming. After Tom told him, the general sighed wearily. "That's exactly what he told me. He's honest, anyhow. He even said you wanted to move up right off, and that after they took it, you wanted to attack before they got settled and offered to lead it yourself. He admits you were right and that he just couldn't bring himself to do it without orders." Carter sighed again. "It's partly my fault. I should have told him to move up at once if the Rebels even threatened that hill, but I thought he'd have enough initiative to do it on his own."

"Yes, I think we could've kept them from taking it if we'd acted promptly, and then maybe have thrown them out before they got organized and settled down."

"You didn't lose your temper and give Pater offense, did you?"

"No, sir. When I saw he wasn't going to do anything, I shut up. I never said anything out-of-the-way."

"I'm glad of that. From the way he acted, I was afraid you had."

"He's probably ashamed of himself and thinks we believe he's a coward."

"Oh, he's no coward. He's just indecisive and afraid to take things into his own hands."

"Yes, sir. You're right. He's no coward."

When Pater came back, Tom could tell he was suffering an agony of shame and mortification. He made a point of being deferential to him, and Carter did the same. It seemed to help.

Pater faced his problem. "We've got to take that hill back, and the only way I can see to do it is bring up the rest of the division and attack the first thing in the morning."

"I'm afraid that's out of the question," replied Carter. "Like I told Colonel Traylor, Hancock won't let my other three brigades go until he sees what he's up against from the west in the morning, and by then it'll be too late."

"Maybe he'll change his mind when he finds out they've actually taken this hill here," said Pater.

"Not a chance. He knows it by now. I sent him word as soon as I found out, and he's had time to do something about it if he was going to."

"Doesn't he know what's going to happen if we let the Rebels keep this hill?" asked Tom.

"He won't admit it if he does," was the glum reply. "He'll claim it's just a diversion or something and sit tight."

"What makes you think that, sir?"

Carter sighed. "Well, when I left here, I was supposed to take my whole division over there, and he gave me the devil for leaving your brigade behind. I didn't dare stay myself, and I wanted to try to talk him into letting me come back here. I told him what would happen if we let the Rebels take this hill, but he wouldn't listen. He's convinced Lee's going to make his big push against that ridge over there from the west and thinks every other move he makes is just a diversion."

"Maybe the Rebels *are* just making a diversion," ventured Pater hopefully.

"No! No!" was the emphatic reply. "They wouldn't send a brigade out just to wander around. They haven't got any cavalry hardly, so they sent that brigade out to scout these two hills here, and they're undoubtedly ready to back them up. They've got a corps north of here that could get here in an hour or so. The best we can hope for is to keep them from reinforcing on this hill here before morning, and that's just putting it off."

"Oh, we'll know if they're reinforced tonight," Pater assured him. "I've got my pickets up so close they'll hear it if they are."

Carter was getting out of patience with Pater. "Like I say," he replied sharply, "that'll just be putting it off."

"Well, then," Pater burst out, "we'll take that hill back ourselves. "We'll attack at first light, and I'll lead it myself!"

"You'd just get your men killed off," replied Carter shortly. "They've got as many men as you have, and they'll be ready for you. They'll shoot you to pieces out in the open like that."

Pater didn't give up. "Maybe we could use the division's artillery to blast them out. It's still over there by that creek."

"Only because Hancock doesn't know it," rejoined Carter. "I left it on purpose when I went over to that ridge in hopes he'd let me come back and didn't tell him. He'd have had a fit if I had." Carter sighed heavily. "Anyhow, the guns wouldn't help much. You could kill half those fellows, and they'd still stop you. They're tough."

An idea that had been germinating in Tom's mind suddenly took form. "I think I see a way we can do it with just our brigade, that is, if they aren't reinforced by daylight."

"How?" asked Pater.

"Attack in column from as close as we can get without being seen. We can move up while it's still dark. If they don't have pickets out and we're quiet about it, we might be able to get pretty close. Then we can attack at first light. If we're reasonably lucky, we can be on them before they're ready for us."

"Sounds interesting," said Carter. "Go ahead, Colonel."

"The lead regiment can drive straight at the middle, and as soon as it hits the Rebels the next two can branch off left and right and go around both sides of the hill. Then the fourth one can follow up the first because it's going to draw most of the fire and may get shot up pretty bad."

Pater was all for it. "That's exactly the thing to do! In fact, it's the only thing to do!"

Carter had his doubts. "It'll be awfully risky. A column attacking a line like that is going into enfilade. If they find it out when you're moving up, you'll get slaughtered."

"I know, sir," replied Tom, "but I can't see any other way to do it, and it's got to be done."

"Oh, it's a dark night," interjected Pater. "They won't be able to see us, and we'll be very careful not to make any noise. They don't have any pickets out of the brush, and I'll have mine drive them back if they send any out." His hopefulness was a little pathetic. "Oh, we'll surprise them all right and drive them out of there." He even chuckled.

Tom could feel Carter's eyes on him.

"Even if it goes off without a hitch," the general began, "those Rebels won't all be asleep, and those that aren't will get off a round or two. That lead regiment's going to catch it. How are you gong to decide which one it'll be?"

"Oh, I'll just have the commanders draw straws," replied Pater promptly. "That way it'll just be up to chance."

Carter made up his mind. "All right. I'll write out your order. Hancock gave me a free hand over here, and Browning heard him do it."

Pater came up with an idea. "Do you think we could get those fellows over there on Culp's Hill to make some kind of a demonstration while we're moving up, something that'll draw the Rebels' attention?"

Tom had the same suggestion on the tip of his tongue but was glad Pater had beaten him to it.

"Good idea," vouchsafed Carter and Tom could almost see Pater's smile of satisfaction. "They'll be expecting a flank attack, and they probably think there's still a division over there. They know you're only a brigade, and they'll never dream you'll go at them head-on in column like that. I wouldn't either if I was in their shoes. They've probably got their right flank refused. They may even face their line that way, and you'll hit them in the flank." He chuckled. "You know, the whole thing sounds harebrained until you get to thinking about it, and then it makes sense." He reined over toward a small fire Anders had burning behind that big boulder Tom had sat on earlier and wrote out Pater's order to attack. He gave it to Pater, then said, "I'll write a note to Greene asking him to commence a demonstration about an hour before daylight and keep it up until he hears you attack."

He scribbled on the pad, then gave Pater another sheet. "Greene's an old friend of mine, and he'll do his best.

"Now," he went on, "I've got to leave. Hancock gave me strict orders to be back in an hour, and I've overstayed already. I don't want to disobey him a second time, or I'd stay. I'll have another try at getting my other three brigades back and bringing them over before you attack, but if I don't show up and you don't get orders to the contrary, go ahead with it and send me word on how it comes out."

He mounted his horse, reined about, and started away. "Good luck," he said as he disappeared into the darkness.

Pater handed one of the notes Carter had given him to Tom. "Here, you take this to General Greene."

"Oh no, sir! I might not get back in time! Just send a courier!"

"I want you to take it, Colonel," said Pater firmly. "You'll know exactly what we're going to do, and you'll get to him. A courier might get lost or something."

He didn't sound like the same fellow he had been a few hours ago, and Tom wondered what had come over him. "Yes, sir. I'll start right now, then." He started to turn away.

Pater stopped him. "Oh, I'm going to need you for a while yet, and there's plenty of time. I want you to go up to our picket line and find out what the Rebels on that hill are doing and if they've been reinforced or anything."

That was something that ought to be done, but it seemed to Tom that Dickens or Marter could do it. He left his horse with Hauser and started out.

After he got away from the fire, it seemed as dark as pitch, but he kept his sense of direction and reached the pickets without getting off course. They were under Captain Hutchinson, a pretty aggressive fellow, and so were very close to the hill. A whispered conversation revealed that the Rebels had their pickets back in the brush if they had any at all. Hutchinson was sure no reinforcements had come up, or he would have heard them. There hadn't been a peep out of those Rebels, and you wouldn't think anyone was there unless you knew better.

Tom guessed they were so worn out they didn't have much spunk left and were depending on reinforcements, but he thought it might be so quiet because they actually had pulled out. He decided to go up closer and try to find out if they were still there, so he gave Hutchinson his sword and scabbard and crept up as close as he dared. He lay down and listened carefully, but all he could hear for a long time was the noise of movement around Cemetery Ridge, now going on for the second night. Then low voices and subdued movement in the growth showed the Rebels were still there. They seemed to be relieving their pickets, or maybe someone was going around to make sure they weren't sleeping on the job. Anyhow, it was soon over and quiet settled down again.

He slipped silently back to the picket line, told Hutchinson what he had heard, then got his sword back and headed for the faint glow of Anders's fire.

When Tom reached the fire, Pater was gone and only Anders was awake. Dickens, Marter, and Hamilton lay sprawled out around the fire fast asleep. Anders said Pater had left word for him to wait there until he returned, and it was a good while before he did. Tom was in a fever of impatience by then and was glad Pater sent him off to Greene as soon as he reported on his mission. He decided to ride, because he was in a hurry, and tied his sword to the saddle with his glasses so it wouldn't be in the way if he had to dismount and go on foot through growth.

He rode northeast until he could see where Culp's Hill blotted out the stars, then turned north. He wanted to enter the open ground enclosed by the horseshoe shape of the hill, but he turned west too soon and encountered the growth around the southern side of it. He expected to be challenged, but he wasn't, and calling out might bring bullets in reply because he didn't know the password. He was on the point of turning right toward the open ground between the two sides of the horseshoe when it occurred to him that General Greene would probably be somewhere along the hill where he could see well and might be found more quickly by dismounting and going along the side of the hill. He dismounted, tied his horse to a sapling, and set off into the brush. He was bound to run into pickets soon and might be able to get a guide.

The going was difficult in the gloom, even after he got through the brush and into the trees. He kept running into low limbs and even tree trunks, because he couldn't see his hand before him in the gloom under the trees. He stepped on loose rocks and had trouble keeping his balance on the steep slope.

Suddenly strong arms seized him and he was borne to the ground. He didn't try to get away, although he could easily have wriggled free at first. "Hah!" exclaimed a voice in his ear. "We've got you, you damned Rebel!" A hand deftly removed his revolver from his holster.

Tom permitted himself to be pinned down. "I'm no Rebel!" he protested. "I've got a message for General Greene, and it's very important!"

A voice grunted in the gloom. "Huh! You sound like a damned Rebel to me, and our men don't go sneaking around in the dark, not if they're couriers anyhow."

The accents showed his captors were New Englanders, and Tom realized he sounded like a Southerner to them, but he didn't have time to argue and tried to break free. He couldn't. Several men held him firmly. "Do you want a bayonet in your belly?" demanded one of them. "Lie still if you don't!"

Tom saw he could only try to talk them into letting him go. "Listen," he said urgently. "Make a light and I'll show you the message I've got for General Greene."

"Oh no, you don't!" exclaimed a disembodied voice. "You've got your friends out there just waiting for something like that!"

Tom protested that he was alone. He identified himself, gave his brigade and division, and pleaded for questions so he could prove who he was.

"So you're a colonel!" came a scoffing reply. "Now listen, Rebel. Maybe we haven't been out long, but we've been mustered in three months now, and any recruit knows colonels aren't messenger boys."

That accounted for a lot of things. These men were new and scared. He was lucky they hadn't spitted him with a bayonet the first thing.

He tried to explain his rank by the importance of the message.

"You're pretty convincing, Rebel, but your accent gives you away."

He blamed that on where he was from, but it did no good. One of his captors said he had gone to school with a fellow from Indiana and he talked just like anyone else. Trying to explain the difference between people from northern and southern Indiana didn't help either.

They were going to bind Tom to a tree with rifle slings. In his desperation, he tried to break away, but there were too many of them and they seemed to have cats' eyes that could see in the dark. He would get loose from one only to be caught by another, or maybe several of them. After a wild, thrashing struggle in the dark, he was pinned down again. They held his arms and legs, and one fellow sat on his chest.

The Yankees were enraged and cursed him heatedly. One of them stabbed at him with a bayonet and pinned his coat to the ground. Another swung a fist that hit a tree trunk and brought forth lurid oaths. Finally they got his hands tied and bound him sitting to a tree trunk.

After that, there was nothing to do but wait until their lieutenant came around with the relief, which one of them said would be right away. If it wasn't long, Greene would get Carter's message in time.

It seemed an age before the relief came, and to Tom's delight, the lieutenant agreed to take him to their colonel. He didn't take any chances, though. He kept Tom's revolver and prodded him along in front.

The Yankee colonel was asleep by a small fire in depression on the hillside. He didn't like being awakened, but once he was, he proved to be a reasonable fellow. Tom showed him the message and explained its urgency. The colonel focused his bleary eyes on it, scratched his head, and seemed convinced it was genuine. He told the lieutenant to take Tom to Greene's headquarters and promptly stretched out again. Tom was glad of it. He had enough of blundering around in the dark and being taken for a Rebel.

General Greene was under a fly made of several shelter halves laced together and hanging down in front. A candle stuck in the neck of a bayonet driven into a tree trunk provided a flickering light. He was hatless and shuffling through a sheaf of papers, pausing occasionally to squint at one. A soldier crouched beside a pair of saddlebags looking through more papers.

Greene was a dark, lanky fellow with graying hair and bloodshot eyes that showed he hadn't slept much lately. Tom saluted and thrust the message on him. "From General Carter, sir, and very important."

The general showed irritation but put his papers aside and took the note. He read it, then laughed with the feverish elation of a man beyond exhaustion. "Carter, the little bastard! Haven't seen him in a coon's age!"

All Tom could do was smile and think the two generals must be very good friends.

"An hour before daylight! It's a little past that now, but not enough to hurt."

Tom felt a wave of panic. He must have lost all sense of time.

The bloodshot eyes twinkled. "Carter's got to do something for me, though."

Tom fought down his panic. "Yes, sir?"

"He's got to send me a quart of that Kentucky bourbon he had the last time we got together. That was the best whiskey I've ever drunk. Oh, we had a time, we did!"

Tom was frantic at the continued delay but managed to smile and say, "Yes, sir, I'll tell him."

Greene got serious. "I'm glad somebody's going to do something about those Rebels on that hill over there. I can't, and I'm surprised they haven't got a corps or two there already. Hancock's going to be attacked front and rear—"

Tom had to break in. "Can the general make a demonstration to help us?"

"All I can do is make noise. I've only got a brigade left, plus a bunch of runaways someone brought in a while ago, the bunch that skedaddled from that hill just before dark."

"Please make plenty of noise, sir; we're only a brigade."

Greene was astounded. "You mean Carter isn't attacking with his whole division? What makes you think you can do it?"

Telling how would take more time, and Tom was getting desperate. "It's got to be done, sir, and with some help from you and a lot of luck, maybe we can do it."

Greene shook his head. "Small chance, very small, but I'll help all I can, and maybe you can surprise them. Now, if they'd left Slocum here with his whole corps, we—"

Tom couldn't stand it any longer. "Excuse me, sir, but I've got to go—"

Greene broke in. "Yes, yes, go ahead. If you don't pull it off, the Rebels will be chasing Lincoln right out of Washington. You can count on me. I'll make those Rebels over there think I'm throwing a whole division at them."

"Thank you, sir." Tom was so relieved he could have cried as he saluted and started to turn away, but Green stopped him. "Wait! Don't forget about that bourbon, now!"

Tom made himself stop and turn around. "No, sir, I won't." As he started away, he heard Greene shouting for couriers.

The Yankee lieutenant had waited for him. He was very apologetic, probably because he was very glad Greene hadn't been told how Carter's message had been held up. Tom took advantage of it and got the fellow to take him down the hill toward his horse by a good path. He went as fast as he could, despite his guide's fears that some nervous sentry would cut loose at them.

Pater would be moving the column up now and Tom listened fearfully for the outbreak of firing that would mean he had been seen, but it didn't come. Just before they reached the foot of the hill, Greene's demonstration began with a great clamor of commands and a moving of men. It seemed too obvious, but if the Rebels were expecting it, they might be fooled.

At the bottom of the hill Tom gasped out, "Thank you, Lieutenant," and struck out for his horse.

"Oh, Colonel! Colonel!" called the fellow after him. "Here's your revolver!"

Tom dashed to meet him, snatched the weapon, then whirled and started for his horse again as he thrust it into his holster. When he reached his horse, he tore the reins loose, leapt into the saddle, and headed for Powers' Hill at a gallop. Its outline was just beginning to take shape against the brightening skies, and the brigade would attack any second. He breathed his thanks that it hadn't been spotted moving up.

He rode directly toward the hill, because he couldn't hope to reach the column until after it attacked. If nothing happened by the time he got there, he could only assume it had been called off and make a run for it, hoping he wouldn't be shot out of his saddle.

He was still several hundreds yards away when startled shouts rose out of the woods on the west side of the hill and a few shots were fired. He slapped his horse on the rump in an attempt to make him go faster while the scattered shots grew into a roar of continuous discharges that lighted up the woods ahead with a yellowish glare. The shooting abruptly fell off as he tore through the brush at the edge of the woods covering the hill and began dodging through the trees.

Suddenly he was passing through a mass of running and yelling Rebels who looked like wraiths in the half-light because of their light-colored clothing. Someone raised the cry of, "Cavalry!" and they seemed to think he was a whole squadron of it. None of them raised their arms against him, and his cometlike passage only accelerated their disorganization and flight.

He didn't see a low limb in time, and a tremendous blow on his head knocked him from his horse to roll half-senseless on the ground. His horse galloped on. The Rebels were streaming away to the east by now and avoided him like he was an explosive shell as he groveled among the dry leaves and dead branches trying to get to his feet. When he finally did and stood unsteadily with ringing head, they were all gone. He felt of his head to see if it was bleeding. It wasn't, so he guessed his hat had cushioned the blow.

There was a great crashing through the growth ahead punctuated by exultant yells and triumphant shouts. It was the head of the column charging around the northern side of the hill, so he broke into a lurching run toward the noise.

As he ran his senses stabilized and soon he was racing along in great, leaping strides, dodging trees and other obstacles with his normal agility. He angled to his left, intercepted the head of the column, then ran ahead of it brandishing his revolver and yelling at the top of his lungs.

Surprised, disorganized, and overrun, the Rebels fled for dear life before the onrush, yelling in fear and panic. Those who weren't fast enough were overtaken and beaten or bayoneted to the ground.

Suddenly a group appeared ahead in a small clearing where the light was better. They stood their ground with clenched faces and upraised rifles, headed by an officer who looked vaguely familiar as he leveled his revolver. Tom's revolver exploded in his hand and the officer fell, but his men got off a ragged fusilade, then swung their rifles as clubs or thrust out with bayonets. Impacts staggered men on both sides of Tom and several crashed to the ground, but the column drove on and overwhelmed the little band that had stood against it. Tom shot two of them from so close that the muzzle flash of his revolver touched them.

He raced on, leading the column on around the northern side of the hill. He didn't fire another shot, because all the Rebels he saw afterward were either down or fleeing for their lives. He slowed the column as it approached the eastern side of the hill. When he got there, the regiment that had attacked around the southern side appeared, driving a few lagging Rebels before it. Pater was nowhere to be seen and there was no time to waste, so Tom started forming a line facing east at the edge of the woods. The regiments were badly disorganized, and it got worse as those bringing up the rear began to arrive.

He was barely started when an uproar from the far left made him think the Rebels might be rallying there, so he yelled to Hartley to take over and ran toward the noise. As he drew closer he heard only whoops and laughter, but he ran on.

The source of the uproar soon appeared. A skinny, rather elderly little Rebel ran into view leading a horse Tom recognized as his. His sword and field glasses were still attached to the saddle. Hauser was chasing the thief like an angry rhinoceros, shouting and cursing in German, while the men in the closest regiment cheered and whooped him on.

The pursuit was so close that the frail little Rebel never had time to mount. Every time he tried, Hauser would almost catch him, and he would have to give it up and run on. The repeated stopping and starting, with Hauser bellowing like a bull and the little old Rebel looking like he was half scared out of his wits, was such a comic spectacle that Tom couldn't help laughing himself.

Finally the frail fellow in gray waited too long before giving up an attempt to mount and was caught. Hauser seized the reins with one hand, the would-be thief with the other, then sent him flying with a mighty kick and a volley of German cusswords. Hauser was making his triumphant way back leading the horse to the cheers of the spectators when he saw Tom and headed toward him. Tom wiped the grin off his face, went to meet Hauser, and soberly thanked him for getting his horse back.

He untied his sword, put it back on his belt, and mounted. He was scarcely in the saddle when a cry went up that cavalry was coming. Hartley had the line pretty well formed, so Tom rode out of the woods to get a better view.

All he could see with the naked eye were the Rebels who had been driven from the hill streaming away toward the northeast, carefully skirting Culp's Hill. He got out his field glasses but could still see no cavalry, only the retreating Rebels. They were sorting themselves out and forming a column, and those strung out back toward the hill were running to catch up.

Finally a party of horsemen emerged from behind the retreating Rebels, cantering away from them to the south. That showed they weren't Rebels, and when Tom focused his glasses on them he saw they were Kemper and his men.

He rode out to meet them. "Rebels a-comin', Colonel!" shouted Zeke Kerns as soon as he was close enough.

"How many? How close?" Tom shouted back.

"Tree deveeson *komm, Herr Oberst*!" called Kemper.

"You'll be seein' 'em in 'bout three-quarters uv an hour, I'd say," said Zeke as they met.

The hill had been captured barely in time, but the situation really hadn't changed. The brigade wouldn't delay three divisions very long.

Kemper went to water his horses, and Tom was left with his problem. The only chance he could see was to try to bluff the Rebels into thinking the hill was strongly held. Then they might not try it. It wasn't much of a chance, but it was all there was, and a certain Rebel brigadier general had shown him how to do it at that bridge last winter. If Greene over on Culp's Hill could make himself look like a threat to the Rebels' flank, it would help a lot.

But Tom had to have the division's artillery he had last seen waiting idly by the creek to the southeast. He couldn't hope to fool the Rebels unless he had it, and he hoped to God it was still there.

Hamilton and Marter sat on their horses well out in front of the hill, so to save time Tom beckoned them toward him and dictated notes to Carter and Greene. He told Carter what had happened and both of them what he was going to try to do. He asked Carter to rush reinforcements in case his bluff was called and Greene to get up whatever he could that would look like a threat to the Rebels' flank. Tom had the messages sent by regular courier, because he was going to need all the help he could get pretty soon, and set off around the hill toward the guns.

Hartley had the line formed and rode out to meet him. Tom was in such a hurry that he was going to ignore him and ride on until he happened to think about Pater. For all he knew, the Pennsylvanian was around someplace, although he would surely have seen him if he was.

He reined toward Hartley and called out as soon as he was close enough, "Where's Colonel Pater?"

"Dead!" was the shouted reply. "Killed early this morning!" Hartley looked like he had something else to say and kept coming, but Tom had no time for him. He turned away and galloped for the creek. Hartley reined up and sat looking after him for a few moments, then turned and went back.

Pater had been killed leading the charge on the hill. Tom now understood his sudden decisiveness of the night before. He made up his mind to prove he wasn't a coward even if it cost him his life. Tom had always liked the fellow. Now he respected him.

To his great relief, the guns were still by the creek, now all limbered up and ready to move. Colonel Wheeler reacted like Tom expected, though. He had no orders to go anyplace and wasn't going to until he got them. Anyhow, he expected to be called to that ridge over there at any time.

Tom's explanation of the urgency of the situation and what he proposed to do didn't shake him. He was a grizzled old regular who obviously regarded Tom as a young whippersnapper who had gulled someone out of a colonel's eagles. "Where's Colonel Pater, anyhow?" he demanded.

"He's dead, and I'm the only man who's commanded the brigade before."

"So you just took it over?" Wheeler was downright hostile.

"Yes, I got us out of a tight spot once before, back last spring, and maybe I can do it again."

Tom was getting desperate when a light seemed to dawn on Wheeler. "Oh, you're the fellow who took over from Rivers when he was killed and smashed up Ramsdell's division!"

When Tom nodded affirmatively, Wheeler went on. "You know, Carter left me back when he moved up then and I didn't get to see it, but I heard all about it." He threw up his hands. "Just tell me where to go, Colonel!"

Tom managed to hide his relief and told him to go on around to the east side of the hill and set up his guns about a hundred feet out in the field in front. He made sure Wheeler understood the game of bluff they would be playing, but the old regular had plenty of nerve and seemed taken up with it. He only hoped they would get the reinforcements Tom had sent for in case it didn't work.

While he was on his way back, the courier sent to Culp's Hill intercepted him and said that Greene had promised to do all he could, although he didn't have enough ammunition to use his guns unless the Rebels actually attacked. The courier sent to Carter showed up next but could only say that Hancock wouldn't let anyone go yet and that Tom would be on his own, for a while anyhow.

The next half hour was one of the busiest he had ever spent. While Wheeler was setting up his guns, Tom took his aides, rode out far in front, and set about making it look like there was at least a division of infantry on the hill from some distance out. He had the line moved back to the edge of the growth and kept his aides and couriers busy spurring back and forth filling open spaces behind it with men taken from where it was hidden by brush and foliage. He never went himself because it might ruin his perspective.

He noticed that most of them kept looking west to see if reinforcements were coming, although the view in that direction was pretty well blocked by the hill. He made a point of never looking himself because it would give a bad impression. Neither did he concern himself about the oncoming Rebels and kept his back turned in their direction. Wheeler and most of his officers had good glasses and would see them as soon as he could anyhow. He knew that any appearance of nervousness on his part would have a bad effect on the men, and they were going to need all the nerve they had pretty soon.

Before Tom was quite done with the line, Wheeler sang out that he had sighted the Rebels, but Tom only acknowledged he had heard and calmly went on with his business. There was quite a hubbub among Wheeler's officers, but a few sharp words from the old regular quieted them.

Tom could see what Greene was doing on the southeast side of Culp's Hill without turning to look. He had moved some infantry around to the southern side and was placing it in the growth where the Rebels would not be able to tell much about it from where they would be. Above the infantry a few guns were being emplaced in a clearing, the gunners manhandling them into position on the steep slope. There were only four guns and not much more than a regiment of infantry, so Greene was leaving enough facing east to look formidable there.

Not until he had the line looking exactly like he wanted did Tom turn to look at the advancing Rebels himself. Before he could get his glasses out, someone shouted, "Cavalry!" and his heart leapt. Sharp-eyed Rebel troopers would see him as the fraud he was if they got close enough. He didn't need his glasses to see a squad of horsemen galloping toward the hill, angling a little south to keep out of range. He only hoped Kemper was back.

A guttural shout and a pounding of hooves showed that he was. The veteran led his men toward the Rebel horsemen at a full gallop, brandishing weapons and whooping. Tom knew he would drive them away, because he had as many men as they did and his were much better armed. Revolvers were a lot better than muzzle-loading carbines and sabers at close quarters.

When Tom raised his glasses for his first look at the advancing Rebel infantry, he saw why Wheeler's officers had been unsettled. Three dense columns were coming from the northeast, looking at first like a great gray cloud low on the horizon because the angle made them overlap. He felt something like the old woman in the fable who undertook to sweep back the sea with a broom.

The commander of a division-sized force would have a large staff, so Tom called his aides around him and sent to ask Wheeler if he could have a few of his officers to impress the Rebels with.

Wheeler came along himself. "If they've got good glasses, we want someone in the bunch who looks old enough to be commanding a division or two," he explained with a wink.

As they rode out farther, a flurry of shots and yells indicated that Kemper had engaged the Rebel scouts. All Tom could see was a cloud of dust and smoke in which weapons flashed and horsemen whirled dimly about. Before he could focus his glasses on the fight, it was over and the gray-clad troopers were streaking back the way they had come, leaving several riderless horses behind. Kemper pursued, but Tom knew it wouldn't be for long.

"Look at them!" exclaimed someone in awed tones. "Just look at them!"

He meant the advancing Rebels, so Tom turned his glasses on them. They were truly an awesome sight. The columns were deploying into line of battle facing directly west, wheeling and maneuvering with smoothness and precision.

A small column angled across the front while the line was still forming. That would be the brigade that had been driven off the hill, and Tom suddenly realized its survivors would undoubtedly be a big help to him. They could be counted on to swear they had been put to flight only by a much larger force, even if some of them knew better.

As it took form and began to move forward, an air of invincibility and inflexible purpose radiated from the great gray formation. It was something like facing a tidal wave. Tom's glasses could pick out individuals, and he noticed that these men were better-uniformed than Rebels generally were. Their line extended back at an angle where the enemy commander had refused his right flank to cover Culp's Hill. Whoever he was, he knew his business and would be a hard man to fool.

"They don't have any guns," observed one of Wheeler's officers in the tone of a man grabbing at straws.

"Oh, they've got guns all right," replied Wheeler. "They're just not up where we can see them."

"They're in too much of a hurry," interjected Dickens. "They know they've got to take this hill before we can get enough men up here to stop them."

"I hope to God they think we already have," breathed Marter.

"A-men!" went up almost like a chorus.

Tom turned to look back at the hill and saw it seemed even more formidable from where he now was. The men in the open spaces back in the growth made the line look several ranks thicker than it actually was, and nowhere did a gap show. The men were keeping religiously to their position. Wheeler's firing line looked impressive, too. The black gun barrels glowered menacingly, and the gunners stood ready to fire. The limbers were spread out between the guns and canted at such angles that they might look like guns from a great distance.

"They've halted!" exclaimed Wheeler.

Tom turned to look and saw that the great gray mass stood still with a group of mounted men out in front. He focused his glasses on them and saw that several were using glasses, too. A thickset bearded officer who rode with his stirrups high seemed to be the center of the group, and his uniform looked more ornate than those of the others. After a while, he turned his glasses on Culp's Hill. He should be able to see enough of the men Greene had posted on the southern slope to know they were there, and also something of the guns above them. There was obviously no intention to move on that hill, so Greene must have done a good job of setting the stage on the eastern side.

The Rebel general turned his glasses back to Powers' Hill and studied it while Tom and the others waited with bated breath. Suddenly a horseman spurred along the front from the right and dashed up to the group. The Rebel general took his glasses down and turned to the rider. He shortly saluted and turned back the way he had come, but only at a canter.

All at once the mounted men in front of the great gray line turned and started back. As they merged into the background, Tom waited for the movement. Would it be forward or backward?

Suddenly he found himself looking at a multitude of gray backs with blanket rolls slung diagonally across them. The Rebels were turning back.

Sighs of relief went up, and one of Wheeler's lieutenants whooped, "Saved, by God!"

"I sure thought we were goners," admitted another. "I never thought they'd fall for it!"

"Well, they did, thank the Lord!" exclaimed Marter.

Everybody started back to the hill, but Tom stopped them. "Wait! They may just turn south and envelop us from the right!" That would avoid any flank threat from Culp's Hill and was exactly what he would do if he was commanding those Rebels. If they did that, it would wreck the elaborate show he had staged, because there wouldn't be time to set up a new one.

That stopped the celebrating and turned all eyes back to the front, but the great gray line segmented smoothly into columns that headed northeast without a hitch. Such skillful handling of that immense mass of men was marvelous, and the drill and discipline that had gone into it even more so. Tom shook his head in admiration. He wouldn't want to come up against those fellows out in the open, even with the odds in his favor. Their direction indicated that they were going west around Cemetery Hill to join the concentration against Cemetery Ridge. If that was where Lee was going to make his grand attack, he had lost the battle already. Hancock and Meade were ready for him.

The jubilation revived as Tom and the others rode back toward the hill, and he was showered with congratulations. He really didn't know if he deserved them, though. That horseman who had come up to the Rebel general while he was making up his mind might have been a courier with orders to countermarch and join the concentration against Cemetery Ridge from the west. None of the others had evidently seen him, probably because their glasses weren't as good as his. He didn't want to say anything that might dampen the celebration, though.

One of Carter's aides came galloping from the west. Tom told the others to go ahead and went to meet him. He was a captain named Howell and had the air of a bearer of good tidings. "General Carter's coming!" he shouted as soon as he was close enough. "General Carter's coming with the rest of the division!" He reined up grinning from ear to ear.

Tom laughed shortly. "Well, just tell him to go back if he wants to. It's all over here. An enemy corps advanced on us but turned back before it even got in range."

Howell's face fell with comic suddenness. He looked off to the northeast where the Rebels could still be dimly seen, sighed, and turned back like a man whose best efforts had come to nothing.

Wheeler followed on Howell's heels. He wanted to limber up and go back to where he had been so they could find him if he was wanted on that ridge over there.

Tom took a look through his glasses to make sure the Rebels were still going away before he told him to go ahead. They were, and their columns again looked like a great gray cloud low on the horizon.

Tom decided to stay where he was until Wheeler cleared out, and not just to avoid riding through the limbering up and getting in the way. He felt very, very tired, and his head was throbbing. He took off his hat and felt of it again. He had a big knot on his forehead and his hat brim was bent up in front, but Hauser could readily steam it back into shape.

After the guns were put back in column and started away, Tom sat and watched them go by. The gunners were chattering cheerily, and some of them waved to him. He waved back and managed a grin, although he didn't feel much like it.

Before the guns were out of the way, he saw Carter was coming from the west. He was alone and as always from a distance looked like a diminutive jockey on a big racehorse. Wheeler rode out to meet him, and they started talking.

Tom knew Carter wanted to see him but decided just to sit and wait for him to come on. He didn't feel like doing anything else. He hadn't had a wink of sleep since the night before last, and it had been a strenuous time ever since.

The general left Wheeler and rode toward Tom. "Well, I finally pried my other three brigades out of Hancock when he heard a corps was actually moving on this hill, but I guess I would've been too late."

Tom nodded. "I'm afraid so, sir."

Carter grew expansive. "Wheeler tells me you ran a big bluff on those Rebels and scared them away."

Tom decided to be completely honest about it. "It may not have been that at all, sir."

Carter showed surprise. "What, then?"

"I thought I saw a courier come up just before they started back and talk to the fellow who seemed to be in charge. They may have been recalled."

Carter laughed. "Now don't go spoiling a good story and keep all these fellows from telling their tales!" He looked to where the brigade was still drawn up along the side of the hill. The men were standing at rest, but they were still where they had been put. "Let's ride out in front a ways and see what it looks like from out there."

They went out a good distance before Carter reined about. He studied the position and laughed gleefully. "I see how you did it. It looks like you've got at least a division there, and then with Wheeler's guns out in front you had enough artillery. That was clever, very clever." He reined closer and stuck out his hand. "Good work, Colonel," he said sincerely. "You saved Meade's neck, and I'm going to see that he finds it out."

"Well, like I said, those Rebels may have been called back, and I don't want any credit I don't deserve," said Tom as they shook hands.

"Pshaw! Take all you can get! That's what I do." He leaned toward Tom and pretended a confidence. "Just watch out that I don't claim credit for the whole thing."

They laughed together and Tom was beginning to feel better as they rode toward the hill. They were getting pretty close when Carter said, "Say, it looks like one of your regiments lost a lot of men, the one that led the column in the charge on this hill, I guess."

He pointed toward the southern end of the line, where von Jagerhof stood in front of what looked like little more than a company of men. Tom had never been close enough to notice it before, and the line had now moved out in the open where it was plain to see. He felt like a bolt of lightning had struck him. His ears rang, the landscape swayed about him, and he felt icy cold. He found himself in front of von Jagerhof but unable to speak.

The Prussian's face was powder-blackened, and ugly rips showed in his coat. One of his cheeks was badly gashed. "I drew the short straw, sir," he said simply. "We led the charge."

Tom's eyes ran over the handful of men behind him. They looked like they had been singed by the fires of Hell, and stared back at him vacantly, like men whose senses had been deadened. Billy wasn't among them, and he heard himself falter, "My . . . brother . . . where is he?"

"He fell in the charge, sir," von Jagerhof replied. "I'm very sorry."

Ab spoke up, his long face unnaturally pale under the grime. "He's dead, sir. I seen him git hit an' fall, 'long with jist 'bout ever'body else." His high, nasal voice rang hollowly, like it came from a tomb.

Tom got off his horse without knowing it, and the animal would have wandered away if Hauser hadn't taken the reins. Shame joined shock and sorrow. He had been so busy playing brigadier general he hadn't even bothered to ask about his brother. Billy had been dead for hours, and he hadn't given him a thought. He bowed his head and stood swaying on his feet.

Carter dismounted and took his arm. "Go see about your brother, Colonel. It's all over here, and Hartley can take charge."

Tom stumbled woodenly back through the trees around the hill. It was a long ways, but he seemed to cover it in seconds. Beyond the western side of the hill he came on the charnel field. The men of the Pocket lay in heaps and swaths, so thickly it was difficult to walk among them. They were all dead. The wounded had been taken away, but there couldn't have been many of them. The regiment had absorbed the fire of a full brigade, and the range had been fatally close. Probably every man who was hit had been struck by several bullets. The regiment had been smashed like the head of a battering ram used to break down a wall.

There lay Pater with his head half shot off. Beside him was Fred Anders, the wooden map case on his back splintered by bullets that had torn through his slender body. Herb Parker lay face down in the grass, sword and revolver near his outflung hands. Cole Burton had been shot in the stomach. He hadn't died easily, because the grass around him had been torn up, exposing the dark, moldy earth, and his hands were blackened with it.

Tom had to force himself to look for Billy, and knew he was close when he began to find the Germans. Schlimmer lay with his handsome face a bloody mess and his blond hair clotted with gore. Nearby was Grabner, his eagle eyes glazed in death. Sergeant Grim's body was so small it almost looked like that of a boy.

A slender fair-haired officer lay on his stomach, a great wound in his back where a bullet had gone through. It was Billy. Tom dropped to his knees beside him. "Billy, oh, Billy," he moaned, "little brother . . . dear little brother—" He touched the body; he moved the stiffened arms; finally he turned it over only to meet the blank, unseeing stare of death.

Tom never knew how long he crouched there until a familiar voice called him back to the world of the living. It was Kemper. Tom never remembered what passed between them, but he thought they both wept. Anyhow, he was sure he did.

After Kemper left, Tom began stalking aimlessly about. He thought of Billy's fine mind and how he was going to study medicine in Germany. He thought of Gerda, who had lost her brother, too. Now Billy would only be a lump of dirt and Gerda a withered old maid.

Enemy dead also lay about, and his eyes happened to light on one of them. He was a small, dark man whose fine white teeth were barred in a frozen grimace and who still clutched a rifle with a blood-streaked bayonet. It was Peachy, the Italian who had stolen the fish while they picnicked with the North Carolina men. Tom now knew why the officer he had shot looked familiar. If he searched around, he might find the body of the boy who had caught the fish for Billy.

It was too much to bear, and his legs trembled under him. He stumbled to a nearby log, sat down and buried his face in his hands. There were no longer any tears. His grief was too great. An awful loneliness came over him, and he wished with all his heart he had died with the others.

A terrible thought pierced the fog of grief. It was entirely his fault. He was the bright fellow who had come up with the idea of attacking in column. That had guaranteed that one of the regiments would be nearly wiped out, and it was his old regiment, the one his own brother and all of his friends were in. He had condemned them to death.

The only thing to do was draw his revolver, blow his brains out, and join the others in death. His hand moved to his holster, unbuttoned the flap, and closed around the grip. Then something stopped him. He thought of Carolyn.

He buried his face in his hands and sat for a long time, as dumb as the log he was on. Suddenly he became aware that someone was speaking to him. It was General Carter, so he got to his feet.

"I can't tell you how sorry I am," said the little man, with a catch in his voice. "Your brother and these other fine men were the best regiment I had, the best—" His voice trailed off, and he pretended preoccupation with the reins he held as he stood by his horse.

Tom nodded dumbly. "Yes, sir, it's gone. They're dead, almost all of them, my brother with the rest."

"If it's any comfort to you," Carter went on, "I believe these men saved the whole army. If the Rebels had kept this hill, they'd have Hancock and Meade over there on that ridge in a nutcracker by now." He shook his head and looked away. "And to think, these men waited back there half the night knowing exactly what was going to happen to them." He looked at the ground. "I doubt if any other regiment in the whole army would have done that."

Carter was right, and Tom wondered what Billy, Cole, and the others had thought of during what they knew were their last hours on earth. The thought overwhelmed him so much that he couldn't speak.

Carter waited a little while before asking, "Do you feel like going on with the brigade?"

"Yes, sir, if you want me to."

"Well, it's yours. No one's going to take it away from you after this. Meade will see to that when he finds out how you saved his neck, and I'll make sure he does." He spat. "Hobson and all the damned politicians can go to hell, Lincoln along with the rest."

Carter mounted. "Well, I've got to go. You can expect orders confirming that you're in command as soon as they can be put out, but I'll tell Browning your brigade isn't fit for any more fighting. I don't know where they'd put you, anyhow. That ridge is packed."

"Yes, sir. Thank you, sir."

Carter started to rein away but stopped. "Since you'll be staying here the rest of the day at least, I believe you ought to bury these men. I'll have my quartermaster send you the tools."

"Yes, sir, by all means. There'll be so many after this is all over they might not get buried for a long time." The thought of Billy's body rotting on the ground made him panicky.

"And they'd only get piled in trenches with a little dirt thrown over them then," Carter went on. "These men deserve better." He answered Tom's salute with a wave and wheeled away.

After Tom got busy again, that icy calm he had felt after the Midlow Massacre came over him again. He was able to go about his business coldly and efficiently, like a machine that had no feelings. It was unreal and a little frightening at first, but he got used to it. He moved the brigade to the west side of the hill to be ready for the worst if the Rebels took Cemetery Ridge. The western side of the ridge couldn't be seen from Powers' Hill, so he sent Dickens and Marter over there to report his dispositions to Carter and watch for any danger of a breakthrough when the Rebels attacked.

When two wagonloads of picks and shovels arrived, Tom faced the problem of burying the dead. Pater's old regiment solved it for him. The men were mostly from the locality, and said those Indiana boys had died defending their homes and families. Burying them decently was the least they could do.

Their new commander went about it systematically. He put his men to measuring and marking out graves spaced in rows in the field west of the hill where most of them already lay. An uncle of his owned the property, so there would be no trouble about it. He had a barn nearby stripped of its sides to make headboards.

Pater's orderly had been a hired man on his farm and wanted to take the body home, which was only a few miles away. When Tom told him to go ahead, he wrapped a discarded coat about the shattered head, slung the body across the dead man's horse, and set out toward the east. Tom shuddered when he thought of what would happen at the farmhouse when the nearly headless body of the husband and father was brought in.

The most the Pennsylvanians would allow the Indiana men to do was build fires and burn the names on the headboards with heated ramrods. They were going to bury the dead Rebels, too, but there would be no headboards for them because nobody knew their names.

Pater's old regiment was nearly up to strength and the men went to work with a will, so it wouldn't take too long to do the burying. Hauser insisted on digging Billy's grave himself and covered the body with a groundsheet so no dirt would fall on the bloodless, boyish face. The sound of the earth falling on the groundsheet sent tremors through Tom's whole body, and his self-control almost deserted him before it was over. He burned the name on the headboard himself, and it was the hardest work he had ever done.

Early in the afternoon a thunder of massed artillery from far to the west began a bombardment of Cemetery Ridge. Tom thought of stopping the work and putting the Pennsylvanians under arms, but their rifles were stacked nearby and it could be done in a few minutes, so he let it go on.

Anyhow, he wasn't much worried. Hancock had been getting ready for three days for just what was happening. Artillery was probably standing nearly hub to hub on that ridge, and according to Carter there was so much infantry it might not need any help from the guns.

Some roundshot and shells with bad fuses hurdled the ridge and landed in the fields beyond, but that was the closest the battle ever came. It was easy to tell the roundshot because it always bounded and rolled much farther.

After an hour or so the enemy's artillery stopped firing and there was a period of eerie silence. Then the guns on the ridge opened up. There were so many of them and they fired so rapidly that it shook the earth and blotted out the western sky with great boiling clouds of smoke that drifted over the ridge and at times almost hid it from sight. Eventually rifle fire in great volume made itself heard despite the roar of the guns, which meant the Rebels hadn't been stopped by the artillery, although it was hard to understand why.

When a few running figures appeared through the smoke and headed down the eastern side of the ridge, some of the men yelled that the Rebels had broken the line and our men were running. Tom thought they were only the cowards and skulkers you could always expect, and he turned out to be right.

Gradually the firing began to die down, first the rifles and then the artillery. Finally it stopped. Tom had no doubt that the Rebels had been thrown back, undoubtedly with great slaughter. Lee had tried the same thing Burnside had at Fredericksburg and gotten the same medicine. When Dickens and Marter came back, they only confirmed this and said that everyone expected Meade to counterattack and finish the Rebels off. The only thing was, Hancock, who had been running things more than Meade had, had been wounded.

Tom didn't think Meade would try it, though. He would probably quit while he was ahead and just let the Rebels go back to Virginia. Then the war would just go on and on. That was the way it had gone from the beginning, and there was no reason to expect any change.

He kept his thoughts to himself, though.

# 50

It was over a month before the brigade went into camp with any chance of staying even a few days, and by that time it was back in Virginia. Like Tom expected, Meade had let the Rebels pull out unmolested after Gettysburg and made no serious effort to catch them as they retreated to Virginia. It was all very discouraging, and there was a lot of talk about it.

Tom welcomed the constant movement and toil of the march because it kept him occupied and gave little time for thought. Fatigue put him to sleep at night, and the keen edge of his grief gradually dulled. Only when something happened, like looking back at a bend in the road and seeing von Jagerhof riding at the head of the handful of men he had left, would it strike him afresh. He came to avoid such things, because they always stayed with him for hours afterward.

The day after the battle he had scribbled brief notes to his father and to Carolyn, all he had time to do. A citizen who happened to be around offered to take them straight to the nearest post office, so he gave them to him along with enough money to make it worth his while. He told his father that Billy had been killed instantly and couldn't have suffered. Although he knew it would be little comfort, he added that Billy had fallen leading his company in a charge on the enemy.

He didn't tell Carolyn about Billy. He only told her that he was alive and well and that he didn't know how he could stand to wait until winter put an end to campaigning and they could be married. He never received a reply to either note while on the march, but that was only to be expected.

Tom dreaded going into camp for even a few days and at first welcomed the paperwork that engulfed him when he did. Little of it had been done since spring, and there was a great deal of catching up to do. He soon saw that it would keep him from more important things and had to call on von Jagerhof and Corporal Stevens from his old regiment for help. Neither minded, because their regiment was now so small they had virtually nothing to do.

Tom got to keep them both when General Carter tipped him off that another understrength Indiana regiment was going to be consolidated with what was left of his old one. The new colonel was senior to von Jagerhof, so Tom asked him if he wanted to be brigade adjutant.

He certainly did. It would be another step up the ladder in Prussia, and another favor he owed Tom. He only hoped he could return them someday. General Carter was more than agreeable. Von Jagerhof was undoubtedly the best man for the job. You just couldn't beat those Prussians. While he was at it, Tom took Stevens as brigade clerk and made him a sergeant.

Von Jagerhof and Stevens immediately took over the paperwork and routine, and Tom could start repairing the damage of the late campaign. Shoes were worn out, equipment broken or lost, and many of the men looked like ragamuffins. He knew he would have to see to it himself because Colonel Brumley, Carter's quartermaster, was a crochety fellow and a stickler for forms and regulations. It took a good deal of persuasion and prodding, even appeals to Carter in a few cases, but he got what he wanted and soon had the men ready to take the field again.

About a week after they camped, Kemper and his men rode by. The veteran was wearing a captain's uniform, so Carter had kept his promise, but he hadn't been able to keep Kemper long. General Browning, the corps commander, had appropriated Carter's scouts for himself, and transferred them all to the cavalry to make it legal. Because of this, no one had seen any of them since Gettysburg.

Browning had outfitted them well. They all had new cavalry uniforms, big black boots, and repeating carbines as well as revolvers and sabers. Tom congratulated Kemper and invited him to visit awhile, but he said they were going out on a scout and couldn't.

Their former comrades gathered around and gaped at them. "My, ain't you-uns a purty sight!" marveled Ab.

"Yah! Yallerlaigs!" scoffed Dan Howard. "I'll bet ye don't do nothin' but ride 'round stealin' chickens an' hawgs an' sich frum pore, starvin' Rebel wimmin!"

"Now lissen hyar, you dum foot sol'jers!" rejoined Charley Evans. "We air Gin'ral Brownin's pus'nal scouts, that's what we air! We don't ans'er t' no one but him, an' he's a majer gin'ral!"

Kemper let the raillery go on a little longer before starting his men on, but a latecomer crowded his way through them as they turned away and confronted Ab. He was a little dark-haired fellow wearing a lieutenant's bars whom Tom was startled to recognize as Zeke Kerns.

"Hey, thar, you big, tall, skeercrow-lookin' feller!" he shouted.

Ab was thunderstruck and could only gape speechlessly.

"Come t' 'tenshun, thar!" demanded Zeke. "An' s'lute! Don't ye know what t' do when an officer speaks t' ye, ye ig'nernt dern hillbilly?"

Ab recovered with a rush. "Why . . . why, you no'count Dubois County ridge runner!" He began to look around on the ground. "Jist lemme find some rocks an' I'll s'lute ye all right! I'll bounce 'em offa yer punkin head!"

Before he could come up with any, Zeke was spurring after his comrades, whooping and hee-hawing gleefully. Ab shied a stone after him anyhow, then joined in the general laughter. Dan Howard laughed so hard he cried, and Tom was hard put to keep from doing so.

Von Jagerhof had come up to see what was going on and laughed as hard as anybody. He and Tom then marveled at how the men could carry on after what they had been through.

The two men went back to the headquarters tent and got to talking about the battle at Gettysburg. Von Jagerhof agreed with Tom that Lee had thrown it away by letting Meade fight a purely defensive battle from that strong position along those hills and ridges. He could have maneuvered him out of it easily, and then there would have been only one outcome. The veteran Rebel commander had no peer in a battle of rapid maneuver in open country. Von Jagerhof thought it was partly due to experience. "You see, he's been commanding for a year and a half now, and none of our generals stays very long. We've had four different ones since he has been in. No one has time to learn to handle the army before he's out."

"Yes, and a lot of it's politics," replied Tom. "McClellan's the only general who ever matched Lee, but they wouldn't keep him because he's a Democrat. If it wasn't for politics, we'd have won the war a year ago. And it goes on down. Look at Hobson and Bixby." He shook his head. "It's cost thousands of men their lives."

Von Jagerhof agreed. "There wouldn't be all this meddling by civilian officials with military matters in Prussia, and men like Hobson would never get field command. Of course we have fellows like him. Everybody does. But in Prussia they only get high rank and ceremonial duties. But then we have no politics, like you do, anyhow, and officers are strictly prohibited from getting involved in anything like that."

Tom sighed. "Politics infects the whole country, army and all. Sometimes I think it'll cost us the war."

"Oh, you people of the North will win," von Jagerhof assured him. "The Southerners don't have the men, or the resources. You've got three times their population and I suppose ten times their industry.

You'll just grind them down and wear them out, even with things going on as they have been."

"Unless the people get sick of it and demand peace," rejoined Tom gloomily.

"I've often wondered if the other party, the Democrats, would do any better than the Republicans. What do you think, sir?"

"I've never thought of that. Now, with things the way they are, I think they probably would. Most high-ranking officers were Democrats if they were anything, so there couldn't be much favoritism or discrimination." He laughed shortly. "But if most officers were Republicans and the Democrats were in power, I doubt if they'd do any better."

Von Jagerhof put a question he had probably been working up to. "Sir, what do you think of going to Prussia and taking service with us, when your war is over anyhow?"

"I've never thought of anything like that."

"Well, there'll be no place for men like you in your army after the war's over unless they're willing to accept a great reduction in rank."

"You're right. Our army will go back to nothing, and I doubt if I could keep a commission if I stayed." He paused. "I don't plan on staying, though. I don't think I'd fit into the peacetime army."

"Oh, you'd see plenty of action in Prussia. Chancellor Bismarck is uniting Germany, and we'll become a united country for the first time since the Middle Ages. The French are sure to try to prevent it, because a united Germany will be stronger than they are and they won't be able to dominate continental Europe like they have for two hundred years. There's sure to be a war with France, and then the English may come in on one side or the other to keep the balance of power."

Tom was intrigued. "I think that's a pretty good picture of what's going to happen over there if Bismarck is able to put Germany together again."

"You'd have excellent prospects in the Prussian service, sir, and what you call good connections from the beginning. My family is very influential, and I'd like to return some of the favors you've shown me."

Tom was a little overwhelmed by the idea, but he had his doubts. "But I'd be a foreigner and German isn't my native language."

"Oh, you speak it well, and you're improving all the time. And you needn't worry about the other thing. We Germans have a long tradition of foreigners in our military." He laughed. "Of course, that's natural. Many of us have had no real country of our own, and we've been mercenaries for generations. Look at von Steuben and de Kalb in your Revolution, and all the Hessians on the other side."

Tom pondered. He hadn't thought of what he was going to do after the war, since all his plans had been wrecked. He didn't think he could go back to Dubois County and take up farming again, but there was Carolyn to consider. She might not be happy as a military wife, particularly in a foreign land. "I'll think about it," was all he could say.

"Please do. If you're so inclined, I can arrange for you to meet an uncle of mine. He's visiting at our embassy in Washington now, on leave as commandant of the *Kriegschule* at Potsdam. That's our war college. You're having the first really big war since Napoléon's time, and there's much to be learned from it." He confided further. "He's looking for military talent, too. There are thousands of Germans in service, mostly on your side, but he's interested in others, too. A war always turns up good men who'd never get a chance to show their talent otherwise."

Tom impulsively stuck out his hand. "All right! I'll have a talk with your uncle the first chance I get! You've shown me what Prussian officers are like, and I'd like to meet one with high rank."

"Oh, he's got high rank," said von Jagerhof as they shook hands. "He's a *Generaloberst*." He nodded and smiled. "I think you might hope to keep your present rank, and look forward to promotion. I know military talent when I see it, and you'd be a valuable acquisition for us, sir."

Tom was a little embarrassed. "Well, I'm entirely untaught, and I'd be in pretty fast company over there."

"Untaught! So were Marlborough and Blücher! Some men don't need to be taught. They know already."

Tom was so bemused he could only shake his head.

Tom didn't have to go see von Jagerhof's uncle, who seemed to keep in close touch with his nephew. A week later *Generaloberst* Helmuth, *Freiherr* von Brandenburg, came to see him, and of course also his nephew. They had known he was coming for several days, and Hauser worked wonders for the visit. He built a plank floor, rigged a tent over it with the sides rolled up, and lined them with aromatic cedar boughs. Von Jagerhof telegraphed a German provisions house in Baltimore for the food and arranged for the perishables to be kept on ice in a nearby town until Hauser came to get them. Tom wondered where his orderly got the planks for the floor, and was astonished when a table and chairs that looked like they had been plundered from a fine mansion materialized on the day of the visit.

The *Generaloberst* must have looked a lot like his nephew when he was young and was still trim and energetic in his fifties. He wasn't at all arrogant or standoffish and his English was impeccable, which he attributed to his English wife. Hauser outdid himself preparing the meal, and the guest said it was the best German food he had eaten since he left Prussia. Even the cook at the embassy couldn't match Hauser, and he was going to steal him if Tom didn't watch out.

Tom laughed and said that anyone with that in mind had better think twice and went on to tell what a tyrant Hauser was. They laughed about it and the *Generaloberst* said orderlies often got that way, like wives, which brought more laughter. Hauser understood them well enough to get red in the face and look sheepish.

After the meal, brandy and cigars were brought out. Tom found the brandy too fiery and only pretended to sip at it until he could covertly dump his glass. Von Jagerhof and his uncle drank the stuff like water, and it made his stomach burn just to watch them.

It wasn't long before the *Generaloberst* got down to business. "My nephew has told me much about you, Colonel Traylor."

"I hope he didn't flatter me too much," laughed Tom.

The *Generaloberst* smiled. "If he did, General Carter flattered you even more. I came by his headquarters and had a long talk with him on my way."

"I owe a lot to General Carter. He's a fine man."

The *Generaloberst* nodded. "My nephew tells me you might be interested in coming to Prussia to take service with us."

"Yes, I am. The chances for action seem good over there, but I'll have to consider it carefully. There's a young lady who'll have to agree to it also."

"Your fiancée?"

Tom nodded. "Frankly, sir, she may not want to go. Her father was killed leading this brigade, and she may not want to be a military wife, or to leave the country. If that's the case, I couldn't go."

"I see." The *Generaloberst* puffed his cigar and looked thoughtful.

"I've told the colonel he might be able to keep his present rank and could certainly look forward to promotion," interjected von Jagerhof.

"I think I can guarantee your entering our service with the rank of *Oberst* on one condition, Colonel," said the *Generaloberst.*

"What's that, sir?"

"Completing the course for field-grade officers at the *Kriegschule.* I have no doubt you can do that. As for promotion, one never knows, but I think you could expect that, too. Our army will be much enlarged when von Bismarck unites all of Germany under our leadership." He nodded thoughtfully. "I expect a war to come of it also."

"Yes," said his nephew. "I told him he would have to fight the French, and perhaps the English too."

"There's certain to be a war with the French. They'll fight to prevent Germany from being united, and the English may intervene, on our side if it seems that the French will win, and theirs if it seems that we will, particularly if they think we might try to conquer Europe, like the French did so often during the past two hundred years. The English were our allies against the French, but they'll take the other side just as readily if they think it's necessary to maintain the balance of power."

The *Generaloberst* flicked the ash from his cigar. "But I think a war with Austria will come first. The Austrians are our rivals for leadership in Germany and they won't give up without a fight, but I don't expect it to be very severe." He nodded thoughtfully and took a puff. "The French are another matter, though, and we may have the English to contend with also." He looked at Tom significantly. "I foresee a period of prolonged conflict, and a young man of talent may go far."

Tom was entranced with the prospect of service on fields where Frederick the Great and Napoléon had fought, but he only said, "I'll think about it, sir."

"I can arrange for you to enter at Potsdam at the beginning of the term in December if you'd care to."

"That's a good deal sooner than I'd expected. I don't know if I should resign my commission before the war's over here."

"Your war will go on a long time yet, at least a year, perhaps two, and I understand your chances of promotion are poor because you are in bad odor with some powerful people."

"Yes, I don't expect ever to be brigadier general, but rank really doesn't mean a lot to me." Tom laughed shortly. "If I would profess a political conversion, I have no doubt I'd be promoted, and I've been expecting an opportunity to do so from the governor of my state. That's the way he does things." He shook his head. "I won't do it, though. I'm just not that sort of fellow."

"I'm pleased to hear that. Men who will trade their principles for promotion aren't the kind of men we want." He paused and puffed his cigar. "You'll have no political difficulties with us. We don't have any politics. The philosophers don't like our political system, but it has its advantges from the viewpoint of a military man."

"I don't know about your *Kriegschule*. I'm entirely self-taught in military matters, you know, and German isn't my native language."

"So were Prince Eugene and Gneisenau. Language needn't be a problem. Look at Karl and I! English isn't our native tongue either."

"The *Kriegschule* worries me. I'll be competing with men who've been brought up to the military and have years of experience."

The *Generaloberst* put down his cigar. "I can ask you a few questions such as you will meet with there."

"Shoot."

The *Generaloberst* smiled. "You mean to begin. I'm not very well acquainted with your American idiom." He went on to put a series of questions to Tom. They got harder as they went along, but he was always able to come up with some kind of an answer.

One that had to do with the use of cavalry on the battlefield led to a disagreement. "The rifle's made cavalry obsolete except for screening, scouting, and delaying action," insisted Tom. "When our cavalry is up against infantry, it almost always fights on foot. That's because we've found out that if cavalry charges infantry equipped with rifles, it'll be taken under fire at six or eight hundred yards and shot to pieces before it can close. It can't be used on the battlefield for shock effect like it was in Napoléon's time, when infantry only had smoothbore muskets." He gave as an example the charge of Jackson's cavalry on the brigade that time in the Shenandoah Valley over a year ago.

The *Generaloberst* was impressed. "I see," he said. "What you say is doubtless true, even if it won't set well with senior commanders. It may be one of the most important lessons to come out of the war."

"Now you see!" interjected von Jagerhof. "The man is actually better off for having no formal military education. He's not bound by obsolete ideas!"

Tom laughed. "Ignorance may have its advantages."

The *Generaloberst* wanted to bring matters to a conclusion. "Well, Colonel, what do you say? May we expect you at Potsdam in December?"

"I'm afraid not, sir. I doubt very much if I'll be able to see my fiancée before winter, when we plan to be married, and I'd want to see my parents, too."

"Perhaps they can come to see you?"

"No, that wouldn't be possible for my parents, and perhaps not for my fiancée. My mother's not well, and I expect my brother's death will affect her a great deal. I'm sure she won't be able to travel, anyhow."

The *Generaloberst* nodded sympathetically. "Your brother was a fine young man. It is a great tragedy."

Tom only bowed his head, so the *Generaloberst* went on. "There is spring term beginning in April. Perhaps you will be ready then?"

Tom nodded. "I'll know by then I'm sure. My fiancée will be my wife by then, and if she'll agree, you can count on it." He felt that he had made the most important decision of his life.

The *Generaloberst* sprang to his feet and extended his hand. "Let's shake on it, as you Americans say!"

They shook hands.

# 51

Two months had gone by and Tom had never heard from Carolyn or his father, so he wrote them again and sent the letters off himself by post rider. A few days later, before his last letter could have arrived, an express messenger delivered a letter from Tom's father.

The letter said that it had been in the papers that Tom had been killed, but one of the men who had written back said it was Billy. He hadn't heard from either of them since that big battle at Gettysburg and begged for a letter, even though he knew it would tell him that Billy was gone. He was worried half to death, and it had given his wife such a setback that he had to put her in the state asylum at Indianapolis. He would rather have died a thousand times, but it had to be done. He couldn't stay with her all the time like someone had to, and he couldn't take her to the Anderses, who were all torn up because Fred had been killed and probably Billy, too. In fact, Mrs. Anders was almost as bad off as his wife was. They weren't the only ones. It looked like the whole company had been almost wiped out, and hardly a family in the county hadn't lost someone.

Tom felt a wave of panic. That fellow who had promised to mail those two notes sent just after the battle had just kept the money and thrown them away. He cursed him and himself, too, for waiting for replies before writing again. All he could do was write two more letters and send them by express. There was a rider at Shoals who would deliver the one to his father, and Carolyn was at her uncle's near Lexington, where there was surely an express office.

He was just starting when a dapper civilian came into the tent. He was a little fellow with oily hair and a small mustache. "Colonel Traylor?" he asked.

Tom put aside his pen and made himself get up. "Yes, sir?"

The fellow extended his hand. "Martin's my name. I'm one of Governor Morton's military agents. We're charged with looking out for the welfare of Indiana troops, you know."

These agents were more interested in politics than troops, but Tom shook hands with him anyhow. He knew what he had come for, and he couldn't have come at a worse time. Tom made up his mind to get rid of him fast, so he caught Stevens's eye and signaled him to leave.

Martin got down to business immediately. "Well, Colonel, I understand there's some difficulty about your promotion, and I've come to see if we can't do something about it."

It was so obvious that Tom could scarcely contain himself, so he only nodded and Martin went on.

"The governor is interested in your case, and tells me all he needs to know is that you aren't hostile to him." He laughed deprecatingly. "You can't expect a public man to help his enemies, you know."

"No, I guess not," replied Tom tersely.

Martin sensed his mood and looked at him appraisingly. "I understand you've always been a Democrat."

"Yes, and I've seen no reason to change my politics." That ought to get rid of the fellow.

Martin wasn't put off, though. "Well, now," he said with some asperity, "I'd think you should have, considering the position your party has taken up back home." He paused and cocked his head to one side. "Perhaps you aren't fully aware of it, though."

"I'm aware of nothing that would turn me against my party."

Martin shook his head and fingered his gold watch chain. "Well, you should know the trouble the governor has had with the copperheads who got control of the legislature last fall."

Tom could contain himself no longer. "Yes, I know all about that, and I resent that epithet you used. You'd have called most of the men in my old regiment copperheads, men who are dead now."

Martin was taken aback and softened his tone. "Oh, you can't expect ordinary soldiers who were only farmers or something to understand things like that very well. They hang onto—"

Tom cut him off. "You talk about the trouble Morton's had with the legislature. It seems to me it was mostly because he tried to run the state single-handed. That's not constitutional, you know."

Martin got angry. "He had no choice!" he insisted heatedly. "Those Democrats, those copperheads, sympathize with the Rebels! They hope the Rebels will win the war. Some of them would take Indiana out of the Union and join the Confederacy if they could!"

"Have they refused to appropriate money for the war or anything like that?" Tom hadn't intended to go this far, but he couldn't stop.

"No, nothing like that. That would show them for what they are and turn their own people against them."

"Did it ever occur to you that they haven't done anything like that because they want to win the war and restore the Union?"

"That's preposterous!" scoffed Martin. "That's the last thing they want! They're always opposing the war. Just read their speeches and resolutions!"

"I have," replied Tom evenly. "They're only against the way the war's being carried on. They're just against things that have been done that have nothing to do with the war. They want a war just to restore the Union."

Martin played his trump. "Haven't you heard about the Knights of the Golden Circle and their conspiracies?" His eyes glittered like a snake's.

"I've read about them in the papers. It all sounds like a fairy tale to me."

"Oh, but it's not! We had a grand jury investigation, and—"

Tom cut him off. "Yes, I've heard all about that. They claimed the Democratic party was controlled by the Knights. They claimed there were thousands of them, organized and armed, ready to overthrow the government and join the Rebels. Yet they couldn't indict a single one of them! And, Mr. Martin, every member of that grand jury was a Republican."

Martin shook his head. "I never expected this sort of thing from an educated and informed man leading our troops against the Rebels."

Tom resisted an impulse to throw the man out. "I'll tell you the way I see it, Mr. Martin, if you want to hear me out."

"By all means," snapped Martin. "I'd be interested to hear."

"It seems to me that you Republicans are making out that honest political opposition is treason. Because Democrats are against things you've done that have nothing to do with the war, you say they're traitors who sympathize with the Rebels."

"Things like what?" demanded Martin.

"The Morrill Tariff, military arrests for only speaking out, the Emancipation Proclamation—"

Martin broke in. "You mean you oppose the Proclamation?" he asked incredulously.

"I certainly do. It's going to cause all sorts of problems in the future, and it's caused plenty already. The men have lost heart, and a good many have deserted. They didn't enlist to free the Negroes. It's the chief cause of all the trouble back home, and—"

Martin broke in again. "It's the war! We're at war with the slave states! Slavery's their cornerstone! We've got to strike at the Rebels any way we can!"

Tom grew sarcastic. "Pray tell me how it's hurt the Rebels. Are the slaves running away or refusing to work? Are they rising up in revolt?" He shook his head emphatically. "No, they're not. They're just going on like they always have, raising food for the Rebel army, driving their wagons, and digging their trenches. It hasn't hurt the Rebels a particle. In fact, it's made them fight harder. They know what they're in for if they lose now."

Martin tried another tack. "I'd think a person who's gone from sergeant to colonel would show a little gratitude to the man who's consented to every promotion he's got."

"You mean Governor Morton?"

Martin nodded grimly.

Tom spat it out. "I don't owe Oliver P. Morton a thing. I've earned every promotion I've got, those that I didn't get just by surviving when other men were killed." He laughed contemptuously. "Consented! What else could he do?"

Martin looked at Tom malevolently., "Well, I guess you aren't interested in becoming a brigadier general, or even—"

Tom overrode him. "I knew all along what your dirty business was!" he spat. "You were sent to find out if I was politically right and would bow down before Morton before my nomination went to the Senate!" He put all the contempt he could muster in his voice. "You fellows are playing politics with the war, all of you, from Lincoln on down. You've sacrificed thousands of lives for nothing but politics!" He was so angry he almost choked. "Good men have been slaughtered like cattle because of it! My brother and most of my friends are dead because of it!" He was shouting, but he didn't care. "Get out, Mr. Martin! Go back and tell your noble governor what I've said, every word of it. I don't care what he does. I'd rather be a private than owe anything to the likes of him!"

Martin shouted back. "I'll do just that, and I can guarantee one thing. You'll get your wish! You won't be wearing those eagles very long!"

He turned away, but Tom seized him by the shoulder and spun him about. "Listen, you little sneak. There's something else you can tell your master Mr. Morton. If he can take my eagles away because of politics, I don't want them! They're worthless baubles!"

Martin was scared and tried to wriggle away, but Tom wasn't done with him. "Maybe he'll give them to you, and you can try fighting the Rebels awhile. Ask him for them! Show your patriotism!" He gave Martin a shove and let him go.

Martin didn't say another word. He just walked out of the tent and away, rubbing his shoulder and looking like a bantam rooster bested in a fight.

The very next day General Carter came to see Tom, who knew what had brought him by the way he looked. "Well, Colonel," he said with a sigh, "you've gotten yourself in a pickle again."

Tom nodded. "Yes, sir, I've been expecting to hear that."

"It's all by the grapevine so far, nothing official yet, but it's coming. You're a goner this time."

Tom wasn't frightened and told Carter what he had said about Morton taking his eagles. "I meant every word of it, too."

Carter sighed again. "I just wish you'd been civil to the fellow anyhow. He went straight to the telegraph and sent a wire to Morton, and it wasn't long before Morton sent one to Stanton demanding your immediate dismissal."

Tom was ready to fight them. "On what grounds?"

"Disloyalty."

"Disloyalty? By God! What proof?"

"Morton's word. That's all Stanton needs. He's done it before." Carter shook his head sadly.

Tom couldn't believe it. "Disloyalty! Why . . . why I've never had anything to do with the Rebels but fight them . . . and kill them!" he bowed his head. "Here I've worked, I've marched, I've fought. I've come within an eyelash of death a hundred times."

"None of that means anything to those politicians." Carter shook his head. "I hate it. I hate it like the devil. I feel like resigning because of it."

"No, sir, don't do anything like that. I brought it on myself. Like you say, I should have been civil to the fellow at least. But I'm going to put up a fight. I'll show them up for the dirty double-dealing skulkers they are."

Carter looked at him with something akin to pity. "You won't get the chance to do that."

Tom was incredulous. "Won't they have to prefer charges? Won't I get a court-martial?"

Carter shook his head. "No. There aren't any charges they could prefer against you, but that won't stop them. They'd do you like they did Charley Stone. He's a friend of mine, and was a brigadier general. You'll be arrested, broken, and confined—"

"Confined? Put in prison?" He couldn't believe it. "But the Articles of War call for charges and a prompt trial before—"

Carter interrupted. "They don't pay any more attention to the Articles of War than they do to the Constitution." He nodded glumly. "They kept Stone in prison six months before he got the chance to clear himself. He did, and kept his star, but he's a jailbird now and ruined for life. He told me he's going to leave the country."

There was a roaring in Tom's ears like when he had led the charge on Ramsdell's division. "Will you help me, sir?"

Carter looked at him directly. "If you ask me to, but it won't do any good, and I'll get the same medicine you will."

"Then I won't ask you. You've spent your life in the army, and we've got to keep some decent men in it."

"There are plenty of decent men in the army, but they lie low and keep their mouths shut when things like this happen, like I've done." The little man looked Tom in the eye. "I'm ashamed of it, though, and if you say the word, I'll stand up with you, and go down with you, too." He meant every word of it.

"No, sir! No, sir! Like I said, I brought it on myself. If I hadn't insulted and abused that fellow, and Morton, too, all they'd do would be block my promotion if I was ever nominated, and I doubt if I ever would be. I don't really care about promotion anyhow. I'll take the consequences on myself, sir. I don't want you to ruin yourself because of my bad temper." He shook his head and sighed. "That fellow just got me at a bad time, I guess." He thought of telling Carter about the letters that hadn't been sent and how it had upset him but decided that it would only sound like he was making excuses for himself.

Carter nodded. "Then I'd advise you to resign immediately and accept that Prussian general's offer. They don't have this sort of thing over there. I'm no admirer of their political system, but you can say that much for it."

"Oh, you know about that?"

"Yes, he told me quite frankly that he was going to try to recruit you, after he'd seen you, on his way back, and I was all set to try to talk you out of it if I had to." He shrugged. "It's the only thing you can do now, though. If you stay in this country, Morton will make sure you're drafted after you're out of prison, and he'll see to it that you wish you'd never been born."

"Will they let me resign to do it, though?"

"If we can get your resignation to Thomas, the adjutant general, before they make their first move, he'll approve it and then you'll be out of their reach."

"But will he approve it?"

Carter sighed. "I'll have to have your pledge of absolute confidentiality before I can tell you about that."

"You have it, sir."

"It was Lorenzo Thomas who sent me word about what's going on, and he risked his neck to do it."

"He must be a decent fellow."

"I don't know about that. I don't see how a decent man could work for Edwin M. Stanton. Let's just say he has his decent moments and he's an old friend of mine."

Tom made up his mind. "Let's do it."

"We'll have to hurry. Go to my headquarters and see Sergeant Weber. Don't say a word to anyone else. Weber will have the papers ready for you to sign, and take them straight to Browning at Corps. He'll sign them immediately. Then Weber will take them straight to a friend of mine at Meade's headquarters who'll see to it that Meade signs them at once. Meade won't know anything about it and always signs anything this fellow puts before him. He'd probably sign anyhow, but we can't take that chance. Then Weber will take the papers to Thomas himself and it's done." Carter nodded. "They won't be expecting that kind of speed, and we'll beat them."

"It sounds like you've been to a lot of trouble over this."

"Yes, I've been pulling wires like mad ever since yesterday."

"I'll be greatly indebted to you, sir," said Tom feelingly.

Carter took his arm and looked him in the eye. "I couldn't live with myself if I let them do you in, after what you did for me at Chancellorsville, and for all of us at Gettysburg."

"I guess you can rely on Sergeant Weber."

"Absolutely. I'd trust him with my life."

"You say the papers are all ready, sir?"

Carted nodded. "Yes, and I signed them, but they're undated. Thomas wants to back-date them, and the endorsements, too, to protect himself and all of us."

Suddenly Tom realized that there was one very important thing he hadn't thought about. "Maybe they won't want me in Prussia after this. They may think I'm a cantankerous rebellious sort of a fellow."

Carter laughed. "Oh, don't worry about that. The general who came to see me knows all about politics in our army. That was his main hope in getting you. If you want to, you can tell him to get in touch with me about it, confidentially of course." He stuck out his hand and, when Tom took it, went on. "You'd better get started, Colonel. I'd better not see you again, so I'll wish you luck in Prussia now." The little man sighed. "Right now I almost wish I was going myself."

As soon as Tom got back from seeing Sergeant Weber, he took von Jagerhof aside and told him all about it. The reaction was totally unexpected. "Oh, this is the best possible thing!" he exclaimed delightedly.

"But, what will the *Generaloberst* think of me now? Won't he get the idea I'm a troublemaker or—"

The Prussian paid no attention and broke in. "You'll have to go to Prussia now! Oh, we've got you! We've got you!" he danced a little jig.

Tom suppressed a smile and repeated his query.

Von Jagerhof scoffed at the idea. "Nonsense! He knows how it is with you of the other party! He's an old friend of General McClellan. They were observers together in the Crimea during the war there years ago, and they've kept up a correspondence ever since. McClellan was the first man he went to see when he arrived last winter, just after he'd been dismissed."

"Well, that might help." Tom sighed. "I'll tell the *Generaloberst* the whole story, and I won't spare myself. He can get in touch with General Carter about it. I'll insist on it." Things were looking positively rosy. Carolyn would see that going to Prussia was the only thing they could do. Maybe everything had worked out for the best after all. "You know," he confided, "I'll be glad to get someplace where there aren't any politics."

Von Jagerhof clapped his hands gleefully. "Go see the *Generaloberst* as soon as you can and tell him you're ready to go! While he's making the arrangements, you can marry your fiancée and settle your affairs. You'll be in Prussia by November!" He danced another jig, then exclaimed, "You know, I'm going to go with you! I'll resign! I think I've learned all I can over here anyhow!"

Tom impulsively slapped him on the back. "Good! We'll go back together!"

"Oh, we'll go places in Prussia!" exulted von Jagerhof. "Thanks to you, I'll jump two grades! I've already got the word! I'll be a *Hauptmann* with my own company!"

They linked arms and began an impromptu dance.

There was a portentous throat-clearing in the background. Hauser had come in on them and definitely did not approve of such antics. *Offizieren und Herren*, he informed them, should not act like schoolboys.

To his astonishment, he was seized and brought into the circle. When he was told what it was all about and invited to come along, he joined in the dancing. He had been homesick ever since he left Germany. He guessed he was just too old to tear up his roots and then put them down someplace else like younger people. He had never taken out any citizenship papers and couldn't be kept to serve out his enlistment if the *Herren* would help him get out.

They assured him they would. The *Generaloberst* would see to it himself. After all, hadn't he admired Hauser's cooking?

# 52

Tom went to Indiana to see his parents first. He could get off the train at Shoals Station, only about twenty miles from home, and see his father. After they went to see his mother, he would go to Carolyn. If the connections had been as good, he would have gone to see her first.

He wrote Carolyn and his father by express so they would know when he was coming. He hadn't heard from Carolyn since they had been together in Washington, although his last letter to her was his third one. His note written just after the battle had undoubtedly gone the same way the one to his father had, though, and he had been moving around too much for any answers to catch up with him.

Things had gone well for him. Carter's shortcuts had gotten his resignation approved by General Thomas before Morton and Stanton could act, and they had evidently decided to let him go. He was now a civilian again, and the only thing military about him was the revolver he wore under his frock coat. He didn't want to go unarmed in these troubled times, especially in Kentucky, where bands of guerrillas and brigands roamed the country.

The *Generaloberst* had welcomed Tom heartily and he had been royally entertained at the Prussian embassy in Washington, where he had stayed over a week. He had been assured that the *Kriegschule* at Potsdam would be awaiting him in December, which gave him over a month before his ship sailed. He planned to spend most of it with Carolyn on a prolonged honeymoon.

If it hadn't been for Carolyn, Tom would have been interested in the *Generaloberst's* daughter Paula. She was a lovely girl, slender and blond and at eighteen too young to hide the fact that she was badly smitten by the brave *Amerikaner* her father thought so well of. Nobody at the embassy spoke English to one another, and Tom had improved his German considerably while there. He also bought books to improve it still more on the voyage.

His father met the train with a buggy. He looked a great deal older, and it wasn't just the lines in his face or the gray that showed in his sandy hair. He had lost weight, and much of the vitality was gone from his big frame. He even walked with a stoop. When Tom stepped off the train, he ignored his outstretched hand and embraced him, something he had never done before.

On the way home, Tom told his father all that had happened to him and about going to Prussia.

"I figured something like that had happened, or you wouldn't have quit on 'em," replied his father. He shook his head and sighed. "I don't b'lieve anyone has ever been done dirtier than you have. There's not a particle of decency in any of 'em, ol' Morton least of all." He shook his head and sighed again. "I hate to see you go, 'way over there 'cross the waters, but I guess it's about all you can do."

"Well, I don't feel so bad about it now that I'm going to Prussia and be in the military there."

His father nodded. "You'll have a lot of rank, and military men set high over there." He bowed his head. "The only thing is," his voice began to break, "I'll be losin' you . . . 'bout . . . 'bout like I lost Billy." He began to weep.

Tom was thunderstruck. He had never imagined his father ever wept. He embraced him and felt tears starting in his own eyes. "Here, sir, Father! Don't; please don't," he choked.

John got a grip on himself. "I'm sorry . . . I'm sorry, Tom." He wiped his eyes with his sleeve. "I'm just not the man I used to be."

"Maybe I should stay here, in this country, I mean."

"No, I don't want you to do that. You've got too good a chance over there to pass it up, and ol' Morton'll find some way to get you here. It'd be selfish of me, and this country's never goin' to be what it was before the war. You'll prob'ly have as free a gov'ment over there as we will, maybe freer."

Tom nodded his agreement. "Things sure don't look very promising over here."

"Yeah, all these things they been doin' durin' the war, they're not goin' t' stop."

"You mean arresting men for just criticizing the government, like Preacher Stevens?"

John nodded. "And puttin' soldiers at th' polls t' keep Democrats from votin', like they've done in Kentucky and Maryland."

Tom pondered. "Do you think they'll do that here, in Indiana, next fall when Lincoln's up for reelection?"

John nodded glumly. "They'll do it if they think that's the only way they can win."

After supper they sat on the porch and smoked. Tom felt so depressed, he was glad they were going to Indianapolis the next day and that he would be going to Kentucky soon afterward. Home without

Billy and his mother just wasn't home at all. All at once he realized he hadn't even thought of Mary Worthington—Stillwell now—even when he had been in Shoals, and was glad he hadn't.

"Say, Tom," his father began, "what're you goin' t' do 'bout your property?"

"Deed it over to you," replied Tom impulsively. "We'll go to Jasper and do it as soon as we can."

"Oh, now, you don't want to do that! You ought to have somethin' to start with over there, and it's yours. You worked for it."

"Come to think of it, you may be right." He paused reflectively. "I'll tell you what. You sell it, and if I need money, I'll call on you for it."

His father sighed. "There's that house me an' ol' Dan Martin built for you and Sally. It's all done but a little finishin' work inside. I went ahead with it even after I knowed you an' her wouldn't never live in it."

"Well, at least take out what the house is worth for yourself. You paid for building it."

"No, I built it for you, and I want you to have th' money if you can't have th' house."

When Tom only nodded, his father went on. "I know a man who wants to buy it off me, too. I may sell most of my land 'long with yours."

"You do that. Just keep enough to give yourself something to do. You've worked hard all your life, and you can sort of retire."

John sighed. "I sure feel like it. I'm tired all th' time. I can't never get rested up."

"You do that, then, and just sit back and take it easy."

"It'll all bring in a sight o' money," mused John. "That's a fine house we built, an' property's high now."

"Yes, you'll have plenty to live on."

John made up his mind. "I'll tell you what I'll do. I'll sell th' land an' th' house, after you deed it over t' me, an' most of my land, too, an' put th' money in both our names. Then you can draw out your part of it anytime, an' when I'm gone it'll all be yours."

"That's all right with me."

John looked at his son strangely. "Tom d'ye reckon I could ever come over there an' see you? I'll have plenty of money t' travel, an' you bein' in their army prob'ly won't give you a chance t' come an' see me, for a long time anyhow."

"Of course. Just as soon as I get settled. Come and stay as long as you want to."

John nodded. "I was a little scared you might not want me 'round, with all them nobles an' high officers you'll be in with. I'm just a plain ol' farmer, you know."

"I'll never be ashamed of you," Tom assured him. "I've met a good many big men since I've been gone—at least, that's what they were supposed to be—but I've never met a bigger man than you are."

John was touched. "Thank ye, Tom." He shook his head "I've always tried t' be th' best man I could. I've always tried t' do right by ever'body, but it ain't done any good." He heaved a sigh. "It's 'nough t' shake a man's faith in th' Lord. Now I ain't got no one but you, an' you're goin' 'way."

"Then I ought to stay over here. I can make out."

"No, you can't stay in this country anymore. You've got to go. I was just a lonesome ol' man talkin' to himself." He paused and shook his head sadly. "It's th' war. It's cost me my family an' my peace of mind. I hope them that caused it burn in Hell through all eternity, 'specially 'cause they're th' same ones that're runnin' you outa th' country."

"Yes, if it wasn't for them, there wouldn't be any war, and Mother, Billy, and Sally would all be here."

It wasn't until he said it that he realized he had spoken of his mother as if she were dead, too.

When they went to Indianapolis and he saw his mother, Tom realized he had spoken more truly than he thought. He would never have recognized her if he hadn't known who she was. She looked twice her age. Her hair was white, her face drawn and wrinkled, and her arms as thin and shapeless as sticks. She didn't know him. She didn't know her husband. She stared at them with blank eyes in which there was not a flicker of interest or awareness. One of the attendants said she was that way all the time. She never spoke or showed any interest in anything or anybody. She had to be told to do everything, even to eat. She wasn't any trouble, though, except for having to be watched all the time so she wouldn't just wander off.

Tom thought of how strangers had been known to take her for his wife or sister only a few years ago. The war had killed her as surely as it had killed Billy. He couldn't stand it and had to go outside. Before he could go back, his father came out and said they might as well leave. You could stay all day, and it wouldn't be any different. He knew because he had done it.

The trip to Jasper to take care of Tom's property came next. It was late in the afternoon when he and his father were done at the courthouse, and they went to see the Anderses before leaving town.

Afterward Tom wished they hadn't. It was terrible. Mrs. Anders scarcely stopped weeping all the time they were there, and Gerda wept a great deal, too. She had lost both her brother and her sweetheart and was no longer the blooming girl Tom had seen on that hotel veranda not so long ago. He wasn't surprised when she said almost the whole town had been in mourning after the battle. Most of Billy's men had been from Jasper or nearby.

The doctor was so downcast he wasn't keeping up his practice and said he was thinking of going back to Germany. His wife stopped weeping long enough to cry that it couldn't be soon enough for her. She wished they had never come to this terrible country where men fought about Negroes and such things. When Tom told them he was going to Prussia, the doctor said he was doing the right thing. Military men stood high over there, and it was hard to tell what things would be like in this country after the war ended, if it ever did.

Both Tom and his father were glad it had been so late when they came that they couldn't stay long without having to travel half the night. Afterward Tom was even more depressed and avoided seeing any other people who had lost someone until it was time to go to Kentucky. He only promised his father that he would bring Carolyn back for a short visit before they went back east to leave the country.

Tom went to Theodore Ridge's law office in Lexington rather than wandering around trying to find his place in the country where Carolyn was staying. Ridge was at the courthouse, but his clerk said it wasn't anything important and went to get him at once. The fellow looked startled when Tom identified himself and acted scared afterward, but he was pretty young and Tom thought nothing of it at the time.

Ridge came back alone. He was strangely reserved and seemed to hesitate before taking Tom's extended hand. When he took him into his inner office and closed the door behind them, Tom knew something was wrong.

"All right, Mr. Ridge, what is it? Is something wrong with Carolyn?"

Ridge looked at him strangely. "Sit down, sir, if you please." His eyes flickered to the bulge of Tom's holster, which showed briefly when it caught on the chair as he sat down.

Ridge sat behind his desk, his face white and drawn. "Carolyn is married," he said simply.

Tom leapt to his feet. "What? Married? How can that be?" The floor seemed to tilt under his feet, and there was a sudden roaring in his ears.

Ridge bowed his head. "It's all my doing. I made a horrible mistake. May God forgive me, for I can't expect you to."

Tom started around the desk toward him, but the anguish in the man's face when he looked up stopped him in his tracks. "All I can say sir," he went on, "is that I tried to play God and made a horrible mistake."

His voice had sunk so low that Tom could scarcely hear him through the roaring in his ears, but his eyes did not waver. Tom found himself in his chair again and heard himself say, "Explain this to me, sir. I can't understand it—how it could have happened—" The roaring in his ears made him dizzy. He bowed his head and suddenly felt weak and sick.

Tom heard Ridge talking as though from a great distance, and the man's voice rang hollowly in his ears, almost like a distant bell, as the roaring began to subside. He forced himself to sit erect and look at him.

"You see," Ridge began, "you made Carolyn pregnant in Washington. I blamed myself for it. I should have known; I just let you fool me, but it all seemed so genuine, your being called back and all—" He stopped and looked down.

Tom could only gaze dumbly at him, so he looked up and went on. "We didn't know that yet when it came out in the papers that you had been killed. I believed it. Carolyn believed it. There it was, your name, rank, and regiment. There couldn't be any doubt about it." Ridge paused and slowly shook his head. "And then we didn't hear from you. I know you wrote her just after the battle, but it never came." Ridge stopped and looked out the window.

"So you got my other two letters, at least the second one!" Anger surged through Tom, and he started to his feet.

Ridge bowed his head. "By that time she was already married and gone."

Tom sat down again, unable to speak, so Ridge went on without looking up, in a voice so low it was scarcely audible. "I destroyed those letters, sir, both of them, and I have scarcely slept a night since." Suddenly he looked like he had aged twenty years.

"Please go on, sir," Tom heard himself say.

"Carolyn was prostrate—worse than when it was her father—after the papers said you'd been killed. I thought she had lost her mind, and she was physically ill, desperately ill. I took her to doctors—even to one in Cincinnati. He was the one who found out she was pregnant." Ridge sighed convulsively and looked at Tom out of tortured eyes. "Then there was only one thing to do: get her married as soon as possible. Do you understand, sir?"

Tom nodded. "Yes, You all thought I was dead. She would have been disgraced—ruined for life." He looked down and saw his fists clenched so tightly the knuckles were white. "And the baby needed a father." Sudden fear knifed through his anguish. "But what kind of a man would marry a woman carrying another man's child? Who is he?"

"It's better that you don't know," said Ridge faintly.

"But I must! She must be provided for, and the baby, too. My baby." Tears came to his eyes, and he had to stop.

Ridge didn't answer immediately. "I can only say," he began chokingly, "she's married to a man who's the purest soul I've ever known. He's very wealthy. You needn't worry. He's a distant cousin."

"Is he . . . does he . . . where does he live?"

Ridge gained control of himself, and his voice sounded normal again. "He's a philosopher. He teaches at a well-known Eastern school, but he's independently wealthy. Carolyn and the child will have everything money can buy."

"But money can't buy love, and happiness!" came from the depths of Tom's soul.

Ridge got up, came around the desk, and put an arm on Tom's stooped shoulders. "It's like I said: he's the purest soul I've ever known. If there are saints today, he's one of them. He's loved Carolyn ever since she was a girl in school at Bardstown." He sighed and sat on his desk. "He never pressed his suit. He's not the sort who would, and he's ten years older than she is."

"But he knew . . . he knew Carolyn was with child."

Ridge nodded. "I told him, and I explained it. He understands . . . understands how it was, that you were on your way to a great battle, and that you, both of you, thought it might be your last time together."

For the first time a logical thought forced its way through the turmoil in Tom's mind. "But she can get a divorce! She'll want to when she finds out, when she understands everything!" Hope began to dispel the black despair of his soul.

Ridge dashed it. "He'd contest it," he said sadly. "He's a saint in more ways than one, like the early Christian martyrs who let the Romans throw them to the lions rather than give up their faith. It'd be a long drawn out legal process with small chance of success. Contested divorces are almost impossible to obtain in Kentucky. I know. I've tried."

"I'll take the chance! I'll fight! I'll spend every penny I've got!"

Ridge shook his head. "And in the meantime the child will be born. It will be several years old by the time it's decided, and if you should win, it'll be illegitimate, a bastard. And Carolyn—"

"Will be disgraced," moaned Tom. "She might not even want to do it."

"I don't know. If she did, it would be an awful ordeal, almost as bad as—"

"What she's already gone through." Tom stared unseeingly at the floor. "Oh, God, it's done, it's done, and it can't be undone."

"It is I . . . it is I who bear the . . . the burden of guilt," Ridge said in leaden tones. "I made a horrible mistake. I tried to play God." He stood before Tom like a man before a firing squad. "Do you forgive me, sir?"

His anguish moved Tom to say, "Yes, I do. You did what you thought was the right thing, and I . . . I accept it as . . . as for the best." He had to look down. "I only wish it was true, what the papers said."

Ridge only seemed to hear his first statement. "Thank you, sir; thank you. Now I have only God to contend with." His voice seemed to come from a great distance.

Ridge resumed his seat. There was a pause during which neither of them could speak.

"I'm leaving the country," Tom finally said. "It'll be better that way."

"Because of this?"

Tom shook his head. "I was going to . . . to surprise Carolyn, so I never wrote her about it. I've already resigned my commission to take service in the Prussian army." He saw no point in making any explanations. It would only prolong the agony that made him want to leap up and rush from the room.

Ridge nodded. "That eases my mind. She's bound to find out someday that you weren't killed, but you'll be across the ocean and she'll think you just . . . just—"

Tom finished for him. "Abandoned her. Got her pregnant and abandoned her!" he exclaimed bitterly. His torture brought him to his feet. "Oh, God! Oh, God! What have I done, that I should be crucified like this?"

Ridge arose also and looked at him ashen-faced. "You are being crucified for . . . for Carolyn, for her happiness, and for the child that is to be born."

"Yes, it's for her happiness," Tom replied as that icy calm he had felt after the Midlow Massacre and Billy's death came over him again. "Someday . . . someday she'll find out I wasn't killed. She'll think I just seduced her, that I'm a faithless wretch, a scamp, and a scoundrel." He nodded as the ice coursed through his veins and objects in the room became glaringly sharp, like they had suddenly been brought into focus through field glasses. "She'll feel only hate and loathing. She'll despise my memory, and that will make her happy with the man who saved her."

With a face that felt like a piece of ice, he faced Ridge and thrust out his hand. "I'll take my leave, sir. Neither you nor any of your connections will ever see me again."

Ridge took Tom's hand. "You're a brave man, sir. You've faced death many times, but I know this is worse, far worse. I count it an honor to have known you."

Tom turned and went out of the building into the late afternoon sunshine, but he didn't see it. The whole world was dark, and the illumination that made things visible seemed to come from within them.

# 53

Tom and Paula stood at the ship's rail only one day from Hamburg enjoying one of the calm, sunny days the climate of Northern Europe rarely allows in November. It was sufficiently cool to make their wraps comfortable, and although the sea only rolled enough to keep his hands on the rail, Paula clung to his arm like they were tossed by a storm. They spoke in German. Tom hadn't used English since before the voyage began and spoke Paula's language almost as easily as his own.

"Oh, I'm happy, so happy, that Father was recalled so we could make the passage together," she sighed.

Tom looked into the blue eyes set in the lovely face that still had in it something of the child. "I'm even happier he accepted my suit when I finally got up the courage to ask him last night. Being both a foreigner and a commoner, I expected the worst."

She smiled knowingly. "I knew he would if you would only ask. Mother saw to that."

Tom pinched her arm. "You women! What chance does a mere man have, even if he is a *Generaloberst*?"

Paula gave a tinkling laugh. "I don't know if I should tell you why—" She cut herself off and looked at him archly.

"Oh, you must! I'm dying to know!"

She tantalized him briefly. "Very well, I will tell. She actually had two reasons." She winked solemnly, the tantalizing look still lingering.

"Tell me! Tell me!" Being with her made him feel like a boy again.

She bowed her head, her gray bonnet brushing the tip of his nose. "One is, was, another suitor."

"Oh?"

She looked up at him timidly. "You aren't angry?"

"No. Why should I be? He has lost and I have won." He pinched her arm again. "I am the victor, and to the victor belong the spoils."

"So it's only spoils I am, like loot from a plundered city?" She tried to look piqued but couldn't and gave it up with a smile.

"Tell me, Paula, please, about this other suitor." He looked into her eyes and felt like he was melting inside.

She sighed. "Well, this other suitor, he was a good deal older than I, a widower, but there were reasons why Mother was afraid Father would insist on him." She nodded sadly. "In Europe many marriages are still made for . . . for reasons other than love, for family connections and such things."

"Oh yes, like was done in the Middle Ages by noble families, for alliances or something like that."

"Mother was afraid Father would do that, and she had a sister who was married to an older man for such reasons. She saw how unhappy she was, and didn't want it to happen to me."

Tom only nodded, so she went on with a sigh. "Now that Father has accepted your suit, that danger is out of the way." She looked at him lovingly. "I was afraid too, for in Prussia the daughter must do as the father says."

"Now, what is the other reason your mother had?" He took a hand from the rail, slipped it into her muff, and clasped her hand.

Paula laughed charmingly. "She says you will become a noble. She can tell it by the look in your eyes and the way you walk."

"The look in my eyes! The way I walk!" scoffed Tom. "They don't give patents of nobility for that!"

She looked at him archly and squeezed his hand. "We women know! We just know! We don't have to think about things like you men do." She nodded and smiled smugly.

"Well, I'll credit your mother with being a seeress if it ever does happen!" he laughed.

She sobered. "And then, Father has his own reason. Otherwise Mother could not have persuaded him, for he is a firm man."

"What is his reason, then?"

"He says you are sure to be a general, maybe even a *Feldmarschall*, someday."

"A general!" he scoffed. "I only hope I can pass the course at the *Kriegschule* and stay what I am, or what I was! I might fail and not even be a *Leutnant*."

"It is all this talking you do about military matters, half the day and every evening." She sighed and shook her head resignedly. "It bores me almost to tears. It just goes on and on."

"We are always arguing, though."

She nodded. "That is what impresses him. He says you have an independent and original mind, that you know theory almost as well as he does, and a great deal more about tactics. Of course, Karl always said you were a natural-born military man."

"I'm afraid the *Generaloberst* has an exaggerated opinion of me, but I'm glad if that's why he accepted my suit for his daughter's hand." He bent to give her a peck on the cheek, but she presented her lips and they kissed. It was the first time and neither of them could speak for a little while. He was glad the bulk of a lifeboat hid them from view.

Finally she said haltingly, "I know . . . I know about the fiancée you had, and . . . and—"

A thrill of dread went through him. "And . . . and my child she will have?"

She nodded silently and turned the full splendor of her wide blue eyes on him, but in their depths he saw only sympathy and understanding.

He was downcast anyhow. "I never wanted you to learn about that." He had made a clean breast of the whole affair to the *Generaloberst*, because he wanted to hide nothing from him. They had talked about it for a long time, and he hadn't been able to hide his feelings.

"Did your father tell you?"

She shook her head, the blond ringlets protruding from under her bonnet catching the breeze. "No, old Fritz told me. He overheard you."

"I knew he did, but I thought we could rely on him. He's been your father's servant for so long."

"Ever since Father was a boy. He told only me. He admires you very much and wanted me to know what a fine man you are."

It all came back on Tom with a rush. He bowed his head and looked at the dark water rushing along the ship's side far below. "I had forgotten . . . almost forgotten," he mused sorrowfully.

She pressed herself to him. "I will help you forget! I will make you forget!" she whispered fiercely.

"But what does it make you think of me? I lose one woman—a woman I loved—and in two months I've found another . . . whom . . . whom I also love—" He hoped to God she never learned about Mary Worthington or even Sally, or she would think he was as changeable as a weathercock.

She got on tiptoes and whispered in his ear, although no one was even in sight. "I only know that I love you, and that you love me, and that I will be with you always . . . always!"

He clasped her slender form to him, again thankful for the shield of the lifeboat, although he would have done it anyhow. "Always, always," he repeated fervently. "Never let me go, never, never. If . . . if

I ever lose you—" He inclined his head at the wild waste of the sea and left it unfinished.

"Always, always," she breathed as she nestled in his arms, "until death do us part."

# 54

Ever since the trouble over Preacher Stevens, Uncle Charley Polson had lived by himself in the log cabin he had built when he came into the country as one of the very first settlers nearly fifty years ago. It was in good shape, because he had always kept it that way and that yellow poplar it was built of lasted forever. His son Jim and his wife were always wanting him to move back with them, but he wouldn't do it, although nothing had come out of the Preacher Stevens business, which was why he had moved out on them. People were always asking him if he didn't get lonesome living by himself. He always told them he didn't, but he never told them why or they would think he was losing his mind.

He didn't get lonesome because he wasn't always alone. His wife, Matilda, often came to him during the long evening hours when he dozed by the fireplace. He would hear her soft voice talking to the toddlers clinging to her skirts as she worked around the cabin, and then she would come to him. They would talk, but he could never remember what they said. Anyhow, they were young again, and the country was young, too, with plenty of deer and bear in the woods and the Indians still coming around sometimes. He never really minded the Indians because they kept a man on his toes and made him feel good.

He had claimed the section of land around the big spring he and the other Kentucky men had camped beside on the march to join General Harrison and go on to Tippecanoe. He had never seen a prettier place and made up his mind to have it after the Indian troubles were over. That wasn't for nearly another four years, because the British pitched in and there was a big war. He had scouted for Harrison and was under Colonel Johnson when they fought Tecumseh's braves and Proctor's white soldiers along that river across from Detroit in Canada.

Then, after it was over, he claimed the land around the big spring, built the cabin, and went back to Kentucky to marry his Matilda. Her folks kicked up a row about her going to live in the wilderness where there were Indians, bear, and catamount, but she loved him and went with him. They lived in the cabin until their children outgrew it and he built the big house where Jim and Mary lived. All his and Matilda's children had been born in the cabin, and the happiest years of his life had been spent there. That was why he had always kept it up and why he would rather live in it than any other place on earth. Matilda loved it, too. That was why she sometimes came down from Heaven to be with him.

He wished he could look forward to joining her in Heaven, but he couldn't. He had too much blood on his hands. It wasn't that he had ever murdered anybody except Mark Dixon, and he had deserved it. Everybody else he had killed had been in war or in a fair fight, except for Indians, and they didn't count. The Bible said: "Thou shalt not kill," though, and he knew how the Lord would look at it. It wasn't that he was afraid. He would face it when it came like he had everything else in life. He had it coming and no one had ever said Charley Polson couldn't take his medicine.

By the time the leaves came out in the spring, he decided he was ready to die. It wasn't that anything was wrong with him. He had never been sick in his life. He was just tired of living. He had lived longer than a man ought to already, and the country wasn't going to be fit to live in much longer. All the young men had gone away to the war, and most of them had been killed. They were turning the Negroes loose, and one of these days they would be all over the country, crowding white men out and taking their women, with the government backing them up. There wasn't any freedom anymore. It was getting to be just like Russia and other countries where men were arrested and thrown into prison just for saying what they thought about the government.

One evening while Uncle Charley dozed by the fireplace, his grandson, Jim, came to him. He was a little boy again and got up on his grandpa's lap to have him tell about fighting Indians and hunting bear like he used to. When he left, Uncle Charley wept. Jim had been his only grandson, the only one who would bear his name when his father was gone. Now he was dead. His bones lay under the sod of Old Virginia not far from where his grandpa had been born. Maybe even one of his relatives had killed him.

The Republicans were to blame for it. Just to get votes, they had carried on about slavery getting into the territories until they scared the South into seceding. Then they started a war to destroy the South and keep themselves in office. They had told everybody the war was just to restore the Union. That was how they had gotten Jim and all the other boys to go fight their kinfolks. Once the politicians got them in the army, they started doing the things they had counted on all along, like turning the Negroes loose. They had lied to the people. They had won their trust and then betrayed it. Now they were going around arresting anyone who complained about it, and if the soldiers quit, they shot them for desertion.

As he dried his tears, a deep and bitter anger began to burn within the old man. He was ready to die anyhow, and he would take some of those Republicans with him when he went. He had lived by the sword, and he would die by it.

He would make them come for him like they had Preacher Stevens and a great many others, but just doing what they had done wouldn't bring them after him. If that were so, they would have come for him already. He was about the only man in the country who had fought King George for freedom, and it would look too bad. Even the Republicans drew back from that.

He knew how to do it, though, and the very next day he stuck his revolver in his belt and went to Paoli. He walked into old man Cartwright's store and told him he wished he had killed that whelp of his on the road from French Lick that time and that now he was going to do it the first chance he got. It scared the daylights out of the old man, and Uncle Charley saw he would get what he wanted. The old scoundrel would send the soldiers after him to save his worthless son, and they would be Republicans. They wouldn't be real soldiers like the ones who had gone away to war, but cowards who stayed behind to do the dirty work, like the old man's son, Tom. Uncle Charley just hoped he would be with them.

He knew they would come at night like they always did, but it wouldn't be for a little while because they would try to catch him off guard. He also knew they wouldn't come to arrest him. They would come to kill him.

He put up a bark shelter along the path from the road to the cabin, in a thicket where no one would see it, and after dark took his blankets and slept in it. He took his double-barreled shotgun and his old horse pistol, both double-charged with powder and buckshot. They would be the best for night shooting, but he took his revolver, too. The moon would be out late for several nights, and he hoped they would come while it was.

The third night he heard horses on the road and got ready. When they slipped past him toward the cabin, he came out and followed them noiselessly along the path. He wanted to wait until they got bunched up before the door and made a good target.

When they did and one of them drew back to kick in the door, Uncle Charley cocked his shotgun. They heard it and whirled with guns upraised just as he let them have both barrels.

The buckshot cut down all of them but one fellow who was a little apart from the bunch. He got off a shot just as Uncle Charley raised his horse pistol. A tremendous blow on the chest hurled the old man over backward to the ground, but he held onto his pistol and managed to raise himself. The fellow fired again, but his bullet went wild and Uncle Charley shot him down. Then he collapsed and died, the smoking pistol still clutched in the gnarled hand that had wielded a rifle at Tippecanoe and the Thames.

Five men had come for him. Only one escaped alive, and he had been left on the road with the horses. The shooting made him think all the copperheads in the country had been waiting with loaded guns. The roar of Uncle Charley's shotgun sounded like a cannon, and its orange flare lighted up the woods. In his terror, the fellow leaped on his horse and galloped back the way he had come as hard as his steed would go.

The next day another party of soldiers came, but this time the Orange County sheriff was with them. He hadn't wanted to go out of his county, but they had prevailed on him to come along, claiming they would all be bushwacked and killed if he didn't.

They found only dead men. Tom Cartwright was lying a little apart from the others, riddled with buckshot like they were. The soldiers threw the bodies across their horses and left hurriedly to get out of this country of dark, looming woods and deadly ambushes.

Uncle Charley's body was gone. Little Johnny Tacker had heard the shooting and come to see about it. He had gone for Jim, and they had taken the body away in the night.

By the time the sheriff came up from Jasper, Uncle Charley was lying beside his Matilda under the stone he had chiseled out himself. Jim told the sheriff what he thought had happened. The soldiers had come for his father, and he had shot it out with them. The sheriff said it was hard to believe that a seventy-year-old man could kill four armed soldiers before they killed him. Jim replied that he just didn't know what kind of a man his father was. After he had questioned little Johnny and several others, the sheriff decided that Jim was right. He took statements from Jim and little Johnny, then went back to Jasper. That was the last anyone ever heard about it.

When Jim went to chisel the death date on the tombstone, he was astonished to find it already there. It must have been on the stone when they buried his father. No one had noticed it because they hadn't expected it. If anyone else had done it, he would have said something, and the inscription was just like the other carving on the stone.

It added up to only one thing. His father had chiseled the date himself. But how could he have known the date he would die? It was unnerving, and so strange that Jim never told anyone but that he did it himself.

The Indianapolis Republican paper put the best possible face on the affair. The next week John Traylor was astonished to read this notice in it:

> We regret to report a tragic occurrence in northern Dubois County last week resulting in the death of Lieutenant Cartwright, who has rendered valuable service at the post here, three of his men, and an old veteran of the War of 1812 named Charles Polson.
>
> The lieutenant and four men went to Polson's cabin on the night of Thursday last, as far as is known only to ask him about the reported presence of deserters in the area.
>
> Old Polson evidently took the soldiers for bandits bent on robbing him and opened fire on them with several weapons. In self-defense, the soldiers fired back. The result was that Polson was fatally shot, but did not die until he had killed the lieutenant and three of his men. The only one to survive had been left on the road some distance from Polson's cabin with the horses.

John was so disgusted that he wrote to stop the paper from coming, although his subscription still had several months to run.

# 55

Congressman Baker rode up to the house he hadn't visited since stopping off on his way back from the meeting at Celestine a few weeks after the war began. That had been nearly six years ago, but the house and grounds looked the same as they had then, flower garden and all. He had expected to find the place run-down and dilapidated. No one came to take his horse, so he dismounted and hitched the animal to an iron ring on a post in front, then walked to the door and knocked.

There was no answer, so he knocked again. Still no one came. He waited, hesitating whether to knock again or leave. Suddenly the door opened and the little old man who had taken his horse the last time he visited appeared in the doorway.

"Oh, hit's Yer Honor Congressman Baker," he stammered. "Th' doctor told me t' turn whoever hit wuz 'way, but he didn't know hit wuz Yer Honor. I'm shore he'll want t' see you."

Baker was doubtful. "Well, if he's that bad off—"

The little man interrupted. "Oh, no, sir, he'd want t' see Yer Honor even if'n he wuz dyin'."

Baker only shook his head and followed the little man. He was led to a back bedroom where an emaciated figure he scarcely recognized as his old friend sat propped up in bed.

Bowles looked at him blankly before recognition dawned in his eyes. "Ben! Ben! How good of you to come—" He paused and gasped for breath but extended his hand as Baker came up to the bedside.

"I'm certainly sorry," Baker said, "to see you bedfast like this. I'd heard you were ill, but I didn't know how badly." He took the doctor's long, bony fingers in his hand. They felt cold to the touch.

"Sit down . . . sit down, Ben," Bowles insisted with a show of energy. As Baker sat in a chair beside the bed, Bowles turned his head to the little man lingering by the door. "Some brandy, please."

"Air ye shore ye oughta?" was the hesitant reply.

"Of course. I haven't had any all week, and I need some strength."

Baker broke in as the little old man left. "Now, Doctor, if my visit's going to be too much for you, I'll leave." He started to rise.

"No! No!" exclaimed Bowles, motioning with his hand. "I want to talk with you, Ben. I must, even if it kills me. I'd despaired of seeing anyone . . . anyone among my old friends anyhow, before I die."

Baker settled back in his seat, so Bowles went on. "People, particularly people of any consequence, avoid me like the plague. No one has come to see me since I've been back."

Baker couldn't think of a suitable reply and was glad to see the little old man appear with bottle and glass. He watched while Bowles heaved himself up in bed and drank copiously, then fell back gasping. He looked helplessly at his visitor. "Just . . . just wait a few moments," he said faintly.

The congressman nodded and looked silently at his old friend. The doctor looked like he was ninety, although he was only a little over seventy. The skin stretched over an almost fleshless head and face but hung in folds on his neck and upper arms. It was unnaturally yellowish and he had the look of death about him.

As Baker watched, a trace of color came to the flaccid cheeks and the eyes gained a little luster. "I can't tell you how much I appreciate this, Ben," he whispered at length. "Like I said—"

"Save your breath, Doctor," urged Baker. "You might exhaust yourself."

Bowles's head moved from side to side on the pillow. "No, Ben, not that I care if I do. It's only a matter of time anyhow, and the sooner the better."

"Don't give up, old friend. You may recover and be yourself again."

"Oh, that brandy will carry me through," sighed Bowles. His head moved negatively on the pillow again. "Recovery is out of the question, Ben." He looked at his visitor sadly. "I'm a physician, and I'm well acquainted with my condition."

"Oh, but, doctor—"

Bowles broke in. His voice gaining strength, and more color was coming to his cheeks. "No, Ben, I'm broken, completely broken down. Those Republicans broke me. Two years in prison, under conditions you wouldn't believe." He laughed gratingly. "They came within an ace of hanging me, and I often wish they had."

"I know how it was. I've seen Stephen Horsey. They let him go a year before you and the others."

Bowles shook his head sadly. "Poor Horsey. He wasn't involved at all. He knew nothing about it. He was just a member of our order, not even the head of his county lodge. He was never even in politics like the rest of us." Bowles sighed and shook his head again. "I guess it took every penny he had. The lawyers bled him white."

"Yes, he's down-and-out," Baker replied. "He used to be pretty well off, and now he's talking about going to the poor farm. He's not able to work anymore."

Bowles didn't reply, so Baker went on. "You say Horsey wasn't involved in whatever you fellows did. Were Milligan and Humphreys?"

"No. Milligan knew what was going on in a general way, but he wasn't involved. Humphreys wasn't involved, any more than Horsey was. He had no connection with any of us."

The doctor gained enough strength to talk almost normally, and Baker was much interested in what he was saying. "From what you say, Doctor, I take it that *you* were involved in that 'Northwest Conspiracy,' as the Republicans call it."

Bowles nodded affirmatively. "I was. I was the only one tried by that military commission who was, after Dodd escaped from military prison anyhow. They never caught Walker, you know. He skipped out to Canada before they could."

"Do you mean that you—and Dodd and Walker—plotted with those Confederates in Canada, with Jacob Thompson, to free those Rebel prisoners of war at Indianapolis and Chicago and start a revolution here in the Northwest?"

Bowles looked reflectively at the ceiling and nodded. "That we did. None of us ever saw Thompson, but Walker saw a lot of Clay, and I a lot of Thompson's two chief lieutenants, Hines and Castleman, and another Kentucky Confederate named Freeman." He looked directly at his friend. "We had it all planned. We were all organized. We had plenty of guns. If Lincoln had tried something—like breaking up our national convention at Chicago or interfering with the elections—I believe we would've succeeded."

"You mean you did it because you thought Lincoln was going to put soldiers at the polls to keep Democrats from voting like he did in Kentucky and Maryland in '63?" Baker nodded and relaxed. "That puts a different face on the thing. I was afraid he'd do that myself, and I believe he would have if he hadn't decided he would win reelection without it."

"Yes, after Sherman took Atlanta and Sheridan stopped Early, he saw he'd win a free election, so he didn't do it." Bowles sighed and looked away. "That's why the others that *were* involved got mixed up in it. They were sure Lincoln was going to do something like that, maybe even arrest whoever we nominated to run against him." He looked directly at Baker again. "But I would have done it anyhow, old friend. As a man who has only a short time to live, I'll be honest with you."

Baker was too shocked to reply, so Bowles went on. "Of course our only chance of actually overthrowing the state governments here in the Northwest and setting up our confederacy depended on Lincoln doing something like that, say, putting soldiers at the polls to keep men from voting against him. It would've taken something like that to rouse our people enough to join our revolution. Nothing like that has a chance unless it's got mass popular support." Suddenly he looked significantly at Baker. "But I was willing to settle for a lot less than that. I was willing to settle for any kind of diversion that would take the military pressure off the Confederates and give them a chance to get back on their feet again."

Baker was incredulous. "You mean . . . you mean you actually wanted the Confederates to win . . . to divide the country permanently?"

Bowles nodded affirmatively. "That I did."

"But why? Why?"

Bowles didn't reply at once. "Don't you remember," he asked at length, "what you said in your speech at Celestine just after the war began, that you'd rather live in a country the size of a postage stamp than—"

Baker broke in. "Yes, I said that, but a lot has happened since then. I guess you could say that freeing the slaves was an inevitable consequence of the war which none of us foresaw. And then we saved the Union." He nodded thoughtfully. "Secession's as dead as the dodo bird, too. We'll be one country, one nation, from now on." He shook his head and sighed. "And then there are the sacrifices we made. I lost one son and have another who'll be a cripple for life."

"You saved the third one, didn't you, Ben?" asked Bowles sympathetically.

Baker nodded affirmatively. "Yes, I did. I used my influence to get him transferred to a safe post in Washington, without his knowledge of course, or he'd never have accepted it." He saw understanding in the old man's eyes. "I'm not ashamed of it. I believe one—and another crippled—is enough. If I hadn't done it, he'd be gone, too. His regiment was almost wiped out at Gettysburg."

"Yes, I understand," was the soft reply. "Our bravest and best, they're mostly gone." When Baker failed to reply, Bowles went on. "I understand how you feel, Ben. No one who's lost what you have could bear up under it unless he could convince himself it was for a just and worthy cause."

"Don't you think it was, Doctor?" asked Baker challengingly.

Bowles nodded slowly, his head crinkling the pillow. His gray mane was so thin Baker could see his scalp in places. "In one respect, it was. You're right about the Union. We're a united country again and always will be." He looked at his friend sadly. "But have you ever asked yourself what kind of a country we'll be?"

"Oh, you're thinking about race mixing and all that," replied Baker complacently. "There'll be none of that. Even if the Negroes do come north, there'll be no mixing. Whites have a natural revulsion—"

Bowles broke in. "How long do you think this natural revulsion will last during a century or so of enforced close association?"

Baker was startled. "Enforced close association? How? By whom?"

"By the federal government. Secession is dead, but so are states' rights. The federal government will rule the states as provinces, like governments do in Europe."

"But no government could ever enforce close association of the races! The people wouldn't stand for it!"

"Oh, it'll take time, much time, a century at least, before it begins." He looked at his friend sadly. "It's like I told you the last time you were here. You'll never see it. Certainly I won't. Neither will our children. Even our grandchildren probably won't." He sighed convulsively. "But it will come, and in a few centuries we will be a nation of yellow people with prognathous faces and kinky hair. We will be without virtue or stability. We will be so convulsed by riot and revolution that only despots will be able to rule us. All it will take will be a century or so of enforced close association. That will take care of that natural revulsion you spoke of."

Baker scoffed. "Now, Doctor, pray tell me how any government can enforce close association of the races and survive?"

"It's already beginning, Ben. The Republicans are giving the Negro the right to vote, and it'll go on from there."

"Oh, that'll pass. It'll soon be over. They're doing it to stay in power, so they won't become a minority again like they were back in the forties when most of them were Whigs. They know that now that the war's over they won't have any hold on the people, no more than they had when all they had to offer were protective tariffs and national banking." Baker nodded confidently. "But we'll put a stop to that when the people finally get this war business out of their minds and we get our old majorities back."

"If you do, it'll be only temporary," was the dismal forecast.

"How's that?"

"The politicians will start bidding for the Negro's vote, and they'll soon learn that the best way to get it is promise him what he wants more than everything else: a legal right to close association with whites, a chance to get a white woman. That means more to him than food and drink."

"But it'll never get that far! We'll see to that!"

The old man went on as though Baker hadn't spoken, and the congressman began to feel he was only trying to convince himself. "If the Negro loses the right to vote, it'll be only temporary, because he'll have help getting it back, and help in pushing on from there."

"Help? Who'd help his own race to commit suicide?"

"The philosophers, the preachers, the literati—the writers. They know nothing of the Negro. Many of them haven't even seen one except from a distance. None of them have any association with them. They fondly imagine he's just a white man with black skin, and they'll hang onto that fantasy like grim death, even in the face of proof that he's something else entirely."

When Baker did not reply, Bowles went on in the same leaden tones. "They'll put it in moral and ethical terms, like they did with slavery. They'll say it violates the basic tenet of Christianity, the brotherhood of man. They'll say it violates the principles upon which this nation was founded, the equality of man as stated in the Declaration of Independence. They'll explain away the Negro's mental inferiority, his instability and criminality. They'll dress him up and give him all the qualities he lacks. They'll make him presentable." Bowles nodded sadly. "And they will keep the pressure on. Upper-class people who won't be affected will join them. It will never let up. It will be like the force of gravity. In the course of time, the people will be convinced that it is morally wrong to exclude the Negro from their society, and they will take him in." Suddenly a fleshless arm came forth and cold fingers rested on Baker's hand. "The day will come," intoned a sepulchral voice, "when the test of a man's virtue will be his willingness to give his daughter to a Negro."

Bowles looked at his friend with a strange glow in his eyes. He could see that Baker was shaken and pressed his advantage. "That's why I did it, Ben. That's why I've done everything I could to help the Rebels win the war since the day it started. If they'd won the war, they'd have kept the Negro in their Confederacy and he wouldn't be free to come north. He'd still be property, like a horse. He could never hope to mix with white people and pollute their blood." He withdrew his arm and waved it feebly. "Ben . . . Ben . . . they failed . . . I failed . . . and the white race is doomed." The old man fell back gasping, the color fleeing his face.

It was all beginning to have an effect on Baker, and he was glad the apparent relapse gave him an excuse to leave. “You've exhausted yourself, Doctor,” he said as he rose from his seat, “and I must leave before you do yourself real harm.”

There was no reply and Baker was on the point of calling for the little old man when he suddenly appeared. “If'n Yer Honor don't mind—” he said apologetically as he rushed to the bed.

“Of course. I'll leave immediately,” he said as he turned to go.

The corpselike figure on the bed rallied and, before Baker could go, extended a stalklike arm. Baker took the cold, bony hand, looked into the dimming eyes, and heard the whisper: “If we don't . . . don't meet again in this world . . . let us hope we will . . . in . . . the next.”

As he rode away, Baker tried to convince himself that what he had heard were only the ramblings of a sick old man whose condition had affected his mind, but he was not entirely successful in doing so.

# 56

It was a cold January night at the institution near Indianapolis, and the snow lay deep on the ground. All was quiet. The arctic cold would keep the inmates bundled in their beds, so the attendant in one of the buildings drowsed by a stove in an alcove at one end. All the doors were locked, and any noise would rouse her.

In a bed at the other end of the building a woman did not sleep. She always sat up in bed and looked out the window into the woods on that side after the candles were put out and the attendant retired. She did it because she was always looking for someone, but he had never appeared to her until tonight. That was why she did not sleep. He had disappeared into the woods soon after she saw him, but she knew he was still there, waiting until she could come to him.

Her mind was yet capable of craft. She knew how to get out. The window near her bed had been made of a green wood and had shrunk over the years until the outside latch no longer held and it moved silently in its frame. For years she had kept a small stick on the baseboard under the window for the time she knew would come.

After a while she got up, raised the window, and propped it with the stick. After she climbed out, she removed the stick and let the window down, all without making any noise.

Although clad only in a loose gown and without shoes, she felt neither the intense cold or the snow into which she sank almost to her knees. She seemed to float effortlessly along, transported by her love and warmed by the cloak in which it enveloped her.

The woods were deep and dark, but he was waiting for her and she found him.

"Billy, my baby, my boy," she breathed.

They embraced and he said softly, "I've come fer ye, Ma."

"I know," she sighed. "I've been waiting so long, so long."

He gathered her in his strong arms and bore her away through the trees, upward and ever upward, back to that happy, golden time when they had been mother and son together, before there had been any Republicans, any secession, or any war.

Had there been an observer and enough light, he would have seen only a withered old woman, thinly clad and shoeless, making her way through the snow and into the woods. Shortly after she was among the trees, she would sink into the soft whiteness and there freeze into icy rigidity.

In a large house in Jasper a very old woman sat by the fire, occasionally babbling senselessly in German. Another woman attended her. Only her trim figure and the way she moved about showed she was the younger, for her hair was as white and her skin as wrinkled as that of the other. Her eyes were very large and sad.

You could tell that they lived alone, that the older woman never left the house, and that the younger one did only when she had to. Certain items of furniture and equipment plus shelves of medical books in an adjoining room showed it had once been a doctor's office. Although it had not been used for many years, it had been carefully kept just as it had been when the man who had used it was alive.

In a less pretentious house on a farm a few miles away a man confronted his wife. She was very tall, a head higher than he was, and very frightened. Traces of bruises on her face showed why, but this time he only spoke harshly and made threatening gestures. Their children hovered in the background, their eyes wide like those of frightened deer.

The man behaved this way for several reasons. Not only was he much shorter than his wife, but he had been virtually penniless until he married her. Also, he had not been away to war like most men his age in the locality. He had left Germany to escape conscription, and had been careful not to take out citizenship papers in this country until the war was over. Thus he frequently felt the need to assert himself in this fashion.

# 57

It was early in May 1945. The war in Europe was ending, and a part of it was the surrender of the German Army Group Center by the *Feldmarschall* commanding to the American general who was his opposite number. The signing of the surrender had been cold and formal. Both men had been grim-lipped and silent, but only for the benefit of the civil officials and war correspondents present. Their hatred of the beaten enemy was not shared by the general. It was not the first time he had been in contact with his German counterpart. During the conditions of static warfare of the late winter and early spring, matters connected with the civil population and the wounded had required exchanges of messages. They regarded each other as highly competent professionals and men who honored the traditions and practices European civilization had established for warfare.

Neither man betrayed his feelings by word or look, the American because he did not want to bring down on his head the wrath of an ignorant and inflamed public. The German did not because he understood this.

That evening after a clandestine exchange of notes, the general donned an enlisted man's coat and cap, took a plain Jeep, and drove away into the darkness.

He entered the room where the *Feldmarschall* waited. As they shook hands and exchanged greetings, an observer would have noted that they looked much alike. They were about the same age. Both were tall, and so blond the gray in their hair scarcely showed. Both had the ruddy faces of men who spent their time outdoors or in rough temporary quarters. Neither had the paunchy flabbiness that sixty years often bring.

They sat at a table, and an orderly brought brandy and cigars. They spoke in German, which the general had spoken before he learned English. For a time their talk centered on their late military operations. The American commended particularly the resistance the German had put up with only a handful of war-worn veterans and raw recruits against the masses of men, tanks, and planes thrown against him.

Eventually the talk turned to other channels. "You know," mused the German, "you and I could easily have been each on the other side. It is strange, most strange, but true."

"Oh yes, if my father hadn't emigrated, I would be in German uniform," agreed the American, "but how could you have been on the other side?"

The German smiled. "My father was an emigrant also, only he went the other way."

"You mean he emigrated from America to Germany?"

The *Feldmarschall* nodded. "Yes. He was of old American stock, English to judge by his name."

"But your name isn't English."

"It was changed to the name of the estate my father was given when he was ennobled. That was the custom at that time in Germany."

The general nodded and puffed his cigar. "Of course. I should have known." He took a sip of brandy. "Please tell me about him. Why did he go the other way? It seems so unusual."

"He became involved in political difficulties toward the latter part of your Civil War. I never really understood it, but he incurred the enmity of some high officials in the government and had to resign his commission."

"Why did he leave the country and go to Germany, though?"

The German enjoyed his cigar briefly. "I hope the general will pardon me, but I won't have anything like this where I'm going."

The American shook his head. "It's a shame, but there's no help for it. You simply cannot talk sense to politicians, or to generals who are politicians more than anything else."

"You mean Eisenhower?"

The general nodded affirmatively. "That's precisely whom I mean. The man has never commanded in the field. His talents are purely political." He shook his head again. "But back to your father. Why did he go to Germany?"

"He was a man of great natural ability. He had no military training at all when he volunteered as a private soldier at the start of your Civil War. In a little over a year he was an officer, and when he resigned he was a colonel commanding a brigade."

The American was impressed. "He surely must have had natural ability, much of it."

"Of course he got books and studied a lot. That undoubtedly helped. Then the man who became his cousin by marriage had taken leave from the Prussian army and took service in your army to get practical experience on the battlefield. He was assigned to the company my father commanded and they became good friends. As my father was promoted, he was, too. This gave Father a connection with the Prussian military, so when he resigned, he went to Prussia on a promise he would keep his rank if he passed the field's officer's course at the old Potsdam *Kriegsschule.* He passed it with honors. Then he married into the von Brandenburg family, one of the first families of Prussia. I think he met my mother before he came over here, while her father was visiting the Prussian embassy in Washington. I know they came back to Europe together anyhow, and were married soon after he finished at Potsdam and was commissioned *Oberst.*"

"Well, how did he do in Prussia?"

"Very well. He did not disappoint those who had stretched regulations to get him. In the Austro-Prussian War, he commanded a brigade. He fought at Königratz and handled it so well that he was promoted to *Generalmajor.* He commanded a division against the French at Sedan in 1870. Acting on his own initiative, he attacked and seized Calvaire D'Illy, the key position that penned up Wimpffen's army there, and held it against the attacks of Ducrot's entire corps until he could be reinforced. It resulted in the surrender of the French army and the capture of Emperor Napoléon III, but the fighting was very severe and he was badly wounded. He nearly died and never completely recovered, although he was on the active list for another thirty years."

"I suppose he was promoted again?"

"Yes. That was when the emperor ennobled him and gave him an estate in Pomerania." The German sighed. "Of course, it's all gone now. The Poles will take that part of Germany—that is, if the Russians do not."

"How far did your father go after that?"

"No farther. He retired a *Generalleutnant.*"

"Was it because of his health?"

The German laughed. "No. He used to remark that men with one leg got more than he did, but he never attached much importance to rank, or to being a nobleman, for that matter. He used the von only officially and was the soul of equality outside the military. He used to get out in the fields with his peasants and show them how he had broken ground and harvested crops in America." The *Feldmarschall* nodded smilingly. "He never made any money off the estate. He indulged his peasants too much, building them better cottages, putting water and sewage systems in their village, and endowing their daughters when they were married. They all loved him. He would go to their dances, drink beer, and frolic with them."

"Why wasn't he promoted again, though?"

"He made himself unpopular with the high hierarchy, civil and military, chiefly by being ahead of his time and being too insistent with his ideas. He had no diplomatic talent, which he was the first to admit."

"Ahead of his time?"

"Yes, he was. After he recovered from his wounds, he was made chief of ordnance because he wasn't able to take the field for a long time. As such, he was the first to take up the magazine rifles, then automatic weapons. I believe he was the main reason our army had such a lead in machine guns at the start of the First World War. He was the same with breechloading artillery with recoil mechanisms, the first really modern guns." The German sipped his brandy and nodded reflectively. "And that wasn't the end of it."

"What else?" asked the American with unconcealed eagerness.

"Infantry tactics. You know we made the first fundamental change in tactics during the First World War, the first adaptation to the new conditions brought about by automatic weapons and artillery concentrations by indirect fire."

"You mean the tactics of infiltration first used by von Hutier at Riga in 1917, and then in your great offensive of 1918?"

"Yes. Father was never credited with them, but he worked them out years before the war and urged them on the high command. They wouldn't hear of such radicalism, and when he persisted he only made himself more obnoxious with the hierarchy. But in 1916, when we were stalemated on the western front, a man named Geyer dug them up, revised them a little and they were glad to get them." The *Feldmarschall* shook his head and sighed. "If we had adopted them when he proposed them, years before the war, we would have won by the end of 1914."

"I don't suppose your father was active yet by that time?"

"No, he died in 1912, but his six sons all served in the First World War."

"You were one of them, of course."

"Yes, but I and my youngest brother were the only ones who survived, and he lost an arm."

Both men looked silently at the floor and there was a short pause. Presently the German went on. "I was not so lucky. I lost all four of my sons in this war."

"You have my sympathy, sir."

The *Feldmarschall* tossed off the last of his brandy and shook his head. "Yes, it is the end for the family founded by my father. You see, my brother never married."

There was a period of moody silence, which the general broke by getting to his feet. "I must go. It is getting late, and I have a busy day before me tomorrow."

The German nodded and rose to see his guest to the door. "I envy you," he sighed. "All I have to look forward to is the prison camp."

They stopped at the door. "Conditions will be better than you expect," the general assured him. "I am not yet ready to revert to the barbarism of primitive times."

"And to think, a hundred years ago we would have openly feted one another!" The *Feldmarschall* shook his head sadly. "How truly we have retrogressed, in our modern age."

The general only nodded his agreement, so the German went on. "It is war," he sighed. "You win and I lose, only this is the second time it happened like that." He laughed bitterly. "Sometimes I wish my father had stayed in America."

The general nodded understandingly. After a handshake and a final farewell, he took the wheel of his Jeep and drove away.

Whenever he passed the camps of his men on the way, he heard joyful celebration, but he did not feel elated himself.